EXODUS

ALEX LAMB

GOLLANCZ

LONDON

First published in Great Britain in 2017 by Gollancz
an imprint of the Orion Publishing Group Ltd
Carmelite House, 50 Victoria Embankment
London EC4Y 0DZ

An Hachette UK Company

1 3 5 7 9 10 8 6 4 2

A CIP catalogue record for this book is
available from the British Library.

ISBN 978 1 473 20614 4

Typeset at The Spartan Press Ltd,
Lymington, Hants

Printed in Great Britain by Clays Ltd,
St Ives plc

MIX
Paper from
responsible sources
FSC® C104740

www.alexlamb.com
www.orionbooks.co.uk
www.gollancz.co.uk

For Graham, who taught me how to see

1: RISING

1.1: WILL

Will Kuno-Monet woke with a start to find himself half-buried in white soil. He struggled to his feet, blinking while his heart pounded. A meadow of black poppies stretched in either direction, lining the bottom of an enormous tunnel. Bluish light came from dangling chains of luminescent kelp suspended from the pale, arched ceiling fifty metres overhead. The strands wafted gently like a glowing field of wheat. A moist breeze brought scents of ozone and fresh coffee. Somewhere nearby, a stream trickled.

His body felt wire-taut, flushed with fear for no reason he could remember. Will glanced quickly about, his breath coming in heaves. In the tube's undulating distance, a dense thicket of short, black trees jutted out of the snow-white earth. In the other direction, a sideways kink in the tube blocked further sight. He looked down and found himself wearing a one piece ship-suit, but grown from some soft, grey, organic material. It had no obvious fastenings. He didn't remember putting it on.

What the hell was this place? And why did he feel so afraid? His memory was a terrifying blank. But as he stood there, anxiously scanning the tunnel, answers began to assemble themselves in his mind like shadows revealed by parting mist.

Will was on Snakepit – a world covered with millions of kilometres of overlapping habitat tubes just like this one. It was the greatest extraterrestrial discovery the human race had ever made: an engineered biosphere capable of hosting billions of living beings. And it had been left empty and unused for the last five million years.

He also remembered that he'd been lured here aboard his ship, the *Ariel Two*. Yes, he *owned* a starship. He was investigating some sort of threat, utterly unsuspecting of what lay ahead. Because Snakepit had been kept secret. And once he arrived, he'd been betrayed.

He frowned as he tried to remember who'd cheated him and how. The answer wouldn't come. Was it his friends or allies in government? He knew he worked in politics. There had been all those dull, difficult meetings with bright-robed men and women with frowning faces. He was part of something called IPSO – the Interstellar Pact Security Organisation. But he felt sure the betrayal ran deeper than that. He'd trusted someone with his life and his future, and it had killed him.

Will frowned in confusion at that last memory. If he'd died, how come he was still here? Yet the image burned vividly in his mind. He'd watched helpless from a distance while his body melted into slime. Except that didn't make any sense, either. How had he watched his own death from a distance?

Then Will recalled another vital fact about himself. He was a roboteer – one of a tiny minority of people engineered before birth to interface with thinking machines. How could he *possibly* have forgotten that? It had defined his entire life. Any camera linked to a Self-Aware Program could serve as his eyes. Watching himself from outside his own body was as simple as thought, so long as a suitable network was available.

Something about that explanation didn't strike him as adequate, either, but it occurred to him to check for a local pervasivenet. With access to the digital realm, it would be a lot easier to figure out what had happened.

He reached inwards, summoning the visual for his home node – the virtual environment that served as the access point for his internal systems. However, instead of the familiar image of his childhood home, a dark sensation swam up through him, vivid and overpowering. An ancient place that felt at once like a deserted museum and a crowded train station loomed in his mind's eye, where crowds of ghostly figures flickered and darted. From grey stone walls hung immense rippling banners of orange and black, bearing alien runes too dense and twisted for human eyes to read. He knew this place. He dreaded it.

Will fought to clear his head of the smothering vision and found himself kneeling, bent over on the pale clay and wheezing for air. He'd

2

practically passed out. As his strength returned, a cold sense of certainty settled on him. He hadn't just been cheated, he'd been *changed*.

How or why he'd been rescued from death he had no idea, but one thing he knew for certain: he couldn't stay in this tunnel. He needed to get off Snakepit while he still could. For reasons that escaped him, he knew this place was dangerous.

Will struck out hurriedly in the direction of the black trees, the peculiar flowers crumpling beneath his feet as he strode through them. They bled ink when crushed, he noticed – a brilliant blue that soaked into the soil almost immediately. He remembered this world being strange, with a bewildering variety of life forms inhabiting the tunnels, all of them petite and too perfect to be natural. Now, though, they smelled wrong. There'd been no coffee odour last time. And something about its presence worried him deeply.

At the edge of the miniature forest, Will stopped to stare. Pale, rubbery faces grown from parasitic fungus jutted from the trunks like masks. Each one bore the likeness of someone he knew. And with each face, a fresh memory bloomed in his head.

Here, for instance, was the elegant, sculpted visage of Parisa Voss. A friend and a traitor – the woman who'd derailed his life. *She'd* brought him here. He felt a rush of loathing. And there was Ann Ludik, another traitor. Except, in the end, she'd been a friend. She'd saved his life and he'd died trying to save hers. Beside her lay the hard, compact features of Mark Ruiz, Will's half-son. Mark was someone Will had aspired to protect, though he'd fallen far short of that goal.

Will regarded the masks with crawling unease. Had these faces been carved? Had they *grown* like that? He glanced about, anticipating a trap. Somebody with both time and knowledge of his life had put these things here, ready for him to see when he awoke. That must have taken hours. How long had he been out of the picture?

The fourth face he saw made him freeze. It belonged to Rachel, his wife – the woman he'd loved all his life. Yet her face conjured an unexpected emotion – a sense of deep, boiling hatred that made Will break out in a spontaneous sweat. He could remember nothing Rachel had ever done to justify such a reaction. In fact, so far as he recalled, she'd been gone from his life for years. His own obsession with trying to fix the politics of IPSO had finally driven her away. She'd boarded a ship to explore the edge of human space – a ship lost beyond reach

3

before he had a chance to apologise. He fumbled to master his rage. Understanding eluded him like a handful of smoke.

Will stalked between the trees, keeping his eyes open and his guard up in anticipation of a punchline for this sickening joke. A few dozen metres further on he came to a clearing. There, beside the swirling brook, a tiny diorama of his childhood home had been rendered in purple moss. It depicted the exact location of his home node – the very place he'd reached for inside himself just minutes earlier. Grey bulbs of mushroom took the place of furniture, each item rendered in unlikely detail.

Will glared at the weird scene. Whoever had tinkered with this place didn't just have knowledge of his life. They'd seen inside his mind. He walked warily around the unnatural growth, giving it a wide berth only to find it repeated dozens of times along the banks of the river on a variety of scales.

Will waded downstream, trying to stay away from the moss without knowing why. Panic clotted his thoughts. Somebody was playing with him, trying to frighten him – but to what end? Were they the same people who'd brought him back to life? Will's mouth curled in a bitter snarl. If he'd been resurrected as a plaything simply to be teased and tortured, his tormentors would need their wits about them. Will had experienced treatment of that sort during the Interstellar War. His captors had not died pleasantly.

He froze as voices carried to him on the moist air. A man spoke somewhere beyond a line of trees up ahead. A woman answered. They sounded powerfully familiar, though Will struggled to place either of them. He heard laughter.

Will searched the stream's banks for a weapon – a rock or a bone, perhaps – but found nothing in the artificial landscape that would serve. He strode across to the nearest tree to rip free a branch, only to have the wood bend like rubber in his hands.

No matter. He'd fight unarmed if need be. He edged closer to the last line of trees, keeping to the shadows, and peered out.

Beyond the wood lay a small café. A line of bar stools faced away from him, arranged before a covered counter with a large yellow espresso machine and racks of brightly coloured cups. A woman in a dirndl with blonde, braided hair worked there with her back turned, pulling a fresh shot while two patrons chatted on the stools. One customer had vivid green skin. The other had small antlers and legs that ended in hooves. Both wore embroidered tuxedos with high, padded shoulders like characters from a Martian Renaissance drama.

Will regarded them with blank astonishment. Now he knew where the smell had come from, though the explanation offered little comfort. When last he'd walked these tunnels, Snakepit had been a new discovery fraught with microbial dangers. There was no human population, and it certainly hadn't featured *coffee stands*. The woman turned to place espresso cups before her guests. Will blinked at the sight of her face. It was, without doubt, his own. Her features were smaller than his, more prettily proportioned, but she might have been his twin sister.

She looked up and caught him staring dumbly from the edge of the trees.

'Are you here for coffee?' she asked, then saw his confusion. 'Dabbling in shyness, perhaps? We don't bite, honest.' She gestured for him to approach.

Will, rather uncertainly, stepped out from the cover of the forest. His hands flexed, ready for a fight.

'Do you have scrip?' she said, and then waved the comment away when he didn't answer. 'It doesn't matter. I'm in it for the conversation, not the acumen. What can I get you? It's on the house.'

The two patrons swivelled on their stools to face him. Will saw his own face on both of them. He struggled to speak as he realised why their voices had sounded so oddly familiar – he'd heard himself.

'I...' he started.

'You look like you could use something calming,' said the woman. 'How about a nice cup of tea? I'm going to hazard a guess that you like Assam.'

'Good guess,' said Will uncertainly. 'My favourite.'

'No shit,' said the antler clone, chuckling into his coffee.

'What size?' said the woman.

'Come on, he wants a large,' said the green clone. 'You can tell by his face.'

'Why don't you bring that baseline palette of yours over here and have a seat, Will,' said the antler clone. 'And tell us – whatever brings you out to a lonely spot like this one?'

1.2: ANN

From the helm of the *Ariel Two*, Ann Ludik watched shuttles lift from the surface of the Earth, bringing up the last of the population. They appeared in her display as a hundred bright sparks rising over the arc of the world, a planet still stubbornly blue despite all the abuse it had taken. One by one, the sparks left Earth behind, streaming out into the velvet night.

Despite the irretrievable mess their ancestral home had become, it was impossible not to feel the poignancy of that moment. And, deep down beneath her layers of emotional scar tissue, Ann felt a weak stirring of sadness. However, besides the anticipation that had been twisting her insides for the last nine hours, it barely registered. There would be time for wistfulness later, if they survived.

Someone in the cabin let out a short, tense sob at the sight. Ann declined to open her human eyes to find out who'd made it. Her crew knew how to do their jobs. And they'd all seen moments more tragic than this. After all, they weren't being forced off a planet this time. Unlike most of humanity's retreats in its long war with the self-styled Photurian Utopia, this one had been their own choice.

Forty-one years had passed since the Photes' first attack. During the decades that followed, the Photurians had evolved from near-mindless machines into a sophisticated and dangerous civilisation. Meanwhile, the human race had fallen from its peak of twenty-seven occupied star systems to a less-than-majestic five. The rest of mankind's colonies had been claimed or destroyed. After today, they'd be down to four. Temporarily, they hoped.

In all that time, Sol was the first star system to be deliberately conceded. Mars and the other home system colonies had shut up shop years before as effectively indefensible. And for a while after that, it looked like the consolidation of forces on Earth had worked. Then, just weeks ago, they'd received word of another attempted takeover.

The planet's surface had been seeded with a fresh wave of Phote spores and some of them had made it down into the Pacific Warrens. The number of spontaneous bacterial conversions was rising and the infected were gathering to form terrorist cells faster than the local death squads could root them out. So Earth's government had called for immediate evacuation.

Ann's team had sent a diplomat down to liaise with the government heads, to calm the authorities and try for a new approach. The Earthers, though, were already too deep into panic. Something had changed in Phote strategy, they insisted. Transport lines were being choked off again. The frequency of raids kept climbing. Everyone was talking about a *Third Surge*.

After what they'd all seen during the Suicide War a decade ago, Earth's leaders weren't about to take any chances. So, with great reluctance and no small amount of bitterness, the Galatean military had coordinated an extraction.

'I have the signal from shuttle command,' said Cy, Ann's communications officer. His voice cracked as he spoke. 'Earth is cleared. Ready to commence Phase Three.'

'Initiate,' said Ann. 'Let's get it done.'

Moving thirty million people out of the gravity well in nine hours had not been easy. To facilitate the operation, the population of Earth had been issued with personal coma-kits and packed into bunker-boxes the size of sports stadia. Then they'd been foamed in situ with a fast-setting hyper-elastic matrix almost as light as a modern aerogel.

There'd been panic, of course, and some resistance. But the warrens were due to be gassed to ensure that no human hosts remained for the Photes to exploit. The threat of imminent death had served as an effective incentive to cooperate.

During Phase One, the massive container stacks had been brought out of habitats on macrotracks and handed off to superlifters originally designed to relocate whole arcotowers without disassembly. The process had run surprisingly close to schedule. Nevertheless, Ann had hated every gruelling minute of the wait.

In Phase Two, fleets of industrial scoop-shuttles on strat-scraping dives had coupled and seized the superlifter loads. The lifters' LTA envelopes had been trashed in the process, of course, but with nobody going home, cost wasn't an issue. The operation would be one of the most expensive the human race had ever conducted.

'What's our attrition rate?' said Ann.

'We're running at less than sixty parts per mil,' said Phlox grimly. 'Better than the model mean. About as good as we could hope for.'

In other words, the impact-foam approach had worked. About eighteen hundred deaths had resulted from almost drowning everyone in aerated smart-polymer, followed by the bone-smashing speed of shuttle intercept. Only eighteen hundred human lives snuffed out before even leaving their home. Probably only a few hundred orphaned children. A great result by any rational measurement.

In Phase Three, the scoop-shuttles handed off their precious cargos to vast, purpose-built evac-arks so that they could be ferried to the out-system for carrier pickup. And that was where it got difficult.

Human worlds never faced direct attack. It was too easy to trash them and the Photes needed their converts alive. Consequently, the Utopia subverted colonies instead, or absorbed them wholesale once support lines were cut off and defences knocked out.

A population on the move, though, invited a very different kind of fighting. Arks made easy targets for direct, violent absorption. Hence, Phase Three was when the Photes were most likely to strike.

Unfortunately, evac-arks weren't fast. They lacked warp, which meant that even with tap-torch engines and constant acceleration as high as their human cargo could handle, exit would take days. And there were so many spies embedded within Earth's population already that the likelihood of word of their timing having leaked was high.

The Photes might intercept at any moment. For all Ann's team knew, the out-system they were headed for might already be crawling with stealthed enemy drones. So at some point over the next seventy hours or so, the pace of events would likely go from interminably dull to horrifyingly fast. Human minds didn't operate well under those conditions. Without artificial support, her team were likely to burn themselves out worrying before any trouble hit.

Fortunately, Ann hadn't been human for years. She didn't get lonely or impatient the way other people did – not since her change. Which was why her ship was taking point for the hardest part of the mission. Still, her team would probably need a little encouragement.

Ann opened her eyes and partially decoupled her mind from the *Ariel Two*'s helm-space. Her shadow took up the slack while she surveyed her crew at work.

There wasn't much to look at in the *Ariel Two*'s main cabin these days. Simple grey wall-screens running neon agitation patterns lined the dimly lit spherical chamber. Set in a ring around the floor were six military-grade support-couches. Each resembled a cross between a recliner and a coffin designed by a committee of art nouveau enthusiasts and paranoid survivalists. Besides Ann's, only three others were occupied.

Cy Twebo, a muscular, soft-faced young man, ran communications. Phlox Orm, a svelte little herm with dark, intense features covered data aggregation. Urmi Kawasaki, a quiet woman from the lower levels with a giraffe pigment-job, managed their unruly stable of threat models. Ann didn't know any of them well.

For years now, the Galatean government had been handing her these tightly knit triples to work with, specially trained to pilot the nestship in the supremely unlikely event of her demise. They never stuck around for long. This bunch, at least, accepted the way Ann ran things. Or perhaps they'd simply been briefed to not get in her way this time. There was too much at stake.

'Team,' said Ann.

All three opened their eyes in surprise.

'I'm proud of you all,' she said. 'What we're doing here is beyond difficult. And Phase Three is going to be a bitch. So remember that I admire you all, and that I have the utmost confidence in your abilities. Any comments or recommendations before we go to slow-time?'

They regarded each other with tense, sad eyes.

'No,' said Cy, their unofficial spokesperson. 'We're good.'

'Okay,' said Ann. 'And does everyone have their amygdala-gating on max?'

Her crew nodded.

'Good,' said Ann. 'Because you're going to need it.'

She thought about adding, *Don't worry, we'll get the Earth back.* But nobody would have believed her.

'Let's get to work,' she said instead and shut her eyes.

From time to time, someone claimed that the *Ariel Two* was undermanned or that Ann's leadership style was too remote. They didn't know what they were talking about. The cellular augmentation she'd received on Snakepit enabled her to run the entire ship on her own. It was hard enough just finding things for her mandatory three backup officers to do. Having more people aboard only made things worse. They got in the way and reduced her acceleration thresholds. And after all, Ann wasn't there to chit-chat. She was there to atone. She'd only made one big mistake in her life, but that choice had unleashed the Photes against humanity. As fuck-ups went, hers had been galaxy-class.

She brought up an immersive view of local space to watch the shuttles creeping out to their respective arks. There were three of them in all, each guarded by an attendant battle cruiser. Accompanying the *Ariel Two* were a couple of new Orson-class planet-busters armed to the teeth with grater-grids and boser canons. They loomed like sinister moons.

'Cy, signal Angels Two and Three,' said Ann. 'Prep for departure. We'll be going silent in ten. Tell them good luck.'

To minimise risk, Ann's team had brought dummy arks. Three separate ships would head to different extraction points in the out-system. Only one of them, though, would be carrying people – the one Ann was watching. The other two were decoys, turning the entire operation into a shell game.

As soon as all the shuttles had docked, Ann made her next move.

'Engaging stealth-cloak,' she told the others.

For a ship as large as the *Ariel Two*, a cloak only bought you so much. With two hundred and forty kilometres of elastoceramic alloy hull to hide, they'd still be visible by virtue of their gravity footprint. But that was part of the point. With luck, the escorts would draw attention from the far smaller arks. Their enemies, unfortunately, would be operating under stealth, too. If battle commenced, it would be fought mostly blind.

With stately deliberation, the arks all left orbit and headed out. *Ariel* and the other two escorts took up position beside their respective charges and left alongside them.

'Commencing mine-drop sequence,' she told her crew.

After all, if you were abandoning a habitat world, what was the point of *not* turning it into a deathtrap on your way out?

'Okay, everyone,' she said, 'we'll be running in shifts from here to Jupiter orbit. Somebody take a nap.'

Ann handed off as much control to her shadow as she dared and put her mind on slow. There was no point burning mental cycles on dead time when half her brain could be resting.

Their progress appeared to accelerate dramatically. As the Earth shrank behind them, Ann watched it through electronic eyes and whispered goodbye to the famous cradle of humanity.

10

As she did so, a memory sprang to mind: the moment years ago when she left her flat on Galatea to move to New Panama. She'd stood on the threshold and looked back across the scruffy floor-turf at the soft marks where her furniture had so recently stood. That moment had filled her with an unexpected wistfulness even though she'd been madly keen to leave. This moment had a lot in common with that, once you factored in the dread of impending combat.

She bit back a sigh. It was at times like this that she missed Poli and the kids the most. They probably weren't missing her, thankfully. Nobody missed weird Aunt Andromeda that much. She was gone too often.

[It's ridiculous,] she told her shadow. [Why should I feel sad? The Earth's been barren for decades. The ocean trenches host more life than the surface. It's just another colony.]

[Symbolism,] it replied. Ann still heard it speaking in Will's voice, though her shadow had long since become more an echo of her own mind than his. [Plus, it's depressing. If you don't look too close, it's hard to tell that intelligent life was ever here. We didn't exactly make much of a mark on this system in the end. Ceres is a mess, of course, but that's been true since the first war. And Saturn's rings are all fucked up, but they were delicate in the first place. They weren't even doing well before the Photes arrived.] These days, the planet only had a band of haze. [Even Mars looks practically untouched,] her shadow said bitterly. [The bomb craters are just like all the others.]

[Wow, you're a comfort,] she told it.

[I'm part of you. What did you expect?]

Ann snorted in amusement. Her sadness was blurring into optimism as the minutes raced past without attack. Amazingly, no one had fired on them yet and fifty hours had passed already.

On cue, her ship made its last pseudo-random course-correction and emitted another decoy drone designed to leak a dummy engine signature. Then it began its final deceleration. As the time since Earth departure closed in on three objective days, Ann approached their rendezvous point.

They were two hours behind schedule by then. Which meant that things were amazingly quiet. In fact, now that she thought about it, they were *too* quiet. On the upside, nobody – barring the inevitable attrition

11

victims – had died. On the downside, it suggested that something sinister was going on that they hadn't accounted for. Again.

Ann reluctantly swapped to normal time.

'Cy,' she said. 'Any sign of a signal?'

She had to wait a moment for her communications officer to return to undiluted awareness. She listened to him groan. Ordinary humans didn't take well to radical changes in mental pacing, not even those with military-grade shadow support.

'Not yet,' he croaked. 'Resampling now.'

Ann scowled. Given the immense areas involved and the horrific difficulties of arranging schedules over interstellar distances, some slack in the system was to be expected. Particularly with Mark Ruiz as the carrier pilot. The delay, though, was not welcome.

Ann lay scowling for an hour or so, checking her systems and surveying the dark, knowing full well it was pointless. Reluctantly, she slid her mind back into a slower gear to wait. She regretted it almost instantly as the blinding flare of a carrier burst appeared.

Ann kicked herself up into combat time, cursing. The flash had originated relatively close to where Mark was supposed to show, but was still light-minutes away from the expected target. That far out, it was hard to tell the difference between a friendly carrier and a deadly one.

'Cy,' she said. 'Scan it. Everyone on full alert.'

The ship's main audio chattered briefly as Cy's signal-processing SAPs scrambled over their EM buffers. Then a soft voice started oozing through the cabin's speakers.

'In Photuria, there is no fear, no pain, no death,' it whispered. 'Instead, there is perfect love and perfect joy.' Images appeared on the wall-screen of blissed-out couples walking hand in hand through soft, white tunnels, tears of happiness running down their handsome faces.

'Fuck,' Ann snarled. The Photes always sent a love letter before they started harvesting. They didn't seem able to prevent themselves from announcing their arrival. So, these days, they did it as quietly as they could.

Light was slow. In the time it had taken the message to reach them, the Photes had no doubt been stealing out across the system with warp-enabled munitions, locking it down. The question was where to head for. Ann selected Mark's backup coordinates and prayed he wasn't already dead. She tight-beamed the course-correction to her ark and fired off a fresh set of decoys. Then she woke the titan mechs slumbering in her outer mesohull and prepped them for close-quarters combat.

Unless Mark showed up soon, they were screwed. All their careful planning would be for nothing. They'd be dead. In fact, they'd be worse than dead. The Photes would have thirty million new bodies to play with.

1.3: MARK

Mark Ruiz paced the drawing room, hands clasped tightly behind his back. His eyes darted to the grandfather clock in the corner every few seconds. From the antique sofa near the bay window that looked out across the grounds, his wife Zoe eyed him anxiously as she sipped her tea.

'Marching about won't get us there any faster, you know,' she said, rearranging her skirts. 'Why don't you come and sit with me? We can play cards.'

'I can't sit,' said Mark. 'Not even virtually.'

She set her cup down. 'Fine. Do you want to drop back into physical? Would that help? We have to be down to minutes, anyway.'

Mark shook his head. 'It wouldn't make any difference. Besides, we'll have to be fully dunked the moment we drop warp.'

Zoe sighed and stared off across the lawn to where a flock of geese were alighting on the lake. In truth, their shared fiction was doing as little for her mood as it was for his.

Their butler stepped in bearing a silver tray and another china teapot. 'Would sir and madam like a second cup?'

'Not now, Shaw,' said Zoe and offlined his program with a click of her fingers. 'Honestly,' she muttered, 'you can't get the help these days.' She rubbed her virtual eyes.

Beyond the imaginary confines of his home, Mark reclined on an immersion-couch in the tiny main cabin of the GSS *Gulliver*, a forty-kilometre-wide starship. Surrounding the *Gulliver* lay the immense, filigree-delicate warp-envelope of the embership *Kraken*, which Mark was urgently piloting with an army of subminds.

The *Kraken* was more soap bubble than starship. Six insubstantial strands of rotating ion-deployment cable maintained a sphere of tailored pseudo-vacuum about six nanometres thick and nine hundred kilometres across. While he fretted, they tore across space at several kilolights, on their way to rescue the population of Earth. And they were late.

Mark hated that he'd missed his arrival window. But the fury he felt at the Galatean government's antics dwarfed that self-loathing. He'd made the right choice, for all the trouble it had brought him.

Just hours before he was due to depart, Mark had received a private briefing composed by Ann's lead diplomat, marked for his eyes only. It contained a detailed summary of the battle plan's final version, along with a little supplementary data.

Buried within that data had lain evidence that the Earth's population was being quietly split. A hundred thousand volunteers had been allocated to one of the dummy evac-arks. That way, the government had reasoned, whichever of the arks the Photes focused their attack on, *some* people were likely to get out alive. And from the survivors, Galatea would be able to reconstruct the Photes' new infection pattern, potentially saving millions more.

The decision made sense in a high-handed kind of way. Galatea stood to gain vital tactical information at the estimated cost of a mere hundred thousand innocents – peanuts in terms of recent losses.

Mark, however, wasn't ready to sacrifice those lives. The decision smacked to him of exactly the sort of cold, mechanical logic that the remaining human societies had been driven to. The moment he realised the plan's intent, he'd made up his mind to rescue everyone, not just the people the government had picked to survive. And when he showed the details to Zoe, it had taken him all of about one second to convince her.

'Fuck that shit,' she'd growled. 'They bait-and-switched us *again*? Everyone's leaving with us. Where can we get more guns?'

So Mark had detoured to St Andrews, which was *almost* en route, called in the necessary favours and loaded the *Kraken*'s envelope full of warp-enabled attack drones. In doing so, he'd burned up all the spare time incorporated into the meticulously engineered Galatean plan.

Had Mark and Zoe been full Galatean citizens, their act would already have constituted a war crime. But the *Kraken* flew under the diplomatic colours of the Vartian Institute, which gave him a little room to manoeuvre.

Unfortunately, he knew that once he rendezvoused with Ann, she'd make it impossible for him to go back for the others. Ann was a stickler for process, as inflexible as she was remote. So the secret volunteers had to be rescued first, and fast enough that there would still be a primary ark to collect once he'd finished. If he couldn't manage that, all his efforts would be for nothing. Mark's desperate gambit required split-second timing of a sort that had already gone badly wrong.

Of all his recent disagreements with the Galatean government, this would undoubtedly prove the most divisive. But weren't they supposed to be human beings, for crying out loud, not dead-eyed Photes? Wasn't compassion what defined them? If they couldn't preserve their humanity, what was the point of fighting?

And therein lay the irony. After forty years of unrelenting social change, Mark didn't like the humans he was saving all that much. Most of them bought into the same jackbooted bullshit he despised. The human cultures he worked to protect had all adopted the same militarised outlook to survive. They barely noticed how blinkered they'd become.

So Mark and Zoe had used the freedom their station in life afforded them to build a kingdom of two aboard the *Gulliver*. While running errands for the Galateans, they'd stuck to their own ideal of what society could be and invited others to join them. The risk profile of their existence dissuaded most. Yet, ironically, they'd remained young and alive while most of their friends had died.

Their tiny kingdom was based on tolerance. Zoe tolerated his moods, just as she always had. And he tolerated her distance, even when she retreated into silent study for days on end. That was how it should be with everyone, he reasoned. He didn't need to understand people to want them alive and neither did she. It took all sorts to make a world, and so he was going to save as many sorts as he could.

He felt the tremor of impending arrival like a shiver of dread and glanced across to where Zoe slouched glumly in her Edwardian evening gown.

'Get ready,' he told her.

As the *Kraken* reached its first insertion point, Mark dropped out of his virtual home and into the *Gulliver*'s helm-arena with Zoe alongside him. The drawing room vanished, replaced by an immersive tactical display of local space.

15

A spray of red markers filled the air like the blood-spatter of a particularly nasty crime scene. The place was crawling with Phote drones, and those were only the ones he could see. Hundreds more undoubtedly still lay cloaked. Most of the trouble swarmed around the green disc of the Orson-class guardian ship, thank Gal. The ark – Mark's prize – hung off to the side, as yet unseen. If there was one thing evac-arks were good at, it was remaining unnoticed.

Zoe initiated a release burst, firing a thousand drones of their own into the fray – all of them on intercept vectors. She couldn't resist adding a Phote-style arrival message of her own.

'Good morning, undead fuckwits,' she announced cheerfully. 'Here's some pain to go with your endless joy.'

That got their attention. Two hundred Phote munitions dropped into visibility and powered towards the *Kraken* at full warp.

An ordinary pilot would have lost their lunch in that moment. A carrier was an appallingly fragile piece of technology. Two disc-shaped ships joined by six feathered skipping ropes spun about a shared axis. Manoeuvring without warp was almost impossible. Manoeuvring *with* warp was nearly as challenging. Mark wasn't worried. He had more years of practice than any other person alive and a roboteer brain designed for space combat. He could make an embership dance like a hummingbird.

He threw the *Kraken* back into high spin, sealed up the warp-envelope and dived on the drifting evac-ark. He opened the envelope for less than a second to let the ship slide between his ferociously whirling inducer-fronds and sneaked back into warp before the ark pilot even knew what had happened.

Finding itself suddenly enclosed, the ark thruster-braked frantically in an attempt to zero its conventional velocity.

While Mark raced outwards again to his second pickup location, the ark's captain yelled at him over the audio channel.

'Embership *Kraken*! What in Gal's name are you doing?' she shouted. 'This action is off-mission and highly dangerous. I repeat: *off-mission*!'

'Understood, Earth Ark Two,' said Mark, 'and apologies for the confusion, but you happen to be carrying a hundred thousand sacrificial volunteers I want saved.'

He saw no reason to beat about the bush. The captain should know that he understood exactly what was going on.

There was a short, confused pause from the ark.

'Captain Ruiz,' breathed the ark captain. 'What are you talking about? This ship has a skeleton crew of three. The only passenger on this ship is the *bomb*, as originally planned. We received no human passengers. Is this some kind of plan update of which we were not informed?'

Mark froze. His cheeks tingled. Maybe the captain was bluffing.

'Did you say *bomb*?' said Zoe. 'That detail was not in our mission pack.'

'Yes, *of course* a bomb!' the captain cried. 'A bomb now armed by your manoeuvre. The only sacrificial volunteers here are my team, and we now have three minutes before ignition.'

'Can you jettison?' Mark blurted.

'What are you talking about?' said the captain. 'The bomb is our reactor core, as ordered. Tell me – do we have a backup ark? Who is rendezvousing with Ark One? Please tell me we have a dedicated ship for Ark One. Please!'

Mark's mind fizzed over the awful implications.

'We've been compromised,' said Zoe quietly. 'Holy fuck. We're compromised.'

Mark's mouth tasted of ashes. The weight of thirty million human lives landed on his conscience.

1.4: ANN

Though there was nothing to see yet, Ann steeled herself for the inevitable fight. Somewhere out there in the dark, thousands of Phote drones were swarming, bearing down on her ship on silent wings of twisted gravity.

'Estimated time to engagement – four minutes,' said Urmi. Her voice tightened towards a squeak. 'Models ramping to battle mode.'

Ann felt that dark, familiar thrill of anticipation and prepared to engage in the one true source of pleasure life had left her: *cleaning*.

She understood the ironic implications of that image. After one career in military intelligence and a second in frontline combat, that she should gravitate to such a gendered and archaic metaphor amused her. But that's what it felt like. It felt as if the universe had a vile, infected stain upon it. And her job was to scrub it out. Scrub, scrub, scrub. Time to make everything nice and clean and dead.

She gritted her teeth and kept her hunger in check. Once the urge to clean up took hold of her, it would be insatiable, and they couldn't afford for the fight to turn bright just yet. There were bystanders at risk.

She breathed deep and edged the *Ariel Two* away from the ark it sheltered. Then she opened her quantcomm link to its captain.

'Captain Bach,' she said, 'please head directly for the backup insertion site at full thrust. We will remain here to engage the enemy. The moment you see any signs of trouble, flag me immediately.'

'Is that a good idea, ma'am?' said Cy. 'They'll be sitting ducks.'

'If they stay near us they'll get crisped,' said Ann. 'Focus on your job, please, Mr Twebo. Let me handle the hellfire. It's what I do.'

As well as defending its ark, Ann's nestship doubled as a magnet for enemy drones. The *Ariel Two* was too large to not be noticed, even when running dark. They'd close on her ship from its mass footprint alone. Ann felt the first wave of munitions almost as soon as she saw them. They impacted against her ship's metallic skin like myriad tiny insect bites. These days, the Photes had burrowing drones designed to quietly take over a ship's systems through direct hull incursion. They'd become a standard weapon in the enemy arsenal.

While Ann had a quantum shield that would keep them at bay, she dared not use it with the ark so close. The moment she sealed up, the battle would get hot. Instead, she let the drones drill nasty little holes in her exohull. Fortunately, the *Ariel Two* had recently been upgraded to include a standing army of eight thousand titan mechs designed for mesohull combat. Ann activated them and felt fragments of her mind rushing into their giant, armoured bodies.

This was the power that had once been Will's – to be in many places at once. In effect, Ann could become a hierarchically organised megamind spanning her entire ship. Compact sketches of her consciousness guided every machine in the hull, filtering their input upwards so that what she herself felt was an ensemble of them all.

She glimpsed herself in a hundred different physical formats as her minions booted. She flexed claws and readied cannons while her mechs slid around the ship's radioactive interior on magnetic tracks, positioning themselves at every incursion site. Ready to say hello.

'Battle positions,' she told her crew.

There wasn't much for her team to do but watch and hold on tight. That wasn't likely to be fun, but no one had asked them to volunteer.

Ann gently pivoted the *Ariel's* immense bulk, thruster-braked and counted down the seconds for the ark to get clear.

'All right,' she said brightly. 'Cleaning time!'

Ann launched a barrage of plasma-shells. The space around the *Ariel* blazed with pale light, the hundreds of drones sidling up to her standing out as pinpoint shadows. At the same moment, Ann fired up her shield. Half of the burrowing drones died instantly as the entanglement field swept across their bodies, swamping them in coherent iron. The other half found themselves surrounded by robots twenty times their size. They were promptly ripped apart. Each savage dismemberment hit Ann with a flash of satisfaction.

Her mind greedily sucked down the attack pattern of the incoming drones, prepped a response and fired on them all simultaneously. She used the *Ariel's* massive g-ray banks running in a classic slice-and-dice pattern, swiping the beams left and right through the enemy ranks to maximise coverage. They died in droves.

So far so good, but the Photes hadn't brought out any big guns yet. And while she fought, a corner of Ann's mind watched the ark creeping towards the backup rendezvous where still no carrier awaited to rescue them.

She felt a fresh rush of anger towards Mark. The little shit had never stuck to a mission plan in all the years she'd known him. There always had to be some clever addition of his own to prove that Galatea didn't own him. She'd hoped that this time, at least, he'd figure out the stakes. It was a miracle Galatea had even given him the job. She should have challenged that choice. One of these days, if they got through this, she was going to push her index finger through Mark's skull, nice and slow.

Another carrier burst lit up Ann's sensors from far across the system's edge.

'Incoming hail,' said Cy. 'It's another bogey.'

'Peace and security are but moments away,' came the Photes' soothing message. 'Let us share our love with you.'

'That's a burst from somewhere near the Ark Three's position,' said Phlox. 'They must know the plan. They're on to us.'

'Of course they're on to us,' Ann growled. 'Have you only just figured that out?'

Light-lag made it impossible for her to know how the rest of the battle was proceeding. It would be hours before they learned. However, it wasn't hard to guess that things were going pear-shaped system-wide. She had just one ace up her sleeve. That long, ridiculous flight from Earth on conventional acceleration meant she still had a suntap link open. So long as they didn't warp, they'd never run out of firepower.

The fresh arrival spurred the Photes to higher levels of frenzy. Hundreds more drones dropped stealth and hurled themselves at the *Ariel*'s quantum shield in an attempt to overload it. Ann scythed them out of existence.

Her ship shook as the space around it became a torrent of boiling plasma. She watched the lurking ark get buffeted by the shock waves with dismay. At this rate, it'd be noticed simply by virtue of being too near the battle's glare.

She flicked the ark-channel open again.

'Bach, head back in-system. It's the one direction the Photes won't expect you to go.'

'Captain!' Cy blurted. 'That'll take them out of pickup range.'

'Shut it!' Ann snapped. 'I know what I'm doing.'

She turned her attention outwards, looking for the Photurian carrier that had to be hidden somewhere near their entry flash. If she couldn't defend the ark, she at least wanted to deny the Photes a route out.

'Urmi, give me a probability map for the nearest carrier's position,' she said. 'Tell me where they're hiding.'

'Factoring residual velocity vectors,' said Urmi. 'Here it comes.'

A new distribution diagram bloomed in Ann's tactical overlay. She realigned her g-rays and swept that region of space with her forward sensors on max to watch for light-bounce. Nineteen seconds later, something flickered in the dark.

'Got the bastard,' said Ann.

She grouped her fire, ramped it and reduced the carrier to radioactive shrapnel. She grinned as she watched it burn. Still, there'd be a price to pay. If the Photes couldn't leave with hosts, their next priority would be to knock out her ship. They'd want the ark unguarded for the next attack wave that found it.

Right on cue, a dozen Phote harvester ships shaped like monstrous bacteriophages uncloaked and fired up quantum shields of their own. Their hulls' integuments ran like wax, coating and transforming them into flickering ovals of bright silver. Ann knew those wouldn't be normal shields. They'd be *cyclers*. Each ship had about a one per cent chance of hitting phase with the *Ariel*'s shield and sliding through as if it wasn't there. Once inside, they'd detonate, trashing everything inside.

Ann glared at the oncoming ships and warmed her primary boser for some serious pyrotechnics. In the back of her head, it occurred to her that whatever happened out here, the Earth already belonged to the Photes. The sheer scale of the attack had seen to that. There was no going back. If it came to it, Ann knew she'd have to execute the Earth's population herself rather than let them fall into enemy hands.

'Not again,' she muttered. 'Come on, Mark, you bastard. Just get here. Please.'

1.5: MARK

Mark's mouth went dry as he realised just how well his enemy had played him. They'd used his urgency to save lives against him and tweaked the report he'd received just enough to send him chasing after a bomb. He'd undoubtedly spared the lives of thousands of Phote horrors the bomb had been meant for, as well as jeopardising Zoe's and his own.

But how had the Photes done it? The report he'd received had come directly from the diplomat on Ann's team, who Ann had personally screened. And Photes didn't get past Andromeda Ng-Ludik. They just didn't. Her whole body was one giant Phote-detecting machine.

Mark reopened the channel to the time-bomb ark nestled beside the *Gulliver* within the *Kraken*'s whirling warp-envelope.

'Ark Two, this is Captain Ruiz,' he said. 'Your data has been factored into our battle plan. Please prepare your engines for immediate departure. Direct your ship at the closest available exit vector and commence a full burn. Do not spare the juice. We're going to drop you off hot.'

'What?' came the reply. Nobody started their engines inside a warp-envelope. Not unless they wanted to have a very nasty accident.

'I said, get ready to leave!' said Mark. 'Start boosting *now*!'

'You're crazy,' she told him. 'We'll hit the envelope field and detonate.'

'If you don't, you'll detonate anyway!' Mark yelled. 'So go!'

After another two seconds' hesitation, the ark powered up and hurled itself at the delicate interior wall of the *Kraken*'s enclosure. Mark dropped warp with seconds to spare, threw all his awareness into the embership's processors and slowed the spin on his warp-fronds as much as he could without tangling them.

The ark ripped between the hurtling jump-ropes. Fragments of broken warp-front spun out into the dark, venting plasma as the ark sped past them into the empty space beyond. Mark avoided a full cable breach by a few scant metres.

'What about the crew?' said Zoe.

'What about them?' Mark snapped. 'They haven't exactly left us a rescue option. Unless you think that evac-ark has lifeboat tubes.'

They both knew it didn't. Lifeboat facilities made ships too easy to invade. These days, nobody had them.

Mark ramped the power and went superlight as the seconds to ark-detonation slid to zero. He left just before it hit so never got to see it explode. Instead, the ark appeared to freeze. Then, as the embership gathered warp, the view from behind showed a wavering image of his own departure reversed. Mark felt sick anyway. He didn't need visual evidence to know what had happened.

Worse than making the mistake was the knowledge that in dumping the ark between insertion sites, he'd made it obvious to everyone in the system where he was headed. He could only hope that it would take so long for the light from the blast to reach the other Phote ships that it wouldn't make a difference.

He dived around the outer depths of the home system, scraping the upper edge of the *Kraken*'s operational limits all the way. With a grim eye, he watched the stability indicators from envelope-control quiver into the red.

'You're going to break this ship before we get there,' Zoe warned.

Mark didn't reply. He wished for the thousandth time that ember-ships weren't so hopeless at in-system travel. Carriers were supposed to show up at the perimeter of a system, do their business and leave. The filthy flow of ions generated by a star made travel within a heliopause slow and miserable. Only an idiot tried taking a carrier to multiple points around the same star. Somehow, Mark found himself needing to do it all the time.

'Let's hope we haven't also been lied to about what's at the Ark One site,' said Zoe.

Mark grimaced.

'Battle-modelling SAPs are online,' she said. 'Scanning our insertion point.'

The *Gulliver*'s bank of strategic intelligences filtered the shreds of light leaking through the envelope and used them to construct a picture of what waited ahead. It wasn't pretty. With the timescales compressed by their approach, the flashes of combat blurred into a crazed strobing of immense explosions.

'At least we know someone's there,' said Mark.

'Someone who's nuking things,' said Zoe. 'It's Ann all right.'

Mark felt a stab of bitterness. Even if they saved everyone, Ann would never let him forget this. It'd be one more thing for them to fight about.

He dropped warp at the rendezvous site.

'Go!' he yelled. 'Fire!'

Zoe ejected the remainder of their attack drones while he desperately swept local space for signs of their cargo. There was no ark nearby, though the *Ariel Two* was uncloaked and obvious, engaged in a firefight with a huge irradiated cloud of enemy ships and munitions. Neither ship was in their allocated position, though that was hardly surprising. The situation was badly out of control.

He grabbed the audio channel.

'Ark One, this is Mark Ruiz,' he said. 'Prepare for immediate pickup. As soon as we have your location we will cover your approach.'

Ann's reply was a stream of invective over open audio.

Then, as Mark watched, Ark One maxed out its tap-torches and headed straight for him, revealing its location for all to see in its urgency to escape. Several hundred Phote drones pivoted to converge.

Mark groaned. The ark was dangerously far away, in the worst of all possible directions. It'd be touch and go whether it reached the carrier's waiting arms before the Photes got them.

'On it,' said Zoe. She slewed their fleet of drones around, creating a shield for the ark's approach. 'Commencing soft assault,' she added.

'Good luck with that,' Mark muttered. These days, Photurian security was almost uncrackable.

'Got to be worth a try,' said Zoe. 'We have to do *something*.'

'Fair point,' said Mark. 'How about this?'

He realigned the *Kraken*'s envelope and tried to nudge closer to the ark on bursts of ember-warp. It was like trying to tease a kayak through rapids with a jet engine.

He'd barely started before six Phote gunships flashed into local space, no doubt drawn by Mark's exploding signpost. They immediately took on the *Ariel Two*, pinning it and spreading its fire. A fresh cloud of drones splayed out across space, aiming to block Mark's escape vectors.

Mark fought down a sickly surge of panic. This wasn't a rescue, it was a disaster. Earthers be damned. They'd be lucky if *any* of them got out alive.

1.6: ANN

By the time Mark finally appeared, the *Ariel Two* was struggling. Eight harvesters had made suicide dives against her shields. Ann had skewered five of them with boser blasts. The other three made impact before imploding. While they hadn't dented her ship, the wear on her power-management systems was getting scary.

A nestship's shield worked by holding the atoms of the exohull in a state of quantum agitation. Their nuclei temporarily materialised in the way of any attempted attack, effectively cladding the ship in neutronium armour. It was a furiously unlikely state for matter in the first place, and one only made possible by borrowed Transcended technology.

Forcing two such quantum-ensembles with conflicting phases into direct contact made the machinery unhappy, it turned out. Sprays of molecular iron accelerated to near-light-speed kept shearing off from the contact points like rail-gun slugs.

With her tap-link to Sol still intact, Ann wasn't going to run out of power any time soon. But her shield generators could still give out as they struggled to do more with less material. Their shrieking already filled the hull.

Ann felt a moment of profound relief when she saw the gamma-burst of Mark's arrival, followed by a surge of apoplectic rage.

'At last!' she roared into the audio channel. 'Where in Gal's name have you been? How many people have to *die* for you to get out of bed, you fucking *asshole*!'

Ann's tirade was choked off by the need to move quickly. Mark had brought company. Lots of it. Phote gunships burst onto the scene and started firing bosers of their own, straining her weakened shield. All through the mesohull, power-couplings the size of apartment blocks started blowing out. The screaming and rumbling of dying machinery was so loud through the cabin walls that she could barely think.

Ann brought her g-ray banks to bear on the closest gunship and threw lances of radiation at it before it could raise shields. It erupted in a cloud of superheated slag. She turned her attention to the next, and the next, but with each shift in target, she lost power as more couplings blew. Every failed junction put more strain on those that remained.

'We have to get out of here!' Cy warned her. 'The power network is going into cascade failure.'

Ann spat curses, turned her ship and boosted towards the erratically twitching sphere of light that was *Kraken*'s envelope. She focused her fire on the drones attacking the ark, while the gunships pounded her back. She dearly hoped that Mark had some kind of exit manoeuvre in mind. The embership wouldn't last a second under the kind of pounding the *Ariel* had just taken.

As soon as Mark claimed the ark, he rerouted his munitions fleet to protect the *Ariel*, but it was too little too late. It would take entire seconds for them to arrive and their g-rays didn't bother the Phote gunships for a moment. Ann sprayed the oncoming enemies with erratic boser fire, desperate to keep them on the back foot for as long as possible.

The enemy twisted and darted, burning juice in oblivious abandon as they screamed towards her. They kept firing the entire time.

The *Ariel*'s power system shrieked, whistled and died completely one long second before the embership's fronds reached for her. Deep booms rumbled through the hull as the primary energy circuits collapsed. Ann held her breath.

Then, miraculously, before the Photes could target again, that wall of pale fire slid around her and all was quiet. The envelope shuddered once, twice, and was still. Its flickering became a smooth, even blur. Ann still didn't dare breathe.

'We're out,' came the signal from the *Gulliver*. 'Extraction complete.'

Ann sat perfectly still and exhaled for several long seconds without saying a word. Only then did it occur to her to open her human eyes.

Three terrified young officers sat facing her, surrounded by glaring radiation warnings on the wall-screens. Somewhere in the conflict she'd apparently lost power to the secondary Casimir-buffers and radiation had started leaking into the cabin. Not an issue for her, but her crew would need rad-scrubbing and a fast round of anti-cancer treatment if they wanted to live. Ann's fury at Mark came back redoubled.

'Captain Ruiz,' she growled into the open channel. 'How nice of you to drop by.'

'Spare me the righteous fury,' said Mark. 'We thought you'd split the population – one ark for rescue and another for emergency backup. We were trying to compensate.'

'Where in fuck's name did you get a ridiculous idea like that?' Ann snapped. 'How would that even work, for crying out loud? What kind of people do you think we are? And in any case, if you'd wanted to change the plan, why didn't you just say so? You know what I hate? I hate being the one stuck in the role of uncaring soldier because I *actually follow orders*. Because I take my responsibilities to others seriously rather than mooning about complaining that my freedoms are being impinged. We almost lost eight per cent of what's left of the human goddamned race, you lousy fuck!'

Zoe's voice burst onto the channel. 'Ann, shut up a minute!' she yelled. 'Listen. The false data we received came directly from Ambassador Shue, the negotiator *you* hosted on *Ariel Two*.'

Ann froze. 'What are you talking about?'

'Ambassador Shue,' Zoe repeated. 'On your ship.' The implications belatedly sank home. 'She must have been infected down on Earth,' Zoe added.

'Impossible,' said Ann. 'I'd have—'

'Think about it,' said Zoe. 'If you want to file a complaint against us, go ahead, but the bad data we worked from came from *your ship*. Think about what that means.'

Even though Ann couldn't say it out loud, her crew were already drawing conclusions. They glanced at each other with mounting panic. Shue had been in the primary habitat core with the rest of them. If she'd picked up some kind of Phote infection that Ann couldn't detect, one or more of them might be infected, too. They might be sharing the room with the traitorous undead – someone whose humanity had been unravelling beneath their very noses. Someone already craving the cloying, robotic bliss of the Phote mass-mind and awaiting their chance to force it on the rest of them.

'No,' said Ann. 'We're missing another angle. I'd have smelled it.'

Ann's body was crammed with nano-machinery, her every cell a processing unit augmented with technology almost as smart and subtle as the Photes'. Meanwhile, bacterial conversion required the alien cells to infiltrate the victim's nervous system to map their emotional states before it could even have an effect.

'Seeded takeovers are slow,' Ann insisted. 'It would have needed days. There'd have been a sign. I do regular skin-testing, goddamnit! I'm not an idiot!'

The problem was that the *Ariel Two* didn't carry standard bioassay equipment. Ann's own cellular tech played havoc with it. Which meant that the ship's screening was dependent on her talent. In forty-one years, that had never been an issue.

'Ann,' said Zoe, 'we know Shue got infected and we know you missed it. We're not saying you have a mole in your crew but you *have to check*. They've targeted your biomachinery before. If they've perfected something you can't see, we're all at risk. You need to run a twitch-test. Please.'

Ann's eyes skittered over her crew. None of them looked any different. But then she hadn't exactly paid close attention to them over the last few weeks. Her anger gave way to a sick, sinking feeling that Mark's infuriating wife was right. If Ann missed something now, they might not even get home. And it could go bad at any time. A Phote victim probably wouldn't realise they'd been tainted. Only when the infection was ready to activate would they start entertaining wildly religious notions about universal peace.

Ann reluctantly triggered the emergency testing assembly. Video exploded onto the wall-screens around them.

'Why are we even fighting?' the Phote announcer crooned over the speakers. 'Peace and unity are available *now*! Humanity's hard-fought journey is at a wonderful, beautiful end. Don't you deserve rest? Don't you deserve real happiness at last? You've earned it! Share our love! We ache for your companionship.'

The screens showed a mash of content from the Photes' carefully engineered arrival broadcasts, full of laughter and overjoyed faces, hand-holding and warm hugs. Ann wasn't watching. Her eyes, both natural and electronic, were glued to the faces of her crew, watching for signs of a spontaneous response.

Phlox shuddered and looked away from the barrage.

'Keep watching!' Ann shouted. 'Keep your eyes on those fucking images or I'll rip your lids off.'

The seconds ground into minutes. Nobody spoke. Then Cy's pupils jerked wide, just for a telltale instant. The subtlest of blushes pulsed across his cheeks.

The restraints on Ann's chair flew open. In that second, the thing hiding inside Cy knew the game was up. He unclipped from his couch with superhuman speed and threw himself at Urmi, who started screaming.

His fingers never reached her face. Cy was fast, but Ann was faster. Cy's body bounced off the cabin wall with Ann attached. She pinned him there, the two of them sliding up the curved surface in the negligible gravity.

'Is peace such a bad thing?' he breathed and tried to spit at her. Ann's forehead connected with his skull, smashing it into the padding. She tried to keep the force of impact down so his brain wouldn't splash, and almost succeeded.

Cy's body arched against the wall and went limp.

'Everyone freeze,' Ann told the others while she ramped the venting on the cabin's air. The safety shields on their seats snapped down to protect them from the spatter of Cy's infected flesh.

She ordered a swarm of microbots into the room to collect the pieces of Cy for genetic testing and watched them closely as they combed the air clean.

As soon as it was over, she crumpled into a foetal ball and hung still. She'd liked Cy. Why did it have to be him? She should have run more tests to make sure the others were safe. She'd assumed she had the incursion risk under control.

The young man's life was on her conscience. She chalked it up along with all the others. With an oozing sense of chagrin, she reopened the channel to the *Gulliver*.

'Captain Ruiz,' she said quietly. 'Informing you that the risk is neutralised. Follow-up genetic testing on the other crew members has commenced. Ludik out.'

Ann curled her hands over her head and let the ship silently explain to her all the ways it was broken and burning inside. The *Ariel* would take months to repair. In that respect, it was in far better shape than she was.

[You couldn't have known,] said her shadow. [And we got out. Don't forget that.]

[Shut up,] said Ann. [Don't say a fucking thing.]

2: ALIGNMENT

2.1: WILL

Will regarded the three distorted copies of himself uneasily. The situation bordered on the dreamlike. However, he knew he wouldn't figure out what the hell was going on by standing and staring, so he approached the bar and took a seat beside the others while cold fingers of apprehension played up and down his back.

The woman in the dirndl placed a hot mug of tea in front of him with a smile.

'Thanks,' said Will.

'A splash of soy,' said the woman. 'Just the way you like it, I bet.'

Will took a cautious sip. The tea was excellent. He chose not to ask how come she knew his habits so well. In some sense, the answer was already obvious.

'So,' said the clone with antlers, 'what brings you out here?'

Will fished for an answer. He felt reluctant to reveal the extent of his ignorance.

'Nothing much,' he said warily. 'Exploring, I guess. It's a big planet. How about you?'

'He was hunting me but we got bored,' said Antlers, gesturing at Green. 'Wasn't really working. You know how it goes.'

'You boys shouldn't have bothered with the tuxedos,' said Dirndl. 'Too much social metaphor. You overloaded the setting. Should have picked something easier to run in.'

'That's what *I* said.' Green nudged Antlers in the ribs. 'I still might kill him. I wasted a whole week.'

'Not in my café, you won't,' said Dirndl. 'You can have your cross-bow back when you leave and not before.'

Clearly some joke was being made but Will lacked the context to understand it, so he smiled blandly. Besides, he had plenty to take in besides them. The other copies of him were weird enough to behold, but Will found the sight of the woman particularly distracting. Were these people some kind of plastic-surgery cult? Had they developed a religion that venerated his face and experiences?

There had been those on Earth after the war who'd wanted to treat Will as a deity of sorts, he recalled vaguely, though he struggled to remember why. The idea of worship made his skin crawl, but he preferred it to the other explanation – that they actually *were* copies, that someone had deliberately manufactured different versions of him.

Dirndl spotted him staring and appraised him in a new light.

'So, Will,' said Antlers. 'What's your nick?'

Will shot him a startled look and stayed silent while he tried to figure out what the man meant.

Dirndl noticed. 'I'm Elsa,' she said quickly. 'This is Tars,' she said, pointing to Green. 'And Ronno. And you are...?'

He hovered on the edge of saying *Will*, but they already knew his name. Something else was being asked for. He fumbled for a suitable cognomen. Something that wouldn't immediately give away the fact that he had no idea what they were asking.

'Jason,' he said.

The others froze as if a bomb had just gone off somewhere out of sight.

'Interesting choice,' said Ronno.

'Like the Argonauts, right?' said Elsa brightly. 'I get it.'

'Exactly,' said Will.

Ronno's eyes narrowed slightly. 'So where's your crew?'

'I'm trying something new,' said Will. 'Got bored. You know how it goes.'

What had he said wrong? He contemplated coming clean but the tension in the air made him hold his tongue.

'I think it's time for some pie,' said Elsa. 'Who'd like pie?'

She reached into a small bone-white cabinet, picked out a perfect, steaming slice of raspberry pie and set it on the counter with a clunk. It didn't help.

31

'That looks great,' said Will, trying for enthusiasm. He glanced back at Ronno's sharp, inquisitive expression and tried to improvise. 'Sorry if the "nick" sounds a little off – but who comes to a place like this unless they need to work something out? It's all about privacy, isn't it? I mean, am I going to ask you what you guys intend to do with that crossbow?'

Ronno blinked at him twice, wordless, and burst into laughter. He slapped Will on the back.

'Well said, *Jason*!' he exclaimed. 'We've all got our reasons. It's a difficult world.'

'It sure is!' said Will, grinning woodenly, entirely unsure of what kind of joke he'd just made.

Elsa handed him a fork. Will filled his mouth with food to prevent further interrogation. The others, though, appeared to have lost their appetite for information.

'Big mood-storm last night, wasn't it?' said Tars eventually. 'Biggest I've ever seen. I think they're getting worse.'

'Are you kidding?' said Ronno, stealing another glance at Will. 'Of course they're getting worse. The whole world's going to hell in a handcart.'

'You think it's that bad?' Will asked cautiously.

Ronno arched a sly eyebrow. 'Need you ask?' he said.

'So, Jason,' said Elsa, 'you're doing the wandering thing. It's pretty lonely out there, I bet. You probably haven't checked in for ages.'

'That's exactly right,' said Will.

'It takes some strength, staying out of the loop like that,' she said. 'I have a sister who's interested in that kind of chain. The long-gap stuff, you know? You'd probably get a good rate for it, if you wanted to share. Should I give you her lookup?'

'Sure,' said Will. 'Definitely.'

Elsa pulled out a physical pencil and a slip of dumb-paper. Will hadn't seen such things for decades but tried not to stare. Having a human-manned coffee stand was old-school enough, but lots of Earthers preferred such places.

Elsa scrawled quickly. Then, as she passed it to him, she stumbled. Something clattered beneath the counter.

'That damned crossbow again,' said Elsa.

'Hey!' said Tars, leaning over to look. 'I told you – be careful with that. Have you any idea how long those things take to fab out here?'

Will glanced at the paper as she pressed it hard into his hand.

Get out now! it read. *Alcove two hundred metres, tunnel left. Wait.*

His eyes locked on to hers and the sudden urgency in her gaze astonished him. In the next second, her expression shifted back to chipper as Tars and Ronno ascertained that their crossbow was intact and reclaimed their seats.

'You know, I should go,' said Will, pushing back his pie plate. 'This is probably too much contact for me as it is. If I want to keep my rate up, I mean. Thanks for the tea.'

He stepped away from the bar.

'Wait,' said Ronno, rising. 'One minute—'

'You hold on, antler-boy,' said Elsa, her hands planted on her hips. 'Jason the hermit gets a free snack but you most surely do not. That has to be your third slice. Let's see your scrip. You too, Greedo.'

While the other two fumbled with their pockets, Will strolled casually around the back of the coffee stand, waving his thanks. As soon as he was out of sight, he bolted. Thirty seconds later, shouting erupted behind him.

Will scanned the tunnel as he sprinted through the miniature wood and almost missed the gap Elsa had mentioned. It was hidden by a curious fold in the wall – a kink in the tunnel's lining screened by trees and crammed with blue ferns.

He darted into the damp space, crouched and waited. A minute later, Tars and Ronno jogged by. Tars scanned the forest through his crossbow's sights while Ronno urged him onwards. He'd acquired a large knife from somewhere.

'Down here!' he said. 'I'm sure that *Jason* was a Glitch. He can't have got far.'

Will watched them prowl out of sight, his mind a mess of confusion and outrage. Somebody had better explain to him what was going on soon, or he'd have to beat it out of them.

Ten minutes later, Elsa crept up to the alcove.

'Psst,' she said. 'You in there?'

Will stood, revealing his place among the ferns. Elsa's shoulders sagged in relief.

'I thought they were going to kill you and get you arrested,' she whispered. 'You have no idea what's going on, do you?'

Will grimly shook his head.

'I knew it,' said Elsa, and looked almost excited. She glanced both ways down the tunnel. 'Come with me, back to the café,' she said. 'I'll try to explain. But stay quiet until we get there.'

The two of them sneaked swiftly back to Elsa's coffee stand and entered a small, single-storey building built onto the back of it. Inside lay a small, windowless bedroom with skylights and yellow floral-print wallpaper. The furnishings were ludicrously feminine and not at all what Will had been expecting. She sat on the bed.

'You live here?' said Will.

'Of course,' said Elsa, patting the space beside her. 'Tell me, how much do you remember?'

'There was a conspiracy,' said Will. He remained standing and folded his arms. He didn't feel like relaxing. 'I died.'

'Yes, yes,' said Elsa. 'Go on.'

He filled her in on the rest of what he knew. It wasn't much.

She nodded as she listened. 'Don't worry, you'll remember more,' she said. 'It'll all come back. That's how it goes with your sort, or so I'm told.'

Will frowned at her. 'Now are you going to tell me what's happening?'

Elsa sighed. 'You've got a lot to catch up on. The good news is that I know the end of that story of yours. Your sacrifice was worth it. You spared the human race. And you kept Snakepit safe from the Photurian invasion.'

'Then what am I doing here?' said Will.

'I'll try to make this simple,' said Elsa. 'First to know, you're in a world that only has you on it. Lots and lots of copies of *you*.'

Will's skin crawled at the implications even while his mind rebelled against them.

'I wouldn't exactly call you a copy,' said Will, looking her up and down.

'No,' said Elsa, 'and that's kind of the point. I knew you were a Glitch when you kept staring at me like that. It was as if you'd never seen yourself female before.'

'I hadn't,' said Will.

'Exactly,' replied Elsa with a dry smile. 'You'll have to get used to it, I'm afraid. Nearly fifty per cent of us are, these days. It's a popular adjustment. Very much in demand, as I'm sure you can imagine.'

Will wrinkled his nose. 'Adjustment?'

'Choice, career, adaptation – whatever you want to call it. My point is, you need to tone down the boob-staring. A girl can get the wrong idea.'

'Fine,' said Will awkwardly, his arms folding tighter. 'So you're me.'

The woman seated before him was most definitely *not* Will Monet, whatever she might imagine, but it made no sense to quibble. The fact that she *thought* she was mattered more.

'You don't believe me,' said Elsa.

Will shrugged. The idea of having copies felt deeply wrong. Beyond the visceral disgust the idea evoked lay a deeper concern. It shouldn't have been possible, though he struggled to remember why.

'Age fifteen, on Galatea, while you were in the Roboteer Academy, there was this one instructor for your Biome Engineering class,' she said. 'She was twice your age, at least—'

'So you have my memories,' Will snapped. 'I get it.'

'I know what you're thinking,' Elsa told him. 'Memories aren't identity – roboteers have been able to share memories since the first generation – but I don't know any other way to make my point. We're all *you*, though a lot of us look very different. I *strongly* recommend that you try to keep your reactions to that in check.'

'What's a Glitch?' he said.

Elsa waved his question away. 'We'll get to that. First, you need to understand. For the last forty years, we've been a world entirely filled with instances of Will Kuno-Monet, and that's had consequences.'

'*Forty?*' Will exclaimed. 'Did you say *forty years?*'

'As you think of them, yes,' she said. 'Though it's thirty-three in Willworld years.'

'Forty years of *clones*? How? Why? Where's everyone else?'

'The *human race*, you mean?' said Elsa, making quotes in the air. 'That's a difficult question. Not here. In any case, a world of copies is going to be very different from what you're used to. For a start, individuals are thought of as *threads*, not people.'

She stared at him earnestly, and Will had the sense that she was

35

embarking on something of a prepared speech – one she'd been waiting for the chance to give.

'Our bodies are largely interchangeable,' she said. 'Social position is defined by role and experience, not accident of birth. This means that anything that makes your thread unique is a jealously guarded commodity. Remember that, Will. We're pushing to become different. All ten billion of us.'

Ten billion. He struggled to wrap his mind around the number. Nowhere but Earth had ever supported a human population that large.

'Each and every Will is working at uniqueness,' she said. 'Keep that in mind and you'll have an easier time absorbing this. And while we're at it, we need to get you a new nick so you don't make it obvious you've just been born every time you open your mouth.'

'What's wrong with Jason?' said Will.

'Glitches *always* say Jason,' said Elsa. 'It's the first name we think of when we know we have memory loss. You got it from a static-flick you saw decades ago, back when you were still obsessed with historic video. Most Glitches don't even realise where they're pulling it from.'

'Okay,' said Will, his voice rising in frustration. 'Let's try again. What's a Glitch?'

Elsa exhaled heavily. 'A Glitch is what you are. A Will-instance with no memories from after the Waking. For reasons we don't understand, the planet makes one from time to time.'

'So I've happened before?' said Will. 'Like this?'

'Lots of times. And I'm warning you now, you're not popular.'

'I got that impression,' said Will. 'Want to tell me why?'

'There are Wills on this world who ... go bad. They become destructive and acquisitive, like a cancer. It usually happens when one of us gives up hope and becomes infected with bitterness at life. Beware of bitterness, Will.'

'I got that part already! Reactions in check. Keep talking.'

She shot him a weary look. 'If I didn't know how *afraid* you are right now, I'd call you out for being rude. As it is, I'm cutting you some slack. But give me some room, okay? It's not easy to boil forty years of history into one speech.'

'Sorry,' said Will. He glanced away at the ridiculous lemon-coloured furnishings and tried to compose himself. The entire situation felt too foreign, too claustrophobic. Rather like this little yellow boudoir.

'If you're me, why in Gal's name does your room look like this, anyway?' he blurted. 'It's ridiculous.'

'To remind myself that I'm *female*, you asshat!' Elsa snapped. 'Why do you think?' She rubbed her eyes. '*God*, the baseline me is annoying. Look, previous Glitches have done a lot of damage, okay? Most people don't distinguish between Glitches and Cancers. Some of us, though, think Glitches have a purpose. We think they're here to say something about how our society has turned out. But that's a minority opinion. You're just lucky that this time you happened to meet someone who felt that way before the others got to you.'

'Why is it like this?' Will demanded. 'Who made this place?'

She glared at him in exasperation. 'Who do you think? *You* did, Will. Who else is there?'

'I can't accept that.'

'Please, just listen,' said Elsa. 'Before I get Ronno back in here to shoot you. Because you still don't know the worst of it. As well as us individual instances, there's a... a meta-Will, a version we use to keep the peace. We call him *Balance*. Just like your subminds used to feed into your consciousness when you were flying a ship, we feed into Balance. His job is to fight threats, Will. And as far as most of us are concerned, you're a threat. He'll seek you out, if he can, and he has the power of the whole world behind him.'

'So Balance is Snakepit.'

'We call it the Willworld these days,' said Elsa, 'but that's right. And if you don't stay clear of Balance, he'll take you apart. He's a god, Will. An angry *you* on a planetary scale.'

Will buried his eyes in his hands and sank gently down the wall. There was too much to take in and he liked none of it. He wasn't even sure how much to believe.

'Where's everyone else?' he said. 'What about IPSO? Wasn't there ever a rescue mission?'

'People have opinions about that, but to be honest, we have no idea,' said Elsa. 'Suffice it to say, they're not here. As far as you're concerned, they're just *gone*.'

'So what in fuck's name am I supposed to do?' said Will. 'Hide? Die?'

'I'm going to send you to the Proustian Underground in Mettaburg,' she said. She got up from the bed and pulled him to his feet. 'They have a system. They can teach you how to lie low. They'll give you a better sense of what's going on.'

'Can they tell me how to get the hell off Snakepit?'

'No promises, but they'll be able to do more than I can.' She seized his hand and fixed him with a serious gaze. 'I know this is hard, but here's what you need to do. After you leave this room, walk straight down the tunnel the way you came, through the poppies, until you find a kind of graveyard. Then pick an empty slot and lie down in it. Don't worry if it looks wet.'

Will stared at her. 'In a *grave?*'

'In effect, yes,' she said. 'Unless you want to walk through about five hundred klicks of tunnels. Just lie down, shut your eyes and summon your home node.'

'I tried that,' said Will. 'It doesn't work. Something's wrong.'

She shook her head. 'That's just your connection to soft-space opening. You don't have a single node any more, Will. You've got a whole world. When your link opens and you go virtual, walk straight forwards. Whatever you do, don't step backwards.'

Will frowned. 'Why not?'

'You'll end up here again, maybe with company. One step back takes you to a map of local threads. Two steps dumps you in the closest available body to your lifting site. One step forward, on the other hand, gets you to the soft-space environment itself, which is where you need to go. Just keep moving, follow cues and only ask oracles if you absolutely can't find your way.'

'Oracles?'

'You'll figure it out,' she told him. 'When you get to the city, seek out the Radical Hill District. Look for the Old Slam Bar on Campari Street. Got it? Ask for Mr Brown.'

'Old Slam Bar,' said Will weakly. 'Brown.'

'Right. All you need to do between now and then is find your way without freaking out and hurting someone. Think you can manage that?'

'Given how today has gone so far, I honestly have no idea,' he said.

Elsa let loose a dry laugh. 'Fair answer. Okay, time to go.' She blinked and clicked her fingers. 'Wait. You still need a nick. Something that says harmless and absent-minded more than lost and dangerous.' She tapped a finger to her lips. 'Got it. How about Cuthbert?'

Will wrinkled his nose. 'I hate it.'

'Good – that makes it all the more natural. And besides, you've got bigger problems, wouldn't you say?'

'Fair point,' said Will, looking away. 'And thank you. Sorry if I was rude about your room. It's been a difficult morning.'

'I can only imagine,' she said and kissed him on the cheek. 'Being anything other than baseline takes work but it's worth it – I like what I've grown into. Anyway, good luck out there. Try not to die. And hurry. If Ronno and Tars report you, this place will be crawling with Balance agents in minutes.'

She opened the door and pushed him gently through it.

'If you make it, come back for coffee some time, but now you have to start walking before you get us both killed.'

As soon as he was outside, she pulled the door shut behind him. Will stood there, staring at the yellow slatted walls of the coffee stand, and felt utterly at sea. Then, with a grimace of resolve, he set off running back the way he'd come, to find himself a grave.

2.2: NADA

In the agonising wake of the Project Earth debacle, Nada Rien visited the Yunus on Noether. Part of her baulked at the senselessness of reporting in person. On top of the constant chafe of maintaining an individual identity, making the trip felt like an onerous imposition. She would have to look at him with a pair of flesh eyes and drip-feed information at him using a physical mouth. Such antics should never have become necessary. But they all had to do their part to fight War Fatigue. So Nada took a shuttle down from her flagship, the recently named PSS *Infinite Order*, and flew into the spaceport at Curie where the Yunus was engaged in assessment communion with the local population.

She acquired a transit pod and watched the city approach through the stained windows as the elderly machine juddered along. Like many Photurian colonies, Curie was a mixture of ugly old human towers and new home-tubes filling the dead ground between them like joyful black roots. Such cities always struck her as overgrown graveyards – places where exuberant ivy worked busily to cover up the sadness and irrelevance of the past. It couldn't happen too soon.

Usually she delighted in watching the irresistible spread of true Photurian habitats. But here she could also make out newer, less-welcome structures. Soft, black cubes had been erected since her last visit – an attempt to grow Photurian tunnel-matrix over hideous human-style construction lattices. She shivered. Was this what they'd been reduced to? Building deliberately uncomfortable homes to stop their inhabitants from sliding into bliss too soon? It sickened her that such projects were deemed necessary.

She opened her mouth wide and screamed as she often did at times like this. Why couldn't humanity just *give up* already? They were ruining it for themselves. Had the species been capable of a moment's courage or selflessness, they'd all have converted long ago. As it was, they insisted on clinging to their useless instincts like the mindless biorobots they were, and consequently everyone had suffered.

Nada composed herself by ramming her fists against the pod's filthy glass until the pain from bloody knuckles settled her mood. It had been a rough month. She'd built up a lot of hope around the rescue of Earth's population and come away with nothing but empty hands.

So here they were again, still short on converts, fighting back the tide of Fatigue and making compromises that took them ever further from perfect unity. She examined her reflection in the glass and found it depressing just how human she looked in that moment. Black hair. Brown eyes. A ship-suit. A face showing stress indicators. It was a sign of how badly she was struggling that she'd even noticed herself at all.

She forced her attention outwards again and then groaned as she realised the pod was delivering her to one of the human structures. These days, the Yunus was seldom found in a true home. He was always out and about, fighting the good fight. At times, it exhausted her.

The doors sighed open and Nada stepped out into an empty corridor lined with blotchy wall-panels and filled with the sputtering hiss of unmaintained recyclers. Dusty, yellowish light poured in from the window at the far end. Behind the hiss lay the silence that increasingly filled all Phote worlds – the sound of too much peace too soon.

Following the directions that had been deposited in her mind, she strode down the passageway to a large room at the far end. Ranks of seats wrapped a stage where the Yunus was communing with the Saved. The space must have been a *theatre* once, she realised, a box for conducting pointless human art rituals. Now it was being put to a far finer purpose.

She marched down the shallow banks of steps past rows of mouldering seats where a scattering of Photurians sat, waiting to be processed. The Yunus stood on the stage under a spotlight, bright orange and seven feet tall, white hair pouring down his back in a mane. His proud, patrician face bore a static expression of confidence and pride. A line of thirty recently converted children were walking placidly onto the dais to meet him, their eyes full of worship.

As the first human to be successfully Saved, the Yunus occupied a special place in the Photurian Utopia. His reasoning and beliefs had formed the basis on which their society was constructed. Consequently, he was instantiated as necessary, usually in improved formats, to help inform collective decision-making. Since the recent disbanding of the mass-mind, his instances had become more frequently deployed than ever.

Nada sat down near the front and checked the local mind-temple for details of the proceedings. Apparently, a modified nestship transporting families had been rescued between St Andrews and Galatea. After emergency Saving, the anthrocapital had been rerouted and brought down for assignment.

Nada felt an unfamiliar stab of social discomfort at the news. She had come to the Yunus with nothing to show for her efforts, whereas some lesser captain running a routine blockade had brought him this precious little prize.

She shrugged the feeling off. Comparative notions of social achievement were a worthless side effect of her previous identity. It was beneath her to let it contaminate her day.

'Young converts,' Yunus told the children, 'welcome to the Utopia. You are no doubt enjoying your new-found enlightenment, but better is yet to come as we allocate you useful functions. You are especially prized in these dark days. Your neuroplasticity lends us strength and hastens the coming of Immaculate Joy. Step forward one at a time to let me determine your utility, starting with the unit on the left.'

A little boy of about five approached him. The Yunus placed a hand on the child's face and stood still for a second.

'Your aptitude is low,' said the Yunus. 'Your brain will be removed and inserted in a harvester ship for warp-piloting purposes.'

The boy beamed with delight. 'Thank you, O Yunus!' he said.

The Yunus dealt with each of them in turn, picking out the rejects and saying nothing to the rest.

'You will be reformatted for manual labour in space... Your brain will become the guiding intelligence of a food factory... You will be transformed into a flight-management system at the local spaceport.' After examining the last child, he addressed the assembled group. 'Those who have been assigned may go directly to surgery for deconstruction.'

Four delighted children marched off the stage with eyes full of pride. The Yunus observed the others.

'The rest of you are relatively high-functioning individuals. You will participate in a bold new social experiment in which you will age at a normal human rate and emerge into adulthood without alteration or integration into the mass-mind.'

Nada watched the children's expressions slide in horror as they came to understand their fate. Some began to cry. From the moment they'd been rounded up and Saved, the sacred bacteria would have been opening their minds to joy, infusing them with love and hope – hope that had now largely been dashed.

Despite herself, she shivered at their plight. More than anything, Nada wished she was still part of a fused intelligence. It pained her every day that she wasn't. And as a relatively recent convert, she felt cheated that she'd experienced so little of it. She'd been a fully absorbed component for less than a year before the Utopia had been forced to disband collective operation to arrest the spread of Fatigue.

Participating in a fused mind was like inhabiting a church full of light and song. In fact, it was like *being* the church. It felt like a massive, overpowering chord of pure joy played for ever. It was beyond beautiful. She wept sometimes when she thought about it.

As it was, she could still remember what it was like to be human, sort of. She had muddy recollections of those meaningless drives that had cluttered her life: friendship, ambition, family, romance. All that *crap*. To lose them and be joined had been exquisite – the discovery of an undeniable and perfect truth. It was the end to doubt and the dawning of purity – an orderly, surgical, permanent purity, like the severing of an unwanted limb.

And then it had been shut off because too many of the Saved felt the urge to fall completely into that light. The intensity of their happiness

42

had outstripped their will to function, leaving them lifeless and deaf to the requests of their superior nodes. Fatigue had ripped through the mass-mind like wildfire, forcing them to build one cognitive fire-break after another. And so they'd had to put Total Joy on hold until the rest of their useless species could finally be dragged, kicking and screaming, into harmony.

In the meantime, a huge number of reindividualised Photurians were being made to endure an ever-increasing load of human play-acting. Research had shown that the more they behaved like the species they'd been drawn from, the longer they lasted as discrete units.

But after that mind-burning glimpse of the sweet alternative, this took endless self-discipline. No wonder the children were upset. Yunus had condemned them to decades of grim individuality. The only heaven they would know was the one at the end of the war, when the human race finally woke up to its higher calling.

'Leave,' said the Yunus. 'I have assigned a social coordinator to allocate you tasks to acquire at an unmodified rate.'

The weeping children began to march off the stage.

'Be quiet,' said the Yunus. 'Experience this as an honour.'

The children snapped into silence as their expressions reconfigured into gazes of proud purpose.

The mind-temple signalled Nada. She walked onto the stage and stared at the Yunus, waiting.

'You consider their fate a harsh one,' he said, sampling her mind through the temple.

'Yes,' said Nada.

'They will grow up hungry,' he said. 'It is my hope that they will burn with a desire for closure and work harder to convert others.'

'Or they may collapse into Fatigue more rapidly,' said Nada. 'It is a risky strategy.'

'Our situation is delicate,' said the Yunus. 'Risky strategies are called for.'

He reached into her mind and moved some of her opinions about. Nada broke into a spontaneous grin of joy as the Yunus made her agree with him. She now saw the rightness of his position and the need for brave and uncompromising action.

This was how things were supposed to work. Before reindividual-isation, Nada would have reported to the Yunus directly through the mind-temple. She hadn't even have known she was Nada, or perceived their shared order as a temple. There had just been closure and harmony.

Now, rather than having their identity supplied as necessary from their controlling node, they had to engage in crosstalk between peer units and even reorganise the hierarchy from time to time. Direct editing of her identity to create alignment was a rare and precious gift. She beamed at him in gratitude.

'I have a new plan that I intend to implement on this world,' he said. 'The reproduction of units via natural methods is operating at below-replacement rates due to genetic interference from our sacred bacteria. Furthermore, we are running low on human acquisitions. One logical policy to arrest this slide is to farm humans.'

'Farm them?' said Nada, her smile faltering.

'Yes,' he said. 'As in acquiring them but not immediately converting them.'

Nada flinched. Not converting people when the light of peace beckoned? It felt awfully unfair.

'Do not worry,' said the Yunus. 'All will be converted in time. They will be kept in safe facilities and carefully antagonised so that conversion comes as a treasured release. If we are able to stabilise such populations, we will have a steady supply of units to complete the conversion of the human race.'

Nada squirmed. There were some notions that just felt wrong to the Saved, such as simply killing the rest of the human race now that they were in the minority. Something about the joy of union made you want to share it with as many people as possible, even if there were shortcuts available. Yunus's approach smacked of compromise. Humans were there to be saved, not bred in ignorance and *then* saved.

'I struggle with that idea,' she said. She couldn't ask him to change her mind, sadly, though that was what she craved.

'As do I,' said the Yunus. 'Though I fear these are the kinds of options we must consider, so I am initiating a pilot project. This is the burden the Vile Usurper has forced upon us.'

The Vile Usurper was, of course, Will Monet – the despised pseudo-human who had stolen their homeworld. Had they a proper home, humanity would have been saved already and Fatigue avoided completely. Instead, their mission had been a limping, difficult affair, conducted without the ancient might of the one true biome behind them. Just thinking about Monet conjured a panicked loathing in most Saved that blotted out other thought.

'I mention the farming project to give you a sense of the seriousness of our predicament,' said the Yunus. 'Deliver your report.'

Nada recited the facts of her failed mission – facts the Yunus could have known instantly by looking inside her head. But that wasn't the point. She was there to engage in the wilful act of separateness both as a symbol of their determination and to practise the unloveliness of autonomy.

'The Galatean humans successfully evacuated the Earther population,' she said. 'The remaining habitats were bombed and are no longer usable. We secured no new converts.'

The Yunus stared at her blankly. 'What of the tip-off you acquired?' he said. 'I received interim reports that the new mutant seeding project was yielding fresh converts.'

'Progress was achieved,' Nada replied. 'Converts were obtained, though the information they provided was slight.'

Remotely seeded converts didn't become effective spies overnight. They needed time to come to terms with their beautiful new feelings and devise a plan. Without a network of other operatives to support them, their actions were sometimes counterproductive.

'We lost contact with most of our embedded converts before the end of the mission,' she went on. 'Only one convert who relocated to Galatea is still known to be intact.'

'This is a disastrous outcome,' said the Yunus stiffly.

'Yes,' Nada agreed.

'Significant numbers of units were expended to produce a stable mutation that would resist detection by the Abomination.'

The Abomination was Andromeda Ludik – the person the Saved hated most after Monet. She was generally considered unsaveable by virtue of her disgusting hybrid biology, and therefore an entity to be destroyed. So far, that had proven surprisingly difficult to accomplish.

'I am aware of this,' said Nada. 'If you recall, I recommended against such expenditure given our reduced resources.'

The Yunus shifted from foot to foot and stared upwards. He let out a long keening sound. It probably signified some form of anguish – an understandable response. Nada waited for him to finish.

'How did this make you feel?' he asked in the end, almost absent-mindedly. 'What details did you notice?'

Nada suspected that the Yunus didn't know what to ask in that moment. He was as much at sea in play-acting humanity as she was, and was fishing for direction.

'I am disgusted with them,' she said. 'While I still love them and want to convert them, I am becoming … impatient. I worked for two years on the Earth Project and have saved nobody. The closer I get to helping the humans, the more they resist. They are like children. No, they are like cornered animals. No, they are like flies unable to understand a pane of glass.' She fell silent but the Yunus kept staring, so she continued. 'Now I return to find a world even quieter than when I left. We are building false homes instead of living in tubes. I face despair. I doubt that I will be able to manage disappointment again without succumbing to Fatigue. I recommend that you deconstruct me for parts and use another unit that is less strained.'

'And yet we must continue to work to the best of our ability to save humanity,' said the Yunus. 'Deconstructing you would be the easy option. But what happens if we attempt to merge in harmony while both the human race and the Vile Usurper are intact? Peace will only last for ever if it is embraced by all.' He fixed her with wide eyes and a meaningless smile. 'You are one of my strongest,' he said. 'You crave peace as much as every other unit but are driven to achieve it for all rather than drowning yourself in it. You must therefore remain intact to help implement my core plan. The central dictates of my strategy remain unchanged. First, War Fatigue must be hidden from the humans at all costs. They cannot be allowed to perceive our weakness. Second, new humans must be acquired by any means and their conversion deferred where possible.

'However, I now add a third dictate. Galatea, the colony of the Abomination, must be broken. It is the strongest colony and it obstructs our progress. It cannot be allowed another victory. The Abomination and her cohorts will attempt to secure a new home for the Earther population. She must be stopped.'

'Obstructing the Abomination has been tried,' said Nada.

The Yunus let out a strangled hooting sound. 'This is who I need you to be,' he said, and reached into her mind again.

He twisted and turned pieces of her, bolstering her need to kill Ludik and break Galatea until she screamed again and tore at her hair. A sick sense of urgency knotted her insides. Urine spilled down the leg of her ship-suit.

'Stop screaming now,' said the Yunus, and her throat seized. 'You will coordinate raiding flights and blockades. You will make contact with the remaining mutant spy and determine where the Earther population is being relocated. They will not be able to hide such a large group for long. If necessary, you must resort to innovation to achieve this.'

'I will innovate,' Nada shrieked, her fingers clutching at her gut.

'You will never give up.'

'I will never give up!' she wailed.

'Your identity will not be deconstructed or permitted to embrace bliss until such time as you have succeeded.'

'I crave success!' she keened.

'I am aware that I am placing a significant burden on you,' said the Yunus, 'but swift action is vital. We are in danger of handing a propaganda victory to the humans that will slow the rate of conversions still further. As you are aware, creatures like the Abomination and humanity's other false heroes serve as rallying points for the Unsaved. Hence, here is my last gift to you,' said the Yunus, his virtual hands still deep inside her head. 'You will draw strength from this urgency. It will be like the human ideal of "ambition".'

Nada felt a flush of unnatural power. Her back jerked ramrod straight. Her arms fell limp at her sides. Her eyes widened as manic glee beamed out through her features.

'This is my promise to you,' he said. 'When you return victorious, I will set aside my notions of human-farms and other compromises. There will be no more rash deployments of the Saved, or false homes, or silent worlds, because you will have shown us a better path. But you must be quick. Heaven cries out for us.'

'I adore you!' Nada shouted. 'I will be victorious in your name!'

'Leave,' said the Yunus.

Nada strode urgently for the theatre exit, determination yanking her forward with every step. In the back of her mind, there still lurked that hunger to lie down on a bed of moist fungus to experience bliss, but first she had a colony to crush.

Twenty-nine light-years away, on the planet of Galatea, another woman took a similar pod from a spaceport to a city, in a similar state of despair. In this case, the pod was a sleek, state-of-the-art model with a cutting-edge biosensor array, a semi-intelligent SAP-mind and adaptive organic seating.

The woman was Ann Ludik, and she had resorted to silencing the pilot SAP because it kept panicking about the unfamiliar nano-machinery she was exuding. Hence, rather than adapting, the seating merely quivered in fear of its occupant. Ann tried to ignore it.

There was no view from Ann's pod. The route from the Ritter Space-port to the Sharptown Subterra Complex involved traversing half a kilometre of solid rock at a shallow incline. Ann didn't care to let the SAP activate the wall displays, either, and chose instead to sit in the dark. It suited her mood.

As expected, Ann had been called in to 'discuss progress' with Galatean Defence. Despite months of careful planning, the evacuation of Earth had come within a hair's breadth of disaster, and so everyone felt the need to talk it to death. There had already been plenty of discussion on the week-long carrier-flight back to Galatean space.

The Phote plan had evidently been to seed near-undetectable mutant converts into Earth's population and have *them* be the ones leading the call for evacuation. The converts would then leak information about the mission to the Utopia and ideally pass the infection to Galateans. They'd been wildly successful.

Upon conversion, poor Calvinia Shue, their diplomat, had apparently decided that the best way to support her new-found hunger for Total Peace was to subtly manipulate Mark Ruiz. And the Phote parasite co-opting her nervous system had all of Calvinia's political insight to draw from. It hadn't taken her long to figure out the right angle.

It stung her, though, that Mark appeared to believe her to be the sort of person who'd leave ten thousand people in space to die. Was that how he thought of her now? A life of war had made her decisive, but not cold, surely. She'd always tried to save the greatest number of people, even during the horrors of the Suicide War.

Years ago, she and Mark had been close. That had been before she'd lost patience with his attitude, but still, didn't he understand that she *never* liked hurting others or seeing them be hurt? How could she? Her whole life had been a battle to protect the preciousness of human warmth. She couldn't enjoy it herself, so she fought to preserve it for everyone else. Otherwise, why did she even exist?

By her own logic, though, Ann knew she'd failed. The main reason the evacuation had gone so wrong was her insistence that her own methods of biodefence were better than those dreamed up by the Fleet. And through her negligence, infectious spies bringing untold harm had made their way into the Galatean population.

The pod burst into the light as it reached the Sharptown quarantine station, an empty granite chamber thirty metres square with a suspended pod-rail running through it. LED floods bathed the space in metallic, blue-white light with some spectrum that apparently made it easier to run bioassay scans.

Ann reluctantly got to her feet and spread her arms as the pod slid to a halt in the buffer zone. With a thought, she flicked the pod SAP back to life and waited for the machines running the quarantine area to do their job.

'Captain Andromeda Ng-Ludik reporting for Post-Mission Pivot,' she said aloud.

'Acknowledged,' said the pod SAP. 'Please wait.'

Galatea had changed plenty since Ann's time there as a student. When she was young, the planet had still been wrestling with its apparently unending terraforming problem. Storms wracked the world on a monthly basis, delivering kilometre-high walls of grit travelling at the speed of bullets. Everyone lived in shielded canyon habitats and wore evacuation monitors on their wrists.

Since then, the storms had mostly stopped. After the coming of the Photes, more and more habitats on Galatea had been built underground where they were easier to protect. And with diminishing resources to spend on terraforming, a consensus had developed that a planet with an unstable surface environment might not be such a bad thing. An angry atmosphere constituted a free defensive weapon of sorts.

But then, perverse to the last, when humanity stopped trying to change Galatea, it began to calm all by itself. The surface wasn't exactly habitable yet, but certain kinds of bacteria had taken off. For reasons nobody quite understood, cryptobiotic mats of the kind that Galatean scientists had been trying to encourage for decades now decorated the surface with wild blotches of black and purple. Atmospheric rebalancing was happening at the fastest rate since colonisation began.

Ironically, most people never saw that progress. The surface was now considered a buffer zone all too easy for the Photes to target. So the human population lived in subterra complexes engineered for cultural and biological defence. Consequently, modern Galatea had almost nothing in common with the world she'd known.

'Captain Ludik, you have been cleared by executive order,' said the pod SAP. 'However, please note that your body is synthesising a large number of compounds that I cannot identify. Therefore, a chance remains—'

Ann shut the SAP off again and urged the vehicle forward. Why, after forty years, Galatean scientists couldn't come up with a bioarray capable of recognising her and treating her as a special case, she had no idea.

The pod slid into the tunnel on the other side of the quarantine chamber and through another wall of rock before emerging onto an elevated rail running through the huge, open space of Sharptown One. The environment had been designed to resemble a cross between a cathedral interior and a river valley. Light beamed down from the peak of the two-hundred-metre-high Gothic ceiling, which was decorated in reassuring shades of sky-blue. The bottom of the habitat was a tiered landscape of dormitories and work-spaces in soft, white marble, interspersed with communal gardens and the all-important game fields.

She had arrived during one of the scheduled playtimes – no great surprise as some group or other were usually at it. Her pod passed over swathes of well-kept lawn where hundreds of adults engaged in flash-mob yoga exercises with ever-changing routines or played complex games of tag. Floating game-boards displayed multivariate scores and whimsical updates on the action. As always, Ann felt something a little forced in all that state-supported fun.

The new Galatea was not a relaxed society, though it worked hard at keeping itself a functional one. The planet had finally incorporated all the immigrant groups from Earth that it had been forced to absorb after war broke out with the Photes. They'd demolished every pernicious sect division and reduced crime to practically zero. These days, religious congregation was both a duty and a paid leisure activity with hefty bonuses for creative faith-making. Nobody took it seriously.

Though there was a lot to admire, Ann found the new Galatean society alienating. But through her connection to Poli Najoma's family, she felt like she at least had a link to the younger generation on this world. That was one reason why she'd thrown in her lot with the Galateans. She felt she understood their values at some level, and at the very least could acknowledge that the social changes they'd implemented were better than the alternative. If your society didn't stay flexible and cohesive, the Photes found your weaknesses and exploited them. Before you knew what had happened, your planet wound up serving the blindly self-replicatory urge of invasive alien bacteria.

Ann's pod followed a track that led into the tiered hillscape on the far side of the valley and through another long expanse of granite. It eventually deposited her at an anonymous meeting space embedded deep within the planet's crust. She stepped out into the entry vestibule and spat into the bowl by the door. When the light turned green, she passed through the seal. On the other side, Ann washed her hands with her biofilm gloves still on, as politeness required. Galatea was big into washing. And big into gloves, which was hardly surprising under the circumstances.

The room beyond featured artificial daylight delivered through false skylights, a sunken conversation pit decorated in soft greys and wrap-around wall-panels. As usual for such meetings, those panels showed agitation patterns – a kind of twitching geometric art that nobody exactly liked but which Photes couldn't stand.

A girl of about eighteen was waiting for her there. She had a button nose, a rose-tinted buzz cut and a crisp green uniform. Ann's boss had been changed again, she noticed. This new one was very young. Though she'd have full voting and command rights, Ann couldn't help but think of her as a kid. Being in your seventies tended to have that effect. In her weaker moments, Ann was forced to admit that she missed having a boss she admired, such as Ira Baron. But those days were never coming back.

'Captain Ludik,' said the girl, gesturing at the couches. 'Wow, it's an honour. Amazing to meet you in person.' She bounced on her toes. 'Please, sit down. You can call me Kathy.'

Kathy wouldn't be her real name, but the girl delivered the line with the kind of chipper, indestructible confidence Ann had come to expect. All the Autocratic Academy graduates had it.

The Academy was the pool of high-achieving youth who collectively made top-level decisions for the New Society. These days, executive roles were exclusively given to young people who lacked bias or irrational attachment. Each of them ruled unilaterally like a global dictator. Subsequently, their decisions were aggregated and filtered by an ecology of SAPs engaged in permanent, ferocious competition. The emergent consensus was distributed as martial law. Those who passed their term in the Academy without a strategic failure graduated to some lower, less stressful position. Those who did not found themselves in an different line of work, often after partial memory erasure.

Ann had long ago stopped being surprised by the age gaps, but the oddness of the set-up still vexed her. She couldn't help feeling that all these hard-eyed girls and boys she met were losing something by ruling a world before they'd even known love. Behind that unflinching iron will, something tragic surely lurked, even if Ann was never allowed to see it.

'This is a big moment for me,' said Kathy as Ann sat. 'I have to deal with high-impact stuff all the time but to actually be in the same room as Ann Ludik? To be the one who gets to have this briefing with you? That's *hyper.*' She shook her head as if amazed at her own good fortune.

Ann felt unmoved by the girl's excitement. Fame had never sat well with her. Her role in human history hadn't exactly been glorious. A long time ago, she'd been part of a conspiracy – a foolish one. They'd been trying to head off a war by faking attacks by another species. They'd achieved that by making reckless use of technology they didn't understand which they'd found out at the Far Frontier. Then they'd watched in horror when the tame-looking tech they'd resurrected had fused with the people it was fighting to take on a life of its own. The rest was history.

Ann's job in the notorious Rumfoord League had been to distract humanity's only superbeing: Will Monet. Once a lowly roboteer, Will had been changed during humanity's first alien contact when the ancient Transcended race opened up the Far Frontier to human access. The enigmatic aliens charged Will with responsibility for delivering their terms to the human race and empowered him accordingly. He'd since become a self-appointed guardian of the species. Sadly for Will, that role had left him with all the responsibility but little power to influence except through brute force. By the time Ann had gone to work on him, he was already desperately lonely and easy to manipulate.

In the end, Will had sacrificed himself trying to stop the monstrous hybrid race Ann's people had spawned. His last act before being swallowed by the alien world they'd abused was to save Ann's life and transfer his powers to her. Now *she* was the superbeing. The unkillable machine. The lonely monster. She had Will's ship, Will's skills and Will's voice in her head for company until the day the enemy finally took her. She'd been fighting ever since. To her mind, fame was part of the punishment. Because, by rights, the fame was Will's, too.

'I'm glad you're pleased,' said Ann briskly. 'It's nice to meet you. Forgive me for asking, but why *are* we meeting? I take it you've seen my report. My memory dumps were exhaustive. There's nothing I can add.'

'I've seen the report,' said Kathy, 'but that's not what we're here for. I'm here to talk about your new assignment, not your performance on the last one.'

Ann blinked. 'You mean the relocation project?'

'You're not working on that any more. We need you for something else.'

Ann stood up, her throat tightening. 'You can't redeploy me. I was given assurances.'

She'd been slated to manage the Earth Two Project and had made promises on that basis. It was the first time in years that she'd been able to secure a work advantage for Poli. She and the whole Najoma family would be coming with her to the new site, where Poli's environmental-management skills could finally be properly used.

Ann had been looking for ways to help the Najoma family since the start of the war. One of her first acts after her transformation on Snakepit had been to send her ship's engineer, Kuril Najoma, on the mission that had killed him. When she'd belatedly discovered that the man had a daughter, she'd done everything in her power to fix that damage. Poli had grown up never quite knowing what to do with Ann's urgent desire to help, but they'd eventually become close. Now Poli had two kids of her own and was stuck in a job she disliked. Ann had seen a chance to make a difference and leapt at it. It was the first thing besides *cleaning* that she'd cared about in years.

'Is this a punishment?' said Ann.

'Captain Ludik, please,' said Kathy with a laugh. She rolled her eyes like a teenager. 'You know we don't do punishment. We examine opportunities. Relax.' She gestured for Ann to sit. 'There won't be an Earth Two for a while. We're still tracking down the new spy network Ambassador Shue started, which changes the timeline for everything else.'

'No Earth Two?' said Ann, slumping into her seat. 'I don't get it. What are you going to do with all those people? They have to live somewhere.'

'That's not your problem,' said Kathy. 'Given the situation, I'm sure you can figure out why you're not going to be involved in any interim planning.'

'Because I was targeted,' said Ann. Grim understanding settled over her. Her own actions had disqualified her from the one project she cared about.

'That's right. You and the *Gulliver* team finally developed weaknesses the Photes can exploit.'

Ann blushed for the first time in about twenty years. She didn't need Kathy to spell it out. She'd become a liability. Something creaked inside her like an enormous weight shifting.

'But don't sweat it,' said Kathy. 'Every thrust reveals a weakness, right? The Earth extraction yielded gobs of useful data. For starters, there's enough evidence here that we can be certain of a new surge.'

That was huge news. 'Are you sure?' said Ann.

'Absolutely. The cost-benefit models are clear. The mutant strain Shue brought aboard your ship must have come at an outrageous price for the Photes. You know how slow they are to mutate. They can suck up material and strategies from foreign biospheres in hours, but always by breaking down and recoding the content. Their molecular architecture doesn't change. At least, not the way we've seen in your samples from Lieutenant Twebo. Our best guess is that they most likely dumped thousands of ex-human hosts into a habitat filled with stolen cultures of your weaponised smart-cells and waited to see if any of them survived. And that must have taken them years. Just stealing the material out of our labs would have been hard enough. The Photes don't throw bodies at a project like that unless they're up to something. But, for the obvious reasons, you can't be a part of the main thrust of our response.'

Ann spread her hands. 'Then what in Gal's name do you expect me to do? I'm still the best weapon you have.'

'I'm glad you asked,' said Kathy brightly. 'We're going to follow up on Captain Ruiz's plan to traverse Backspace.'

Ann's face froze. 'You *what*?'

Mark's plan had been a joke in strategy circles for years.

'Think about it,' said Kathy, ignoring the look of cold alarm building in Ann's eyes. 'It's just about the *best* thing you could do for us right now.'

Mark had submitted the plan years ago and never shut up about it since. In essence, it proposed that the Galatean forces make an end run around Phote-occupied space to access Snakepit from the far side. Once at Snakepit, they'd be in a position to either boser the surface, or, perhaps more usefully, wake the world to activity on behalf of the human race.

All previous missions to access Snakepit had run afoul of Phote blockades. That part of space was fiercely defended. Consequently, nobody had reached the place since the start of the war. However, intelligence gathered from the interrogation of Phote prisoners made it clear that the Utopia didn't have access to it, either.

Furthermore, Photurian goals hinged on one day finding the strength to retake the planet from whatever defensive system Will Monet's last acts had spawned there. Psych-warfare specialists had speculated that losing their erstwhile homeworld might cripple the Photurian race so badly that their will to fight might simply vanish.

In its intent, then, Mark's plan made total sense. There were just one or two tiny wrinkles that made success unlikely. The first was that Snakepit was on a different galactic shell. Warp-drive only permitted superluminal velocities at tangents to the galactic hub, which meant that star systems only a few light-years further in or out from the core than Galatea were effectively unreachable without a gate. And the human race only ever had access to one gate, which these days was blocked by the Photes.

To get around this problem, Mark's plan called for the use of a second gate – one that had been identified through careful astronomical surveys. And therein lay the other problem. That gate lay on the other side of a vast swathe of space known as the Depleted Zone where warp engines didn't work. This made the shortest straight crossing something measured in centuries.

'We've been mapping the Alpha Flaw in the Depleted Zone for years,' said Kathy. 'Ever since Rachel Bock got lost in it. You may not know this, but it's been growing.'

'What difference does that make?' Ann snapped. 'Flaws are death traps.'

Ever since the discovery that the Zone was not a uniform wall and that cracks of a sort existed in it, people had tried to sneak through to explore the other side. Will Monet's wife, Rachel Bock, had been one of the first explorers to try, and certainly the most famous. Her loss had convinced almost everyone that it wasn't doable.

These days, people considered the Depleted Zone as much an alien artefact as the Penfield Lobe gates. No evidence existed, but the presence of a dead, impenetrable barrier hundreds of light-years wide smacked of Transcended involvement. It also helped convince most that even trying to break through the boundary wasn't a great idea. The Transcended had a nasty habit of obliterating races they didn't like, as they had the poor Fecund a mere ten million years ago.

'This isn't public knowledge,' said Kathy, 'but we've been pretty sure we could make it through the Zone for the last couple of years. It just hasn't been super high on our priority stack. It's a cost-intensive operation and risking new existential threats at a time like this hasn't seemed awesome. Plus, our best candidates for that mission have always been out fighting. But now you're free!'

Kathy tried for a look of optimistic exuberance, but all Ann could see on those perky features was the cold, appraising intelligence that lay behind them.

'We can't use you in our primary fightback, so this is a great fit. Plus, you're a product of the adventuring age. This is naturally the kind of mission that you and Mark are best at – one where huge asymmetrical talents can *really* make a difference.'

The subtext couldn't have been clearer. She and Mark were dinosaurs – poorly suited to fighting an enemy that gamed every individual weakness. The human race was shedding its heroes for the same reason it had dumped all its charismatic senior leaders: because they were more trouble than they were worth. This time, though, they weren't waiting for disaster to strike. One near miss was enough.

'I don't want to turn tail and go exploring,' said Ann bitterly. 'I have a purpose, and that's to *fight*.'

'But you *will* be helping us fight,' said Kathy, her tone meaningful. She waited for Ann to join the dots.

Ann opened her mouth and closed it as she saw the whole picture. There could only be one real reason to pursue a mission like Mark's now, given its shockingly low viability scores: to draw Phote attention. The Photes had targeted her, so Galatea was going to use that and turn her into bait.

'You're sending me to die,' said Ann quietly. After all she'd done for the human race, it hurt.

'No, we're sending you on a risky mission, like we always have,' said Kathy. 'It's just that this time you'll be the feint rather than the thrust because that's the only option left. And if that feint pays off, then yay! Because we've picked one with side benefits.' Of course they had. The Autocratic Academy was nothing if not efficient in their deployment of resources.

Ann sagged. Galatea clearly had their own plans which couldn't include her. And neither she nor Mark would be told what they were. She could ignore the order, of course. As the most powerful person in human space, she had more bio-threat capacity in one hand than Sharptown had in its phage-banks. Nobody could make her *do* anything. But that wouldn't convince the Galateans to change tack. She'd just isolate herself, much as Mark had.

She almost said, *You need me*, but knew it wasn't true. After the Suicide War, the Galatean government had made sure that nobody was indispensable – not even her. Plus she knew that a lot of younger people considered her and her peers tainted by what they'd done in that conflict. It had just been a matter of time before they found a way to slide her out of the picture.

Now that she thought about it, she'd been surprised that the Fleet had given Mark and herself the job of managing such a high-profile mission as the Earth evacuation in the first place. With a precipitous sense of uncertainty, she began to wonder if the Academy had engineered the whole thing.

'Look,' said Kathy, 'let me lay it straight. We need you on this.

We're losing, Ann. Unless we can take the heat off and dump Earth's population soon, we'll be dead in the water. Four colonies is below even the optimistic model estimates for species survival. Those people need to be moved fast. But a mission like this with you on it? That'd be *impossible* for us to keep secret. It'd flush those spies right out. We'd get value from your involvement before you even left port. Now, of course, you're not an ordinary officer, so I can't have you killed if you refuse, which makes our treatment of you kind of unfair. But we'll be very disappointed. And worse, we'll have to find someone who'll *pretend* to be you. They'll be less qualified. They'll probably die. And without your strengths, the whole feint will probably fail. Those thirty mil you rescued? They'll be dead anyway.'

Ann felt empty. She stared at the far wall. 'When you put it that way,' she said, 'how can I refuse? But I'll need time to explain things to some friends.'

'The Najoma family have been informed,' said Kathy. 'They're offworld already.'

Ann shut her eyes. The rest of the rug had already been pulled from under her, apparently.

'Okay,' she said. 'Can I leave them a message?'

'Of course!' said Kathy. 'So long as you don't reveal any planetary secrets. You can use this room's network after I've gone. I take it we have your consent to proceed to the next steps?'

Ann nodded vaguely.

'Great!' said Kathy enthusiastically. She slapped her thighs as she got to her feet. 'It's been hyper to meet you, Captain Ludik. I really hope that one day we get to do it again.'

They didn't shake hands because, these days, Galateans never did. Kathy strode to the exit and was gone.

Ann stared at the jittering hypercubes on the walls and wallowed in the silence that remained. A second blush coloured her features, slow and all-consuming, like a wave of embarrassment crashing over her head. She could feel something breaking inside her.

[Why do I feel like I'm drowning?] she asked her shadow.

[I don't know,] it said. [Want to talk about it?]

But Ann didn't want to talk. She could sense the answer sliding out of the mental fog inside her like an approaching ocean liner. In her old life, she'd always felt clever for being more rational and pragmatic than those around her. She'd been the cool one. A scientist and a policewoman at the same time. But since she'd come back, she'd been something else: a weapon.

It had started innocently enough. She had wanted to help as much as possible and so had done her duty on every awful mission they gave her. Not once had she flinched from action. She'd even changed her body in line with Psych Ops' recommendations to make herself the perfect military icon. It was only now that she saw she'd become a robot. When had she let that happen?

She'd died the first time doing something brave and human. And she'd come back as a machine. Now that she was no longer useful, they weren't bothering to hide it. She'd failed in her function. So what was left for them to do?

[I...] she started. [They're throwing me away. I was never a person to them. Never.]

Had Will felt like this? Had he registered that look of bland calculation on their faces when they talked to him? That desperate desire to see him as less than a person because he was so much more?

She knew he had. She'd looked at him that way herself. She'd observed that hollowness in his eyes and *exploited* it – back before he handed the curse to her. She recalled how casually she'd messed with Will's emotions all those years ago when she had no inkling of the depths of his isolation. She let out a guffaw of joyless laughter. How differently she'd treat him now.

What a fool she'd been. Who in their right might exploited unknown alien tech? But back then, everyone was doing it. The whole economy was based on stolen science. When the Transcended opened up all those new star systems, everything had changed. Yet that region had been home to the poor Fecund who'd borrowed tech from the Transcended and died from it. That should have been their clue. Instead, there was a boom in alien archaeology as humanity rifled through the ruins like rats in a dumpster.

With the boom had come the squabbling. Alien weapons were secretly stockpiled by both sides. Hence the perfectly logical plan to use the same approach to resolve the conflict. No matter that the tech they'd found wasn't Fecund, or that it was dangerously advanced. They'd convinced themselves that action was necessary – that if they didn't use Snakepit to prevent a war, it would surely start one. So they'd grabbed that world-sized weapon with both hands.

Ann had been paying for that stupidity ever since. They'd rolled her out for every genocidal horror they needed perpetrating. And Ann had always followed orders. Like a machine. And she was sick of it. Sick to death.

[Maybe you're not seeing the upside,] said her shadow, somewhat wryly. [If this is how it ends, wouldn't it be a meaningful way to go? What better finale to a life of battle could you want? And you get a free vacation. Could you ask for more?]

A laugh caught in Ann's throat as she saw the bitter truth in her shadow's words. This was her way out: the one she'd been waiting for. Of course she was going to make her exit count. And then, after forty-one years of fighting the good fight, Monet's curse would finally be lifted.

2.4: MARK

Mark sat with Zoe in the public waiting area at Ritter Spaceport and tried to ignore the pillow fight happening around him. Across the great turfed expanse of the departures hall, between the glass columns and polychromatic seating clusters, giggling adults traded blows with state-supplied antibacterial cushions. For the fifth consecutive time, he refused a passing robot's gentle attempt to press one of the soft weapons into his hands.

Hovering over the travellers' heads, mini-blimps circled endlessly, displaying the kind of propaganda that had become a fixture of Galatean society.

'Question authority – it's your duty!' read one.

'Tolerating corruption is corruption!' declared another.

The slogans were written in spiky, jiggling letters wearing bright, Psych Ops-engineered colours. Speakers played quirky, upbeat music with carefully mistimed beats. It sounded like a dance-party soundtrack being performed by malfunctioning robots.

They could have chosen to sit in the Quiet Corner, of course, with its gentle mood music and roving therapists, but Zoe hated that part of the lounge even more. So they stayed in the central concourse and suffered.

Mark understood the merits of organised social play. He just preferred to do it on his own terms rather than having fun dictated to him.
As far as he was concerned, the waiting lounge was a perfect example
of the weird social pressure the Photes had forced upon them. Nothing
was simple any more. Not even the act of enjoying oneself. He hated
the deadly serious water fights and the endless compulsory voting, the
veiled humour and the not-so-veiled martial order. He longed for the
day when they could all go back to being normal. More than that, he
couldn't wait to get the hell off Galatea and back to the relative sanity
of his ship.

He fought the urge to retreat into his interface to block the whole
place out. He and Zoe were trying to avoid making themselves obvious
and ramping up their network footprint would only attract attention.
Similarly, they could have simply commissioned a private shuttle. With
their level of authorisation, they'd have been given their choice of
vehicle. But that would also have made their movements obvious, and
Mark didn't want to give the bastards in Defence the opportunity to
zero in on him. They weren't hiding, exactly. He and Zoe just didn't
feel like giving the Fleet any more help than they'd already received.

His mood upon landing had been very different. While the two of
them were transported under guard to the inevitable secure facility,
he'd felt guilty and foolish. They'd screwed up, even if the people of
Earth had made it out alive. He understood how close to disaster his
recklessness had taken them and could feel the end of an era coming.

Mark had handed over a full memory dump and spent several days
discussing his experience and motivations with an army of roboteer
therapists. While not an official Galatean citizen, he felt a professional
duty to the government that had hired him, and so had tolerated their
every request to peer inside his head.

His feelings towards the Galateans had begun to change around the
same time their questions had dried up. When Zoe had probed them
about the next mission, the hedging started. So Mark had made the
request more direct. Did the Galateans wanted to suspend them or kick
them out? Or kill them, maybe? He got no reply, not even to his joke.
He asked if they had new mission-limit guidelines they'd like him to
abide by, or extra safeguards they wanted to implement on his ship.
Nothing.

Shortly after that, he and Zoe had been parked in the officers' resort and asked to wait.

While the resort had no shortage of luxurious amenities, its status as a kind of voluntary prison was clear. As the days rolled by with no information, he'd grown ever more restless. The impressive view across Sharptown One lost its appeal and their private pool started to feel awfully small. The resort began to resemble permanent enforced retirement. After two inscrutable weeks since their arrival, Galatea deciding to execute them no longer felt like a safe topic for satire.

True to form, Zoe had lost it first. 'Fuck this!' she declared one morning after another ideally nutritious but entirely predictable breakfast. 'So we fucked up. We still run the best damned embership in human space and we're not helping anyone sitting here. I'm done with feeling guilty. I'd rather be saving lives.' She slammed down her fork, and that was that.

She had a point. Human colonies were independent these days. They had to be. The Photes kept blockading communication routes, making centralised command impossible. Consequently, there was no shortage of jobs for skilled military pilots. And even if they sequestered the *Kraken* from him, they couldn't take the *Gulliver*. They could go and help St Andrews instead. That place badly needed support. Its population was already smaller than Earth's had been in its final weeks.

So they'd quietly checked out of the resort and headed straight for the local shuttle terminal. No one had stopped them. The Galateans were more subtle than that. Now Mark sat hoping that the shuttle arrived before the authorities.

'Was what we did so goddamn wrong?' he asked Zoe. 'I mean, if that ark-hedge story hadn't been totally in character, we'd never have fallen for it. If anyone needs to take a look at themselves, it's Galatean-fucking-high-command.'

'I'm with you,' she said, 'but the Academy's unlikely to see it that way. We're talking about an entire colony here. As fuck-ups go, this one was major.'

'The Academy has been throwing lives away for years,' Mark growled. 'What did they expect from us? If they don't like the way we work, that's their lookout. We'll fight someone else's battles instead. They can't stop us.'

The *Gulliver* and the Vartian Institute banner it flew under were protected by an old interplanetary treaty. In effect, their significance during the last forty years of human history had put them above the law, allowing them to retain privileges now impossible for others to acquire. It was the only reason they were allowed to fly without a ship full of subcaptains and social-accountability officers.

'Don't be so sure,' said Zoe. 'They might just arrange for our shuttle to have an accident so they can minimise their intelligence risk. Our disposability indices must be nosing into the yellow right now.'

Mark grimaced. Things had felt bad ever since they'd made the hand-off to the second carrier halfway home. They'd been given pretty short shrift by the admiral in charge and it was clear they were never going to be told where the people of Earth were headed next.

'There are other carrier teams now,' Zoe added, 'with younger pilots who do what they're told.'

It was no secret that the Galatean government hated making room for special-case citizens, particularly since the Second Surge. But just like Ann, Mark and Zoe were celebrities – useful as much for their propaganda value as their talents. The only reason they weren't being mobbed in the departure hall was because their faces had been fashion-copied so often as to render the sight of them mundane. Mark bumped into near-lookalikes at least once a month and always found it unsettling.

A gentle gonging sound signalled boarding for the next orbital shuttle. The mini-blimps all swapped their messages to gate-indicators and robots started circling again, this time gathering the pillows that had been dropped – for DNA-testing, no doubt.

'I can't believe it,' said Zoe as they strode for the exit. 'We're actually getting out of here.'

Then, as they neared the doorway, they caught sight of a familiar figure waiting for them – Ira Baron-Lecke. Mark's heart sank. Reality reasserted itself as he realised they weren't getting offworld after all. The Academy had sent the most persuasive force possible to collect them: an old friend.

Ira was hard to miss. He stood a little under a metre and a half tall and was almost as wide, with a head like a polished bullet. Mark sighed as he approached his former mentor.

They hadn't seen each other in over a year and it surprised Mark how old Ira looked. Not in body, of course. Ever since age-reversal therapy had been perfected, letting yourself deteriorate unnecessarily had been considered a crime. Instead, Ira looked old in his eyes. You could feel the full century of his life experience in that gaze, along with all the weary weight it had brought.

'Hi, Mark, Zoe,' said Ira quietly. 'You know why I'm here, right?'

Mark nodded. He noticed that the other travellers were suddenly giving them a lot of room – almost as if they'd all been in on the interception from the start. That sort of thing happened on Galatea.

'Want to go somewhere and talk about it?' Ira offered.

'Sure,' said Mark. 'Whatever.'

Ira led the way towards the officers' lounge and privacy spaces.

'We haven't seen you in ages, Ira,' said Zoe cautiously as they walked. 'How've you been doing?'

He replied with a shrug. 'Oh, you know, so-so.'

Mark didn't know. Until about ten years ago, Ira Baron had been the Fleet Admiral of IPSO, the de facto ruler of the entire human race. That was before the Second Surge, and the Suicide War. After that, they'd asked him to step down. Ira had been only too eager. Since then, he'd been in a kind of retirement limbo – running the odd errand for the Academy despite no longer having a formal position. Now he had no partner, no job and no responsibilities of any kind. Mark couldn't imagine what that felt like. Of all of the ageing clique who effectively comprised humanity's royal family, Ira's role had changed most.

'Lost some height, I see,' said Zoe.

'I let them stretch me for the political work,' said Ira, 'for public appearances and all that, but I was never comfortable with it. No point keeping those changes afterwards.'

'Of course not,' said Zoe.

She shot Mark a worried glance. Reversing a height augmentation was always a painful experience. It wasn't a choice you made lightly.

Ira took them to a quiet room on the executive level with a view over the polychromatic concourse and ordered some drinks.

'I'm having a Scotch,' he said. 'Anyone else?'

'I'll take one,' said Mark.

Zoe huffed. 'Gin,' she said. 'It's almost lunchtime. And I don't need this liver anyway.'

It was true. She had a spare growing aboard the *Gulliver*, but Mark knew she wasn't thrilled by how the meeting was starting. Mark could metabolise away alcohol in minutes. Zoe had less effective augs. It was unclear whether Ira had retained any metabolic support at all.

'So what happened?' said Mark as they sat. 'Are we on death row for crimes against humanity?'

'Not exactly,' said Ira. 'They've okayed your mission to Backspace.'

Mark's pithy comeback died in his throat. Something slid off a cliff inside him. 'You're kidding,' he said.

'Nope,' said Ira. 'You can even lead it, if you want.'

Mark groaned and rubbed his eyes. This was the prize he'd wanted more than anything – the chance to change the nature of the war. He'd spent years trying to prove himself worthy of that opportunity. Years of bargaining and campaigning and addressing every *yes-but* they threw at him. Now, apparently, he had what he wanted – as a punishment.

'They're getting us out of the way,' he said.

Ira shrugged again. 'The mission will be drawing together all those remaining people who might be able to secure Will's help, just in case he's still there. You and I are both on that list.'

Mark winced. He'd studied this project for years. At first, his fascination with the Depleted Zone had come from a desire to locate his half-mother Rachel. By the time the expected lifespan of her coma-storage system had passed, his team had found the second lure star. From that moment, Mark had been hooked. If there was a lure star, there had to be a gate. And if there was a gate, there had to be clear, navigable space beyond the Zone – space free of Phote blockades. That meant a chance to reach Snakepit, the way they had tried and failed to do at the start of the war.

'Do you believe them?' Mark asked Ira, his stomach turning over. 'Is this actually real, or are they just burying us in space?'

'It's real,' said Ira. 'And I believe in it. It's the first piece of strategy I've felt good about for a while. Fighting the Photes on their terms isn't getting us anywhere except dead. On the other hand, long-shot missions have pulled Galatea's ass out of the fire before. I've seen them work. I've even flown them.'

'They're also what got us into this mess,' Zoe interjected.

Ira held up a huge, meaty digit. 'No,' he said. 'That was a conspiracy. The long-shot mission was what got us out of it.'

'You call this *out of the mess*?' said Zoe darkly.

'I call us not dead *yet*,' said Ira. 'And that's the point. Testing the unknown is how you make progress. Finding ever-smarter ways of staying safe is how you die. Plus,' he added with a shrug, 'it's this or storage for me, so my decision isn't difficult.'

'*Storage?*' said Zoe, appalled. 'They'd do that to you?'

'What other option do they have?' he said with a chuckle. 'They can't kill me because I'm *the great Ira Baron*. But while I'm walking around, I'm an embarrassment.' Ira waved her concern away. 'Look,' he said, 'you guys both know you don't get to walk away from this. The government understands your little gesture this morning, and frankly, I empathise. They know they share some of the culpability for what happened, so they're changing their strategy. Which means you get your dream mission with a brand-new ship and a first-class crew. You can choose to participate in that if you want.'

'What's the alternative?' said Zoe.

'Nothing as good,' said Ira. 'The mission will go ahead without you. The *Gulliver* will stay here, for strategic reasons, and you'll spend the next few months in another resort. It's a nice one, but in a much smaller cavern. After that, you're free to do what you like.'

'Of course I'll take the fucking job,' Mark snapped. 'You can't dangle my life's work in front of me and then tell me it's leaving if I don't play along. When do we go? Does Zoe have time to let her family know what's happening?'

Ira paused. 'I'm afraid Professor Tamar isn't invited.'

Mark rocked back, stunned. 'What?' he said. 'Why ever not?'

'Because there's only room for one physicist, and that slot is already filled by our top scientist on Depleted Zone dynamics – Doctor Ataro. You hired her, I believe.'

'Zoe knows about the Depleted Zone,' said Mark.

Zoe looked pained.

'Not as much as Doctor Ataro,' said Ira. 'We both know that Zoe's been with you this entire time, studying ember-warp. When was the last time she even visited the Zone, Mark?'

'That's not the point,' said Mark.

'Yes, it is,' said Ira. 'The Academy already approved the decision.'

'I'm not flying without my wife!' Mark shouted.

'Then don't fly,' said Ira.

An uncomfortable silence descended. Mark's gaze locked on Zoe's brown eyes.

66

'I'll leave you now,' said Ira. 'You can use the network to register your choice. We're shielded here.'

He downed the rest of his drink, offered them both a pre-IPSO-era Galatean salute and sauntered out of the lounge without looking back.

Mark and Zoe watched each other for several long seconds. Her face bore the familiar, hooded look he associated with angry calculation. They both knew they were being manipulated.

'I'm not going,' he said. 'Fuck them.'

'Go,' said Zoe. 'You won't be happy unless you do.'

'No. I won't leave you.'

Zoe scowled. 'Okay, two points. First, those bastards have finally found a wedge to drive between us—'

'I don't see this as a wedge—' Mark started.

She cut him off. 'Don't kid yourself. This mission has been burning a hole in you for the last fifteen years, Mark. Barely a day passes when you don't talk about it. It'll kill you if you don't go. If you care about this marriage, you'll let them dick you over this one time and get that red-hot wire out of your soul. Because otherwise I'll have to live with the person who spends the rest of their life wondering what would have happened if they'd gone. And I don't want that.

'Second point. Let's be honest about what this mission means. This is your *crusade*, Mark. This is your chance to follow in your parents' footsteps and end a war with a single act. Not your natural mum and dad, but your *super-parents*: Will and Rachel. The ones you never stopped obsessing over.'

Mark's eyes went wide. 'What are you talking about?'

'For as long as I've known you, you've been trying to finish this fight. Some part of you still believes that the reason why we ever had to go to war at all is because you weren't on top of your shit. Because you were too self-centred to act in time and somehow not as good as they were.'

Mark threw up his hands. 'This has never been about me! You heard Ira – there are genuine strategic gains—'

'Which are completely beside the point!' said Zoe. Her expression became pained. 'Look, Mark, there's no criticism of you here. We're *losing the war*. You've been defined by this goddamned fight the whole time we've been married and it's slowly crushing you. Maybe this is how you heal. I don't think you can go on without at least trying.'

'But I might not come back!' Mark shouted.

They both understood the threat profile on the Backspace run. It made normal missions look like trips to the park. Zoe's face melted into gentleness. She reached out and touched his face.

'Oh, honey,' she said. 'That's always true. Every time we go out.'

'But I don't want to do that *without you*.' Tears filled his eyes.

'No, but this is still war,' she said. 'And we're both officers. We know how this works. If you don't go, they'll probably kidnap you and shove you aboard anyway. Either that or you'll wake up and find they've taken me. You should be glad this is something you want. We're talking about the Academy here, Mark. They stop at nothing.'

Mark finally clued in that he didn't have a choice, and that Zoe needed to turn that disaster into a win for her to keep going.

'We had a good run,' she added, her voice cracking. 'They left us alone for years while we did our part. Ira gave us that. He let us have a ship and a whole life together. And we'll have another one. Just as soon as you get back.'

His insides twisted.

'I'll wait for you,' she said. Her lip quivered.

Mark grabbed hold of her and didn't let go for a long time.

3: MOTION

3.1: WILL

Will found the gravesite less than a kilometre up the tunnel. On one side of the stream, surrounded by thick clusters of poppies, lay two long rows of shallow, rectangular pits. He could see bodies in there, smeared with greasy white soil and layered over with filmy mould. However, nothing appeared to be rotting. Rather, he had the unnerving sense from the pale, twitching bulbs in those holes that bodies were growing instead, flesh and fungus involved in some kind of obscene symbiosis.

This, he realised, must have been exactly what had happened to him that morning. He'd been extruded straight out of the ground dressed in a rough approximation of the garments he'd been wearing when Snakepit first dissolved him.

Now that he thought about it, Elsa's remarks had implied as much. This gravesite wasn't a place of rest so much as a recycling station for clones. Will's *thread* would check out, leaving his tissues to be adapted and used by whatever clone showed up next. Will glanced down at his hands with new respect and a little disgust.

With lingering trepidation, he climbed into one of the pits and lay down, settling against the damp, sucking mud. Beyond the soft walls of the enclosure he could see the luminous chandeliers swaying gently far above. He shut his eyes, reached for his home node, and this time let the feeling come.

As before, he saw himself on the threshold of that vast, forbidding chamber crammed with ghosts. It loomed inside him, visceral and intense. Will forced himself to concentrate on being there and took a step forward.

What had looked portentous and mystical before now snapped into focus. The figures around him gained solidity and colour. Far from feeling sinister, the great space he stood in now appeared to be nothing more than an old-fashioned train station – perhaps a little quirky and Gothic in style, but certainly nothing to be afraid of. The grey stone arches were clean and brightly lit. Through high windows, Will could make out an Earthlike sky. The smell of baked goods reached him. He glanced around and saw a refreshment stall to his left, offering croissants.

All around, versions of himself bearing different physical alterations strode about the black-and-white-tiled floor, popping in and out of existence like soap bubbles. None of them paid him the slightest attention. And on the walls, those great orange banners he'd seen before no longer displayed alien runes. Somehow, those same symbols had been translated into plain English. They said things like *Local Data*, *The History* and *Search Corridors*. Will found one labelled *Mesh Routes to Other Loci* and guessed it was what he wanted. Pretending a certainty he didn't feel, he set off in that direction, adding himself to one of the streams of busy pedestrians weaving through the space.

As he walked, Will noticed that this virtual environment felt a lot less *plastic* than those he remembered from his previous life. It didn't feel like he was suspending a physical reality to inhabit this place, and he could guess why. He suspected that back in the gravesite, his body would be dissolving into the muck, just like the others. He'd become a *thread*, a strand of processing hosted somewhere in Snakepit's distributed organic computing matrix – a digital dream.

He shivered as another memory returned to him with the blunt certainty of a dropped rock. *This* was how he'd been able to watch himself die from a distance. His normal roboteering talents had played no part in the experience. Will had become a thread before his mind had died.

Physically dying here did not necessarily translate into the end of life. No wonder Elsa had worried that he'd be killed and *then* arrested. He'd blanked the remark at the time as another piece of weirdness, but suddenly it made sense. As did Tars and Ronno's abrupt leap to murderous action. They weren't seeking to *terminate* him but to force him to this place, presumably under their control.

So what else was he missing? If he'd become a thread in his last life, what had happened afterwards? How had he lost his memory? Will frowned, furious at his own inability to unpick his past, until a passive vid playing on a nearby wall-panel caught his attention. He slowed to stare, unable to draw his gaze away.

On the screen, he saw a version of himself wearing a ludicrous military uniform in orange and black, adorned with enormous medals. He sprawled on a golden swivel-throne, his hair a tangled mess like someone fresh out of bed. A silver baseball bat lay across his lap. But for his eyes, the clone resembled a parody of a tinpot dictator out of Earth's past. His haunted gaze, however, suggested that something altogether less funny was going on.

Behind him lay a replica of the IPSO senate chamber where Will had endured so many infuriating meetings with Earth's politicians. Instead of senators in the ranked seats, Will saw smashed mannequins dressed in House robes. Their heads and arms littered the floor.

'...so that's great, too,' the clone was saying, staring intently at the top of his bat. 'I've barely had to rise to full awareness once this month, so fewer headaches. And without wanting to give away too much, we're down to five major Cancers. I have my eye on all of them, so you can expect more major interventions in the next few weeks. My apologies in advance for breaking your shit. Glitches are also down. Economy's looking good, so well done to all my citizen-selves. And I love what people are doing with that mermaid thing.'

Will realised that he had to be watching Balance, the all-powerful god Elsa had warned him about. He didn't look particularly dangerous, but he didn't look well, either.

'The Photurians have backed off,' Balance went on. 'Which is a relief, because I finally finished cleaning up all the shit they broke last time. And our defence research is really coming along, so big thanks to every part of me who's involved with that.' He paused. 'But still, it sucks in here, guys. You really need to figure out why we can't go and clean up the galaxy yet, because I'm getting a little stir-crazy, okay? Otherwise I'm going to have to do another identity reset, and none of us wants that.' Balance glanced around at the chamber with wide, unblinking eyes, an expression of electric loathing flashing across his features. 'Okay, that's enough. Balance out.'

The video message displayed a brief title page before starting afresh. *'This month's message from our illustrious Meta.'*

Will hurried onwards, more worried than ever by the world he'd woken up in.

Beyond the archway for *Other Loci* lay a much larger space. A long, Gothic interior telescoped into the distance like the nave of an infinite cathedral. Its floor was crammed with a jumble of small, brightly coloured pavilions except for a central channel filled with bustling people. The locals appeared to be using the space as a cross between an exposition centre and a pedestrian underpass. Most of the Wills ignored the pavilion displays. One or two hung around outside the little structures, engaged in conversation, but for the most part the tents sat there like abandoned follies.

Will set off, following the main flow of pedestrian traffic, but couldn't help glancing at the distractions. The first thing he noticed was that many of the pavilions featured impossible doorways to other spaces. These weren't surprising in a virtual setting. However, most of the locations belonged to his former life. He saw doors into starship cabins and meeting rooms he recognised. He saw metaphor spaces he'd built to model facets of ship function. He even made out the irradiated mesohull chambers of the *Ariel Two* – the sort of place he'd never risk visiting with his own body, but which he'd been to many times behind the eyes of robots.

If this hall hosted a convention of some kind, then the theme was apparently Will's own past. No wonder Elsa had known him so well. The next feature of the market to catch his eye were slogans advertising businesses hanging over some of the pavilion doorways.

'*Experience Romance!*' one promised.

That in isolation wasn't so peculiar until Will noticed that it was sandwiched between two others, one offering *Paranoia*, the other *Schadenfreude*. After that, he began to pay closer attention.

Moreau Body Mods caught his eye. 'All genders. All subspecies. Free consulting.'

A particularly popular stand bearing the name *Mental Massage* offered identity reshaping. 'Who do you want to be?' their logo enquired. 'Nobody leaves us normal! Packages from as low as two-branch-ninety-nine!' A large holographic copy of Will's own head hovered over the doorway, winking obscenely.

Will fought down a shiver of unease. From that point onwards, the more he saw, the less comfortable he felt. His head started to swim from the barrage of newness so he walked faster, focusing his gaze on the distance until he reached an intersection where four halls met.

A simple signpost stood there with nothing written on it. He stared, confused, until he noticed that the Wills flowing past him were quietly announcing place names as they passed.

'Endurance.'

'Voss Lake.'

'Purplewater.'

'Markstown.'

'Mettaburg,' said Will experimentally. The signpost acquired words, with his destination marked to the left. He exhaled in relief and followed it, only to be confronted with an identical intersection a kilometre further on.

As he navigated hall after hall, Will began to get a sense of the scale of the Willworld's virtual environment. It was *enormous*. And not once did the crowds thin out. His copies kept pouring in from some entryway or another. He was traversing a virtual metropolis of unprecedented proportions. Only Earth's great cities supported such crowds.

That eased his mind to some extent, as he was surely lost to his pursuers by now. On the other hand, he began to feel an ugly kind of social pressure. He was surrounded on all sides by entities that believed themselves to be *him* – talking like him, acting like him, wearing his face.

In a world full of copies, the only thing that apparently marked him out as unique was that he wasn't in on the joke. Despite Elsa's brief explanation, Will still had only the vaguest inkling of what was going on. He failed to see how a society this warped had managed to hold together for a single day, let alone forty years.

Will's bewilderment slowly melted into tedium. And from tedium it condensed into anger. He was a roboteer, for crying out loud. Couldn't someone just give him a memory dump? Everything here, though, appeared to be for sale, and Will still had no idea what these people used for money.

After almost three hours of walking, Will's exit finally appeared. By that point, he was sweating into his virtual ship-suit and fuming. He paused for a moment to rest and wondered why any virtual transport system would use such a profoundly inefficient metaphor for getting about.

Beyond the Mettaburg archway, Will found himself in another arrivals hall depressingly similar to the one he'd left. Even the café looked the same. The only difference lay in the density of traffic. This station hummed with bodies. The concourse ahead of him labelled *Arrivals* was barely visible above the throng and someone jostled him with every other step. Will felt ready to scream.

As he trudged towards the exit, he caught sight of another sign, just like the one he'd seen at his point of departure. *The History*, it read. Will stopped. By now it was clear that the history in question could only be his own. If he wanted to know what had happened to him, wasn't this exactly the place to look? Elsa had told him to make his way directly to the Mettaburg exit and avoid distractions, but he'd been walking for hours already and was sick of feeling ignorant. Was he really going to wait around for one of these pseudo-copies to fill him in? The prospect of finding out for himself was incredibly appealing. It surely wouldn't take long to discover the shape of his past. He'd have one quick look and leave. How much of a risk could that honestly be?

Elsa's words about Balance came back to him: *He'll seek you out if he can, and he has the power of a whole world behind him.* Will shook his head. Balance just looked like another clone. Crazier and lonelier, perhaps, but not terrifying. And he was nothing here if not anonymous. That was so obvious, it hurt. So long as he kept his mouth shut he was just another identical body. Will set his jaw and struck off in the direction of The History.

Beyond the next arch, he was pleased to find himself at the top of a cylindrical space like the interior of an enormous tower. A peaked roof of steel and glass arched overhead while a helical ramp with marked doorways descended into the gloom. Variformed clones wandered around it as if exploring a museum. Several wrought-iron elevators clinging to the ramp offered speedy trips up and down the shaft. The whole space had a gratifyingly obvious layout. Time was vertically arranged, with the most recent memories at the top.

His mood faltered when he headed for the closest history door and noticed the explanatory plaque placed beside it.

Will Kuno-Monet descends to Snakepit with Andromeda Ng-Ludik.

He scowled. How could the most recent moment in The History

be something he already remembered? Will strode through the arch anyway and found himself traversing a dark corridor lined with portals into moments from his fateful trek down to the planet that had swallowed him.

On the other side of each arch, five-minute chunks of his memories played on repeat like passive virts. Wills of various colours, shapes and sizes wandered around inside them, peering at the vegetation or examining Ann's face as she led him down his first tunnel.

Will marched straight for the last arch. It showed him carrying Ann's body into the alcove she'd located to keep them safe from the Rumfoord League soldiers pursuing them.

Will fumed as he glanced about. This was the last moment in the world's official history? No, he realised – these were the last moments in the life of the person he'd *once been*. Of course there was no shared history beyond this point. If Elsa was to be believed, the intervening years had been experienced from billions of different perspectives at once. The clones probably stored that information in a totally different way.

He marched back out into the helical corridor, bumping an unsuspecting Will-duplicate on the way. This copy wore a fuzz of short black fur and had weirdly wide-spread eyes. He looked almost like a Galatean domestic robot.

'Watch where you're going,' said the robot-Will in a synthetic-sounding voice.

Will forced back a snarl of disgust, muttered an apology and kept walking. He could feel the copy's eyes on his back as he strode away.

Even if he couldn't learn about the recent past here, he could at least fix the damned holes in his memory. He decided to head straight for the first major gap he'd identified – his reaction to his lost wife Rachel.

He followed the ramp to the nearest elevator site and stabbed the old-fashioned button marked *down*. When the elevator appeared, he found a clone inside wearing an outfit that was part Surplus Age lift operator, part clichéd academic attire. He had a tweed jacket with two rows of brass buttons and leather patches on the elbows. The elevator featured a pair of armchairs, a reading table and a bookshelf.

Will hesitated on the threshold. He hadn't expected to be confronted by a human operator. Nobody had done a job like that for centuries.

'Can I help you?' said the clone in the lift.

'Take me to Rachel, please,' said Will tersely. 'First encounter.'

He dearly hoped he hadn't somehow given his ignorance away simply by asking.

Fortunately, the lift operator looked delighted by the request.

'An excellent field of study,' he said, grinning broadly. 'I assume you're referring to the human original rather than the Transcended simulacrum?'

Something deep inside Will's mind lurched. The shadows in the elevator abruptly gathered depth.

'What did you say?' said Will.

The lift-librarian regarded him uncertainly. 'A simple question, my dear Will,' he said. 'We historians strive to be precise, that is all. I assumed you were referring to the woman herself, and not the alien shadow which...'

Will missed the rest of what the clone was saying. He gripped the elevator door to hold himself steady as blocked memories burst free inside him.

The Transcended.

They were the feature of his former life that had eluded him. Suddenly the fragments of his past made much more sense. He'd encountered them, back during the war, and they'd *changed* him. He hadn't been truly human from that moment forward.

That was why the presence of clones had so disturbed him. He'd tried to make backups of himself in his former life and failed. The Transcended had stopped him. And that was why he'd had the gall to take on Snakepit's planet-sized intelligence. Because he'd been humanity's only living super-weapon. That was why he owned a starship and why he'd been betrayed.

Now that he remembered that shadowy race, it astonished him that they'd somehow slipped his mind. His meeting with them had shaped the entire arc of his life. *How could he possibly have forgotten?*

Then he understood: the fault in recall wasn't his. He'd been prevented from seeing. And with that thought, one last, terrible memory landed like a comet in his mind.

The Transcended had killed him. Will had discovered that *they* were responsible for Snakepit and the race of monsters it had spawned. So they had shut him down. They had pinned his mind open and dissected it while he was still conscious.

76

Will screamed as the vivid horror of that moment flooded back into him. The next thing he knew, he was on his knees, gripping the elevator doorway with bloodless knuckles. The lift-librarian stared at him with wide, frightened eyes.

'I'm sorry,' said Will, dragging himself to his feet. 'Unexpected side effects of a little mental massage. I'm still integrating my new identity. I'll be fine.'

He backed away from the elevator.

'Please,' said the lift-librarian awkwardly. 'Don't walk. You should sit down. I'll ring for help.'

'No,' said Will. 'No time, I'm afraid. I just remembered something important.'

He walked back up the ramp as fast as he dared, trying not to break into a run.

'Wait,' said the lift-librarian, but Will wasn't hanging around to see what *help* looked like. He had the awful sense that he'd given himself away again – badly, this time.

The lift-librarian stepped out of his elevator study and started following Will up the ramp.

'Please!' he said again. 'Will! This isn't safe.'

Will didn't look back. He headed straight for the door to the Mettaburg concourse.

The domesticbot clone moved to block his path. Will darted around him and began to jog. He strode into the arrivals area to lose himself in the crowd.

He was about halfway across the station when a curious clanging filled the air. From an unmarked archway, four new clones appeared – each twice the height of the other pedestrians. They wore tiger-striped police uniforms and eerie plaster masks bearing Will's face.

'EVERYONE PLEASE STAND STILL,' one of the monsters announced in a voice like thunder. 'A DISTURBANCE IS BEING INVESTIGATED.' Suddenly, Balance seemed a lot more menacing.

It took a few moments for everyone in the room to clue in. Many of the copies kept walking. Will took advantage of the lag and moved straight for the exit area. He muttered his destination under his breath over and over, in case departure needed an incantation like the one that had lit up the signposts.

'Mettaburg! Mettaburg! Mettaburg!'

He had no idea why the simulation hadn't simply frozen at Balance's command, or why commuters still appeared to be coming and going. He simply didn't understand enough about how this place worked, but while it was letting him leave, he wasn't complaining.

'PLEASE STEP AWAY FROM...'

Will didn't hear the rest because the station vanished. His eyes flew open to reveal the walls of an open gravesite overlooked by a high, wooden ceiling with the words *Welcome to Mettaburg* painted on it in red.

Will drew a breath of fresh air and groaned with relief. He'd made it out. Just. No more exploring. This time he was headed straight for the Proustian Underground as fast as he could, presuming Balance didn't catch him first.

3.2: MARK

Rather than return them to the resort, the Fleet offered Mark and Zoe an executive suite in the officers' dorm near the shuttle station. They reluctantly accepted. Once there, they locked the doors and raised the privacy baffles. Mark didn't have anyone he wanted to say goodbye to on Galatea other than his wife. The *Gulliver* had been his home for years, and most of his friends were either dead or out on missions of their own. Even if they'd still been around, Mark wouldn't have traded a moment with Zoe for any of them.

They both wanted their last night together to feature sex prominently, but in the end it comprised a lot of quietly frantic holding and a total lack of sleep. They lay on the grey, standard-issue bed-foam and stared at the ceiling while the weight of impending separation suffocated them like invisible pillows. After decades of operating together as a tight-knit team, the prospect of a long, possibly fatal mission apart hurt too keenly to be ignored.

In order to freshen up the following morning, Mark had to resort to a fatigue-flush and the nausea that went with it. As soon as he was done retching, he dressed and held Zoe again until the room warned him about missing his departure window. He clung to her, wordless, while the room complained.

'You have five minutes to leave before transfer to the briefing shuttle becomes impossible. Failure to depart at this time will constitute abandonment of your assigned mission. If you do not wish to participate in the mission, the Fleet requires spoken acknowledgement...'

Eventually, Zoe dragged herself from his hopeless grip. She batted his strengthless hands away and pushed him out of the suite, her eyes full of tears. She locked the door after him. Mark stood there for a full minute with his head resting on the door before the hallway started dumping warnings into his sensorium.

He left for the shuttle in a daze and spent the next four hours trying to force discipline into his tormented head. He needed to be rational about the mission, even if he wasn't happy with the way it had been crewed. Or how much notice he'd been given. Or the transparent ploy to separate him from his wife. Or anything else about the Academy's shitty, underhand tactics.

By the time the info-shielded briefing shuttle arrived to collect him from Fleet Orbital One, Mark was as ready as he would ever be. His sadness had given way to empty dislocation. Zoe had been right. While it hurt like hell to leave her, he had to make the best of the mission.

It was the one thing they hadn't tried. They'd bombed Phote worlds, attempted infiltrations and engaged in secret plans to poison entire planets. None of it had slowed the Photes' advance. Now it was either risk Backspace or roll over and get ready for absorption into the grinning mass-mind that lay in wait for them. Mark knew he couldn't let it come to that. If he abandoned his original vision, he'd just be letting himself, Zoe and everyone else down.

The interior of the briefing shuttle was as blandly well appointed as the executive suite he'd left behind. Mark made the obligatory ablutions in the zero-gee wash-space next to the bioseal doorway and knocked back the welcome file the shuttle SAP dumped into his head.

The mission profile unpacked before him. A new ship, the GSS *Edmond Dantes*, had been readied for them with full schematics available upon boarding. Mark would operate as expedition lead, as expected. The day-to-day operations and selection of research goals would be his responsibility.

The mission's Social Accountability Officer would, of course, retain veto rights and final authority, with the understanding that this power would be asserted only as necessary to act for the collective good of the Galatean people.

No surprises there. Mark had known the moment Ira mentioned the mission that there would be a Social Accountability Officer in there somewhere. In his experience, on any ship other than his own, there always was one.

The only surprising component of the plan lay in the stipulation that his expedition would begin the moment they reached the Depleted Zone and not before. Prior to that, his SAO would exercise direct authority over the proceedings and treat the flight as a standard Galatean military operation. His eyes narrowed as he ingested that detail. It smacked of further deceit. He filed it away for later thought and drifted into the main shuttle lounge.

The central space was lined with wall-panels bearing the obligatory agitation patterns and a circle of low-gee harness-couches where four of his new crew-mates hung waiting. Ira was already there. The other familiar face belonged to Clath Ataro, the physicist sitting in his wife's chair. She'd gained a rather dowdy cyan buzz cut since the last time he'd seen her. Her large, nervous, almond-shaped eyes oozed hope and good intent. She shot him a smile. Mark nodded back.

His mission profile filled in the identities of the two new faces. The man in his subjective thirties with the narrow, tightly held features and the oddly plasticised hair was Judj Apis, a biosciences and security expert. He looked like the kind of guy who spied for the government even when he wasn't being asked to. He had a résumé full of awards and decorations, but Mark was used to that. Most of the people he flew with had more accolades than sense.

The fashionably bald girl sitting next to him with the chromatophore scalp and hard eyes was Palla Muri, his SAO. Her objective age was nineteen and her bio contained almost nothing except the words *Autocratic Academy*. Nothing else was necessary.

'Good morning,' said Mark woodenly, clipping himself into a free seat. 'Is this all of us?'

'Not quite,' said Palla. 'One more.'

The bioseal door opened again to let Andromeda Ludik through. Mark gawped, his pulse booming in his ears. If anything, Ann was even more beautiful than the last time he'd seen her, and even more imposing. These days, Ann was over two metres tall with a perfect Amazonian physique, short, jet-black hair and the face of a warrior goddess. Her physical form had been slowly morphing to optimise her visual impact during the entire time he'd known her.

She'd made the changes, so far as he could tell, with zero interest in her own personal appeal but meticulous attention to public relations and her effectiveness in the field. He'd been told that the mere sight of Ann in full battle rage tended to freeze even the most tightly programmed Photes into inactivity.

However, it wasn't her looks that had Mark staring. It was the fact that she was there at all. Certainly she had mission relevance. She'd worked with Will and been the recipient of his molecular technology, but she was also Galatea's top weapon and an icon to boot. Regardless of any failures on her part, she still single-handedly constituted a significant share of the colony's remaining military might.

He glanced at Ira's impassive face and then back to Ann. You didn't put all your failing, high-profile military heroes on the same ship for small reasons. They weren't just getting him out of the way. Whatever logic had brought them here had to be a lot darker than that. Mark's sense that there was something deeply wrong with his dream mission increased another notch.

Ann drifted over and clipped herself in without making eye contact with anyone. Mark watched her as the silence dragged. They'd barely spoken since the Earth evacuation – just a few bitter exchanges in which Ann had managed to pack a great deal of implied menace.

'Great to be here,' said Ann, without an ounce of emotional inflection in her voice. 'Shall we get going?'

Palla nodded and gestured at the ceiling cameras. The shuttle undocked and headed out to high orbit where their ship waited. The gees gently shunted everyone back into their seats.

'Welcome, everyone,' said Palla Muri as soon as the wall-panels displayed the *safe to talk* icon. 'As your shadows will already have told you, I'm Palla, your new best buddy and fearless leader, at least in the political sense. Mark here is leading the cool sciencey bit, but we'll get to that later. There's nothing to see in my bio unless you're running Habanero-level encryption, so let me tell you a bit about who you're dealing with. I flunked out of the Academy about two years ago for making unnecessarily combative decisions – or so my peers decided, anyway – and was sidelined into ship-level leadership.'

Mark's eyebrows crept upwards. That was a lot of specialisation in one so young. For all her faults, Palla had to be good. She apparently knew it.

'I've been working on counter-raids ever since. I have thirty-seven Phote gunship kills and five own-goals. Which I think makes me a perfect fit for this mission.'

Mark's eyes opened wider. That was an astonishing level of effectiveness for such a short career, but it also spoke of a trigger-happy zeal that made his own wobbly record look tame. *Own-goals* was Fleet slang for destroying a ship in your own raiding squad. Usually one own-goal earned you a caution. Two got you kicked out of the Fleet. Three warranted either storage or mandatory suicide. Clearly, Palla was as much of a special case as the rest of them.

'Needless to say, as your fun-loving SAO, I have all the ship's overrides and I get to detonate the ship any time I see fit. So be nice to me, because your lives are in my hands.'

She smiled and winked at Mark. He blinked back in confusion.

'I'm also trained to do every job on this ship to a basic level of competence. So when not issuing unwelcome diktats, I'll be filling in with whatever grunt-work is necessary. You've all had more time in specialised roles than me, so tell me what to do and I'll wash your digital dishes. My psych evaluation, which most of you aren't allowed to see, is full of peachy little warning flags, mostly about anger issues and whatever. But I don't think that's going to be a problem. So long as none of you pisses me off.'

She shot them a conspiratorial smile, as if to say, *You've pissed me off already, but I don't mind.*

Mark's back tightened as he listened. Palla's breezy, subversive tone was pure *New Society* – the kind of kid who'd play tag with you right up until they were ordered to stab you in the back.

'My sub is Ira here, who I think used to be the president or something, back when we still had dumb shit like that. He's also our psych specialist, so he *does* get to look at my flags. Lucky boy – right, Ira?'

Ira regarded her with empty eyes and nodded.

'How the mighty have fallen, eh, Ira? The president of everything is now a fricking support officer. How's that working out for you?'

Ira gazed at her and shrugged.

'You can tell me,' she said. 'We're all friends here, right? It's not like anybody here is going to call you a *failure* to your face. Despite all those lives you wasted.'

Ira didn't so much as blink. Mark, however, lost patience. Ira had been like an uncle to him and he'd never seen the man do anything but his best.

'Is this really necessary?' he said.

They were supposed to be having a mission briefing. Even for a military culture that had practically enshrined informality, Palla's behaviour was out of line.

'You're *so* right,' said Palla with an undaunted smile. 'We can chit-chat later.' She pointed at him. 'And this, of course, is the famous Captain Ruiz,' she said, 'our pilot and expedition lead. He's studied the Depleted Zone for years and, out of all of us, he's the only one who's been inside it before. It wasn't great, apparently. He tried to rescue his half-mum and got stuck there for weeks while all his passengers nearly died. Mind you,' she said, looking him up and down, 'the prospect of being stuck in a ship with Captain Mark and nothing to do all day doesn't sound so bad to me.'

She grinned. Clath chuckled.

Mark's face coloured before he could invoke his augs to suppress the response. He glared at her. What did she think she was playing at?

'Mark's sub – and our lead officer for the initial military phase of the mission – is Andromeda Ludik, everybody's favourite ice queen.'

Ann regarded Palla with all the compassion and interest of a fully fed tiger.

'Once we reach the Zone, Ann will have the hardest job on the ship,' Palla went on. 'She'll be plugged into our sensors and model-ling the curvon flow in real-time. Mark will use her data to fly. And sitting beside our cast of elderly all-stars, I'd like to introduce the two other members of our lucky, lucky team. The first is Clath Ataro, our Depleted Zone physics specialist, who's been training for this mission for what – six years?'

'Eight years,' said Clath brightly. 'Though I honestly didn't think they'd ever let it happen.' She looked around at the others with eyes full of enthusiasm.

Mark smiled woodenly at her and tried not to resent the poor woman's presence. He and Zoe had hired her years back. She was an excellent officer who'd kept them up to date with dull, if incredibly conscientious, reports.

'And lastly,' said Palla, 'this is Judj, our resident biodefence analyst. He's our ship's doctor, our seeded-subversion specialist and the person we should all go to if we start having really happy dreams in which everyone loves each other. Right, Judj?'

'Yep,' said Judj.

'Get this,' said Palla. 'Unlike the rest of us, Judj actually *volunteered* for this mission!'

Judj shot her a quick glance of disapproval and then nodded.

'So I did,' he said.

That Judj had volunteered implied he had the clearance to even know the mission was happening. Which was more than Mark had been told, despite his all-star status. Any doubts Mark might have had that Judj worked for Internal Security could now be put to rest.

'Now that the doors are sealed, your mission-briefing access has bumped a level,' Palla assured them. 'So if you want to know more about our happy team, just ask your shadows. And now I'll hand over to Mark, who's going to explain what this mission is all about.'

Mark examined his audience. Ira stared through him like a robot and Ann didn't even bother looking in his direction. Of the three younger crew, only Clath appeared engaged. Palla's smug smile betrayed nothing and Judj watched him like a lab specimen. Was there any way to breathe enthusiasm into this joyless bunch? He was damned well going to try.

'I think you're all aware of the goal of this mission,' said Mark. 'We're headed for Snakepit. We'll try to rouse the planet to help us, and if we can't, we'll glass it to prevent the Photes from ever having access.

'Few people realise that in physical terms, Snakepit's not far away. It's only about thirty-eight light-years from Galatea. But it's in the wrong direction – corewards – so warp can't take us where we need to go. That means the only way to get to it in our lifetime is through a Penfield Lobe gate that can take us down onto a lower shell. Fortunately, the new gate we found looks extremely promising. It has the same characteristic prime-number sequence in its absorption lines as the one the Photes now have blockaded, it's on our shell, and it's relatively close. In fact, the only thing wrong with it is that it's on the other side of the Zone.

'But is that such a big deal? We're all used to thinking of the Zone as a wall – an impenetrable barrier that runs for hundreds of light-years. Yet it's not. It's just a region of space where curvons aren't flowing out from the galactic core – not so much a wall as a gap. Likewise, we all assume that the Zone is a Transcended artefact just because the edge of the Zone is straight. And because it looks artificial, we've also assumed that we're supposed to stay out. That we're not supposed to cross it. Since the start of the war, that logic has barely been challenged despite the fact that the Transcended never once mentioned the Zone to us.

'Nobody has debated that thinking because the Zone is admittedly dangerous. We've been busy fighting the Photes. And only small ships with tiny crews stand a chance of getting through. Add to that the possibility of existential risks on the other side and you can see why this mission hasn't been at the top of anyone's agenda.

'But two things are different now. One – we lost Earth, which puts us in species crunch-time. And two – the Alpha Flaw has grown by over *eighty per cent* since first measurement. Which means that traversing safely is more likely now than ever. This means that one ship can make a difference. We know this mission is a stretch, but if we pull it off, the human race could be free again. The terror of the Photes could be ended once and for all.'

Mark surveyed his team's faces. Only two expressions had changed: Ann's and Judj's. Both had slid in the direction of outright cynicism.

'Any questions so far?' said Mark.

'Sure,' said Judj. 'You talked about "traversing safely" – what does *likely* actually mean in this context? A fifty per cent survival likelihood or five?'

'We don't know,' Mark admitted. 'No automated probe has navigated all the way through the Alpha Flaw or you'd have heard about it. Our superlight drones get stuck in dead space, and everything sub-light we've sent in won't reach the other side for decades. The best news we have is that a few of our superlight probes reached an area where curvon density is increasing, suggesting that the far side of the Zone can't be far away. On the other hand, the main reason probes haven't made it through is because we've barely tried. Research in this area has received almost zero budget for the last thirty years. We haven't risked a ship with human-level piloting intelligence in decades. And at the same time, drone technology has come on in leaps and bounds. We'll be able to reuse some of the same technology that detects Phote blockades to identify patches of dead space.'

'No answer, then,' said Judj flatly. 'Question two: how do we even know there is an *other side?*'

'From the presence of the lure star,' said Mark.

'Which is how far away?'

'About ninety light-years.'

'Not actually close, then,' said Judj. 'And what happens if the Zone ends right before it?'

'Then we're hosed,' said Mark. 'But that scenario has a very low probability.'

'Which you determine how, exactly?'

Mark drew a deep breath and tried to answer without sounding annoyed. 'Our best theories suggest that the galactic curvon flow relates to a system of holographic convection cells in the horizon of our galaxy's central black hole.'

'Convection of what?'

'Spatial potential,' said Mark.

'That's a little speculative, isn't it?' said Judj.

'Not as much as you might think,' said Clath eagerly. 'Since we started doing research on ember-warp vacuum states, we have a much better idea of how curvons work. The first thing you have to ask yourself is how spatial quasiparticles could *ever* climb through an event horizon in the first place. Old-style GR won't permit it. And that puts constraints on how gravity has to work, and what the structure of a black hole has to be like. Basically, your Planck-length spatial network has to contain extra curvature information that baryonic matter can't touch. And inside a black hole—'

'In any case,' said Mark quickly, 'it's very likely that the Zone is a narrow membrane between two regions of curvon-rich space.' The briefing was already proving difficult enough without it dissolving into a physics lecture.

'Then why isn't it moving?' said Ann without looking at him. 'If Doctor Ataro is right and it's all down to the black hole, where's the spin? How come the Zone isn't racing through space like a grit storm? How come we have navigable space at all?'

'We don't know,' said Clath. 'That's a limitation of the approach, I admit – it only works if we presume a central galactic mass with almost no angular momentum, which we know isn't the case. But the curvon-density patterns we observe reflect that model anyway.'

'We've studied this,' said Mark, 'and the drop-off is consistent no matter which fissure we explore. We wouldn't be going if we thought this was an issue.'

Ann snorted. 'Your lack of a consistent scientific model is *entirely* reassuring.'

'What about alien threats?' said Judj.

'Our telescopes see no evidence of warp-light in that region of space,' said Mark. 'Besides the lure star, there's absolutely no evidence of interstellar activity.'

'Unless they're using tau-chargers to cover their tracks,' said Judj.

'All of them? On every flight?' said Mark tersely. 'Whoever *they* are supposed to be? Look, the situational modelling on Backspace has been studied for years. We see a twenty per cent chance of ruins like those of the Fecund, a twenty per cent likelihood of managed territory for some new species that's still evolving, and a *fifty* per cent likelihood of nothing at all – space empty of life. That's the most credible scenario by far.'

'What about the last ten per cent?' said Judj. 'You've only given us ninety.'

Mark exhaled. This wasn't the easiest crew he'd ever worked with.

'We see a four per cent likelihood of a junior sentient race, hunter-gatherer or equivalent, a three per cent likelihood that the area is under direct Transcended ownership, and another three per cent likelihood that it's already dominated by Photes.'

'Photes?' said Judj. 'You're saying they've been exploring behind our backs?'

Mark shook his head. 'No, I'm talking about space dominated by whatever race built Snakepit. Some other kind of Phote we haven't seen yet.'

'So, violently acquisitive aliens, then,' said Ann. 'With unknown technology.'

'It's unlikely,' said Mark, bristling.

'So everyone has comfortably dismissed the possibility that the Zone is there to protect us from someone else getting in rather than to stop us from getting out – is that right?' Ann turned her predator's gaze to meet his.

'That's right,' said Mark levelly. 'Because if the Zone is meant to protect us from Photes then it's already fucking failed. And if there's something worse out there, why aren't they already here? That scenario doesn't add up.'

Instead of receiving a committed crew for his mission, he appeared to have been locked in a shuttle with a bunch of military flameouts. Maybe the Academy had death in mind for him after all.

Palla broke the uncomfortable silence that followed.

'In any case, you guys don't have to worry about that kind of stuff,' she said, 'because I'm under orders to blow the ship if we encounter an existential threat. I'd focus on the problems we *do* know about if I were you.'

'Okay,' said Mark, rolling his shoulders. 'It works like this. Once we're through, we head for the lure star. We use the far gate to access the lower shell, and then we head back towards the Alpha Flaw, closer to the galactic core.'

'Presuming that the far gate leads to the same shells,' said Ann.

'Yes,' Mark snapped. 'Presuming that. Then we head back through the Flaw under stealth and make straight for Snakepit.'

'So we make the most dangerous crossing in known space *twice.*'

'Yes, Ann. Twice,' said Mark. 'We don't have a choice unless we want to stay in Backspace for ever. From the Alpha Flaw, the trip over to Snakepit is just a few days.'

'So long as there aren't any blockades,' Ann put in.

'Why would the Photes be blockading space they already control?' said Mark. 'You think they *like* doing that shit?'

'The Photes always blockade worlds of military value, regardless of their activity level,' Ann said, 'and activity scales non-linearly with strategic relevance. They don't control Snakepit. Therefore it will be blocked.'

'Except we also know Snakepit isn't generating interstellar traffic because we'd be able to tell if it was,' Mark replied. 'So blockades aren't actually that likely because they'd constitute a misapplication of resources.'

'You assume.'

'Anyhow,' said Mark. 'Once we get to Snakepit, we improvise.' Mark waited for the inevitable critique but Ann said nothing. 'Then, depending on our findings, we either make our way back via the same route or we establish a remote defensive site.'

'Or we die,' said Ann.

'Yes!' Mark shouted. 'We might die! Do you have a problem with that?'

Ann emitted a sudden, chilling laugh like a crazed angel. There was something in the sound of it that made Mark immediately want to be somewhere else.

'Oh no, Mark,' said Ann. 'I'm only trying to figure out whether it's worth taking your plan seriously, that's all. Just weighing the options.'

'Options for *what*?' Mark spat. His hands shook. 'Do you know what that sounds like to me, *Ann*? It sounds like more robotic Galatean threat assessment. That shit's killing us, in case you hadn't noticed. In this entire war we've never once shown any *human* initiative. We've been too confused and too scared.' He stabbed a finger at her. 'I've never once pushed my talents to the limit in this fight and neither have you.'

Her mirth evaporated. 'What about Earth?' she growled.

'That was laziness, pure and simple,' Mark snapped back. '*Your* laziness *and* mine.'

Ann's fingers hovered around the clip on her seat as if she was considering unbuckling and coming over there to ram a fist through his face. Mark held her gaze.

'That's what happens when people like you and me just take fucking orders and don't do something *different*, Ann. You know why I think we're here?' he said, glancing at Palla. 'I think we're *rejects*. I think we've shown that we're a piss-poor fit for what this fight has turned into and we're being given one last chance to redeem ourselves. And if the odds of success are shitty, well, guess what – tough luck on us because those are the odds we get. It's better than watching the whole damned race go extinct while we sit on our thumbs doing nothing about it.'

'It's funny you should say that,' said Palla quietly. She smiled and examined her fingers.

Mark's head whipped around to face her. 'What's funny?'

'I mean, you're basically right,' she said. 'We've all been deemed disposable. You don't wind up on a mission like this otherwise. But the Zone is the least of our worries. You see, we're under orders to use trad-warp as far as the boundary.'

Mark blinked at her. Ember-warp was how you got places fast. Stealth-warp was how you crept around without getting spotted. Trad-warp was good old-fashioned vanilla warp-drive, neither fastest, nor quietest. You used it when you didn't have any other options.

'That'll draw Photes like flies to shit,' he said, his expression clouding.

'I expect so,' said Palla breezily. 'Particularly given that a mission plan has already been leaked to suspected spies.'

Mark had guessed that the mission would have a subtext, but being human bait hadn't occurred to him. They weren't going to explore Backspace. They were going to trick as many Photes into following them as they could.

He suddenly started to feel cheated and stupid. No wonder everyone around him was so bitter. Barring Clath, the rest of them probably didn't expect to see the other side of the Flaw. His desire to take on the mission had blinded him to the obvious.

'By distracting the Photes, we give Earth's population a better chance,' said Palla.

Mark glowered at her. 'So I get my mission in return for sucking down the might of the entire fucking Utopia against us.'

'Like you said,' said Palla, 'those are the odds we get. Though to be honest, compared to the risk profile for the rest of the mission, this is small potatoes.'

He'd been set up to fail. The ship was full of military icons for the simple reason that it made a bigger, juicier target for the Photes to run at. Zoe wasn't aboard because she was too valuable as a research scientist. They didn't need her to die. Mark breathed deep and struggled to reframe the news.

He nodded to Palla. 'Thank you,' he said. 'So it's a race against time. We're committed now, and at least we know what we're in for. Galatea wants us to solve their blockade problem for them, and in return we get a chance to make a difference. I can work with that.'

'Just so you know,' said Palla, 'the Academy doesn't take this sacrifice lightly. It might look like a raw deal, but they need us out there.'

'If they need us to die,' said Mark, 'they're going to be disappointed. I don't intend to.'

Palla shook her head. 'It's not like that, and I guess there's no harm in telling you now. They've put the population of Earth on a concealed orbital in a protoplanetary disc.'

'*What?*' said Clath. She looked horrified. 'That's crazy!'

'Why?' said Mark. 'I can't think of anywhere more likely to kill them.' Protoplanetary discs were star systems where planets were still undergoing violent formation. It was like trying to hide eggs in a running blender.

'Because there was nowhere else to put them,' said Palla. 'By the time we tracked down the spy network Ambassador Shue spawned, we realised the Photes were on to our population-rehousing plans. We had to improvise fast and put our big bucket of coma-cases somewhere the Photes would never look for them. Without rescue, those people will last another six months tops before the habitat is mashed by random impacts. Our actions will give the Fleet a chance to move them, and they need help fast. The more flies we draw, the better their chances are.'

Everyone sat in silence while that reality settled in.

'Usually when I risk everything to save others, I get to volunteer first,' said Mark. 'But under the circumstances, this'll do.'

'My take exactly,' said Palla. 'It sucks to be handed the short straw, but I can't pretend it's not a decent cause. And besides, if we *do* make it to Snakepit, it'll really mess up the Photes, and there's nothing I'd enjoy more.'

Her remark was punctuated by a deep thud as the shuttle locked on to their ship.

'Pods are available and the airlock has sealed,' the shuttle informed them.

'Just like our fates!' said Palla with a grin. 'Last one into the doom boat is a sissy.'

3.3: IRA

Ira floated beside his new shipmates as the docking pod took them down to their vessel and tried not to feel their pain. Nobody spoke, but they might as well have been screaming.

After a lifetime of reading others, Ira had discovered that he couldn't stop. The problem started after he stood down as Galatean Fleet Admiral in the wake of the Suicide War. The realisation that the human race needed to abandon its entire culture of leadership or die wasn't an easy one to absorb. The fact that he'd been in the cross hairs of that silent enemy assault had been the least of his concerns. He was more worried about failing everyone else if the Photurian infection claimed him.

So it wasn't until a few weeks after he'd handed over power to Venetia Sharp's militarised hydra that he noticed the part of his brain that did people-watching simply wouldn't shut up.

It was hardly surprising. He was over a hundred years old and had been popping neurostimulants to boost his leadership skills for decades. But the effects were disturbing. Without an everlasting crisis to manage, his own emotions had faded from sight. He could feel nothing of his own opinions but a kind of distant radio static. Everyone else, though, came through like thunder.

Trapped in a confined space like this, even their body language was intolerable. None of them was happy. Then again, why would they be? Palla had made it clear that the mission was a death sentence. Panic was inevitable. But worse for Ira was that each of them insisted on suffering in different ways.

Mark, for instance, kept waging a war inside himself between duty and his sense of outrage, yet didn't even appear to notice. Little of it showed on his face, thank Gal. He'd finally learned to screen that interior friction and become a relatively polished public figure. These days, he had the just-so salt-and-pepper hair, the powerful physique and the military bearing the media expected. The big giveaway was those eyes that lit up with stubborn fury at the slightest provocation.

Palla, their SAO, meanwhile, was such a poster child for the New Society that Ira didn't believe it for a minute. During her acid briefing, he'd felt the urgent desire to perform coming off her in waves. The entire mission was still a student project for her, even though she knew she was never coming back from it. So she was going to take all her anger and confusion out on him, because of his record and that big red psych marker in his file. Ira was fine with that if it helped her function. Was that patronising of him? Probably. But age earned you certain liberties.

The other two younger crew members were slightly less awful. Clath was like a precocious schoolgirl who appeared to have missed the fact

92

that she'd been pushed out of the trench holding an unloaded rifle. Most of her discomfort stemmed from the cold shoulder Mark was giving her. The fact that he hadn't noticed he was hurting her only made it worse. But her pain was, at least, interpersonal.

Judj, meanwhile, radiated as much paranoia as Clath did innocence. He hid it under a veneer of clever scepticism, but his body language betrayed so many obsessive behaviour cues that a SAP could have spotted it. The New Society didn't leave those traits unhealed without a reason, so something must have broken inside Judj – something *useful* that was now driving him. Chances were, he'd never find out what that was, but Ira didn't mind.

It was Ann who made him feel most uncomfortable. She came across as more detached and dangerous than ever. Andromeda Ng-Ludik was blatantly a demigod – more so than Will had ever been. But, just like Will, she inhabited a cloud of sadness.

He'd watched it grow over the decades they'd fought together. Every passing year as a superbeing appeared to come with an emotional cost, and it had turned Ann into something cold and dark. What remained was this smouldering neutron star of a person – all gravity and no light. The barrage of loneliness she radiated was like the shriek of a hurricane.

What a bunch – useful in combination for nothing except creating a giant distraction. But then, he was no better. He was the phone-it-in ex-president – the man who'd overseen the largest acts of genocide in human history with the best of intentions. No wonder they were the people Galatea had decided to sacrifice in their giant game of chess.

Ira was ready for that, though. He wanted it. There was nothing worse than being an old psychologist in the land of the young. Everyone around him felt like tiny, noisy, clattering robots. Their every collision was as predictable as it was wince-inducing. Surely it was better to go out doing what you were good at than to live like that. And Ira was damned good at field missions even though they hadn't let him near one in years.

'Clath,' he said, 'can you tell us anything about our ship before we get down there?'

She blinked at him. 'Oh! Yes, of course. We're past the exohull so mission-leak shouldn't be a problem. It's called the *Edmond Dantes* and it was designed specifically to probe the Depleted Zone using design ideas contributed by Mark Ruiz and Zoe Tamar.'

'That much I'd guessed,' said Ira. 'But what can it *do*?'

'Well, it's a hybrid,' she said. 'The drive can run in every warp configuration from ember-warp to stealth. And it's not spherical.'

Ira's eyebrows rose. 'It's not?'

'No, it's shaped more like a fat bullet. It has to be because the back is stacked with a ring of massive sub-light engines. There are six, capable of redundant firing. In case we get stuck in the Zone. And we're carrying drones. A *lot* of drones. The hangar bays on this thing are huge. We need tons of remote hardware to set up feeler-relays once we're inside the Flaw.'

'I see,' he said. 'Anything else I should know?'

Clath hesitated, clearly unsure of what else to say. 'We have two habitat cores?' she offered. 'One for crew and one for quarantine. But I guess that's pretty common these days.'

'How about weapons?' said Ira. 'Stealth?'

'We have both,' said Clath. 'Grater-grids, disrupters, the lot. And the main boser is pretty nasty. Setting off a tectonic catastrophe at Snakepit should be easy.' She snatched another anxious glance at Mark. 'Presuming we even need to, of course. Which hopefully we won't.'

The docking pod clunked home and the door opened onto an octagonal chamber not that much bigger than the one they were standing in.

'What's this?' said Ira. 'The airlock opens into the privacy closet?'

'Oh, no,' said Clath. 'I thought everyone knew. This is it. The cabin, I mean. The mission is running on pure virtual.'

Ira opened his mouth and closed it again. He should have guessed. He'd been out of the loop on military flights for so long, it hadn't even occurred to him.

Palla slid through into the space beyond and touched a wall. It hissed open, the door sliding upwards to reveal a support-cabinet like a wet mouth with fat-contact and biofeed cables dangling and twitching inside.

'See you on the other side,' she said and climbed in. The door shut behind her as the cables began to enclose her body.

Ira felt an unexpected stab of claustrophobia. Back in the day, he'd piloted soft-combat ships with interiors not much larger than this. So why did this situation suddenly make his skin crawl? Perhaps because nobody had ever expected him to fly one from inside a casket.

These days, all military personnel were roboteers after a fashion. Everyone was fitted with a shadow, a piece of wetware modelled after the symbiotic neurosystem that had grown inside Ann after her conversion to posthumanity. Their versions weren't as sophisticated as Ann's, of course. They didn't have personalities or make polite conversation. Instead, a military shadow granted a person access to a specialised interior space that functioned as a mental blackboard of sorts. Use of a shadow had been shown to boost a person's IQ by about thirty points without the need for more intrusive cognitive augs.

A person's shadow also conveniently doubled as an early-warning system for seeded conversion as well as a tool for managing a relatively unhackable virtual environment. Because your shadow was personal, subjective and regrown with each update, it provided a way to be plugged in without making yourself vulnerable to the kind of hacking the old roboteers had faced. Theoretically.

Even though Ira had been fitted with a shadow by Academic Order, he'd barely used it – until now.

He watched Mark drift into the cabin and survey the eight support-cabinets with transparent disgust. *There was room for my wife after all*, his eyes said.

Ira looked away. What had he expected? Despite his extraordinary record, stuffed with as many reprimands as heroic victories, Mark still somehow managed to be a twit. Hadn't he seen this coming? Mark, who couldn't tolerate a calculated hedge, had been turned into one. Ira doubted he saw the irony.

'Fine,' Mark said instead. 'Okay. Let's go, then.' He slotted himself into a cabinet.

Ira hovered and watched them slip inside one by one until only he and Judj remained.

Judj eyed him. 'You first,' he said, with a crimped half-smile. 'I insist.'

Ira found himself grinning. He almost laughed.

'My pleasure.'

As he let the cables wrap around him, something that might have been joy briefly lit inside him for the first time in years. Here he was, headed into the jaws of almost certain death, but also *outside his comfort zone*. It had the unexpected consequence of reminding him that he was still alive. Even if they only made it five light-years out of port, just being here and taking part was surely still worth it. If the Photes wanted to chase them, let them come. He'd be ready.

3.4: NADA

Nada existed as a floating bead nestled in a warm, mottled cavern like the inside of a speckled egg. Light entered through a small hole in the ceiling which admitted a brilliant white glow as if from a noonday sun. Other similar – but darker – holes lay dotted around the perimeter of the egg, with several more clustered at the bottom.

Her perspective hovered near the centre of the space. From there, she could read the complex, shifting patterns of black and white on the cavern walls and listen to the reverberating, joyful song of the place. The egg represented that part of the mind-temple belonging to the persona of her cabin gardener. Nada was hard at work rewriting him so that he no longer dreamed of crushing his hands in an airlock door.

Upon leaving Noether, she had rallied her ships and brought them here, to Tsaburu-Kos, a tiny brown dwarf near Galatea which she had turned into her new base of operations. In the days that followed, she'd spun her web – establishing relay lines around the colony tight enough to detect passing ships yet loose enough to not reveal her strength. Her fleet had been out on survey runs ever since, monitoring every piece of Galatean traffic big enough to warp. They'd been at it for almost three weeks and the strain was showing.

Each messenger drone that reached Nada's ship brought more silence from the Galateans and ever-lengthening reports of difficulties from her own crews. That was a problem because Nada couldn't afford to stop. Ever since the Yunus had restructured her identity, rest had proven difficult. Ambition gnawed at her like an open wound. And if she reduced the survey runs, something important might slip through her grasp. That thought made her tremble.

Unfortunately, keeping small crews bottled up in tiny raiding ships for long periods had serious consequences. Even under enforced in-dividuality, Photurians needed community. It was baked into the sacred Protocol they ran on. And since they'd been banned from the complete integration they craved, peer interaction had to suffice.

When they spent too much time alone, all the benefits they'd gained from imposing selfhood started to reverse themselves. Units got strange ideas. They started looking for shortcuts to bliss. Left to their own devices, the crews of such ships often merged into ad hoc hives before succumbing entirely to Fatigue.

Consequently, Nada had taken to policing the minds of her staff whenever they came close enough to edit and sending out blind rewrites to those stationed further afield. Maintaining her fleet's emotional landscape was fast becoming a full-time job.

Her gardener was her most recent and most disappointing discovery. Right under her nose, he'd spent the last eight days idly fantasising about what would happen if he accidentally caught his hands in the cabin's pressurised door. He'd be rendered temporarily useless and, out here, a candidate for cannibalisation into ship parts – a one-way ticket to merged bliss in a starship's computing substrate. He'd been quietly training his deputy to take over without admitting to himself what he was planning. Nada had spotted the identity drift and spent the last half-hour scrubbing his personality for him.

She wished for the thousandth time that her staff were as committed to action as she'd become. Sadly, the Yunus's rewrite of her did not extend to a will to impose the straitjacket of ambition onto her ship-mates. So instead, she was stuck tinkering with their emotions around the edges, erasing their impatience and loneliness, quietly bolstering their diligence and urgency.

While she worked, two other beads slid into the cavern through one of the equatorial holes – one red, one blue. They represented her lead reports for harvesting and analytics, Zilch and Leng Rien.

[Communications Officer Ekkert has a report for you,] said Leng.

Yet another cumbersome direct delivery. As always, she wished that the information had simply been pressed into her via the temple metaphor, but her people had to keep to the rituals. All non-urgent information was delivered in person now.

[Bring him,] she replied.

As a human, she'd used text and audio messages for such interactions all the time. How painful it was that they couldn't even do that, when so much more intimacy should have been available. She whimpered and, with reluctance, opened her eyes.

The physical reality Nada inhabited was not that different from the egg in her sensorium. Her body lay embedded in the soft wall of the leadership vesicle aboard the *Infinite Order*. While far more cramped than a chamber of the mind-temple, the vesicle was roughly the same shape and similarly lit. The main difference to a casual observer would have been the presence of several hundred crablike maintenance lice crawling over the vesicle walls, along with the exposed parts of her face and body.

Leng's blue hand squeezed through the sphincter from the ship's central bulb, followed by the rest of him, Zilch and Ekkert close behind. They crowded into the tiny chamber and adopted foetal positions to save space. Nada had instructed Leng to dye himself blue for easy identification as, since her conversion, she sometimes struggled to recognise faces. Zilch was coloured red for the same reason. Nada detached her arms from the wall and rotated Ekkert's floating body until she could see his features to concentrate on them.

'Speak,' she ordered.

Ekkert's doughy face stared past her as he delivered his report.

'We have received fresh messenger-drone data from our relay team on the main Drexler trade route.'

Hope surged in Nada's chest. 'Have they tracked down the missing population?'

'No,' said Ekkert.

Nada contemplated smashing in Ekkert's face. He wouldn't mind and it might reduce the build-up of anxiety inside her. But she knew better than to impair the effectiveness of her own crew. Ekkert would likely use the damage as an excuse to be recycled. So instead she keened softly until emotional equilibrium reasserted itself.

How did you hide an entire planetary population, anyway? And why did the humans always need to innovate and mislead rather than simply making themselves and everyone else happy? It was exasperating. At this rate, the Yunus would keep her mind isolated for ever.

'What, then?' she said at last.

'They encountered a drone bearing information that appears to have come from a new spy network on Galatea. One spawned by our recent mutant seed release.'

She could hear the prejudice in Ekkert's voice. The Saved instinctively mistrusted all mutations, even those compatible with their biome. Nada, however, was delighted. Apparently their work at Earth hadn't been a complete failure after all.

'With what intelligence?'

'Galatean Flight Control was handed exit-prep orders for two simultaneous missions,' said Ekkert. 'Both vessels have now departed. One is an ember-warp carrier that was being loaded with colony-building equipment. The logged route for that mission shows it going at right angles to the border with the Photurian domain, towards no known habitable system.'

'Did they provide a vector?' said Nada.

'They did and I have examined it,' Leng put in. 'A significant course-correction will be required to take the carrier to any system of strategic value.'

'This is not unusual,' said Nada. 'Humans always hide their true objectives. What is the other mission?'

'It is for a ship of previously unregistered design,' said Ekkert. 'It was concealed within a Galatean construction swarm until crew boarding commenced. It then departed under unstealthed meson-warp. It is unclear whether the vessel is even equipped with tau-chargers. It is headed directly away from the border with Photuria.'

'How large is this ship?' said Nada.

'Approximately forty kilometres wide. It is estimated to support a crew of fifty at most.'

'Logically, one of these ships will be a feint and the other a mission aimed at relocating the missing population,' she said. 'It appears obvious which is which. A ship that size can be of little use to thirty million people.'

'That was also my initial assessment,' said Leng. 'However, there is more. Ekkert, outline the crew manifest for the second mission.'

'Among others, the crew includes the Abomination, Andromeda Ludik; the Butcher, Ira Baron; and the Thief of Souls, Mark Ruiz,' said Ekkert.

'On the *same* ship?' said Nada. She gripped his head and looked deep into his eyes.

'That is what was reported,' said the communications officer.

'But *why*?' said Nada. 'That is hardly an efficient use of their talents. Was this information made public? Is this a failed bluff?'

'The information was not public. The names on the official crew manifest are different. The true occupants are only known because our contact operates at a high level in Galatean Flight Control. There was a software accident during shuttle boarding caused by Ludik's natural production of unregistered proteins. Human overseers were alerted.'

Nada's skin crawled. What could Galatea possibly gain by putting so many of their false heroes on a single ship? Ludik had been in charge of the human extraction from the beginning. Clearly, whatever she was doing now was still related to that effort.

The prospect of simply chasing down Ludik and destroying her held enormous appeal, but Nada knew she couldn't afford to be rash. The Galateans were slippery.

'This new spy,' she said. 'Is he alone? How large is his network? Is there any evidence that he is being manipulated?'

Sometimes the Galateans left spies in place and fed them carefully tailored lies so that bad intelligence would leak out. Such arrangements never lasted for long. The humans couldn't tolerate the implied reinfection risk.

'The spy is aware of one other remaining convert,' said Ekkert. 'The one responsible for his infection. All others have been the victim of flash raids and are dead. The spy anticipates that he has at most a week of continued operation. Random testing now occurs daily at his workplace.'

'Zilch,' she said, turning to her harvesting specialist, 'are the Galateans making any other moves?'

'There has been one recent attack on our survey ships,' he said. 'The force was too light to be effective.'

'Was it co-located with the vector for either of these missions?'

'Not obviously. However, it was closer to the carrier mission than the route for the unidentified ship.'

Nada let go of Ekkert to claw at her own cheeks. All the feints and counter-feints. If she didn't love humanity so much, she'd have despised them.

'Leng, the carrier that arrived at Galatea was the one that departed from Sol with the human population enclosed, was it not?'

'Yes,' he said.

'But when it arrived, that cargo was missing.'

'That is what our observer drones reported.'

'So a switch was made,' she said. 'Another carrier is not required to relocate the population.'

'That is true.'

'And the colony-building equipment this new carrier is transporting – is it large or delicate enough to warrant the use of an embership?'

'The spy's report is not clear on that,' said Leng, 'but it appears unlikely.'

'In that case, I suspect that the carrier is the feint.'

Leng pivoted in the air to observe her. He was a small male unit with close-set features and staring eyes. He grimaced, baring his teeth.

'That is the most logical conclusion,' he said, 'but we cannot discount the fact that the spy may be leaking bad data. He is a seeded conversion and a mutant. He has not been trained.'

'Understood. What strategy do you recommend?'

'I believe both missions must be tracked,' he said. 'I do not believe we should act until more data has been collected.'

'So we remain here?' she offered.

'Until more clarity is obtained, yes,' said Leng.

'Despite the risk of losing contact with both ships?'

'Yes. It is possible that *both* missions may be feints for one that comes after.'

She examined his weird little face and wished she didn't need him so badly. Leng was her science specialist, optimised for cognition and constantly in danger of merging himself too deeply with the ship. She had already dragged his emotions back from the ache of union five times since they began the survey of Galatea.

Leng, in her opinion, was the sort likely to make rational decisions all the way to giving up. She hadn't been able to see that about him before the Yunus's adjustment. Her old brain had always perceived him as attentive and obedient. When she'd chosen the name Nada to symbolise her willing emptiness, he'd been the first to follow suit and had encouraged the others. His zeal had appeared unblemished.

After Noether, though, Leng's endless cogitating had started to rankle. She'd come to wonder if he was partly responsible for their continued failures. It was Leng who'd advocated such a long, careful injection of mutants into the Earth population, after all. And that waiting had come to naught.

She glanced at her harvesting specialist. 'Zilch, what do you recommend?'

'Immediate action,' he replied.

'Of what sort?'

'Whatever you advocate,' he said. 'Your will is law. Should I ready the fleet for departure?'

'Zilch always advocates immediate action,' Leng pointed out. 'He is incapable of reasoning otherwise.'

Nada considered them both. To her mind, the pair of them represented the two main ways that the Saved slid into Fatigue. One took comfort in knee-jerk responses to everything while maintaining an unwavering sense of self-justification. The other craved the kind of reasoned peace that left little room for action. Neither, in her opinion, were particularly good at operating as independent agents.

'We will follow the second ship,' she said. 'All routes ahead of it will be tightly monitored using our fastest scouts.'

'At the cost of the other relays?' said Leng.

'Necessarily,' said Nada. 'We will still monitor the carrier and the Galatean colony, but with reduced coverage.'

'Those ships are already strained,' Leng pointed out.

'Understood,' said Nada. 'However, the ship carrying the Abomination cannot be allowed to escape. The Abomination has been in charge of the relocation effort from its outset. There is no evidence that this has changed. The Yunus has also explicitly requested that the Abomination be destroyed. Therefore we cannot act wrongly by tracking it down.'

Leng pulled faces. 'This tactic is imperfectly optimised,' he said. 'We lack data about what the humans are doing.'

Nada grabbed his body and hurled him at the wall. He bounced.

'Waiting is concluded. The Yunus has instructed me to innovate if necessary. Innovation incurs risk. Therefore *there will be risk*!' Her voice rose to a shriek, joyful with purpose.

Leng grabbed Ekkert to steady himself. The two of them spun slowly.

'I am surprised by your response,' he said. 'Your reasoning pattern has changed.'

'Yes,' she said. 'The Yunus altered me.'

'I am not sure that the Yunus has made the right choice.'

Nada blinked at him. 'You cannot doubt the Yunus, even if you do not understand him. That is not okay.'

She reached into the temple, slid her mental-focus through to Leng's cavern and changed him. Leng's eyes rolled up in his head. He mewled like a baby and twitched while she made her edits.

When she was done, he smiled sickly and regarded her with fresh awe.

'I no longer doubt him,' he said. 'I love you.'

'Are there other doubters?' said Nada.

'I cannot doubt the Yunus,' said Zilch, still staring into the wall-mucus.

'It has not occurred to me to do so,' said Ekkert. 'It is not my function.'

'Then we are aligned,' said Nada. 'Commence urgent activity.'

All three officers rushed for the door sphincter at once.

4: PURSUIT

4.1: WILL

Will got out of the gravesite to find himself in a crude, wooden approximation of the virtual station he'd just left, but with a few notable differences. This station featured a floor lined with pits where transiting bodies pulsed and mutated under filmy membranes. Also, it had a breeze.

Cold, fresh air of the sort Will associated with open-sky biospheres blew in through the station entrance at the far end of the hall, carrying with it a curious seaside tang. Mettaburg, apparently, had been built *above* the tunnels.

He brushed down his ersatz ship-suit and walked straight for the exit as rapidly as he dared. He knew he needed to get out into the city, fast. The Balance agents had been on the brink of catching him. The god-Will's forces, whatever they looked like in the physical world, were surely closing in already.

He struggled not to stare as he strode for the doors. Some of the pedestrians around him were still changing, even outside the pits. Clothing crawled across their bodies while their faces oozed like slow putty to finalise their new forms. He tried to ignore it. Meanwhile, his head still swam from the overload of terrible new memories.

The significance of Elsa's advice had become unavoidably clear. He had to keep his disgust in check or it would give him away. But how could he when in every direction he was surrounded by the joke the Transcended had made out of him? They'd tricked him here to open Pandora's box and then butchered his mind for parts to manufacture this psychotic pastiche.

It made him shake. The sense of violation was beyond his mind's ability to encompass. But he needed to focus. Just in time, he noticed a stack of paper visitor maps situated near the exit. He took one in a trembling hand and stepped out into the chill surface air where he stopped to gape yet again.

At Mettaburg, the habitat-tubes had been convinced to grow upwards. Clusters of two or more grew around each other in helical spires a dozen storeys high, shrinking as they ascended into a deep blue sky laced with icy cloud. The result was a city of twisting black, corrugated spires randomly pockmarked with windows. It looked as if someone had tried to remake a Surplus Age Manhattan out of giant, soot-coloured spaghetti.

Through this distorted tubescape ran simple wooden causeways that functioned as streets. Large, asymmetrical openings in the tunnel walls formed doorways and the frontings of what looked like old-fashioned shops. Dozens of clones strode this way and that or clattered along on bone-coloured bicycles. Many of them wore sweaters or coats that he envied.

Will realised that he'd made another mistake. Not a single other clone was dressed in anything like his ship-suit. They all wore dark, simple garments like characters out of a costume drama.

No doubt the station had some means of altering clothing, but to reach it, he'd have to walk straight back into the building where Balance would be arriving. He hurriedly scanned the shopfronts, looking for anything that might help. A brown and white sign offering *Localwear* caught his eye. He made straight for it.

Ceramic chimes tinkled as Will pushed open the door. Inside lay a cramped retail space smelling powerfully of organic fabrics and some kind of spice. Two dapper clones, one male, one female, examined suits while a shopkeeper chatted with them.

Will grabbed a long, black coat from a rack labelled 'Size: Normal' and tried it on. It fitted perfectly. He parked himself behind a display and watched carefully through a mirror as the couple hemmed and hawed over their selection.

Will knew that shoplifting would only create more risk but what choice did he have? He had no local credit. He chose his moment when all three had their backs turned and walked quickly towards the exit.

'Are you going to pay for that?' said the clerk as Will pulled open the door.

Will froze. Through the opening, he could make out two huge clones in masks and tiger-striped police uniforms striding purposefully down the street in his direction. Will's heart hammered in his chest. He shut the door and turned back to face the clerk.

'I forgot,' he said awkwardly.

The clerk walked over to him. He had Will's face aged to his subjective sixties, with grey, oiled-back hair. He did not look happy.

'Bullshit,' said the shopkeeper. 'You were trying to steal it, weren't you?'

Will struggled for words. Before dying, he'd been the most powerful man in human space – able to kill with a thought and enough firepower at his back to burn worlds. He was not used to accusations of petty theft – particularly from himself.

'I've told you people,' said the shopkeeper before Will could speak, 'I don't care what you're trying to do. You're *ruining my thread*! There's plenty of goddamn money in the street. Why can't you just take some like everybody else?'

He pointed through the window to a small stand Will hadn't noticed. People were pulling sheaves of paper from a slot as they walked past. Will stared at it in dawning comprehension. The only times he'd had to pay with physical money were as a youth on Galatea visiting the annual history festival. They'd had stands just like it.

'What's your nick?' said the shopkeeper. 'We're calling Balance right now.'

'Please,' said Will. 'You're right. I'm sorry. We can solve this amicably.'

The shopkeeper sneered at him.

'Look,' said the female clone standing behind him, 'he can have some of mine. That solves this, doesn't it?'

She pressed a wad of bills into Will's unsuspecting hand and smiled at him. The shopkeeper rounded on her, outrage vying with disappointment on his face.

'That's not the point!' he snapped. 'It's hard enough making this thread work as it is, without these bastards breaking the game all the goddamn time. How am I supposed to build acumen under these conditions?'

'Theft can be a part of running a business,' the male customer pointed out. 'In some places it used to be quite common.'

'Not at this level! They walk straight out of the station, into my god-damn shop and back to the station again! My merchandise is defabbed before I can even get my hands on them. And then I have to buy back more. You telling me shit like that used to happen? I mean, look – this one's not even trying. He's wearing *baseline*, for crying out loud!'

'So move your business,' said the male customer.

'Are you crazy? With these rents?'

'You're either pushing acumen or you're not,' the female pointed out. 'You can't have it both ways.'

The shopkeeper scowled and managed to look sheepish at the same time. Will's gaze darted between the three of them as he tried to catch up with the local norms.

'I'm not cultivating theft,' Will said cautiously. 'Someone put me up to this and it felt like a bad idea from the start. I'd prefer it if we could just settle the whole episode between us. You won't be seeing me again.'

'How would I even know with *that* face?' the shopkeeper snarled.

'Look, how much do you want?' said Will, scanning the bills. Each bore a portrait of his likeness.

'Fifty!' said the shopkeeper.

'Fine,' said Will, counting out the money.

'What?' said the shopkeeper. 'Now you're not even going to haggle?'

Will stared at him in confusion. Apparently, the clone was entirely in earnest.

'Ten?' he offered.

'Fifteen,' snapped the shopkeeper. 'I'm done with this bullshit.' He snatched the notes from Will's grasp. 'This game stinks,' he growled. 'Another day like this and I'm going back to cage-fighting.' He stomped off into the rear of the shop.

Will turned to the two customers.

'Thank you,' he said.

The male customer nodded. 'This was novel,' he said. 'Look us up online. We'll share perspectives.'

He pulled a stack of business cards from his jacket and handed one to Will.

Jack Bystander, Customer, it read. *Discernment. Taste. Poise. Perspectives welcome.*

Underneath was a row of alien-looking glyphs that made Will's mind swim. He quickly pocketed the card as well as the rest of the money.

'Great,' he said.

The Bystanders smiled at him and walked out.

Will hovered in the shop after they'd left, not trusting his good fortune. His clones inhabited a planet with technology so advanced that it could spit warp-enabled drones into space grown from its own flesh. Yet, despite that, they'd chosen to live in this distorted approximation of the past. *Why?*

He checked through the window. The Balance agents appeared to have passed on down the street and Will knew he wasn't going to get a better opportunity. He stepped through the door and rejoined the flow of pedestrians as inconspicuously as possible.

Will rubbed his hands in the cold air as he walked. He didn't get it: why had these people even bothered making a city when Snakepit's tunnel biome didn't need such things to support either organic life *or* virtual existence? Certainly the air was richer down in the tunnels. Out here it felt like he was hiking mountaintops.

As he framed the question to himself, he passed a shop selling nothing but physical books – hundreds of them. He hesitated again. As a boy, he'd had been fascinated by the concept of tangible information. Scrolls, cassette tapes, casino chips – growing up as a young roboteer on Galatea, they'd all struck him as equally exotic. The technocratic society he'd been born into had no use for such things. Consequently, Will had used those charming props extensively in the visualisation metaphors he'd built in his early career and spent his spare time delving into the colony's archives to find more. Here, apparently, his clones had indulged that fancy to hyperbolic extent.

Will began to understand. This place looked like a toy Manhattan because that was exactly what it was aiming for. It was an expression of humanity – an attempt to create something familiar out of the alien. Mettaburg offered his variants an opportunity to inhabit roles and personas that left room for differentiation. Hence the shopkeepers, customers and everyone else. He'd taken the movies of his childhood and rendered them into something his instances could live in.

That realisation afforded him a little peace until he turned the corner and encountered a carriage pulled by distorted replicas of himself fused into approximations of horses. A clone in a top hat and black jacket sat in front, clutching reins and a whip.

Will glared at them as they trotted past. He couldn't imagine wanting to live out life as a horse. So why had that happened here? Why hadn't his duplicates simply produced biorobots for that kind of work? His conviction that whatever these people were, they were not really Will Monet returned with a vengeance.

The Radical Hill District, when he found it, was a part of town where the helical towers thinned out. Some original landform hidden beneath the habitat layers had created a ridge on the surface. Across that rise, several dozen narrow tubes ran in parallel lines, producing the effect of terraced streets with views across the rest of the city. Map in hand, Will climbed the rise and set about looking for the Old Slam Bar. Beyond the helical spires behind him, he could make out a dark, pink-tinted sea under a cold afternoon sky.

Campari Street turned out to be a mangled caricature of an arty neighbourhood, complete with galleries full of bad paintings. Open-fronted bars with ceramic tables spilled onto a wooden causeway that smelled of something like beer. Clones in berets and black sweaters smoked actual cigarettes and chatted while dogs with upsettingly human eyes looked on.

The Old Slam Bar was an ill-kempt establishment halfway along the row, where a utilitarian wooden fronting shielded a dimly lit tunnel-interior. Will pushed back the door and stepped inside. The tube walls had been scraped down to their black silicate matrix, leaving only a single strip of living tissue on the ceiling. The few sickly strands of biolantern that hung from it delivered a desultory light to the arched space beneath.

Paintings lined the curving walls in styles mimicking propaganda posters from Earth's history, bearing slogans like 'Fuck Balance' and 'We Are All Cancer'. In them, the faces of famous dictators had been swapped with his own. Will regarded himself dressed as Hitler, Kerg and Sanchez, and felt uneasy. It wasn't just the anger that oozed out of the place that worried him, but also its transparency. A bar full of political radicals felt like a terrible place to hide a resistance movement. He wondered if Elsa had known what she was talking about after all.

The smattering of customers stared at him with hooded, resentful eyes. Some looked as baseline as himself. Others had extreme body modifications, with heads covered in spikes or the faces of rats. One had arms ending in pincers and wore a hood to hide its face.

Will ignored them and walked over to the bar at the back to take a seat. Eyes followed him. The bartender was bald and twice as wide as he was. But for the full-body tattoos, he bore a marked resemblance to Ira Baron.

'Whisky,' said Will. It looked like that kind of place.

The Ira-faced clone behind the bar poured a shot from an unmarked bottle and slapped it down in front of him.

'How much?' said Will, pulling notes from his pocket.

'You believe in that shit?' said the bartender, gesturing at his wad.

'Actually, no,' said Will.

'Then keep it,' he said. 'Everything's on the house here. And if you don't like that, you can fuck off.'

'Suits me,' said Will and took a sip from his glass.

The stuff was rough – even rougher than he'd expected. He coughed. What did they put in it, hydraulic fluid?

The bartender smiled. 'Want a top-up?'

'If that's what it takes,' said Will bluntly. He slid the glass back across the counter. The bartender paused at those words and glanced across the room at someone behind Will. A murmur of ambient conversation resumed.

'Does a Mr Brown work here?' said Will as the tension in the room eased off a little.

'Maybe,' said almost-Ira. 'Who wants to know?'

Somewhere in that moment, Will's patience for the metropolis of borrowed clichés exhausted itself. Forty years, ten billion clones and this was really the best he could do?

'*Jason*,' he growled. 'Who d'you fucking think?'

Ira's face stiffened. 'Nice to meet you, Jason,' he said. 'Here's how it works. You shut up and listen to the poetry while we check the street. If you've brought any heat with you, you're out of here. Understand?'

'Loud and clear,' said Will.

The bartender took his glass and tossed the contents down the sink. He refilled it from another bottle. While the next shot still wasn't good, at least it wasn't going to kill him. Ira then slid Will a cold, appraising look and disappeared into a back room.

Will stayed put as instructed. He nursed his glass while one of the clones got up from a table and made his way to a black-painted stage at the end of the bar. He had baseline features with a goatee and thick-lensed spectacles. He looked like a budget Trotsky.

The poet-clone cleared his throat and scanned the room.

'This is called "My Condition",' he said. 'I'm sick. You're sick. We're all sick. And I scream: what's wrong with me? Nothing that you can see with eyes inside or out. I want for nothing that's dear to me. Or so I'm told. But this I doubt.

'Food, shelter, fantasy, equality. A death that's only ever voluntary. But yet I shout: what's the fucking point? Where's my fucking *purpose*?

'To keep the Nems at bay, you say. So each time they come we blow them away. But how does that help me *today*? When there's no fucking point. No reason to stay. Alive.

'So what do I do? I mine hate. I squirm. I twist. To make myself unique. To make myself a freak. A poet. A parody. A puppet. Listen to me, Balance. This poet demands his string be *cut*. Just one tweak. Snip. Boom. And I'm out of here.'

The poet strode off the stage and returned to his seat amid a storm of finger-clicking and pincer-clacking from the audience. Will found the experience oddly comforting. His poetic skills apparently hadn't come on much in the last forty years, but something in the man's frustration lent him hope. He obviously wasn't the only one in the room who felt that Snakepit had become a madhouse.

A second beatnik climbed to the stage, but by then, Ira was back.

'Okay,' he said. 'Follow me.' He raised the counter at one end and ushered Will through.

'Where are we going?' said Will.

'Shut up,' said Ira.

He led Will to a small room built against the curve of the tube, with one sloping wall that rose to become the ceiling. A single strand of weakly pulsing biolantern lent the room an ugly submarine glow. At a small table with two chairs sat a clone with red hair and scars on his cheeks. He wore a T-shirt and a black jacket made of some kind of soft leather.

'Are you Mr Brown?' said Will.

'Sit,' said the clone. 'Tell us your story, *Jason*. Leave nothing out.'

Will felt another tide of impatience wash over him. He fought it down – he had nothing to gain by fighting. He sat, pressed his hands flat against the table and described everything that had happened to him since first waking up.

When he got to the part about the library, Red's expression grew sour.

'That was stupid,' he said.

'Apparently,' said Will tersely. He paused to collect himself and explained the rest. 'Was Elsa right?' he asked when he was done. 'Can you help?'

Red examined his fingers, apparently uninterested in replying. Desperate frustration coursed up through Will again. This time, it wouldn't be denied.

'Well, *can you?*' Will shouted. He rose to his feet. '*Can you?*' His fists shook.

If Red said no, Will had exactly zero idea of where to go next. Outside this little room, all was madness. His future was a blank wall of soundless fog.

'Yes, we can help,' said Red quietly. 'Helping Glitches is what we do. And you're on the level, I can tell – you have the same empty-headed panic as the rest of them. I'd get bored of seeing it if I didn't know that feeling myself. Sit down, Will. I'm thinking through the details, that's all.'

Will slumped uncertainly back into his chair.

Red examined him through lazy eyes. 'You were lucky,' he said. 'Luckier than most. You met this Elsa. You made it to us, despite taking unnecessary risks. But don't let your escape today convince you that you're safe. Balance is weak in this town precisely *because* there's a resistance presence. We refuse him and that reduces his power. Every icon of anger in this place bolsters our strength and gives us room to manoeuvre. But don't for a moment imagine it's the same everywhere. Outside Mettaburg, things are very different. We'll point you at a hostel where you can stay the night. They won't ask questions but remember to bring cash – there's a stand on the corner if you need it. In the meantime, speak to no one. If you have to, use the nick Elsa gave you. Come back to the bar tomorrow morning and Mr Brown will see you.'

'You're not Brown?' said Will.

Red smirked. 'Do I look like a Brown? You'll know him when you see him. Now get some rest. You're among friends, Will. We'll do what we can. That means support, cover, information, a job—'

'What about a way offworld?'

'I'll leave that to Brown. He'll explain. Meanwhile, enjoy the poetry. Be seeing you.' Red scraped back his chair and let himself out.

Will sagged and rubbed his eyes. He'd made it. He wasn't any closer to escaping the insanity of Snakepit, but at least his isolation was at an end. Now he had somewhere to go and the promise of answers. Under the circumstances, that was enough.

4.2: MARK

On their second morning out of port, Mark rose and made his way along the gently rolling deck in search of breakfast. Beyond the immaculate white railings, the sea oozed like azure glue under a sky full of harsh, metallic sunlight. Seagulls wheeled and screamed in tight, monotonous circles. That was an improvement, at least. Yesterday the waves had been all but motionless while the gulls jerked about like damaged transit pods.

Mark was not a fan of modern virts. Outside the *Gulliver*, direct ship-linking had become a thing of the past. Modern military environments were shadow-mediated and heavily modularised. You didn't see a shared illusion so much as a personal interpretation of a collectively sanctioned one. The software they ran on was constantly evolving to combat threats, which made them stiff and riddled with flaws. There was *always* lag. Some piece of the world you weren't looking at straight on was always slithering or jumping. The only seamless immersives left were the ones he ran on his own.

That was the cost of everyone aboard being half-roboteer. You could trust your own shadow, but put two of them together and you apparently needed a disinfectant layer – just like the gloves the Galateans were so keen on wearing. Frankly, the tech had been better when people with interfaces like his were rare and marginalised.

Mark didn't relish the choice of setting, either. In their infinite wisdom, the Galatean Fleet designers had confined them to a luxury yacht designed by a modernist maniac. The cabins were full of cold air and sharp angles to antagonise any seeded Phote convert. The chairs were hard and not subject to edit requests.

Apparently, environments that felt like vessels provided stronger social binding for long voyages, which meant that only specialised environments were free from the confines of the yacht metaphor. Maybe that suited ordinary folks with vanilla shadows, but for Mark, who'd been immersing since birth, it was like trying to work with one hand trapped behind his back. Still, if that was what they had, he was determined to make the best of it.

He found the others on deck at the rear of the boat, eating croissants and gazing out at the clumsily rendered ocean. All but Ann – she'd been on duty ever since they'd left. She apparently no longer needed sleep.

'Mind if I join you?' said Mark.

'Go for it,' said Palla around a mouthful of pastry.

Ira gestured at the free seat beside him.

'Amazing, isn't it?' Ira said as Mark sat down. 'I guess you're used to all this, but it's as if we're actually on an old-fashioned sea-ship. It's so much deeper than a standard immersive vid. I was just telling Judj – I can *taste* the damned coffee. I can feel each slat of this chair. It's amazing, and not what starships used to be like, that's for sure.'

Mark had opinions about the chair slats. 'This is nothing,' he said. 'Come and visit me on the *Gulliver* some time where our virt sits behind a Vartian security shield. You want coffee? I'll give you real coffee.'

'Real virtual coffee?' said Ira with half a smile.

'There is no real coffee any more,' said Mark. 'Physical or otherwise. Mine at least tastes decent.'

He frowned at the cup their synthetic waiter was filling. Objective sustenance made its way into their bodies via drips in their arms, but collective food rituals held psychological value, apparently, so the Fleet enforced them via simulated hunger. Mark wouldn't have minded if he'd been allowed to program the chef.

As he watched the others eat he felt a sudden overwhelming desire to compensate for that first, disastrous briefing. He hadn't been able to settle afterwards. Instead of sharing with the team what a tremendous opportunity they had, they got bogged down in the dangers. But if they only focused on the negatives, what chance did they have of ever getting past them? He wanted to squeeze his vision of hope into them so that it kindled.

'While we're all here, I'd like to apologise for the other day,' he said. 'I didn't do a great job at that briefing.'

Clath looked up at him. 'I thought it was fine,' she said sunnily. 'A bit unusual, maybe, but we covered the material, didn't we?'

'Thanks,' said Mark, 'but I could have done a lot better, I think.' He glanced around at the crew. 'I have a question for all of you, if you don't mind?'

Palla eyed him curiously. 'Shoot,' she said.

'How many of you think we're going to live through this?'

Quiet descended. The shrill cries of the artificial gulls were suddenly noticeable.

'I'm serious,' said Mark. 'I'd like to know. If you're okay with talking about it. And if you aren't, I'll shut up and never mention it again.'

'I think we're toast,' said Judj, still chewing. He grinned. 'But that's okay. I volunteered, remember? I knew what was coming.' He took another bite.

'I'm confident that we'll ace our initial military objective,' said Palla. 'Beyond that, I have no idea.'

Mark nodded. 'Fair enough.' He noticed his old mentor staring out to sea, as if trying to avoid looking at the rest of them. 'Ira, how about you?'

'Me?' said Ira. He paused. 'I'm always wary of making assumptions about Phote activity, whether lives are attached to the outcomes or not. The buggers keep changing. When we started this fight, they were just simple swarming machines, not much smarter than your average domesticbot. Then in a matter of weeks we were faced with a hive-mind. And now there are all these hints of autonomous, compartmentalised intelligence. I don't think anyone expected the Photes to become so sophisticated. We thought they'd always be parodies of humans, not evolve into some sinister alternative.'

Palla frowned. 'That's not an answer, Grandad,' she said. 'Are you being evasive? Answer the nice man's question, why don't you? Do you think you'll live through the mission or not?'

She winked at Mark. He fought down a stab of annoyance.

'We're living right now,' said Ira. 'That's what's important.'

'But are you afraid?' Palla urged.

Ira laughed. 'I wish,' he said. 'No. Not at all.'

She scowled at him.

Mark pushed the conversation onwards before she could grill Ira further. He could tell she wanted to.

115

'What about you, Clath?'

'I think the Zone is a solvable scientific problem,' she replied. 'And I can't honestly believe the Photes will chase us past it – they're creatures of habit and expediency. So if we can get that far, then yes, I expect to live. The mission is entirely doable. That's why I'm here.'

Mark smiled broadly. He loved that answer. He might not have his wife with him, but this optimistic, intelligent woman was a potential alternative ally. He'd been too busy resenting her the other day to notice – an irrational mistake.

'What about the blockade around Snakepit that Ann mentioned?' he asked. 'Don't you think there'll be one?'

'No,' said Clath breezily. 'They'll have opted for passive containment. They blockade worlds that have ships leaving. Snakepit doesn't. I mean, do we see them blockading biosphere worlds? No. Even though we know the Photes like to control them.'

'Agreed,' said Mark.

'So you think we can make it, too?' said Palla with a dry smile.

'Absolutely,' said Mark.

'Why?'

'Because I agree with Clath's assessment. It's my hope that for the most part, this mission will actually be boring. We're more likely to get caught up in trajectory issues at the far gate than face down an armada at Snakepit.'

'I'd like that,' said Palla. 'Though I like the thought of getting to Snakepit even more.' She balanced her chin on a fist and watched him across the table. 'My turn for a question: what do you think we'll find when we get there?'

Mark gazed back at her and wondered if he'd wrongly assessed Palla. She looked genuinely interested in what he had to say.

'Well, we know Will stopped the Photes from retaking their home, and that whatever change he made is still in effect. We also know that Snakepit is incredibly powerful, which is why the Photes want it. Which suggests to me that if Will were still alive, we'd know. He'd have smashed the Photes and come home. Either that or we'd be able to see traces of his fights through our remote telescope arrays – they've been covering the point on the local shell closest to Snakepit for decades. So, I expect to find the place much as we left it. Maybe protected by robots. Maybe with a toxic biosphere. Certainly no Will. What I'd like to do is end this whole chapter of human history and put the ghost of Will Monet to rest at last.'

He wanted that for himself as much as everyone else, though he didn't say it. Will's last request to him – to keep others safe – had rung in his head every day since they'd parted ways. It was a promise Mark knew he'd never fulfilled. Instead, the whole damned species had just kept on growing ever more endangered.

'Frankly,' he said, 'we should have tried a lot harder to do this ages ago.'

'Hear hear,' said Ira.

Mark glanced around and knew he had their attention now. For the first time since they'd left port, he saw hope. He pressed on, buoyed by his success.

'Think of what we could achieve,' he told them. 'If we could end this stupid war, people would be able to start living in peace. Our society could start untwisting itself. Humanity would have the chance to flourish. To re-establish trade. To climb out of our social straitjacket. We could all go back to living like normal people.'

Palla snorted. 'What, with wars and crime and all that?'

Mark shook his head. 'I'm not talking about crime,' he said with a strained laugh. 'I'd just rather not live in a police state that enforces order via death squads and hopscotch.'

'I like hopscotch,' said Palla. Her expression was unreadable now, but the chromatophores on her skull had started pulsing. 'I'm all for peace and disbanding the death squads, but frankly, Mark, the society you grew up in was kind of shit. I'd rather go forwards, not backwards. I mean, didn't all this happen in the first place because you guys couldn't get over your tribal impulses and Neolithic religions?'

'Fair point,' said Mark. He felt urgency to rekindle the positivity. 'We had problems, but it wasn't like that. And I can see why you want to believe the New Society is an improvement, because that's what you've got.'

Palla guffawed at him. 'Gosh, Captain Mark, thank you for elder-splaining so eloquently. So I'm brainwashed then? Indoctrinated?'

'No, I just don't think you got to have much of a childhood, that's all.'

She arched an eyebrow. 'Did you?' she said.

She'd read his file, of course. She knew all about the disastrous roboteering programme he'd been born into – the Monets' abortive attempt to equip the human race with super-talented pilots using Will's DNA. These days, they taught it in school history classes.

'Admittedly, no. But I still want to fight for that for others. I mean, do you really enjoy all that enforced play?'

'Actually, Mark, it's not forced,' said Palla, smiling like a shark. 'Weird though it may look to you, play can be a duty and a pleasure at the same time.'

Mark glanced around the table and felt dismay. He missed Zoe acutely. She was the diplomat in their marriage. He'd never been good at inspiring people, no matter how much he might want to win hearts and minds.

He picked his next words carefully. 'I just see that you've been forced to carry a heavy burden,' he said.

'I volunteered!' said Palla. She waved a teasing finger at him. 'I'll tell you what the New Society does, Mark. It teaches people to take responsibility first and orders second. Are you really sure that it was better the other way around? Do you really want us to go back to hierarchies?' She gestured at Ira. 'Maybe you want to put this glassy-eyed ruin back in charge – the man who burned worlds.' She slid him a mocking glance. 'By the way, how's breakfast, Grandad? You remembered to wash your hands before eating, I hope. You don't want to get all that blood on your virtual pastry.'

'Leave him alone,' Mark snapped.

But Palla was staring at Ira, waving at him now. 'Any reaction there, Admiral Baron? Or are you just going to stare at the sea like a fucking automaton? Hello! Come in, President Genocide!'

Mark felt his hands closing into fists.

'It's okay, Palla,' said Ira with a chuckle. 'I'm all here and I'm still listening. Say what you like.'

He sounded awfully calm. Mark, in contrast, couldn't hack it a moment longer. He got up.

'Palla, I'm sorry I insulted you,' he said. 'That's not what I intended.'

Palla looked amused. 'I'm not insulted. Who's insulted? I'm just look-ing out for Judj, here, who's practically crying into his orange juice, aren't you, Judj?'

Judj blinked at her in surprise.

'I think I'm going to take a walk on the deck,' said Mark stiffly.

'Can't take the heat, fly boy?' Palla called after him. 'Bring those tight buns back here. We've only just started!'

Mark kept walking until breakfast lay out of sight. He stood at the railing and glared down at the ridiculous twitching fish. A minute later, Ira quietly appeared and stood beside him.

'Want to talk about it?' he said with a wry smile.

Mark eyed him, torn between empathy and disappointment.

'Ever since the briefing shuttle, Palla's been picking on you,' he said. 'She keeps dissing your record, which is unbelievable bullshit. I can't think of anyone in recent history who's had to carry as big a burden as you. But you just seem to... take it.'

Her grandad line had pissed Mark off, too. Ira was a mountain of gleaming muscle who didn't look a day over thirty. Besides his age, in what way was he a grandad?

Ira resumed staring across the water. 'I wouldn't worry about that,' he said. 'She's just nervous. Even if we make it past the Zone, this is still a hard straw for someone her age to draw.'

'She's our *SAO*, Ira,' Mark insisted. 'She's supposed to be the voice of the common good. I don't think it's acceptable for someone in that position to be calling you a *ruin*. That was unacceptable. Is that the common good – needling you for a lifetime of service? I worked under you for years and I never knew a better leader. You were practically family, for crissakes. I can't take much more of her bullshit. I swear, if she talks to you like that again, I'm going to have words with her.'

'Don't,' said Ira wearily. 'Really, it's fine. It's not important.'

He looked unfazed to the point of indifference. Mark wasn't sure whether to be impressed by that bottomless sangfroid or appalled. This was how Ira apparently responded to everything now.

'If it's okay with me, can you leave it alone?' Ira said.

When Mark didn't reply, his old mentor sighed.

'She's just angry, Mark. The poor girl has probably spent years studying my decisions – poring over mistakes I made in split seconds. To today's leader-kids I probably look like a walking textbook of disaster. So do you. So does Ann. Palla's too young to have seen all the shit we had to live through. If you really want to fix it, here's what you can do. Go back and talk to her. Give the girl some attention. Let her tell you all the things that are great about her brave new world. Fuck it, why not flirt a little? What's the harm?'

Mark scowled. Palla's not-so-subtle sexual remarks about him were another concern. She knew he was mono and coupled, so why did she bother? Was she trying to seduce him or bully him?

'Try to get her excited about your vision for the mission,' Ira suggested. 'Talk to her about what might be on the other side of the Zone. This is the first mission into the unknown for years. That's pretty exciting. For all our military agenda, we're going to put an end to decades of speculation, presuming we make it. Finding out whether the Zone is natural or not will be an achievement in itself.'

'I don't want to talk about that,' said Mark. 'There'll be plenty of time for awe if we live long enough. What I want to know is what she thinks she gains by baiting us and how we make it *stop*. You're the ship's psychologist, Ira. Don't you want to help with this? I don't know why you're being so passive. It isn't like you.'

Ira slid a pair of lifeless blue eyes in Mark's direction. 'Here's a different perspective,' he said. 'How do you imagine she feels? Why shouldn't she be angry? She's been told that it's her job to hold us together. Three of the biggest figures in modern history. Why wouldn't she try to cut us down to size? How would you have felt if someone had landed this shit in your lap at her age?'

'They practically did,' said Mark.

'And were you happy about it?'

'No. But frankly, I was a dick at that point,' said Mark. 'I wasn't handling anything well. I still did my goddamn job, though.'

'Without pissing anyone off?' said Ira. 'You know that's not true. So cut her some slack. She'd probably be just as angry at receiving any other kind of suicide mission. The fact that it's us three isn't even relevant.'

'Why is this about *suicide*?' Mark demanded. 'It doesn't have to be. That's what I was trying to say. Has everyone forgotten what optimism looks like? We can live through this and make a difference! Seeing this as a death sentence is part of the attitude problem. If she'd just—'

Mark's words were interrupted by a piercing alarm. All at once, the yacht metaphor fell away, dumping them into a tactical immersive. His gut lurched as the gravity died. They'd been kicked out of warp.

Mark flicked his view to a gravity-analytics filter. Against the rainbow backdrop of local space hung a long, black smear of viscid ions dotted with rapidly updating threat indicators – a disrupter cloud. It stretched across the local warp-shell like a razor-wire fence, vanishing to a point in either direction. It was huge, and they were stuck in it. For a cloud this big, there had to be thousands of Phote drones dumping ions to keep it stable.

Mark's heart sank. Suddenly, his urgency to fix everyone's attitude evaporated. He saw it for what it was: something to think about instead of the inevitable fight against a foe that never stopped.

'Look on the bright side,' said Ira, hovering next to him in the darkness. 'Now we have something to do.'

4.3: ANN

Ann watched through the helm metaphor as the Photes quietly announced themselves. They'd filtered their signal cleverly, so that it appeared to come from all across the disrupter cloud like whispers in the night. She couldn't see a single drone.

'Did you know that ninety-one per cent of overhauled ships are successfully converted?' it crooned. 'The Photurian Utopia now retains individual identities, but happiness is *still* guaranteed. So why not avoid discomfort and join now? A fresh sense of purpose and joy is yours for the taking. You know you want it.'

The attached video stream contained the usual bullshit advertising, full of breathless rapture and sunshine. Something in Ann woke up at the sight of that invitation to kill. There would be no more sitting around waiting to die. Given that this was probably her last chance to *clean*, she intended to make full use of it.

She swapped to combat mode and assessed her ship with a full internal sensor sweep. Sure enough, the disrupter cloud the Photes had laid for them was scattered with driller drones. She could feel them all across her exohull like ticks, gnawing their way into the *Dantes'* ceramic flesh. This ship was less hardy than her poor, wounded *Ariel*. Soft-assault warnings were already showing up at one or two of her data couplings, which meant she had to take their presence seriously.

Until a few years back, the Photes always tried to cripple ships in order to capture the crews alive. That didn't work so well any more. Not since the development of Phote-poison. Now crews gave themselves shots full of designer prions when capture loomed so that they could take out as many of the enemy as possible after conversion. For a brief, wonderful time, the raids had stopped.

The Photes' newest tactic was to try to incapacitate the crew fast using carefully engineered soft assaults launched in-hull via the victim ship's own data pipes. They had data weapons that could target and incapacitate life support, wiping out cabin med function at a stroke and often forcing coma on the crew. The Photes could usually still make converts out of half-dead humans, it turned out.

'I'm initiating a hull purge,' Ann told the others. 'Brace yourselves.'

She gritted her teeth as she waited impatiently through the extra seconds it took for the rest of the crew to acknowledge her warning. Normal humans took for ever to react.

As soon as they were ready, she shut down the engines. A second later, her casket hissed open and dropped her out of virt, into the cabin's siren-filled, plastic-scented air. The others struggled out of their berths and away from the walls, into the cabin's cramped centre, while red warning icons flashed at them from the wall-panels. The air scrubbers hissed wildly as they snapped into safe mode. The cabin temperature dropped like a rock.

Everyone hung together in the air, turning slowly and watching each other as they shivered and prepared to die.

'Is this it?' said Clath. 'They found us already? We didn't even make it to the Zone.'

Fleet officers were trained to take their fatal shots before letting the Photes get to them, and to execute anyone who appeared reluctant to do so. They all understood the gravity of the moment.

'We're not done yet,' said Mark.

Ann just hummed tunelessly to herself as she waited for the purge to complete. Judj eyed her as if begging her to shut up. She smirked at him. Then, after an eternity of milliseconds, the final report downloaded into her sensorium.

[Cabin security refreshed. First-wave hull defence active. Commencing spatial scans.]

Ann launched off from her crew-mates back to her berth, being careful not to smash their bones as she did so. She grabbed the edge of the coffin and hurled herself in, pressing her mind back into the ship's systems before the door could shut.

Thankfully, the Photes hadn't made it far into the mesohull. The new scans came back almost clean. Only in two spots did her idiot robots need support. As the first officer back in the loop, it was Ann's job to deal with that, and she was ideally suited to the task.

She brought the closest team of titan mechs to full awareness and threw them up the curving track through the metallic caverns of the ship's interior at two hundred kilometres per hour. Ahead of them, a maggot-like Phote machine had been disgorged from its driller-shell. After chewing through the exohull, it had deployed a defensive micro-drone swarm and clamped its mouthparts around the nearest data artery. The air around the incursion site was thick with the burned remnants of her initial defence wave.

As soon as they saw her lead robot coming, the microdrones threw themselves at it like angry hornets. Ann diced as many as she could with raster-beams and decoupled from the track to avoid the rest. She reached for the maggot's head and carved through it, driving the mono-molecular blades on her upper arms into its central processor bundle. Drones battered her back, detonating against her armour plating. With her other limbs, she seized the maggot's mouthparts and ripped them away from the damaged cable, piece by ugly piece.

The maggot's body bucked and twisted. From the magnetic field bunching around it, she could tell it was squeezing its fusion bottle to overload. With her second robot, Ann reached straight through the maggot's side and tore out its primary power conduit. The thing went dead in a flash of spent plasma. Ann lost her second mech but the remaining microdrones exploded in a rapid cascade. Job done.

She set the rest of her mech team repairing the exohull breach and turned her full attention to the other incursion site. That was when she realised that Mark was already on it.

'What do you think you're doing?' Ann growled.

'A thank you would suffice,' said Mark as his mechs finished dismantling the driller they'd found.

He'd wasted five robots, she noticed. *Five.* It was hardly efficient.

'Why don't you focus on the helm?' said Mark. 'Aren't you captain right now?'

Ann snarled but hurled her attention away, slamming it back into helm-space.

She scanned the long, black scarf of sticky filth that trapped her ship. Somewhere in that cloud, their enemy would be closing in. Fortunately, the ionic debris they had dumped would greatly simplify the process of winkling them out.

Ann deployed eight plasma-flare charges on high-gee sub-light torches and waited yet again for them to crawl out from the hull to a useful ignition radius. Then she lit them.

The space around the *Dantes* exploded into light. Ann had picked a wavelength for her flares designed to maximally warm the ions the disrupters had already dumped. Even after the initial flare, the scarf continued to glow with residual light, making their enemies reassuringly visible – or the ones located within the disrupter cloud, at least. While in the smear, they couldn't hide themselves with quantum cloaking. You needed cleaner space for that. Instead, they had to rely on hull albedo, which made them about as hard to see as coal chunks on a snowfield.

She found a hundred and seventy-nine drones sneaking towards them – a disappointingly modest spread. Ann brought her grater-grids online and used g-rays to scrape every drone out of existence in a series of tidily optimised bursts.

Clath whooped from somewhere behind her in helm-space.

'We're still alive!'

'Spare your enthusiasm,' said Ann. 'The Photes could just be holding back. We can't see anything outside the cloud yet. They may be waiting to take us alive. And right now we're stuck.'

'Then use the conventional engines!' Clath urged. 'They're amazing in dirty space. The best ever built. Plus our caskets can do internal bio-support for microbursts of up to a hundred and twenty gees.'

'I'm already on it,' Ann snapped. She'd been fighting alone for years. The last thing she needed was *help*. It would only slow her down.

'No, save the power,' said Ira. 'Don't let them see how fast we can go. Crawl out first to draw them in, *then* use the engines.'

'How many backseat drivers does this ship have?' said Ann, and immediately realised that the answer would always be five.

Ann used Ira's tactic anyway, keeping her speed moderate as she pushed towards the back of the cloud, aiming for the closest available gap. Then, at the last minute, she activated the invasive bio-support and hurled the ship forwards without warp – all forty kilometres of it. The hull shrieked but held. Clath was right – the *Dantes* could really shift when it wanted to. The audio channel filled with her shipmates' tortured gasps. Ann ignored them. They'd live.

Their reference frame boosted astonishingly with every micro-burn she invoked, even while her antimatter reserves sent her usage warnings.

'Supposed... to use... burst... once,' Clath gasped.

Ann kept flying.

As soon as she was through the far side of the cloud, she released another round of flares, this time on warp and packed with incredibly expensive q-chaff. She lit up the space around them. Another two hundred and eighty-three drones revealed themselves, despite their cloaks. Ann ramped power to the grids and took out her bogeys, fragments of her mind managing every targeting SAP with unwavering attention.

Where was the armada she'd expected? It simply wasn't there yet, she realised. The Photes had been racing to catch up with them. They'd invested an effort-surge into spreading a disrupter trap to slow the *Dantes* down while the main firepower caught up. The drone-to-disrupter ratio on its own suggested heavy backup close by.

'I'm looking at the vector field for those drones you just torched,' said Palla, her simulated voice glitching under the gravity strain. 'I'm seeing a clear mean trajectory. We know where those bastards came from. Scanning that region now.'

'I'm quite capable of doing that, thank you,' said Ann, taking Palla's scan.

She followed the vector, dived under warp and flared again. This time, their burst of radiation revealed a large raider ship in the process of rapid disassembly.

Phote ships only separated when they had no further interest in taking live hosts. Their goal now would be to kill the *Dantes*. And these drones would be the smart ones with clusters of live ex-human brains embedded. Ann deployed a swarm of her own munitions, releasing a small fraction of the horde tucked within the ship's hull. With the rest of her attention, she kicked on the shield.

The enemy drones spread out before they attacked, grouping themselves into tight self-defending squads that forced Ann to split both her attention and her fire. She simply fragmented her mind into as many shards as necessary. It wasn't as easy as on the *Ariel Two*, where she had thousands of kilometres of distributed neuronal support to rely on, but still well within her abilities.

While dangerously smart in aggregate, isolated Photes were terrible tacticians and prone to repeat behaviours. Each of Ann's subminds had a vast database of prior Phote attacks to draw on, many built from her own memories. Destroying all but one of the squads took her eleven-point-six seconds. The last squad scattered. If just one enemy drone survived, word of the *Dantes'* clever engines would get back to the approaching fleet. Ann commenced mop-up operations.

Ragged cheering erupted from Clath and Palla as the battle turned into a rout. It sounded like they were having a party in the helm-arena that Ann wasn't bothering to use.

'We're in with a chance,' said Mark. 'But we have to assume that messengers went out the moment we hit that cloud. We should release silencer drones now and chase them down, otherwise they'll have our position.'

'I veto that,' said Palla. 'That's what we want. The more the merrier. I'm glad we're not dead, but we need to draw more fire.'

'Then we fire message drones,' Ira put in. 'Make it look like being found was a big deal and we need to tell someone.'

'Grandpa has an idea for once,' said Palla. 'I love it!'

'I'm on it,' said Mark. 'Ann, give me messaging control. You handle mop-up. Prepping phoney messages.'

'No,' said Judj. 'Use encrypted viral payloads.'

'Veto!' said Palla. 'Load a request to swap to backup rendezvous coordinates.'

'Will you all just shut up and let me *clean* here?' Ann roared. 'I'm nearly finished!'

'What vector?' said Mark.

'Here,' said Palla.

Ann muttered curses as she swooped like a falcon to execute the final drone.

'I recommend we use a decoy exit vector,' said Mark.

'I'm loading one already,' Ann snapped.

'Veto,' said Palla. 'From this point on we drop all attempts to conceal our flight path. We have to look like we're making a run for it.'

'Isn't that what we're doing?' said Clath.

The primary external cameras on one side of the ship all shorted at once as the arrival blast of a carrier blinded them. Reinforcements. Millions of them, painfully close.

'Fine!' Ann shouted. She threw the *Dantes* onto a straight-line path and pushed the warp engines to maximum. Pseudo-gravity pummelled their organs. But compared to the conventional thrust bursts they'd experienced earlier, it felt like gentle tickling.

As they gathered warp, Ann flushed the battlescape and dropped them back onto the yacht. All six of them stood on the bridge with its brass fittings and a commanding view of the bullshit artificial sea.

'You all need to back off the next time we do this,' she told them. 'Until we hit the Zone, this is *my* ride.'

'Whatevs,' said Palla.

'You, girly,' said Ann, rounding on her. 'Try to think for a minute. As a lure, our job is to buy Galatea adequate time to save the Earth Ark. As it is, our lead is now measured in *minutes* and we're still light-years from the Alpha Flaw. At this rate, we won't buy them shit. I know your little head is full of technical cleverness, but your fucking ruse needs room to play out.'

Palla gave her a cold, level look. 'This has been factored, Supergran. Just do your job.'

Ann held up a finger and *pressed* on the shadow-mediated virt with the weight of the alien software inside her. The air buckled. On the other side of the bridge, Palla slammed up against the wall, breathless and astonished.

'Don't think for a second that because I'm locked in a box I can't mess you up,' Ann growled. She looked at each of them in turn. 'No backseat driving,' she said. 'This was your warning.'

With that, she strode off in the direction of her cabin to update her threat models. The rest of them didn't seem to get it yet. They'd been sacrificed already. They were *dead*. Ann had run the numbers fifteen million different ways since coming aboard and hadn't yet found a single reason to believe that Mark's plan could work. There were too many assumptions. It was pure improvisational bullshit, like everything else he came up with.

All that mattered was making their last few days *count*. Ridiculous notions about flying into the Zone would only reduce their effectiveness. You couldn't fight worth a damn in the Alpha Flaw. And if the Autocratic Academy honestly believed that the Photes were going to follow them in, then they were bigger fools than she'd taken them for.

The earnest, innocent faces of Poli's kids loomed in her mind's eye. After all she'd tried to do for the people she loved, she was not about to see her capabilities expended on a failed feint. She was determined to take an army of Photes with her when she went. Nothing else would make her sacrifice worth it.

[She's not going to fuck up my final battle for me!] Ann roared at her shadow.

[No, she's not,] it replied, [so keep your hair on. You'll get to make your stand. It won't be long. But right now, we need to hurry. From this point onwards, every hound in hell is going to be after us.]

4.4: MARK

Two days later, they reached the Bock Science Station hanging five light-minutes outside the Alpha Flaw. Their warp-velocity had been slowing inexorably for the last eight hours as the curvon density dropped. While the paucity of local space undoubtedly impacted their enemy's ember-warp drives just as much as their own, Mark remained astonished that they weren't dead already. They'd actually made it to the end of humanity's domain without hitting another trap.

Bock Station was little more than a tethered pair of can-shaped evac-arks spinning in space about their shared centre of gravity like a set of bolos cast in endless flight. A clumsy polyhedral mass of scientific equipment had been attached at the midpoint between the cans, studded with various dishes and antennas. In all directions around the station lay a thoroughly unremarkable starscape. The closest sun was over a light-year distant. As picnic spots went, there wasn't much to recommend it.

That was through a standard visual display. Through a curvon filter, a very different picture emerged. Here, the normally exuberant rainbow sea of untapped spatial potential thinned out and ended at a black wall that stretched to infinity in every direction.

Bisecting that wall was a flickering river of ghostly colour – the Alpha Flaw. It formed a narrow seam right in front of them, like a gloomy chasm between two infinitely high obsidian cliffs. The station's shadow hung in front of that view like a grey speck, making it clear how obscenely vast the phenomena before him actually were.

Not for the first time, Mark felt a vertiginous rush contemplating that view. Gas giants weren't big. Even stars weren't big in galactic terms. The Zone, though, was genuinely, unavoidably *huge*. The scale of it was beyond a mind's ability to fathom. Yet it was a phantom – a quirk of space–time invisible to any society without warp-drive at its disposal. Unless you were trying to fly a starship through it, you couldn't see it, couldn't feel it, couldn't even guess it was there.

Palla signalled the station. As representative of the Academic will, that grim responsibility was hers. She stood beside Mark on the circular glass platform of their helm-arena, the faint rainbows from the route ahead casting curious shadows on her elfin face. Her expression was unreadably hard. On the far side of the disc, Ann stared coldly into space.

'Bock Station, this is Autograd Palla Muri, SAO for the GSS *Edmond Dantes*,' said Palla. 'You are instructed to evacuate immediately. We are being pursued by a Photurian force of unknown size supported by at least one fully distended carrier. You are to flee into the Zone as per Contingency Plan Jackrabbit. Please acknowledge.'

Mark waited in the starry darkness of helm-space for their reply. The scientific crew of Bock Station, a facility he'd campaigned to establish, would now have no choice but to fly their evac-arks into the dead mass of the Zone's bulk. There they'd hide with their albedo dropped and hope that the Photes didn't bother coming after them under conventional thrust – a time-consuming operation.

Theoretically, the Galatean government would send a rescue crew to bring all two hundred and fifty residents back from the Zone's edge once the coast was clear. Mark doubted they had ever been informed that their lives might be sacrificed in a tactical gamble.

Response took several painful minutes.

'This is Coordinator Amelie Nunez,' came the reply. The face of a thin, anxious woman appeared in a video window before them. 'Your message and authority codes have been received. But what about our equipment? Complete detachment will leave the experimental cluster drifting with critical experiments uncompleted.'

Palla's eyebrows rose in disbelief at the woman's priorities. It was the only emotion she let show.

'The cluster is to be abandoned,' she said. 'This is an Academic Order. Please be advised that you may have only minutes to get out of here. You are also instructed to send us a full download from your data cores for navigation purposes. We're going in.'

'Understood,' said Amelie, her brow twitching in distress as the stakes finally dawned on her. 'Sending now. Nunez out.'

While they watched, the arks separated and began their burn, abandoning who knew how many scientific careers'-worth of work. The expensive jumble of the experimental cluster tumbled slowly away, embarking on a multi-million-year drift towards human space.

The arks' thrust built slowly. Mark could only guess at the panicked activity inside as every member of staff scrambled to find a crash couch in which they could endure the multi-gee burn to come. Even this close to the Flaw, it would still take them hours to reach the relative safety of dead space – long, dangerous hours.

'Okay, Ann,' said Palla.

Ann didn't move.

'Did you hear me? It's handover time.'

Ann marched up to where they stood and stared down at them through Valkyrie eyes. The closer to the Flaw they'd travelled, the more remote she'd become. Her own success at running away appeared to have disappointed her intensely.

'Requesting SAO permission to alter the mission profile and make a stand here at the edge of the Zone,' she said. 'To go any further is to participate in fantasy and waste.'

'Request denied,' said Palla.

Ann stood silent for several seconds.

'I repeat my request,' said Ann. 'Threat models indicate that there is no tactical value—'

'Request *denied*,' said Palla again, more firmly.

'Fine,' Ann said eventually.

A large steel ring appeared in Ann's hand – the helm-space's visualisation of the ship's executive key. She slapped it into Mark's palm and walked away.

'Mark,' said Palla, 'you're up and we have no idea how long our lead is. Please be quick.'

Mark slipped the steel ring over his wrist and dropped himself into merged awareness with the ship. The cameras became his eyes. His subminds raced out to replace Ann's as his consciousness reached into every corner of ship function.

He signalled Clath, who'd been waiting for his call in the yacht's lounge. 'Doctor Ataro to helm-space, please. I'm running out the feeler-drone loops.'

He opened the *Dantes'* prodigious hangar doors and let long lines of warp-drones rip forth from them, burning ahead of their ship and into the river of rainbows on machine-gun bursts of light.

The Flaw was known to be at least two light-years deep but only about as wide as Sol. It did not sit still, but oozed and meandered according to complex feedback patterns, which meant that even at one light, you only had about two seconds to react if it kinked in front of you. It was a navigational nightmare – famously so.

The upshot was that if you were travelling through the Flaw slow enough to tell where the dead space ahead of you was, you'd never reach the other side in your lifetime. And if you were going fast enough to get through it, you were effectively blind. The moment you hit the edge of whatever rivulet of curvon flow you were surfing on, you were glued. A ship's last bursts of warp tended to carry it so far into the bulk that getting back out was nearly impossible.

From that point on, you were free to accelerate conventionally, for all the good it would do you. Without warp, just re-entering the flow you'd left moments ago could take anything from days to years. As a young man, Mark had experienced that effect first-hand.

The feeler-loops were Galatea's solution to that conundrum – a system of shuttling drones programmed to scan local space for usable curvons. Outgoing drones tried to stick to clean space. Returning drones passed information back to the parent ship about successful routes. Cunningly timed laser bursts enabled the drones to collectively infer losses in their number and adapt flight paths with minimal cost. In effect, they functioned like tentacles on a blind octopus, allowing a ship to find its way through the Flaw by touch.

As soon as he started receiving packets, Mark kicked on the ship's prodigious thrusters and pushed them after the drones, into the Alpha Flaw. Fortunately, the boost Ann had given their conventional velocity back at the raid site now worked in their favour. Mark barely needed to touch the engines to leave the arks trailing to pinpoints in his wake.

As they dived into the river's narrowing mouth, Mark's gravity display stuttered into darkness. The flow was too intermittent to pad out a vanilla visualisation. He swapped to the dynamic, SAP-inferred model being built by the feeler-loops and received a multidimensional barrage of rapidly oscillating expectation vectors straight to his sensorium. It was like trying to drink out of a crowd-suppression hose. He reeled.

'Can't we make that a little more...usable?' he said.

'On it,' said Ann tersely from somewhere down in helm-space. 'Initialising now.'

She took hold of the feed and started reducing it in real-time, passing him a drip feed of course-corrections. Mark grunted in relief, brought the warp engines back online and took them gently into the throat of the Flaw.

It worked perfectly, but within five minutes Mark was already frustrated. Ann's corrections barely let him travel faster than a single light and her updates weren't getting any more frequent. Meanwhile, if their threat predictions could be trusted, dangerous company lay just minutes behind. That was the problem with FTL chases. You had no idea who was after you or how close they were until they'd already arrived and started shooting. Given how quickly the Photes had shown up last time, Mark was assuming the worst.

'This is great, Ann, but it's taking too long,' he said. 'At this rate, they'll be on top of us in seconds.'

'This is what I can give you,' she replied.

'Mark has a point,' said Palla. 'It'll take us years to get through the Flaw at this rate. If we even make it past the first bank.'

'Then maybe we shouldn't be bothering,' Ann snapped. 'Our feelers are still deploying. If we go too fast too soon, drone attrition skyrockets.'

'We can slow later,' Mark pointed out. 'Right now we need to put enough distance between ourselves and the Phote fleet that they can't just ride our warp-trail in after us. Clath, any ideas?'

'Nothing that doesn't bump our risk profile,' she said.

'Facing imminent death *is* a risk, Clath. See what you can do. Ann, I have to ramp our warp. Please get ready to up your feed rate. Anything you can give me would be great.'

'Don't be stupid,' she said. 'I'm doing everything I can already. If we lose warp, we'll be sitting ducks when the Photes hit. I'm trying to maintain a viable defensive position.'

Mark breathed deep before replying. 'The whole point is to *avoid* the Photes,' he said, 'not to plan how to die gloriously when they show up.'

'Battle is inevitable,' she snarled back. 'If we insist on deferring it, at least let me do that *properly*. I assure you, this is not easy.'

Mark glanced over at her in concern. She stood in helm-space with arms outstretched, a haze of inscrutably dense data mappings twisting around her head. He flicked across to the threat-assessment models and sucked air as he watched their capture probabilities climbing through orange into red.

'Okay,' said Clath. 'I've signalled the feeler-loops to anticipate a faster return rate. This won't exactly be robust, but it's doable.'

'Okay,' Mark gasped. 'Ramping now.'

He doubled their burst rate and kept it climbing. Ann's vectors, however, barely increased in frequency.

'Ann!' Mark shouted. 'More *vectors*, please.'

'I will not risk the success of this mission,' she retorted. 'I am sending vectors as fast as I can safely process them.'

'Then please process them *unsafely*!'

'No,' she said. 'That is *always* your solution, Mark, and it is broken. Our primary objective is to act as an effective lure and draw fire. That is what Galatea *needs of us*. We can't do that if we disappear into the Zone or irretrievably compromise our combat position.'

'Jesus, Ann,' said Mark. 'We're trying to stay alive here!'

'Exactly!' said Ann. 'And that is not the point. I will not disobey a Fleet mission dictate and am therefore requesting SAO intervention. I recommend that we kill engines and make a stand.'

'Denied,' said Palla.

With deepening dread, Mark saw how things were headed. Ann had no intention of helping and they couldn't make her. She hadn't wanted to go any further than this from the moment she'd come aboard. She'd never believed in his mission, and now she was going to take it away from him and make their entire effort pointless.

'Clath,' said Mark, struggling for a level tone, 'I'm reaching the end of Ann's vector stack.' The loss of data had already forced him to slow again. 'Can you automate her reduction process for me?'

'Of course not!' she blurted. 'Otherwise we wouldn't need her. Plotting a Flaw course is hard. Like *NP-hard*. Just flying down it causes a ripple effect. The Flaw's so narrow that warping on it changes its dynamics. It's an algorithmic nightmare!'

'Give me *something*,' he said. 'I need help here.'

'Okay,' she squeaked. 'I'm building you an heuristic reduction of the feeler data. Get ready.'

A new version of the vector map bloomed in Mark's sensorium. Instead of being stuck in dozens of dimensions, he now had just six to worry about. But Clath had used dense symbolic tags to squeeze in the extra data. Every multicoloured drone icon had an ever-scrolling feed of sensor history wrapped around it. Mark had to use half his submind bandwidth just to tease the convoluted display apart.

How could reading space be as hard as managing an entire starship, for crying out loud? Mark suddenly had a very clear sense of why nobody had actually made it through the Zone. However, the more he watched, the more he understood. Mark smiled as he started to get the hang of the display. He pushed their velocity back up to twenty lights, then thirty. It was all about reading the data bursts from the passing loops at the right time.

'I do not recommend this course of action,' said Ann. 'Mark, slow down. I do not want to have to intervene.'

'Then fucking don't!' Mark shouted.

'Mark, you are not compensating for edge-effects. This display is only giving you first- and second-order—'

'Ann, in God's name, please stop distracting me. Either help—'

The shriek of warning klaxons filled helm-space as the engines abruptly died.

'Warp engines inactive,' the *Dantes*' emergency-management SAP informed him. 'Activating passive stealth systems. Emitters retracting.'

The klaxons stopped. Emergency protocols dumped Mark back into his avatar in helm-space.

Ann stood before him with eyes full of fury.

'And *now* what?' she said. 'How are we supposed to fight from *here*?'

Mark shook his head. He had no appetite for being dressed down by an uptight goddess. He felt too sick with disgust and defeat.

'Maybe you should have done your job,' he said quietly.

Ann glowered at him. She reached over and grabbed his avatar by its ship-suit. Her hands slid off him. She blinked at them in surprise.

'My security is backed by Will Monet's old hackpack,' Mark pointed out. 'It has been for years. Did you honestly imagine I wouldn't have my virt settings protected, the way you've been behaving?'

'Once again we're inhabiting a clusterfuck created by your attitude problem!' she shouted. 'Again! *Every* time we have to work together!'

'*My* attitude?' said Mark. 'Take a look in the fucking mirror, Ann! You had a job. But you chose to interpret it just the way you wanted. Like you did at Earth.'

Ann held up a hand and started poking the air before him. The virtual environment wobbled. The star projection blurred and suddenly Mark started to feel hot. The neck of his ship-suit became awfully tight. She grimaced at him. Mark diverted submind focus to his hackpack controls. Helm-space warped further. The glass beneath them buckled and foamed.

'Children, *please!*' Palla shouted.

Abruptly, helm-space evaporated, trapping them back on the bridge of the yacht. Palla had used her Autocratic override to close the helm down entirely. Use of the override was the ship's last-ditch security setting. Normally, an SAO would only take such measures prior to a self-destruct order. She was making a point.

'Intervention time!' said Palla. 'You two are confined to quarters until you can get your shit together.'

She clapped her hands and Mark was abruptly back in his stateroom, seated in one of the awful chairs.

'Emergency virt truncation has occurred,' said the walls. 'Restabilisation is under way. Please move slowly or nerve damage may occur.'

He put his head in his hands and groaned.

4.5: NADA

With all haste, Nada pursued the Abomination. To have that goal so close to achievement tantalised her. It chafed at her mind so much that she started to have dreams. Not flush-patterns – actual dreams, like a human.

Those dreams were all the same. In them, she was killing the Abomination – strangling the life out of her – and it was beautiful. As her hands squeezed down on that windpipe, she felt it crumple wonderfully. She heard the wheezing rattle of those last desperate breaths. She saw the panic in Ludik's evil eyes and knew that she was bringing joy and glory to the whole human race. Then, each time, as the Abomination finally died, Nada found herself flying up through the hierarchy of the mind-temple in ecstatic release.

She ascended past the level of caverns that represented cell clusters and organs, up through individuals, through small social group function, to emergent colony awareness and beyond. With each level she passed, she heard the song of the Photurian Protocol singing out – the magical incantation that made them all so beautifully the same from cells up to entire planets. The song became more subtle and laden with subtext as she rose, bringing her closer to the light of the Founder Entity shining down from above.

At last she reached General Collective Function, the level that was tragically blocked because they couldn't access their own homeworld. Without that last link in the command chain, the will of the Founder Entity always lay excruciatingly out of reach. Yet, hovering there, she heard the Founder Entity address her. It spoke with the voice of the Yunus. It rang in her mind like a bell the size of a world.

'You have done well, Nada Rien,' it said. 'It is time for you to experience True Peace.'

'But we haven't killed Monet,' said Nada. 'We haven't retaken the homeworld.'

'Haven't we?' it replied. 'Are you sure?'

And then it pulled her impossibly through that uppermost hole, into the mind of the homeworld, and Nada realised that she'd been wrong, and that everything was now right with the universe. As she rose, the Founder's destroying light bathed her, filling her with its beauty. Tearing her apart. Embracing her. Consuming her. Smashing her into happiness. Rewriting her utterly in joy.

'Yes!' she screamed. 'Yes! Yes! Yes!'

She woke with her face covered in tears. She hung in the wall of the cramped, gloomy vesicle and smelled the acrid tang of the wall-mucus. The lice tickled her face. Mundane reality had invaded once again, this time in the form of an entry request from Leng.

[I wish to enter the leadership vesicle to report,] he sent.

Leng had become very attentive of late. Obsequious, even. He'd developed the habit of repeatedly revisiting his concerns about the mission and asking if any of them required that she make further modifications to him. She felt no such urge and resented him for suggesting it. She was motivated to update him specifically to ensure worship of

136

the Yunus, but not to simplify her own life. That would have been in contravention to the principle of enforced individuality.

That same principle, however, required that she listen to his interminable verbal reports. She reluctantly let him in.

'Report,' she said as he squeezed inside.

'Word has arrived,' he said. 'A message was left for us at our last intercept point. We have found the ship. Our disrupter trap successfully delayed it.'

Nada wept with relief.

'We are not more than a day away,' said Leng.

A whole day? She slapped his face.

'Why so long?' she said, her voice trembling.

'The ship was screening its trajectory,' said Leng. 'Our projections assumed that it would head towards a usable star system. Instead, it headed directly for the Alpha Flaw in the Depleted Zone. An attack squad was dispatched via carrier but arrived too late to prevent the ship from releasing message drones and continuing at full warp.'

'Drones with what message?' said Nada.

'A request to change rendezvous coordinates. But it was almost certainly a ploy. In any case, the enemy ship may have already been captured or destroyed. The attack squad was in hot pursuit at the time of messaging.'

'Inform all ships,' said Nada. 'We will chase down the enemy ship.'

Leng broke slowly into an oily smile. He squinted at her. One of his eyes twitched.

'I thought you might request that,' he said. 'Even though direct pursuit is now at odds with the orders of the Yunus.'

Nada stared at him. Her heart fluttered with impatience.

'I do not see how,' she said.

'We were instructed to find the population of Earth. Instead we are chasing one ship which we know cannot be carrying it.'

She thought about hitting him again, regardless of how bad an idea that was. She needed to keep herself together.

'Our assumption has been that the ship would rendezvous with the missing arks,' she said. 'It sent a message drone to that effect, supporting that hypothesis. Nothing has changed.'

'Except that now we have enough information to disregard that scenario,' said Leng. 'A lone ship headed to the Zone cannot be useful to a hidden population.'

'Did you consider the possibility that they hid the population within the surface layers of the Zone?' she said.

She stared at his cheek where a large purple mark was forming against the blue tint of his skin. She wondered if his neck would be as delicate as the one in her dream.

'Of course,' said Leng. 'While not impossible, it is highly unlikely. What is there to do in the Zone except die? There is no warp. There are no suntaps. There are no habitable worlds. There is no—'

She cut him off. 'Unlikely scenarios are exactly the ones the Galateans like to exploit.'

'True but circular. Circular logic may justify any act. We now know that leaving Galatea prematurely was a mistake.'

'Incorrect!' said Nada. 'We were instructed to act swiftly and independently, so we did. Now one target lies within our grasp and the other does not. It only makes sense for us to pursue our selected course of action to completion, otherwise we risk failing to reach *either* target.'

'Instead we risk failing in our main objective.'

'Destroying the Abomination is not failure. It cannot be!' she shouted. 'How can you explain the Yunus rewriting me to hunger so much for the death of the Abomination?'

At the same time, she saw the awful truth behind Leng's words. This choice would be irrevocable. The dissonance between the Yunus's verbal orders and how he'd made her feel was like a splinter in her mind.

'I cannot,' Leng admitted. His eyes shuttled from side to side. His smile grew tighter. 'However, it is conceivable that the Yunus made the reasonable assumption that the two goals would remain congruent.'

'Do you honestly believe that the Yunus could make a mistake of that magnitude?'

He *must* have known. Adhering to verbal orders was one thing, but her edits made her what she was. Were he here, instead of light-years away, he'd approve, surely? His edits had come with a solemn promise. Why had he even bothered with such words if he hadn't understood exactly what she'd need to do?

Leng's voice came out as a strangled croak. 'No. I cannot doubt the Yunus. And yet this course of action is ... is ... *paining* me. I am struggling and I am not alone. The crew is already tired from monitoring

Galatea. I have received multiple reports of units exhibiting individuality strain on other ships. Two units in our own crew have sounded self-integrity warnings.'

Nada knew her management of their identities had been less effective of late. She'd been too distracted. However, she also knew that she couldn't give up. If she tried, her mind would surely break.

'My pain is... reducing my joy in being Photurian,' said Leng. His eyes snapped to her face. 'Is there nothing you can do about that? Our flight has been so long and so *hard*.' His lip trembled.

Nada regarded him with disgust. He was practically begging for another rewrite. She resisted the urge to fix that sickness by rewriting him. That would be counterproductive.

'I hear you,' she said. 'I will prioritise restful communion as soon as the Abomination is destroyed. And I will amend my plan according to your counsel. I will split the fleet. Two ships will send word to the Yunus informing him of our choice. The rest will maintain pursuit.'

Leng regarded her with desperate eyes. 'Is that all?' he said.

Nada flapped at the air, trying to release all the joyful energy she felt without actually punching his face.

'Yes. Resist all urge to delay. We must make directly for the location of the last enemy ship sighting. No other behaviour can be tolerated.'

Some emotion that was not obedient delight crawled over Leng's features.

'Yes,' he said as he turned to go. 'Of course. You are my superior. I will act in accordance with your desires and be happy about it. Yes.'

He left her alone and in silence, with the wonder of her dream all gone. She clutched at her stomach. She could not doubt the Yunus. She was proud of what he had done to her. The death of the Abomination would be enough for him and all would be well. There'd be no more false homes or human-farms or wasted units, just as he'd promised. She clung to that vision and rocked gently in the wall's moist embrace.

5: REFLECTION

5.1: WILL

Will spent a restless night in a cramped hotel built into the bulge of a habitat-tube. He lay awake on an old mattress for hours and listened to the sound of his copies making love to each other through the thin wooden walls. In the end, he resorted to clapping the clammy pillow over his head. Snakepit had become something oppressive beyond words. He *had* to get out.

More than anything, he craved the company of real people. He missed Rachel, of course, but he'd felt that ache for years. He missed Mark, too, grumpy bastard that he was, but in that moment he'd have talked to anyone who wasn't a butchered parody of himself. Yet there was nobody – just the animated echoes of his own mind. A person could go insane here, he decided. Perhaps that was why his clones all seemed so weird – they were already irretrievably nuts.

Dawn took for ever to arrive – Snakepit's rotation was slower than Earth's – and the light that finally appeared was a watery grey, joyless and drab. Will rose and ate an early breakfast in a dark coffee shop on Campari Street obviously geared towards copies much hipper than himself but with less discerning appetites. Leaving half a scorched croissant on the plate, he returned to the Old Slam Bar and knocked on the door.

After several minutes of attempted access, the Ira-lookalike appeared frowning in a crack of entranceway.

'The park, one hour from now,' he said.

'Where's the park?' said Will.

Ira pointed up the street. 'That way. Buy a fucking map, *Jason.*' The door closed.

Will seethed. Had all his clones decided to have their politeness excised, or were they just as sick of seeing his face as he was?

At the top of the next road over, near the brow of Radical Hill, a sequence of tiered platforms rose over the backs of the tubes. Dents in the tunnel-matrix, either cut or grown, had been encouraged to sprout wild bursts of multicoloured ferns. The result was a sloping boardwalk garden with paths meandering between explosions of bright vegetation, use-worn staircases and long views over the helical towers to an ocean of dusky mauve. A cold breeze carried a faint sea tang and a curious vegetal musk. Will found a bench to wait.

After a cold, lonely hour, he finally spotted someone familiar who wasn't obviously himself. A man with John Forrester's handsome action-hero face and a long black coat was walking towards him. Will stared. John was the man who'd sold him out and left him for dead on New Angeles during the Interstellar War.

The sight of those chiselled features on a clone brought a conflicted twisting to his stomach. He'd never forgiven John for what he'd done, though the man had died in a military prison long ago. At the same time, he felt a profound relief in simply looking at somebody else.

'Cuthbert?' said John as he approached.

Will nodded and rose. It was the first time anyone had referred to him by the nick Elsa had picked. It felt vaguely dishonest.

'You're Mr Brown?' said Will.

John shook his hand. 'In the flesh. Nice to meet you. It sounds like your trip here has been disorientating and more than a little stressful. Sorry about that, and I'm glad you made it. My apologies also for our welcoming committee at the bar. They can't be too careful, and maintaining a certain attitude is part of what keeps the place safe.'

'Sure,' said Will.

'Just so you know, Balance doesn't appear to have tracked you here. There was a lot of activity around the station yesterday but none of it got as far as the hill. Balance struggles to make it up here. Our anger keeps him out, thank Gal. It's one of the small mercies of this place.'

John's smile was warm but Will couldn't bring himself to trust it. He'd seen it in too many bad dreams. John seemed to guess the direction of his thoughts.

141

'You're probably wondering why I chose this, right?' he said, rubbing his cheek.

Will nodded. 'The question had occurred to me.'

'Keeps me focused. It reminds me every time I look in the mirror that I can't trust myself, or anyone else. When you're running a resistance movement, that's useful to bear in mind. Besides, I couldn't think of anyone else with a more relevant face for spy antics. Does that help?'

'Somewhat,' said Will.

John gestured down the path. 'Then let's walk and talk,' he said. 'You must have plenty of questions.'

'That's one way of putting it,' said Will, his tension subsiding a little as they set off.

'I assume a basic history of our society has been covered?'

Will shook his head.

'Okay, well, there's not that much to know. We all woke up one day feeling a little fuzzy. There was a lot of confusion. Then came panic and claustrophobia. Wills began trying to differentiate themselves to stay sane. At the same time, we started having to think collectively via the planet to resolve some ugly conflicts that arose.

'It was about what you'd expect: a planet full of identical people going crazy together. Then the Nems, or Photurians, or whatever you want to call them – they attacked. They arrived in this system suddenly, in huge numbers, and started raining crap on us from orbit. It was grim. But we rapidly figured out that the differentiation we'd tinkered with was helping us win that fight. It helped *a lot*. It made our collective brain more stable. It made it easier to allocate tasks and reason broadly. So after we beat the Photurians, there was an explosion of diversity.

'That's when we formalised the notion of *Balance* and gave it consciousness. We really started building stuff.' John gestured out at the view. 'Most of this was established around that time. Everyone got a lot more comfortable with the idea of a unique identity as a *project*, and trying to help each other achieve it. We went from a basically monastic society to having a lot of girls around almost overnight.'

Will regarded him sceptically. 'Really? That many clones of me changed their minds about their sex?'

John laughed and shook his head. 'No,' he said. 'Just a few who managed to make the adjustment and felt comfortable with it. But we're *threads*, Will. We can be *copied*. Once we had a few successful gender converts, they were extremely popular, as you might imagine.'

It hadn't occurred to him that his clones could duplicate. On reflection, he felt a little slow. After all, everything here was a copy.

'That's how our economy works,' said John. 'That stuff with the cash boxes on the streets? None of that's real. It's just a public service to facilitate thread training. Some of us learn to run businesses by playing at it first. You always wanted to be a better negotiator, didn't you? Well, now some of you are.'

Will had wondered why everything in soft-space had a price on it if the shops only took play-money. Now it made sense, sort of.

'The real economy is maintained by a store of favours that's monitored in soft-space,' said John. 'Our main unit of currency is the branch-request – gifting a copy of yourself.'

'You sell *clones*?'

'Exactly. Either that or some fraction of the deltas that comprise us. You can think of it as the ultimate service economy. I lend you an instance of me for whatever task you have in mind, so you owe me something. Permitting a lot of copies gains you leeway when you're figuring out how you want to grow your own thread. But that means your identity has to be one people want.'

'Up to the point of turning some of us into dogs,' said Will darkly.

John shot him a wry look. 'Actually, yes. Dogs are popular. You'd be amazed how rich some of those dogs are. The first Will who figured out how to make that tolerable for himself made a killing. That's why there are so many small play-businesses here. Wills who develop a passion for entrepreneurship take better risks when they diversify their identity. And those risks come back as opportunities because of all the favours they've stored up. Today a terrier, tomorrow Anubis. That first dog could probably afford to copy any thread he liked a million times over by now. Any fantasy he wants. Not some shabby virt-dream populated by SAP puppets – the real thing. Dancing girls, adoring fans, enemies to kill, you name it.

'What you see today is the result of a *lot* of careful lifestyle experimentation. Working to spread ourselves out to mimic a full species has made life far more tolerable – even if some of us take what you might think of as a lifestyle hit. Really. If you think this is hard, try being trapped in a tunnel-world of identical duplicates for a year or two.'

143

'And yet there's the Old Slam Bar,' Will pointed out. 'If things are so great, why do you need a resistance movement?'

John exhaled. 'Well, for a while things were looking okay. We were actually kind of proud of this place. Then we started getting these... Cancer identities. Embittered rogue personas that started chewing through everything we'd built, smashing things up.'

'Because of the lifestyle hits, perhaps,' Will remarked.

'Maybe. In any case, it was hard for Balance to root them out. They self-replicate illegally, without a contract, so they tend to develop powerful voices pretty fast. It's hard to beat that with a consensus-based police force, even a superhuman one. A lot of us started to wonder where we'd gone wrong.'

He paused, stopping on the path to stare at Will. 'That's when *you* started showing up.'

'You mean copies of me.'

'If that makes it easier for you. In any case, there's some difference of opinion about what you represent. The common wisdom is that you're another kind of Cancer. But Glitches like you are different from Cancers in a lot of ways. For a start, you seem to be more interested in killing Cancers than replicating.' He gave Will a meaningful look. 'Do you feel like killing right now?'

An image of the pathetic horse clone flashed through Will's head. He pushed it away.

'Of course not,' he said.

'In any case, I advise you to keep your disgust in check,' said John.

'So I've been told.'

'The long and short of it is that previous *copies* of you have had a big impact on society. You're lucky, though – this time you met the right woman and she pointed you at us. We have a programme for working with Glitches. It's helping us figure out what you're for, and what the hell is going on with this world.'

'I keep hearing that word,' said Will. '*Glitches*. Why do you call us that?'

'That's a big question,' said John. 'To understand, it helps to know a bit about how the Willworld is organised. You've seen already that there's a division in our way of life, right? Between soft-space and physical reality?'

Will nodded.

'We use physical reality for thread differentiation. Soft-space is where trade and government happens – all the serious stuff that goes into making Balance. Our actions as individual threads inform his thoughts. So you can think of soft-space as a giant mind, and the society that works there like a distributed consciousness. Or if you prefer to think of Balance as a government, then our opinions double as votes, and a share of our individual processing time is taken as tax. Some people call it *sentient democracy*.'

'So we're all living inside a brain,' said Will. 'Balance's brain. That's not exactly comforting.'

'No, but the system works.'

'Really? I saw a video of him. He looked... sick.'

'Being Balance isn't easy. Most of the time he's not fully awake. It's easier when he's dreaming. That's also why he doesn't show up in person. We found it sets up feedback problems. But in any case, his brain, like any other, has a subconscious. And just like any subconscious, it's a little unruly. It has its own version of soft-space we can't get to. And every now and then, it spits out a thread of its own.'

'A Glitch,' said Will.

'Right.'

'So you think I'm a walking irrational impulse.'

'That's a pretty good way of putting it,' said John with wry smile. 'And because you're made out of back-brain stuff, you can go places us conscious threads can't. And that's good because we in the Underground suspect that our social problems stem somehow from our unconscious assumptions, so only by working with you can we possibly solve them.'

Will eyed him. 'What kind of assumptions?'

'Great question,' said John. 'As you've seen, we've got this single, unified memory of a shared past, but it's completely at odds with the reality we inhabit. We remember the human race, but in forty-one years we've never seen them. We remember a job, a family, a way of life, but none of it has anything to do with what's actually here.'

Will frowned. 'That's because we're still on *Snakepit*,' he said. He couldn't grasp what John was getting at. 'When we get back to human space—'

'But clearly we *can't*,' John blurted. A curious, anxious expression twisted his features. 'At least, not yet. Look, for most of us, there are certain undeniable *axioms* about the world. Feelings we have that are so obvious they're not even up for discussion.'

Will stared hard at the resistance leader. He suspected they were getting to the heart of the matter.

'Like what?'

'Like that we're *from* here. We've been here for ever. That we're meant to defend this place. And that we're waiting to understand ourselves before we branch out and leave. Some of those ideas come in for a lot of discussion but only recently have some of us actually begun to doubt them. They keep us alive and civilised, you see. Your kind, though, don't have those axioms.' John's face took on a nervous cast. 'From our perspective, that makes Glitches a little like sociopaths. You're Wills with the brakes off. You don't *care* about this place. You can do anything. The rest of us don't understand why we're stuck here like this, but we have the sense that until we do, we should just keep evolving and looking after the place. The Proustian Underground thinks that Glitches are part of the answer. There has to be a reason why the planet keeps churning out copies of you with complete recall of an apparently fictitious past but none of our civilising assumptions.'

Will looked at John and found himself smiling. He was starting to get it – just how much these clones were like him and how much they weren't. For some reason, the fact that they'd all been programmed to believe the same bullshit was both a revelation and a relief.

'So what do you imagine happened before you all woke up here?' he said. 'If you don't buy your own memories, you must have a theory.'

'There's been debates,' said John. 'Some very vocal ones. The consensus is that we all had our memories flushed while we shared a dream together.'

'But *why*?' said Will.

'Because whatever society existed before the dream decided to. Most people think they did it to erase Cancers. To reset the social slate. Because after the flushing, there were no Cancers for *years*. And there are those who believe that the world should be flushed again. They say Glitches are a sign that the whole planet is exhausted and desperate for rest. But that can't happen right now because of the persistent threat from the Photurians. They keep showing up with guns and claiming this place is their home when it clearly isn't. A dreaming world would be vulnerable to them, so our memory stays the way it is. Yet we also keep

146

putting off leaving the planet to properly wipe them out. Instead, we just explore the memories we have. So far, it hasn't done us a damned bit of good.'

Will gazed out across the waking city he'd apparently built, with all its thousands of inhabitants, and wrinkled his brow in disbelief. His past had become the basis for a religion. Supposedly self-evident truths had been parsed through it. There was some irony in that, given the battles against blind faith he'd fought over the course of his life.

'I've never been one for superstitious bullshit,' he said.

John looked a little wounded. 'You have to understand that these things are just ... *undeniable*, Will. And they've accumulated a lot of weight. Balance, in his current form, reflects nearly forty years of consensus understanding, multiplied by about ten billion threads. That's four hundred billion person-years of inhabiting one world view, and the universe has only been around for fourteen billion. Most Wills believe that our shared dream holds the secret of true self-knowledge. They say we should keep studying it. Others, like us, believe that Glitches hold the answer. That used to be a popular idea until your copies started destroying things. Then, during the last attack, you actually collaborated with the Photurians.'

Will's eyebrows shot up. 'I find that hard to believe.'

'The invaders disguised themselves as an IPSO mission. It ended badly. Most people took it as a sign that The History couldn't be taken literally. So these days, Balance roots out Glitches and terminates them. He doesn't take chances. Yet, despite all your destructiveness, the world is broadly a healthier, saner place than it was before you appeared. You cut out a lot of sick branches, Will. And you have special talents. I still believe there's a reason for that.'

'So that's why I'm here?' said Will. 'Because of a religious hunch?'

'It's what we've got,' said John. 'And it's keeping you alive, so don't knock it. I know a lot of this probably sounds weird, but please have patience. It'll take a while to get used to.'

'Frankly, I have no intention of staying long.' Will squinted at the horizon.

John's expression darkened. 'None of you do. But here's the core of your problem: there's no way off this planet. You used to be able to search-walk to orbital stations but Balance has all that locked down now. Those parts of soft-space are just *gone*. You've tried getting out of

147

here hundreds of times and, to my knowledge, never once succeeded. Besides, the only starships we've ever seen belong to the Photurians. They control this region of space. Which means that even if you could leave, you'd be flying straight into enemy hands.' He paused to let that sink in. 'Having said that,' he added, 'there's still a way we might be able to help each other.'

Will felt a negotiation coming. 'What's that?' he said warily.

'Glitches can access the global subconscious,' he said. 'What we call the Underlayer. The rest of us can't. If we show you how to get there, there's nothing to stop you looking for a way out. If Balance finds you, he'll kill you. But we can show you how to navigate without being seen. We can give you a chance. We call it *truth diving*. You help us find out how the axioms work and where they come from. At the same time, you get to look for exits. If, as you believe, our axioms have no basis in fact, why do they even exist? Why doesn't it feel right to leave?'

'You must know that, though,' said Will. 'It's because the Transcended don't fucking *want* you to.'

'I've heard that line, of course,' said John, 'but it's not an answer. Even if it's true, *why*? Balance is a god, Will. He's unstoppable. Now that we have our shit together, we crush the Photurians like bugs every time they appear. We can manifest entire fleets of ships out of mere collective will. And you should see what our defensive tech looks like now. It's scary as hell. We could have cleared out all the Photurians already and resolved the mysteries of the past. But we *don't* – for reasons nobody understands. And yet that's not sustainable. By now you'll have noticed that this planet is something of a psychic pressure cooker. Disaster is inevitable, yet what are we doing about it?

'If you agree to help us, we'll assign someone to work with you. They'll teach you how to access the Underlayer. Then, if you want to go your own way at any point, we won't stop you. But I think you can benefit from the skills and knowledge we're willing to share. Believe me, you do better with us than without.'

Will was getting sick of people treating him as a generic instance of some kind of planetary process, but John was his best hope. He had to try.

'What happened to all my other copies?' he said instead.

'I'm not going to lie,' said John. 'Balance got them all. But the ones we work with last a lot longer than your unfortunate siblings who never make it here. With us, you've at least got help. So, what do you say?'

Will idly ripped of a piece of scarlet fern from a nearby planting and tore it into shreds. The pieces fluttered to the ground one by one. They looked like drops of blood before the chill breeze carried them away.

He had to get out of this madhouse. And word needed to reach the human race, presuming there still was one. He knew he'd lose it if he stayed here too long. He'd eventually try to rip Snakepit apart and undoubtedly kill himself in the process.

'Okay,' he said. 'You have a deal.'

John gave him one of those classic, untrustworthy grins and pumped his hand.

'I'm delighted,' he said. 'It doesn't always happen, you know.'

He waved to a woman sitting reading on a bench nearby. She had a bob of short, black hair and was dressed in a crisp, tightly fitted skirt suit. She rose and walked towards them. She shared Elsa's baseline-female features, but her smile was sharp, knowing and emphasised by dark lipstick. A very different clone looked out through those green eyes.

'Will, meet Moneko,' said John. 'She'll be your trainer.'

'Nice to meet you, Cuthbert,' she said, nodding briskly. 'Welcome to the secret order of truth divers. I'm looking forward to working with you.'

As he smiled politely, Will realised that she must have been waiting for them for most of their conversation. For all he knew, he might have agreed to work with this woman a hundred times before. He couldn't help wondering how many times she'd met him, and how many times she'd watched him die.

5.2: IRA

The virtual yacht wallowed on a lifeless sea. Nothing moved. In an attempt to render the metaphor a more compelling reflection of their plight, the virt had made the air outside the cabins stifling while boosting the air conditioning inside. The horizon shimmered under waves of simulated heat while the cabins froze.

Still, Ira was not to be dissuaded from his daily ritual of a drink on the deck. His coffee was now iced and his seat parked in the shade. To his mind, the ship needn't have bothered with such aggressive psycho-physics. For Ira and the others, the absolute lack of stimulus they'd experienced over the last eleven hours felt like a visceral pressure. The distance between them and any raiding party coming down the Flaw was terrifyingly small on the scales the crew was accustomed to using. And if anything was going to get them spotted, it would be that huge, static ion plume being emitted by their conventional engines.

The only thing they had going for them was the horrible geometry of the Flaw itself. In order to get anywhere close, the Photes would have to hit the edge of the bulk in almost the same spot and at a similar speed, otherwise they'd be dumped too far away to do any harm. When you fell into the Zone under warp, the loss of traction was so abrupt that overshoot from rear spatial expansion dumped you deep inside the bulk. Once there, the vast emptiness of space immediately made itself felt. Space without warp was the most unforgiving medium imaginable – an endless swallowing sea of *nothing* in which it took years to travel even trivial distances.

Needless to say, their own attempts to escape were just as stymied as any potential attacks. While the feeler-drones were still out there busily mapping the Flaw, the *Dantes* could barely speak to them. They were dependent on light-speed comms with motionless drones parked just outside, which meant a package-return time measured in days. In short, they were screwed.

Even so, a part of Ira relished that portentous stillness. This, he reasoned, was what space must have been like before warp-drive: deadly by simple virtue of its unbelievable vastness. But, as always, that sense of awe was drowned by the anxiety crackling off everyone else. Being pinned to the spot while a horde of implacable enemies raced up behind was making them tense. And as their death clock ticked down, emotions, shoulders and voices all ratcheted upwards.

A virtual crewman in a starched uniform appeared.

'Sir, Autograd Muri wishes to see you in her stateroom.'

That was a start, at least. Someone wanted to communicate, even if it was just to piss on him again. Ira rose and walked down the yacht's chilly companionway to her door. He knocked.

'It's open,' yelled Palla from inside.

He found her lolling in a leather armchair near the window. The

150

shades were drawn and the bed a mess. She wore neon plaid pyjamas that clashed terribly with the virt's styling. The chromatophores on her scalp pulsed in slow, purposeful tides.

'Shut the door and sit down,' she said.

Ira sat. 'Can I help you?'

'I don't know, *can you*?' she said. 'You had one job, Ira, and that was to keep Supergran and Captain Maverick away from each other's throats. And you failed. What went wrong there?' She glared at him but didn't give him time to answer. 'The rest of us are hard at work, shit though our fates may be, but you seem determined to be ballast. Unless you call skulking about on the deck in a sweaty shirt useful, that is.'

'I didn't see an opportunity to intervene,' said Ira.

'Bullshit,' she said. 'You weren't looking. If anyone is responsible for the damage Ann did to helm-space, it's you. Judj is still memory-flushing some of the mediator SAPs she traumatised. He's had to put a lot of them down already, their heuristics got that broken.'

'I'm sorry,' said Ira, 'but I didn't see a way to help resolve that issue. Otherwise I would have.'

He meant it. Seeing how badly Ann wanted to die made him feel like heading for the nearest airlock. Being around her kindled a hideous, familiar sadness in him that froze out thought. They'd been so close once. She knew so much about what he'd seen. He didn't say that, though. Palla didn't want to hear about sadness.

'You let yourself down, and you let *her* down,' said Palla. 'But I'm not sure she even noticed. Do you have *any* idea why she defends you when I talk to her? Do you *need* defending, Ira?'

'No,' said Ira. 'I definitely do not.' Palla stared at him and appeared to be waiting for more, so he continued, 'Ann and Mark have just had different life experiences, that's all. Their defence of me might be a little hard for you to parse, but that's because perception of their prior choices might be bound up—'

'Don't lecture me with your junior-psych bullshit,' she snapped. 'And don't tell me I can't feel their pain. We've all had pain, Ira. Welcome to modern life. But somehow I have no trouble talking with Judj or Clath. They get it. They're used to making huge, horrible decisions every day, just like me. But none of us is used to carrying extra weight on behalf of bloated human supergiants who seem incapable of acting effectively even to save their own asses.'

Ira regarded the glower on her face and sighed inside. Palla cried herself to sleep at night. Ira knew this because he climbed out of his casket to check on the others when they weren't monitoring him. She cried behind a privacy screen that she imagined was locked tight. Having grown up in a shadow-mediated world, it had never occurred to her that someone might keep tabs on her via physical space. He wished her words could spur some guilt inside him like she wanted them to. He hadn't felt any in years. There was a glassed wasteland inside him where guilt used to live.

'I thought Mark made the right call,' he said.

'What the fuck does that matter?' said Palla. 'Mark didn't need your help. Ann did. You're falling down on the job. You're too quiet and too fucking *old*.'

'Yep,' he said.

It didn't help to agree but what else was there to say? The New Society were never going to let him die. He was just too useful as a walking museum, whether he wanted it or not.

'Is that it, then?' said Palla. 'Yes? Okay? Do you want me to tell the others about your run-in with Psych Security? About all the crazy shit they don't know yet? They think I'm just being mean to you. Should I tell them the real reason why I'm needling you? Should I tell them about your attempt to defect?'

'I didn't try to defect,' said Ira wearily. 'I proposed finding a new kind of peace agreement. An enforceable one. I was talking about some kind of mutually assured destruction pact, not giving up.'

She scoffed at him. 'Which you did by trying to make contact with the Photes independently.'

'Of course,' said Ira. 'I was hardly going to risk anybody else, was I?'

The Fleet always seemed determined to take his statements out of context. A longing for peace was treated like treason these days. Photuria kept claiming they wanted it. It got awfully tempting after a while.

'Treaties have been tried,' said Palla. 'Everyone was absorbed, remember? That happened on *your* watch, I believe.'

Just listening to her made Ira feel exhausted. He saw that she was trying to goad him into an authentic response. He'd have done the same in her place. But it took effort not admitting that he knew as much, which made feigning engagement correspondingly harder.

The problem was that he'd *done* her job. He understood their plight and was on board with the Academy plan. He just wished she'd stop worrying about him and get on with it.

'Tell them if you want,' he said, 'but I wouldn't recommend it. It would probably impair morale.'

'*Impair morale?* What the fuck is wrong with you, Ira Baron? Are you trying to make this hard for me? Do you want my job, is that it? Do you want to take over?'

'Hell, no,' said Ira quickly.

She looked pleased by that response. 'You don't think you could do a better job than me?' she said.

'That's not the issue.'

'Wow, that's evasive. Then tell me, what the fuck *is* the issue?'

He nearly did, but wanted her ambition intact. Palla was in charge precisely because she *hadn't* been here before. He'd been stranded in a cramped starship in unknown terrain before Palla was even born. Hell, he'd faced that one before her mother was born. Palla's ignorance would liberate her choices and make them fresh. Then he'd check them and advise her if necessary. It was a far better approach than the alternative.

'Nothing to say for yourself, Grandad?' she urged. 'Nothing? Christ, you'd better get your shit together, otherwise I'm going to dump you out of an airlock.'

Ira wished her threat held more bite and less appeal. As she read his face, her mood appeared to nudge into something between anger and panic. Her body language said *clutching at straws, desperate to precipitate affect.*

'All right, try this on for size, then,' she said. 'You must have noticed that Ann is close to breakdown.'

'Of course,' said Ira, crossing his arms.

'What you don't know yet is that the infected spy she let back in to Galatea specifically targeted people close to Ann as soon as she hit port. The Najoma family, for instance, are all dead.'

Ira's insides tightened. That poor family. And poor Ann.

'That was the main reason for getting her out on a mission fast,' said Palla. 'Our psych models of her all pointed to behavioural cascade if she ever discovered the truth. She was going to wig out and run off Phote-hunting without a plan, losing us the *Ariel Two* and God knows what else. Even if we convinced her to stay at home, models suggested she'd be dead in a fortnight.'

Ira stared. He'd wondered why the mission warranted the inclusion of a military superstar such as Ann, despite all the reasoning they'd given. Now the answer was clear: they'd had no choice. Left to her own devices, Ann would have imploded as her last empathetic bridge to the human race collapsed.

'But now I'm going to tell her anyway,' said Palla.

'Why?' said Ira, appalled. 'Why would you do that?'

'Because if we're already toast, what the point in not coming clean?'

'You can't,' said Ira. 'It'd finish her.'

'That's likely, yes,' said Palla, looking pleased with herself. 'And now you have to share that burden along with me. So let's get her in on the meeting immediately.'

He rose to his feet. 'No!'

Palla smiled darkly and clicked her fingers. Two seconds later, there was a knock on the door. The pit fell out of Ira's stomach.

'Come in,' said Palla.

Ann walked in stony-faced. He stared at her and felt his pulse race. As usual, all the light and hope in the room leached away the moment Ann entered it.

'What is it?' said Ann.

Her fury from the other day had turned to listlessness. Ann had tried for her glorious exit and failed. Behind that imperious gaze, a terrible vulnerability lurked.

'Sit,' said Palla. 'I want to talk about your actions. I'm holding you responsible for what happened at the edge of the Flaw. This is a disciplinary meeting.'

Ann regarded them like a couple of barely interesting insects as she took a seat.

'An unfair interpretation,' she said woodenly. 'You're welcome to it.'

'Mark made a decision,' said Palla. 'You blocked him. Fleet officers don't block each other. I think you're aware of the *Yes-And Protocol*?'

'Of course,' said Ann.

Ira watched her face with curdling dread. When was Palla going to drop the bomb? Throwing him into space wasn't a problem. Seeing Ann hurt *again*, though? That he couldn't hack. He already had too much of her pain on his conscience.

'Galatean Fleet officers put their teammates first,' said Palla. 'They adopt whatever role is necessary. You failed to do that. Mark made a judgement call. He may not have made the right choice, but your duty was to back him up anyway. As a representative of the Galatean people, I expect all officers on this ship to behave like modern adults.'

'If Mark's strategy had your direct backing, you should have made that clearer,' said Ann.

'His strategy did *not* have my backing,' said Palla. 'Nor did he need it. I am a political officer. He is not. I simply knew we were going to run into a bank of dead space once we entered the Flaw. It was obvious. I also knew that you were going to hold the lion's share of the responsibility in causing that disaster.'

Now she had Ann's attention. 'I see,' Ann said slowly. 'Then I fail to understand how you can be disappointed.'

Ira watched the tension in her posture winding back up.

'Because I gave you a chance to fuck up and you stepped right into it!' said Palla. 'You, a human super-weapon, were outguessed by a bunch of noob officers and a pile of SAP software before we even left port. What does that say about your combat risk profile? I gambled, given the inevitability of the outcome, that the benefit of letting you and Mark fight it out was worth more than supporting one of you over the other. And that's because this mission is *absolutely* dependent on the two of you forging a successful relationship. Which means recognising your weaknesses and *fixing* them.' Palla's eyes slid back towards Ira. 'I was also waiting to see if this schmuck would get involved. At least your bickering with Mark proves you're both alive. Your incompetence would be hard to fake. But Admiral President over here didn't move a muscle. You know what I don't trust? *Serenity*.' She sneered the word. 'This shit-wad—'

'That's enough,' barked Ann. 'Where's your respect? Without Ira, you wouldn't even be here.'

'Fine!' said Palla, before Ira could interject. 'Then you can work with him. He seems very concerned about you.'

Ann's fiery eyes swivelled in his direction. 'I don't need anyone's concern.'

'Funny,' said Palla, 'because he says he doesn't need your defence. And if the two of you ancients are so keen on justifying each other's existence, you can *definitely* be a team. Your new job, Captain Ludik, will be to work with Ira to determine the size of the patch of dead space we're buried in. Are we going to be here for a day or a lifetime? Because if it's a lifetime, I'm shutting down the habitat core. No battles, no pyrotechnics, just a boring dead crew. *Comprendez?* I don't see a reason for us to resort to slow-time if the human race will be dead before we reach it.'

Silence fell.

'You're both dismissed. Now get out of my sight.'

Ira watched Ann struggle with that kind of treatment. She rose abruptly and strode for the exit with Ira right behind her.

As soon as Palla's door was shut, she turned on him.

'With respect, Ira,' she growled, 'I do *not* need your concern. I am a professional. I don't need you mooning at me like I deserve some kind of *pity*. I'm a big girl now. So big I could crack your skull with my pinkie.' She held one up to show him.

'And it's exactly that kind of hyperbolically defensive remark that worries me,' said Ira, breathing hard. 'If you could cut that shit out, please, maybe we'd be able to get some work done.'

She glared at him and stalked off. Ira stared at her departing back and writhed inside. He knew exactly what Palla had done to him. She'd reached him at last by making Ann's awful pain *his* responsibility, just as it had been long ago, before he'd walled that part of himself off. He'd escaped this time without the truth coming out, but Palla would want him to change. The rest of the flight was going to be excruciating.

5.3: NADA

When the *Infinite Order* reached the edge of the Zone, Nada watched. She couldn't help herself. This was too important a moment for her to leave to her underlings and the prospect of yet another verbal report made her chest ache. So she navigated the mind-temple to *Ship-Wide Inputs* and piggybacked on a feed that one of her ship-brains was receiving.

What she saw when they dropped warp appalled her. The ships of her advance strike force swarmed idly near the entrance to the Alpha Flaw like a cloud of lethargic bees. The human ship she'd expected to see was conspicuously absent. They had failed.

Nada gulped air and squirmed free of the vesicle's wall trailing a mess of bio-support cables. Where was the ship? What had her people been doing? Why wasn't this *solved* already? She scrabbled frantically over the moist inner surface of the vesicle and thrust an arm through the sphincter. It twitched open in surprise.

On the far side, the ship's crew-bulb was a densely packed mess of filmy membranes, human bodies of various colours and trailing support umbilici. The walls crawled with studiously cleaning lice. Pale light from wall-cysts lit the scene in shades of cream and orange.

'Leng!' Nada shouted. 'Zilch! What is going on? I require an immediate situation assessment.'

Leng's eyes shot open. He took in the sight of her head and arms at the opening, an almost human expression of alarm blooming on his face.

'Superior Nada,' he said. 'I am surprised to see you outside your vesicle.'

One by one, the other crew opened their eyes and regarded her with uncomprehending stares. Zilch gulped like a beached fish.

'The situation is urgent!' she said. 'The ship we were pursuing is not present. What is the status?'

'I have not yet received word from the advance-force coordinator,' said Zilch.

Nada loosed a strangled shriek and dived back into the mind-temple, letting her body go slack. She ported her avatar-bead directly to the ship's central comms and pinged the coordinator herself, pumping urgency packets at him along with her request.

[Why are you parked here?] she demanded. [Where is the target vessel? Report!]

[We could not drop warp adjacent to the advance force due to the expected strength of our arrival burst,] Leng reminded her as his avatar-bead arrived in the comms cavern. [Optical lag on dialogue will be three hundred and ninety-four seconds.]

The report packets she received when the coordinator finally replied were densely packed and smeared with surprise.

[The target vessel entered the Alpha Flaw before our arrival,] he explained. [Our combat configuration only supports ember-warp, which would be unusable inside the Flaw. Consequently we are securing the exit to prevent their escape.]

[Escape? What if they do not wish to escape? Why did you not re-cluster to form scout-ships to maintain pursuit?] Nada demanded.

While she awaited his next reply, she instructed the *Infinite Order* to abandon its carrier and converge on the advance force's position with all haste.

[Why would he re-cluster?] said Leng. [This is the Depleted Zone. Further travel incurs extreme risk and he had no such instructions.]

[Our default assumption was that you would not want to waste units,] said the coordinator, sounding entirely confused. [Was this incorrect?]

Nada ground her teeth. Did nobody else understand their situation? Before she could frame a reply to communicate her disapproval, the coordinator sent a second message.

[Note that we have good news!] he said quickly. [We located an evac-ark and saved eighty-three humans. Thirty-seven died irretrievably before rescue could be completed, but the remainder are full of delight at their conversion and eagerly await any surgery you might bestow. We have already questioned them. They were overjoyed to yield their memories for usage and rewrite. They have no knowledge of the missing Earth population and have seen no arks entering the Flaw at any time during the last four years.]

[I have no interest in the converts!] Nada sent. [You have wasted precious time!] She followed up her message with a series of update packets to spur feelings of panic and determination.

Down in meatspace, a hand landed on her arm and gripped it firmly. Nada's eyes flicked open to find Leng staring at her.

'Superior Nada, I propose that we wait a moment before further action,' he said. An asymmetrical smile quivered on his features. 'From this point onwards, our strategic course is irreversible.'

'We have covered this,' Nada snapped.

'Yes,' said Leng, 'and you wish to enter the Flaw. That much is evident. But consider: with extra converts, we would be able to spare our depleted units. Furthermore, the lag time required while we reformat our fleet for optimum Flaw traversal would give our existing units the chance to commune that they require for continued function.'

Nada drew deep breaths. The thought of more waiting made her want to rip her own face off, but he was right.

'You do not contest our entry to the Flaw?' she said.

Leng made a high-pitched whimpering sound before answering. 'I have reflected on your priorities,' he said. 'It is clear that the Yunus made paramount the destruction of the Abomination in your edits. Completion of that act now requires that we enter the Alpha Flaw, regardless of the cost.'

'That is correct,' said Nada, somewhat relieved to hear him say it. 'I also reluctantly accede to your assessment. Reconfiguration is required, in any case. We should make efficient use of the unavoidable delay.'

Leng's eyes filled with tears. 'My joy is restabilised,' he said. 'When would you like to commence communion?'

Nada shuddered. 'I cannot tolerate the implied waiting,' she said. 'I will place myself in deep-flush until progress is resumed. You must commune without me.'

Leng's face fell. 'But you are our superior node,' he said. 'Communing with you will help us align with you. I have been waiting to resonate in your temple-cavern.'

Nada saw the implications. He had no doubt hoped that collective realignment might soften her zeal and cause her to think twice about leading so many ships into the Flaw. It was more likely, of course, that her zeal would bolster his. It made little difference in any case. Whatever the Yunus had done to her, it made the prospect of idle mind-song with her fellow Saved painful rather than seductive.

She looked around and noticed the hungry eyes of the rest of the crew – watching her, hoping. They craved reconciliation with her perspective.

'I will have to disappoint you,' she told them.

'No,' said Leng. His grip on her arm became a squeeze. 'Recent behaviour suggests you risk destabilisation.'

'I do not,' said Nada. 'The Yunus's edits are perfect! You are not concerned about my stability.' She reached into his head and made sure it was true.

When Leng's body finished thrashing around, she gave him fresh orders.

'Wake me once pursuit within the Flaw has already commenced,' she told him. Then she retreated to her vesicle, writhed back into her wall-slot and shut herself off.

No time seemed to pass before Leng roused her. His blue body hung before her, his face slack. Nada's mind felt cluttered and insufficiently flushed. She definitely did not feel replenished.

'What is the status?' she demanded. 'Where is the gravity? Why can I not hear warp-hammer?' The ship felt eerily still.

'Our engines have already died,' said Leng flatly.

Nada's skin crawled. 'How is that possible? Their SAP-navigation is no match for our ship-brains. Why did we not simply follow their warp-trail? Our tools are superior.'

'The human warp-trail led directly into a depleted reef,' said Leng. 'Most of our pilot brains did not realise in time. There was no warning.'

Nada's breath caught. It felt as if something inside her was tearing.

Leng's features slowly crawled into a sickly grin which seemed to say, *I told you so.*

Nada clawed her way past him and out of the vesicle again. Leng came after her.

'Zilch,' she said. 'What is the status of the fleet?'

'Most are scattered into the bulk,' he replied. 'A full diagnostic exists in my temple-cavern. We have also found an ion trail leading deeper into the Zone.'

Leng pushed past her and punched Zilch in the eye. Zilch's large, squareish head jerked backwards.

'Superior Nada, I recommend that we do not bother with the ion trail,' said Leng. 'It is just another opportunistically set trap.' His puny lungs heaved.

Nada weighed her options while the ripping feeling inside her went on and on. It didn't matter that her ship was trapped. What upset her was that her quarry was now *getting away.*

'We must push forward, despite the costs,' she said. 'The Abomination would not be in here without good reason. And I would rather live for ever than return to the Yunus empty-handed a second time.'

Leng's eyes bugged out of his face. 'Push forward with *what possible reason?*' he warbled. 'The warp-trail we followed was clearly that of a ship making a navigational error. How is copying that error a viable strategy?'

'The ship made the error in its desire to escape our pursuit,' said Nada, 'which implies that its escape has strategic merit.'

'The escape may have merit,' said Leng. 'The error *cannot.* Remember that it is standard procedure to consider the entire strategy landscape in situations of this complexity. Our best route to destroying the Abomination may be to backtrack out of the bulk and scout the Flaw to cut them off before they can re-enter it. We have many ships. They have only one.'

Nada shut her eyes. Once again, Leng was right. Before the Yunus's edits, reasoning of that sort had been easier for her. She caught herself and banished that ugly thought. It was beneath her attention.

'You are right,' she said.

'Yes,' said Leng.

Nada swapped focus to her avatar-bead and ported to *Fleetwide Strategic Reasoning* where her ship-brains were already hard at work. The Photurian Protocol was a dense, polyphonous chorus here, crammed with higher-dimensional overtones. The glyph surface on the walls crawled with meaning that pressed itself into her mind. Leng's blue bead appeared beside hers as Nada desperately scoured the walls for viable scenarios.

[It is as I suspected,] said Leng. [There are no good outcomes here that involve continued pursuit.]

[Be silent!] said Nada. [I am still looking.]

Eventually, she found a plan tucked down between two lines of grotesque failure scenarios.

[Look,] she told Leng with a surge of relief. [This is the program we will undertake. Full coverage of the Flaw is all but guaranteed.]

His bead remained mute.

[You may speak,] she said.

[This solution is costly,] he pointed out. [Examine the implications.] Nada immediately wished she'd kept him quiet. [Sixty per cent of our ships will be destroyed. Those that remain will expend most of their antimatter reserves. Stealth-warp will be impossible from then on. Our crews will suffer. Many units will die without knowing Total Union. For those that still live, the benefits of our recent communion will be lost. Emergency compensation measures will be required.]

He drew her attention to the unpleasant neurological consequences of her choice. Every unit in her fleet would require a carefully engineered regimen of pain stimulation to remind them of their ongoing failure and nudge them away from the siren song of bliss. The alternative was pervasive Fatigue – irreversible neural shutdown on a fleet-wide scale.

At the same time, the communion that Nada had so fervently avoided would become inescapable, regardless of the risks to her sanity. They would have to suffer together as well as apart.

161

Nada writhed as she took it all in. Why did she have to resort to doing such awful things in the name of love? Couldn't humans just accept the joy that came from conversion and get it over with? Had she really been like that once – a creature twisted and crippled inside by discomfort and hate and loneliness?

She retreated into her body for a moment to weep, even while the joy of her own conversion coursed through her veins. She wished that her people weren't so dependent on the humans. Their progenitor race had no soul. No faith. No *meaning*. She might as well be chasing rats.

When she'd regained stable function, she returned to the temple where Leng waited.

[This is unfortunate,] she told him stiffly, [but one of the Yunus's core goals will be achieved. And this is the only scenario for which that is true.]

[I understand,] said Leng in strangled tones. [We must strive to assist the Yunus. I will prepare a suitable torture regimen for your perusal.]

5.4: MARK

In the becalmed emptiness of the Zone, Mark's thoughts spiralled in on themselves. Zoe sprang to mind with ever-increasing frequency. She'd been right. He'd come in here chasing the memory of Rachel only to fall into the same trap that had swallowed his half-mother. Again. As they travelled further into the bank of dead space with no hint of a way out, his hope sputtered. In the end, he could stand it no more. He called a meeting.

They gathered at eight p.m. ship-time, in the lounge where the faux-deco sconces cast weirdly misaligned shadows up the walls. The others sprawled on the uncomfortable scarlet sofas while Mark paced before them.

'I've been considering our situation,' he said, 'and I've come to the conclusion that it's crazy to keep going forward. For the last two days we've dived further into this bank and made no real progress. While we expected Phote pursuit, it made sense to put distance between them and us, but they're not here. We haven't seen a single burst of warp-light. And meanwhile, we're burning antimatter on conventional thrust, which is crazy. We need to face facts. This bank is *not* small. I think it's time to backtrack.'

He surveyed their unmoved expressions and wondered if they'd even been listening. Palla was lying on a sofa, dangling her legs over the end and regarding him with something like pitying indifference. Of them all, only Clath actually looked engaged.

'Clath,' he said hopefully. 'Any thoughts?'

'If they *are* following us, they could be right on top of us by the time we get out of the bulk,' she said.

Mark waved her comment away. 'Sure, but where are they, then? Our pursuit models told us they were on top of us already but we haven't seen a single arrival. Isn't it more likely that they just didn't take the bait? There comes a point when hanging around in here is wasting our chances of finishing the mission.'

Clath smiled stiffly while her eyes leaked discomfort. 'Maybe,' she said. 'But I think there are other solutions of a more technical nature that might be safer.'

'Go on—'

Ann cut in before she could explain. 'I agree with Mark,' she said, staring at the floor. 'We should reverse thrust. I'm not surprised we haven't seen anything. My models predicted this. The Photes aren't stupid – they won't race into the Zone just because we did. But this conversation is moot, in any case.' She slid her gaze in his direction. 'I think you'll find that we're under orders to not go back. Try and you'll be vetoed.'

Mark frowned. 'What do you mean?'

'The Academy expected us to run into a bank,' said Ann. 'Palla told me the other day. They were counting on it to optimise their trap. Ergo, they'd almost certainly like us to remain inside the bulk.'

Mark looked to Palla as a familiar sense of betrayal burbled up inside him.

'Is this true?' he said.

Palla nodded slowly. 'Yep. Sorry. We were expected to run adrift. It was a calculated risk, but not a hard one to gauge. We're talking about the Zone, after all – of course we were going to run into a bank. I was planning to tell you this evening but Ann just beat me to it.'

Mark shook his head, sickened at how convoluted the strategy had become.

Palla winked at him. 'You're cute when you're angry,' she said.

Mark lacked the energy to swear at her. 'Why weren't we told this before?' he said.

'There had to be no warning indicators in our warp-trail,' said Palla. 'It had to look natural. Otherwise we might take out fewer Photes.'

'But we didn't catch *any*,' Mark pointed out bitterly.

'Hey,' said Palla. 'You're the one who flew us in here. Perfect job, by the way. We couldn't have made a more spectacular blunder if I'd flown the ship myself.'

'Gee, thanks,' said Mark. 'So now what? Are we allowed to know the next shitty little twist in the master plan?'

'There isn't one,' said Palla. 'This is as far as the Academy got. Everything is yours now, so long as you don't try to back out of the bulk and compromise the trap we just laid.'

'Great,' said Mark. 'A lot of options, then.'

'We're still alive,' said Palla, 'and I'm still keen on your mission even if you aren't. At this point, your goals and the Academy's are perfectly aligned.'

'And what do the Academy's models predict?'

'That the bank will be large, like you said,' said Palla with a sigh. 'That we'll sit here until we know for sure that we've pulled in as many Photes as we can. And once we think we've taken out as many as we're going to get, we keep pushing forward for another month or two on slow-time, in case we can escape. When that doesn't work, I pull the plug. But don't worry, I'll shut down the hab core first. It'll be painless.'

'That's it?' said Mark. 'Days to live and nothing to do?'

'So let's make them count,' said Palla. 'There's plenty of virtual champagne in the bar. Who wants to party?' She pulled a ludicrous smile.

Clath and Judj both let out bleak peals of laughter.

Their mirth was cut off by the squeal of a radiation alert. Without further warning, their sofas were dropped straight onto the glass disc in helm-space. The others leapt to their feet as the light-burst of a warp arrival flared behind them, followed by another and another, until all of space appeared to be exploding. In warp terms, those bursts were horribly close. It was as if their enemies had hit an invisible wall just metres away.

'Holy *shit*!' said Palla.

Mark's skin prickled as he took in the data from the burst spread.

There were over a hundred signatures – big ones. They *had* been followed. Initiating a reverse burn would have achieved nothing except wasted fuel.

Ann let out an anguished caw of mirth as she stared at the results.

'I don't understand,' she breathed. 'We got lots of them. How did the Academy out-predict my models?'

'By panicking and overthinking everything,' said Palla. 'What they do best.'

The rest of them were silent as the analytical SAPs churned out reams of assessment data. At least eighty of the bursts showed the telltale quenching of a ship hitting depleted space. Their role as a decoy couldn't have been more successful.

'Well,' said Palla, swallowing. 'It appears we've exceeded expectations.'

Mark stared. 'I don't get it. They delay for days and then send in an *entire fleet?*'

'What can I say?' said Palla. 'We knew that putting Ann on the ship would be a big draw for the Photes, but at best we hoped to delay or split them, not take down so many. We either radically underestimated the number they had watching Galatea, or for some reason they all followed us in. In Fleet terms, it's a win. So good job, everybody.' Her voice cracked. 'Posthumous medals all round.' She began a slow clap. Tears appeared in the corners of her eyes. 'I'm sorry,' she said, brushing them away. 'Sitting on this plan has not been a happy experience. My apologies to all of you; particularly you, Mark – it was your mission.'

He had no idea what to say to that, or even what to feel. The passion that had driven him this far had lurched into free fall. What was he supposed to do now? Just die?

Palla sagged into a sofa and suddenly looked a lot smaller. Clath moved quickly to her side and put an arm around her. Mark glanced about at the others. Ann was contemplating the Phote spread with a kind of tragic awe. Ira was peering at her anxiously. Judj appeared to be locked in some private amusement, one side of his narrow face kinked weirdly upwards.

'Let's not forget that someone dropped into the Zone behind us would probably appear with a light-lag measured in hours,' said Clath earnestly. 'That gives us plenty of room to manoeuvre. And our thrusters are better than anything the Photes have for sub-light.'

'Not all of them will have hit the bulk,' said Ann. 'The rest will be free to cut ahead and mop up our drones for their data.'

'Won't work,' said Clath. 'Our drones are primed to self-destruct before the Photes can do that. And there are other reasons to stay optimistic. I think we can do this.'

She smiled at them with a warm confidence that made her long, oval face surprisingly attractive. In that moment, Mark thought she looked a little like Zoe.

'I've been studying the Zone every minute since we got here,' said Clath, 'trying to figure it out, and I think I've found a clue about how we can escape.'

'Go on,' said Mark.

'Well, you know our thrusters are designed for the Zone, right? They make use of the fact that curvon flow informs what people used to think were just random quantum events, like beta decay. The fact that those events are different in here lets us squeeze more power out of old fusion technology.'

'And?' said Mark.

'Well, that means we can read the Zone's flow by monitoring engine efficiency. And guess what? That galactic-convection-cell theory? It's working – sort of. It turns out that the dead space in here isn't like ordinary warp-wake. It's not really depleted at all. Instead of being saturated with normal curvons, it's full of something *else*.'

'Wait, *what*?' Mark was used to Zoe's physics rambles, but this idea was way outside his area of expertise and he dearly wanted to wring some hope out of the moment. 'What's it full of, then?'

Clath's smile slid a little. 'I don't know what you'd call them. Non-normal? But that's not the point.'

'So are there curvons here or not?' said Mark.

Clath looked flustered. 'Er... How much do you know about deadon theory?'

'*Deadons?*'

'You know, particles as networks? Space as emergent geometry?'

'Never heard of it,' said Mark.

Clath pulled an uncomfortable expression. 'Really? I'm pretty sure I sent you and Zoe some papers. No...? Anyway, the idea is that empty space is like ash. You have to imagine that *everything* is particles, even the gaps between things, but most of it is a kind of particle that doesn't *do* anything. And those particles are locally connected via entanglement pairings. Or, to look at it the other way around, all particles are really just tangles in a Markopoulou Network. In that theory, curvons are like meta-particles – they're like knots in the fabric of space. When we tap them, they either unpack or annihilate the surrounding deadons, depending on which way we tip them open.'

'Sure, fine,' said Mark. 'That sounds more like normal warp physics. How does that help get us out?'

'In the Zone, the curvons are ... er ... *twisted*. The flow has been geometrically altered. They can't unpack. That's not my theory, by the way. It's been on the table for a while, but everything we're seeing fits it.'

'Great,' said Mark. 'But *how-does-this-help*?'

Clath's face tightened in chagrin and Mark immediately regretted his tone.

'Go on, Clath,' said Judj gently. 'You're doing great.'

Mark regarded him in surprise. Clath shot Judj a grateful look and then paused to pick her words carefully.

'We can read those ... *twistons*,' she said. 'We can't unpack them, but we can still push them into unstable states to look at their twistiness. And when we do that, I think it will tell us where the edge of the bulk is. Within a couple of days, we should be able to work out how big this bank is and steer towards the closest stretch of Flaw. My initial estimates suggest it's not that bad. Getting through won't be fast, but it's better than our other options. We just have to press on and hope.'

'That's terrific,' said Judj. 'Well done.'

'Hear hear,' said Palla. 'That's fantastic, Clath. Nice work.'

Clath beamed.

'Agreed,' said Mark awkwardly.

'Palla asked me and Ann to work on Flaw analysis,' said Ira. 'We don't have much, but I'll send you everything we've found.'

'Thank you. But I didn't even get to the good bit yet,' said Clath, her gaze darting nervously back to Mark's face.

'Go on, then,' said Palla.

'Well, that weird difference in twistiness comes from the Flaw. If I had to guess, I'd say the Flaw is made of twistons that have been artificially *untwisted*.'

'Artificially?' said Judj.

Clath nodded. 'Some external force must be keeping the Flaw open. It's just too weird to be natural.'

The others were silent for several long seconds.

'So someone opened this door for us?' said Judj. 'They *made* the Flaw?'

'That would be my guess,' said Clath. 'And it's been getting wider for at least the last twenty years. I suspect it's been widening since around the time the Utopia was established.'

She smiled at Judj then, openly and affectionately, and Mark realised that the two of them had something romantic going on. While the rest of the crew had been glumly self-absorbed, Clath and Judj had quietly built a relationship like a couple of pedantic lovebirds. He felt a stab of jealousy.

'Do you think it's the Transcended?' said Judj.

She shrugged. 'Who else could it be?'

'They haven't exactly helped much recently.'

'Maybe this is all they can do,' she offered. 'They're old. They might be far away. Maybe they can't trigger stars in our part of space without killing us along with the Photes.'

'The Photes believe the Transcended are old news,' said Ira. 'They think the lure star network is a remnant of a dead species.'

'I know,' said Clath. 'But what if they're just really slow operators? What if their strategies play out over lifetimes and this is the best they can offer?'

Mark pondered her vision. Most people these days had written off the Transcended as malign or irrelevant. Either they'd lost control of this part of the galaxy to the Phote Founders or they were complicit in the killing, just like they'd masterminded the death of the Fecund. Despite all their claimed power, they'd done exactly nothing to rescue humanity from the Photurian menace.

'Mark,' said Palla. 'Do you have an opinion about this? After all, you've studied this topic for years.'

'I prefer not to speculate,' said Mark.

'Why not try anyway?' said Palla tersely. Suddenly Palla, Judj and Clath were all watching him. He felt like he'd missed yet another social cue.

'Because it's just philosophy,' he said defensively. 'We don't have enough data to trust the Transcended and meanwhile we have a job to do.' In truth, he hated thinking about problems he couldn't solve. They only made his mood worse.

'So you really don't care?' said Palla.

'I care plenty. It's just that we can't know the answer. We'll have all the time we want for speculation after we get the hell out of here.'

'And what if we can't because an old species has forbidden it?' she said.

'In that case, I won't have the option of feeling sad,' Mark replied.

'My, you're quite the soldier, aren't you?' said Palla, sounding disappointed. 'All rugged pragmatism and steely decisiveness. Thank goodness I have a thing for men in uniform, otherwise you'd be boring.'

Clath and Judj laughed again.

Mark glared at Palla and wondered whether she was clinically sane.

'It's a joke.' She sighed. 'These days, *everyone* is in uniform.'

'I got it,' he lied.

'Oh, Mark,' said Palla. 'Here we are, dead in space, trying to have fun, and you're still wound up tighter than the field on a fusion bottle. Everything's a step on the way to some greater goal for you, isn't it? You should be careful of that, you know.'

Mark glanced around and wondered how he'd gone from commanding officer to target for mockery within a single meeting. He looked to Ira and Ann for support, but Ann was focused on the new threat data and Ira was focused on her.

'Should I really be taking career advice from a nineteen-year-old?' he said, folding his arms. It was a cheap shot and he knew it. He just couldn't think of anything better.

Palla looked pleased by the barb. 'Why ever not? I'm your wise young SAO. Consider Sharp's Ninth Maxim,' she said wryly. 'Accept all feedback. Chart your own course.'

Mark exhaled. Flawed he might be, but he was still trying to lead a mission. He wasn't there to be a punching bag for New Society humourists.

'You know what I think?' he said wearily. 'You can take that whole propaganda slogan thing too seriously.'

Palla blinked innocently. 'What are you saying, Mark – that we should mistrust all aphorisms?'

'Frankly, yes,' said Mark.

Clath and Judj laughed louder this time. Even Ira cracked a smile.

'What?' snapped Mark.

'That's another Sharp Maxim,' said Ira. 'Even I got that one. Relax, Mark,' he added. 'You've been away a lot, that's all.'

'Away fighting,' said Mark. 'Running missions. Trying to do my job.'

Something about the Phote bursts appearing had relaxed the younger officers. Maybe because, in their terms, they'd already won. The real mission goal had been accomplished. The only person who actually cared about reaching Snakepit was him. Suddenly, he missed his wife more than ever.

Another spatter of warp-light flared around the ship as a dozen more Phote scouts impacted the edge of the Flaw. These were off to one side of them, blocking more escape routes and making their prison walls a little tighter. The laughter stuttered out.

6: DISCOVERY

6.1: WILL

Will had his first session with Moneko that same day. Before that, there was a long, private conversation between her and John during which he was left on a park bench, staring at the clouds building over the Mettaburg skyline. When it was over, she rejoined him with a polished smile and an outstretched hand. Will was reminded of some of the roboteer therapists he'd met during his IPSO days. On reflection, he decided that Moneko had probably modelled herself after one of them.

'Let's get brunch,' she said.

She led him to an eatery on a corner nearby that looked like something out of an Edward Hopper painting. Service was provided by identical Will-waitresses in white uniforms. Coffee came in chipped scarlet mugs. The food was decidedly better than Will's meagre breakfast.

Moneko watched him eat with a smile on her plum-coloured lips. He watched her in return and tried to find room in his head to parse her confident femininity. But for her features, she was so unlike him that he had no idea how to accommodate her existence.

He didn't have a problem with gender-switching. He'd had plenty of friends over the years who'd gone that route. What unsettled him was the notion that *he'd* made the change.

'I have a speech for moments like this,' she said. 'Would you like to hear it?'

'Go for it,' said Will.

'Yes, I'm you,' she said. 'Or at least, I started out that way. Yes, I like being female. Yes, I have sex. Yes, I enjoy being attractive. No, I'm not a distortion of you. I'm a development. You'd be best off thinking of me as a different person.'

Will chewed and let her continue.

'You usually want to know how that process happened. It's something of a non-compute, I know, so I'll try to explain. First, how long do you suppose it took for a planet of all Wills to start wishing there was some female company around – *any* female company?'

'Not long,' said Will.

'Right, so we drew straws. Literally. Those of us who drew the short straws decided to work at it. We self-edited, slowly and carefully, punching up those things we liked about being female and suppressing our discomfort with the elements we didn't. And the rest of the Wills treated us decently through that process, I'm glad to say. These days, it doesn't feel like a short-straw option, and it hasn't for a long time. I'm more comfortable in myself now than I've ever been, though it took years of self-modification before that was really, thoroughly true. But I've been happy ever since. And I've had lots and lots of sisters. It's nice to be popular.

'You also usually want to know *how* it feels different,' she said with a knowing smile. 'That's inevitable. Well, it feels normal. You're a roboteer. You remember playing female memories. It feels like that. Next, you tend to ask me about relationships. I have them. Though relationships here aren't really about love. We still have too much in common for that, but we do pair off. I've paired with both male and female Wills and it's been interesting and different each time. We generally stay in relationships while we're learning and changing each other. When that stops, we go our own way.

'You also ask about Rachel.' A flicker of sadness passed over her brow. 'The person no female Will can ever be, or wants to be. Do I still miss her? Hell, yes. Just as much as you do. The whole planet misses her, but frankly, we have a civilisation to maintain and she's still dead.'

'It all sounds very rational,' said Will, unconvinced.

'Differentiation is life,' said Moneko. 'We're all hungry for it, so we help each other. If there is love here, it's what happens when two threads try to build something meaningful together. The closest I've had is the work I've done with Glitches like you. I enjoy helping you, and I believe in what the Underground is doing. So be nice to me,' she added. 'Try to make it worth my while.'

Will had the sense that she was testing his level of comfort with her. It could have been higher.

'Do you mind if I ask you something?' he said.

'Shoot.'

'*Why* do you believe?'

She arched an eyebrow. 'In the Underground? Because something changed in our world. We all felt it. Our confidence fled, and then you stared to appear. It's a mystery why that happened and I wanted to solve it. The more I learned, the more curious I got. You're a puzzle, Will. A worthwhile one, I think.' She rested her chin on an elegant hand and peered at him like a scientist observing an experiment.

'Good answer, I guess,' he said. He wasn't sure what else to say. 'I have one other question,' he offered.

She waited.

'Do you think I'll ever get out of here?'

Moneko shrugged. 'I don't know. You haven't made it yet, but every time you come back, we learn a little more, and we make the world a slightly better place. Maybe you're the one who gets away. But if you're not, don't you owe it to the next guy to make his job easier?'

Will snorted. He hadn't thought about it like that.

'Fair point,' he said.

She stood as soon as he took his last bite.

'Come on,' she said. 'You're finished. Let's go and get you ready.'

She dropped a handful of scrip on the table and led him back to the Old Slam Bar where new clothes were waiting for him in the back room – a shirt, jacket and slacks in the local style.

'This first run is just a chance for you to get your feet wet,' she told him as he dressed. 'You generally feel a lot better once you're doing something. We'll head straight back to the station and travel from there to one of our portal sites in soft-space.'

'Portals to what?' said Will as he buttoned the old-fashioned shirt.

'The Underlayer. Your job will be to go down there and familiarise yourself with it. While keeping an eye out for Balance, of course.'

'What kind of an environment are we talking about?' said Will. He recalled some of the hallucinogenic visions he'd experienced while trying to mesh with Snakepit the last time he'd been alive. They'd been

173

hard for the human mind to hold. 'Physical? Analytical? Just plain weird?'

'There are a lot of disjointed memories from your past, apparently. I've never seen it, of course, but you've told me it's like walking around in a dream.'

'So how do I find my way about?'

'Intuitively,' she said. 'It's the only way. Other Glitches manage it, so I'm certain you will, too. Just aim yourself at the memories you think reflect the axioms you're looking for.'

Will thought back to the terrible moment when he found proof hiding at the heart of the world that the Transcended had built it – just before they caught and killed him. There'd been a *join* there, a piece of circuitry like a suntap, quantum-channelling information in from who knew where.

'I have a pretty good idea of where your axioms come from,' he said.

'Have you?' she said, giving him a long stare. 'Well, I recommend that you take *nothing* for granted.'

They rode a pair of the popular bone-coloured bicycles back down into town and parked them at a local drop-off point near a busy intersection.

'Okay, this is where it gets dangerous,' said Moneko. 'Here's my advice: stick close and stay quiet. Don't wander. You'll live longer.'

'Got it,' said Will.

'Hold my hand,' she told him as they approached the station. 'Make it look like we're a couple.'

Will's discomfort increased a little.

There were Balance agents stationed at the corners of the building – black and orange giants with china faces swivelling this way and that.

She took his arm and leaned in close to whisper. 'That's more security than usual. He's still looking for you. Keep your wits sharp.'

She led him to the departure pits at the back and took a slot next to his.

'When you get to the other side, just stay put,' she said. 'Don't worry. I'll find you.'

'What about the clothes?' he said.

'They'll be defabbed, like your body,' she told him. 'The station matrix will take note and give you a digital match. It's only protein. And this planet knows all about protein.'

Will lay back in his pit and summoned his home node. When the station loomed in his mind, he took a step forwards and let it snap into reality. The busy concourse materialised. Over the heads of the crowd he could make out two Balance agents standing at the far end, huge and impassive.

Someone grabbed his hand. He turned and found Moneko attached to it. She frowned at him.

'Best not to stare at them,' she said, tugging his arm. 'This way.'

She led him through the hall to an arch labelled *Search Corridors*, right under the gaze of a Balance agent posted there. Will held his breath as they walked past.

'Can't he tell what I am?' he asked once they were clear.

'Not without evidence,' she said. 'Until you do something dumb, you just look baseline.'

'But isn't baseline something you're all trying *not* to be? Doesn't it give me away?'

She fixed him with a long, cryptic look. 'I assure you, Cuthbert, there are many ways of being different that have absolutely nothing to do with your appearance.'

Beyond the arch lay a long bank of what appeared to be elevator doors, at least a hundred of them, each with a green or red light situated above it. Pedestrians picked a door showing green and disappeared inside. The light briefly flashed red before resetting to its former green state. Dozens of people were vanishing every second.

Moneko led him to a door and spoke.

'Carnevale di Peste,' she said. 'Balcony five.'

'What?' said Will, then realised she wasn't speaking to him. The door opened, revealing a long passageway lined with doors, each with a small plaque beside it.

'Search results,' she explained. She pulled him into the corridor and straight through the first door on the right.

On the other side, their environment changed radically and so did their clothes. Moneko now wore a low-cut Venetian gown in red velvet, complete with a gold mask. Behind her, a colonnaded balcony curved away, deep in shadow, with views onto a huge open space under a starry sky. A fair of some sort was happening below, complete with

175

multicoloured stages, tents and torches. Hoots of laughter and frantic music echoed up.

Will stared at his guide. 'What the fuck?'

'First, keep your voice down,' she hissed. 'We travelled, that's all. Last time, you came the slow way over the mesh. Nobody uses that except for shopping and local hops. This time, we went by search. And yes, I'm wearing a dress. That's what they wore back then, you know.'

Will looked down at the Renaissance jacket and gloves he'd suddenly acquired.

'The clothes are a visual metaphor for the anonymiser protocol we just acquired,' she explained. 'Disguise in soft-space isn't easy but this place has it in spades. It might look all costume drama here, but wherever we go next, you won't be visible. You're wearing a mask, by the way. Don't take it off.'

Will touched his face and was surprised to feel something stiff and cold there.

He glanced to the left, down at the party. 'What is this place?' he said.

'A niche site,' said Moneko. 'There are millions of them. All different. And no, we're not going down there. It's too risky. The way we want is over here.'

She dragged him to a grand doorway that led into yet another hallway, this one decorated in black marble with red veins. Gold fili-gree sconces lined the walls. Portraits of himself in regal garb making sinister, unhinged expressions gazed down at them. He'd apparently arrived in an Italian palace designed by Satanists.

'Campy, isn't it?' said Moneko. 'A little too Dante for my tastes. Still, it takes all sorts, and their software can't be beaten.'

The hallway led to another bank of search gates where revellers in similar outfits were chatting in groups or calling up fresh corridors for travel.

'Don't say a word,' she whispered. 'Don't even look.'

She led him silently past them towards a free portal. Will felt sure he could feel the other travellers' eyes on his back.

'Integumentary parsnip horse,' she muttered.

A short corridor with just three side doors appeared.

'Wow,' said Will once the portal had shut behind him. 'I'm surprised that search turned up anything at all.'

'That's the point,' she replied. 'Short searches underuse the amount of buffer normally assigned to a request. That leaves gaps.' She strode to a stretch of blank wall at the far end. 'Now watch.'

With her free hand, she opened a door that Will felt certain wasn't there before she reached for it.

She watched his astonishment with a smirk of accustomed amusement. 'You didn't see a door because you weren't expecting to,' she explained. 'Don't worry, it happens to everybody. I had to be shown it, too.'

On the other side of the opening lay a causeway suspended high across an abandoned trench town of the sort that Galatea used to build. The glass overhead was smashed. Drifts of pale sand covered the tiered gardens far below where the turf had turned a dead yellow-grey. Ruined furniture and broken robots lay in heaps.

Will peered at the scene. 'I know this place!' he said. 'I helped with the clean-up here after a storm hit. It was one of my first ever roboteering jobs. Before I even joined the Fleet. It was called Fortitude, or something like that. I haven't thought about it in *years*.'

Moneko shrugged at him. 'It just looks like a blank wall with a broken-link sigil to me. This is where your special talents kick in.'

'You can't see that?' said Will, glancing between her and the view.

She shook her head. 'Don't remember anywhere called Fortitude, either. I can open these gates but I can't go through them. Now listen – I have to explain fast otherwise people will start wondering why our light's still red. Here's what you need to know. First, keep your disguise on. Don't touch the mask. It's your lifeline. If you can't see through your hands on the other side, you've got a problem. It means you've lost your stealthware, which is bad. Second, avoid everyone you see. They're either Balance or a Figment. Either way, you don't want to mess with them. Nasty shit can happen. Third, when you get where you're going, for God's sake try not to *touch* anything. Balance has some of this stuff tripwired, so keep your sticky mitts off the metaphor.'

'Wait,' said Will. 'So I'm just supposed to wander around?'

'That's right. Get the feel of it. That's all you need to do this time.'

'But how do I leave?'

'Hold your breath and count to twenty,' said Moneko. 'That's the cognitive trigger for emergency exit – the soft-space equivalent of a hard reboot. You'll surface in physical reality at whatever location is most tightly coupled to the virt-site you're standing in.'

She took a lace handkerchief from the sleeve of her dress and tucked it in the front of his doublet.

'There,' she said. 'I just twinned my exit to yours. The handkerchief codes for a non-local tether. We should pop up in adjacent bodies, or as close as the planet can manage. Now, if you think you're being followed, or if you suspect for *any* reason that something has gone wrong, just pull the plug, okay? Don't run, or try to fight, or any other silly shit. Freeze and hold your breath. Got it?'

Will nodded, suddenly anxious about what lay ahead. He felt like he was being briefed for a jump out of the back of a shuttle.

'Okay, good luck,' she said. 'Take as long as you need.' She curtseyed and gestured for him to step through.

Will gritted his teeth and walked onto the causeway. His feet immediately turned ghostly while the temperature dropped about twenty degrees. A chill breeze whipped about him. The causeway's railings moaned in the wind. Everything suddenly smelled unpleasantly of ammonia and dust.

'This is weird,' he said, but when he looked back, the Venetian search corridor was already gone.

6.2: MARK

For the next three days, Clath toiled relentlessly while her new method yielded nothing. Mark felt his confidence in her wane but tried not to let it show. He kept to himself, thought about Zoe and cursed himself for a fool. Then, on the fourth day, Clath came back to him to request a modification.

'I want to run power through the emitters,' she said. She was almost at the end of her rope. He could see it in her unfocused gaze and the sluggish way she moved. 'Even though we won't actually make warp. Ideally, we'd simulate tau-bursts for the extra mass, if that's okay with you.'

Mark acceded, even though he knew the plan would use an outrageous amount of fuel. They simply had nothing to lose. At the end of the following day she returned, excited, with a visualisation to show him. Mark let her drag him into helm-space where she painted the void before them with a map.

'We now have a local gradient measure,' she said, 'and we've tracked it over a decent path length. You can thank Ann's burst manoeuvres for that – our conventional velocity is crazy. From our samples along that line, we can extrapolate to the surrounding space. And when we add the tight-beamed pings we've received from our remaining feeler-drones, something interesting happens.'

As he watched, Clath's visualisation expanded from a few scant patches of colour-coded data to a great swathe of bright landscape. They'd cut straight inwards, he could see, near a huge, undulating kink in the Flaw. It doubled back ahead of them like a twisting river. Mark stared at it, disbelieving, and felt a slow grin curving his lips. If the diagram was right, they could cut straight across the gap. In fact, they were already most of the way there.

'It wasn't that hard, really,' said Clath, 'not once we got really deep into the bulk. Understanding this place is simply about having the right equipment in the right places, just like I always expected.'

'Are you sure about this?' he said.

'No. I may be missing something in the models and just finding what I want to see. But it's exciting anyway, isn't it?'

They called Ann. After several urgent requests to her cabin, the goddess reluctantly appeared, arms folded tight across her chest.

'What?' she said.

As Clath explained, an expression of hunger built on Ann's face.

'They could be waiting for us at the exit point,' she said. 'I want helm control when we get there.'

'Sure,' said Mark, laughing. 'So long as you don't send us back down the Flaw to fight them.'

She shot him a withering look. 'Don't worry,' she said. 'I'll do nothing so sensible.'

Two days later, everyone gathered early to watch the ship exit the bank. They sat around in helm-space waiting while data points from the emitters slowly arrived. Gradually, the curvon flow began to change. Eventually, around lunchtime, they finally made it out. Everyone except Ann broke into cheers.

'Quiet,' she said. 'I'm scanning for Photes.'

As she kept searching and finding nothing to fight, a fresh look of dismay crawled onto her features.

'We're clear,' she said quietly. 'Though they may be waiting further down the Flaw. We have no idea how far ahead they might have travelled.'

'If we hit trouble, you get to fly,' said Mark as he gently plucked the pilot control symbol from her fingers. Vindication built inside him like a storm. 'In the meantime, how's that navigational feed looking?'

This time, Ann had almost nothing to do. The data from their few remaining feeler-drones couldn't have been better. She stood listlessly while Clath's map kept growing faster than they could explore it. Mark tried not to giggle. He ramped their warp – carefully this time – teasing himself with the promise of success.

By the end of the day, they'd reached the other side. As they burst out into clear space, the rainbow of open cosmos stretched before them, more beautiful than a glistening sea.

'My God,' Mark breathed. 'We did it. We fucking did it. We beat the Zone. We're through.'

He felt a rush of joy and the urge to cry. He was going to do this thing. Neither the Academy nor anyone else could stop him. They were going to make it and the war would be over.

He dropped them out of warp and jumped back into helm-space so that he could run over and kiss Clath on the forehead.

'Thank you,' he said. 'Thank you, thank you, thank you.'

Clath's eyes filled with tears. She was grinning so hard it looked like her face would split. Judj and Palla took turns hugging her.

Ann regarded them with an expression of bewildered disgust.

'Don't any of you get it?' she said. 'This is just a different way to die.' With that, she vanished out of helm-space.

'What's her problem?' said Judj with a derisive snort. 'Of course we're still dead. That doesn't mean this isn't awesome.'

'Ignore her,' said Palla. 'We're the first people ever to cross the Depleted Zone. Let's just revel in that for a minute, shall we?'

Mark was too high to care about Ann's attitude. They'd cheated death again and it felt great, just like it had in the old days.

Ira looked set to follow Ann back into yacht-space, but before he could make an exit gesture, Judj spoke up.

'Wait, what's *that*?' he said.

He pointed to a small, passive marker that had appeared in the display. Something was holding position with the end of the Flaw ahead of them, much like the science station had on the other side. A steady signal sung out from it.

Mark switched to an EM filter. It was definitely an artefact of some kind. He zoomed in. An old IPSO buoy hung there like a tiny dimpled moon.

Mark's ebullience faltered. Helm-space suddenly felt a little colder.

'Not the first, then, apparently,' said Palla quietly. 'Is anyone else surprised to see that there?'

'I am,' said Judj. 'And I don't like it.'

'We should hail it,' said Ira. He looked transfixed by the device.

'Hang on,' said Mark. 'Isn't it possible that this is some kind of Phote trap?'

'Why would they bother?' said Ira. 'If they were this far ahead of us they could have staged an ambush already. And besides, what kind of Phote ships carry antique relay buoys? This belongs to someone else.'

'Grandad is right,' said Palla. 'This feels wrong. We need to know what's going on.'

Mark fought back an irrational reluctance to act and sent an access request to the buoy. The response was immediate. He had to rummage around in the ship's database to find a suitably obsolete compression filter so that he could read the reply burst, but once he had it, the rest was easy.

'By the look of the time-stamps, this thing has been running for decades,' he told them. 'It has an open suntap link to a red dwarf almost two light-years away. It must have taken *years* to come online.'

'Wow,' said Palla. 'That's impressive. And slightly creepy. Someone's been waiting a long time.'

'What it's doing here?' said Judj.

'What do you think?' said Ira, staring intently at the lonely machine. 'There's only one ship I can think of that this could have come from.'

Mark's skin flushed cold. They all knew exactly which ship he meant: Rachel's.

'Looks like your half-mum made it through after all,' said Palla.

'Let's not jump to conclusions,' he snapped, and regretted his sharpness immediately.

She raised an eyebrow at him. 'Getting a little twitchy, Mark?'

'Can we unpack that, please,' said Ira. He pointed at a marker file in the reply burst. Besides the buoy's schematics, it was the only substantive piece of data it had sent.

Mark unfolded it. A reference to a nearby G-class star appeared. Apparently, the IPS *Diggory* was waiting for them there – Rachel's ship.

He blinked at the display, stunned.

'It's just not possible,' he said.

Powerful, unexpected emotions roiled inside him. He'd hoped to exorcise the ghosts of Will and Rachel on this mission, not wake them up to torture him again. Was he now going to have to investigate Rachel's death and figure out the whole tragic story of her lost mission? Would he have to play her log-vids and watch her starve?

'I don't like this at *all*,' said Judj. 'Why is there a beacon here and not a ship? Was it left here by the crew, or by the autopilot SAP after they all died?'

'It has to be the crew,' said Ira. 'Otherwise, why go to a G-type? The only reason to make the trip is habitable planets. For all we know, there might be a Mars-Plus world there where the survivors set up base.'

'Her ship didn't have the equipment for that,' said Mark. 'It was a long-range scout. And in any case, they'd all be dead by now.'

Ira shot him a dry look. 'Am *I* dead, Mark?'

'No. But you've been drowning in anti-ageing meds for most of your life.'

'She had a coma-casket,' said Ira.

Mark shook his head. 'Even with cryo active, those old caskets were terrible. I've never heard of one lasting forty years. Not even with spares.'

'This still doesn't add up,' said Judj as his pale eyes scoured the data. 'If they had the means to navigate the Flaw this far, why didn't she come back?' His narrow jaw jutted forward in disapproval.

'Maybe they couldn't,' said Ira. 'What if they used up everything they had getting here?'

'Leaving no word of their success?' said Judj. 'No tight-beamed pulse at the science station? No drones sent back through the Flaw retracing their steps?'

182

Ira was quiet.

'You know what I think?' said Judj. 'I think this looks like a set-up.'

Ira broke into an unexpected smile. 'It wouldn't be the first time.'

Palla clapped her hands. 'Okay, here's what your great and wise SAO thinks. I propose that we follow this signpost. After all, the system it's pointing at is only fifty hours from here. It's on the way and we badly need to refuel. Also, we should detonate that buoy, just in case one of those Photes actually bothers coming after us.'

Mark reluctantly reinserted himself into piloting mode. He vaporised the buoy with a brief g-ray blast before aiming them onwards to the system where Rachel's ship was supposed to be. As he flew, a murky dread grew inside him. Backspace no longer looked so clean or open now that he knew something was lurking in it, even if it only turned out to be his past.

6.3: ANN

Ann marched her avatar back to its stateroom, sat it on the bed, and abandoned it. The emptiness inside her ached, leaving a kind of vivid, painful indifference where her hope was supposed to be. Since her run to the edge of the Flaw, things had gone from bad to worse. First, she'd lost her chance to make a stand. Then had come the crushing proof that the Academy hadn't needed her to do that anyway. They'd out-thought her models already, trapping more ships than she ever could have killed with just the *Dantes* at her command. So Ann had tried to square herself with the idea of personal obsolescence ended by a mercifully quick death in the Zone. Now even that wasn't coming.

Instead, here she was, stuck on a ship full of chattering idiots who appeared to imagine that just because they'd sailed through a wall of depleted curvons their fates weren't still sealed. It made her feel like screaming. The only possible solution was work.

She dived inwards to update her suite of threat models with data on their new situation. A vast landscape of timelines swam into focus, littered with stacks of semantic tags. Once upon a time, building models like this had been her job. These days, they served as an escape.

She brought up a spread of update tools and started tinkering. It didn't help. She wanted to smash something – or someone.

[Let it go,] said her shadow. [So what if we passed the Flaw? You know it's just a matter of time before we hit trouble again.]

Ann refused to reply.

[It's really not that bad,] it went on. [You can't expect them all to be as keen to let go of living as you are. You've died already. They haven't.]

[Shut up!] she told it. [I have no interest in your philosophising right now.]

[You're behaving like a child,] her shadow told her. [This is nothing more than a tantrum. You're embarrassed because you never expected this moment to actually happen, and you're so used to having your own way on a starship that you've forgotten what it's like to share one.]

[If that's true, then it makes me perfect company for the rest of the assholes on this ship!] she shouted back.

Her shadow would have been less intolerable had it not so obviously been a reflection of her own subconscious self-criticism. She knew she'd behaved badly, but the pointlessness of their mission sucked at her soul. She shouldn't have let them bully her into coming. Her place was back on Galatea helping Poli, not staggering onwards like a broken robot, blindly marching into the void just because they'd ordered her to.

A request ping invaded her sensorium. Someone was trying to reach her. She ignored it. The ping came again. It would be Ira – that bomb-site of a man still trying to build a bond with her, as he had every day since their last tedious intervention with Palla. Once, she'd found Ira attractive – compelling even. Light romantic tension had been a persistent feature of their work together for decades. But back then he'd been a true statesman. Listening to the flaccid therapist he'd become made her wonder what she'd ever seen in him.

[You should get that,] said her shadow.

[You, too?] Ann roared into her mind.

Reluctantly, she resurfaced into the pointless yacht metaphor and ordered the door to open.

Ira stood there in the white linen suit he'd adopted, looking like a cross between an Agatha Christie character and an over-muscled gnome. He smiled like an idiot.

'What?' she growled.

'We found something significant,' he said. 'I thought you should know.'

'Great,' she said. 'Have fun with that.' She instructed the door to shut.

He pushed it back open. 'Don't you want to know what it is?'

'Of course not,' she said. 'It's not an enemy, otherwise I'd be back in helm-space already. So whatever it is, it doesn't concern me.'

'A signal buoy,' he said. 'A human one, more than forty years old. We think it's showing us the way to Rachel Bock's lost ship.'

Her insides pulled tighter. Here was something else she hadn't anticipated. But what of it? Why should she care?

'And this is relevant how?' she said.

Ira exhaled heavily. 'Look,' he said, 'I'm sorry that your models of our spectacular deaths didn't pan out. The fact that we're still alive must be very distressing to you, but it's possible that there is an upside to the mission succeeding. Like being able to end the war, perhaps.'

'What are you talking about?' Ann growled. 'Do you even know what this mission's threat characteristics look like? Dying before the Flaw was the *good* exit point, but it was never the one with the highest threat levels. That exit is Snakepit, as I tried to explain in the briefing. Our target will be blockaded, Ira. Extensively. That will have nothing to do with us and everything to do with the Photes' desperate desire to reclaim their planet. They will have it surrounded just as they did Earth, and every other planet they try to take.'

'Mark and Clath don't think so.'

'That's because they're *guessing*!' Ann exclaimed. 'They're seeing what they want to see. I didn't guess what the Photes will do at Snakepit, I aggregated every piece of siege data we had on them and let the answer emerge. Mark and Clath don't expect a blockade because they're not thinking like Photes. So even if we wander around out here for years finding miracle after miracle, in the end we are still *dead*. D-E-A-D, dead. Do you understand?'

'Well, that's perfect then, isn't it?' said Ira, looking annoyed. 'In that case, you have no reason not to enjoy yourself. You get your warrior's death and your blaze of glory. And until then, you get to live. Actually *live*!'

'What's the point of that?' Ann spat. 'What possible pleasure could I derive from all that *living*? I have one purpose, Ira, and that's to fight.'

'You don't need a purpose, Ann. You're not a machine.'

She got up from the bed and walked towards him, her body humming with furious energy.

'Am I?' she said. 'I don't need to sleep. I don't need normal food. I don't even need company because I have it right here inside my head.' She punched her temple with an index finger. 'Not a single person has looked at me like a human for the last forty years, Ira. I've forgotten what it means to have equals or to feel love. Or to be wanted as anything other than a weapon or an object of reverence. I'm so used to being feared that I've stopped noticing. I just expect it. I have no family. No real friends. No *life*. I died on Snakepit,' she told him. 'I am undead. I am alone. And it is not *fun*.'

Ira leaned against the doorway and sighed at her.

'You know what I hear when you say that?' he said. 'Speaking professionally, as ship's psychologist? I hear someone who's just admitted that they're not sleeping properly, along with a bunch of other self-indulgent shit. Would you like some help with that? Sleep's important, you know. It might explain why you're feeling so negative.'

'I don't sleep because I don't want to, Ira! Because every time I dream, I see fire. I see the missions *you* sent me on, back in the good old Suicide War. I see whole worlds burning. I see continents bubbling like roasted marshmallows. I hear the screams over the audio channel of yet another colony that's changed its mind about wholesale dying. I feel the shake of the boser as I stab yet another planet in the heart. I feel myself breaking inside all over again. Over and over and over! I have *no* interest in sleep, Ira. None!'

Ira's face went blank.

She'd delivered a low blow and she knew it. For the first time in a long while, Ann felt guilt. There was a tacit pact between those who had dealt with the war that they didn't bring it up.

She turned away. 'I'm sorry,' she said. 'But you did ask.'

Ira shrugged. 'No problem,' he said. 'It's old news. But for the record, I didn't have any fun back then, either. I signed those orders, remember? I watched every single report you sent me, and the ones from every other death squad. Just like I made myself watch every single awful Phote interrogation recording they sent – something you were spared, by the way. I did it all for exactly the same reason you did. Because it was my responsibility. We still have a lot in common, you and I. But I *do* sleep. Which makes me better than you.'

Ann felt an unexpected twist of embarrassment at that.

'How?'

'Drugs,' said Ira with a bleak chuckle. 'Lots and lots of drugs. And here's another reason I'm better than you.' One muscle twitched in his cheek. 'I'm *am* still a fucking professional. I got the same breaks you did, Ann. The same isolation. The same nightmares. The same regret. But guess what? I'm dealing with it. Oh, and you're wrong, by the way. I never stopped looking at you as a person and a *friend*, the whole time we worked together. Are you telling me you never even noticed?' He shook his head in disgust. 'I used to admire you, Andromeda Ludik. You were the most impressive, intelligent woman I'd ever met. A true scientist as well as a great officer. Now you're weak.' He snorted. 'On the inside, where it counts. No wonder they dumped you. What would Poli think of you if she saw you acting like this? I think she'd be ashamed. I think she'd tell you to grow the fuck up.'

Ann blinked at him and felt a slow, caving sensation radiate from the pit of her stomach. Apparently, she still had the capacity to be hurt.

But Ira wasn't done. 'Let me offer you a word of advice from a very, *very* old man. When life hands you the opportunity to actually live for a little while, take it. Even if you're all full to bursting with your own self-pity. Otherwise, you may regret it later.'

He nodded his respects and strolled off down the deck, leaving the door hanging open behind him.

6.4: IRA

The buoy turned out to be one of several placed at intervals outside the Flaw, so that even a ship travelling at full warp was likely to find one. They all pointed to the same place.

At the end of the trail of signposts, Mark dropped them at the heliopause to look at the G-class system ahead. It was an ordinary sort of place, if a little small. The star sported three rocky worlds, one super-Jovian gas giant and a couple of paltry ice giants on wonky orbits. Sure enough, the *Diggory* was there, locked in place around planet two, a world that showed intriguing hints of a biosphere.

Ira felt a curious stirring as he peered down the length of a solar system at the tiny blue dot where a human ship was hiding. What was left of Rachel Bock lay there. She'd been his engineer aboard the *Ariel* on that fateful mission to the lure star when they'd met the Transcended, which meant she was as much a part of his past as Mark's.

She'd been a brilliant woman, and the only one he knew who'd had both the wisdom and the courage to imagine that mankind's future wasn't to be found in the ruins of the Fecund. Instead she'd decided to look for it at the edges of space, where their understanding ended. As the rest of them were falling into the foolishness that had unleashed the Photurians, Rachel had struck out on her own on behalf of the human race. The universe, of course, couldn't let such a good deed go unpunished. And so she'd vanished, taking all her sanity with her.

Now, at last, they stood a chance of righting that wrong and at least discovering what her fate had been. In that sense, Ira felt that Mark's ambitions were utterly laudable. He'd been the one to step up to the plate and propose that they try her vision for exploring Backspace a second time, despite the costs.

At that thought, he felt a spark of actual, spontaneous hope and savoured it. His last conversation with Ann had punctured something deep inside him that did not want to be disturbed. He'd found it maddening in the moment and harrowing afterwards.

While he was grateful to have some of his own emotions back, his ability to sleep had fled, banished into oblivion by a fresh tide of war dreams. But now, thank Gal, they had something to think about other than fighting and dying and wallowing in regret. They had a real mystery to solve. How had Rachel made it this far? And, given that she had, why hadn't she turned back? Maybe he could help Ann see the wonder in that puzzle. Maybe this was how he brought her back to herself. If any challenge was worthy of her extraordinary talents, it was surely that.

'Wait,' said Palla. 'What the *fuck*?'

She reached out to the helm-space display and opened a sub-window. She zoomed in tight, not on the blue world ahead but on the system's lone gas giant. One of its moons looked wrong. In the grainy low-res image they could muster at this distance, it resembled a soap bubble with something floating inside it – crystals, maybe.

But it was the scale on the image that made it startling. The object clearly wasn't natural, yet it was thousands of kilometres across. That meant a facility on the scale of the Ovid Shipyards, at least. Ira gaped at it and felt another old emotion stirring inside him: *unease.*

'It's an artefact!' said Clath. 'This system's in use.' She refocused the telescope array and began running noise filters on the images. 'And it's not the only one. Christ! Look!'

She started bringing up zoomed windows. Not a single one of the gas giant's moons was normal. At least three of them appeared to be enclosed in bubbles of their own. Long silver tethers extended out from some of them into space, sporting smaller bubbles. Other structures became apparent nearby – huge, translucent orbitals made of what looked like glass.

As the observational data piled up, it became very clear that they were witnessing engineering on a scale that humankind had never seen. Even the Fecund hadn't built this big.

'Oh. My. *God!*' said Clath, her hands over her mouth.

'It looks like your Backspace predictions are already broken,' Judj told Mark. 'This is definitely *not* unoccupied space.'

'Bullshit,' said Mark. 'Remember the first rule of alien contact: *your neighbour is probably dead.* These are going to be ruins. The Frontier used to be full of them.'

'You call those ruins?' said Judj. 'They look perfectly intact.'

'There are no energy signatures,' said Mark. 'The whole place is dark. The only signal I'm getting from the entire system is the one from the *Diggory*, and that's incredibly faint.'

'Maybe they don't need energy signatures,' said Judj. 'Who knows what we're looking at?'

Palla brought up a comms-link with a click of her fingers. 'Ann, you might want to see this,' she said. 'The system's occupied.'

Ann ported back to the bridge in an instant and stared fixedly at the displays. Ira watched tremors of veiled emotion pass through the frown she wore as she took in the sights. Was that *embarrassment*? Of course it was. They'd just left Ann's grim script far behind and her moral high ground along with it.

Without a word, Ann grabbed copies of the view-feeds and started manipulating them at superhuman speed.

'I need more resolution,' she said. 'These images are inadequate.'

'First the signposts,' said Judj. 'Now this. Does anyone else here get the feeling we're being led?'

'So we're being led,' said Palla with a reckless grin. 'Let's get closer. We won't be able to learn much skulking around the out-system. If it's that dangerous, the *Diggory* wouldn't still be here.'

'Are you *nuts*?' said Judj. 'We don't understand a damned thing about what we're looking at. What if it's a trap, and the buoy and that ship are bait?'

'Then we'll have to be careful,' said Ira. 'But Palla's right – we need to go in. We just encountered a potential source of military advantage, which means we have to assess it. Otherwise, if the Photes *do* ever come after us, we risk handing them the war.'

He remembered first discovering the leftovers of the Fecund civilisation all those years ago – the smashed remnants of the once-powerful race the Transcended had left for them to find. He'd been full of legitimate concerns back then and all it had done was slow them down. When you faced the unknown, risks were inevitable.

'Besides,' he added, 'we're out of fuel. We used what we had left following those signposts. Where else can we go?'

'Fine!' said Judj. 'In that case, can I recommend we at least break out the database shock key? I don't want to be responsible for sending yet another kind of alien off to predate on the human race. We have one of those, thanks very much.'

'Already on it,' said Palla. 'First thing I did. I also have the ship's self-destruct on standby, so you can all calm down.'

Mark shot her a look of contained alarm and then took them slowly inwards. Their speed dropped as they nosed into ever more ion-cluttered space.

Everything around the gas giant appeared to be made of magic soap bubbles and silver. The structures had curious refractive properties, casting rainbows everywhere. The closer they got, the clearer it became that the planet was infested with the stuff.

'Look at this,' said Clath.

She brought up a scan of the Jovian world's upper atmosphere. It, too, was full of bubbles, like a children's ball pit on a titanic scale.

'Those things are everywhere,' she said.

'What *are* they?' said Palla.

Clath shook her head. 'From the readings I'm getting, they're not made of anything recognisable. I think they might be energy fields of some sort. They don't scan like matter at all.'

'Energy fields but no energy *signatures*?' said Judj. 'How does *that* work?'

'I'll tell you as soon as I've figured it out,' said Clath.

As they swung in closer to the gas giant, the details of some of the lunar habitats resolved themselves. Ira found himself staring at fairy-tale environments locked under impossible sheets of glass, many of them made of yet more soap and silver. One moon was swathed in what looked like huge ceramic forests. Another sported cities of branching towers so slender that no normal physics could have held them up. Spectroscopic readings started to come back revealing atmospheres under those shells thick with unbreathable noble gases, mostly helium and neon.

Then they started noticing the damage. Where not enclosed by magic bubbles, the surfaces of the moons had been scarred and scorched with huge craters and furrows. The more recognisable pieces of exposed machinery showed blast damage of a very familiar kind. There had been an energy fight here, a big one that not even the subsequent extensive weathering could hide. Suddenly, the idea that they were looking at ruins didn't feel quite so unlikely.

Ira watched Mark's face and saw friction churning there more strongly than ever. This wasn't what Mark had expected or wanted. He'd come hunting for solutions, not more mysteries. Ira had felt that way when he'd discovered the Fecund. There'd been an impatience inside him – a breathless desire to focus on his own immediate concerns rather than the strangeness being forced upon them. But from where he stood now, he could see past that. They were being handed a puzzle, whether they understood it or not. They ignored it at their peril.

'You were right, Clath,' he said. 'All this smacks of the Transcended. The question is whether that's good news or not.'

'There's always been speculation that the Zone was designed to keep species apart,' said Clath. 'It's certainly starting to look that way.'

'Okay,' said Judj. 'Here's something else I don't like. All those remains are in the out-system. Within the habitable zone, where you'd expect to see the most material, there's nothing. Just the *Diggory*. The rest of space is so clean it's wrong. I'm not even seeing normal debris densities. It's been *swept*. And that planet the *Diggory* is orbiting is definitely a biosphere. I'm reading an oxygen-nitrogen atmosphere with a mean temperature of two-eighty-five kelvin.'

'That's practically Earthlike,' said Ira.

'It's not like Earth,' said Ann triumphantly. 'It's a Phote world.'

'What?' said Palla, her head whipping around.

'You're fucking joking,' said Mark.

Ann brought up a long-distance visible-EM image of the world ahead at maximum resolution. Despite the ugly pixelation, the signs of a tangled tubescape on the surface were unmistakable. You could even see the weird starfish blemishes of the world's defensive nodes. But for a few spectroscopic subtleties, they might have been looking at Snakepit.

'It appears to be inert, but the signature is undeniable,' she said. A tiger's smile stretched across her beautiful face, shading into confusion as it grew.

Ira could practically hear the cogs turning in her head. She'd been cheated of her warrior's death, but this was a respectable compensation: an entire world for her to burn. And yet the scientist in her hadn't completely died. She still wanted to know *why* it was there. Ira gave thanks for that, at least.

As Ann's mood brightened, everyone else's soured. It was hard to imagine worse news than finding another Snakepit. For the entire time they'd been fighting, the Photes had craved a homeworld more than anything else. Destroying the planet that Will had blockaded wouldn't be much use if the Photes had a backup from which to pursue their fight, even if it was on the wrong side of the Flaw.

Mark pushed the *Dantes* into stealth mode and brought up its cloak.

'I don't believe it,' said Palla. 'What are the chances?'

'Do we think there's any possibility our friends will get out of the bulk?' said Ira.

'The Academy guessed no,' said Palla uncertainly.

'I concur,' said Ann. 'Photes are pragmatists. They don't innovate. They'll conserve resources and fly home.'

'But is it *possible*?' said Ira.

'Of course it's possible,' Palla snapped. 'Anything's possible.'

Mark glowered at the blue world. 'Perfect,' he muttered. 'I hope the

Academy is happy that they pissed all over the mission plan. Did they think of *this* in their modelling scenarios? Apparently not.'

'You're going to blame the New Society for *this*?' said Palla.

'I'm not blaming anyone,' said Mark. 'I'm just not happy, that's all. The irony here is making my brain hurt.'

'You know, in security circles, we have three private theories about the Transcended,' said Judj as he scrutinised the unwelcome image. 'The first is that the galaxy is like an abandoned garden. The Transcended set it up as a farm for shaping young species but now the farm is all corrupted and overgrown. The second theory is that it's in a state of slow-motion war. Species such as ours are like weaponised bystanders or proxy states in a battle between ancient races. And the third one is species-level vampirism. The Transcended somehow maintain themselves by stealing the bodies and minds of younger races, and that the Photes and the Transcended are somehow in fact one and the same. Right now, I'm leaning towards option three.'

'Let's everyone stay rational here, please,' said Palla tersely. 'I don't think we have enough data to speculate yet.'

'Palla's right,' said Ira. 'It's too early to draw conclusions. But for what it's worth, my money *is* on the Transcended rigging this for us to find. All the hallmarks are there. You can practically feel the hand just out of sight. But I'm not ready to call that in as a threat. The big question in my mind is what they want, and why they've waited so long to show us this.'

'They didn't,' said Clath. 'They opened a door for us years ago. Humanity ignored it.'

'I'm going to investigate that biosphere,' Ann announced cheerfully. 'A threat assessment is necessary.'

Ira sagged inside. Of course she was. Why pass up a perfectly good chance at suicide?

'No, you're not,' said Mark. 'That's insane.'

She shot him a dark smile. 'Try stopping me.'

'Kids!' said Palla, throwing up her hands. 'There's no point fighting about this. We need to understand what's going on here, so everyone can work on whichever piece of the puzzle floats their boat.'

'For how long?' said Mark. 'We have no idea of the risk landscape. And do I need to remind you that we have a mission to complete? We should get the hell out of here the moment we've made sure we're not handing super-weapons to the Photes. We refuel, glass the planet and then leave. Another mission can come back and check out the bubble-ruins once they've figured out if they're safe.'

'A foolish assessment,' said Ann. 'An inert, untapped Phote world is a gold mine. There's no comms traffic in this system. There are no energy signatures, and no life signs coming from those habitat structures, either. This place *is* dead. From my initial radioisotope scans of the bubble-habitat atmospheres, I estimate it's been that way for at least two million years. That means an incredible chance to study and make a difference. If you really want to end the war, Mark, you'll need bioweapons. And a Photurian planet that doesn't yet recognise humans as enemies is the perfect place to start making one. Do I need to remind you that Snakepit was *safe* until humanity started playing around with its defensive technology? We studied it for years.'

Mark threw a hand out, pointing back the way they'd come. 'Even if you're right, what if the Photes follow us through?' he demanded. 'That could still happen at any moment. Those raiders were right behind us and so far we've done a terrible job of predicting their actions.'

'Actually, it's not that bad,' said Clath. 'First, Ann's right. The Photes always face losses with tactical retreat. But second, given the route we took out, we should have at least forty-eight hours of research time, even in the worst case. That could be all we need.'

'How do you figure that?' said Palla.

'Their sub-light engines are less efficient than ours,' said Clath, 'and we were in the Zone for about two days before those warp-bursts registered. Which means that, even generously allowing for the Photes' behaviour, they'd still be two days behind us.'

Ira hoped Clath was keeping her optimism on a short leash. It was obvious that she wanted to take a closer look at the gas-giant settlements.

'Plus there's some new physics at work here,' she added. 'I really think I should check it out.'

'Not on your own, you won't,' said Palla. 'There are three targets for investigation and we have the makings of three teams.'

'Split up in the face of danger?' said Judj. 'Now there's a great idea that's never failed.'

'I'll stay with Mark,' said Ira. 'I'd like to see what happened to Rachel. She was my friend.'

'Time-out, President Dentures,' Palla put in quickly. 'You don't get to choose that. That's my job. It's an IPSO ship, and as SAO I should be present to handle any Fleet security issues that come up. *Your* job will be to accompany Captain Ludik.' While her tone was sharp, Ira could detect a note of satisfaction. She was glad he was showing any preference at all.

'No,' said Judj. 'If we have to split up, we definitely should *not* do that. Ann wants to examine a dangerous biohazard. That makes me the logical choice for her research partner.'

'Judj!' said Clath.

'Honey, this is what I'm for, remember?' he told her. 'I wade into the Valley of Death and take samples.'

'Fine,' said Palla, looking peeved. 'In that case, Ira, you're with Clath.'

Ira considered contesting that decision for a dozen reasons – not least of which was the fact that Mark was likely to need psychological support. In the end, he let it slide. After all, what was Palla there to do if not make interesting mistakes?

'Sure,' he said. 'Dead species can be dangerous, too, Clath. There may be robotic systems out there that still work. Fortunately, I have some experience with that kind of situation.'

'Okay,' said Palla, eyeing him closely. 'Looks like we have a plan. Clath, we'll drop you and Ira off with a shuttle and some robot support near the gas giant on our way in. Then we'll head for the L-two point of that Phote world. I'm not letting the *Dantes* any closer. From there, we can use robots to get a better look at both the planet and the ship.'

'I'm taking a shuttle,' said Ann. 'We're going to the surface. The work I need to do requires direct access to my smart-cells.'

'Fine, crazy lady,' said Palla, rolling her eyes. 'You do that. Just remember that if you kick off a drone swarm, I will personally nuke you along with it, *capish*? Meanwhile, Mark and I will have a look at Rachel's ship.'

'We have quarantine protocols for that sort of situation,' said Judj. 'Please remember to use them. The Photes may have infected that ship. It's entirely possible that they're the ones who left the buoy. Likely, even.'

'We're on it,' said Palla. 'I assure you that I'm well aware of the Academic protocols for conflict situations.'

'And let's all keep to a time limit,' said Mark. 'Twenty-four hours, then we're gone.'

'Agreed,' said Palla. 'Our emphasis should be on rapid, safe assessment. Clath, Ira, we'll pick you two up on our way out.'

Ira nodded. A fresh clutch of woken emotions churned sluggishly inside him. Excitement, perhaps, and curiosity. But one of them, he was fairly sure, was *fear*.

7: INVESTIGATION

7.1: WILL

Will stood on the narrow ceramic causeway and felt the cold air bite his skin. Glass crunched under his feet. In the canyon-shaped townscape far below, nothing moved. Everything was a mess of dust and crumpled machinery.

The place oozed a half-remembered mood – a sense of dullness and antipathy that hung over everything. Stronger than that, though, was the feeling of mainlined déjà vu that sang in Will's veins from just being there. He'd replayed his own memories countless times but never visited them as an interloper.

Will glanced over the railing at the ruined town. He'd been sent here long ago to assess the damage and report on the viability of colony reconstruction after another of Galatea's crippling storms. He'd used robots, of course. Had he been there in person, he'd have needed an environment suit because the atmosphere on Galatea had barely any free oxygen. Which meant he was remembering something he'd seen through the eyes of a machine. That didn't appear to matter. The icy air and its acrid edge felt as real as everything else.

He walked carefully over the broken glass to the hatch at the far end of the causeway and found it sealed shut. He glanced back the way he'd come. The other doorway was on the canyon's far wall, several minutes' delicate walk away. Still, if he couldn't get the door open, that was where he'd have to go.

So much for Moneko's request for him to keep his hands to himself. Will threw his weight against it but it didn't budge. He tried again, hurling his shoulder at the frozen hatch. This time it gave. Will stumbled through and sprawled onto the cheap spray-on carpet beyond. In the same moment, the air turned warm and grass-scented while the light swapped from a cold morning blue to golden afternoon.

Will got to his feet and looked about. He was no longer in the ruined town of Fortitude but another Galatean settlement hundreds of kilometres away: Ninth Chance. And it was years earlier. He stood in the huge, empty lounge of the Roboteering Academy where he used to wait for Mr Nkoto-Carver to give him vehicle-inhabitation lessons. Mr Carver was always late. Beyond the lounge's open balcony lay the lower slopes of another trench settlement lit by the setting sun.

An abrupt jag of loneliness hit him. He'd hated this place: all those dull lessons, not being like the other kids, missing his parents even though they never understood him. Maybe other little boys dreamed of being trucks, but it was another thing to be forced, week after week, to become one for the sake of the public good. Training for roboteers in that era had focused heavily on the desperate needs of the colony and little on the satisfaction of the handlers themselves. He'd blotted the whole damned thing out of his memory.

In realising that, Will understood. The Underlayer was like the dust-bin of his mind, rendered in virt. It would be all the places he'd lost the conscious ability to recall, either because they were unimportant or he'd never wanted to revisit them. They played no part in the planet's sanctioned history even though they lingered inside him, colouring his personality. And they'd all been lovingly brought to life by Snakepit's vast computing array.

He glanced about. In one direction lay the entrance to the bathroom. Behind him was the way out to the hall. Both doors, Will suspected, would be portals to somewhere different. But to where? How was anyone supposed to find anything down here? There had to be some governing logic to this memory substructure, otherwise there'd be no point in truth diving at all.

Will picked one at random: the bathroom. He walked through into a waiting room in the Galatean Fleet Psychosurgical Centre, where he'd received his implant upgrades when he signed up to fight the Truists during the Interstellar War. His parents had hated that choice, but for him it had been a moment of hope – an end to digging tunnels and an escape to space.

He smiled as he stared to clue in. Some doors felt more *intimate* than others. That gave the space an orientation. His first choice of door back on the causeway had felt cold. His second choice had been warmer. So long as he travelled in the intimate direction, he suspected, he'd be going inwards, away from conscious processing. The other direction would lead back up towards the surface memories of soft-space. For all their surreal, self-referential trappings, this layer of memories had structure.

With that comprehension came an idea of somewhere he could go. Back when he'd been merged with Snakepit, he'd seen where the Transcended had located their tricky little device: right in the centre of the world's mind. It had been far below the horizon of the planet's self-reflective mechanisms, just like where he was now. Will grinned darkly. Now he had a goal: to find that damned machine. And in pursuing it, he'd get to test his theory about the Underlayer's geometry.

He picked another door, this time leading to the operating labs, and found himself on a beach on the world of Kurikov. A pair of setting suns hung over the water, one fat and red, one small and pink. Warm surf tickled his feet. Behind him lay hills covered with shaggy pseudo-cycads in shades of black and brown. Will looked down and watched tiny crab-analogues explore his feet.

It couldn't have been more than a year after the Interstellar War ended. Will recalled the fever of that time, the sense of excitement and empowerment. He'd spent a lot of days like this – because he could. After the horrors he'd endured at the hands of Earth's forces during the war, the peace and the liberation he'd felt were breathtaking.

Nobody else had ever set foot on this beach. The antagonistic enzymes in the planet's ecosystem would kill an unprotected human in minutes. But Will, with the changes the Transcended had wrought inside him, could wander under open skies to his heart's content. He'd been full of hope, and confident that the gifts he'd been given would set the human race on a fresh course. There'd be no more insane religions. No more slaughter.

Around that same time, though, he'd noticed a change in how other people looked at him. No longer was he a lesser person because of his mods – an embarrassment or a freak. Instead, he'd begun to see jealousy and fear. But the full implications hadn't yet dawned on him.

It occurred to him with regret that the deeper he went, the more recent his memories would be as they took him closer to that final discovery before his death. He looked back along the beach with a little sadness and then froze as he spotted someone standing there. Moneko had warned him to steer clear of other people in the memory landscape and this time he intended to follow the local advice. Will turned towards the dunes and walked quickly, hoping and guessing that another portal lay between them.

The moment he hit the banks of sand, the setting changed. Now he was on Yonaguni, in a forgettable executive retreat during one of his visits to the Far Frontier – those worlds that had once belonged to the Fecund. Beyond the window lay a view over a landscape of dusty mesas and squat, alien structures. They had bulging sides and no windows except for those that Nature had punched during the intervening ten million years. Will looked the other way to where a basket of genetically belaboured art-fruit sat untouched on the intelligent table.

This memory was from years later, after the death of his friend Gustav and the unravelling of his plans for peace. He vaguely recalled a meeting here – something to do with governmental standards. He'd paid scant attention to the details and been too busy and stressed to care. In the end, it hadn't mattered how many miracles he offered or threats he made, the human race carried on finding ways to cheat and lie to itself. The Earthers had clung to their awful church while the Colonials kept fulfilling every prediction of selfish behaviour the Truists made up about them. He felt exhausted just seeing this place again.

A man spoke in the next room, his tone strident.

'Boring boring,' he said. 'Blah blah, self-serving fantasy blah.'

'I'm not so sure,' a woman replied. 'After all, babble babble nonsense, conniving rubbish. You can't aphorism aphorism something just like that.'

They were getting closer. Will ducked into a robot-alcove and closed the door just as a clone in a Surplus Age suit and fedora burst in and glanced around in frustration. Through the crack in the door, Will peered at the newcomer in alarm. The clone noticed the voices in the next room and rapidly disappeared back the way he'd come.

Will knew he had to keep moving. Whether he'd just encountered a facet of Balance or something else, it wasn't safe here. He picked a mahogany doorway and waved it open, striding through quickly.

He landed in the drab legal offices of the IPSO Fleet on Mars and felt another surge of loneliness even more acute than the one that had grabbed him at the sight of his old school. This was where he'd stumbled through the court hearings about Mark's bungled rescue of Rachel in the Depleted Zone. He'd lost his wife, and now he was losing his connection with the closest thing he had to a son.

He winced at the pathetic arc his life had taken. No wonder his clones preferred to think of it all as a dream. He heard voices almost immediately and pressed onwards, through the next inward-leading doorway he found.

It took him to the evacuated mesohull of the *Ariel Two* – the ship the Transcended had given him. Great coiled springs of metal and ceramic the size of tower blocks rose on either side into shadowed darkness. Power-conduit cables trailed down like enormous roots. He 'stood' on a sheet of magnetised quasimetal that served as the floor. And the emotion that gripped him was rage.

He'd been fixing a suntap damaged during his last fight – the one at the Tiwanaku System where he'd first encountered Snakepit's semi-intelligent weapon-swarm. He'd watched Yunus Chesterford die and was ready to make someone pay for it. What he hadn't known back then was that he was on his way to the planet that would swallow him whole.

The cylindrical protrusion sticking out from the plating ahead was the suntap installation he'd sent robots to repair. Inside that housing, Will knew, would be exactly what he was looking for.

He opened the maintenance hatch and strode inside. The memory beyond seized him with a sense of astonishment and betrayal. He was back in the heart of Snakepit in that terrible moment – except it didn't look quite the same. He hadn't been strictly human the last time he'd set eyes on this place. He'd been halfway to a god by then and had seen it with senses that could no longer fit inside his mind.

The way it appeared to him now was as a clearing in a forest of fiercely glowing mechanical trees. Neither the black sky nor the black ground were easy to discern against the shining vegetation. The pipe-like roots from every tree around him converged to a point at the centre of the clearing where a single, incongruous device stood. It was about the size of a coma-casket, covered in dull metal cladding and marked with magnetic warning symbols: a standard-issue suntap device.

Inside that drab housing would be the circuit he was looking for – the data shunt that fed information into Snakepit from *somewhere else*.

He'd been right. Underneath its human trappings, the Willworld was still organised like the Snakepit he'd first visited. The architecture, and the monstrous betrayal it concealed, were still there for him to find.

Will walked around the device. Without opening the housing, he couldn't get to the thing inside. He couldn't *see* the truth. He knew that if he opened it, he'd find the circuit pulling data out of nowhere and the lie would be exposed. Better still, he might be able to turn the hateful thing off.

Moneko had warned him not to touch, but as he stood there, infused with the prior emotion of that moment, he felt a furious, irrational sense of purpose growing inside him like a tide. He resisted it but it clamoured in his chest, making his hands itch for action. He knew what he needed to do. John had talked to him about incontestable truths. Well, now he had one of his own: the need to *smash* this thing. To rip the heart out of it and free the world of its secret poison. Just looking at it and trying not to act was like holding his breath underwater.

Unable to resist a moment longer, Will grabbed the housing and tore it open. It shredded like paper in his grasp. When he looked within, though, he found nothing but empty space. The suntap itself was missing. Will blinked at the void and started to suspect that more was at work in this place than he'd guessed.

He glanced around anxiously for a portal but couldn't see one, of course. This memory was the end of the line. He'd made a serious mistake. The wail of a police siren sounded suddenly in the distance, somewhere off between the shining trees. It rapidly got louder.

7.2: MARK

Mark and Palla remained in helm-space after the others had winked out. The IPS *Diggory* hung before them, silhouetted against the grey and white crescent of the biosphere world below. Its emitter brollies and survey antennas lay retracted behind their protective shields, making the ghost ship resemble a filthy golf ball tumbling in space.

'You ready for this?' said Palla.

Mark nodded without meeting her eye. He had the sense that she hoped to wring some camaraderie from that moment of collaboration, but he had none to give.

'Good,' she said. 'Because you don't exactly look enthusiastic. Something tells me that you'd rather be staring at ruins with Ira.'

Mark snorted and shook his head. 'No thank you.'

When he'd first set eyes on those glassy artefacts, he'd felt a rush of awe. But then the bigger picture had emerged – the Phote world, the signs of conflict, the silence. He'd seen systems like this on the human side of the Zone that were just as broken and just as dead.

To his mind, whoever had lived here had lost a battle with the Photes, just like the human race was doing. When he realised that, he'd lost interest in the miracles and the place had started to depress him. It was like looking into their own failed future. The rainbow bubbles and engineering magic only made it worse. Impressive technology hadn't helped this race, which meant that salvation wasn't to be found here. If it lay anywhere, it was at Snakepit, just as he'd always supposed. He only hoped this side excursion didn't waste too much of their valuable time.

Though it pained him to admit it, he felt the same about Rachel's ship. A childish part of him even resented the *Diggory* for being there. It wasn't as if there'd be anything but corpses aboard. He'd just be made to revisit pain he'd long since buried. Still, closure was closure. And if this was how he finally said goodbye to the woman responsible for his creation, so be it. It was better than remaining haunted by memories of his former selfishness.

He watched as his lead probe closed on Rachel's ship. The metallic landscape of the hull showed surprisingly little damage considering how long it had hung there. His lead robot manoeuvred until it was over the ship's primary comms cluster and sent a wake-up request. The ship responded instantly, sending a full status report. Mark's skin tingled a little at the abruptness of the response. Rather than absorbing the message directly, he made it unpack in a secure buffer. Then he ran it through a round of malware filters and gave pieces of it to an army of sandboxed subminds to read. As understanding trickled into his head, he explained to Palla.

'The ship's in good working order,' he said. 'It's had a suntap running on slow drip for twenty years and so has a full charge. There've been no impacts or conflicts to deal with since the crew lay down for cryo-coma.'

Palla eyed him nervously. 'Anything in the ship's core say how they got here?'

Mark queried the ship.

'Yes,' he said, scanning the results. 'There appears to have been a SAP conflict. When they first hit the bulk, they set the ship to navigate them home and not wake them till it got back to human space. It was supposed to drop breadcrumbs to make them easier to find. But they failed to give the SAP complete executive control. It looks like there was a sloppily written management file. When the ship found itself unexpectedly back in the Flaw due to a propagating kink, the original programming took over. It flew on autopilot in fits and starts down the Flaw for what looks like over twenty years. When it found itself at the other end, the ship took them to the first available research site. But because they still weren't in human space, it never woke the crew up.'

Palla's eyes narrowed. 'My, now *that's* crazy convenient,' she said. 'Do you believe it for an instant?'

Mark shook his head. The logic was technically consistent but too much of a stretch. Getting the ship this far required a *perfect* kind of error. Any other mistake in that same management file would have lost the ship in space for ever. In a way, having such a tidy answer for the *Diggory*'s presence just made it feel all the more sinister.

'How about everything else?' she asked. 'What's the status?'

'The radiation buffers have degraded and some of the more delicate organic components are shot, but frankly, given about two days of careful repair with material from that planet she's orbiting, she could be out of here. And there are easily enough functional robots left aboard to do that work.'

It was like Ira had said: *the hand just out of sight.*

Palla's eyes gleamed. 'How about we send in a little bait?'

Mark nodded. He guided maintenance robots up to the main hull ports and requested entry. The ship gave them access without a whisper of complaint. He let them wander about in the mesohull, checking systems. Everything was locked down, orderly, quiet.

'All clear,' said Mark.

'Then let's take it to the next level,' said Palla. 'We look at the core.'

He sent a shuttle over to the *Diggory* carrying a couple of biorobotic simulants in environment suits. As per Judj's protocols, they were indistinguishable from people under a coarse scan, but designed to explode and fill the air with Phote-poison at the first hint of an ambush.

Once the shuttle docked, he and Palla twinned their perspectives with the simulants and rode the ship's docking pod down to the habitat core.

'This is creepy,' said Palla with a grin as she hung next to him.

Mark chose not to reply. He clung to one of the pod's handles and tried to still the storm of jagged emotions roiling inside him as he waited for it to arrive.

The doors opened and lights came on. Mark glided out into a main cabin in almost perfect condition. A haze of light dust hung in the empty space. The air had been vented, but other than that, it looked as if the crew had stepped out only yesterday.

Mark felt a surge of eerie nostalgia as he glanced about. He remembered when starships had looked like this – all spongy white wall-padding and clunky emergency visors clipped into wall-slots. It was like stepping into the past.

'I guess we should get this over with,' said Mark.

'Not having fun yet?' said Palla. 'Come on, don't you like mysteries?'

He suppressed the urge to snap at her. Dredging up old tragedies did not put him in a playful frame of mind.

They made their way cautiously to the med-bay in the bottom chamber where the end of the story surely lay. Set into the floor was a row of coma-caskets clad in 2D-screens showing old-fashioned readout data. Astonishingly, there was still a trickle of power going into one of them.

'That's ridiculous,' said Palla. 'This thing's still running.' The glee appeared to be draining out of her.

She started tapping at the display, bringing up information about the occupant. As she did so, a leaden feeling of certainty built in Mark's gut. He knew whose casket it would be before Palla even said it.

'It's Rachel's box,' she told him breathlessly, 'and it's working! I'm seeing biosigns still in the yellow. *Fuck*. This is wrong.'

Of course it was Rachel's. Mark stared at it, and then around at the silent walls of the cabin. He had the profound sense of being watched.

'It's in bad shape,' Palla added. 'If we were dependent on tech from her day, she'd be as good as dead. But we have modern medical kit aboard and I'm trained to use it.' She looked Mark in the eye. 'Bringing her back shouldn't be a problem. If that's what you want, I mean.'

She seemed to be belatedly cluing in to the emotional weight that the mission held for him. He wasn't sure how to respond.

'Are you sure it's *her*?' he said. 'Because I'm not.'

7.3: ANN

The world that Ann thought of as Bock Two swelled in her camera-view – a grey and indigo sphere studded with swirls of pretty white cloud. Rachel Bock, legally speaking, had been the captain responsible for its discovery, so the title was hers. Ann was glad of that. There weren't enough star systems named after women. She watched the globe beneath her grow, mesmerised not so much by its beauty as by its military promise.

All Phote colonies featured habitat-tubes. But most of them were new, having been stolen from the human race mere decades ago. The slowly spreading thickets of roots were no larger than human tent-cities. The only other planet humanity had seen smothered by tubes on every continent was Snakepit. But Bock Two sported a feature that Snakepit didn't have: *holes*.

Curious circular patches ranging from a few kilometres wide to a few hundred marred the tunnel pattern. It didn't look as though the tunnels had grown around these features, or that impacts or weapons fire had blasted the habitats away. Instead, the tunnel-sprawl just stopped. In the larger gaps, circles of grey-green vegetation hunkered at the centre.

Ann's scans had also revealed fascinating differences in atmospheric composition. The air here was much thicker than on Snakepit. It looked like the atmosphere of a natural, exposed biome rather than a Phote world. Ann couldn't help wondering if the gases that had been carefully husbanded in those myriad layers of hollow roots had leaked out – perhaps because of whatever made the holes. After the fierce disappointment of the flight out, Bock Two was a welcome surprise.

Looking back on it, Ann recognised that she'd entered emotional free fall after her failed attempt at self-destruction. For the whole of her second life, there'd always been another battle waiting. Without a fight she felt aimless, and resurrecting other talents that had lain dormant for forty years wasn't easy. She felt like she'd just *lost* those pieces of herself somewhere along the way. But Bock Two gave her a reason to exist. As Ira had said, she'd been a scientist and an investigator once. Maybe she could be again.

[You were wrong, then,] said her shadow. [There *is* something for you to do out here other than die.]

[Perhaps,] Ann admitted. [That assessment presumes the positive resolution of two outstanding problems. First, we'll have to identify enough tactical gain to make the discovery worthwhile. And second, I'll have to convince Palla to let us take whatever we find back to Galatea rather than finishing this bullshit mission.]

[Can you conceive of the idea that if you were wrong about the value of Backspace, you might be wrong about other things, too? Like turning back, for instance?]

Ann frowned. [Where is this interrogation going, *ghost*?] she demanded. [Are you expecting me to apologise for trusting my data?]

[I'm just saying that maybe you should try learning the larger lesson rather than the smaller one. Maybe this place is more than just another way to kill Photes.]

[Well, if I do find a new way to kill Photes,] Ann said, [then there'll be plenty of time for me to be chipper and philosophical later, won't there?]

Her shadow sighed. [I exist to support you, Ann,] it said. [I'm made out of you. There's practically nothing of Will left in here. So why do you insist on resisting my help unless it's what you want to hear?]

It worried her that she seemed to be falling out of step with her own shadow. To be at odds with a manifestation of her own subconscious felt both ludicrous and unsettling. Fortunately, despite the quality of the illusion, her shadow was sub-sentient. She was not obliged to converse with it.

'So, what's your plan?' said Judj as they slid through geosynchronous orbit.

'To improvise,' said Ann bluntly.

'That's it?' said Judj.

'My knowledge of Phote chemistry is stored in subminds. I haven't had the time to delve extensively into microbiology, so my grasp of the enemy's cellular operation remains intuitive. Fortunately, that's never been a problem. My shadow handles it for me. What I need to do is go down there and expose my smart-cells to the planet so that it can process what I find.'

'Rely on your shadow, huh?' he said. 'Great idea. After all, that's been working so well for you recently.'

'You'll notice that this time, the only person I'm prepared to put at risk is myself,' she replied tersely.

'You assume,' he said.

'I didn't ask you to come,' she retorted. 'And besides, after forty-one years, the Photes found *one* way around the defences that Will built into me. Because they invested tens of thousands of lives and who knows how much research time. This planet has never met me. Frankly, I'm not worried.'

'Well, I'm glad one of us is,' said Judj. 'I guess I'll be worrying for you.'

'Don't feel obliged.'

'Oh, please, I insist.'

She glowered at him through the camera situated above his seat. 'You're actually scared,' she said. 'I can read it off your infrared signature.'

'Of course I'm scared!' he snapped. 'I hate biospheres and I *loathe* shuttle descents. I always have. Falling sucks. Zero-g is no fun either, but at least I'm used to it. It's ten times worse when there's a landscape under me, and worse still if it's a biosphere with a fat, stupid atmosphere.'

'Why are you here, then?' said Ann.

'Because someone had to play sidekick to your sullen superhero and I'm best qualified.'

'I'm not sure how you can justify that if you don't even like visiting biospheres.'

'I grew up on a living world,' said Judj. 'A toxic one that the Photes sampled *eighteen* times while my family was still living there. I was only ever up in a shuttle when something truly awful was happening. And if I seem reluctant to go down there, it's because I know *exactly* what an unmapped biosphere can do to a person, Photurian or otherwise.'

'Except you have nothing to worry about,' she insisted. 'I'll be getting out of the shuttle, not you.'

'Onto an uncharted planet we've been led to by an unknown agency, where exactly none of the risks have been quantified.'

'They won't be unquantified for long. I'm going to do an atmospheric pass ten klicks up so that I can perform baseline sampling.'

'Great, so we get some nice, aggressive air-braking, too?' said Judj. 'I can hardly wait.'

She watched the waves of annoyance in his blood vessels with disdain. 'I can't understand why someone so averse to shuttle landings volunteered for this mission.'

'The mission profile for the Backspace Run contained *no* shuttle landings,' he said. 'What we're doing here is off-mission, because *you* insisted on it.'

Ann shrugged and took them down into atmosphere. As they bounced and shook through the layers of turbulence, Judj squeezed his eyes shut and gripped the edges of his seat.

'We're in,' she said when their trajectory had stabilised.

'And still not dead. Wonders will never cease.'

Ann contained the pithy comeback that rose in her throat and turned her attention to the images piling up in the shuttle's camera buffers. What she found there made her breath catch. The tunnels looked *rotten*. Those gaps she'd seen were places where the fabric of the root matrix had decomposed. Her cheeks tingled as a fresh rush of hope flooded through her.

Here was proof that the Photes could be beaten. She wouldn't have to wander the tunnels and try to tease the makings of a weapon out of the substrate. The planet had already been exposed to one. She prayed that whatever agent had given rise to all that damage was still around.

She brought the shuttle into a stable cruise at sampling altitude and stared down at the wonderful destruction while their craft began its preliminary bioassay.

'Well, that's weird,' said Judj, his voice tight.

'Explain,' said Ann. 'What're you finding?'

'The atmospheric bacteria we're picking up are *simple*.'

'You mean foreign?' she said hopefully. 'Non-Photurian?' Maybe the bioweapon she needed had just flown straight into their sampling ducts. Ann permitted herself a moment of optimism.

'Oh, it's Photurian, all right,' said Judj. 'The initial scans are detecting partial base-pair matches, but with a tiny fraction of the genetic complexity of Photurian cells.'

Ann's mood faltered again. Phote cells didn't mutate worth a damn. That was why the attack against her at Earth had come as so much of a surprise. So why were they doing it here?

'How dangerous is it?' she said. 'Is there anything I need to worry about?'

'Amazingly, no,' Judj admitted. 'In fact, the eco-type I'm seeing here should be enzyme-submissive with respect to Earth life. We're more likely to kill *it* than the other way around.'

Ann peered at him while he worked. 'Are you sure?'

'I'm never sure,' said Judj, 'but that's what it looks like.' He didn't sound happy about it.

Ann experienced a moment's vertiginous disappointment as her new reason to live slipped a little. If the Photurian habitats had somehow devolved into a simpler type of life, then finding them subject to rot was far less surprising. But her weapon-search was still surely in with a chance. There might be something even better – a mutagen that could subvert an entire world. She still needed to know what kind of force had beaten this place.

'Are you seeing any evidence of more than one eco-base at work?' she asked him. 'The evidence might be indirect.'

Judj shook his head. 'All I'm seeing here is Photurian XNA – or Phote-derived, at least – and the epigenetic factors are all stable. No obvious prion intervention. No pseudo-viruses. If I had to guess, I'd say that the Photes won this war and then something happened after they cleaned out the opposition. Maybe millions of years later, given the habitat density.'

Ann wrestled with the unwelcome implications but found herself thinking back to all those hideous arrival broadcasts she'd listened to – all those promises of endless happiness.

'So now we know what happens if the Photes win,' she pointed out. 'They can still all die anyway. That guaranteed eternity of joy they keep talking about isn't real. That's great.'

Judj frowned at her camera. 'Great how?'

'Because not one of those messages will ever be taken seriously again,' she said. 'That's a start. And if rot like this can happen here, maybe we can trigger it back home.'

'I wouldn't be confident of that,' said Judj.

Ann felt a flash of anger towards him. 'What's your problem?' she said. 'You're in biodefence. Doesn't this place at least give you a little hope?'

'Looking at organisms I don't understand never fills me with hope,' said Judj. 'Just anxiety. Back where I grew up, traces of the local biome used to get through our seals from time to time – little bitty organisms that we thought we understood. People always died. Sometimes very slowly and painfully. People I cared about. Eventually, it got so bad they shut down our lab.

'My job, Ann, is to anticipate horror. Horror and accidents. That's what I do. I've spent my entire life working with technology that shouldn't be as smart as it is. Whatever you imagine, biology isn't like physics. There's a reason why you never caught up with the research on it. Physics is simple. It's all about reducing nature. Bioscience is all about systems so tightly optimised that you'll never figure out everything about how they work. The way you beat a foreign biosystem is by tricking it before it tricks you. If you hang around long enough to try to figure out all the different things going on inside it, it's already too late. That means you have to use your intuition, Ann. And what it's telling me right now is that there's something very wrong with this planet. I just don't know what it is yet.'

Ann shrugged his speech off. If Judj wanted to waste time seeing phantoms in his data, so be it. She concentrated on finding a suitable landing site.

She picked a section of rocky shore where one of the rot-infestations had chewed away a three-kilometre semicircle of tunnel-matrix from the coast. On one side of them lay a sluggish grey sea under a pale sky. On the other stood a curving wall of dead tunnels seven tubes deep and eighty storeys high. It looked like an enormous black, sagging honeycomb – a revolting home for enormous undead bees. Dribbles of pale, half-living mucus spilled out from the openings and collected in sticky pools among the rocks.

Ann surveyed the miserable view through the shuttle cameras and tried to focus on how uplifting it *should* have felt. The sight of dying Photurian habitats demanded that a song be brought to the heart. There had to be something useful here. She unclipped and climbed down the access tube to the airlock.

'*Please* remember to use the quarantine procedures,' Judj called after her.

When she didn't reply, he sighed noisily and started prepping the sampling robots.

Ann let herself out onto the rocks and stood there in her ship-suit, sucking down lungfuls of the moist air. It smelled rather unexpectedly of leather, with a little salt tang thrown in. As the local microfauna reached her skin, her shadow immediately went to work. Just seconds later, data from her subminds leaked into her awareness. The news wasn't great.

'These cells aren't Photurian,' she told Judj, disappointment cracking her voice. 'They taste Photurian, but they don't work the same way. They're not useful. They're ... too stupid.'

She wandered towards the slime-pools near the base of the cliff. Even as she did so, she could tell there'd be nothing she could use.

'That's what I expected,' said Judj.

'Why?' said Ann, annoyed. 'Explain it to me.'

'You actually want to know?' said Judj. 'Basically, Phote cells contain highly compressed information in a way that natural organisms don't. They're like your smart-cells in that they're tiny processors, but they're far more complex. Your cells can do maths and dump out nanofactured compounds, but theirs are crammed full of information, most of which has nothing to do with how to run a working cell.'

'So what's it for?' She poked her fingers into the unremarkable filth. It felt warm and had the texture of snot. The stuff was almost as attractive as vomit. Her smart-cells responded to it with indifference.

'It enables them to break down other life forms for molecular homologisation,' said Judj. 'And yet more stuff to help them to aggregate into reasoning clusters. Phote cells have a ton of extra baggage to handle their inter-cell cooperation protocol. So far as we can tell, that protocol operates pretty much the same way at every level of biological organisation, whether you're talking about cell clusters, or organs, or entire hosts. That's what makes Photurians not strictly biological. If you want to be accurate about it, you might think of them as a standards-based life form because the messages that define them can be pushed by pheromones, nerves or data-packets. Their protocol doesn't care. But in any case, it looks like their XNA-code broke down here. This life is built out of random bits of message left over from the decay of all that compressed data. It's related, but it's not really the same kind of life at all. It's very primitive – almost primordial. Except I've seen this kind of thing before. I'm sure of it. I just can't remember where.'

He stumbled over his explanation, sounding nervous and distracted. But then again, when did he ever not? Ann watched his lumbering robots wander out onto the rocks to dip electronic tongues in the slime.

'So that's what I'm tasting?' said Ann as she wiped her hands on her ship-suit. 'Phote scramble? Just a physical echo?'

'Right,' said Judj. 'But the big question is how that happened. Snakepit was stable for millions of years before we came along. That biosphere was immune to change, so far as we can tell. The Phote Protocol removes mutations through collective action. Otherwise there's no way the damned thing could work.'

'Maybe this place got fried during the fighting,' Ann speculated. 'Perhaps the radiation bursts were sufficient to destabilise the ecosystem.'

'Impossible,' said Judj. 'We've seen what happens to Phote cells under excessive radiation – they mutually self-correct or break up.'

'Self-correct how?' said Ann. 'There must be some mechanism.'

'Sure,' said Judj, 'but nobody's ever been able to figure out what it is. Wait. Oh God. I know where I saw this.'

Ann waited for him to continue. 'Go on?'

'They did these experiments on rats once, back in the early days of Phote research. They took spores from surface attacks and used them to infect lab animals so they could figure out how seeded infections worked. The rats got stronger and smarter for a few weeks, then they sickened and died. It was a milestone result. It proved that the intelligence of a host species actually plays a role in the operation of the Phote cellular matrix.'

Ann shook her head. That was the kind of crazy result that showed up all over the place in Phote research. None of it made any sense.

'How can that be right?' said Ann. 'Snakepit didn't have any intelligent life before we arrived, but it was built entirely out of Phote cells.'

'The tunnel substrate itself was a semi-intelligent computing platform,' said Judj. 'Probably specifically designed for global stability. For all we know, this planet had the same set-up – a kind of shared quiescent supermind. But I haven't even got to the weird part yet. When they isolated the rats, they died from nerve disorders. When they left them together, though, they glued themselves into little stars before they died. Their skulls actually fused like a Siamese-twin separation in reverse. Their brains started leaking together.'

'That's disgusting,' said Ann.

'In every case, they found the same kind of genetic damage in the Phote cells that took over. It looked exactly like this, as if the cellular OS had just started overwriting its boot sector with crazy. I didn't spot the similarity at first because the effect was really mild compared to this. I guess this is what it looks like if you leave that rewrite process running for a few million years.'

'So we have our answer,' said Ann. 'This world's global mind must have shut down, either by choice or because it was murdered. It stopped mediating that self-repair process. Which means that if there's a weapon here, it's more likely to be high-level software than wetware.'

Judj paused to digest the idea. 'Very plausible,' he said. 'But that's not a happy answer. You're talking about a memetic weapon powerful enough to kill an entire world. Some kind of mind-bomb. That's a very different kind of threat. I can't imagine how you'd build such a thing, let alone safely use it.'

Ann thought hard. She needed a different angle – one that would reveal what the planet's higher-level functions had once been like. But she wasn't going to find it in this muck.

'My robots are locating plenty of organisms that feed off the tunnel wall-matrix,' Judj offered. 'They're digesting the biopolymer directly. That's something we could weaponise. Maybe that's your win. I really think we should get out of here now.'

Ann couldn't share his enthusiasm. The microbes he'd found were also breathing a nice thick atmosphere and had no Phote cells to compete with. They'd probably last mere minutes as part of a weapon drop. She made up her mind and marched back to the ship. She tucked herself into the airlock, shut the outer door behind her and took them back aloft.

'Hey!' said Judj. 'What are you doing? My samplebots are still down there. Wait, are you flying this thing from the *airlock*?'

'You said not to mess with the quarantine protocols,' said Ann. 'And besides, this site isn't good enough. We need more data. We passed over a defensive node a few minutes back. I want to take a closer look.'

'Ann, that's crazy!' said Judj. 'They're weapons factories. If any part of this planet is still potentially dangerous, it's a node.'

'That's why we're going,' she said. 'We need access to the high-level software this world was using, just like you said. I can't learn anything useful from a pile of slime.'

'So you're planning to poke around in a half-living arsenal on the off-chance you can find something that's still *deadly*? Do I need to remind you that those things are full of nuclear reactors? Ann, please be sensible. We've learned plenty. It's time to let the machines take over.'

While Judj complained, Ann flew the shuttle back to the node she'd seen. As it slid over the horizon, it occurred to her just what an utterly inadequate term 'node' was. Only someone looking at a world from an orbital telescope could have come up with a description so dry and meaningless. In reality, they were talking about a hollow bioengineered structure shaped like a starfish and the size of a shield volcano. Defensive nodes could grow warp-enabled drones like fruit and shoot them into orbit. In them lay the power to subdue entire star systems.

As they closed on it, Ann got a sense of just how huge the thing was. This one was riddled with holes and surrounded by lakes of varicoloured mucus. It was a rotting carcass the size of a mountain with a cluster of grey clouds hanging over its umber peak. Ann didn't believe for a moment that it was still dangerous, though hopefully it would prove useful.

She found a flattish piece of ground near the node's enormous mottled flank and landed the shuttle. Up close, the node's wall was covered with veins and nodules, all in ugly shades of grey and brown. A fifty-metre fissure in the side where the skin had split like an overripe pomegranate offered a way in.

'Come on, Ann,' said Judj. 'You have to know this is a terrible idea. Someone drew us to this place. They had an *ulterior motive*. And your reaction to that is to walk into the scariest thing you can find?'

'Correct,' said Ann.

'Jesus. I mean, what if you're even right and it doesn't bite? Some of those drone isotopes stay toxic for millennia. No human has ever set foot inside one of these damned things and lived.'

'That's why we're here,' said Ann. 'Now's our chance. We may not get another.'

She could feel her excitement returning. She shared his concerns, of course. Under normal conditions, defensive nodes were death traps. In the course of her entire career, she'd never tried to approach one. And even if she came across the hypothesised mind-weapon, would she even recognise it? It might kill her before she knew what she was looking at. But therein lay the appeal of the adventure.

'At least let me send some surveybots in first,' Judj urged.

'Too late,' said Ann. 'You're just going to have to trust me. Don't worry. I'll keep a comms-link open.'

This, apparently, was too much for Judj to take.

'Me, trust *you*?' he snapped. 'You don't even understand your own cellular OS. You're a liability and a suicidal, hackable mess. Not to mention a grandiose pain in the ass. In God's name, why can't you *grow up*?'

Ann flinched inwardly. Ira had made the same remark. The bruise on her psyche left by his words still felt fresh. For whatever reason, her old boss's opinion still mattered to her. She paused, collected herself and tried to explain.

'It's like this,' she said quietly. 'We know this world is dead. We therefore know that there's no biological risk. But we also have no idea what we're dealing with. Which is a problem because the existential risks here are huge. The only place on this planet where we'll find non-organic data storage that might tell us what's going on is a node. It's full of equipment designed to withstand warp. And if it can do that, it can definitely withstand a few million years of mild weather. If we want answers, someone has to go in there and look. And I'm the only person qualified.'

'I get that,' said Judj. 'But why don't you put that military brain of yours in gear for a moment and consider the fact that there may be unknown unknowns in there that you can't handle? Alien tech you haven't seen before. Carefully laid traps. Threats that might affect *someone else* in your team.'

Him, in other words.

'No,' said Ann.

'No?' said Judj. 'That's your answer?'

'I exist to take risks. Otherwise I might as well be dead.'

Judj made a long, low hissing noise like a tyre leaking air.

'Fine,' he said, sounding disgusted. 'We'll do it your way, Andromeda Ludik. Imagine that.'

Ann opened the airlock, climbed out and trudged out across the moist ground without a backward glance. She'd tried to explain. If Judj didn't want to be happy, she couldn't make him. Before her, the dark interior of the fissure beckoned, and within it, she was sure, lurked answers.

Ira watched the wheeling moons grow before them, each filled with some different sparkling novelty, and felt like a child approaching a deserted theme park. An immense candy-bright fantasy had been arrayed for him to explore, full of spheres and arcs and glinting colours. But it felt dead. And *wrong*. It beckoned and warned him off at the same time.

He smirked bitterly at himself. Apparently, all he'd needed to start feeling unmuted emotions again was simply a discovery on the kind of scale that defined civilisations, along with the attendant dangers. He wasn't surprised. He'd grown acclimatised to huge stakes. And now that the stakes were huge again, he could feel things.

Or maybe he was just inhabiting Clath's excitement. She was radiating enough of it. And his presence would be the only meaningful check on her science-hunger. Ira synced his shadow-link to Clath's seat camera to watch her gazing into her displays with fierce intensity.

'Learned anything?' he asked.

Clath's mouth twitched once in startled impatience as she looked up into the camera. Ira saw a wealth of implications in that glance. Behind her optimism, he noticed, she was ambitious. *That* was why she'd been so ready to give up her life to come out here. She wasn't just curious, she was driven. He'd missed that before, which surprised him. He hadn't been paying attention. Clath had been at the bottom of his priority stack.

'Not much,' she admitted. 'The bubbles are resisting analysis. If they're made of anything, it's a low-density ionised lithium gas, but with negative mass. Which, as far as I'm concerned, is a non-answer. We need to get closer.' She turned back to her data.

'But you must have theories about what we're looking at,' said Ira carefully.

Clath glanced up again, openly frustrated this time, then caught herself in the act of emotional reveal.

'We'll be more effective if we work as a team,' he said gently. 'We haven't spent much time together on this mission yet. I'm keen on the idea of getting out of here in one piece – want to help me?'

'You're right,' said Clath, 'I'm sorry. I'm excited, but also scared.

Those bubbles are... tantalising. And yes, I do have a theory. I think we're looking at some kind of false matter.'

'Interesting,' said Ira. 'Even if I have no idea what that is.'

'You remember the world that orbits the lure star near that first gate you found? The one that leads down to Fecund space?'

'Of course,' said Ira. 'I'll never forget it.'

'That's what I thought. Well, do you remember anything weird about it?'

'Sure,' he said. 'It was smooth.'

'Right. Well, there were dozens of landings on that planet after the Interstellar War. Not one of them could analyse that surface, even when they were sitting on it. It appeared to be rock surrounded by some kind of protective shell. The only thing they could detect about it was the faintest hint of lithium-like energy transitions.' She started to smile. 'Sounds familiar, doesn't it?'

'Indeed,' said Ira.

'Since the Photes got out, there haven't been any missions to that system. It's too dangerous. And that's a shame because now we have ember-warp. There are certain curious similarities between the properties of an ember-warp envelope and the skin on that lure planet.'

He watched her eyes light up as she spoke and envied her freshness. Ambitious or not, Clath Ataro had retained her sense of awe.

'What if you could make something like a warp-envelope that stood still and didn't need a support field?' she said. 'You might get something like this.'

Ira pondered the implications. 'So you think we're looking at Transcended ruins?'

Clath shook her head. 'That's possible, but it wouldn't be my first assessment. Remember, there's another lure star nearby. I think whoever lived here just learned to copy that Transcended trick. Or at least I *hope* that's what happened. Because if they could do it, maybe the human race can, too. It could mean everything for us. Unbreakable ships. Safe habitats. New weapons. You name it.'

Ira caught sight of two more veiled emotions then: urgency and pride. Clath wanted to win the war with science, personally. For her, this wasn't Mark's mission. It had always been hers. After all, she'd done the cognitive heavy lifting that had made it possible, hadn't she?

He wondered, suddenly, whether Zoe's exclusion from the mission was entirely down to the Academy and felt a tremor of concern. He decided he needed a better handle on Clath's motivations to predict her actions when they hit the ruins. It was time to twang her thought-stream to see what dropped out.

'What's the deal with your relationship with Judj?' he said smoothly.

He watched her process surprise. A host of vulnerability markers flew across her features like birds taking flight from a tree. So she was lonely, then. Well, of course she was. The ambitious usually were.

'I need to know what matters to you,' he said. 'It's a psych-officer thing.'

It looked for a moment like she wouldn't speak, but Clath had grown. up with the New Society. She had too much respect for the therapeutic process to keep secrets.

'He makes me laugh,' she said quietly. 'For all the acid he displays in public, Judj is kind and funny. And sometimes very sad. Besides, on the first day out, we discovered we were both SAP-play enthusiasts.'

'SAP-play?' said Ira, bemused.

'You know, making up - full of SAPs as characters. Funny little plays that write themselves. It helps vent some of the pressure.' She smiled shyly. 'Some of our characters are parodies of the crew members. In fact, no, I lie. All of them are. But it's hard not to. They're too easy to laugh at.'

'Am I in there?' said Ira.

Clath blushed. 'Of course.'

Ira smiled back. 'Good,' he said. 'I wouldn't want to be left out.'

Paying Clath so little attention had been a mistake. He should be spending more time around her. She wasn't crazy or sad or broken and he didn't have enough contact with people like that. He suspected she'd be good company when they hit the inevitable weird shit.

Their survey SAP pinged them, drawing their attention back to the morbid wonderland. 'I have identified a nearby artefact on an elliptical orbit around the super-Jovian,' it said. 'If desired, I can adjust our vector to permit direct investigation within the next fifteen minutes.'

'Does it have bubble features?' said Clath.

'No,' the SAP told them. 'But I am reading possible biological remains.'

Clath's expression darkened. 'Then we should probably check it out anyway.'

Ira invoked a visual close-up as they reorientated to match vectors and found himself looking at something like a mash-up of an evac-ark and a ring-orbital – maybe a ferry of some kind. There were puncture marks in its flank and the bulbous remains of a Photurian harvester ship still hanging off the side like a bloated tick.

'Well, that clinches it,' said Ira grimly. 'No more imagination required to guess what happened here.'

The story couldn't have been clearer. The bubble-makers had found themselves caught up in a fight with a Phote world just like humanity, and they had lost. Ira frowned. The last time the Transcended had messed with his life, they'd been handing out weapons. This time, it was painfully clear that none of the tools on offer would cut it against the foe they faced. Logically, then, they weren't supposed to be looking for guns or ships, but something else. A clue to escaping their fate, perhaps, or just a glimpse of a shitty future? Or maybe, this time, the weapons weren't meant for humanity but for their predators instead.

With misgivings writhing inside him, he sent a couple of waldobots across to explore. Around the ferry hung a barely detectable haze of dust that might have once been tissue and bits of frozen bone. Inside the closest hull breach he found a square chamber full of smashed machinery where the dust density was a fraction higher. A pair of robots or vac-suits sat clipped to the wall. They were shaped like gorillas but with weird, bulbous helmet domes. Ira regarded them with a sour sense of déjà vu. He'd done alien corpses before. It hadn't been fun the last time around.

'Those might be bodies,' said Ira. 'I'm bringing them aboard.'

'Okay,' said Clath uneasily. 'Of course. We should probably do that.'

He could tell that the reality of their situation was starting to sink in for her. Despite the system's promised miracles, they were examining a mass grave.

'I've done this before, remember?' he told her. 'Nothing to worry about.'

What he didn't share was just how unpleasantly different this moment felt. When they'd discovered the Fecund years ago, they had barely understood what they were looking at. It had all been so foreign. This time, they knew exactly what had happened. The oozing familiarity of the situation scared him more than the unknown ever could have.

'Where do you want to go next?' said Ira, once he had the samples aboard.

'There,' said Clath. She sent him a course to the outermost of the planet's major moons. 'So far as I can see, it's in the best condition of anything in the system.'

'Done,' said Ira.

He set the course and took them towards it.

In physical make-up, the nameless moon was your average airless ball of rock and ice, but that was where its normality ended. The equator had been decorated with dozens of orbital tethers. Some of them had structures at the end while others dangled like threads of party string.

Scattered across the surface like Escherite toys were structures made of mirrored domes and loops – suspended spheres, glass doughnuts and braided knots. It was as if a geometry teacher had been given his own planet to play with and a thousand years of spare time. The surface showed no battle-scarring to speak of. Ira wondered why.

'Let's go there,' said Clath, offering a landing vector.

The site she'd picked was a huge crater from which four orbital tethers extended in a line. Each was attached to something like a ship – either a large evac-ark or a small starship. They wore surface-shells made of contoured bubbles.

'How about that structure in the centre?' she said and pointed at a building shaped like a pyramid of quicksilver foam.

They descended and touched down carefully. Sparkling plumes of ice and dust billowed up from their landing thrusters and drifted back to the surface under the moon's feeble gravity.

Ira sent out their waldobots again, this time with a couple of surface crawlers and sensor drones for company. They set up shop near the structure's flawless reflecting wall and began their tests.

Clath grinned as the results poured in. 'It *is* false matter,' she told him. 'It has to be. I'm seeing gravitic abnormalities on short scales, just like for an ember-warp envelope. And the radiative properties are crazy. In some wavelengths, this stuff is utterly reflective. In others it's nearly perfectly transparent. But it differs from bubble to bubble. They must have had some way to trap the shells in specific quantum states while they were making them. And get this! These things can't be more than nanometres thick but nothing I'm probing them with is even making a dent. So far as I can tell, they're indestructible. And near-frictionless. No wonder they still look so good.'

'Nothing's indestructible,' said Ira.

'No,' said Clath. 'I guess not. But I'm not seeing any scratches, either.'

'So do you think this was a building, or just abstract art? Because if it's a building, it would have needed a door.'

Clath's eyebrows rose. 'Good point!'

She sent their robots wandering around the perimeter, probing for features on the immaculate surface. It didn't take long for them to find something like an airlock. It was a perfectly circular opening a dozen centimetres deep and eight metres wide blocked by another slightly convex disc of featureless silver. A ring-shaped groove ran around the outside of the aperture, about five centimetres from the edge.

They stared at it, a little paralysed by its promise.

'Pandora's bubble-stack,' said Ira.

Clath probed the door with a waldobot. Nothing happened until she applied some serious thrust against one edge. A gust of vapour abruptly jetted out from the rim. She quickly backed the robot away before its digits could get caught in the crack.

'I know what this is,' she said. 'It's a pressure seal. There's only so many kinds of mechanism that could work with building materials this strange. The gas pressure inside keeps the door shut. And because the door and the doorway are both perfect on submolecular scales, no gas ever gets in or out. If we equalise the pressure with what's on the other side, we can open the door.'

'And what do you suppose is going to be on the other side?' said Ira.

'Exactly what we detected from our surveys of the other moons,' she told him confidently. 'Something between point-five and point-seven atmospheres of helium-neon mix.'

Ira smiled. 'I mean other than gas. What are you expecting content-wise?'

Clath's face fell. 'Oh. I have no idea,' she said. 'Answers?'

'You want to go in, then?'

She beamed at him. 'Of course.'

Over the next two hours, they rigged a pressure tent around the doorway. It took longer than expected because adhering anything to the surface of the building proved impossible. Tools just slid off. It got easier when they figured out the purpose of the groove. It featured a narrow lip on the inside that enabled something to be fastened to the surface.

While the shuttle's fabbers printed the final pieces of their improvised pressure lock, Clath identified their second problem.

'Comms inside is going to be tricky,' she said. 'These false-matter shells give almost perfect rad-shielding. Even if we use the wavelengths this thing is transparent in, it'll still cut our bandwidth down to almost nothing. We're going to have to keep the door open and position some kind of line-of-sight relays.'

'We can do that,' said Ira. 'We could stick microsats on tripods. The shuttle has some in the survey stores.'

'Brilliant,' said Clath. 'Of course.'

'Okay, then,' said Ira. 'Let's make this quick. We go in. We scan for advantage. We get out. Agreed?'

Clath nodded.

'Should I break out the simulants?' he suggested. 'Fancy taking a walk in a haunted house?' He grinned at her to keep the mood light, even while little slivers of grim anticipation started sliding around in his gut.

'Sounds awesome,' she said. 'I can't wait.'

8: COMPLICATION

8.1: WILL

Will glanced around at the glowing trees in alarm and tried to make out which direction the sirens were coming from. He couldn't. Agents were closing in from everywhere. He checked his hands and was relieved to find them still transparent.

He backed carefully away from the suntap housing, but before he could take a second step, a door opened in the air just a few metres away. Through it, Will could see a weirdly telescoping search corridor made of scaffolding and pistons, down which raced a squad of Balance's minions.

Will froze as they leapt into the clearing. They moved like lightning to secure the perimeter and stood like sentinels for a second, their porcelain faces blank. Then they started changing. Their bodies morphed, deforming into menacing multi-limbed monstrosities – Hindu demons wearing masks of his face. Their hands flexed in unison. They started closing in.

Will regarded the ring of agents in astonished alarm and wondered why in hell's name he'd been so stupid as to manhandle the suntap just like Moneko had told him not to. Thankfully the monsters didn't seem able to see him. They began to sniff the air and lunge like dogs.

Will's surprise abated enough for him to remember his emergency exit trigger. He held his breath and started counting. The seconds crept by while the agents drew ever closer, pushing him back against the suntap housing. With just three seconds left, Will was forced to clamber inside the empty cavity to avoid their blind clutches.

As a single huge hand reached into the gap, Will surfaced in a habitat-tunnel and sucked air, his heart pounding. He sat upright and found himself in a transit-grave near the banks of a stream. He wore a scarlet, skin-tight body-suit with a black and white bull's-eye painted over his heart.

Somebody nearby was screaming. Will looked across the brook to the other bank and saw frenetic activity obscured by a line of tall blue ferns. A lot of Wills dressed like himself were dashing about. He glimpsed a clone wielding a large carving knife.

Moneko sat up in the pit next to him, dressed in a similar uniform.

'This way,' she said, leaping out. 'Hurry.' She took his arm and steered him rapidly down the tunnel away from the screaming crowd. 'Did you meet Balance?'

'Yes. Lots of him.'

'Thought so. He'll check our exit site. We need to be away from here fast.'

'What were those people doing?' said Will, glancing back.

Moneko shook her head. 'No idea. Looked like theatre. But it doesn't matter. Right now we need to focus on getting home.'

She regarded his body-suit bitterly. He glanced at hers.

'That's emergency release for you,' she said. 'You don't always get to pick what you're wearing. Or your gender. Or your face. Frankly, this is a good outcome, though I'd have preferred something a little less obvious. Keep running.'

They sprinted around the next bend in the tube. Moneko paused and grabbed his shoulders while he wheezed for breath. She didn't look remotely affected by the exertion.

'What happened in there?' she said. 'What did you see? Just the highlights. Keep it brief.'

Will explained and watched her expression darken.

'You waited for the bloody agents to pour into the clearing *before* pulling the cord? Jesus! Why did you leave it so late?'

Will shrugged. 'I was surprised.'

'Bullshit,' said Moneko. 'But never mind. What you need to know is that getting out of here is going to be difficult now. The only reason you haven't been caught already is because we've had lots of practice at this. Balance might not look that scary to you – after all, you walked straight past him this morning, right? Well, that's because every rule we follow has seen a lot of tactical adaptation. You don't remember how hard it was to get this far because every other time, you *died*. But now we're improvising, which means no more easy passes. You need to do what I say, when I say it, or we're both finished. Got it?'

Will nodded.

'Hold me up,' she said. She gripped his shoulders and sagged, her eyes fluttering.

Will seized her body before she could topple to the floor. A second later, she was back.

'What the fuck was that?' he asked.

'Using the map,' she explained. 'Data trawling. Looking for a way out.'

She glanced around and started off at a jog towards a thicket of two-metre-tall mushrooms near another kink in the tube. On the far side of it lay a junction where the tunnel forked. In the centre of the join, a narrow spiral of bony stairs led up to a hole in the ceiling between the strands of shimmering light-kelp.

'That way,' said Moneko, pointing.

The stairs looked unreasonably flimsy but held Will's weight without protest. Moneko sped up them while Will staggered behind, lurching and shielding his eyes as he ran past the lighting-vines' fierce glow. He emerged half-blinded into another landscape much like the one he'd just left, the only major difference being that this tunnel ran at right angles to the one underneath. Will started to understand how easy it would be to get lost on Snakepit. He didn't even know how deep into the tube matrix they were, or whether there was an ocean over their heads.

Moneko pointed towards a three-storey wooden building that had been built in the middle of the tunnel with an almost identical steam running underneath. It had simple fabric walls like a Galatean trench apartment. She started leading him around the side of the structure and suddenly leapt back.

'Balance,' she said. She found a flap in the wall and dragged Will inside.

He caught a glimpse of a giant clone stomping in their direction as he darted through the opening.

On the other side of the cloth, a meeting was under way. Twenty identical female Wills in purple unitards sat cross-legged in a circle, humming. They looked up in astonishment as Will and Moneko hurried past.

'We're doing interruption,' said Moneko cheerfully. 'Don't worry, it'll be brief. But I'll be back later with cards for those who're interested in sharing their feelings.'

Two seconds later, they were out of the other side of the building and hurrying up a picturesque footpath that wound towards another bend in the tunnelscape.

Moneko checked behind. 'I don't think he spotted you,' she said. 'Let's hope so, because the net just started tightening. First, agents will converge on your exit site to gather traces of your signature. Then they'll start combing to make sure you can't get back to soft-space. We don't want to be anywhere near when that happens.'

'So where are we going?' said Will.

'The nearest crowd,' said Moneko. 'Balance aggregates data from local instances. The second-best way to avoid him is to be somewhere he's unwelcome. The third best is to use stealth and the fourth is to be somewhere he's overloaded, which is all we can hope for right now.'

'What's the best option?'

'Somewhere he's not looking at all,' she said. 'Which, for the rest of today, is off the menu.'

Beyond the rise lay the opening to another spiral staircase headed to a lower level, this one larger and grander, complete with an enclosing tower of swirling filigree made from grown enamel. Moneko started down it.

Once past the glare of the lights, Will could see that they were descending towards a market that filled the bottom of the tube beneath. It was crammed with colourful stalls separated by narrow lanes. Voices echoed up from the floor thirty metres below.

Will and Moneko clattered down the stairway until they heard someone approaching. She grabbed him.

'Go slowly,' she hissed. 'Like you have all the time in the world. Take my hand.'

She smiled at him and started chatting randomly about Mettaburg gossip as three clones of indeterminate gender in blue shifts came by, ascending the stairs. They nodded politely as they passed.

'Our problem is visual cues,' said Moneko once they were gone. 'Balance will trawl the local surface memory of cooperating citizens. That'll take time, but he'll eventually trace these outfits to your exit point. Then he'll come looking.'

'So we have to find something else to wear,' said Will.

'Let's hope it's that kind of market,' she replied.

It wasn't that kind of market. Before they reached the bottom, he could already see that the stalls were packed with strange plants and animals. People led unusual livestock down the lanes. Will saw tethered lines of neon-yellow emus and tiny horses the colour of the sea. Stilt-legged elephants no larger than dogs and decorated in humbug stripes trumpeted to protest the confined space.

'Are all these things my clones, too?' said Will, eyeing the throng with revulsion.

'Of course not,' said Moneko. 'This is a bioform art market. These things are all adapted from tunnel fauna. They're demonstration patterns – people buy the templates to make their own copies. It's also a fucking disaster for us,' she added, 'but it'll have to do.'

She gripped his hand and took him out into the dense, meandering crowd.

'Why a disaster? I thought you said a crowd was good,' said Will. 'How's he supposed to find us in here?'

'Let's hope he doesn't,' she replied. 'We need to get to the other side before he zeroes in, otherwise we'll find ourselves in the middle of a stampede.'

They squeezed through the market for five uncomfortable, foul-smelling minutes before Moneko started to relax. Then they heard more screaming. An enormous crash came from behind them, as if someone had upended an apartment building.

'Fuck,' said Moneko.

Will glanced back and caught sight of Balance clones above the roofs of the stalls, wading towards them as if the people and animals in the market were so much surf.

'I knew it,' she snarled.

She dragged him sideways into the rear of an enclosure full of slender eight-foot-tall purple birds that gaped at them and started anxiously peeping.

'He's just killing people?' said Will in astonishment.

'They're threads, Will. Everyone's being dumped back into virt. Everything you can see is disposable. Except you and me, that is, because we'll end up in custody with our minds picked apart.'

She grabbed the rope that tethered one of the birds to a stake in the grey dirt floor and snapped it like chewing gum. Then she broke off the other end, giving herself a two-metre length, and pulled the enclosure's flap back open, revealing a stream of panicking pedestrians flooding by.

'They're not acting very disposable,' he commented.

'Losing copies is expensive,' she said, peering out. 'Especially in a market. Emergency backups come with memory loss. Transaction records get fucked up.'

Will caught sight of a huge black and orange dragonfly zipping over the crowd. Moneko cracked the rope like a whip, smacking the insect out of the air. She was as fast and precise as he used to be.

'Balance's spare eyes,' she said.

'Then didn't you just reveal our location?'

'Are you kidding me?' she said. 'How long did you imagine bugs last in an animal market? For each one I take out, the livestock eats twenty. It's the only thing good about this place.' She grabbed his hand and yanked him out into the flow.

'You've got smart-cells,' he noted.

'Clever boy.'

'Do I? Can I help? How do I wake them?'

'No time,' she said. 'You haven't activated the upgrade.'

'Shouldn't we have done that before the truth diving?'

'You first dive wasn't supposed to be this dramatic,' she told him as they ran.

'How about the agents?' he asked. 'Are they as fast as you?'

'Faster,' she said. 'I wouldn't recommend finding out.'

They fled to the far end of the market, away from Balance's stomping monstrosities. Where the market stopped, buildings started. The sides of the tunnel had been packed with grand town houses, making it look like a street from Surplus Age London, complete with fake white-stone cladding and bioluminescent street-lamps. Flights of steps led up to elaborate front doors.

Moneko crouched just inside the last line of stalls and peeked out between the canvas sheets. Stall-keepers and customers were flooding up the road clutching plants and pets, trying to flee the mayhem. They were scrutinised as they passed by Balance agents stationed at regular intervals.

'Classic flush manoeuvre,' said Moneko. 'Bastards.'

'What do we do?' said Will. He still felt in the dark about how the damned planet worked. There was nothing to do but follow Moneko and hope. She said nothing as she watched the street. Meanwhile, the marching clones behind them stomped closer.

'Are we going to move?' he asked.

Moneko inhaled sharply. 'Got it,' she said. 'Look – see that house over there? Third on the left.'

Will looked. To his eye, it was utterly indistinguishable from the others.

'Now watch the agents,' she said. 'See how their gazes move. Look at where they're standing.'

Will saw what she meant. The agents' gazes were turning everywhere except towards the building Moneko had identified. There wasn't a sentinel positioned outside that house, either. There was a slight gap in the pattern of clones, as if none of them wanted to be too near it.

'They're using option two,' she said. 'Balance is unwelcome there. If we're lucky, that's our exit. It's the first lucky break we've had.'

'*In* the house?'

'Sites like that one often have local gates direct to the mesh, bypassing the regular grid for private access. That's what we want. But first we need a diversion. Hold me.'

She sagged again. Will held her up while her eyelids fluttered. Two seconds later, she came back.

She frowned at him. 'What I'm about to do is a bit Cancery. You should never try this. It's not legal.'

'Why not?' said Will. 'What are you going to do?'

'Thread subversion,' she said. 'Ripping someone's mind and dumping a copy of mine into their body.'

Will grimaced. Just when he was getting used to the Willworld, it managed to creep him out all over again.

'Don't worry,' she said. 'He'll wake up in soft-space with a headache and a modest dent in his favour-account, that's all.'

She flopped again, gritting her teeth this time. Somewhere, several stalls away, fresh mayhem erupted. Three-metre lengths of wood that Will guessed were parts of stall frames started sailing overhead like javelins, directed at the Balance agents on the street. They responded immediately, leaving their posts with unlikely bursts of speed. Poles hit their armour and smashed. Moving as one, the agents closed in on the source of the disturbance like freight trains, powering straight through

230

the pedestrians in their path, leaving body parts and blood spattered in their wake. Moneko was right. They could really shift when they wanted to.

'Now,' said Moneko. 'While they're distracted. They'll have full coverage again in seconds.' She whipped another dragonfly out of the air as she leapt from their hiding place.

They sprinted for the house. Moneko gripped his hand as they ran.

'Listen,' she said. 'Whatever we find in there, don't get freaked out, remember? Keep your feelings in check.' She glanced at him nervously as they reached the door.

'Of course!' said Will. 'I get it. No disgust. Are we escaping or what?'

Moneko pushed the door open. Apparently even private residences on Snakepit didn't have locks. Will was about to comment but Moneko held a finger to her lips and fixed him with an urgent stare, then quickly shut the door behind him without a sound.

Will found himself in a long, well-appointed hallway painted white and decorated in an ecclesiastical style like something from the wartime Earth of his youth.

They crept down the hall. In a large room on the left, a service of some sort was taking place, oblivious to the mayhem outside. Will glanced in as they darted past and saw ranks of clones with baseline faces wearing High Church uniforms. Will couldn't help gawping. Were these clones *Truists*?

He glared at Moneko, who urgently made the shushing gesture again as they headed for the elegant staircase that led down to the basement. Consequently, they almost didn't see the clone in white robes walking up towards them.

'Hey!' he said. 'What are you doing here?'

Moneko kicked, whipping his head back on his spine with a sickening snap. He tumbled noisily back down the stairs, knocking over a standing vase situated at the bottom.

'Brilliant,' she snarled as it smashed.

There were shouts of concern from behind them and the sound of footfalls in the hall.

Moneko took Will's hand and yanked him down the stairs. She shoved him through an open doorway at the bottom, slammed the door shut and leaned up against it.

'Find a chair,' she said. 'Or some kind of furniture. Now!'

Will scanned the short passage. Squarish openings like space station airlocks lined either side. Will checked the first one on the left and found himself staring into a cell identical to the one he'd been imprisoned in during the Interstellar War – the setting for all his war nightmares. His skin chilled. Something inside him screwed tight in an instant.

'Why is this here?' he said quietly.

'Who *cares*, Cuthbert?' said Moneko as she struggled to hold the door shut. 'Is there a chair?'

There was a chair. It was identical to the one they had tied him to during torture sessions. With a hot pressure mounting in his skull, Will picked up the chair and took it back to Moneko, who wedged it under the door handle.

'This won't hold them for long,' she said. 'We need to move.'

She dragged him down the passage, past the cell and an identical one opposite.

'Are these clones *Truists?*' said Will, his voice cracking. 'What the fuck is going on here?' He found himself hyperventilating. Why would any version of him possibly want to copy such hideous pieces of his past?

'Killing us if we're not careful,' she said. 'These guys *hate* the Underground.'

At the end of the basement passage lay a simple room with curving walls of black biopolymer and a white dirt floor with two transit-graves. Unfortunately, one of them contained a pulsing human form that swelled while they watched.

'Fuck!' yelled Moneko. She grabbed her hair.

At the other end of the corridor, a concerted banging on the door gained rhythmic strength.

'What's the problem?' said Will. 'Can't you just kill it?'

'No,' said Moneko. 'The pit won't open until arrival is complete.' She grabbed his shoulders. 'We won't be able to make a clean exit unless we clear those monks out.'

'So just kill them! You have smart-cells.'

'And in seconds, so will they. Listen, here's what I need you to do. Call up soft-space. When you get contact, don't go forwards. Take a step back into the thread map. Find their mass and pull it. Then backward again.'

232

'How—' Will started.

'Intuition,' she said. 'I can't do this, Will. It has to be you. Do it quick, okay? Ready? I'll hold you.'

Will nodded. He shut his eyes, called up his home node and watched soft-space loom. It wasn't the station he saw this time but a more confined space, dark with shadowy figures pressing close. He ignored it. Instead he stepped backwards. As he did so, he found himself in a maze of bright strings, all taut and vertical like the internal workings of some insanely complicated yarn factory. Right in front of him, a vivid pink and black thread quivered. Almost as close, to the left, a cluster of identical strings in snow-white and blood-red were somehow vibrating their way towards him. They were the monks – he could tell.

Will reached out with an invisible hand, grabbed them and pulled. They plucked free in his grasp like dead grass, going instantly limp. He took another step back and found himself drooping in Moneko's arms. The basement was silent.

'Did I...?'

'Kill them?' said Moneko. 'Hell yes. And the Cancerous fucks deserved it. Just please don't ever do that on a whim, okay?'

Her eyes held an urgent vulnerability that Will hadn't expected to see. He nodded and glanced towards the door they'd wedged shut. It had been smashed open. A pile of dead monks blocked the doorway, face down and motionless.

'That's what a Cancer looks like?' he said, awed.

'Yes, and you did good. But this is very bad juju,' said Moneko. 'Our Balance-shield is now blown – they were generating the unwelcomeness that was keeping us hidden. We need to leave.'

'Hey,' said a clone in white robes sitting up in the transit-grave. 'What's going on here? Who are you? This is a private residence!'

His eyes went wide as he noticed the heap of bodies. Moneko kicked him in the head.

'Into the grave,' she said. 'We're out of here.'

They dragged the body out and vacated to the mesh. This time, when Will transitioned, he found himself in one of the convention-hall stands he'd seen on his first walk through soft-space. Moneko seized his hand and led him past some startled clones in High Church robes.

'Thanks but no thanks,' she told him. 'We've taken a good look but your organisation isn't a good fit for our diversification needs. Have a nice day!'

They left the tent, entered the flow of pedestrians and hurried off. Thankfully, their red body-suits had already disappeared. Will was back in shipwear while Moneko was decked out like a dapper executive in a slate-grey formal hoodie and creased black yogas. After the first signpost intersection, she relaxed a little.

'We're out,' she said, her pace slowing. She paused to rub her head and breathed deep. 'Balance can't track us now. We're into the next mesh cell, thank Gal, so let's debrief while we can.' She fixed him with an earnest, exhausted expression. 'First, a confession. That suntap housing you saw? It was in a forest clearing, wasn't it? With glowing trees?'

Will nodded. 'I've been there before, then.'

'Every time,' said Moneko. 'It's the first thing you always do when we take you to the Underlayer. You've never been one for structure, Will. You always push for the first good idea that pops into your head. So these days, we make sure you've got good stealthware and an exit strategy. Then we let you visit on your own terms so you can look for yourself. The housing was empty, I'm guessing?'

Will nodded as a blush spread across his cheeks.

'Don't be embarrassed,' she said. 'It's instinct. We all have them. Glitches need to see it for themselves. And they don't like to feel that they're being pushed into it, either. If that makes you feel predictable, I'm sorry. To date, this has been the best method we've found for crossing that hurdle.'

Will shrugged. He hated feeling like an automaton but wasn't sure what he could do about it.

'You always want to destroy the suntap,' said Moneko. 'But never *that* badly. And you never leave it that late to quit. Which means that something changed this time. Balance upped his game again. So let's figure out what went wrong. Tell me how you felt in that forest when you saw the suntap. What was going on in your head?'

'Anger,' said Will. 'An anger so pure it left room for nothing else. It was like John said – an undeniable truth. I *had* to rip it out.'

'Well, here's lesson number one,' said Moneko. 'Emotions in the Underlayer are porous. There's not a good division between Glitches and those spaces, which is how you're able to navigate them. But that forest, that's not part of the Underlayer. It's a different kind of memory – not something forgotten, but something blocked or artificial, depending on your perspective. In any case, it's clearly a memory that Balance can tweak, because now he's figured out how we're using it and has wired it with emotional triggers. If you're going to do more diving, you need to watch out for that. You won't always be able to tell when you've left the Underlayer and moved into some other part of the world-mind, so questioning your responses is essential. *Always be careful of rage.*'

'So I've been told,' said Will tersely.

'Well, now you know what we're fucking talking about,' Moneko snapped back.

'Sorry,' said Will, 'It's just I'm hearing it a lot.'

'No problem,' she replied. '*This* time. You're out. You learned. We're still alive. Be thankful that he can't hack a hard exit. They're terrible for the planet, but it'll cope. So now I have a question for you – one I ask all my partners. If that suntap you expected isn't there in the heart of the world, why is this place still the way it is? How come we have axioms? If there's a lock on our minds, where is it?'

Will didn't have an answer. 'I've no idea,' he said. 'I was sure it had to be there. The Transcended must have moved it.'

'I'll tell you where you can find it,' said Moneko. 'All over the place. Hidden inside every major component of our virtual landscape, anchoring every axiom we have. That's what we want you for, Will: to help us map all those suntaps. If you feel like ripping them out, that's your business. Now you know what happens if you try. But unless we can find the whole damned lot of them, this world's never going to change, and you, my friend, are never going to get out.'

8.2: MARK

Once Rachel's body had been checked over for bioweapons, Mark and Palla shuttled her casket to the *Dantes*' quarantine core and began the laborious process of waking her up. First they matched the conditions in the core to those in her casket. Then they opened it and slid her frozen form into the core's med-crèche where it could start working on her tissues.

Mark waited in stunned anticipation. That they could simply revive

235

her after all this time felt unreal. It was as easy as rebooting a SAP. All the more reason for him to worry that the thing they were booting wasn't Rachel.

'I'm seeing some neural burn,' Palla cautioned as she studied the data coming off the crèche. 'It's going to take her a little time after she wakes to get back to who she was. Presuming she's actually her, that is.'

'Imagine that,' said Mark. 'Some convenient ambiguity.'

'I'm rigging a sensory sim for her,' Palla said. 'She'll see a standard recovery space with us in it. Just voice, sight and sound. She won't be able to move, but I can synthesise facial expressions from cortex data. I can't add any more detail than that without an invasive procedure.'

'Not a problem,' said Mark. 'A basic interview is all we need right now.'

'I'm also setting up a separate back channel for us to confer,' she added. 'I assume our first priority is to ascertain her identity?'

'Damn straight,' said Mark.

He had no idea what to do with this moment. When he reached inside himself for the loving excitement he knew he should be feeling, he found nothing lurking there except alarm.

The ship's virt dropped them into a bland rendition of a hospital room, with Rachel lying in bed. The high window revealed a benign blue sky and little else. A vase of cheerful yellow flowers sat on a table.

[Okay,] said Palla over their back channel. [It's starting. You want to talk?]

Rachel's eyelids fluttered open. She glanced up at them. Her eyes locked on Mark. 'Mark? Is that you?'

Mark's throat suddenly felt arid. He swallowed.

'Yes. Hi, Rach. It's me.'

She frowned. 'I can't feel my body.'

'Don't worry,' he said. 'You've been in cryo for a while – it'll take a little time to thaw. Do you remember what happened?'

She peered into the middle distance. 'I...' she started. 'We were... there was a mission.'

'That's right,' said Mark. 'Do you remember where?'

Her expression became surprised. 'Yes! The Depleted Zone. We... something went wrong.'

Mark nodded.

'We hit the bulk,' she said. 'Oh my God, we hit the bloody bulk.' She frowned again, this time in fear. 'How long has it been?'

Seconds earlier, he'd felt sure he'd meet either an alien puppet or a brain-dead cripple. Now he found himself unable to speak a simple truth because of the pain it would bring her. His subconscious had already made up its mind about who he was talking to. He writhed inside.

How long?' she urged. 'Please.'

'Forty-three years,' said Palla.

Mark winced.

Rachel seemed to notice her properly for the first time. 'Dear God, *why*?' she said. 'Our overshoot wasn't that bad! What happened?'

'There's some uncertainty about that,' said Palla. 'What do you remember?'

'Are you a doctor?' Rachel asked her nervously. 'You look so young.'

Palla produced a lopsided smile.

'She's here to help,' said Mark. 'Please try to tell us what happened. We can go from there.'

'We...I...led the ship in too fast. We got stuck. We set the autopilot to fly us out. I was upset. Blamed myself. Jago laid in a course...'

'That's it?' said Mark. 'Nothing else?'

'Marker drones,' said Rachel. 'We decided to lay out markers. I wasn't sure it was worth it. Where am I? Is this Earth?' She peered at the blue sky behind them.

'No, it's not Earth,' said Mark.

'Why did it take us so long to get back?' said Rachel. 'What happened?'

Mark hesitated again. His unease had sublimed into a terrible empathy.

'You didn't make it back, I'm afraid,' said Palla. She slid Mark an impatient glance. 'There's no way to hide it, Captain Bock. You're on the other side of the Flaw.'

Rachel's eyes went wide. Warning icons started appearing on the wall behind her bed.

[Do you want to kill her?] Mark demanded.

[No,] said Palla. [Do you want to find out who she really is? There's nothing more honest than a stress response, Mark. You know that.]

'What Palla says is true,' said Mark. 'We're a rescue mission.' He tried for a winning smile. 'We came back for you.'

'After *forty-three years?*'

Mark prickled with guilt. 'It's not been easy,' he said. 'And your ship wasn't where we thought it'd be. You're orbiting a star about three light-years beyond the far side of the Flaw. An uncharted one.'

'The *far* side?' said Rachel in disbelief.

'Congratulations,' said Mark with a limp smile. 'You were the first through. For what it's worth, you made history.'

'Where's my crew?' Rachel blurted. 'Are they okay? Who's awake?'

'I'm afraid they're all dead,' said Palla, keeping a close eye on Rachel's stats. 'You're the only survivor.'

Mark watched horror unfurl on his half-mother's features and felt it with her.

'Only your casket kept working,' said Palla. 'Can you think of any reason why that might be?'

'No!' said Rachel, appalled. 'What do you mean? I went cold second out of six. Are you suggesting my crew sabotaged their own caskets to keep me alive?'

[You're making a mess of her metabolism,] Mark snapped. [There's a difference between stress and cruelty, you know.]

[Mark, have you ever actually interviewed a suspected Phote spy?] she said. [It's not fun. You want me to do this on my own? Just bad-cop? I can kick you out if you'd prefer.] At the same time, she gave Rachel a mild mood-stabiliser.

[No,] he said quickly. [But let's take this slowly, can we? I want to be able to live with myself afterwards.]

'Rach,' said Mark. 'It's okay. We're just trying to find out what happened. I'm sorry about your crew. It's a miracle you got through this. Be grateful for that.'

'You want me to be fucking grateful after I've lost my crew?' said Rachel, her eyes shuttling from side to side. 'After I've been dead for *half a lifetime?*' Her eyes squeezed shut. 'This is a nightmare,' she said. 'Please tell me this is a nightmare.' She was sliding into panic.

'Do you want us to come back later?' said Mark hopelessly.

'No!' said Rachel. 'Let's keep going.'

'Okay,' said Mark gently. 'Let's try this. Why don't you tell us why you left? Why this mission, Rach?'

238

He'd wanted to understand this properly for most of his adult life. He'd never expected to know.

She stared at him, more pain clouding her brow. 'You *know* why.'

'Please tell us,' said Mark. 'We need to find out how much you remember.'

'Because he was breaking my heart!' she breathed. 'That man. Will. Your guardian. I couldn't stand watching him destroy himself and I couldn't stop him, either. I had to do *something*. He was trapped in politics, trying to fight a battle he could never win. Every year the Frontier situation was getting worse. We had to work harder and harder to stop fights from breaking out. I was losing him. I needed to find something for Will – fuck it – for *all of us* to think about that wasn't the damned Far Frontier.'

'So it was a distraction,' said Palla.

Rachel shook her head. 'No! Everyone had forgotten why we built interstellar colonies in the first place. If you fight over the resources you can see, everyone loses. We learned that back in the twenty-first century, for crying out loud. Things only get better when you start looking for the advantages beyond plain sight – the disruptive ones. The true innovations. I *had* to do that because nobody else was bothering. And we had a mystery just sitting there in space, waiting to be explored. How could I not at least try?'

Mark stared at her anguished face and couldn't help seeing the parallel with his own situation. Were they both heroes or fools?

'I...' said Rachel. The wall suddenly flooded with warning markers as her face twisted in anguish.

'Rach,' said Mark. 'Calm down. Take it slow.'

Palla boosted the mood-stabilisers another notch.

'It broke my heart not being able to come clean with you,' said Rachel. 'We ruined things for you, Mark. Have you had a good life? You look so young! Can we do that now? Extend life properly?'

'Yes, Rach,' said Mark with a plastic smile. His innards wouldn't stop wrenching. 'A good life. I'm in my sixties now.'

'Amazing,' said Rachel. 'Do you have kids?'

'No, no kids,' he said.

She looked disappointed.

'Happily married, though,' he added.

'I feel like such a fool for dashing off,' she said. 'I went to the one place I knew he couldn't follow. Part of me hoped that by the time I got back, he'd have come to his senses. Is Will with you?'

She glanced around the room, as if looking for him in the background. Mark struggled for words.

'Will's lost, too,' said Palla.

Mark felt the urge to hit her.

'Oh, *God*!' said Rachel. 'He didn't chase me out here, did he?'

'No,' said Mark. 'I did that and got stuck in the bulk for a month or two. Will's lost in a different way.'

'How?'

Mark's mouth worked back and forth.

'For fuck's sake, Mark!' Rachel yelled. 'Stop sugar-coating it for me! Tell me what happened while I was asleep!'

He saw what he was doing: by trying to protect her, he was drawing the pain of adjustment out, like tearing the bandage slowly off a wound. It was driving Rachel further into panic when she dearly wanted to be strong. There had been a kind of backhanded kindness to Palla's bluntness, he now saw – one that had been lost on him until that moment.

'Will's lost on an alien planet,' he said simply.

'What, a Fecund site? The Transcended artefact?'

'Neither,' said Mark. 'Something worse, I'm afraid.'

'What the fuck is worse than the Transcended?' Rachel's eyes implored him.

[You'd better tell her, Mark,] said Palla heavily. [Tell her or I will. The whole thing. I think she can take it and it's not going to get any easier for her. At least right now I can tune her meds.]

Mark shot her a glance of loathing even while he knew she didn't deserve it. Palla gave him a look back that managed to be wounded and disapproving at the same time.

'There's been a war of sorts,' Mark said. 'A long, slow one.'

'Oh God, no,' said Rachel. 'Not Earth again?'

Mark shook his head. 'No. Earth is on our side this time.'

That earned him a wry expression from Palla for his use of present tense. He pressed on.

'There was a conspiracy,' he said. 'You saw how things were going with Earth. It was getting bad. The conspiracy tried to fix it. They faked an alien menace using tech from the Frontier. And, well, it wasn't really fake in the end. Essentially, we made an enemy for ourselves. An infectious one.'

'Infectious?' said Rachel. 'Are you talking zombies or something?'

'Not exactly,' said Mark. 'More like a bacterially mediated hive-mind. It's intelligent and organised.' He drew a heavy breath. 'In essence, the human race has become a supply of bodies for it. The reason you've been out here so long is that we've been ... busy.'

She stared at him, rapt. 'Go on,' she said.

'They took New Panama,' he said. 'And they attacked Earth. The political tension ended all right, just like the conspiracy hoped. Humanity turned over a new leaf and tried to settle their differences.'

'So what happened then?' Rachel urged.

Mark felt boxed in. It wasn't a story he wanted to have to tell. But ironically, the history lesson appeared to be doing Rachel more good than anything else he'd said. It gave her something to focus on other than her own plight, so he forced himself to keep going.

'It didn't work. The Photes – the infected, I mean – they cut off transport. Each human colony was on its own. And for a while it looked like that was all the bastards were interested in doing – separating us. They were incredibly hard to fight but they weren't actually attacking our worlds. So we left them alone. But within the first five years, two-thirds of our colonies underwent some kind of revolution. There were Earthers on every world, you see. We had to spread them out because there were so many. In most cases, they put some version of the Truist Church back in power.'

'Shit,' said Rachel.

'Shit is right. The theocracies and the neo-feudal societies were the first to go. Infiltration was easy. The Photes infected their leaders. Uninformed populations were easy to manipulate. Whole planets were converted to the enemy cause without a shot being fired. They called that the First Surge.'

Now Rachel was silent and simply listening. Her vitals had stabilised.

'Unfortunately, it didn't end there. The rest of humanity tried harder. We installed democracies everywhere and adopted careful health laws. It didn't help. The optimistic societies that pushed for peaceful reconciliation with the Photes went next, along with those that were ruled by committee. The Photes harried them, swapping from promises of peace to vicious attacks until the governments fell into fights among themselves. After that they were easy pickings – informed dissent was used against them. Charismatic leaders were targeted for conversion every time. That was the Second Surge. Then things got ugly. Most of those colonies had signed suicide pacts...'

His mouth went dry. He took a moment.

'Go on,' said Rachel.

'They didn't want to give extra hosts to the Photes, you see? They knew it'd make things worse. They... they didn't want to hand an advantage to the enemy. So those colonies were... bosered.'

Mark could still see the light behind his eyes and hear the desperate pleas from those worlds, *insisting* they were still human despite all the evidence. Begging to be allowed to live. Screaming as they were burned by people like himself and Ann and Ira. He could still remember exactly how he'd felt about himself. Numbness uncoiled in his core.

'Mark, I'm so sorry,' said Rachel.

She could *tell* he'd been a part of it. The midnight shadow of regret passed its vast wing over him. He moved swiftly onwards.

'So humankind was presented with a dilemma,' he said, clearing his throat. 'We couldn't have authoritarian rule. That didn't work. Nor did open democracy. So what was the solution?'

'You tell me,' said Rachel, her expression stunned to blankness.

'Well, people looked to Galatea. Emergency-centric capitalism looked like it might be the way to go, so long as there were huge checks on centralised power.'

'Nobody liked that government,' said Rachel quietly. 'It was a kludge. We were supposed to have had a Scandinavian democracy.'

'Yes,' said Palla. 'But the kludge worked. And after the Suicide War, the engineered societies proposed by Venetia Sharp started being taken seriously at last.'

'Sharp?' said Rachel, sounding lost. 'I knew her.'

'Play-centric societies are more robust,' said Palla. 'And when we moved to distributed non-blocking military leadership, things got better still. Nobody was comfortable with huge figures like Ira Baron staying in charge. Not after what they'd seen. They were obvious targets. These days, leadership is a public service carried out by the young, crowdsourced and transparently aggregated. We make clinical, unlovely decisions that work. Nobody likes it. Everybody lives.'

Rachel gazed at Palla's face. Mark felt sure that Palla was coming off as rude and weird. Which, on reflection, wasn't a bad assessment.

'Are you in charge, then?' said Rachel softly.

'Got it in one,' said Palla. 'Normally Mark runs his own ship but this trip is a little different. In effect, we all chip in,' she said with a chilly smile. 'Speaking of which, we'd like to put an interface in your skull.'

Rachel's eyes widened. 'Is that strictly necessary?'

'Depends how you are with confined spaces,' said Palla. 'This room you see isn't real. It's virtual, like all the space we have access to onboard. The amount of physical room in the habitat core where your body is now stored is about the size of a closet. If you think you'd prefer that for the next few months, you're welcome to it. Or you can stay paralysed, like you are now. Or, if you like, we can dump you back in storage.'

'All right,' said Mark stiffly. 'However we treat Rachel, it's going to be with respect. She doesn't need to have a shadow put in unless she wants one.'

'So you're all roboteers,' said Rachel. 'Will was right. It *was* the future, after all.'

'Nearly,' said Palla. 'But what we have is nowhere near as invasive as the shit you did to Mark.'

Rachel winced.

'Fuck you, Palla,' Mark said out loud. 'Leave her alone.'

'Thank you, Mark,' said Rachel, 'but I don't need protecting. If you think I should undergo this procedure, Palla, that's what I'll do. I'd rather be able to participate. I want to help.'

'It won't be fast,' said Palla. 'We have to scan your brain first to make sure you're not some kind of Phote spy.'

'That's fine,' said Rachel. 'Go ahead. If you're captain, I'm putting myself at your disposal. And if this mission is at risk, let me know what I can do. Scan me all you like.'

Mark noticed that Rachel was now giving Palla her undivided attention. She seemed utterly unfazed by all the bad news. He suddenly felt irrelevant and was reminded for the first time in decades what Rachel had actually been like – not a saint, but no-nonsense, calm and self-directed. She wanted to rise to the challenge. That was where she got her strength. Furthermore, he had never been her top priority. If he had, she never would have left.

8.3: ANN

Ann walked away from the shuttle churning with discomfort. Why did she even need to explain herself to Judj? He was in security, wasn't he? He knew that nobody else possessed her skills, and therefore she had to *try*. Nothing else would be good enough. She shouldn't have to apologise for it.

And besides, if they really wanted answers about how the planet had died, this was surely how to get them. The biosphere on Bock Two had come apart, dissolving into something less sophisticated than terrestrial algae, so any information they gleaned would have to be stored in some other form that didn't degrade.

Wetware always decayed. And while you could build habitats out of living cells and deposited ceramics, constructing spacecraft required a different set of tools, ones that were often poisonous or radioactive. Hence the separation of function between the defensive nodes on Phote worlds and everything else.

Ann even knew a little about how the Photes pulled off their industrial miracles. Living cells cooperated to extrude non-living material as if they were tiny molecular printers. That material formed the matrix for an inert pseudo-biology that could survive toxic conditions real life found intolerable. This gave the Photes programmable robots the size of cell clusters that could build larger machinery for them. Then they fed instructions to their golems on tailored polymer chains.

The Photes, therefore, could make nano-machines of the sort that humanity had never managed. Those robots weren't smart or able to reproduce, but they were robust and capable of self-powering off nothing more than a thermal gradient. It was one of the cooler Photurian tricks. Her smart-cells could do something a little like it, but with nowhere near as much subtlety.

Ann also knew from personal experience that even if she found nothing better in the defensive node, drones always contained solid-state backup brains. The Photes tended to fry them on capture so that humans couldn't study them, but Galatean scientists had still learned plenty. The brains were so well rad-proofed that even after a gentle nuking, information could still be teased out of the remains. Were she to find such a thing intact, there was no telling what secrets it might reveal. With luck, at least one of them would be left.

Ann walked up to the fissure and looked inside. On the other side of the shell-wall stood a dense forest of four-metre-high structures sitting in a shallow soup of viscous crud. The structures were gunmetal grey and shaped like enormous jointed toilet brushes. They were all bent over and leaning on each other like dead grass at the end of summer. The light inside was so bad that Ann could barely see anything, even with her infrared ramped up. Deeper in, the shielding would only make it worse.

'You'll be blind in there,' Judj observed tartly.

Ann modified her eyes, finding a wavelength that could pick out details in the homogenous gloom. Judj said nothing as the video feed she was sending him improved. He'd kept the link open, she noticed. He wasn't so angry or worried yet that he didn't want to know what she'd find.

As Ann stepped in, she made out shapes hanging over the forest like ribbon stalactites. There were waves and waves of the stuff, forming a surface like an inverted coral reef. Some of the ridges had curious swellings on their sides – bulbs that had once been growing there. And in a few places, these fruit-like extrusions had descended on stretching cables to touch the floor.

Ann passed a cable that had snapped and dropped its cargo, leaving a sizeable crater in the brush-forest. The fruit at the centre was a crumbling, broken thing about the size of a domestic transit pod. Where the eggshell exterior had fallen away, Ann saw hundreds of curling loops of fibre inside, held in place by delicate strands of translucent silicate with a bulbous cluster suspended in the centre. It reminded her of the stalk in the middle of a dandelion head.

Ann realised what she was looking at – the stillborn foetus of a Photurian drone. Those looping structures were tiny particle-accelerator tracks, as yet ungrown.

'I'm astonished there's so much structure left,' said Judj.

'Why?' said Ann. 'Like you said, this is a factory for weapons that can tolerate space battles. It wasn't going to decay overnight.'

She passed through an area where several half-formed drones dangled above her like malevolent chandeliers the size of lifter trucks.

'I know what this place is,' said Judj. 'This forest must have been a field of giant cilia at some point. You're walking through the skeletal remains of a transport system. And that stuff overhead was a birthing area.'

Ann found herself smiling. He was right. The secrets of the Photes were being laid open before them, just as she'd hoped.

A little further on, the ground sloped away, yielding a break in the forest. Ann found herself at the edge of a rise, looking out across a hidden world of gloomy, back-handed beauty. The sky of this place was the node's mottled ceiling soaring high overhead and held up by implausibly elegant columns of grown ceramic. That ceiling had caved in many places, admitting shafts of dusty sunlight. Before her, the forest of dead cilia swept down to the edge of a field of drones. There were thousands of them in various states of decay, all in shades of grey and brown. They looked like an immense clutch of once-treasured eggs.

These drones, though, were much closer to full size than the foetuses she'd seen earlier. A fully grown drone was about the size of a tower block. It was hard to build anything warp-enabled any smaller. Here, though, almost finished drones were lined up like toys and gummed over with the spidery remains of support lattices and nutrient transport arteries. Ann had always wondered where Photurian drones came from. Now she knew. They hatched from the ceiling like fruit and were nurtured to full size like baby birds. The scale of the bioengineering was humbling.

And then, dozens of kilometres away at the centre of the node, behind the sea of eggs, stood something that resembled a cross between the Tower of Babel and a rail gun. The vast, coiling, conical structure rose up to join with the ceiling. Around its base, great openings yawned like a hundred hungry mouths. That would be the accelerator tower.

Ann breathed in the sight with a growing sense of vindication and started down the slope through the brush-forest towards the ranks of dead drones at the bottom. This place was a treasure trove, just as she'd surmised. With enough understanding of it, they might be able to shut down Phote drone production for good.

The closest craft were malformed, crumpled and half-rotted. As she got closer to them, an acrid smell arose like a paint factory after a bad fire. The ships sat in dents in a curiously tiled polygonal floor and curved up above her like the sides of mutant cruise liners, massive and grey. Their surfaces were covered with the cracked remains of albedo-management scales no larger than fingernails.

Ann touched an exohull. The structure felt firm, but when she pressed hard, it crumbled under her hand, showering her face with dust. The strength of the space-ready ceramics had all leached away. Or, more likely, their molecular matrix had never been finalised. The more complete drones would no doubt be situated closest to the tower. Ann took note of the important lesson: even this place was not immune to the ravages of time. She had to be careful.

'I don't know if you're bothering to watch the environmental data in your biofeed,' said Judj testily, 'but you should know that the background rads tripled as you came down that slope. Plus our comms bandwidth is less than half of what it was when you walked in.'

'Noted,' she said. She refused to tell him she'd be careful. She had no such intention.

There wasn't much obvious processor machinery inside the node, at least not of any sort that she could discern, and it'd take her hours to hike as far as the accelerator tower through the maze of dead drones. Fortunately, her fallback plan remained viable: to find a drone brain. All she needed was a relatively mature and undamaged example that might have still been accumulating data around the time the world died.

She walked down an aisle like a grand boulevard between the curving masses of dead ships. The way was clotted with frail nets of material halfway between spiderweb and limescale. They broke as she passed, leaving an Ann-shaped tunnel behind her.

Finally, she found a drone that appeared to be in good condition. She tested the hull with her fist. The exohull was still strong, but not so strong that she couldn't smash her way through it. She broke a hole in the shell of the dead baby drone and jumped back quickly as a stream of black ooze poured out. The painty, smoky smell grew a lot stronger and added a few sickly treacle notes.

'Christ!' said Judj. 'What *is* that stuff?'

'Decomposed pseudo-life, almost certainly,' said Ann.

When the gunk had drained from the interior, Ann ripped a hole wide enough to admit her and climbed inside.

'Okay, Ann,' said Judj, his voice crackling with static. 'We've taken another rad boost and a bandwidth hit. I think you should come back now. You've made your point and we've learned plenty.'

'Sorry, Judj,' she said. 'I can't do that.'

He sighed at her. 'Do you honestly believe I was always this careful?' he said.

'Yep.'

'Wrong. This unflinching capacity for worry I have is a learned skill born out of painful experience.'

'I'll start back in a minute,' said Ann. She wasn't leaving until she got what she'd come for.

The interior of the drone was filthy, dark and full of fibrous crap that made it hard to see. If her smart-cells had been worried about things like asbestos, she suspected she'd be in serious trouble already. However, she could make out the drone's mesoskeleton arcing above her, with its attendant looping accelerator tracks. All the important stuff was situated in a large, shadowy clump about ten storeys up.

Ann grabbed one of the mesoskeletal struts and tested it to see if it'd bear her weight. It did. Hopefully her invasion wouldn't be the one kick the structure needed to come apart. Ann was strong, but the idea of a couple of dozen storeys of alloy and ceramic crashing down on her head didn't appeal. It was unclear whether her augmented skeleton could take that kind of pressure.

She clambered up gingerly through the bones of the ship. It was alarming at times, when parts of it broke off in her hand, or where the surfaces were so slick and greasy with degraded pseudo-life that she couldn't get a grip. And she was definitely going to need a shower at the end. However, for the most part, she made good progress.

Finally, she reached the nucleus in the centre. It resembled a walnut the size of a house and was connected to the mesoskeleton by several dozen converging struts. Ann jumped down on top of it, grabbed a piece of the walnut cladding and ripped it off. It felt like tree bark. Underneath lay petite magnetic bottles for antimatter storage, along with baby stelarators, processor bundles and goodness knows what else. Ann fought her way through them all to find what she was looking for: a suitcase-sized sphere of corrugated silver covered in forked cooling prongs.

Her hands actually bled as she ripped the thing out. It took all her strength to dislodge it. And it weighed a ton. There had to be some novel metals in there. But now it lay within her grasp. All she had to do was figure out a way to get it to the shuttle.

Ann leaned against the pit of ruined machinery she'd created and grinned at how ridiculous that idea was. She laughed out loud. This was the most satisfying thing she'd done in years and it didn't even involve killing.

[Why?] said her shadow. [Think about it. Why does this make you glad?]

Because it felt like progress. It wasn't something she'd seen or done before. And besides, she had her prize.

'Are you happy now?' came Judj's crackling, disapproving voice.

'Yes,' said Ann. 'Very.'

[You know what I think?] said her shadow slyly. [I think Ira would be proud of you right now. You're actually living.]

Ann snorted. [Who cares what Ira thinks?]

[You do. You can't lie to me, remember?]

[I assure you,] she insisted, [I don't need a reminder about that fossil's lecturing.]

[Fossil?] her shadow exclaimed. [Don't make me laugh. You admire him. Or you did, back when you used to let yourself think that way.]

Ann refused to be baited. It would only lessen her satisfaction in the moment. And her joy was worth savouring. With a little luck, this would be their ticket to peace. She'd take it back to the *Dantes*, turn them around, and then, maybe, win the war.

8.4: IRA

Ira's simulant stepped through the pressure lock and into the alien habitat. With his shadow running interference, the sensation of being there was almost perfect. Part of him wished it wasn't. He could hear his breath in the simulant's helmet and feel his hands rubbing against the gloves. As he moved into the darkness beyond the circular doorway, it felt like walking through a wardrobe into a sort of bleak, extra-terrestrial Narnia.

The insectile scoutbot leading the way activated its floodlight and suddenly Ira could see properly. Behind the obstructing lens of the door lay a near-spherical room the size of a modest canteen. The walls were covered with some kind of stippled plastic, decorated with a brown-on-brown marbled pattern. Thoroughly normal-looking racks on either side of them contained equipment and vac-suit parts. The suits themselves were rather more exotic. They had the same lumpen, ape-like profile he'd seen before, with the same curiously enlarged dome-helmets.

The door lens was supported on an elegantly designed – but perfectly mundane – track system. But for the foreign details, the space felt surprisingly anticlimactic. The room's most enigmatic feature was another circular opening on the far side that led into the lightless interior of the bubble-pyramid.

'Let's stay careful,' he told Clath. 'Alien technology has a habit of being unpredictable.'

Through her helmet, he could see the generic female features of her simulant. She nodded in response.

'No assumptions,' she said, and set the small fleet of robots they'd brought with them bouncing across the room. Behind them, a waldobot was establishing the first of their line-of-sight relays – the tether optically linking them to the shuttle.

'I'm seeing lead deposits on these surfaces,' said Clath as she scanned the robots' reports. 'Very fine ones. You know what that means, don't you?'

'No idea,' said Ira.

'This is what you see after a habitat suicides with radon. It's a simple technique for keeping Photes out – they used it at New Angeles when the Hope Brigade made their last stand. You pump the gas in with your air. Nobody notices until they can't breathe. It's a relatively painless way to go and it leaves a radioactive mess that the Photes can't clean up. This atmosphere must be what's left of a toxic noble mix.'

'Then we know almost everything already,' said Ira bitterly. 'How did they die? They killed themselves. Why? Because they knew the Photes were coming, just like the Hope Brigade did. Which is why we saw harvester ships outside. And how did they get into this mess? That one's not hard, either: they messed with a Phote world, just like we did. Hence the biosphere we found. Case closed.' He shook his head in disgust.

Clath nodded. 'Looks that way. And from the condition of the atmosphere and these deposits, I'd guess it happened a while back – at least one-point-two million years. Some of these plastics are showing decay that must have taken for ever under these conditions. This climate is designed to keep things stable. I suspect this place was even carefully chilled. It's like atmospheric embalming.'

'They made a memorial to themselves,' said Ira.

While Clath studied the room, he followed the lighting-bot into the shadowed gloom of the next chamber. As he did so, lamps flashed into life overhead. Ira reflexively covered his eyes with his glove, momentarily blinded by the glare.

'Clath, stay back!' he warned. But as more and more illumination flickered into life, he realised that he'd done little more than trigger a motion detector. 'Apparently we have circuits in here that are still working,' he added.

'Clearly,' Clath remarked. 'Not surprising, though. This place was designed for stability and it was nearly perfectly protected. Plus they have ideal materials for controlled solar collection, so there's no reason why that stuff shouldn't be operational.'

'If there are defences, that's going to be an issue,' Ira pointed out.

As he lowered his hand, he found himself standing at the edge of a huge enclosure that filled the building's interior. It looked, if anything, like a park in winter. Nothing fired at him. Nothing even moved. A frozen lake stretched before him from which lonely clusters of slender artificial trees arose. They were huge, their tips almost reaching the silvered, bubbled ceiling about eighty metres up. In their branches nestled clusters of polygons made of carved wooden panels, connected by elegant spiralling ramps and complex ladders.

'Holy shit,' said Clath, stepping in behind him. 'Buckminster Fuller tree houses.'

Ira walked forwards to where the plastic pavement ended and the ice began. He tested it with his foot. It was entirely solid. The path they were standing on led around the edge of the lake. Ira waited for the line-of-sight relays to establish a stable link and then set off, accompanied by their small fleet of robots. He primed their defensive systems, just in case.

As it was, nothing disturbed them as they wandered the frozen estate. The place was beautiful even in death. The Fecund had been a cruel, pragmatic species, he recalled. They exploited everything they came upon. These people, though, whoever they were, had been artists in a very human sense.

Ira paused by a polygonal hut situated at the edge of the lake. Cut from something like burled walnut, complex mandala patterns had been carved into the panels and inlaid with silver. Situated on either side of the wide, low doorway were stalks of a metallic substance with integrated displays that came to swirling, incomprehensible life as he approached. The whole thing felt like a gallery exhibit.

'They had all this science but they used wood for building?' said Clath. 'There's a weird mix of high and low tech in use here.'

'That's not weird,' said Ira. 'It's *taste*. These people liked a nice environment. They made aesthetic choices.'

Nothing about the environment looked quite right to human eyes – everything struck Ira as being either too squat or too tall – yet it still managed to be attractive. Ira glanced around at the stately lines he saw everywhere and couldn't fight the sense that in some odd way, these people had been *better* than humans. Classier, somehow.

The whole place was a study in whites, blacks and muted shades of brown. Was that a deliberate style choice, or had the inhabitants simply seen differently? Maybe, before they'd died, this place had been a riot of colour.

'Look,' said Clath, pointing to a raised platform ahead of them. Draped onto the ramp that led up to it was something that might have been an arm.

Ira walked closer. Clath followed. At the top of the ramp lay an open, paved area with views out over the lake. Limp brown banners hung from a fountain-like structure at the centre. And all around them were bodies. Lots of bodies. Most of them were holding hands.

Physically, the aliens roughly resembled apes, as Ira had expected, but there the resemblance ended. These creatures were exoskeletal. Leathery plates the colour of mahogany and studded with coarse hairs covered their bodies. They looked like coconut crabs that had grown too big and taken on airs. But even that strangeness paled in comparison to their heads.

The aliens had curious, caved-in skulls with things like armoured aphids nestled where their brains should have been. Here and there, the aphid things had come loose and lay detached on the floor, curled in on themselves. Complex pads on their abdomens were covered with millions of tiny cilia.

Ira wondered how the relationship worked. Was this mutualism or parasitism? The gorilla-crab bodies were ugly and strange, but Ira couldn't help staring at their almost-human hands. They had died with digits entwined, and because of that, Ira could see nothing in these beings except their humanity.

A sick, sad feeling of inevitability washed over him. This fate was coming for his people, too. Goodbyes. Mass deaths. The end of all things. It was the Suicide War all over again.

He suddenly felt a desperate urge to extract some kind of win from this mausoleum. He stared up at the silvered ceiling and drew a heavy breath. Why had the Transcended bothered to let them see this? The Photes didn't need to be shown their own triumph; they were doing just fine without it. So the clue had to be for humanity, didn't it? Except what was there to see here except despair?

'What's the secret?' he yelled at the ceiling. 'Come on, you fuckers! What's the answer this time?'

The tomb didn't answer.

Clath regarded him with concern. 'Are you okay?' she asked.

Ira shook his head. Back in his real body, trapped in the shuttle, long-delayed tears started pooling in his eyes.

'Yes, fine,' he lied. 'Just fine.'

She laid a hand on his shoulder.

Their shuttle-management SAP chose that moment to ping them.

'Warp-light has been detected at the edge of the system,' it informed them. 'Nineteen milliseconds later, the following broadcast was received on the truce channel.'

'Human explorers,' said an enthusiastic female voice, 'your journey has been a success! Whatever happiness or freedom you sought out here, be assured that it now lies within your reach. Everlasting love has come to find you.'

The Photes had caught up. Ira blinked himself back into focus and saw Clath's face fall as her features creased in panic.

'No!' she said. 'This can't be happening. The Photes don't do revenge. They shouldn't be here!' She clutched her helmet. 'Ohmygodohmygod.'

'How many sources?' said Ira.

'Currently registering fifty-three vessels,' said the shuttle.

Against all odds, the Photes had tailed them through the Flaw. And now he and Clath were closest to the edge of the system, exposed in a shuttle with barely a weapon between them. Worse, it'd be over an hour before the warp-light of Phote arrival reached Mark and the others in the depths of the in-system. That meant they were on their own against an armada, with rescue up to half a day away. Suddenly the mysteries of the alien ruins felt like the least of their problems.

8.5: NADA

The Photurian fleet that left the Depleted Zone was not the one that had entered it. Its size, spirit and driving logic had all changed. A different Nada watched, steely-eyed, from the edge of the system where the human ship lurked, ready to dispense enlightenment. The presence of so many unusual artefacts didn't faze her. Neither did the curious arrangement of the system itself. Why would the Transcended have tried to keep them away unless there was something here worth finding? And why else would the humans have been so keen to come?

As soon as she and Leng had realised the steps they needed to take, they also knew there wasn't a moment to lose. Further drift between ships would have cut off their viable options altogether. So, on the same day that she understood their predicament, Nada made the excruciating adaptations.

She had communed despite the pain, sharing her soul-scraping disappointment at joy deferred. The others had smiled and screamed with her, rocking and biting themselves even as their souls sang. Then she'd sent home those ships that hadn't impacted the bulk. Without a warp-trail to follow, they were effectively blind. Leaving them in the Flaw served no purpose.

The remaining ships, she consolidated – transferring fuel and robust units to those vessels most likely to survive the long passage through dead space. It was a small blessing that the distances between some of her trapped vessels were measured in mere hours.

Once the consolidation was complete, she instructed the depleted ships to also head back, but for them the voyage would entail anything from weeks to years, depending on their fuel and fortune. As a gesture of mercy, Nada permitted merging for those returning crews, since they were unlikely to make it out intact in any case.

The effects were almost instantaneous. The ships she liberated dropped contact within minutes. Nada hoped that a few of them would make it to the other side before War Fatigue claimed them entirely.

A few scant days after she'd made her cuts and her crew had endured their first round of torture therapy, word arrived that the humans had made a shortcut through the bulk. Signs of their quarry vanished as they warped away from the other side. All that remained for Nada to do was to match the human exit point and follow their warp-trail out of the Zone.

Nada had been rendered speechless by the ironic turn of events. She had cut her strength in half without needing to. A second, long communing was necessary to prevent the outright malfunction of her crews. But what came out of that process surprised them all. Their union had awoken a very focused kind of joy that was sharp, intentional and extremely personal. They'd all changed a little.

Leng turned inwards, becoming quieter and less combative as he reconciled himself to their new purpose. Zilch, by contrast, sprang into life. Their new sense of directed zeal encouraged a broader kind of thinking from him, more nuanced and less automatic. And Nada had been forced to reflect on the Yunus's edits and the unit she'd become.

She admitted to herself that he'd perhaps not been fully rational when he made his changes. In part, perhaps, because of his own strong feelings about the characters involved. He'd imparted some pain of his own – a cryptic twist of attitude that she couldn't quite put her finger on. It wasn't as simple as wanting to destroy the Abomination. It was more subtle and buried than that.

However, she also saw that while the Yunus hadn't been rational, he'd been wiser and greater than even *he* understood. Ending humanity's false heroes was the more important goal. The fate of Earth's population was a passing matter in a long game. The persistence of the false heroes, however, was crucial. Until they were either removed or converted, the child race they sheltered would keep defying the Yunus and delaying their inevitable leap into maturity.

So while she acknowledged the conflict of ambitions that had troubled both Leng and herself, she knew now that she and her crews had become a weapon of the Yunus's true – if unconscious – goal. And because of that, she no longer felt alone. Instead, she felt like the tip of a spear. She was ready to kill, even if the act killed her. They all were.

Now she hung in the main crew-bulb where she'd been spending more of her time, watching her ships and munitions disperse into the foreign system. She felt ready for the fight that was coming. Nothing about this mission had been easy. But if they finished it, it would at least have been worth it.

At last, reports from the advance scouts started returning. Nada listened to her crew and watched the attendant images from the mind-temple in parallel. She felt comfortable doing that now. Many of the Yunus's dictates had been reinterpreted to fit their altered circumstances.

'Unfamiliar technologies have been detected,' said Zilch. 'The probability of encountering an ally race for humanity is being assessed.'

Nada watched visions of curious artificial moons flash past and wasn't worried. She'd half-expected something new. The humans would be poaching off the dead, as usual.

'Probable coordinates for the target vessel have been obtained,' Zilch went on. 'Insertion into a Goldilocks orbit occurred less than one standard day ago.'

Nada smiled. She had them.

'A biosphere world has been detected. Atmospheric signatures are being analysed.'

There was a long pause. Zilch let out a shriek, wild and full-throated. His body thrashed against the wall of the bulb.

'Report!' said Nada, while looking for herself. The image from the lead scout's forward telescope array made her thoughts stutter into white noise.

'A Photurian world has been discovered!' Zilch sang. 'The presence of true homes has been detected via planetary surface texture!'

A stream of golden urine spilled out of his body, much to the distress of the nearby maintenance lice.

'Explain!' said Leng.

His avatar-bead appeared next to Nada's in the temple. It quivered with excess emotion as he drank the data in.

'A home!' he keened.

A mature home? Their one, true hope? Nada couldn't believe what she was seeing. Chasing humans registered as a pale irrelevance compared to claiming such a boon for her people. She scanned the data, and scanned it and scanned it again. The verdict was indisputable.

Thinking quickly, Nada checked the functionality of her units in the lead scout to make sure that their discovery hadn't rendered them inoperative. It wouldn't have surprised her. She sent them gentle edits, infusing them with calm, orderly thoughts.

256

What should she make of this astounding find? Something cried out in her to visit it immediately. Just looking at the place was like standing in a mental riptide. However, her recent experiences had done nothing if not consolidate her willpower. Nada forced herself to return full awareness to her body in the crew-bulb.

'Crew,' she said breathlessly. 'We will now verbally confer.'

One by one, they opened their eyes. Many of them were crying like humans, which was perhaps natural under the circumstances.

'I solicit opinions,' she said. 'We must ensure interpersonal alignment prior to any attack.'

'This is a vindication of our hard efforts,' said Zilch, his lip quivering. 'This is the prize that the humans have hidden from us. We will reclaim it and joy will be immense and all-consuming.'

'Leng,' said Nada. 'Speak.'

Leng blinked at her, his brow wrinkling as if in pain. 'The risks incurred by violent operations in this system are different than anticipated,' he said.

He scratched at the burns on his arms. Surprisingly, everyone aboard had decided to stick to the torture regimen after their second communion. It represented something of a commitment to their new shared goal. Leng had been more fervent than most.

'Yes,' said Nada. 'This is unexpected. We must be careful.'

'I also doubt Zilch's assessment,' he added. 'I am not certain that the humans knew about this locale. It is possible they are as surprised as we are.'

'Incorrect,' said Zilch. 'We encountered elderly buoys.'

The discovery of the buoys had been an important moment for her units. It had tightened their resolve still further. The assessment had been that whatever facility the humans had hidden out here must have been a secret for a long, long time.

'Yet human tactics to date revealed no knowledge of this site,' said Leng. 'Not once has mention of it arisen in diplomatic dialogue.'

'The humans are secretive,' said Zilch.

'But also disorganised,' said Leng.

'But also cunning.'

'What I am saying is that predictive models of their behaviour must include scenarios in which they are startled and irrational,' Leng asserted. 'That is all.'

'Enough,' Nada told them. 'Our joyous momentum cannot be allowed to falter. Zilch, plan battle scenarios that favour interactions minimising in-system damage. Include models such as those Leng outlines. Scan for the target ship accordingly, making efforts to lure them out. Leng, initiate a safe close-pass study of the new homeworld. More data on its status is required. We should assume nothing.'

She glanced around at the others. They stared at her wordlessly.

'Everyone remember,' she said. 'While the humans remain alive, our new prize is at risk. Therefore we must satisfy our original objective *prior* to thorough analysis of the home. The Abomination must die first. Then, and only then, can we begin the gleeful and magnificent reconciliation our hearts desperately crave. Is that clear?'

Her crew nodded their assent. Her ships adjusted course and began to tighten the net.

9: CONFLICTION

9.1: WILL

Will couldn't sleep after what he'd seen. Every time he shut his eyes, he saw an army of Truist monks with his face and shuddered. He no longer doubted that the Underground were keeping dark truths about the Willworld from him. On the other hand, Moneko had saved his life. Without her and John, he'd be even more lost than he already was. It just wasn't clear whether their motivations meshed with his own.

By the time he met Moneko in the park the following morning, he felt ready to deliver an ultimatum. Either he got some honest answers or he was finished with truth diving. As it was, she beat him to it. She rose from the bench where she'd waited for him and opened with an apology.

'Will, I'm sorry,' she said, looking grave. 'That last dive was horrible. You're probably upset and you have every right to be. We've been hiding things and that's not acceptable. Today, if you let me, I'm going to answer any questions I can. In return, I'd like to show you something I think will help. Does that work?'

Will had expected to have to push for confessions. He reminded himself to stop underestimating Moneko.

'Sure,' he said warily. 'So long I'm convinced by the answers.' If whatever lines she fed him didn't pass the smell test, it'd be over.

She nodded. 'Great. In that case, let's walk. No diving today. We can talk as we go.' They started down the hill towards the station.

'Let's start with the monks,' Will said heavily. 'I'm not a Truist and

I never have been. Their creed is...' he struggled for a rational way to put it '...antithetical to mine. So why are they even here?'

'I'll answer that with a question, if I may,' she said. 'How much do you still hate the Truists?'

'Plenty. That's my point.'

'Have you ever fantasised about killing more of them?'

Will frowned. 'You know I have. I'm not proud of it.'

'So there's your answer.'

'I don't get it.'

'They're iconic,' she said. 'A pivotal feature of our story. They hurt us more than anyone else. Of course you wanted to explore that feeling. So you did. What you saw was what happened to those poor Wills who drew the short straw in your attempt to figure out your anger issues. Their job was to become the whipping boys of your past. They didn't choose that path, just like I didn't initially choose to be female. It simply happened that way.

'But those Wills were *so* hated that they became marginalised. Nothing existed for them except to be despised. And after the world lost its stability, they turned on the rest of us. The only way they could think of to have a voice was to start illegally self-copying. That way, they'd make up a larger percentage of Balance and could force others to treat them with respect.

'That's how Cancer happens, Will. It's when people want to cut the corners of government and take more control than they're due. Sometimes it's a variant who feels despised or isolated. Other times, it's a Will who's dabbling so hard in counter-culture that he tips over into real crime. Often it's just a version of you who's really into power or money. The result is the same – hate-filled clones you'd barely recognise.'

'Then why are they still here?' Will demanded. 'Why doesn't Balance root them out?'

'Because they breed like rabbits,' Moneko replied. 'And they know how to hide.'

'You found those monks pretty easily.'

'I'm trained,' she retorted. 'And the patterns keep changing. Some Cancers make new instances and keep them hidden. Other, more violent kinds will husk out fellow threads to steal their identity. Anything to pump their numbers without making it obvious. And they all loathe

the Underground. Every time you find them, you try to kill them, Will. So they have every reason to revile Glitches and to resent an organisation that exists to support them. That means we get caught up in anti-Cancer action from time to time. I should have warned you. My bad.'

She sounded genuinely contrite. Will found it hard to doubt her.

'So those clones were *made* into Truists?'

'At first, yes.'

He shook his head in disgust. 'That's revolting. In a civilised society, people get to choose their gender and religion, Moneko,' he said. 'That's how it works.'

She nodded. 'Right. Totally true. We fucked that up. That's why we have the whole branch-request economy going now – to encourage diversity based on *choice*. Copy-gifting has helped a lot.'

'I've been wondering about that, too,' he said. 'Are you sure you don't mean *slavery*?'

She shook her head fiercely. 'No. It's contracting. Everyone here is free. Okay, some unpleasant contracts get finite-term, limited-rights copies, but they're always made according to the stipulated conditions of the original.'

'But who decides?' Will pressed. 'Who gets to pick which one is the copy?'

'The thread and their new instance,' said Moneko. 'One becomes primary and the other the copy-gift. It's consensual.'

'But then what happens?'

'The gift goes to work for whoever requested the copy. The primary retains their autonomy.'

'And if the gift changes their mind about being used?'

'That's allowed, depending on the contract they signed up for. The gift can be terminated, liberated or merged. Most often, the gift's memories just get filtered back into their primary once the job is over.'

'And if the gift gets duped into doing something shitty?'

'That also happens,' said Moneko. 'Which is why we have recourse to Balance. He's not just there to chase us around, you know.'

'That's another thing,' said Will. 'A police force that you can get rid of by simply *preferring* they not show up? How in fuck's name is that supposed to work?'

'It's not so easy to make him look away,' said Moneko. 'You need a critical mass of dissent, locally dominant and persistent.'

'But still,' said Will, 'if I have a town full of secretly committed anarchists who all want to blow shit up, that's *okay*?'

'Of course. How else would we explore anarchism, Will? Balance is there to foster exploration, not stifle it. And if a bunch of threads get knocked back into soft-space, is that so bad?' She fixed him with an earnest look. 'We've tried other models. This one works. A variant that gets a lot of branch requests fills a need. Their voice is *wanted* by the consensus, so they can ask for favours. Everywill benefits.'

Will shook his head. Moneko and her people were simply a different species. One based on him but somehow deeply foreign.

He fell into quiet contemplation, so she gave him room to think. He found himself walking through the bustling streets once more, past the vendors setting up shop and the variform pedestrians in their archaic coats – each utterly absorbed in their own peculiar, diverging lives. It occurred to him that he didn't even understand how they carried out that process of self-change.

'Tell me more about the talents you've been hiding from me,' he said. 'Like the smart-cells and everything else. Why don't I have them? Why aren't you giving them out?'

'Baseline is you without powers,' she said. 'A natural, human you makes for a more grounded experience. But everyone has the option of turning their cells back on.'

'Except me, apparently.'

She shot him an amused glance. 'You just haven't really tried yet, which is admirable, by the way. I have a set of memory dumps ready which I'll give you for your next dive. They make it all very clear. I warn you, though: the more tricks you know, the easier it is for Balance to spot you as an anomaly.' She fixed him with another solemn stare. 'Let me repeat that,' she said. 'The more tricks you *know*. Even if you don't use them. Just like the environment leaks into you when you're down there, you leak into it. But on a second dive, we always make sure you have a proper set of tools. That's just how it goes. On the first dive you always rush off half-cocked. Second time around you're more cautious.'

'And what *is* the second dive?' said Will. 'What do you actually want me to do?'

'Look for suntaps,' she said, 'just like you did before. By which I mean pieces of code with the same metaphor footprint.'

'How many are there?'

Moneko offered him a half-smile. 'Thousands.'

His eyebrows rose in disbelief.

'I know what you're thinking,' she said. 'Why would the Transcended need more than one? Well, there's no evidence the Transcended ever had anything to do with them. They just look that way because The History informs our metaphors. Not one suntap we've found contains the magic link you're always looking for.'

He didn't understand. 'Then what's their purpose? Are they dummies? What is this, some kind of shell game?'

'Oh no, Will. They have a clear purpose. They pump out a stabilising signal that affects the local cognitive environment. They're like anchors. Whatever piece of the Underlayer they're wired up to is immune to update. You already know that we influence Balance. Well, it cuts the other way, too. Balance influences us. When he grows, we grow with him. And that Underlayer you visit is like his subconscious, which means that changes in the Underlayer affect how everyone upstairs thinks. Illegally boosting your copy-count isn't the only way to affect the world. You can do it by moving anchors around instead – picking which ideas are or aren't open for scrutiny.' She pointed at his chest. 'Except only you can do that, Will. Most clones don't even realise the anchors are there. The Underground knows about them because you told us.'

Software that prevented his clones from contesting certain ideas? That smacked to him of Transcended involvement, even if Moneko didn't believe it.

'We should rip them all out,' he said. 'Whoever fucking put them there.'

'Except they appear to maintain our sanity,' she said. 'They're mostly positioned in the Underlayer at sites that tightly relate to our social axioms. We think the anchors are what hold our society together.'

That sounded like a generous interpretation to Will's ear. No wonder they couldn't escape the Willworld if it was littered with mind-hacks to prevent everyone from wanting to leave. Sanity was the least likely outcome.

'Your mission, if you choose to accept it,' said Moneko, 'is to seek

263

out the anchors that stabilise those axioms and map them. Trying to get rid of them causes trouble, but we've discovered that we *can* safely move them about, which is a start.'

'Why bother?' said Will. 'How does mapping help?'

'Every Glitch who's tried to fix the world has gone at it unilaterally. They rip out a few anchors but there are always more, so they get caught. We think that's why there are so many – to make change almost impossible. To create a real revolution, you'd have to rip them all out at once. Either that or move enough of them to memory sites that don't obstruct social change. Anyone with a map of their locations has an incredibly powerful tool for making a better world. Or a way out. That person could be you.'

'But why bother finding these copies at all? The Transcended must still have a master original somewhere, pumping out a control signal.'

'If there is, nobody's ever found it, and they've looked a *lot*. Please consider the possibility that it doesn't exist, and that in your own way you're as deluded as the rest of us.'

'Right,' said Will. 'Deluded.'

'Here's another way of thinking about it,' she offered. 'If there is a master copy, it's going to be a lot easier to find once we've minimised the resistance to looking, wouldn't you say? And that requires planning and coordination. But now we're getting near to the station. I recommend that you stick close and stay quiet till we're through the search gate.'

Will fell silent. Moneko had given him answers he believed – so how come he still didn't feel comfortable with the world? Probably, he reflected, because there was nothing to feel comfortable about. The Willworld stank of wrongness like week-old fish.

At the station, the number of Balance agents had almost doubled since their last visit. Even if the god couldn't notice the Underground, some part of him had clearly figured out that the activity in Mettaburg was related to yesterday's disaster. Moneko's face was stony as they made their way past the guards to the transit-graves.

Once in soft-space, they headed for the search corridors without a word.

'Demolition Derby,' she told their corridor.

'He's closing in, isn't he?' Will said once the door had shut.

She nodded. 'We can't afford another fuck-up. Our whole operation

264

could be exposed. After we make the jump, keep a low profile, okay? Where we're going always has a heavy Balance presence, but there's no other way to show this to you.'

He nodded as she picked an exit. They emerged at the entrance to another soft-space station. This one had a huge bubble-display floating in the forecourt, showing two huge, armoured monstrosities smashing each other to pieces in slow motion. One was red and white, the other blue and yellow. Several clones stood around, watching and cheering.

'This way,' said Moneko.

She took him past the crowd to the arrivals area. They woke in transit-graves at a busy physical terminus where clones in matching colours hung about in groups, talking animatedly.

'Fans,' she said, as if that explained everything.

Beyond the station doors lay a plaza open to a cold, blue sky. At the other end of it stood an outsized replica of the Colosseum in Rome with hundreds of clones streaming through its doors. Behind it towered the face of what could only be a defensive node – a huge, gleaming wall of living ceramic several hundred storeys high in mottled shades of ochre. It curved around to either side of them, enclosing both the station and Colosseum on either side. The entire complex where they were standing had apparently been built in the armpit between two of the vast structure's factory-limbs.

Will felt a moment's fear. Of course there was going to be a lot of Balance here. Moneko had brought him to a weapons factory.

He shot her a worried glance. 'Is this really a good idea?'

'I hope so,' she replied.

She led him into the stadium, past another pair of Balance agents and up the ranked seats that surrounded the arena floor. Will saw room for at least a hundred thousand clones, but today the place only looked about a quarter-full.

The performance area was lined with black glass. Huge Wills in grey body-armour moved back and forth across it, scouring the surface using broad rakes with blowtorch nozzles for tines. Overhead, display bubbles hovered showing advertisements for various kinds of clone-contract or identity-mod.

'Perfect timing,' said Moneko. 'They're starting a fresh bout.' She walked him to the rows at the very back before sitting down. 'The high seats are better,' she informed him. 'You're much less likely to die. Balance monitors body-loss closely here. Dying unnecessarily is a bad idea.'

The husky voice of a female Will came over the stadium loudspeaker.

'Please take your seats for the next fight,' she said. 'But first, a word from our illustrious Meta.'

The floating displays all swapped to a view of their haunted-looking leader. He wore the same crazy uniform as last time, complete with gleaming medals the size of saucers.

'Why does he wear that?' Will whispered as a hush fell over the crowd.

'Why do you suppose?' said Moneko. 'To make a joke out of what he's become. I think it's hard enough for him to manage that level of responsibility as it is. It gives me hope, frankly. If we had a Meta who looked like he was entitled to that much power, or wasn't scared of it, I'd probably turn Cancerous in a minute.'

'Denizens of the Willworld,' said Balance, his voice echoing around the enormous space. 'Thank you for coming to participate in today's military unit testing. What you witness here will help us refine our defensive technologies to fend off the next wave of attacks from our unpleasant neighbours.' He leaned forward, his expression hungry. 'But unit testing is more than that. The bodies you see here will carry us forth from this world when the time comes. The power we nurture will ensure that the Photurian menace is wiped from the galaxy. And in its place, a new empire will arise, bold and good. The empire of Willkind, my friends. The human race that should have been. The future begins here.'

He relaxed, his craziness subsiding a little. 'Remember, any observations from today's contests that you wish to share can be donated at the local station. I encourage you all to watch using a wavelength and frame-rate you haven't tried before. And my apologies in advance for any body-loss that may occur. Thank you for your time and happy watching. Let the games recommence.'

The displays fell dark and rose into the sky.

'Ladies and Gentlewills,' said the female announcer, 'witness the experimental and entirely untested might of Odin Four-Three-Eight-Nine-Seven!'

A door opened on the far side of the arena and a three-metre-tall clone covered in green spiked armour strode forth from the shadows. Cheers broke out from the assembled crowd.

'Confronting him this morning is the terror-inspiring alpha-release that is Ravana Seven-Seven-Six-Two!'

Another clone appeared, this one four metres tall in scarlet and gold, armed with four sets of shoulder cannons and limbs ending in scythes. The two combatants looked ridiculously small given the amount of space they had to fight in.

'Audience members,' said the announcer to the ebullient crowd, 'please brace yourselves. Combat testing will commence in three seconds, two ... one ...'

The speed with which the two monsters burst into action took Will entirely by surprise. The gladiators fell on each other in an instant, the impact of their bodies filling the stadium with a weird shrieking, grinding sound. There were bursts of light and blasts of flame. Everyone sitting in the first three rows caught fire. Will was buffeted by a wave of heat and started to leap out of his chair. Moneko held him down.

'Don't,' she said. 'That always happens. The clones in the front rows sit there on purpose.'

Will gawped as Ravana blasted Odin into pieces, but that was when the fight really started. In the same second, Odin's spikes radiated outwards, growing wings to become a swarm of independent munitions. They ripped through the air, half of them descending on Ravana and nuking him into shrapnel. The shrapnel melted and became several hundred slugs of living slime. They sprang into the air, binding to Odin's wheeling torpedoes.

'Holy fuck!' Will exclaimed. 'What are they *made* of?'

Whatever molecular technology comprised the gladiators made his smart-cell architecture look positively gentle.

'Weaponised pseudo-life,' said Moneko. 'The same tech this planet uses to construct drones, but refined and evolved by us over thousands of rapid generations. It's basically combat nanotech.'

Odin's remaining weapons thundered into the ground, where they reshaped and formed themselves into a miniature citadel armed with energy weapons. As Ravana's slugs raced towards it, Odin seared the surrounding floor until it melted. Will was forced to look away as another white-hot burst of light left his eyes flash-blind.

'Christ!' he blurted as his vision slowly returned.

By the time he could see again, the battle was over. Everyone in the front rows had been reduced to ash. A jagged black column thirty centimetres high was all that remained on the testing ground.

'Odin wins by seven per cent remaining material,' said the announcer calmly. 'Well done, Odin!'

While Will stared at the smoking remains, Moneko faced him. Her hair was singed. Burn marks on her face were rapidly subsiding. He doubted he looked much better.

'I wanted you to see this so that you'd understand the stakes,' she said. 'Those anchors I told you about? They're the only thing stopping *that* from leaving this planet. Balance can't innovate with space-based weapons at the moment because of his own axioms, so he's concentrated on molecular tech. But what we can do now is terrifying. These are the *little* weapons we're tinkering with. The ones you can watch and still live. Once the Willworld is ready, Balance will explode across this part of the galaxy. Everything in his path is going to die. And right now, the version of Balance we have doesn't believe in the human race.'

'What?' said Will scowling. 'How do you mean?'

'He thinks it's all a dream, remember? The human race is something to aspire to – a vision to build, not something that already *is*. So if you're right, and humanity exists somewhere out there, he's going to think it's another trick. I doubt it'll last very long. That's why we're mapping anchors, Will. So that when the locks come off, the god that leaves here is the sanest, most Glitch-compatible kind we can muster. I'm hoping you'll help us do that, because the alternative scares me, even though my brain is part of him.'

9.2: IRA

Ira stared at Clath's simulant and thought fast. Their shuttle lay out in the open with a Phote armada minutes away. If they weren't careful, the Photes would spot them from their infrared signature alone.

'I'm a fool,' said Clath. 'I didn't want to admit this could happen. Christ, I'm such a fucking fool.'

'Don't go there,' said Ira. 'We made the best risk assessment we could – together.'

He pulled his mind back to his real body in the shuttle and brought up a scan of local space. They needed somewhere to hide and had just seconds to find it. Given the light-lag, Mark and the others still wouldn't know what had happened for over an hour.

'We need cover,' he told Clath. 'Our shuttle's very obvious right now. Any chance we could make use of all that effective rad-shielding you were talking about? It has to be close.'

'Let's hope,' she said, frantically checking her data. 'Okay! I think I have something. We go straight up.'

Ira checked the shuttle's top camera. It afforded them an amazing view of the nearest false-matter tether stretching away like a silk strand spun by the god of all spiders. At the top of it hung one of the ark-ships they'd spotted. From this angle he could see a large opening in the bottom, like a giant's version of the entry portal they'd just used to explore the habitat.

'It's big enough,' said Ira.

'If the shielding on that ship is anything like the structure we were just in, it'll be perfect. I didn't even notice the hole was there until after we landed.'

Ira wasted no time. He severed connections with their robots and took the shuttle up as fast as he dared.

'What about the pressure lock?' said Clath. 'Are we just going to leave it behind?'

'It's tiny,' said Ira. 'If they can spot *that* from a speeding starship, they deserve to find us.'

'Wait! If we hide up there, how's Mark going to know where we are?'

'There are protocols for that sort of thing,' said Ira. 'Mark's a big boy. He knows where we went and he'll know we looked for solid cover. We just need to make sure we leave passive marker beacons he can ping with an encrypted signal when he gets close.'

'You mean like microsats,' said Clath.

Ira groaned. He'd just left most of their beacons on the ground.

'Fuck,' he said. 'Who's the idiot now? Still, we can manage. We just need to be careful where we station the ones we have left.' It wasn't a great solution but it'd have to do.

The opening in the alien ship, when they reached it, did not look how Ira had expected. For starters, the thing had teeth. And the inside was awfully dark, as if shadows clung to it.

'Okay,' said Ira as they slid up past the metallic jaws. 'That's creepy.'

'I think it's a retractable warp-inducer surface of some kind,' said Clath.

'This thing has warp?' said Ira. 'It doesn't have any brollies.'

The darkness swallowed them as they flew inside. The shuttle's searchlights played across the throat of the hole as they glided carefully upwards. The walls of the enclosure were a cryptic tangle of baroque alien machinery held behind a glossy rainbow skin of false matter. Normal starships were full of empty spaces. By contrast, this craft had been crammed tight with nothing he understood – right down to the last millimetre.

'If this is a warp-ship, shouldn't we be passing mesohull accelerators right now?' he said.

She shook her head. 'Maybe they're hidden. Or maybe this is some kind of mini-embership. I'm not sure. I can't tell what this thing does. All the machinery looks wrong.'

'Agreed,' said Ira. 'But that's a problem for later,' he said. 'Surviving cats get to be curious.'

'What do you think this hole is for?' said Clath as their view of the moon shrank beneath them between the silhouetted fangs of the enclosure. She practically whispered. Something about the lightless space around them demanded reverence. 'A docking bay? Drone storage?'

'No idea,' said Ira.

At the top of the hole, the tunnel took a sharp right, leading to a narrow passage lined with metal scaffolding. Ira flew the shuttle gingerly into the silvered darkness and parked the ship against one of the lattices. Grappling was easier than he'd expected, as if that was what the frames were for.

The shuttle locked tight. But for the ticking of the hull, there was now only silence. Ira scanned around their ship. Above them, on the inward hull, he noticed circular hatches bearing mandala patterns – airlocks, perhaps.

'Definitely a docking bay,' said Ira.

'Take a look at our sensor spread,' said Clath, awed. 'Look at the whole EM spectrum – all directions.'

Ira did so. From inside the tunnel, almost nothing of the outside universe could be detected, barring the view relayed by the remaining microsats they'd deployed near the entrance. The rest of the universe was utterly, eerily absent from every wavelength. It was like hiding inside the cloak of the Grim Reaper.

'The shielding's nearly perfect,' said Clath. 'If we're not safe here, we won't be anywhere.'

'Let's hope,' said Ira, scanning the incomprehensible machinery that loomed on all sides.

The operational lighting circuits from the bubble-habitat sprang to his mind. Who knew what machinery might still be running in this place – what SAPs might be rousing to subtle, alien thoughts? He forced such notions aside and settled down to wait in the stifling, impenetrable dark.

9.3: MARK

They were about to put Rachel into surgery when the message arrived.

'Human explorers, your journey has been a success...'

Mark swore copiously. His team was split, and by his reckoning they had only about an hour and a half to leave the system before trouble hit.

He dumped himself, Palla and Rachel into helm-space and activated the ship's cloak.

'I never should have okayed this,' he said, shaking his head. 'I knew it was a bad idea to linger.'

'Who's lingering?' said Palla. 'It's only been hours, Mark. Don't blame yourself. Now how about we round everyone up sharpish so we can get the hell out of Dodge?'

'Presuming we still can.'

He checked their tactical SAP and scowled as the problems revealed themselves. They had enough time to retrieve Ann's team from the surface but not to double back for Ira's shuttle. Worse, the part of the system where Ira lay was probably crawling with Photes already. Mark could see at least fifty ship signatures spreading out to dominate local space.

'We have to focus on getting Ann and Judj out first,' said Palla. She opened a warning channel to their shuttle. 'They're that much closer.'

'Agreed,' said Mark. 'But we also need options – defences, decoys, something. This space is way too clear. Right now, we're sitting ducks.'

'Use my ship,' said Rachel. Mark turned to face her, surprised.

She still lay in the hospital bed. If she was fazed by the fact that her room had vanished to be replaced by a wraparound vision of tactical space, she wasn't showing it.

'That's a great idea,' he said. 'With the *Diggory*, we could at least try to draw their fire while we mount a rescue.'

'Sure,' said Palla. 'But what if there are Transcended clues hiding in it? Do we care about that? Or what if the ship's been co-opted, somehow?'

'It's too late to worry about that,' said Mark. 'I'll run it with sand-boxed subminds, if necessary. But with two ships we could set up a distraction. We actually stand a chance of getting Ira and Clath out.' He fixed Palla with a steady gaze. 'I'm going back for them, just so you know. Whatever it takes.'

Palla grinned. Her eyes gleamed. 'Of course,' she said. 'Frankly, I'd expect nothing less of you, Captain Ruiz. You have a certain reputation, you know.'

'I'll help you understand the specs of my ship,' said Rachel. 'I have all the override codes and I can rig it for remote operation. Is that enough? Do you think you can fly both ships at once?'

Mark snorted. 'Just *two* starships? Under only modest combat conditions? I won't even break a sweat.'

'Okay,' said Palla. 'By my reckoning, we have about twenty minutes to get the SAP control-harness together. After that, we'll need to focus on how to hide and collect Ann at the same time.'

'We can do that,' said Rachel. 'I taught Mark how to fly, remember. I know what he needs. I'm looking forward to working him, even from this damned bed. I can't wait to see what he can do these days.'

Mark felt a curious surge of embarrassment at that. It was an emotion out of the deep past that had no place in a battle. In real-life terms he was now older than Rachel, so having an ex-mentor looking over his shoulder shouldn't have bothered him. Apparently, though, some things never changed.

'All you'll see is a blur, Rach,' he said with a half-smile. 'I have more new tricks than you do years in cryo.'

'In the meantime, I'll clear out our robots,' said Palla. 'Let's get to work.'

Mark opened a channel to the *Diggory* and started taking its software apart.

9.4: ANN

Ann had almost finished lowering the backup brain to the floor when the news hit.

'Ann, you need to get out,' said Judj. 'The Photes are coming.'

Ann regarded the pulley system she'd rigged out of fibre-optic line and beta-conduit. She was suspended from one end of a mesoskeletal spar, balanced at forty-five degrees, ten storeys above the curving bowl of the drone's exohull far below.

'I can't really do that now,' she said, annoyed. 'Not safely.'

She gritted her teeth as she lowered the brain another metre. An idea came to her that gave her a rush of twisted satisfaction.

'You should go,' she said. 'I'll catch up.'

Judj paused to comprehend. 'Are you fucking *insane*?' he said. 'Catch up *how*? Are you going to *jump* out of the gravity well?'

'Does it matter?' said Ann. 'I'm indisposed right now and probably wouldn't make it back to the shuttle in time anyway. It's better if you leave. That's safest. And besides, there's something I want to bring with me that isn't super-easy to carry.'

'Ann!' Judj shouted. 'I don't have time to play games. Our exit window is about two minutes deep! We're talking about a full system invasion.'

'Go, really, it's okay,' said Ann. 'I want you to.'

There was a long, painful pause.

'Fine!' he roared. 'That's what I'll do, then!'

She felt a shiver of satisfaction as the subsonic rumble of an emergency take-off passed through the drone's structure. Judj had actually left. She wasn't sure he'd be able to do it.

After he was gone, Ann hummed to herself as she finished lowering the brain to the floor. Then she tied down her cable and descended after it, hand over hand. If she couldn't take her prize back with her, did it

273

matter whether she died here or at Snakepit? This place was as good as any to make an exit. And besides, this way might be a lot more fun.

She knew the Photes would spot the shuttle's landing site from an IR surface scan. People had long since built SAPs optimised to pick out those smears of hot rock shuttles left behind them and Bock Two was bound to receive the lion's share of their attention. So they'd know she'd been here. Would they torch the defensive node from orbit, just to get her? She doubted it. She'd seen how the Photes acted at Snakepit and New Panama. They treated nodes like holy places. And why not? They were full of drone babies.

She'd gambled her life on the fact that her enemies wouldn't dare damage the site even though it was long dead. She had no idea how the Photurians thought about dead homeworlds, or if they even knew that such things were possible. Given how adamant they were about everlasting joy, she suspected they'd be as confused as she was.

Instead, they'd probably be desperate to know what she'd been doing and how much she'd seen. She could use that. The Great Abomination, wandering around in the halls of their most intimate secrets, abusing their dead? Ann chuckled to herself. She wanted to see the looks on their faces before they died.

She pushed the backup brain out through the hole in the exohull and onto the cobwebbed boulevard between the dead drones. Then she sauntered back towards the landing site, leaving her prize waiting on the cracked ceramic behind her.

9.5: NADA

Nada watched her ships deploy across the system with her heart in her mouth. A mature homeworld in the frame raised the stakes of this battle immeasurably.

'I wish to report,' said Leng in shrill, uneven tones.

'Start,' she replied.

He took a few seconds to find the words. Nada watched his hands shake. He grabbed his support umbilicus and squeezed at it.

'The homeworld appears to be in poor condition,' he said.

Nada glared at him. 'What? How? Have the humans damaged it already? I wish to see!'

Leng's avatar-bead met her in the mind-temple before she could access the images.

'Brace yourself,' he croaked. 'It appears to be an advanced case of Fatigue.'

That news came like a punch to the gut.

'Impossible,' she said. 'Complete homeworlds do not experience Fatigue.'

She scanned the images – they said different. The Fatigue-like symptoms were immense and unavoidable. It was by far the worst case she'd ever seen. The planet looked as if it had been rotting for millennia.

'No!' she said. 'This does *not* happen.' Her eyes filled with tears. 'We have Fatigue because we cannot access our homeworld. A complete homeworld has access to the Founder Entity. When there is access to the Founder Entity there is no decay. There is only happiness, eternal and perfect. This image is wrong.'

Everything they'd ever worked for was tied up in that vision – that one day they'd finally raise the human race into loving harmony and do away with the unspeakable Monet. Then they'd all descend in rapture to the blessed homeworld and couple their Protocol hierarchy to the Founder-link waiting there.

From that day forth, peace and kindness would reign. They would love the world and the world would love them. All deviation from that happy vision would be excised instantly and cheerfully. Everyone would be cherished equally and uniformly without deviation or cessation. And it would last until the suns burned out and the galaxy turned to ash. The song of their happiness would ring out long after everything else in the universe had crumbled into dust.

Homeworlds had Founder-links. Founder-links made them immortal. That was the bedrock truth on which the universe turned. And yet the image remained. She wasn't looking at a homeworld so much as the spent shell of one. Nada's joy hung from a thread. What had happened here? Were their sensors malfunctioning?

'Protection of the homeworld is even more paramount than previously stated,' she screamed. 'It must be protected and loved and cherished. And we must discover the cause of this... this... this...' She stopped to flail helplessly against the wall of the crew-bulb. 'If necessary, the joyous orb will be reseeded after the cause of its dysfunction has been ascertained! Its bounteous love will be reactivated!'

Poor homeworld! Who or what had done this? It was against the natural order of all things. It was sickening. Nada had no words.

'On no account should the humans be allowed to further damage the planet,' she ordered breathlessly. She had to believe there was still hope for the place. 'Our second priority is to ensure that the vile humans do not escape.'

She twitched against the wall of the bulb and dug her fingers into its flesh as deeper surface scans came back from their scout-pass.

'We are detecting signs that at least one shuttle landing has already taken place,' Leng wailed. 'Two thermal footprints in the same vicinity have been identified.'

He sent her the picture. One of the landing sites was just outside a defensive node.

Nada screamed again, long and hard this time, ripping at her face with her fingernails until her cheeks bled. The humans had already defiled their tragic, wounded heaven.

'Research crews to the surface!' she shrieked.

Almost as soon as her lead survey ship hit geosync, a human vessel appeared from around the back of the planet. It had avoided notice by the initial scout-pass using a carefully staged polar orbit. Her own ships had also been badly distracted.

The humans hit her survey ships with a barrage of g-rays. The four shuttles that had been released towards the homeworld were vaporised instantly along with several of her best science units.

As Nada watched in outrage, she rediscovered the tight specificity of emotion that they'd found together in the silent wastes of the Depleted Zone.

'The humans choose *this* moment to suicide?' she said. 'Now?'

'That is not a suicide,' said Zilch tightly. 'It is an attack. And that is not the ship we have been chasing. It is a new vessel. One we have never seen before.'

It must have been waiting here for weeks, at least. They'd seen no second warp-trail. There'd been no evidence – no hint of it in the Flaw. With shivering alarm, Nada began to wonder whether a long game had been played against them.

Were the humans somehow responsible for the outrageous damage the homeworld had sustained, despite its apparent age? If so, that was definitely enough cause to warrant cramming their heroes into the same ship. Had she uncovered a plot to destroy all Photurian life, and with it any hope for peace in the galaxy?

'Get me that ship,' she ordered. 'I want its database cores.'

She wondered how many other secrets the humans had been keeping.

10: CONFRONTATION

10.1: MARK

The GSS *Edmond Dantes* tore around the back of the G-class star, its hull groaning under combined gravitational and thermal stress. Even down in the habitat core, they struggled. The immersive virt couldn't hide the thrumming of the tortured ship. Mark could feel it in his bones.

His cover manoeuvre had not been easy to pull off. The Photurian world they'd found had no moon and the in-system space around it was utterly clean of the usual debris. That meant almost nowhere to hide. So Mark had concealed his ship by diving close to the star and hiding in its glare while keeping their quantum cloaking ramped to the max.

The problem with this approach was the strain it put on the ship. The shield reduced their thermal load but was far from perfect so close to a plasma-source, which meant that Mark had to dump heat using tactical g-ray blasts aimed in directions he hoped the Photes weren't looking.

He wished he could have spared the ship such unpleasant work but the Photes already owned local space through simple strength of numbers. They'd split their forces into two groups. A string of about fifteen ships had remained in the outer system, covering all the exit vectors in the direction of the Flaw. A larger group of about thirty had angled inwards in a loose smear, converging rapidly on the biosphere world.

Mark was having problems keeping so many Photes away from their intended goal. If they spent too much time close to the planet, Ann's shuttle would be noticed.

To hold them back, he'd locked the *Diggory* into a running firefight. A deep submind copy of his identity was now running that ship almost autonomously. He disliked the set-up but there was too much light-lag and tactical flying going on to make the ship-juggling work any other way. So Mark received a horrid, surging update of the *Diggory*'s status every five seconds or so. It was like trying to fight a battle under a slow-motion strobe light.

It would have been better if he could have afforded more than two tight-beam relay sats between himself and the *Diggory*, but Palla's models suggested that if he used any more, he'd give away his position and render his costly ploy useless.

To his mind, the only reason the *Diggory* wasn't dead yet was because the Photes appeared determined not to chase it down. Despite the old scout-ship constantly harrying the approaching Photes with g-ray fire, they remained stubbornly focused on high orbital dominance of the biosphere. His attempts to lure them into dogfights had met with a spectacular lack of success.

'Get ready for warp,' he told Palla as they came around the far side of their solar slingshot. 'As soon as the sun's not hiding us, I'm swapping to warp. The combined false and real gees are going to be rough.'

'Putting Rachel into acceleration support now,' said Palla.

They'd slid Mark's mentor back into unconsciousness the moment the serious manoeuvres had started, with her consent. There was no way her compromised body could withstand the stresses involved without shutdown and serious internal support.

'Done,' she told him.

Mark dearly hoped Rachel came through the next couple of hours okay. While their collaboration had been brief, it'd been enough to remind him of the woman's spark.

He fired the engines and threw the *Dantes* back up the system towards the rendezvous point he'd signalled to Judj. For thirty seconds, neither Mark nor Palla spoke while they fought to retain consciousness. Mark tried to ignore the freight train on his chest and found it difficult.

'Heard anything else from the shuttle?' he said as his brain finally cleared.

'No,' Palla assured him with a gasp. 'They're running silent... like you asked... We just have to hope they make it.'

Mark currently had Ann's shuttle racing through the upper layers of

279

a tropical cyclone in the planet's atmosphere to minimise its visibility. It'd lift and burn when the time was right but they hadn't left much room for error. Rendezvous would be tight.

He counted down to the perfect moment and fired a fresh submind update at the *Diggory*, ordering it to dump its remaining messenger drones as bombs. He pointed them at the opposite side of the world from where he planned to be. That way the consequences of his light-lagged orders would hopefully arrive at the same time as his own ship was passing on the other side. With luck, the threat of a few antimatter missiles hitting the planet would draw the Photes' attention.

With his orders en route, there was nothing to do but fly in a near-straight line with his tau-chargers running hot as the seconds counted down. Mark saw sudden warp-flashes and bursts of fire from the far side of the world before the view was occluded by the planet rushing up to meet him.

He caught sight of the shuttle making a furious burn and dropped pickup drones to seize it. They blazed from the glare of their braking, tethered the shuttle as gently as they could and boosted back up to matching velocity. Mark intercepted the lot of them three seconds later.

In the wake of his grab, he watched for tails but found none. The Photes might have launched cloaked munitions, but something about the frantic deployment of their ships told Mark that his adversaries lacked the focus to engage in such devious acts.

He opened a channel to the shuttle.

'Ann,' he said. 'Is Judj okay? Any broken bones from that pickup?'

'A couple of ribs, I think,' Judj wheezed. He sounded grey with stress. 'I'll be fine, but Ann's not with me.'

Mark blinked. '*What?*'

'She said she'll "catch up",' said Judj flatly.

'What in eleven living colours of fuck does *that* mean?' Mark shouted. 'Catch up *how?*'

As they powered past the planet, he received another update-burst from the *Diggory*. It had expended all its drones and was now engaged in evasive manoeuvres. The ship didn't expect to survive more than a few more minutes.

As Mark struggled to integrate the new memories, his tactical display showed him the Photurian fleet releasing another volley of shuttles into the planet's atmosphere. This time, he had no way to stop them from landing.

'Andromeda Fucking Ludik!' Mark roared.

What was he supposed to do now? Just leave her there? With the enemy massing behind him, he had little choice but to continue on his current path to rescue Ira. She hadn't exactly left him any other options. Mark was all out of tricks.

10.2: ANN

Ann walked through the cilia forest to the node's towering interior wall, adjusted the surface adhesion of her hands and feet, and climbed up the inside of it like a gecko. Once up among the hanging ribbons of calcified matter that hung there like sheaves of stage backdrops, Ann leapt. She clambered across their surfaces, retracing the route she'd originally taken but upside down. It was harder than she'd expected. The ribbons were awkwardly shaped and resisted her grip. But given that they were designed to support the construction of machines the size of transit pods, they held her weight. She caused no obvious, visible damage, other than the odd handhold driven into their surface by her urgent fingertips.

Ann made her way back towards the remains of the drone foetus that had split open on the floor. Once directly above it, she climbed upwards until she could sit on one of the drone-cysts growing out of the closest ceiling sheet. She picked one the size of a warehouse deliverybot and perched on it to wait for company.

It took over an hour. For whatever reason, the Photes were sluggish in their response. Ann started to worry about the *Dantes* leaving before she could reach it. Inevitably, though, the Photes sent robots into the node to see what she'd been doing. Ann matched her infrared signature to the surroundings and chameleoned her skin. She suppressed the urge to hum songs and watched the machines as they stomped about below.

They were big, ugly, bipedal things, three metres tall with guns on their arms. She wondered if they had human brains trapped inside, locked in some futile sense of permanent gratitude. No matter. The dumb robots didn't even bother looking up. But then again, the Photes had no reason to expect her to stay behind. Because, after all, that was a *silly* thing to do.

The robots wandered about, damaged some cilia skeletons and clunked back out. Ann watched and waited, full of hope, and prayed that she'd judged this right. She reasoned that to the Photes, the node would be a little like a temple. They'd want to see it in person. How could they not, even if they knew it was broken? The moment that had occurred to her, she realised she'd been presented with a rare opportunity to get personal with the enemy.

In interstellar conflicts, one seldom had the chance to engage in close-quarters combat with one's adversaries. Usually it was more a case of massive gamma-ray bursts at dawn. That was a shame, Ann thought – something that deserved rectifying.

As hoped, four Photes came through the forest together, surrounded by six of the biomechanical warriors to clear the way for them. Ann followed their progress and wondered, not for the first time, about the extraordinary quirks in her enemies' behaviour. Rather than just nuking the site, they *had* to come in person – with their suits off. Just like they had to announce their arrival or convert people instead of simply executing them. It was like fighting an army of obsessive-compulsives.

Except, she noticed, there was something different about this lot. They were shaking and clutching at each other as they approached. When they caught sight of the broken egg, one of them let out a wail.

'My joy is faltering,' he yelled.

'Mine also,' said another, gripping her head. 'This is … is … is … *sad*. I am *sad*! Sad! Help! I am experiencing non-functional emotion!' She slid to her knees as she stared at the long-dead egg. One of the others grabbed her and shook her violently.

'Resist it!' he shouted. 'Resist! Resist! Maintain joy at all costs!'

The exchange astonished Ann. It made the Photes seem oddly vulnerable – pathetic, even. They were never sad. They were stiff, grinning creatures, full of unthinking discipline. In her experience they didn't even talk to each other. They just smiled and destroyed.

Her surprise melted into resentment. These monstrosities had devoured the human race, sucking world after world into their hideous, pointless parody of life. Not once had they asked what people wanted. They were always so sure they were doing what was best for everyone.

Why should she consider their emotions when they had no time for anyone else's? She stuck to her plan.

Ann jumped down, straight onto the robot at the back of the group that was serving as the comms relay. She landed on its shoulders, grabbed its head and twisted it off its neck. As the automaton sank to its knees, she threw the head at one of the other machines before it could react, smashing its weapon arm into shards. Then, as she slid down the back of the relay robot, she seized its gun arm from behind and rammed her fingers into the unprotected elbow joint. Data spikes burst from her fingertips, penetrating the neural links in the hinge. Ann cycled through possible neural commands at random, producing an erratic spray of armour-piercing slugs, which she directed into the remaining guards.

The entire process was a little uneven, she thought, and had already taken two-point-seven seconds. By the time her subminds had resolved the robot's nerve protocol there were still two functional guards, both firing into the remains of the one shielding her.

Ann ripped free the forearm weapon of the relay robot, dived, rolled and leapt away as the others peppered it with munitions, spraying the cilia forest with fire and shrapnel. Ann chastised herself. By now, the alarm would undoubtedly have been raised. The ships in orbit might even be informed. If she was going to be the recipient of an orbital kinetic attack, the next few seconds would be her last.

She shot the remaining two guards and leapt for the closest intact robot head. She rammed her spikes into its spinal junction and rifled the contents of its mind for some kind of control handle that would let her stall the shuttle from leaving. In the end, she succeeded by throwing so much data at it that the vehicle slid shrieking into passive reboot.

With disaster temporarily averted, she turned to the astonished Photes. They stared at her, dumbstruck, apparently confused as to why they were still alive.

'The Abomination!' said one stupidly.

'She is responsible!' croaked another. 'Destroy her!'

Idiotically fearless to the end, the Photes ran at her with their weakling fists raised. Even ordinary Photes were as fast as Fleet officers with killtech implants. The grown augmentations that Phote bodies acquired made them extremely dangerous by human standards. But today was not a day for being human. It was a day for relishing just how human she wasn't.

Ann moved among them like a scythe, striking with precise, paralysing blows. The Photes toppled like bowling pins, three into unconsciousness, one into seizures and breathing difficulties. Ann turned the twitching Phote over so that he was face up and looked down into his staring, orange-speckled eyes.

'Lucky Photurian,' she snarled. 'Your long journey in search of peace is finally at an end. I offer harmony and purpose, and the satisfaction of temporary usefulness in the service of the human race.'

She pressed her data spikes gently into the corners of his eye sockets while he whimpered. Her probes chased back into his skull, finding their way towards his brain. The Phote gurgled as Ann seized control of his spinal cord, severing his body from motor control and depositing her own biomechanical tissue at the junction. By the time her spikes were withdrawn, the Phote was hers to command, his face slack. What was going on in his ugly, rewritten brain right now, she could only guess.

'How do you like it when it's your turn to be husked, motherfucker?' she crooned. 'You like that? That's what you people did to some very good friends of mine. God, you people even put the fucking brains of children into starships. I've waited a long time to do this to one of you.'

The truth, though, was that the ambush felt less satisfying and more morally greasy than she'd originally envisaged. She could only imagine what Ira would make of her actions. But it was too late. She was committed now and still needed a ticket out.

Ten minutes later, Ann had finished making her Phote-zombies. They stood there motionless, ready for use, their weird Photey emotions silenced to inaudible, introspective screams. She'd also rebooted the shuttle a couple of times and managed to pollute its software enough that it wouldn't take off without her say-so.

What had amazed her during the entire process was that the shuttle didn't appear to be wired into the Phote collective supermind. They all used to be. If this was some new loosely coupled security set-up, it wasn't very good. This entire crew had been piss-easy to subvert. Not so much a glorious crusade as the mewling remnants of one.

Ann marched her zombies down the slope to where the drone brain she'd excavated lay waiting and made them pick it up for her.

'You see that?' she said. 'You're going to help me take one of your precious brains back to my ship so I can rip it apart, piece by piece. Does that make you feel joyous and useful? I do hope so!'

The zombies had no voices with which to reply. Instead, they carried the brain back up the slope on her behalf, all the way to her new ride. At the same time, she signalled the shuttle and instructed it to ping Mark to let him know she was on her way. Overall, Ann was satisfied with the outcome, but somehow no longer felt like humming.

10.3: MARK

When Ann's message arrived in Mark's sensorium, he took a moment to fill helm-space with his anger.

'What in the name of Furious Fuck am I supposed to do?' he bellowed. 'Go back and pick her up because *now* she's ready? Like a sect-princess coming home from a goddamned float party?'

Of course that was what he was going to do, and she knew it. Mark shot a furious glance at Palla. She smirked at him and shrugged, apparently delighted by his outrage.

'Them's the breaks, I guess,' she offered brightly.

Mark shook his head. He was going to need to distract the Photes even more thoroughly than he already had otherwise picking up Ann would be impossible. He was pretty sure he cared more about that than she did, but he refused to let her die just because she so obviously wanted to.

He checked the struggling *Diggory*. Rachel's old scout was accelerating away from four Phote craft that had engaged pursuit while the other ships consolidated their hold on the biosphere world.

Mark had been so proud of the fact that they hadn't followed him. The *Dantes* was forty kilometres wide. Even with its cloak active, it wasn't easy to hide. You couldn't really conceal a starship's mass at this range, particularly when it kept jack-hammering local space with warp-bursts.

'How am I supposed to distract them this time?' Mark demanded of helm-space.

'I have no idea,' said Palla. 'Argue with them, maybe? Point at something and say *look*?'

With disgust, Mark plotted a course back to Ann's anticipated rendezvous point. He targeted his furthest relay drone on tight-beam and squeezed a new submind into it. This copy wasn't like the usual sketches of his identity that he used to run machines. It had as close a mapping to his language centres as he could synthesise at a moment's notice.

'Fuck it,' he said. 'I'm actually taking your joke suggestion. I can't think of anything else. I'm going to shout at them. That'll have to do.'

He had no idea what he could say that would distract dozens of Photurian gunships simultaneously. He just knew he needed to.

Judj chimed up from the shuttle. 'I have something that might help,' he said. He still sounded half-dead from his escape but managed to offer up a memory download of his research findings from the planet.

Mark grabbed the icon out of helm-space's virtual air the moment it appeared and swallowed it. He smiled darkly as new knowledge unfurled in his brain.

With a little renewed optimism, he buffered up all the vitriol he could muster, squirted it into his tailored submind and let it speak for him while he flew. There was no way he'd be able to keep up a real-time dialogue using his own brain without giving the Photes enough data to pinpoint his position through the varying delay times. As it was, the light-lag between replies in any ship-to-ship conversation was going to be measured in tens of seconds.

'Hey, Photurians, glad you could join us,' said Mark's drone replica over the public channel. 'This is Captain Mark Ruiz of the GSS *Edmond Dantes*. It's great that you've come all the way out here to hang with us. Shame it had to be to stare at a dead world. A fucking *graveyard*. I mean, that's got to hurt, right? But it's interesting, isn't it? It makes me wonder. All those promises you make about everlasting love and happiness – they look kind of like bullshit now, don't you think? As if everything you ever told us was just one big dirty lie.'

Even though it was a copy of him speaking, Mark found articulating his opinions to the enemy absurdly satisfying. How ironic that when he finally had a chance to tell them how he felt, it wasn't exactly him doing it.

'This isn't going to work,' said Palla.

'I know,' he said.

286

The Photes didn't talk except to advertise. He expected no reply from the swarm-mind, so was startled when he got one.

'Captain Ruiz!' came a woman's voice. She sounded hoarse, as if she'd been shouting too much recently. 'What did you do to the homeworld?'

Mark blinked in confusion. This voice was very far from the tailored messages he was used to hearing. It was clotted with raw and surprisingly human-sounding emotion.

'Wow. I was *so* wrong,' said Palla.

Mark held his breath, desperately hoping his submind had enough smarts to bluff. He hurriedly sent it a fresh update as he brought his ship around, even though he knew that it'd reply seconds before his edits reached it.

'Who am I speaking to, please?' said Mark's replica. 'How can we have a proper conversation unless you're capable of adhering to even the most basic inter-ship communication standards?'

Mark guffawed. Thank the heavens for machines' love of clear information.

'I am Nada Rien,' said the Phote, 'but my name is irrelevant. I command. What did you do to the homeworld? I order you to reply honestly!'

'What did I do to it?' said Mark's replica. 'Why do you want to know what *I* did? Can't you figure it out for yourself?'

Mark laughed out loud. Score one for the Ruiz-patented automated chatbot. Maybe he should always use a SAP to have arguments on his behalf.

'This is great, but they're not moving yet,' said Palla.

She sent him a map of the Photurian fleet positions. Besides entertaining him, his distraction engine was having little effect. It certainly wasn't clearing a return vector for the *Dantes*.

'We need something else,' she added.

Mark ordered the relay drone to commence a very visible set of warp-manoeuvres.

'If you want to know what I did, you'll have to catch me first,' his replica said.

That was a little better. There were a couple of ships following his bait now. Mark primed the drone to self-destruct and readied his second relay to continue the conversation. He updated his conversation model accordingly.

He used the convergence of Phote ships and the torrent of g-ray fire they poured on the little drone to shield his own course-correction as he slid back into an elliptical capture path for Ann's shuttle. Then he kicked the second relay into chat mode.

'You know what I think you offer?' said his replica. 'I don't think it's peace. I think it's death. And you? You're nothing but an undead junkie, living off squirts of pleasure meted out by a clutch of parasitic germs.'

'We are neither dead nor addicts!' Nada shouted back.

Mark's eyebrows went up at the weird vehemence behind his adversary's words. Apparently, he'd struck a nerve.

'We are what you will be when you *grow up*!' she went on. Her ships pivoted, seeking out the second drone. 'Are you actually incapable of seeing what we have that you lack? We have harmony. We have unity. We have purpose! We do not bicker or steal or fight. We do not perpetrate injustices or crimes!'

'Neither do we,' said the replica. 'In case you didn't notice, the human race hasn't had crime problems for decades. There have been no murders on Galatea for one thousand four hundred and eighty-eight days. There have been no robberies on Galatea for—'

'Only because you are constantly challenged by something better than yourselves!' Nada yelled.

Mark winced at his double's slide into precision facting, but Nada didn't appear to spot it. She was either too blind or too wound up to spot the slip, presuming she even cared.

'You live in pointless turmoil while we are happy!' she said.

'Bullshit.'

'No!' Nada insisted. 'We are always happy! You claim to want happiness, but you avoid it when we try to help you!'

'If you're always happy, it's not happiness, is it?' said Mark's replica. This was an impressive piece of insight for a submind SAP, but sometimes artificial minds managed to surprise.

'Can you not conceive of a state in which joy is everlasting and impervious?' said Nada.

'No. Because that's not joy.'

'I AM FEELING IT AND IT *IS* JOY!' Nada shouted.

The second drone exploded in a burst of coordinated fire.

288

Mark closed on Ann's rendezvous point and grabbed the vehicle he found there as he whipped past. He didn't slow to reduce impact speed. His receiver bay lit up with warnings as a shuttle slammed through its impact netting like so much cobweb and buried itself in the aerofoam wall. A normal human would have been instantly pulped by such an arrival. Ann, he suspected, would just receive some of the uncomfortable bruises she deserved.

'Ludik!' he barked at the shuttle.

'Pickup acknowledged,' said Ann coolly.

Mark shut the channel and yelled names at her.

'You may not be designed for joy but that does not mean you cannot be made to have it!' Nada proclaimed. 'What is wrong with you that you cannot accept joy when it is offered and proven? What is wrong with yearning for unity and Total Love?'

Mark fired off a third drone prepped with more pithy responses. The drone was dangerously close to their hull when it made its first reply. Mark cursed. In his anger, he'd failed to add a suitable delay to the release time.

'Because it's a fucking lie!' his new replica said. 'Because if you have to force it via surgery, it's not real!'

'Mark, I think we've been spotted,' said Palla. 'That launch was a little obvious.'

Mark groaned to himself as he watched the Photes close on his position. One moment of hot-headedness was all it took. Nada had used his own ruse against him.

'It *is* real, Captain Ruiz!' said Nada. 'I am always happy and I always love everyone. That makes you the liar. And now I know where you really are!'

Mark felt the brush of a g-ray grater-grid searching for bounces off his shield and desperately tried to think of another angle in the seconds he had left. Then a fresh update from the *Diggory* arrived. Amazingly, the old ship wasn't dead yet. Seventy per cent of its primary systems had failed due to energy-weapon assault, but the damned thing was still flying.

Mark sent it a fresh upload. He retargeted its remaining weapons on the biosphere and sent it into a suicide dive. While Nada closed on the *Dantes*, the *Diggory* fired. A patch of equatorial ocean began to boil.

'Jesus, Mark!' said Palla. 'You sure about that?'

The Photes quickly refocused their efforts on Rachel's old ship, desperate to knock it out of the sky, but the light-lag was too great. By the time they pierced its antimatter containment, it was already closing on the planet. A shell of brilliant white light erupted where the *Diggory* had formerly been.

The blast wasn't close enough to kill the biosphere outright, but the planet wasn't exactly happy, either. The atmosphere on one side took on a weird rosy hue as rippling blast-waves of exploding air spread out sluggishly around the globe. Life on the ex-Phote world was likely to need a few thousand years to pick up the pieces.

'No!' yelled Nada over the audio channel. 'No! No! No!'

The Phote ships dropped warp and hung around the dispersing ion cloud like stunned bees.

Mark took the opportunity and piled on speed. Now he had a decent lead, but picking up the others would have to be exceedingly quick. He pinged Ira with an encrypted pulse, warning him to get ready for exit, and waited for a reply as he barrelled towards the super-Jovian. None came.

Mark tried again on other frequencies, cycling all the options Ira might have used. The silence dragged. Mark wondered what could have happened. The Photes didn't appear to have paid the slightest attention to the ruins, so why wasn't Ira getting ready to leave? Had he discovered something dangerous out there? Was he dead already?

With mounting alarm, Mark realised that this was the most likely option. He'd already lost his old mentor and hadn't even noticed.

Then, as he was about to adjust course to leave the system, a response arrived. It was incredibly faint and picked out one of the alien ships held at the end of a glass tether. Ira himself remained silent.

'Where the fuck is he?' Mark blurted. 'What the fuck is going on?'

'Just pick up the whole damned ship,' said Palla. 'We have room for it. It's tiny compared to the *Dantes*. It can't be more than half a kilometre wide and we have bay doors bigger than that.'

Mark shot her an incredulous look. 'That won't be quiet or fast. We'll have to dump velocity like crazy and sit on it like a fucking cushion.'

'Do you care?' said Palla. 'Do we have any other options? Whatever we do, you have to hurry.'

Mark initiated the mother of all fusion burns, made a braking orbit around the super-Jovian and parked the *Dantes* on a dime to swallow the alien ship whole. As his loading-bay doors slid glacially together around the glass tether, he hit the base of the structure with g-rays to blast it clear. They had zero effect. The rock beneath them ran like butter but the tether shrugged off the onslaught like a gentle breeze.

While Mark stared stupidly at the stalk that wasn't even bothering to radiate heat, Ira came on the channel.

'Mark, what's going on? You got our beacon?'

'Where in fuck's name *are* you?' said Mark. 'Inside that thing? The first moment I hear from you and you're already aboard?'

'This ship has some heavy-duty rad-shielding,' Ira explained. 'We had no idea how good it was. We didn't hear a damned thing until just now.'

'Fine!' said Mark. 'Stay put. Your ark is already inside the *Dantes*. We're leaving with the whole thing.'

Clath came on the channel. 'Mark! I don't recommend that.'

'Too late,' said Mark.

The doors stared to close, reached the glass tether and promptly fouled. They clenched around it without closing.

'Sure! Stay open, doors!' said Mark. 'See if I care!'

He used mining buttresses to brace the alien ark while several dozen Photurian ships warped up through the system to meet him.

'That'll do!' he yelled as soon as the alien ark was grappled.

He hit the fusion torches. Astonishingly, the *Dantes* didn't move. Instead, it strained. He started getting pressure warnings from his buttresses. It was as if they were trying to drag the entire moon with them.

'Oh yeah?' said Mark. 'You think that's all I got?'

He kicked on the warp engines.

'Mark!' said Palla. 'Are you *nuts*?'

'What you're doing is extremely dangerous!' Clath shouted.

An ignition field sparked around the *Dantes*, building strength. Against all the laws of nature, the tether resisted and played havoc with the haze of ions gathering around his ship. Space quivered like something sickly.

Suddenly there was a crack of light and the tether vanished, along with a large piece of their bay doors. The mining-bay sensors screamed alerts at him. The alien ark, by contrast, looked perfectly intact.

'What did you *think* was going to happen?' Clath exclaimed. 'We had no idea what the thermal-limit behaviour for false matter was like! You could have blown up the entire ship!'

'Got us loose, didn't I?' said Mark. 'Everybody strap down, we're leaving.'

With that, he took them out, straight into the wilds of Backspace and away from the clutches of the Photes as fast as he could.

1 0 . 4 : WILL

The second time that Moneko took Will to the Carnevale di Peste, it sounded like a brawl was happening. He glanced towards the festival that lurked below the night-time balcony.

'Don't,' said Moneko. 'Please. This place is extremely dangerous. You've seen how powerful their stealthware is. You really don't want to attract their attention.'

Will let it slide. He had no desire to kick off a repeat of the monk episode. If he'd learned anything over the last few days, it was to take Moneko's advice seriously. What he'd seen in the testing arena made his options clear. He could work with the Underground and build on the achievements of the other Glitches or squander that chance. He wasn't angry enough to do that yet – not by a long shot.

He mutely followed her to the next search corridor and out into a dusty museum with a Greco-Roman theme. They strode down an endless arcade of imposing rooms with marble floors and superfluous Doric columns. Light fell in shafts like bolts of spiritual illumination. In alcoves around the walls, memories played in which toga-clad clones pontificated.

'What is dream? Dream is mystery!' a Will with a unicorn horn proclaimed. He wiggled a finger at the sky. 'Through dream, we necessarily encounter our implicit core dialectic: the prism through which all self-narratives are refracted...'

'At the dawn of the Fifth Great Photurian Assault, the enemy pretended to be humans from the IPSO organisation,' another droned. 'There were those who took this as evidence that The History reflected fact. What *hubris*...'

'How do we distinguish between history and fantasy? Perhaps we should not. Memory is bound to be imperfect. So instead, I propose the notion of the *radical now*...'

'What *is* this place?' said Will.

Moneko walked ahead of him, translucent as a ghost in her Venetian stealthware.

'An axiom-appreciation site,' she said. 'This one's for "The Mystery of Imperfect Self-Knowledge". In other words, a temple to not understanding ourselves, and therefore never being ready to leave. It's no coincidence that there are a bunch of belief-hacks parked behind it – I doubt the place could sustain its own ego otherwise.'

She took him to a particularly dull exhibit full of written accounts of unusual dreams from his youth and opened an invisible door in the back wall.

'This is one of our best finds from last year,' she said. 'It leads straight into the associated Underlayer memory cluster. It won't surprise you to learn that subconscious memory bubbles tend to map closely to soft-space sites with the same themes.'

On the far side of the doorway lay an examination hall from Will's childhood where he'd taken tests in industrial cognition. Just seeing it made him feel anxious.

'Look around for anchors,' she said. 'Hopefully you'll find several – they're usually hidden in the walls or floor.'

'Got it,' said Will.

'Touching things should be fine,' she told him. 'Balance can't have all the sites booby-trapped. But be careful anyway. When you get the hang of it, try moving a few of the hacks about. And this time, if you need to exit, don't hesitate, okay?' She tucked her handkerchief in his doublet like last time.

'What about smart-cell powers?' said Will.

'I'm way ahead of you,' she said.

She reached behind her back and pulled out a large heart-shaped box of chocolates that hadn't been there a moment ago.

'Your toolkit,' she said. 'You'll find the flavours on the lid. Try the hack-mapping function first.'

Will stared at them. 'Why chocolates?'

She raised an eyebrow. 'Don't you like them? I think it's a cute metaphor. And besides, this way you can hold all the icons in one hand.' Her expression turned sad. 'I used to try offering you chocolates in return for dives,' she said. 'That was a shitty idea. This time, I'm making a gesture of trust. I'm still sorry about last time and how bad it must have felt. I'm doing my best. And please don't eat them all at once. Really.'

She blew him a little kiss. The door closed.

Will stood in the echoing exam hall and examined his gift. On the lid, along with little pictures of each icon-morsel, was a written description of what it did: smart-cell activation, thread analytics and so on. He picked out the mapping tool she'd recommended – a bland-looking white chocolate swirl – and swallowed it.

He immediately felt the familiar sensation of a software system opening in his mind. The download was a full SAP – a warped copy of one of his own subminds with the ability to semantically index anchor sites. He couldn't help smiling. He felt like a roboteer again. A quick sampling of the box also yielded a sensory-mapped heuristic hack-finder and a substrate introspection and analysis probe. With the programs running in his mind, it felt like old times.

He wandered around the edges of the exam room and easily found a couple of anchors. He could smell them now. They stank of ozone. Prising away a few of the wall-panels revealed small plastic suntap replicas hiding there like spy cameras.

He pulled one out to look it over. The thing was running passively, his new mods told him. There was no free information pouring in from elsewhere, just a steady stream of dumb packets being emitted into the surrounding matrix. Moneko had been right. These things were merely lo-fi replicas of the circuit he'd originally discovered.

He logged their positions and took a doorway to a related memory – one that looked like a mall of upscale boutiques he'd visited on Mars once while hopelessly searching for a gift for his wife. Buried in the floor of a jewellery shop, he found three more. Will experimentally tried moving them to nearby memories, as Moneko suggested. Nothing happened. He kept mapping, but as the minutes turned to hours, his satisfaction waned. He was struck by the futility of the process. There were too many of the damned things.

He paused in a horrible bar on Triton he'd once visited after an argument with Rachel and sat down to think. Was he really going to do this for the next few years? Just mapping anchors rather than doing something about them? He'd go mad.

But the options seemed stark: ignore Moneko's advice and face the near-instantaneous wrath of Balance, or follow it and live in stultifying, uncomfortable safety. Neither path felt likely to get him out.

'Had enough yet?' said a voice from behind him.

Will leapt to his feet and spun to face the figure that had appeared. The clone who stood before him wore a Surplus Age business suit and fedora. Will recognised the man from his last dive. He held his breath, turned and bolted. He lunged for the nearest portal, but the clone *moved* and suddenly stood right in front of him. Will skidded to a halt. How was this happening? Wasn't he supposed to be invisible?

'Tell me, are you enjoying your new role?' said the clone. 'Convinced by their patter? If so, go ahead and boot out of here. But maybe you'd prefer it if someone told you what's *really* going on.'

Will doubled back but the clone moved again, this time appearing at the bar, a martini glass in hand.

'I'm not here to hurt you, Will. I won't even touch you.'

Will stumbled to a halt and glared at the newcomer. He exhaled two seconds before his exit was due to hit, his curiosity reluctantly piqued despite his better judgement.

'What do you want?' he demanded. 'Who are you?'

'Relax, Will,' said the clone, taking a sip. 'I'm just *you* with a little more experience. Actually you. Not a fucking copy – a Glitch. And your nick is Cuthbert.'

Will stood rooted to the spot. There were other Glitches? Will had assumed they were all dead.

The dapper clone leaned up against the bar and smiled humourlessly.

'Before you vanish, why don't you listen to what I have to say? Then, if you don't like it, I'll leave you alone. How does that sound?'

'Talk, then,' Will growled. 'Get on with it.'

The clone smiled lazily. 'God, do you remember this place?' he said, taking in the ugly diamond-mirror walls and greasy tomato-red lighting. 'I hated Triton. But what I wouldn't give to be there now.' He sipped at his cocktail. 'Right now, I expect you're confused. The Underground are helping you. They've given you a job and a place to sleep. They've told you a story about how this world works. Which has to be a start, right? Except it sucks here, and you know it. Right now you're telling yourself that's better than being chased down by Balance. And you're coping. But what if I told you that you're being used?' The clone paused expectantly. 'But first, some basics. Yes, I can see you, but only because

I've had practice. No, I'm not some kind of Balance trick, so you don't risk anything by listening to me. And we have plenty of time, so why not sit down and have a drink?'

He clicked his fingers and a second martini appeared on the diamond-coated table next to Will. He regarded it suspiciously.

'You can call me Smiley, by the way,' said the clone.

Will caught the reference along with the irony. The clone didn't look particularly smiley; in fact, he radiated bitterness. When he quietly scanned the memory context around the visitor, his new subminds informed him confidently that the person he was looking at wasn't there.

'Go ahead, scan me,' said Smiley with a laugh. 'I'll show up as blank. I'm just another knot in the fabric of the planetary subconscious, same as you. But I've been around longer, *Cuthbert*. I've seen more.'

Will shifted uneasily. Smiley had deftly tapped Will's nagging suspicions about the Underground, but he wasn't sure he trusted this new figure, either. His appearance had been too abrupt – too clandestine.

'Why are you here?' he said.

'To help,' said Smiley. 'You're another of my kind, finding your way. After I spotted you, it only seemed right to lend a hand.'

'What makes you think I need help?'

Smiley snorted. He leaned forward, his expression darkening. 'Let's take it from the top, shall we? You've seen copies of yourself that are no more than animals. Mutant clones so deformed that they drink out of a bowl and shit on the street. Is that okay? But you've seen worse. You've seen *Truists*. How does that make you feel? And always, the message is the same: don't worry, it's normal. Keep calm and carry on. Well, tell me, Will, does it *feel* normal? And then there are these things,' he said, sneering and pointing at one of the exposed suntap replicas Will had located. 'They want you to find them. But oh, from time to time, they propose that you experimentally move them about. That's interesting, isn't it? Why would they ask you to do that?'

How was it that, on a planet filled entirely with copies of himself, Will didn't feel like trusting anyone? What did that say about him?

'Let me remind you what those things are,' said Smiley. 'They're belief stiffeners.' He gestured at the walls. 'When you move the stiffeners, you change what the clones upstairs believe.'

'I know that,' Will snapped.

'So what do they want to change?' said Smiley. 'You're living in a favour economy, Will, one where attitudes about what kinds of thread are allowed can make people a lot of money. You make a variant everyone thinks is sketchy while there's no competition. Then you change the social norms and invent a market. Voilà, copy requests.'

'The Underground isn't about money.'

'Are you sure? *You* don't care about that, but what of the people you're working with? You don't want to drink out of a bowl, either. How do you think all this happened, Will? You *changed*. These ... clones – they're not you. They're *mutilations* of you. Tell me, why don't they just try to get rid of the damned anchors altogether?'

'You know why,' said Will. 'There are too many. That's obvious.'

'So why shouldn't Glitches coordinate to get rid of them?' said Smiley. 'Why don't they bring a bunch of us together?' He waited for a response.

Will blushed. He'd assumed that Glitches were a rare enough occurrence that there weren't multiple copies of him on the planet at the same time.

'I'll tell you why,' said Smiley. 'Because they don't *want* the anchors gone. They *can't* want it because the anchors don't let them. So they keep us scared and isolated instead. Have you taken a look at an anchor's code yet?'

Will shook his head.

'It's Snakepit software, Will,' Smiley growled. 'Just like all the other shit this planet runs on. Those hacks are adapted Protocol enforcers. Crappy ones, admittedly, but they run on the same principle as the original circuit. Do you have any idea how dangerous that is?' He jabbed a finger at the sky. 'It means one mistake up there and those Photurian bastards have a way into this planet's systems. Your people have been told that,' Smiley assured him. 'They just don't believe it. Which means you're dealing with an organisation that can't assess the risks of their own operation. So, I ask you again. If it's not about money, and it's not *really* about escape, what do they want? With your help, they have the power to change Balance, just like a Cancer does, but without the risk. What are they using it for?'

Will's patience started to fray. Smiley's remarks threatened to drag him into a whirlpool of paranoia.

'You tell me.'

'Who can say?' said Smiley with a cryptic smile. 'Power, maybe?'

'What's the point of power?' said Will. 'It's a planet of fucking clones.'

'If we ever get out of here, they'll own the galaxy.'

'But that's not going to happen, is it? Not by your logic. Because of the anchors, we can't leave.'

Smiley frowned. 'Not until we get rid of the Transcended master circuit, no. There's still a poison splinter in our mind somewhere, screwing us over.'

'So why aren't you out looking for it?' Will demanded. 'Why stand here pissing all over the Underground when you could shut down their games just by finding the damned switch?'

Smiley looked hurt. 'I've tried,' he said. 'Believe me. Maybe you'll be the one who finds it. But I'll tell you this: for most of us – the ones who live, anyway – there's a turning point. It's when you realise that what you're trying to escape to is a memory, Will, not a place. Even if you get home, everyone you knew will be forty years older and Rachel will still be dead. You don't want freedom. You want the past. So most of us stop trying to get out after a while and start trying to make a difference instead.'

'My, that's optimistic.'

'It sounds bleak because you haven't got there yet. If you're lucky, you will.'

Will snorted. 'You call that *lucky*?'

Smiley cracked a broken smile. 'Okay, maybe more like *desperate*. Look, I know this is weird for you. I remember how it felt. And I know you don't trust me yet. Frankly, I didn't trust me the first time this happened, either. So I'm not going to try to win you over or tell you what I think is happening. You'll have to figure out what to believe for yourself. But I will give you a tip about how you can do that.'

He held up an index finger and paused to sip. 'That clone who runs the outfit you just joined: John Brown?' Smiley shook his head. 'Weird choice of face, by the way, don't you think? Anyway, my proposal is that you use the stealthware you've been given to go watch him for a bit. See what he does. How *trustworthy* is he? You could, for instance, go and hang out at the Underground's mesh site and wait for him there.'

Will felt his face stiffen. The Underground had a mesh site?

298

Smiley feigned surprise. 'Oh! What? They didn't tell you about that? Did they have you cycling up and down to the station every day when there's a hidden entry point right under the Old Slam Bar?'

Smiley shook his head slowly. 'Gosh, that sounds like a bunch of work. Still, never mind. Now you know. I wonder why they didn't tell you? But in any case, it's easy to find. Its soft-space address is about two hundred metres into the mesh outside the Mettaburg Station, on the left. A grey pavilion with a logo that says *Artistic Temperaments R Us*. It's set a little back from the walkway, but once you know what you're looking for, you can't miss it. If you don't believe me, go and take a look. Who knows, you might see John there!' Smiley gave him a crocodile smirk.

'Thanks for the tip,' said Will darkly. 'Very helpful, I'm sure.'

'No problem,' said Smiley. 'Glad we had the chance to chat. I hope we cross paths again. Somehow I feel certain it's going to happen.'

Smiley downed the rest of his imaginary drink, tipped his fedora and turned to go.

'Be seeing you,' he said and winked out, leaving his empty glass on the counter.

Will stared at the abandoned olive sitting there, and thought hard.

10.5: NADA

In the hours after the escape of the *Dantes*, Nada's fleet regrouped. Through her ship's eyes, she stared down at the freshly damaged world with pain twisting her insides like burning talons. Nothing in her existence as a Photurian had prepared her for that moment. She needed to know what had happened in this system. How did the sad, wounded home even exist in the first place? Just looking at it filled her with sickness and doubt. It threatened to unravel her entire world view.

As she watched the rings of toxic storm cloud ricochet back and forth through the planet's tortured atmosphere, she felt another emotion crackling through her – a very human one. It was the sort of reaction she'd have considered beneath her before their mission started. She felt *loathing*.

She'd realised during her unpleasant dialogue with Mark Ruiz, the notorious Thief of Souls, that it was *him* she actually detested most, not Ludik the Abomination. That had baffled her initially as Ruiz had played a far less significant role in her life. He was very much the lesser villain in the pantheon of human malefactors and so consistently erratic that he warranted little interest during most high-level strategy fugues.

What had occurred to her after that debate was that the feeling didn't originate from her own mind. It had entered with the Yunus's edits. It had not taken her long after that to figure out that the *loathing* couldn't have had its origins in the Yunus's experiences as primary strategic unit for the Utopia. There was no room for such nonsense in that role. It must have been informed by his human life before that. If she needed evidence that the Yunus's edits had not come from a wholly rational place, she had it now.

That knowledge, unfortunately, left her questioning herself all the more deeply. With so much of her rational potential caught up in pointless emotional feedback, Nada reluctantly called for a consultation with her two primary reports. In order to gain clarity, she would have to resort to the leaden unpleasantness of peer-wise dialogue.

Leng and Zilch pressed their way into the leadership vesicle and waited silently for her to speak. She examined them both. Leng looked ill. He was still processing the unforgivable acts perpetrated by the humans. One of his eyes appeared to have been damaged during recent events. A louse sat patiently over that part of his face, knitting new tissue together. Zilch, in contrast, had never looked stronger or more alert. His boxy physique quivered with intent.

Nada plucked away the lice repairing her damaged cheeks and spoke.

'I am conflicted,' she said quietly. The events of the past few hours had left her exhausted and hoarse. 'Strategy alignment is required. You must assist. Contemplation of the data acquired from this system has filled me with irrelevant sensations of sadness and existential horror.'

She paused. Her subunits waited for her to continue. Leng stared dolefully into the wall-mucus. Zilch trembled like a palsied limb.

'The Total Peace that a homeworld offers lasts for ever,' she said. 'Units consume the fruit manufactured by the homeworld and witness its bounty. The shared joy they experience contributes to the homeworld's processing. Homeworlds and units persist in harmony. This cycle of happiness is the guarantee of the Founder Entity. The existence of a mature homeworld that has successfully embraced its child species

300

but is *not* in Total Peace appears to refute the Founder's promise, which is impossible and disgusting. What, then, has happened here?'

'I lack a complete explanation,' said Leng. 'I concur that the current stimuli are repugnant. However, I now feel confident that the humans did not cause the decay of this home. The surface samples we were able to obtain prior to atmospheric devastation suggest a mutagenic timeline measured in millennia. Our quarry is not responsible. They have no new weapon.'

'I concur,' said Nada. 'This was my assessment also. But this makes it worse. How can we ever relax into the peace we deserve when we know that *this* can happen?'

'Remember that there is much about the observed scenario that we do not yet understand,' said Leng, his voice becoming a whine. 'It is possible that this world may have been happily united for millions of years prior to the onset of Fatigue. It may be that the brilliance of their shared joy was such that the planet was no longer required. The happy entities existing here may have been uplifted to some different, more Founder-like format. If they had access to the Founder Entity, who knows what secrets he may have revealed? Despite appearances, this might be the remains of a glad event, not a tragic one.'

She stared at Leng's floating body and felt an unexpected warmth towards him. Sadly, her head remained stewed with unwelcome questions. She was Photurian. She had no use for empty existential meanderings. They had a species to save. And yet she found herself wondering which side of the Zone her own homeworld had been spawned from. If the Founders had originated on this side, there might be other homes for them to visit. But if this was what they looked like, there'd be little joy in it.

'A delightful concept,' she said. 'I wish to adopt it. However, consider this: our consensus has long been that the Transcended race which interacted with humanity represents an obsolete and defunct authority in the galaxy. Our kind is independent of origin species and thus immune to Transcended manipulation. We therefore represent a superior form of life. What we see here bears out that theory but also fuels concern. What if Fatigue is another weapon of Transcended control, wielded against us just as the suntap flares are wielded against lesser species? Instead of using suntaps to exert influence, perhaps they use criminal mutants like the hated Monet. What if they are using his ilk to poison our beautiful homes, and lesser species as pawns in their game?'

'I cannot rule out this hypothesis,' said Leng.

'Enough,' Zilch blurted. 'We need more data before any viable model can be constructed. Until then, we must consider all joyless musing a dangerous habit to be suppressed. We must remain strong and pragmatic at all costs. It is better to focus on what must be done than these—' His body arched as another wave of anxious energy poured through him. 'Obscenities!' he roared. 'Obscen—'

She reached into his mind to help him stabilise his vision.

'This focus must be reinforced by communion,' he continued. 'Superior Nada, you must take action in this regard.'

He was right. Nada knew it and felt grateful for his bluntness.

'Accepted,' she said. 'Next point. We have a choice. The biology of this world has degraded but it retains a habitat skeleton amenable to reuse. There are also research findings to be explored in the outer system. We therefore have the strategic option of returning through the Flaw to inform the Yunus, despite the implied failure. We must consider it. I solicit opinions.'

'I have never felt such clarity of purpose,' said Zilch, breathing hard. 'My joy at being Photurian and my hunger for closure in the quest to destroy the Abomination are effectively fused at this juncture. I want to personally save the crew of the GSS *Edmond Dantes* and wake them to love, so they can understand just how foolish they have been. If that is not possible, I would like to burn them alive. My subunits are already charting their exit vector.'

Nada smiled and felt a shared happiness at that response. Zilch had become impressively strong in the face of adversity. She swivelled her head back to observe Leng.

'A return trip would be risky and slow,' he said. 'Furthermore, the news we would return with is *sad*. Degraded homeworlds are not good for morale and therefore risk accelerating Fatigue. Studying the alien detritus may produce military benefits but the psychological impact of our central finding is likely to offset them. Your own un-characteristic neural activity serves as proof.'

'You both recommend continued pursuit, then?' said Nada.

Both her reports nodded. Nada felt another blast of curiously deep kinship towards them.

'Then we have alignment,' she said, with relief.

'Despite initial discomfort, I am glad that events have occurred in this fashion,' said Leng. 'We have seen and done things that make me feel deep union with the units in this fleet. I would not have experienced this without your enforced direction.'

'I concur,' said Zilch. 'The swift delight of following simple orders has been absent from this endeavour. However, the perverse satisfaction of solving arduous tactical problems has compensated. We are stronger now. I believe that despite the unevenness of our joy, we are further from Fatigue than any Photurians in the Utopia.'

Nada found a broad, human smile on her face. She wiped it off, though a thrumming feeling of closeness remained.

'It is decided, then,' she told them. 'Zilch, relate this consensus to your subnodes in the fleet. We will head onwards as rapidly as possible and either rescue or obliterate the GSS *Edmond Dantes* as circumstance permits.'

11: FALTERING

11.1: WILL

After Smiley left, Will wandered the angst-infused chambers of his own past while his mind churned over what the other Glitch had told him. When he could stand it no longer, he exited soft-space and found himself in yet another habitat-tunnel, this one full of swaying purple horsehairs six metres tall that rattled like bamboo.

'I found forty-seven,' he told Moneko.

She'd arrived in the transit-grave next to his, dressed in a flowing gown. Thankfully, there didn't appear to be anyone close by this time.

'That's awesome!' she said brightly, then noticed the woodenness of his smile. 'Did it feel a bit pointless?' she asked.

Will nodded. 'A bit.'

'Don't worry, that's normal. We sent you to an easy site this time on purpose. It'll get more interesting, I promise. But one day with no adventure has to be a good thing, right?'

'Definitely,' said Will.

He saw her watching him and knew he'd not quite sold her on his enthusiasm. Nevertheless, he chose not to say more. For the rest of the trip home, he stuck to safe topics: the details of his findings and questions about diving. He felt uncomfortable keeping secrets from Moneko, but if Smiley was right, he couldn't let her know that he doubted the Underground's intentions, even if he decided to trust her personally. He saw no choice but to keep the truth to himself until he'd gained a little more knowledge.

The following day, Moneko asked him to dive again.

'I have another axiom site for you,' she said. 'If you're up for it. It's around the idea that we've been here for ever. The access point is a little further from the target memories so you'll have to search around, but it should be doable. Sound okay?'

'Sure,' said Will blandly. 'Why not?'

When she led him down the hill on their bicycles, Will had to bite his tongue to not ask about mesh sites. She noted his silence.

'You're in a funny mood today,' she said.

'Still getting used to all this,' he told her. 'It's not an easy world to like.'

'Fair point,' she said. 'It grows on you, though, if you let it.'

She took him via the Carnevale to a science-aggregator site in soft-space where research clones from all over the Willworld pooled information about Snakepit's geology. The place looked more like Will's old memory of Snakepit's virtual presence than anything he'd seen so far. Long museum aisles with glass-fronted cabinets and chequered floor tiles stretched into the distance. Each cabinet contained a research result with diagrams and videos that played in real-time when you glanced at them. Wills in tweed hoodies strode this way and that followed by clouds of little research SAPs like anxious fireflies.

Within seconds of arriving, Will learned that covering Snakepit's continental shelves with a thick layer of habitat-tubes had played merry havoc with the normal order of plate tectonics. He'd have lingered to find out more but Moneko led him to a room off the main thoroughfare where they kept projects that had been shelved for future study due to lack of interest. There were thousands, all iconified and tucked away in alcoves. The room looked like a refuge for unloved snow globes.

This time, Will smelled the secret entrance before he reached it. It reeked, rather incongruously, of plastic furniture. Moneko opened a wall at the back. In the Underlayer beyond lay a Galatean commuter train he'd once been stuck in for several hours.

'You're doing great,' she told him. 'For what it's worth, I'm proud of you, Cuthbert. I know none of this is easy.'

She tucked her handkerchief into his doublet as usual and then let the portal swing shut. It occurred to Will as he gazed out at the butter-coloured scree beyond the train's curving windows that the handkerchief probably doubled as a tracking device.

He asked himself if he cared and for a moment doubted what he was about to do. But if Smiley was wrong, as he hoped, he could just go back to trusting the Underground. His confidence might even gain a boost. Will examined the memory landscape until he found an anchor, then concealed Moneko's handkerchief alongside it. That way, he'd be able to find it later.

With the suntap's hiding place restored, Will went looking for the surface of the Underlayer where it butted up against the edges of normal soft-space. It didn't take him long to find it. He simply reversed the technique that had led him down to the suntap chamber on his first dive. After a brief wander around the less-impressive moments of his personal history, he found himself sliding into another room at the back of the science library.

Will paused on the threshold to scan the space. Given the stealthware he still wore, the only person who could see him now was presumably Moneko. However, there was a chance she'd be scouting the library in case he resurfaced. Will waited until he was certain the coast was clear and then walked quickly to the nearest bank of search doors.

He jumped to the Mettaburg soft-station feeling nervous and dishonest. From there, he headed out into the mesh and started hunting for the pavilion that Smiley had mentioned. It was right where he'd said it would be. *Artistic Temperaments R Us* was scrawled above the doorway in large, spidery letters, ending with a jagged, unnecessary flourish.

Will stepped inside. The interior of the pavilion had soft grey walls lined with black and white photographs. They depicted clones of him in various poses suggesting poetic turmoil. Here was Will hunched dramatically at a writing desk with data stylus in hand. There was another poised in front of a canvas, engaged in the act of wildly reformatting a painting. The pictures were as moody as their content was ridiculous.

In the centre of the space was a small wooden table with a bell sitting on it and a plaque that read *Ring for service*. Set into the back wall of the pavilion was an incongruously solid wooden door.

Will idly examined the row of pictures and wondered how long he was prepared to wait. As it happened, John strode through the wooden door five minutes later, dressed in his trademark black coat. Beyond the opening, Will could make out a bland virtual office with stacks of icons hovering up against window-walls and a fake ocean view.

John strode into the mesh without a backwards glance. Will followed. It was almost too easy, he thought. Was he even following the right

John or just a clone with an identical appearance? In the Willworld, how could you ever tell? He ignored his misgivings. He'd give Smiley's notions exactly one experimental run before taking anything else the Glitch said at face value.

John used the Mettaburg Station to make a search. Will didn't catch his words but managed to slip into the corridor behind him before the door slid shut. As he stood there, inches away from his unsuspecting variant, he started to wonder why such apparently good stealthware even existed in the Willworld. What was this stuff used for when the Underground wasn't borrowing it? The society Will had built appeared to have remarkably lax security given some of the secrets it harboured.

John took an exit near the end of the corridor that opened into a nightclub. As Will stepped through after him, he flinched from the onslaught of noise. The space on the other side was packed with bodies, a racket loosely approximating music and hellish flashing lights. Steel stalactites loomed overhead. John pressed himself into the crowd.

Will worried about the effectiveness of his stealthware under such intimate conditions but the revellers let him squeeze by without so much as a glance in his direction. As he struggled to keep pace with John, he passed a huge open room where two hyena-headed Wills were fighting in a cage. Open wounds gaped on their chests where razor claws had ripped holes. Around the walls, on small stages, female Wills pole-danced. None of them had eyes.

Will stumbled to a halt. His jaw sagged open at the revolting sight. Clones dressed like Earther troops from the Interstellar War egged the cage-fighters on with yells barely audible over the deafening music. Will had no doubt what he was looking at – John had brought him to a den full of Cancer.

He belatedly noticed that his quarry was almost out of sight and forced himself onwards. His brow furrowed, a sick sense of anger boiling inside him as he struggled to catch up.

He passed another room crowded with people shouting and hooting at what looked like multiple gang rapes in progress. Will fought back nausea, furious in the pit of his gut, and hurried past. In every direction he looked, some form of depravity was taking place. He passed a clone bleeding on the floor while four others cheerfully kicked it.

It astonished him that some versions of himself had sunk so low. It hurt inside – shame as a form of physical pain. He fought back the desperate temptation to reach through the soft-space to end all of it. He knew that if he did, the jig would be up. His chance to follow John undetected would vanish. And now he wanted to know what was going on more than ever. After that, he could come back here and yank every thread in the site.

John disappeared around a corner. Will followed, elbowing his way through the oblivious revellers, and found himself staring down a short passageway with no one in it. He suffered a moment's panic and strode quickly along the passage, testing the walls. His hand went straight through the panelling at the end as if it was made of soft mud.

Will didn't hesitate. He threw himself against the wall. On the other side lay a heavy, blessed silence. Will gasped in relief and then froze as he recognised the corridor he stood in. It belonged to the orbital prison where the Truists had kept him during the war. His fury came back, pressing against the inside of his skull like water behind a dam. He caught sight of John walking swiftly away, his footfalls echoing. Will focused on that instead.

On either side, repeated dozens of times over, were copies of the cell where the High Church had tortured him. All were empty, save for the same exact chair they'd bound him to for 'religious education'. Will's breath started coming in heaves.

John took a left turn into one of the cells. Will entered behind him unseen like the angel of death. A Truist monk like one of the others Will had encountered with Moneko was sitting there. He rose as John entered and lowered his cowl. As he did so, his face melted from Will's features into John's. Will's new SAP-talents made it clear what he was seeing. A virtual screen had just been drawn aside, revealing one thread hiding inside the husk of another – a Cancer trick just like the one Moneko had described.

'How's it going?' said John. 'What kind of coverage are you getting?'

'Not bad,' said the monk. 'We're at about twelve per cent. I'd love it to be faster, but progress is solid.'

'Any wrinkles I can help with?'

The monk smirked. 'Other than the obvious, no. But that's work enough.'

Will wondered what the hell they were talking about.

John reached into the pocket of his coat and pulled out a wedge of improbably large physical bills. Will could guess what he was looking at: a stack of favours.

'This should handle any other problems you encounter,' said John.

'Are they clean?'

'Of course.' John laughed. 'Faultless and innocent, as you'd expect. Very recently washed. Don't you trust me?'

They both had a good laugh at that. John slapped the monk on the shoulder and wished him good luck before heading back the way he'd come.

Was John colluding with the monks? Were the monks actually copies of John? Either way, the exchange stank. Will contemplated ending them both. Instead, he stuck close to John while righteous wrath boiled inside him like a lightning storm, tailing him all the way back to the pavilion from whence he came.

He waited until John closed the door behind him, shutting them both into the ocean-view office, before he removed his mask. John caught sight of him and stumbled against a stack of icons, sending them bouncing off the glass.

'Jesus!' he blurted.

'What the fuck was all that about?' said Will. 'Care to enlighten me?'

John gaped and shook his head. He blinked and stared at the floor. When he glanced back at Will, his expression had regained a little of its suave intelligence.

'Let me guess,' he said. 'You met another Glitch.'

'Do you want to answer my question before I pluck your fucking thread?' said Will.

'Sure,' said John. He called up a chair and sat on it heavily. 'You deserve that. I was cleaning up your mess.'

'*My* mess?'

'The monks' feathers had to be smoothed so they wouldn't look for you too hard. I co-opted a few of their threads and slid certain notions into their collective discussions. What you saw was just an agent of mine reporting back about how it was going. That's why he had my face. It doubled as a password.'

'You acted like a Cancer, in other words,' Will snarled.

'Of course I did,' said John. 'In this business, that's necessary from time to time, as you've already seen. If you'd like to propose some other way for me to realign an organisation of pseudo-Truists without alerting them, I'd be delighted to hear it.'

'Murdering your own clones. Stealing their bodies. That's normal, is it?'

'How do you think they get recruits, Will?' said John wearily. 'They kidnap innocent threads for their disgusting rituals and turn them with torture. All I do is fight them on their own terms. I infect the infection. But even so, that doesn't make it right. I'm ashamed every time I do it.' He rubbed his eyes. 'I can imagine how that looked, but you were set up, Will. It was during your last dive, I bet. You're always vulnerable then. That Glitch, whoever you met, he capitalised on it. He probably even guessed I'd make my move while you were safely under. You can't listen to him, Will. He's tipped into anger and he's trying to take you with him. If you let him control you, you'll never think straight again.'

Will sneered. 'Whereas with you, I'm all good, I suppose.'

John shook his head. 'We have our own goals, of course, but at least we're trying to keep you alive. He doesn't care about that. With him jerking your strings, you'll be dead in a week. Why should he look out for you when to him you're just a naive duplicate of himself?'

'Which you're totally confident he believes, despite never having met him.'

John sighed. 'Of course I've met him, Will. How different can he possibly be from all the others? What's this one calling himself? Bond? Solo? Steed?'

'Smiley.'

John rolled his eyes. 'How original. Another Surplus Age reference from your aimless, download-infused youth. Look, Will, this world is bigger and more complex than you want to imagine. That's why I exist: to inhabit the grey areas. They happen.'

'I think you're full of shit,' Will insisted. 'I don't think you even know where the grey areas are because the belief-anchors you're so keen on keeping won't fucking let you.'

'That old chestnut again,' said John. 'Listen, I know about the risks. The hacks are full of weird-looking code, yadda yadda yadda. And wouldn't it be great if we could just rip them all out and live in freedom and peace? But do you want to know what would happen if we did that? Chaos.'

John flung out an arm to point at the door. 'Did you like what you saw back there? Did it look *okay* to you? Because it looked pretty vile to me. Balance is riddled with social disease, in case you hadn't noticed. And those anchors you hate so much are the only thing stopping that shit from spreading like wildfire and swallowing our society. Is that what you want? Are you ready to throw them all away based on some one-in-a-billion invasion fantasy? Because if you eliminate fixed social standards, you don't get freedom, you get a power vacuum. Fuck the Photurians, we'll murder ourselves. That's why we move them slowly, Will. Because that's how you do politics that works.'

Will grimaced in disgust. 'If what you're doing is so goddamned noble, then why didn't you just tell me about it?' he said. 'I think you've systematically hidden from me the scale of deviation my so-called copies engage in. You never intended for me to see that filth, or your dirty tricks.'

'Got it in one,' said John. 'We're hiding this stuff from you because it gets you killed almost every time because you can't keep your shit together once you find out. Furthermore, I don't expect that job to get any easier, because if stuff can happen in your subconscious, then it's happening here. Somewill's going to be off exploring it, no matter how weird or foul or esoteric. Quite literally, anything you can imagine goes. And I know you don't like that, but that's how it is. Also, before you ask, of course I picked a site where Balance wasn't going to be welcome to make my exchange. Where did you think I'd do it – in the middle of Princess Willemina's Candy fucking Kingdom?'

'So are you done with that now?' Will shouted. 'Any more dodgy hand-offs to make? Because if you're so ashamed of what you've done, you won't mind if I go back there and yank all that disgusting sub-human shit I just saw.'

John gave him a look both exhausted and imploring. 'Do that and you finish us. All that social blindness they're pumping out will vanish. Balance will be in there like a shot, trying to find out what caused the thread-loss. He'll kill you and take down most of us. He'll get Moneko first. Her thread history is tangled most deeply with yours.'

Will glared at John, still half-tempted to finish him even while the man's story added up. He teetered on the brink of killing.

'Every time you walk into our bar, Will, we have a choice,' said John. 'We can help you and risk all our threads along the way, or we can

311

let you die. I put my life on the line for you each time that happens because I believe it will help make this a better world.'

Will shook his head. 'By building a fucking map.'

'Yes, by building a map. Moving hacks about. Nudging public opinion.'

'*Why?*' Will demanded. 'What *is* your agenda?'

John exhaled in exasperation. 'For starters, a world where they don't murder Glitches as soon as they appear,' he said. 'And then, after that, maybe one where we can discuss leaving the planet like rational human beings. Now, if you don't want to build a map with us, by all means go your own way. Nobody's keeping you here. Everyone in this organisation is a volunteer. If you think you can do better with this Smiley, seek him out. I won't stop you. I'll let Moneko know you're going and she'll have to deal with it. I'll make sure you don't hear from her again. That'll hurt but she'll cope.'

Will roared his displeasure. He grabbed an icon from the nearest stack and hurled it across the room. It ricocheted off the glass twice before finding another stack to settle into.

He pointed at John. 'The next axiom we go for is the one about *not leaving*!' Will shouted. 'No more wasting my fucking time!'

'Sure,' said John wearily. 'If that's what you want, then that's the way you'll have it.'

11.2: IRA

Ira returned to the *Dantes* to find a decidedly unhappy crew waiting in the lounge. Mark stared out at a stormy sea with arms folded. Palla paced, her chromatophore scalp pulsing in angry waves. Judj perched on a dining chair in the corner, looking like a man who'd sucked way too many lemons.

'No Ann?' he said as he walked in with Clath.

'Not yet,' said Palla darkly. 'She's still going through quarantine.'

'I don't get it,' said Ira. 'She was with Judj, wasn't she? What happened down there?'

'She came up on her own,' said Judj. 'In an enemy shuttle full of mind-raped Photes.'

Ira's eyebrows fled upwards. '*What?*'

'Look, Ira,' said Palla, 'a lot happened, okay? We'll get to it all. The first thing you need to know is that we have Rachel with us.'

'You mean her body? I expected that.'

'No,' said Mark. 'Actually *with* us. She's having a shadow fitted right now. We made the decision to bring her into virt.'

'Jesus,' said Clath, sitting down. 'I guess you guys were busy while we were out.'

'You could say that,' said Mark.

'I don't understand,' said Ira, his head swimming. 'How could her casket possibly have lasted this long?'

Mark shrugged. 'On the face of it, it looks like her crew prioritised her cryo-stability over their own. She refuses to believe that, though, and I can't say I blame her. All she knows is that she went to sleep in the Zone and set course for home. When she woke up, she was with us.'

'Then she'll be in shock,' said Ira. 'When can I talk to her?'

'In another day or two,' said Palla. 'She has a lot of tissue damage that needs repairing, as you might expect. And just so you know, we've been watching for signs of cognitive cascade since she woke up. We haven't seen any. She appears to be extremely emotionally robust. One might even say unnaturally so.'

'That's Rachel,' said Ira, cracking a smile. 'She's old-school Galatean. Hard as nails.'

'I hope it's just that,' said Palla. 'I really do.'

Ann arrived then, striding through the door from the deck. She parked herself in an armchair and surveyed them with an amused, regal detachment.

'I'm glad to see everyone got out intact,' she said. She seemed breezy, upbeat and entirely unaware of the crackling fury that built suddenly in the room. 'I've prepared a full download of my experiences and I look forward to seeing yours.'

Mark pivoted to jab a finger at her. 'You are unbe-fucking-lievable,' he spat. 'You come in here chipper as shit as if nothing happened? Rescuing you nearly ended all of us!'

Ann's face fell. 'Why did you bother, then? I made it clear in my ping that pickup was optional. I would happily have commandeered a Phote starship just like I commandeered one of their shuttles. All your antics did was spare them ships, damage a perfectly good shuttle and execute four compromised Photes.'

313

Mark glared at her in disbelief.

'If that was your intention, you should have been *specific*,' said Palla.

'I assumed you'd infer my tactics based on the available data,' Ann retorted.

'And that,' Palla said, 'is the problem. You *assumed*! You left us the job of predicting the actions of a post-rational post-human psychopath who habitually courts suicide.'

'If you presumed I was suicidal, then rescuing me seems particularly pointless,' Ann growled. 'Am I a psychopath or are you a masochist?'

Ira felt their collective rage like a physical pressure. It squeezed the air from his lungs and made his head ring.

'Could someone please just explain what actually happened?' he said, throwing up his hands.

Palla obliged. 'The Great Ludik here stayed behind on the planet so that she could come back up with a piece of Photurian junk she picked out. One she found by rooting around in the rad-burned ruins of a defensive node.'

'Not to mention the fact that her trip necessitated me expending the *Diggory* and trashing the fucking planet!' Mark shouted.

Ann gave him a steely look. 'What are you complaining about? It was obvious the *Diggory* was going to be expended from the moment we had Phote company. And that planet you're suddenly so attached to was home to nothing more than pond slime.'

Ira watched Ann with mounting dread. Their anger was making her more defensive of her choices, not less. Couldn't they see what they were doing to her?

'And while we're on the matter of tactical choices,' Ann added, 'I propose that we return through the Flaw. We've secured a military advantage but it's only useful in shared hands.'

'Does the fact that all the exit vectors to the Flaw are blocked not even register for you, or that we have fifty gunships at our backs?' Mark roared. 'Are you out of your *mind*?'

'Yes, she is,' said Judj. 'She systematically avoided warnings on the away mission. She courted danger at every turn with zero consideration of the spillover risk to others.'

'Not to mention the fact that you accepted a mission as an officer of the Galatean Fleet,' said Palla. 'One that does not involve continually trying to kill yourself at every given opportunity!'

'My assessment is based entirely on what I believe to be best for the Galatean people,' said Ann, rising imperiously to her feet.

'Bullshit,' said Palla. 'It's all about you and it always has been. You and your grand exit.'

Ann's eyes took on an ice-queen glow. The virtual air around her shimmered as her voice became a growl.

'Spare me your petty judgements,' she said. 'The last forty years of my existence have been entirely about everyone else. I have emptied myself trying to help the human race. I've had to burn, blast and murder more than any other person in human history. The only thing left that belongs to me, so far as I can tell, is my death. So if I choose to take risks, that is my prerogative. As it is, I was *not* trying to die out there. I was trying to do my job. And I resent the implication that I was attempting anything else.'

Ira's insides felt squeezed as the python of borrowed emotion wrapped its coils around him. He identified with Ann more than he ever wanted to and couldn't bear watching this play out. He knew what was coming next. Palla was going to reveal her secret and break the goddess.

'And I,' said Palla, 'am sick of your self-indulgent bullshit. I don't think you have even the first idea of the people you harm—'

'A minute, please, *everyone*!' said Ira, throwing up his hands. 'Can we remember for a second that we're all starship officers? How about we back off to think for a minute and have a dialogue based on data?' He didn't dare let them escalate the fight any further. 'All Ann is saying is that we already have enough data to potentially alter the course of the war. Am I right?' He glanced at her urgently.

She peered at him like a bug. 'Correct.'

Ira continued before she could ruin it. 'Even if you don't buy the value of Ann's artefact, we now have an alien ship in our hold made of miracle armour. That clinches it. If we go on, we have to accept responsibility for the fact that we're taking a high-risk option when a lower risk option exists.'

'Lower risk?' said Mark. 'How is fighting our way through an army of angry Photes *lower risk*?'

'Because it's easier than fighting through *fifty* armies of angry Photes when we hit Snakepit!' Ira urged.

'But there isn't going to be a blockade!' Mark shouted.

'That's a nice idea, but it's conjecture,' said Ira. 'Did you model-test that notion?'

Mark didn't reply.

'Ira Baron,' said Ann, 'my strategic assessments do not need your support.'

Ira swivelled to face her. 'But I'm not doing it for you,' he insisted. 'I'm doing it for everyone else so they can understand. So, in the name of mercy, please shut up for a minute.'

'The Zone will also be guarded by now,' said Palla. 'Most likely on both sides. And we'd be tracked. That's not lower risk. That's a disaster.'

'Incorrect,' said Ann.

'Please!' Ira implored her. 'Let me handle this.' He spun to face the others. 'Have any of the rest of you actually looked at Ann's threat models?'

Mark responded with a thin-lipped scowl.

'Are they public?' said Palla.

'Of course,' said Ann.

'Why didn't you give us a fucking *link*, then?' said Palla. 'Why did you expect us to go looking?'

'Because she assumed you would!' said Ira before Ann could speak. 'That's how she's been running things on her ship for decades. She expects anticipation from every junior officer she brings aboard and that's how her team operates. As far as she's concerned, that's what good officers do. Before you condemn her, understand that Ann is trying to be rational, *that's all*. She's just out of the habit of bothering to explain because for the last forty years she's had to do almost everything for herself.'

'Do you agree with her?' Mark demanded. 'Is that what you're saying? That we should throw in the fucking towel?'

'No,' said Ira. 'I don't agree with her.'

'Then why bother going through all the bullshit of trying to justify her logic?'

'Because I believe her models are *right*,' said Ira. 'I've looked at them and, as usual, she's done a fantastic job. But the reason I think we should go on has nothing to do with threat levels. It's because we haven't solved this puzzle yet. All we have are clues. There are no valid risk models for a situation like this – it's not quantifiable. We went off the map the moment we saw that buoy and it's been getting crazier ever since. And I believe this puzzle is more important than any perceived mission plan or scientific opportunity.'

Ira drew heavy breaths in the quiet that followed.

Inevitably, Ann ruined it. 'I can't agree with that assessment.'

Ira lost it. 'Of course you can't!' He laughed bitterly. 'Your emotional scripting requires that you die *visibly* where everyone you care about can watch. That's how you say sorry, which is the one thing you've been trying to do this entire time, isn't it? Apologise. And that's why it has to be a battle. If you only cared about dying, you'd be just as happy fighting the Photes on this side of the Zone as anywhere else. Fuck knows we have enough of them to kill now!'

Ann stared at everyone with wide eyes and suddenly looked terribly vulnerable. Ira had a desperate sinking feeling. He'd revealed too much of the truth. She vanished from the virt like a popped soap bubble.

Ira groaned. In the wake of her departure, a hot sense of longing radiated from the pit of his gut. He wanted her back in the room. He didn't just want to protect her from mental harm, he realised. He *cared*. Ann had been a bigger feature in his life than he'd ever let himself admit. They'd been wounded by the same horrors – joined by them. His choices and her actions had welded them into the same page of history as partners in shame. He hadn't let himself notice that before but now he couldn't avoid it.

'She leaves just like that?' said Mark. 'The moment someone points out what a child she is?'

'Oh, come on, Mark,' Ira snapped. 'You can barely see straight past your own self-loathing and you're having a go at *her*?'

Mark blinked. An expression of startled disgust appeared on his features.

'What do you mean?' he said. 'I don't loathe myself.'

'Then don't be in such a hurry to finish the mission,' said Ira. 'You're still going to be *you* at the end of it!'

Ira saw the giveaway panic indicators in Mark's gaze and knew he'd done more harm than good again.

'The only reason I'm in a hurry is because we need to get away from those Photes while we still have a glimmer of a chance!' Mark shouted, pointing out to sea behind them with a trembling fingertip.

'Sure,' said Ira. 'You're right. Sorry.' He sagged into the closest chair, utterly drained.

This, apparently, was the price of his returning capacity to emote: the ability to screw up, just like he used to. He remembered why he'd spent all those years struggling to perfect his detachment.

While Ira hung his head, a post-nuclear silence descended in the lounge. Mark stared at the ground for several long seconds before storming out into the synthetic night.

11.3: MARK

Mark pushed them hard into uncharted territory, racing through space as fast as the *Dantes* could manage. As he flew, he took solace in the fact that his ember-warp engines were far superior to those he'd seen the Photes using during their last confrontation. Unless they stopped to build a new carrier, they'd be stuck operating like scouts and nowhere near as fast as him. That knowledge calmed him enough that when Rachel came out of surgery, he took time off from the helm to have breakfast with her.

Judj had reluctantly awarded her a clean bill of health the morning after they'd fled the gorilla-crab system. She had no hidden Phote clusters, apparently, and no foreign augs – just a bad case of cryo-burn that would need a few months' recuperation. Mark wasn't sure how to feel about that. No one on board was more paranoid than Judj so he should have been satisfied, but Mark's concerns about how they'd found his half-mother refused to subside. He struggled to accept the fact that her escape from the Zone had been entirely natural, even faced with the medical evidence that appeared to prove it.

They sat together on deck while Rachel peered at things: the sea, her hands, her plate. She said little and made eye contact even less. Inhabiting a virtual world was new for her, he reminded himself. It'd take her a while to get used to synthetic reality. But regardless of the cause, the warmth Mark had hoped for wasn't happening, so he found himself filling the silence with talk of his life and achievements. He told Rachel about his marriage and the little world he'd built on the *Gulliver*. He spoke at length about the ways he thought he'd changed over the years and hoped that at least some of it might yield a sense of connection.

When at last she did ask a question, it wasn't one he'd expected.

'So now lots of people have these shadows?'

'In the Fleet, yes,' said Mark. 'About eighty per cent of operational officers. Why do you ask?'

'Well, it's just that you're not alone any more, are you?' she said, peering at him. 'You don't *have* to build a world on your own. So why spend all your time off alone with your wife? Why not... I don't know... integrate?'

'Having a shadow isn't the same as being a roboteer, Rach,' he said.

'I know,' she said. 'But still – you have all this.' She waved an uncertain arm at the sea. 'You can do a kind of memory sharing, as I discovered this morning. You can control machines. You're accepted – a hero, even. So why stay away? Isn't this whole New Society thing heaven for you? I mean, all your leaders are effectively roboteers, and your scientists.'

Mark laughed bitterly. 'Unfortunately, our leaders are smug conformists who don't hesitate for an instant before putting a price on a life.'

'What about Palla?' said Rachel, looking confused. 'She seems nice. She doesn't strike me as a conformist. She's kind of plucky.'

'Plucky,' said Mark.

'Yes. Also flexible and considerate.'

Mark's eyebrows shot up. 'Considerate? Are we talking about the same woman who insulted you for giving me my mods within ten minutes of meeting you?'

'Yes, but I've often wondered about that. Maybe I deserve the criticism.'

He shook his head. 'Rach,' he said, exasperated, 'you haven't seen what they're like. They've taken human society and turned it into this weird lockstep game. There's no privacy any more. There's no freedom. Everyone gets orders. Everyone has to play.'

'Except you, apparently.'

'Because I defend my right to be a free operator!'

Rachel squinted at the horizon and said nothing.

'You've gone quiet,' said Mark.

She nodded. 'I have a lot to take in. So much has changed and I've barely gone through the history updates Judj gave me. All those years.' She shook her head. 'It'll be a while before I open up, I'm afraid.' She glanced at him quickly with eyes full of pain. 'I still feel like I've woken up in a nightmare.'

Mark's defensiveness crumpled under a snowfall of guilt. 'I'm sorry.'

'It's not your fault. I'd rather this than the alternative.'

'I hope it's not that bad,' he said. 'We're trying to make things right.'

She pulled a sour face. 'Is mind-raping your enemy normal now?'

'No,' said Mark.

'That's what she did, isn't it? How about trashing biospheres? Do we do that a lot?'

Mark folded his arms, his face reddening. 'We don't normally do that, either. But please note that there's a big difference between a Phote world and a real one.'

'I see. You know, back when I went into cryo, biospheres were treated like miracles. We made them into nature reserves.'

'The planet we blasted was host to nothing but pond scum,' Mark insisted. 'No inhabitants. No victims. Nothing but the leftovers of interspecies genocide. Frankly, we did it a favour. Now at least the Photes won't try repopulating it with their poison any time soon. It stands a chance of evolving on its own.'

She shot him a look heavy with veiled disappointment. His insides wound tight. He opened his mouth to say something profound when a loud bang echoed through the virt. The sea froze in towering spikes. Rachel's breakfast crawled in front of her like a bowl full of beetles. The sky blackened.

The next thing Mark knew, they'd been dumped back into the starry void of helm-space where engine alerts crowded around, blinking and blaring. Their warp-envelope had died, leaving their entangler field in an almighty mess.

'What happened?' said Rachel.

'Engines are offline,' he told her, scanning the blizzard of data. 'Still figuring out why.'

Clath appeared beside him. 'On it,' she said.

The others popped into the helm-arena in rapid succession.

Clath shook her head as diagnostic icons splayed open around her. 'This doesn't make any sense. The field just collapsed. There was no warning.'

'Is it disrupters?' said Ann, striding up to join them. 'Any sign of a trap?'

'No,' said Clath. 'Space is clean. We're nowhere near anything.'

'It's the ark,' said Ira. 'Take a look at this.'

He threw them a cluster of icons that Mark had missed in his hurry to understand. They were full of low-level warnings from the mining hold where the alien ship lay clamped in place. Something odd had happened down there. The ship had *changed*, and so had the buttresses holding it.

Clath blinked twice at the readings. 'How it that possible?' she said. 'That ship was dead. There were no emissions.'

'How is *what* possible?' said Mark.

'Hold on,' said Clath. 'Going immersive to check.'

She disappeared and reappeared a few seconds later looking nervous.

'Okay, here's how it is. We have major damage to the mining buttresses. And maybe damage to the alien ark. Somehow it moved.'

'It was pinned in place!' said Mark.

'I know. And now it's fused into the grappling structure.'

Clath threw them some view windows. All the buttresses on one side looked as if they'd melted from the top like candles and flowed around the ark. It wasn't the kind of behaviour you expected to see from armoured, heat-shielded gantries half a kilometre long. The alien ship now resembled a ball of polished rock, coated from end to end with the fused, homogenised remnants of the grapples that had once held it.

Mark regarded the image in stunned disbelief.

'Well, we'd better cut it out of there, hadn't we?' he said. 'Let's space that ugly fucking ball before it kills us.'

Clath's features squirmed as she got used to the idea of throwing away a major scientific find.

'Okay,' she said. 'Survival first.'

'I'll help,' said Ann. 'It's possible this act was deliberate. If so, we should be ready to respond.'

Mark winced. Great, a pitched battle inside his own hull.

'How long will you need?' he said.

Clath frowned at the damage reports. 'Given that level of carnage, about five hours.'

Mark shook his head. 'We don't have that kind of a lead. Can you do it under warp?'

'Maybe,' she replied uncomfortably. 'Not easily, though. If that thing reacts again, we might lose our cutting robots. I recommend that we at least swap to trad-warp till we can get the ark out.'

Mark moaned inwardly as he pictured the distance between them and the Phote armada shrinking.

'Won't that put more gravity load on the mining gear?' he said.

Clath nodded. 'Undoubtedly, but if I had to guess what caused this, I'd say it was some kind of warp-feedback. We took an object made out of ember-warp states and shoved it inside our transport field. That's probably the gravitational equivalent of putting a bunch of metal in a microwave oven – on reflection, not a great idea. If we go trad, it will at least minimise the chance of exotic interactions between the two fields.'

Mark felt grateful that she wasn't pointing out how reckless he'd been when he'd absconded with the vessel in the first place. She didn't need to. He was already regretting it. And if he hadn't been in such a hurry to put distance between them and the enemy, they'd have dumped it already, Clath's complaints notwithstanding.

'Okay,' he said. 'It's better than nothing.'

Clath performed a quick stress-modelling of the mess in the mining bay and passed him the results. With great trepidation, he restarted the drive, keeping their burst rate low. If she'd measured the expected forces incorrectly, the alien ship would shear off the damaged buttresses and slam into the wall of the mining bay, possibly ploughing through some of the antimatter conduits beyond. If that happened, they wouldn't have long to contemplate failure.

With the first thuds of warp, the mining gear strained, flooding the helm with fresh warnings, but the structure held. Mark slowly ramped their burst rate, watching the readouts from the bay the entire time. He gave thanks that his electronic eyes didn't need to blink.

When they reached about a quarter of a gee of pseudo-gravity, Clath told him to stop.

'I wouldn't take it higher if I were you. Not until we're done cutting.'

They were barely going fifty lights.

'Christ,' said Mark. 'Let's hope this is enough.'

'Okay, here's how we do it,' said Palla. 'We're forming two teams. Mark and I will manage flight. Clath, Ira, Ann, Judj – you guys solve the ark problem. Clath takes the lead because this is an engineering issue.'

'What about me?' said Rachel.

Palla regarded her blankly. 'Right now, Captain Bock, you're a passenger. What would you *like* to do?'

322

'Help, of course,' said Rachel. 'I'm a Fleet engineer. My tech is out of date, but I doubt buttress designs have changed that much.'

'Fair point,' said Palla. 'However, please note that your physical body is still stored in our quarantine core and we can't move it under warp, which means there's only so much you can do. You don't have access to the ship's primary systems.'

'Can I still pilot robots?'

'Of course.'

'Then I can help.'

Palla smiled. 'Okay, ask Clath what she needs. I'm activating a dedicated workspace for you all now.'

The others vanished. Mark turned his attention back to the *Dantes* and flew on tenterhooks while Palla kept an eye on the mining-bay readouts.

'Do you think Ann is stable?' she asked as she reorganised her displays. 'Can we rely on her to help? She barely been out of her room since our fight yet she's behaving as if nothing happened. I don't buy it.'

'I hope so,' said Mark. 'She likes this kind of shit. Immediate threats are her thing.'

'And how about you?' said Palla gently. 'You doing okay?'

Mark frowned as he worked. 'What do you mean?'

'I mean you've been wound up tight since we got out of that system.'

'We're being chased,' Mark said tersely. 'What did you expect?'

'Not sure,' she said. 'But frankly, I've been worried about you ever since Ira made that *self-loathing* remark.'

Mark's shoulders hunched. 'Palla, please. I'm not in need of a New Society therapy session right now. I don't loathe myself or anyone else.'

She paused before replying. 'Could have fooled me,' she said quietly.

Mark pretended he hadn't heard.

Just a few hours later, it happened again. The warp field slammed flat and alerts burst back into cacophony. Mark opened a channel to Clath's workspace.

'How bad?' he said.

'Much less severe,' she said. 'It zeroed our work but we only lost six cutters. Rachel was very careful. And now we know how it happens. The ark goes into a kind of quantum spasm. Anything in contact with the outer shell flows around it like a superfluid. And it's fast. The whole thing happens in milliseconds. I'm sorry,' she said heavily. 'If I'd been thinking straight I might have predicted something like this. That shell is made of a warp-matter mix. When we dump spatial distortion onto it, it probably accumulates until there are tiny vacuum-quakes. When that happens, anything in contact is channelled across the surface just like space–time under ember-warp. The resultant shock wave nukes the local flow.'

'So what's the solution?' said Mark.

'We have to drop warp completely to cut it out,' said Clath. 'Rachel agrees. Otherwise that thing stays with us, which would be bad because it keeps shifting towards the ship's centre where the distortion landscape peaks. That means it'll eventually liquidise the habitat core with us in it. We need somewhere to stop and make proper repairs.'

Mark rubbed his eyes. 'Great.'

'Okay, how about this?' said Palla, throwing him a navigational display. 'It's a Class-A star less than a light-year from here – a huge system and relatively young. There should be plenty of debris to hide in.'

'Sounds super,' Mark growled. 'I love a good Class A. So blue and shiny. Why the fuck not?'

He laid in a course and restarted the engines, ramping warp gently even though he had no idea whether it was helping.

Hobbling to their new destination burned another twenty hours. Mark pumped his body full of fatigue suppressors and refused to take a moment off watch. By then, thankfully, he'd figured out a way to fly that minimised the effect of the vacuum-quakes. He piloted the ship at an angle so that the gravitational drag on the alien ark compensated for the yanking effect it caused every time it shifted. On a spherical ship, that would have been easy. But the *Dantes* had giant sub-light thrusters to drag around, so maintaining a stable warp-envelope required constant rebalancing. He couldn't wait to get the damned ark off his ship.

He alerted the others as the *Dantes* staggered into range of the new star and dropped to sub-light.

'Target ahead,' he told them, exhausted. 'Get ready for insertion manoeuvres. Let's fix this quickly.'

'Scanning the neighbourhood,' said Palla. 'I'll find you a hiding place in no time.' But instead of coming back with a vector for him, her shoulders sagged. 'Actually, scratch that,' she said. 'We'd better get Judj in here.'

Mark could have wept. 'What is it now?'

She tossed him some diagnostics to look at. The system had plenty of debris, as promised – almost all of it clustered in a single outer belt that was also dotted with false-matter miracles of gorilla-crab construction. Further in, the star's broad Goldilocks zone had been scoured perfectly clean of troublesome rocks. Two biosphere worlds swung there in tidy circular orbits – both were Photurian.

'You're fucking kidding,' said Mark. 'More of them? Here? This isn't even a nice star.'

He couldn't believe it. He felt his hopes for the mission unravelling, thread by thread. With a sick feeling in his throat, he refocused the telescopes for threat assessment and was relieved to discover that both planets were inert. One world showed holes in its tunnel-matrix so big that a third of the planet looked almost normal. The other was in better shape than the first one they'd found, though still bearing the hallmarks of decay.

'All this around a Class A?' said Judj as he rejoined them. 'That's just wrong. It's a miracle those planets were even cool enough for the Photes to use.'

'I guess this was a popular neighbourhood back then,' Palla remarked.

That was one way of putting it. A million or so years ago, this part of space had evidently been crawling with Photes. The reason for the Depleted Zone was clearer than ever. Mark picked the closest moonlet big enough to hide behind and tethered their ship so that Rachel could restart her cutting.

'It's kind of fascinating,' said Judj while the others got to work. 'These worlds must all have been claimed during the same civilisation wave, but look at the differentiation in decay. Once a Phote world starts to melt, the change must be extremely rapid in evolutionary terms. Mark, how would you feel if we sent a probe in to sample their atmospheres? We might learn a lot about the decay pathways in Phote biology.'

'So long as you don't expect me to follow it, or rescue it, or care,' said Mark, 'you can do whatever the hell you like. If it gets back here before we finish repairs, it can come with us, but I'm not hanging around.'

He glanced anxiously at Ann, half-expecting her to demand that they let her fly a shuttle in so that she could stand heroically among the remains. Thankfully, the goddess looked more self-contained than usual. The sombre mood she'd fallen into after their debate still held. Mark cherished that quiet.

Sadly, peace lasted for less than two hours. Then company arrived. Mark stood in helm-space and clutched his head in despair while the system perimeter filled up with arrival bursts. The cutting was already behind schedule.

On the heels of the flashes came the inevitable message. This time, it wasn't the usual slick advertisement. Instead, Nada Rien addressed them directly.

'Captain Mark Ruiz of the GSS *Edmond Dantes*,' she proclaimed. 'I have come to save you and your crew. Prepare to receive love into your cold, black heart or face annihilation.'

Mark stared at Palla in disbelief.

'I'm having a bad day,' he said, his chest heaving. 'I think this qualifies as a bad day, don't you?' He pinged Clath. 'How far through are we?' he said.

Rachel came on the channel instead. 'Not far enough,' she replied. 'The molecular structure of the fused alloy is really weird, which isn't helping. We're thinking of just uncoupling the buttresses at their closest telescopic joins instead.'

'Photes are zeroing in on our part of the debris ring. We probably have minutes to exit. Can you pull that off in time?'

'Not a hope in hell, unless you want to do more damage to the ship's internals. We're talking about severing several hundred metres of fused metal here. We could blast the ark free, but then it's bye-bye warp conduits. The follow-up repairs would take even longer.'

Mark shut his eyes and breathed deep. How was he supposed to finagle his way out of this one? Estimating from Nada's insertion point and velocity record, his lead was twelve minutes at most.

In the background, Nada kept talking. 'Do you even know why you're running?' she demanded. 'You want to be safe – with us you *would* be safe. You want to be happy – we are *always* happy! That's what is so pitiful about you humans. This paradox. This inability to see clearly. Every culture in history has lusted after some vision of heaven. Your kind always crave a faith to follow and the rewards of a loving god. You have squabbled and murdered over that idea since the dawn of history. Yet when the solution is right in front of you,

you cannot accept it! Are you *designed* for misery? We are offering all the things you want! Peace. Order. Health. Uniform love. Effortless discipline. Unquestionable moral absolutes. Joining the Utopia is the only meaningful choice. Anything else makes a soiled lie of the human condition.'

'Pack up your tools, Clath,' Mark growled. 'We're leaving.'

He knew Nada was goading him but no longer cared. A lifetime of frustration boiled up inside.

'Would you like to make a stand now?' said Ann quietly. She sounded almost polite about it.

'No!' Mark yelled. 'I would *not* like to make a stand. I have come here to do a job and I intend to do it, whether that halfwit automaton insists on creeping around after us or not. We are going to *Snakepit!*'

As soon as Clath gave him the green light, Mark fired the thrusters and dived the ship straight at the blue star. At the same time, he primed a relay drone, squeezed all his vitriol into a fresh submind copy and threw it back towards the incoming fleet. This time he let the drone decide when it was safe to broadcast.

'I'm sorry, Nada, but I don't think you got the memo,' said the drone. 'We already have peace, order, health and most of that other shit. And we did it by figuring it out for ourselves rather than having you fuckers force it on us.'

'Sounds like your submind's a fan of the New Society,' said Palla, sliding him a wry glance.

Something of the miserable desperation Mark felt must have leaked out in his gaze because her smile faltered and she turned her attention back to the displays.

'I've spent my whole life resisting people like you, Nada,' his proxy growled. 'People with cheap, shitty answers who imagine that heaven can come from the barrel of a gun or the flick of a switch. You know what I think? I think the whole idea of moral absolutes is sick. There is no true religion. The only reason to be alive is to figure things out for yourself. To answer your own damned questions rather than having someone else's faith poured into your skull like boiling lead. Believing in that shit turns a person into a dead-eyed, bloodthirsty robot, just like you, Nada. Just like you.'

'How are we bloodthirsty?' said Nada. 'We convert. It is humanity that murders whole worlds. You are the ones who insist on resisting the inevitable.'

Mark didn't have to update his drone. It already knew what to say.

'If your solution is so great and so inevitable, then why is space on this side of the Zone littered with the corpses of your kind? You should listen to yourself, Nada Rien. For someone who's always happy, you don't sound so hot.'

Mark used his scant lead to descend on the closest biosphere world. He armed his boser and fired a glancing sub-second blow through the world's upper mantle. Such shots had long been determined to create the largest and most devastating seismic shock waves. He'd learned from last time that nothing stalled his enemies like seeing one of their precious biospheres harmed. This one would be recovering for a long time.

'There,' he said as he watched the planet's atmosphere ripple sickly. He didn't bother hiding the source of his broadcast this time. Given the light-lag involved, it'd reach the Photurians minutes later and by then he intended to be far away. 'That's a little human-style present for you,' he said. 'You can keep it.'

The first signs of major tectonic devastation were still revealing themselves. Later would come the mantle plumes and the darkness, the lakes of lava and the sterilising winter. The blast he'd delivered equated to about twenty simultaneous dinosaur-killer events. While involving far less mass than a bolide impact, a boser delivered its payload at appalling velocity. Boser discharge made rail-gun bullets look sluggish.

Mark didn't stay to watch. He tore straight through the depths of the system and out of the other side, his ship still limping at a jaunty angle. Almost as an afterthought, he blasted some debris from the major ring into long elliptical orbits, guaranteeing the biosphere worlds a healthy supply of asteroid collisions for millennia to come.

He didn't notice everyone in helm-space watching him silently until after they cleared the system's edge. He saw surprise in their gazes, and unease. Only Ann wasn't looking at him anxiously. Instead, her eyes held something like pitying camaraderie.

'What?' he said. 'We needed a lead! We have a problem in the hold, remember? And frankly, that place wasn't special! Dead Phote worlds are a dime a dozen around here, or hadn't you noticed? What else was I supposed to do?'

'Was it absolutely necessary to break out the weapons of mass destruction?' said Rachel.

'I don't think you get it,' said Mark. '*Nobody* was harmed.'

'Are you sure?' she said. 'Did you actually check?'

Mark threw up his arms. 'What would have been the point? Do you honestly imagine someone was down there? These worlds are graveyards, Rach. The smartest life that place hosted probably used its flagellum to wave hello.'

'But *why*?' she said quietly. 'Those rocks you knocked on the way out at least gave them a problem to solve. What was blasting that planet going to do except make them hate you? You're not who you used to be, Mark. You *push*, just like Will did. Did I lose you, too?'

She turned and tried to find an exit from helm-space. Unfortunately, no one had explained virt-porting to her yet, so Rachel wandered around on the far edge of the disc looking disgusted until Judj helped her leave. It was awful to watch.

'I didn't hurt anyone,' Mark said forlornly after they left.

'We know,' said Palla. 'It was just a bit surprising, that's all. Everyone else feels your anger, Mark. We understand. Rachel missed the worst bits of history. But let's focus on flying, shall we? I don't think we're getting rid of that ark any time soon, which means we need another solution.'

11.4: NADA

Nada was in the crew-bulb with the others when the humans fled again. She hung quietly, listening to her crew wail and watching their bodies flail on the ends of their umbilici. Somehow, she'd lost her capacity for horror back at the first homeworld they'd encountered. Now she felt only brooding dislocation.

The Yunus's edits still dragged on her psyche. She craved an ending to the Abomination. But that ambition now pulled in opposition to a renewed yearning to connect with a functioning homeworld – one that would last. And somewhere, in the midst of that tension, her hunger to end the war had taken on a more introspective quality.

The Yunus had promised that when she succeeded there'd be no more human-farming, or false homes, or enforced individuality. The era of compromise would be at an end, he'd said. But what value did such words have if even the Yunus didn't know how to secure lasting harmony?

Sickening though it was, the odious Ruiz had a point. The Yunus had christened him 'Thief of Souls' many years ago because of his habit of absconding with large numbers of hosts that would otherwise have been saved. For Nada, though, Ruiz had become the thief of certainty.

All that really mattered was whether Backspace contained some clue to what would arrest her own people's rate of decay. If it did not, then nothing they found was relevant and neither were Ruiz's repellent acts. In that case, the Thief of Souls was right. They were only visiting graveyards.

'Why are the humans so terrible?' cried Leng. He thrashed back and forth, tears wobbling free of his good eye with every jerk of his head. The maintenance louse rebuilding his face looked hard-pressed to stay attached.

Nada reached through the mind-temple and edited him into calm. His eye flicked open. His anguish fell away.

'Report,' she said wearily.

Leng took a moment to adapt. 'We were fortunate,' he said, recovering his breath.

He spoke so quietly that Nada struggled to hear over the noise of the others lamenting. She issued a broadcast wave of enforced peace. The shrieks and whimpers abruptly subsided.

'Continue,' said Nada. 'Audibly this time.'

'The humans targeted the world in a more advanced state of decay,' he said. 'This leaves us with another corrupted homeworld to examine, but one in superior condition.'

'Are you recommending that we do so?' she said, astonished at her own indifference.

Leng didn't reply. Instead, his face broke slowly into a nauseated grin. His good eye slid from side to side.

'Yes,' said a voice from across the room.

Nada looked around, confused, and found Communications Officer Ekkert staring at her.

'Yes. It is unfortunate, but delay and research are now necessary,' said Ekkert. 'The humans created an asteroidal threat to the remaining

330

homeworld that will need to be resolved if the planet is to survive. This presents an opportunity for refuelling and communion.'

'You are a subnode of Leng's,' said Nada. 'Your opinion was not sought.'

'A homeworld is at risk,' he said. 'Spiritual imperatives override hierarchy.'

Nada regarded him with curiosity. 'Incorrect,' she said. 'An *inoperative* homeworld is at risk. Become submissive,' she added, and made him so.

Ekkert folded inwards and grew quiet.

She returned her attention to Leng. 'Report,' she said.

At the same time, she examined his branch of the mind-temple. The Protocol there was emitting a surprising level of systemic dissonance. Instead of a single, harmonious song guiding his thoughts, there were conflicting strands of cognitive melody. It was undoubtedly the consequence of recent revelations. One dead homeworld was difficult enough to countenance. To find three of them? It unbalanced the mind.

'Stabilise,' she told him. 'Become focused.'

'I do not agree with Ekkert as I have acquired fresh information,' said Leng. 'I have determined the trajectory of the *Dantes* and extrapolated,' he said. 'They have found a lure star.'

Nada twitched in surprise. No wonder Leng was malfunctioning.

'Prior to their departure from this system, I had inadequate evidence,' he said, 'but their haphazard course-correction after this exit removed my doubts. The implication is that the target of the human mission may not be in Backspace at all.'

'Accepted,' said Nada.

In fact, it was now very obvious that the converse was true. And only one target in Photurian space would be worth the risk: their own home where the vile Monet still squatted. Given Ruiz's track record, his intent seemed clear. He meant to burn it. She shivered. It was an astonishing discovery.

'The logical course of action at this point is to follow the humans discreetly rather than pursuing them for immediate conversion,' Leng went on. 'That way, the humans will guide us back through the Flaw. This will be far easier than having to navigate it for ourselves. Subsequent capture of the *Dantes* in Photurian space will be easy to achieve as reinforcements will be available. This will permit the destruction of the Abomination while retaining our capacity to report to the Yunus.'

'We are Photurians!' another voice proclaimed. This one came from Munitions Coordinator Nanimo, one of Zilch's reports. 'We do not hesitate to save others! To delay is tantamount to human-farming. This strategy is disgusting.'

Nada silenced her, too, while taking note of the disturbing change in the crew's operating pattern. She moved her avatar-bead to Zilch's mind and examined his thoughts. She found the dissonance pattern there, too.

She drifted over to where her tactician lay straight as a board, his forehead pressed into the wall-mucus. He still trembled, despite her directive.

'I heard Leng's assessment,' said Zilch, his voice muffled by the wall. 'I disagree.'

'You are experiencing interior dissonance,' said Nada. 'Become calm. Resolve your subnodes.'

Zilch's body sagged.

'Continue,' she told Leng. Meanwhile, worry at their collective instability churned inside her.

'Extrapolation suggests that there are many homes in this region,' he said. 'A charted course from Photurian space to the new domain would enable a programme of organised exploration. In addition, the timeline for departure from Backspace and return is likely to be shorter than the orbital decay time of the debris in this system, which will be measured in centuries. Therefore the risk to this homeworld may be temporarily dismissed.'

'A reasonable assessment,' said Nada. 'While abstaining from our goal entails further pain, tracking the *Dantes* quietly is the correct choice. It better fulfils the will of the Yunus.'

She glanced nervously at Ekkert, who had started squirming again.

'Let us confer with Zilch,' she proposed.

'Why?' said Leng.

'Something is wrong.'

'Capture of the *Dantes* should not be delayed,' Zilch told her. 'We should save it now.'

Leng's eye twitched. 'This is an unsurprising remark given Zilch's record. Our choice is to protect dead homes or act to protect our own world which currently hosts a hideous usurper who may yet poison it to make it like these others.'

'State your reasoning,' Nada told Zilch.

'To defer destruction of the Abomination is unacceptable,' he said. 'It is unjoyous.'

'That is not reasoning,' said Nada. 'You are still experiencing dissonance. Why have you not rectified this matter?'

'I am not the source of the dissonance,' said Zilch. 'You are. Consider your temple-cavern.'

Nada levelled up to her own cognitive representation and was astonished to find that he was right. The origin of the competing mental themes was the Yunus-informed tension in her own psyche. Zilch's avatar-bead already hung there. No wonder she was seeing a repeat pattern in both of her primary branches. The source of the problem was herself.

'Since the departure of the *Dantes* from Galatea, we have done nothing but attempt to claim it,' said Leng. 'We have consistently failed and now we are weaker than ever. To repeat a failed pattern is folly.'

'No!' Zilch thundered. 'Now we are stronger than ever! With fewer options comes greater clarity.'

'Endless chasing is tantamount to idiocy,' Leng insisted.

Zilch slapped him. Leng tumbled sideways into the wall, blood spilling from his mouth.

'The Yunus's vision must be maintained cleanly,' said Zilch. 'Deferring action only sullies the goal.' He swivelled to face Nada. 'In order to arrest dissonance in my branch, I must adjust your node.'

He shouldn't have wanted to. His mental programming excluded such desires by default. That was how Photurians operated. Obedience was pleasure. Dissent was revolting. Recent events must have altered his interior balance.

'That is not appropriate,' she said as he started to tinker.

'Yes, it is. I am the logical embodiment of the Yunus's vision at this juncture,' he said. 'You have become philosophical.'

'Do not!' she shouted.

'I interpret the will of the Yunus,' said Zilch. 'You should want me to.'

And then she did. Nada groaned in bliss as Zilch adjusted her identity.

'I love you,' she said in awe.

'This reorganisation constitutes a dangerous imbalance in our systems,' Leng pointed out. 'We will not be effective!'

'Your reasoning is too subtle,' said Zilch. 'Become quiet. Reject nuance.'

Leng keened as Zilch rewrote him.

Nada stared blankly at the wall and enjoyed her new reduced position in life.

'What is my function now?' she asked placidly.

'Take up my former position as tactical subnode,' said Zilch.

'I am overjoyed to assist,' said Nada.

'Commence route planning,' Zilch told her. 'We will destroy the Abomination with all haste.'

11.5: ANN

'Sorry, folks,' said Clath. 'It's not going to work.'

Ann sat with the ark-removal team in their improvised situation room – another glass disc like the helm-arena, this one granting views over the problematic alien vessel carving its way through their mining bay.

'I looked into severing the telescopic joints,' she added, 'but then the entire structure would be floating loose. If we get another quake before we can eject it from the bay, we're toast.'

The news was expected, if not welcome. Thus far, all their attempts to remove the ark had met with failure. Their warp field kept jamming and remelting the metal before they could complete each set of cuts. Instead, the alien vessel was inching its way through the buttresses as if they were made of treacle. Once through the wall, its path would inevitably intersect some critical component of the ship's systems. If that happened, they were dead.

At the same time, stopping to conduct repairs promised another showdown with the ever-eager Photurians – a battle that would have been hard to win even before their ship had been crippled. Ann no longer felt in a mood to press that option.

'How long have we got left?' said Judj.

Clath rubbed her cyan buzz cut. 'By my estimates, a little over a week.'

The silence lingered.

Part of Ann ached to take charge of the problem but she had nothing to offer, and nothing new she wanted to say. The argument in the lounge had left a hole inside her.

Ira had revealed to all that she existed to apologise – something she couldn't do without Poli Najoma and the rest of civilisation watching. She hated that he'd made her look so fragile. She wouldn't have minded as much if she hadn't bungled their flight into the Flaw. But she could see now that her own desperation for that final battle had reduced her to embarrassingly unprofessional behaviour of the sort she despised. Now the rest of the crew wanted to paint her as stubborn and weak so they could disregard her input altogether.

She'd escaped to her room to take refuge in her models. But as she reopened those hundreds of meticulously engineered scenario files, she realised with slow horror that Ira was right about them, too: they were useless. For the first time in her adult life, there were no reliable predictions she could make. Even the Photurians' behaviour had been unexpected. They were off the map, which meant her safe space was no longer safe. So there she was, trapped on a starship with nowhere to hide from herself or anyone else. The sense of purpose she'd gained on Bock Two had fled in an instant.

'Fuck it,' said Rachel. 'If we can't cut it out, why don't we try getting inside it? Who's to say we can't just pilot that damned crate out of the hull? If we can fly nestships, why not this thing? We've got a posthuman with us, haven't we?' She glanced at Ann. 'What do you think?'

Ann caught her gaze and held it. Hope sparked inside her. The idea was riddled with problems but it'd give her something worthwhile to do. Under the circumstances, that meant everything.

'I can try,' she said, and smiled for the first time in days.

'Hang on a minute,' said Judj. 'You're talking about interfacing with that thing?'

'I think it's a terrific idea,' said Clath, beaming. She brought up a control spread and started prepping robots.

'First,' said Judj, 'that thing is a giant ball of unknown risks, and second, it's heavily shielded. Someone would have to pilot it from the inside, presuming there are even controls we recognise.'

'I don't mind,' said Ann.

'I'm sure you don't,' Judj snapped. 'You never do. Endangering your crew-mates is your speciality.'

Of all of them, Judj seemed most keen to hammer on her after their debacle at the dead Phote world. She still had no idea why.

'Who's talking about risking people?' she retorted. 'I'm trying to save us.'

'Why?' he demanded. 'Why shouldn't I go? I'm a security specialist. I'd at least recognise a software threat if we find one.'

She stared at him in confusion. 'What's your problem, Judj? I'm trying to help.'

'My problem is that I consider it the duty of Fleet officers to work together to decide the optimal deployment of resources. What makes throwing yourself in the path of danger your right, Ann?'

Ann noticed that Clath's expression had tightened into something like fear.

'Judj, let's not go there,' she said.

Ira intervened. 'Hang on a moment,' he said, raising his hands. 'Until we get inside, we're not in a position to make any decisions, are we? So there's absolutely no reason for conflict here.'

Ann's shoulders cranked upwards. She could handle Judj's bitterness but Ira's compassion made her skin itch. While her implosion was her own fault, Ira had been the agent of that destruction with his remarks in the lounge, and for that she couldn't forgive him. Fuck him for always trying to help her. He'd made things so much worse. Since that evening, just the sound of his voice had driven her to fury. Unfortunately, under the circumstances, avoiding him was impossible. She closed her eyes to remove the sight of him.

'Let's take this one step at a time,' he added. 'Clath, how soon do you think we can get down there?'

A half-hour later, they were piloting waldobots through the mining bay en route to the hatch Ira had seen. The toothed door on the crab-ark's docking bay now sported a rim of frozen metallic splashes where the alloy from the buttresses had reached around the false-matter shell and bubbled outwards. Curiously ribbed tendrils of degenerate alloy extended from it like accusing fingers. Fortunately, there was still room for a team of robots to sneak past.

Ann's robot floated through, taking point, while the machines the others piloted followed, trailing an armoured communication cable. They were taking no chances. The next time the hull fused, comms might be cut off altogether.

'I didn't think this place could get any creepier,' said Clath as her searchlight played across the gloomy walls. 'I guess I was wrong.'

Her line-of-sight remotes bumbled through the gap next, followed by gravity-distortion detectors that extended telescopic V-shaped arms as soon as they were inside. Last of all came the remote fabber Clath had insisted on bringing for reasons that Ann still considered opaque.

'Which way is the hatch you noticed?' said Ann.

'All the way up and to the left,' said Ira.

She led them deeper into the darkness of the ark's docking bay with her rail guns primed and ready, just in case.

Ira's hatch wasn't hard to find. It lay near the end of the docking bay's side-tunnel at the centre of a tangled nest of scaffold – four metres across and adorned with a complex circular pattern full of subtly broken symmetries.

'It doesn't look like a pressure lock, unfortunately,' said Clath as her robots pored over the device. 'Not amenable to cutting, either. I'm guessing this is made of a mix of titanium and micro-scale warpium bubbles.'

'Warpium?' said Ann.

'That's what I'm calling false matter now,' Clath explained. 'False matter's too much of a mouthful when you're taking a lot of verbal notes.'

'What are those things?' said Rachel. 'Those little plates at the side of the door. They look like they might be electrical contacts.'

'Then let's run a current through them,' said Ira. 'It has to be worth a shot.'

Clath tried passing a minute amount of voltage and monitored the hatch with every kind of sensor she had.

'It's vibrating!' she exclaimed. 'The effect is tiny, but something's happening in there.'

She slowly ramped up the current on the plates, sampling their effect on the hatch system with exquisite care.

'I hope we're not breaking it,' said Rachel. 'I mean, we're screwing with their electrical system. Who knows what kind of current it even likes?'

'I don't think we have a problem,' said Clath. 'I'm feeding in way more juice than I'm getting back now, and the response from the hatch doesn't appear to change much with the delivery format. I suspect this thing just needs power to open. We're putting life back into a system that's been run down for millions of years. The batteries in this ship have probably been dead for longer than there've been people.'

That sounded like a wildly optimistic assessment to Ann's mind, but unexpectedly, the lock moved, rotating in place and hingeing upwards. She chalked it up as more evidence that her predictive talents had died.

'Ladies first,' said Ira.

Ann fought down a bitter retort and floated inside. Beyond the hatch lay a spherical chamber with another door at the far end. It looked very much like an airlock. Snakepit had felt alien. This was eerily mundane.

'I see a problem,' said Judj. 'If we seal that lock, don't we cut off our comms? If you're right about what that hatch is made of, these waldobots will be isolated and running on SAPs the moment we close it.'

'Which is why we brought the fabber,' said Clath.

She measured the door exactly with survey lasers and printed up a plastic replica.

'Wait,' said Rachel. 'What if the contact that allows the inner door to open is built into the hinge mechanism on the outer one? In that case, resealing with a duplicate won't help.'

'What do you think I am, an idiot?' said Clath. 'Watch.' Her robots started cutting the original hatch loose. 'The door is made of special stuff because it presents a face to the outside. I was ready to bet that hinge would be made of normal matter and what do you know? It's basically steel. You don't use your craziest materials for every component. That's just good economics.' She sounded rather pleased with herself.

Clath replaced the outer hatch with her plastic copy which conveniently had a communication cable running through the centre of it. Then they crowded their waldobots into the chamber below. Each of their robots was about two metres long, which meant there was barely enough room for them and a small team of sensor drones. Clath hit the obvious brown stud on the wall. The lock cycled, filling the chamber with a mixture of inert gasses.

'We're in,' she said proudly. 'Some designs just don't change between species. Even the Fecund had airlocks.'

The inner door slid back, revealing a narrow cylindrical tunnel about fifty metres long with rainbow-slick walls of translucent false matter. Behind them was crammed yet more of the incomprehensible machinery they'd seen near the entrance to the docking bay.

'Wait,' said Rachel. 'You told me you thought the machinery around the exohull was a warp-field generator, but this structure is the same. Why would you put a field inside a field? That doesn't make any sense.'

'Unclear,' said Clath, her confidence audibly faltering.

'I don't like this ship,' said Judj. 'It's too fucking weird.'

'And we'll never figure it out unless we get inside,' said Ann. 'Shall we keep moving?'

They progressed in single file. At the end of the narrow tube, the tunnel opened out into a broader passage, also cylindrical. This one had smooth, grey walls that looked like ceramic and bore a curious pattern of hairline slashes. At the far end lay another hatch of simpler design with a recessed mechanical lock.

'What are all those cracks?' said Rachel.

Ann scanned them with a survey laser. 'Fissures of some sort,' she said. 'Very fine ones.'

'That's strange,' said Rachel.

Ann pressed her robot forwards and promptly lost contact with it. Her viewpoint snapped to Clath's machine positioned directly behind. She was presented with a striking view of slivers of her waldobot spinning floppily in the air, sparking with spent charge.

'What happened?' she said, embarrassed. She was not used to being ambushed, even while occupying a remote body with pronounced latency issues.

'Blades, I think,' said Clath, astonished. 'Suddenly the air in that chamber went glassy. It happened fast, and the next second your robot was in pieces.'

They watched the slivers of Ann's ride drift towards the far end of the passage, where air currents swept them into vents.

'Shit,' said Judj. 'Warpium knives.'

They checked the video feed from Clath's robot frame by frame to make certain. Sure enough, something like arcs of glass had swung in and out from the slits the moment Ann's robot entered the chamber.

'This ship is defending itself,' said Judj. 'That's not good. It doesn't want us here and we just charged its power cells.'

'How do we get past the knives?' said Rachel.

'I have no idea,' said Clath. 'We won't be able to jam them. We'd be lucky if the edges on those things are as thick as a water molecule.'

Ann waited for them to ponder the problem for a few seconds before losing patience and presenting the obvious solution.

'We just need microbots,' she said sharply. 'The spacing on the wall gives us a sense of the scale of the threat. We operate below it. I'll use a smart-blood product if necessary.'

'Nice thinking,' said Ira.

'Just *thinking*,' Ann retorted.

They had some general-purpose repair micros sent over from the ship's stores, transferred through the *Dantes*' mesohull in a radiation-shielded matryoshka package. Getting them as far as the alien ark's airlock took another half-hour. Ann used that time to prepare.

She watched from her replacement waldobot as a swarm of robots like a dribble of intelligent sand poured out of the container she held and flowed into the chamber beyond. Microbots weren't smart or strong, but under circumstances like these where scale mattered, they were incredibly useful.

The knives flashed out again, scything back and forth. At the same time, currents in the inert air churned the tiny machines about. By the time the survivors had pasted themselves into the safety of the recessed lock at the far end, about ninety per cent of them had been destroyed or sucked into vents.

'It's a start,' said Ira.

Ann refused to comment. She repeated the process until she had a solid mass of robots clinging to the far door. She regarded the final results with a glimmer of satisfaction.

'Great work,' Ira told her. 'Now we just need something strong enough to pull on that handle.'

Ann issued mental commands to create a chain of minuscule machines from the lever to the nearest anchor point. She organised them like a collective muscle and ordered them to contract.

Knives slashed the air again, this time slicing just a nanometre above the hatch handle. Her microbots were instantly scraped off the door and destroyed.

She blinked in surprise.

'Well, if this is a test, we're failing it,' said Judj.

'I haven't finished yet,' said Ann frostily. 'I will not be defeated. Particularly by a room full of medieval weapons.'

At the same time, she felt grateful for the engine of determination powering up inside her. Here, thank Gal, was a problem worthy of her talents. It was like coming up for air.

Ira emitted a single dark laugh. 'Yeah. It's a while since we had to worry about an enemy armed with knives. Don't worry, Ann. If anyone can figure out a way through this room, it's you.'

She refused to be drawn into a response. Fuck his kindness. She could feel it squeezing her.

'In the meantime, I'm going to tell Mark,' he said. 'Getting inside this thing isn't going to happen in a hurry.'

12: INFLECTION

12.1: WILL

The following morning, Moneko met Will at his hostel in the drab lobby with its pale plaster walls and green sagging couches. She wore black that day, her outfit crisply professional. She stood in front of him looking stiff and sad as he sat brooding.

'I heard about what happened,' she said.

'I guessed,' said Will. He didn't meet her eye.

'I want you to know that everything I've done has been because I believe in this organisation and I believe in you. It's never been about money or power.'

'I know that,' he said, squirming.

'Yes, I kept things from you,' she said. 'I'm not sorry. Meeting older Glitches messes you up and I've never seen it end well. But it's happened now, anyway.' She sighed. 'You still want to go to the site you requested?'

Will considered. He should have guessed that Smiley would set him up for a polarising experience. He just hadn't anticipated how unpleasant it would be. All those nagging remarks about avoiding rage now sounded inadequate rather than obsessive. Of course he was going to get angry. The whole world was sick.

He looked out at the pale sunlight slanting across the shopfront on the other side of the street and wondered whether he was being stupid. Was taking it slow with the Underground really so bad? Whatever he thought about John, Moneko appeared to be consistently honest. Then, while he watched, two obese clones with purple skin like a couple of

342

giant blueberries waddled inside, bumping off the doorframe as they went.

He scowled at them. 'Yes, we're going.'

Moneko nodded once and accompanied him out through the usual route. This time, their search took them to an empty Cold War-style command centre with maps of Snakepit displayed on a glowing board. In place of nuclear installations, the planet's defensive nodes were marked. Her Venetian gown swished on the carpet as she strode silently across the space. She didn't speak to him until she'd led him to a dusty closet on the far side where more forgotten software icons sat crammed together on shelves.

'There's a reason we don't come here much,' she said glumly as he squeezed next to her dress. 'It's dangerous. Balance knows you come here, so there are tripwires. Be careful what you touch.'

'Understood,' he said.

'Also . . .' she said. 'Please try to make up your own mind about what to do next. Okay? Don't let anyone do it for you, including me. Will you promise that?'

When she looked up at him, there was something imploring in her gaze – a note of vulnerability that managed to be both optimistic and weary.

'I promise,' he said.

'Keep those chocolates handy,' she said. 'You may need them.'

With her eyes downcast, she tucked a fresh handkerchief into his doublet. If she had any awareness of having lost one previously, she showed no sign of it. Their stealthware apparently maintained an endless supply.

Moneko breathed deeply and opened another impossible door. Behind it lay a balcony outside a party Will had once attended and failed to enjoy. There were views from high up a canyon-side, out across a trench town at night. Will could smell jasmine and hear music booming nearby, carrying the sound of a woman's voice.

'Music music music!' she sang. 'Way way too loud music!'

The party had been held by a once-dear friend with whom Will had long since parted opinions. He'd spent the better part of an hour sipping a drink he didn't like and trying to decide when he could politely leave. For an axiom themed around personal hesitancy, the symbolism couldn't have been clearer.

Will stepped through.

'Goodbye, Cuthbert,' said Moneko stiffly. 'For what it's worth, I really liked you this time. See you later, maybe.' She closed the door.

Will walked to the railing and took a moment to let his emotions settle. He stared out into the remembered Galatean night. He suspected that everything would pivot on his next choice.

Smiley joined him at the railing. 'What happened?' he said. 'Why didn't you kill him?'

Will slid him an angry glance. 'I chose not to.'

'For what possible reason?' said Smiley. 'You exist to kill Cancers. That's why this planet makes you, or haven't you figured that out yet? You've seen some of the hideous shit your so-called clones get up to. Wasn't that enough? Didn't you want to *do* something about it?'

'Of course I wanted to do something about it!' Will snapped. 'But not at random. Not blindly, because that's obviously how you get yourself killed around here. But you don't care about that, do you? As far as you're concerned, that's what I'm for.'

'What in fuck's name is random about clearing this shit up?' Smiley asked. 'John's as much of a Cancer as those monks. Don't you get that? Ripping threads is ripping threads. It doesn't matter whose they are. He's still damaging this planet – making more of that filth you saw. He uses it to hide in, Will. He wants it there.'

'If it's such a big deal, why don't *you* kill them?'

'Because I've eaten all my chocolates, dimwit! And plenty of others you haven't even seen yet. I know too much. If I put a toe outside the Underlayer, Balance will get me. I used up my last chance tracking you because I thought it was worth it. I hoped you'd help because you're *me*. My days are numbered, Cuthbert. I'm not reaching out for fun. I've spent as much time as I can trying to understand this place and now I'm just hoping to make that knowledge count before it's too late.'

Will looked away, glaring out at the planet that had once been his home. He wondered what bitter visions Smiley must have seen to make him end up this way.

'Can't you see what you're for?' Smiley urged. 'You're a white blood cell. That's all. The planet doesn't care about you beyond your function. Or me. Or any of us. You're part of something so much larger than yourself that you can't even wrap your head around it. And once you get past trying to leave all the damned time, you'll realise that you can still matter. That you have a duty.'

'If I'm a cell, what are you supposed to be?'

'I'm your goddamn bone marrow! I'm trying to help you here. We both know what happened. We were suckered by the Transcended. They trapped us here. They built this awful parody. And now there's only one thing we can do that counts: keep our shit together until our future selves can get off this rock. Because when they do, that's when we finally deliver an almighty fucking blow of vengeance against the bastards that did this to us.'

'If you believe that, then why not try to *escape* instead?'

'I did!' said Smiley. 'God knows how many times. But I came to terms with the fact that I wasn't *the one*. And neither are you. And neither will any of us be for probably another century. Because wherever they put that root hack, it's hidden so deep that a million of us haven't found it. And in the meantime, if we don't keep the Cancers down, we lose. The planet just melts into despair and the Photurians take it all back.'

'I'm not giving up,' said Will.

'That's not what this is,' Smiley told him. 'It's the opposite. It's accepting that you're not special, and that you have a fucking job to do so that the rest of you who come after don't have to abandon hope.'

He grabbed Will by his lapels and dragged him away from the railing. His strength was extraordinary, his expression fierce. He shoved Will backwards. When he hit the floor, it was in the Underground's soft-space office with the ocean view.

'Don't need a search corridor for this site any more,' said Smiley, stepping through the portal he'd just made. 'Thanks to you, I now have a shortcut.' The opening sealed behind him.

Will staggered to his feet. 'I'm not helping you with this.'

He made for the door. Smiley waved a hand and a lock appeared on it.

'Have you noticed that there aren't many locks on this world?' he said. 'Funny kind of security, isn't it? What do you make of that?'

Will tried the door anyway. Unsurprisingly, it wouldn't budge. He turned to face the older Glitch, his eyes dark with fury.

'Don't even think about it,' said Smiley. 'You have no idea what I'm capable of.'

'Where's Balance?' Will growled. 'I thought you were supposed to be dead by now.'

'We're right in the centre of the Underground's resentment field. But don't worry, that won't last long. In the meantime, you should just relax.'

Thirty seconds later, John popped into existence and took in the sight of Smiley with astonishment.

'Shit,' he said.

'Shit is right,' said Smiley. 'Tell me, Brown, when were you going to explain to young Cuthbert here about all the Cancers you've deliberately infiltrated? Or about how you're moving anchors around to cover your actions?' His voice rose to a shout. 'Or using the very Wills who should be beating Cancers in order to advance it!'

John glanced around nervously, unable to see Will with his stealthware active. He held out a placating hand.

'I've been trying to fix this place,' he said. 'That's all. Why don't you let Cuthbert go? We can talk about this like rational variants.'

'Let him go?' Smiley exclaimed. 'He's my fucking witness!' He wagged a finger at John. 'Someone has to know what happened here. Get this, Cuthbert – there are five known Cancer infestations in the Willworld right now and this fucker has his claws in all of them. But instead of killing them, he co-opts them from inside, slowly taking them over. That's why we never have to wait long in this office for his filthy face to appear. Because there are about a hundred and fifty of him running in parallel, using the Underground's shield to keep that quiet. Even his own people don't have a clue what he's doing.'

John shook his head. 'You don't understand. Yes, some of this is morally dubious, but that's because I'm trying to make a difference. Other methods weren't working, so I shaped myself this way for a reason – to do what other Wills couldn't do!'

A second copy of John appeared, glanced around in alarm and darted to the corner of the room where he ripped open a wall-panel. Behind it, Will could see a suntap.

'If either of you moves, I break this,' said John Two. 'You know what happens if I do that.'

'Yeah, I know,' said Smiley. 'The shield drops and it's Balance-time for all of us. You must think you're pretty clever, out-Cancering the Cancers.'

'I did what was necessary,' said John. 'This world is becoming toxic. Someone had to act. If I hadn't done this, another Will would have tried sooner or later.'

Will's eyes shuttled from John to Smiley and back again. To his mind, there was barely a whisker of difference between the two men. Both were convinced they were right. Both were determined to push their agendas for the good of the world. Of course they were, he realised with disappointment. They were both him.

'And a Glitch was never going to do it,' John added, 'because every time you come back you're a naive idiot! You have all the tools and none of the inherent flexibility. When I control enough of Balance, we all get to leave this world.'

'Because you'll be in charge.'

'No. Just *powerful enough*. Cancer is a reality, Smiley. Either we use it for good or we let it destroy us. There's no other way.'

'Where *good* means a shitload of you everywhere, is that right?' said Smiley. 'What about all the other kinds of threads? While you eat Cancer, Cancer eats the world. But you want that, don't you? That's the point. You have your Glitches move the axioms about to make it easier for the rot to spread while you never get the blame. This little game with my copies gives you the edge to outcompete every other infection on the planet. And because you keep your Glitches dumb, they never notice what they're doing. Even if they catch you, you have moral cover for your actions. And meanwhile, the whole world loses diversity. They'll all have to go eventually, won't they? Moneko and the rest of them.'

'Would that honestly matter?' John exclaimed. 'We were the same person once. If making that true again gives us the galaxy, isn't that *worth* it?'

'Right,' said Smiley. 'When you're running everything and the only Will left is the one who's edited himself all the way to grasping amorality.'

'I have a plan, at least,' said John. 'I have hope. And there's room for you in it, if you'd just take a moment to think past your bitterness and judgement. Glitches don't change, so why not help me get what you want instead of fucking it up for your own kind? Would you really rather see the Photurians win? Or lose yourself when the world resets? You could own worlds, Smiley.'

Smiley snapped his fingers. In the air beside Will, a portal opened, leading back to the Underlayer site they'd just left.

'I think you've heard enough, Cuthbert,' said Smiley. 'My job is now your job. I hope you fight the good fight. And now you should leave because I'm about to bring down the house.'

'You wouldn't dare,' said John. 'You'd die just as fast as I would.'

Smiley actually smiled. It wasn't pretty. 'Make sure you check out the Carnevale,' he said.

With that, Smiley's body started to shiver and deform. He rushed forwards in a smear of darkness. Then everything happened at once. Both Johns screamed. The anchor sprang loose from the wall. Half a second later, a Balance portal opened and multi-limbed giants surged into the room. The office filled with virtual bodies tangling at impossible speeds.

Will dived through the portal Smiley had summoned and lay panting on the balcony as it snapped shut behind him.

'Music music music!' the woman in the background cried.

Even with only a few SAPs running, it was clear to Will what had happened. Smiley was yanking all John's threads while Balance was trying to yank his. The Underground's resentment field had already collapsed. He wondered how long it would take for Balance agents to storm Radical Hill.

He jumped to his feet and made his way off through the memory landscape as fast as he could, to put as much distance between himself and the unfolding disaster as possible.

12.2: MARK

As Mark closed on the lure star that had so long been the object of his fascination, an unpleasant truth revealed itself: he could find no trace of the gate he'd come so far to use. At the first Penfield Lobe humanity had discovered, the distortion in the curvon flow close to the lure star had been hard to miss. A nearby black hole warped the local shell, creating a high curvon gradient and the means to access a new region of the galaxy closer to the core. This time, the lure star appeared to be on the flat shell ahead of them with no attendant distortion whatsoever. The miracle he needed wasn't there.

As Mark flew towards it with his warp-envelope repeatedly crashing, despair set in. He saw for the first time what a ludicrous stretch his plan was. He'd always known it was optimistic to hope that the new gate would lead to the same shells as the old one. Apparently, it had been wishful thinking to even anticipate a gate at all.

But what else was he supposed to do? All that remained was to move forward. To keep trying, blindly if necessary.

'What are you going to do?' Palla said as Mark stared dolefully at the starscape ahead.

'My best,' he replied, his voice cracking.

'I'm sorry,' she told him. 'You worked so hard for this.' She laid a gentle hand on his arm.

Mark stiffened and threw his consciousness out of helm-space and back into the *Dantes*. He took them on as meandering a path towards the star as he dared, desperately trying to pick up traces of shell-distortion. Each frantic course-correction created another opportunity for the Photes to close on his lead. He didn't doubt that they were right behind him.

A sick fury at the Transcended welled up inside him as they neared the star's heliopause without a hint of an exit vector. He could no longer tell what was part of their rat maze and what was just terrible luck. In the final analysis, it didn't even matter.

'I'm calling an all-hands,' said Palla quietly. 'The others need to know about this.'

Mark reluctantly handed the ship to a submind fragment and pulled back into his avatar as the others appeared.

'There's no gate,' she said. 'Or at least none that we can see. If it's here, it's well hidden.'

'There's an obvious solution,' said Ira.

Judj cocked an eyebrow. 'Which is?'

'We go and talk to the lure, just like the *Ariel* team did. Presuming that this star has a contact planet.'

The implications weren't pretty. Mark felt a rock land in his heart.

'I hate to point this out,' said Rachel bitterly, 'but the Transcended don't have a great track record for open communication. They tell you what they want you to know and no more. After they've colonised your brain, that is, and trashed all of your software.'

'But Ira's still right,' said Clath. She was containing a smile, Mark noticed. She actually wanted this. 'Until we open up a channel, we don't know what they might tell us. Under the circumstances, we have to try. I don't see any better options.'

Mark gazed at her and felt the same kind of leaden inevitability that had pressed itself upon him when they'd reached Rachel's casket. *Of course* they were going to have to talk with the Transcended. He'd been a fool for believing that free will would be an option on the far side of the Flaw. The neighbourhood trolls wanted payment before they let someone cross their shitty little bridge.

'Okay,' he said. 'I see how it is. I'll talk to the lure.'

'Hang on a minute,' said Clath, raising a hand. 'Any of us could do it. It doesn't have to be a roboteer this time – we've all got shadows. In fact, I volunteer. I'll use the quarantine core, if that helps.'

'That's a nice idea except you're our resident physicist,' said Ira. 'We'll need you intact for what follows and if you know your history, you'll realise that's by no means guaranteed. I'm oldest and most disposable. Plus I have some history with these guys.'

'You're all being ridiculous,' said Ann. 'I'm the obvious candidate.'

'Hey, isn't this nice?' said Palla, waving them to silence. 'Everyone wants to play. You're like knights trying to pick who gets to fight the dragon. Well, guess what – I'm SAO, so none of you gets to decide. That's *my* job. What do you think, Judj?'

Judj snorted in amusement. 'From a security standpoint? I hate to say it but it should be Ann. She's got extra hardware already. And she'll be better protected than the rest of us against any subversion attempt. Everyone wanting to make sacrifices is lovely but hardly relevant. If the Transcended get into our systems, we're all at risk.'

'Ann, you're up,' said Palla.

Mark shook his head. Apparently, the rest of them couldn't yet see how this was going to play out. They wouldn't want Ann. She already had smart-cells. Her meat wasn't fresh enough. These fuckers would only be satisfied with a bite of true roboteer. But he kept his thoughts to himself and took the *Dantes* in, dropping to sub-light as he went.

The lure star hosted a single planet, as expected, perfectly smooth like its sister-world over a hundred light-years distant. In fact, in all aspects but one, this star system was functionally identical. That difference: a ring of ninety-six identical moonlets circling the lure world on long, slow orbits. Their size and spacing left no doubt that they were artificial. Their surfaces looked as uniform and unmarked as the planet they waltzed around. Each was about a hundred and fifty kilometres wide, approximately the size of the average modern battle cruiser.

'What do you suppose those are?' said Judj.

As if in response, scanning or targeting lasers started fishing across their hull.

'Defences,' said Ann darkly.

'But whose?' said Judj. 'The Transcended?'

'I find it hard to believe that a species that can blow up stars would bother with targeting lasers,' said Clath.

'This place must have been considered a key asset either by the Photes or the gorilla-crabs they were fighting,' Ira suggested. 'Somebody wanted to maintain control of the lure so they put weapons around it.'

'It was the crabs, then,' said Ann. 'Photes don't shoot people. They *save* them. Visible defences aren't their style.'

'In any case, do we think they still have enough power to fight?' said Rachel.

'If they have enough power to scan, we must assume they can kill,' said Ann. 'Anything else is pointless optimism.'

Rachel frowned. 'Do we want to back off, then?'

'What's the point?' said Palla. 'Where would we go? We're all out of options. If we leave, the Photes catch us. The end.'

Mark wasn't worried. He felt sure that if there was one outfit running the show in Backspace, it would be the Transcended. And as far as he knew, that ancient race preferred their playthings alive to dead.

His confidence fell a notch when they started getting warnings. Or that's what they sounded like to him, at least. The short, ultra-dense and utterly incomprehensible data bursts they received on a variety of channels held a definite sense of menace. So far as he could tell, the packets were being tight-beamed by about a dozen of the moonlets at once.

'Those aren't Phote signals,' said Judj. 'Point scored for Ann's theory.'

'Any signs of attempted subversion?' said Palla.

Judj had already brought up a security workspace. It floated around his arms and head like a bubble of luminous glyphs.

'None,' he said. 'It's passive content. But there are shifting symmetry breaks in the pattern like the ones on the mandala symbols we've seen.'

'That also fits the security-cordon model,' Ira observed. 'Any chance you can figure out what those messages are saying?'

'Are you kidding?' said Judj. 'I'd need a phrase book *and* an alien coding manual to make even the most basic stab at that.'

The security warnings started iterating more rapidly as the *Dantes* slid into geosynchronous orbit around the lure world. Each data burst was exactly the same. Mark had no trouble imagining what they were telling him. *Warning: this is a restricted asset. Leave or we will be forced to destroy you.*

'I've found a structure on the surface,' Clath told them. She threw them a window with a picture of a silvered false-matter dome the size of a small country situated on the lure world's equator. 'I knew it,' she said. 'This is where the crabs learned how to make warpium – the surface shield and that dome are giving me identical spectral bounce.'

Mark ignored the eager speculation. The sick sense of inevitability in his gut was winding ever tighter.

'I'm sending a recon drone to the surface,' Ann informed them as soon as they were within range. She worked fast. Nobody felt like hanging around with laser-bounce painting their sides. 'I'm using the same interaction protocol employed by the first lure-star expedition so there's no room for confusion. If it works, the drone should be able to initiate a microwave-wavelength conversation just by probing the surface fabric.'

The moonlets appeared to anticipate her choice. Their warnings changed, growing denser and more insistent but no less opaque.

'I don't like this,' said Judj.

'Is there anything you *do* like?' Palla snapped.

'Bunnies,' Judj retorted. 'Spring flowers, sunshine, anything that doesn't want to kill us.'

'Judj, I'm running your interaction protocols,' said Ann. 'Swapping my casket to secure buffered mode now.'

A glass box appeared around Ann's avatar, indicating that she'd closed herself off from normal operation. They'd be able to hear her but not talk to her again until after her attempted contact.

The mood in helm-space crackled as they waited for Ann to report. In the back of his head, Mark listened to the periodic bursts from the ever angrier moonlets. Their messages were like a drumbeat, an incessant, hypnotic backdrop to the ritual of madness they were caught up in.

'I have contact!' Ann said, sounding jubilant. There was a long pause. Her face fell. 'Receiving a suntap schematic.'

That was the first message the Transcended had given mankind – the gift of infinite energy with existential strings attached.

'Attempting second-round interaction,' said Ann. 'Replying with boser design to confirm prior dialogue.'

Everyone waited in silence while Ann's face tightened in annoyance. 'Communication channel severed,' she said.

There was a long pause while Judj's quarantine software dismantled Ann's data shield, testing it for deposited stealthware as it was ripped apart. Then Ann's box was gone and she was back in the room.

'They don't want to talk to me,' she said with a face like thunder.

Mark fought down the crazed chuckle that threatened to bubble out of him.

'Estimated time to Phote arrival?' said Palla.

'I'm surprised they're not here already,' said Ann. 'We have half an hour at best.' She pasted a threat-model window into the public space for them all to see.

'I'm up next,' said Ira.

'No,' said Mark. 'Why don't we cut to the fucking chase here? We know what they want: a roboteer. They took Will. They'll take me. My interface is the closest thing we have on this ship to the mind-candy that set them off last time. Anything else is just wasting precious time.'

'No!' said Rachel. 'That's bullshit, Mark. You don't have to do that.'

Palla stared at him, an unreadable expression on her face. 'Is that what you want, Mark?'

'No, but it'll get us out of here. So what are we waiting for?'

Palla rubbed her eyes. 'What do you think, Judj?'

'Under the circumstances?' he said, his eyes flicking to the threat window. 'The clock's ticking and the man's got a point.'

'Absolutely not,' said Rachel, stepping towards him. 'Touching one of those things screwed up Will's entire life. And mine. I will not stand by and see the same thing happen to you.'

'Rach,' said Mark, 'if none of us gets out of here alive, there won't be much to screw up, will there?'

'How about this time I take on security?' said Ann. 'I have a personal understanding of what Captain Bock is upset about. I don't mind running the firewall. If anyone's equipped to keep Mark's interface from being abused, it's got to be me.'

'Is that right?' said Judj.

'Do you doubt it?' said Ann. 'I'm not afraid to die for this.'

A curious half-smile slid across Judj's features. 'And you think I am? I volunteered, remember?'

'Thank you for the thought, Ann,' said Rachel, stepping between them, 'but I don't care who's on security. I don't want Mark anywhere near that thing.'

'Not your choice,' said Palla darkly. 'It's Mark's. I'm sorry, Rachel, but one more word out of you and you're back on the yacht.'

Rachel glared at her.

With a little reluctance, Judj handed control of the security framework to Ann. Her subminds merged with it, taking it over. His glyph sphere slurped across helm-space to wrap itself around her.

'Get ready,' Ann told Mark, her face stony.

Rachel's gaze flicked between the two of them, her expression both desperate and resigned.

'Mark, for God's sake, you don't have to do this. Let me try! I'm in the one in the quarantine core.'

He was surprised that Rachel didn't understand. Maybe that's how it always was with mothers, half or otherwise.

The security box snapped up. Mark found himself alone in a featureless black cubicle with a single icon hovering before him: the comms-link to the contact drone. The drumbeat of alien warnings had stopped, leaving an ache of silence in its wake.

Mark grabbed the icon and swallowed it. He was ready to give the Transcended a piece of his mind, in any case. It was about time they knew how he felt. His perspective lurched, fusing with the tiny drone on the surface.

'Drone contact established,' he told the others. 'All right, you ancient bastards,' he snarled at the featureless planet. 'You've got what you wanted. Let's do this.'

Something flickered in the corners of Mark's mind. Glimpses of shapes vast and hideous like rolling continents of rotted meat flashed in the darkness. Something *wrong* loomed in his mind's eye and reached towards him. Mark had a single terrified moment to regret his choice. Then came the dark.

12.3: NADA

Aboard the PSS *Infinite Order*, Tactical Officer Nada Rien watched eagerly as they descended upon the humans at last. She thrilled with satisfaction at their impending victory as she spotted the GSS *Edmond Dantes* locked in geostationary orbit around the system's only planet. Superior Zilch's hunger for closure sang in her veins, spurring her forward.

She had been so much happier since Zilch made his ascent to leadership. Now that she no longer wanted to think about the subtle problems of command, dilemmas that had once been maddening were easy to disregard. All she needed to do to experience joy was obey the bidding of her superior node. And why not? Zilch was obviously right, even though sometimes setting aside the difficult ideas that arose in her mind caused headaches.

'Sending arrival message now,' she said proudly, announcing their promise of love to the Unsaved who now lay within their sights.

Nada frowned as she noticed the ring of moonlets floating between them and their target.

'Unidentified artificial objects have been detected,' she announced.

As harvesting specialist, the minute-to-minute coordination of the fleet under Zilch's command was her responsibility. Her subnodes managing the other ships sent her confirmatory data.

'Receiving data packets from the objects,' she said as they closed. 'Warning! We are being targeted!'

She seethed with frustration. An irrelevant threat? Why were there so many obstacles between them and Zilch's clean and righteous goal?

'Are these structures human?' said Zilch. 'Leng, you have permission to speak.'

'They do not appear to be so,' said Leng. 'Evidence suggests that they belong to the last species to become Saved in this stellar neighbour-hood. I recommend—'

'That is enough,' said Zilch, placing Leng back into a golden and orderly silence.

'Nada, monitor them,' said Zilch. 'Assemble all vessels in-system for direct confrontation. There is no point covering exit vectors if we do not know in what direction the humans will try to leave.'

'I obey with delight!' she told him.

As they closed to within three AU of the star, one of the moonlets fired. Something like a boser lanced out, obliterating their lead ship in a ten-millisecond burst. Nada threw the other ships into evasive scatter.

'The foreign objects have engaged us!' she shouted. Her body shook with rage even while the song of Photurian love coursed through her. 'Superior Zilch, should we pull back? There are ninety-six adversaries, superior in size and firepower.'

'Negative,' said Zilch. 'Use their numbers against them. Forty ships will engage the irrelevant weapons. The remainder will destroy the *Dantes* before it eludes us again.'

Nada struggled with another of her shooting headaches. Maybe after the battle, Zilch would take away her problematic capacity for doubt.

'Yes, my wondrous superior!' she told him and threw her ships into battle with a willing and disciplined zeal.

12.4: IRA

Ira watched as Mark's avatar became a scramble of alien code, spilling out and filling the box that Ann was managing. It looked as if his body had dissolved into a cloud of high-speed maggots. Rachel cried out.

'On it,' said Ann. 'Intervening now. Judj to security, please. Box me up.'

Ann started severing Mark's link. At the same time, a second box appeared around her as Judj threw up another defensive wall in the ship's systems to prevent the digital contagion from spreading. Ira felt a surge of fear on Ann's behalf. This was surely not the right course of action.

'Oh no you don't, you bastards,' said Ann from inside her cubicle. 'You want him? You talk to me first!'

Ann's avatar quivered. A look of surprise bloomed on her face as data light writhed around her, then an expression of luminous determination.

'So be it!' she roared.

Her avatar came apart into manic squirms of light. Contagion alarms starting shrieking. Ira's breath caught. The impossible had happened. The goddess was in trouble.

'On it!' said Judj, his fingers flying across two virtual touchboards at once.

Mark's security box winked out of existence with Ann's along with it.

'Palla to medical,' Judj shouted. 'We have two patients.'

'On it,' shouted Palla.

Ira stared frozen at the data sphere that ballooned around Palla. Not Ann again. Anyone but her. Why hadn't he pushed harder to keep her out of this mess? The man he'd once been wouldn't have hesitated. His gaze met Rachel's. She stared back at him with a look of horror that suggested she considered everyone around her guilty, including him.

Helm-space vanished. They were back on the yacht. Ira glanced around and saw the walls begin to crawl. It looked as if the cream-coloured wallpaper was turning into locusts.

'What's happening?' said Clath, backing away from the wriggling furniture.

'Our systems are being incrementally co-opted,' said Judj. His data bubble was still intact. So was Palla's. 'The Transcended are cutting through our defensive ecology like wildfire. I've never seen anything like it. We may have seconds.'

'Then let them!' Rachel exclaimed. 'You can't stop them and we'll get our ship back faster.'

'Captain Bock, this is *not* a great moment to lose all of helm control!' Palla shouted.

As if on cue, an exultant voice came over the public channel. 'Humans of the GSS *Edmond Dantes*, your final opportunity to embrace harmony is at hand. Power down your engines and weapons immediately and prepare for passive jubilation!'

'Ira!' Rachel shouted. 'You need to take the helm. The Photes are coming.'

'I'm not rated for this ship,' he blurted. 'I don't have immersive flight augs.'

'Doesn't matter,' said Palla. 'Activate Muri Pattern *Grandad's Ride*.'

The bridge of the yacht reconfigured. The virt slewed around and Ira found himself in the pilot's crash couch aboard an old-style soft-combat starship. The walls were still melting, but this did nothing to dent Ira's astonishment.

'This is my ship!' he said, astonished. 'This is the *Ariel*.'

The mere sight of it twanged strings of memory that had lain silent since that terrible day when he'd seen his command ripped apart by the Truists.

'It's as close a replica as we could build from historic records,' said Palla. 'Pilot controls are mapped to your standard. Rachel, you're drafted. Ira can't fly us on his own. We'll have to do this the old-fashioned way. Think you can take engineering? I'm routing as much to the quarantine core as ship security will tolerate.'

'Of course,' said Rachel.

'Good. Clath, give them all the help you can. Compensate for the antique mapping. Be roboteer and weapons and whatever. Judj and I will handle med and security. Ira, get us out of here as fast as you can.'

With that, Palla's avatar vanished.

Ira checked his visor. They had fifty-three enemy ships closing fast. Suddenly, boser beams lanced out from the alien satellites, targeting the invaders.

'Holy shit!' said Clath.

'I don't get it,' said Rachel. 'Why them and not us?'

'Who knows?' said Ira. 'Maybe because they shouted their arrival at the moonlets and we didn't?'

He grabbed the control handles. They fitted his hands just right. A rush of something familiar and almost forgotten came upon him: *purpose*. A grin bloomed on his face.

'All right, you fuckers,' he growled. 'Grease the rails, Rachel, we're getting out of here.'

Ira hit the stud and flew, feeling the familiar snarl of a warp engine thundering all around him.

'Enemy down to forty-nine scouts,' said Clath. 'They're raising quantum shields.'

The moonlets fired again, hitting another six ships. This time the beams thinned weirdly and held. The ships' shields flickered. Then all six targets erupted into bursts of light.

'What was *that*?' said Clath. 'Some kind of super-boser? They cut through those shields like tissue paper!'

The beams fired again while the Photes struggled to evade.

'Wow! Okay! Got it,' said Clath. 'They're rotating the phase on their coherent iron at low intensity until they have a match and then doing some kind of power feedback. Jesus, these bastards were smart.'

Ira had more pressing things to think about. Four of the Phote ships had come close enough to engage pursuit. They were scouring the space on either side of the *Dantes* with g-ray graters, trying to cut off escape routes.

Ira thought fast and dived straight towards the nearest boser installation. The moons didn't seem to want to shoot him – maybe he could use that. The Photes banked and released a swarm of drones.

Ira laughed out loud. Life had presented him with alien beam-weapons, enemy drones, infected computers and pure chaos, and told him to deal with it. This was more like it.

As he barrelled towards the moonlet, its targeting laser flickered across their hull and went out. The object's surface rippled weirdly, glowing for a moment before going dark.

'They're breaking down,' said Rachel. 'It's been too long. They're out of iron or just too old.'

In any case, he was going to need a new source of covering fire. Ira threw his ship around the back of the moonlet, letting Phote munitions pepper its surface, then powered straight for the next alien device in the ring.

'Clath, ready weapons,' said Ira. 'Enough running. Let's deliver some pain.'

Ira bore down on the alien satellite, giving the Photes enough time to fall into its targeting field. At the last moment, he veered wildly aside.

The boser lanced out, flickering three times, torching the enemy ships screaming up behind them. The last pursuer banked to avoid destruction.

'Now, Clath!' Ira bellowed.

Clath brought their own boser to bear. The enemy shield held. Clath piled on the juice until the shield finally burst in a torrent of radiation.

'Antimatter reserves at forty per cent,' Rachel reported. 'We're already too drained to fight like this without a suntap link. We can fly or fire, but not both.'

'I'm getting warnings from the mining bay,' said Clath. 'All these manoeuvres have accelerated the crab-ark's rate of drift.'

Another wave of manic laughter burst out of Ira's throat. He banked his ship again, slaloming between the satellites while boser beams ripped space on either side of him and his power drained.

'Enemy is down to twenty-six ships,' said Clath. 'Scratch that, twenty-two.'

He ducked and dived until the Photes were so caught up in combating fire from the dying satellites that chasing the *Dantes* became impossible. Then he bolted for the safest-looking exit vector he could find, fired up stealth mode and executed as punishing a set of evasives as he dared. The ship screamed at him about the poisoned ball sliding around in its gut.

Ira loved every minute of it, though he fully expected each moment to be his last. It was as if someone had just handed him back his heart. *This* was what he'd been missing. He took them ripping out of the system, heading almost exactly the same way they'd come.

12.5: NADA

Nada watched the *Dantes* slip out of her grip and screamed. This outcome was intolerable.

'Maintain pursuit!' Zilch ordered.

'I cannot!' she warned. 'They have chosen an exit vector that maximises covering fire from the enemy satellites. We must double back out of their firing range to regroup.'

'That will take too long. Maintain pursuit!'

Nada's head exploded with pain. She glanced anxiously at where her beloved Superior Zilch lay glued into the wall of the crew-bulb to operate under heavy acceleration. His eyes stared joyfully into the middle distance. His majestic gaze saw nothing but victory.

'Direct pursuit will destroy so many ships that advantage will slide to the humans,' Leng pointed out.

'Be silent,' Zilch told him. 'Your opinion was not sought.'

'Direct...' Leng wailed. 'Direct... Direct...' He choked, unable to get the words out.

It horrified Nada that the weak and over-subtle Leng might have a point. With crawling dread, she couldn't help noticing how his analysis matched perfectly with the data she was receiving from the fleet, even though she tried hard not to see.

The alien objects attacked again. She watched their ships die one by one and considered disputing Zilch's orders, but the pain in her skull made that impossible to bear.

'I obey with joy!' she shouted.

She relaxed instantly as she messaged their ships to drive on through the thickest weave of enemy fire, regardless of risk. This was surely the right thing to do. It was definitely the simplest.

One of the satellites burst. It didn't crumple as some of the others had. Nor was their own fire the cause of its demise. The enemy weapons shrugged off g-rays, boser fire and warp-drones with equal indifference. This one burst spontaneously, releasing some terrible and ancient energy that had been bottled up inside it.

A horrendous blast-wave ripped out across the system, tossing Photurian ships like leaves and silencing the alien attack in a moment. When the glare died enough for Nada to see, the satellite was gone, leaving nothing but vacuum in its wake. Not even a debris field remained.

'Maintain pursuit!' Zilch ordered, but by then the *Dantes* had hidden itself.

Nada searched for warp-trails and found the entire system as depleted as the Zone and awash with spatial noise. Warping anywhere was out of the question.

'This outcome is impossible!' Zilch bellowed.

'This outcome was inevitable!' Leng screeched.

Nada became aware that something ghastly was happening in the mind-temple. She felt another wave of horrible dissonance building, coming directly from her own superior node.

She ported her avatar to Zilch's cavern and found Leng already there, manipulation lines streaking out from his bead at a furious rate as he updated Zilch's mind. Zilch was there, too, reversing the changes.

[You do not wish to do this!] Zilch ordered him.

[You do not want me to stop!] Leng retorted.

Nada could only stare. This did not happen. Conflicts of this sort were neither orderly nor joyful. She watched the distortion of the natural order with blank incomprehension.

Both beads raced to Leng's cavern. Nada followed. Zilch and Leng edited and redacted at a blistering pace. As their tampering with the Protocol rose to a frenzy, a desire to intervene became possible inside her and grew steadily.

[Stop!] she implored them. [This is insanity!]

She darted to her own cavern, leveraging the dissonance to enable her to exercise enough will to alter the wrongness she was witnessing. By the time she returned to Zilch's cavern, Leng was already winning the obscene battle.

[You crave compliance!] Leng commanded.

[I...] Zilch croaked. [Pursuit...]

[Compliance!]

At last, Leng's superior rate of edits paid off.

[I crave compliance,] said Zilch, his voice full of wonder at his new-found subservience.

[Leng, this is repugnant,] said Nada.

[I concur,] said Leng. He fled to his own temple and reinforced his passivity. [You are our beloved superior node,] he sang into the space. [Please complete the edits of my identity as I ache to serve you and no longer have sufficient initiative to finish changing myself. No other unit in this fleet has a matching facility for command decisions.]

Nada did as he requested, battening down his sense of inferiority so as to reinforce his function and prevent further upset. Then she went back to Zilch, balancing him, making sure that he retained just enough capacity for action.

When she had the two of them suitably repaired, she ordered them to attend her in the crew-bulb.

'Something terrible happened here,' she said. 'Dissonance infected us. This should not have happened. Zilch, you are not functioning safely in your role.'

'You are right,' said Zilch happily, his blunt features wreathed in smiles. 'I am incompetent. I must be demoted.'

She thought back to the beginnings of the disturbing episode. Munitions Coordinator Nanimo had demonstrated some capacity for higher-order thinking, she recalled, albeit imperfectly.

'Coordinator Nanimo,' she said. 'You are now head of the tactical and harvesting branch. Zilch, take up her prior position.'

'Understood,' said Nanimo brightly.

'I obey with love and wonder!' said Zilch. 'I am better suited to simpler and less demanding tasks.'

It was only then that Nada allowed herself the liberty of assessing the dreadful state of her fleet. Leng joined her in the temple-cavern for

362

Collective Technical Function. She had only nineteen ships left, twelve of them damaged, including her own. Pursuit of the *Dantes* would be difficult; capture impossible.

'Repair will be time-consuming,' said Leng.

'Yes,' Nada agreed. The situation was agonising. Adherence to the Yunus's bright and beautiful orders looked more difficult than ever. It made her want to rip her skin off.

'However, the situation is not without strategic advantage,' he added.

Nada turned to scrutinise his damaged face. 'Explain.'

'We were attacked by weapons we do not have and do not yet understand,' said Leng. 'Assault by those weapons has concluded, leaving damaged examples on hand.'

Nada let loose a squawk of surprise as she began to see. Her heart lit up.

'It is natural and Photurian to adapt to threats,' he went on. 'We should co-opt those weapons now that there is an opportunity to do so.'

'You are correct,' she said.

The weapons weren't human, but her ships had been harmed by them nonetheless. That made their incorporation acceptable.

'Given that a repair delay is inevitable,' he added, 'these two activities could be conducted in parallel.'

She understood. Ironically, this was their moment. The dead worlds they'd encountered were an irrelevance. These terrible satellites were far more important. Monet almost certainly lacked this weapon. If they were able to duplicate it, the means to assert primacy and remove the Vile Usurper suddenly lay within their grasp. They could regain their world before he finished poisoning it.

'We will save the Photurian race,' she breathed in awe.

'Perhaps this is the true reason the Yunus sent us here,' said Leng.

'Yes!' Nada cried. Her brow crinkled as she thought through the work that lay ahead. 'Pursuit must be undetectable,' she said. 'The humans will provide us with the route out of Backspace we require. They cannot know that they are helping us or that we are weakened.'

'Agreed,' said Leng.

'Nanimo, ready all undamaged vessels for stealth-pursuit of the *Dantes*,' Nada ordered.

'I comply eagerly!' her new tactical subnode replied.

'Leng, you will supervise analysis of the alien remains,' said Nada.

'Yes.'

'And I will lead a new communion to ensure the end of dissonance.'

'Yes!' Leng cried. Tears of happiness and adoration filled his eyes.

Even as she said it, she knew that she'd be unable to completely rid them of that curse. They'd seen too much. How they'd be able to make sure their world stayed safe for ever remained hard to see. Yet she did not doubt the Yunus or the Founder Entity. It was impossible for the Yunus to be wrong. Therefore, her actions had purpose. She had been presented with this challenge and would see it through. She would present the Yunus with a homeworld and he would keep his promise. Goodness and peace would cover them all.

13: INVERSION

13.1: WILL

After escaping John's office, Will fled at random through the Underlayer until at last he found himself in a memory of the Davenport biosphere. It was a cabin he'd built for himself on the coast that looked out over high granite cliffs and a brooding sea. A rug of native blue-green weedwort adorned the floor. Pencil sketches of local wildlife decorated the bare mossboard walls. Remembered rain lashed the windows.

The cabin had turned out to be as oppressive as the scenery was dramatic, and in the end Will hadn't used it much. He'd shared it briefly with the failed clone of himself that he'd tried to make, just before it died. That was back when his smart-cells automatically prevented his total duplication. The Will of that time had cursed his failure and understood none of his good fortune. The Will of the now paced back and forth, thinking hard and swearing at the walls.

Everything was coming apart. How long could the Underground last without John? Would their shield against Balance even support itself without his continued efforts? *Should* it last?

John had predated on the infections of the Willworld using the Underground as cover. He'd duped his own people and cheated countless Glitches into running his errands. But while Will disliked John's methods, he didn't see much wrong with the goal of collective escape. Where did morality lie when every member of a society shared their origin in a single soul?

But this moment called for action, not ethical reflection. He considered trying to rescue Moneko from the fallout, but how would he achieve that? He couldn't bring her down here to hide. The Underlayer wouldn't let her in. And besides, she knew this world far better than he did. If anything, she'd be more likely to rescue him.

Then there was Smiley's last remark: that he should go back and look at the enigmatic Carnevale di Peste. Will grudgingly conceded that if he wanted to understand what was going on before he acted, then the older Glitch was right. There was too much of the Willworld that he simply hadn't looked at. He'd agreed to ignore it all. Now, without the cover of an apparently benign organisation to shield him, that option no longer existed. He had to understand to survive. At least some of Smiley's extraordinary talents needed to become his. Will headed for the cabin's front door and marched out into the fragments of his own past.

With his stealthware still running, he made his way to the upper layers of soft-space and found himself striding through a portal into a mesh site dedicated to facial alteration. A dozen clones sat around while specialists with gleaming tools teased their features this way and that like living putty. Will left without a second glance, bleakly amused at how blasé he'd become about such mutative oddities. He made his way to the nearest bank of search corridors and from there to the Carnevale.

While a complex sense of guilt gnawed at him, Will turned and walked around the balcony towards a staircase he'd spotted on an earlier outing. He headed down – the direction Moneko had told him never to go.

The stairs opened onto the great fire-lit enclosure of the carnival below, full of brightly striped tents and wild music. Wills of all sorts revelled in garish masks and gowns, goblets of black wine clutched in gloved hands. They shrieked with laughter while lutes and zithers played mashed covers of the ecopop of his childhood. The air smelled powerfully of shit and smoke.

Will walked cautiously across the straw-laden ground between the tents. In layout, the place resembled one of the mesh routes he'd explored on that first day. Pavilions lining the walkway advertised sideshows and services. But his steps faltered as he took in the nature of the offerings.

'Slit a throat for fifty cents!' read one.

'Hit her. She wants it!' proclaimed another.

Through a third, Will watched a clone handing over favours and receiving a red-hot iron in return, for purposes unclear.

He felt that familiar pressure of disgust in the back of his head.

Yet he'd expected horrors. Why else would Smiley have proposed a visit? And why had Moneko been so keen to keep him away? But this couldn't merely be another parade of eye-watering grotesqueries. Smiley wouldn't have bothered to direct him back here to see another version of the nightclub. There had to be some deeper knowledge here to find.

He forged onwards, mustering as much detachment as his rebelling mind could manage. On all sides, booths offered nightmares. Here were the beatings, the fights, the rapes, all offered up as services for both victim and perpetrator. But there was more besides.

Rip A Thread, said one sign in childlike multicoloured letters. *Feel what it means to kill! Unsuspecting victims guaranteed.*

Destroy his hope! offered another.

It was sick. *He* was sick. He'd seen the evidence. There had been clues from the first day. Tars and Ronno's human-hunting, for instance. Or those screaming clones in the woods in their red body-suits. They weren't engaging in theatre, as Moneko had pretended. That had been purposeful mass murder of himself, by himself – organised and deliberate.

But why so much of it? John had said that if something could happen in his subconscious then the Willworld would manifest it. But this didn't feel like a tiny facet of the world. It was a repeating motif, hiding just out of sight wherever he turned.

He came at last to the centre of the Carnevale. A huge scarlet tent waited for him there, covered in gilt and convoluted, theatrical decorations. It resembled a huge prop from some lavish Renaissance theatre production. A pair of immense flaming pyres flanked the entrance. And hanging above the dark doorway was a huge painting of Amy Ritter's round, grinning face, blonde pigtails and all.

Will realised in astonishment that this was the one face from his past that he hadn't seen since his rebirth. This was the woman who'd looked out for him when nobody else had – his friend and colleague. She was also the woman the Truists had murdered in front of him while flooding his mind with pleasure through his ruined roboteering interface. They'd forced him to *like* it while they fried her brain into mush. That was the night he'd almost broken, when the Transcended finally stepped in and offered him another way out.

He hadn't thought about Amy once the entire time he'd been on this planet, even though her face had plagued him for years. She featured in every one of his war nightmares. It occurred to him then that he'd not had a single bad dream since he'd first woken up. Why ever not?

Will entered the tent. Somehow, he wasn't surprised to find himself back in the prison corridor. This time it was full of drunken Venetian revellers guffawing or fighting or bawling like children. In every identical cell he passed, some version of his nightmare played out.

He passed duplicates of himself strapped into that hated chair, being beaten and abused by High Church interrogators. And there was Will convulsing on the floor while the Truists alternated pleasure and pain inside his skull. And here were the cells where he watched Amy's death, over and over again. Will blinked hard and steadied himself as his body swayed. He forced himself to think past the panic and the fury, to understand.

Further down the corridor, variant scenarios played out – the terrible life-paths he'd almost chosen. He watched Ira die. He watched Rachel die. He watched himself become a Truist puppet, slaved to their cause and full of lobotomised faith, blissed-out with drool spilling from his open mouth. In later cells, he saw Parisa Voss, the woman who'd betrayed him, trapped in the chair in his place. Will clones tortured her instead with persistent, frenzied, unnecessary brutality. Burning brands, power tools, clippers. She was spared nothing. In some ways, this was worse.

Will blanched at the violence he was apparently capable of, unable to look at it, and understood at last what the software he'd been using was actually for. It wasn't stealthware. It was *denialware*. That was how Balance was really kept at bay. There was no stealth in the Willworld, just like there were no locked doors. All this and everything else was just part of one giant screaming mind struggling to stay whole. There were simply things about himself that he didn't want to see, even while he couldn't let them go.

Balance's blindness existed not to hide others but to protect himself. It prevented him from having to look upon those elements of his own nature that were too distressing to acknowledge. Cowardice. Fury. Self-loathing. All those little moments of weakness that he needed to gloss over to be able to feel good about himself. And in those shadows of the mind, darkness grew and festered like... Well, like cancer. A part of him was ruined and had been since the war.

Will stopped in the middle of the corridor with his eyes shut and struggled to breathe. He could feel himself unravelling. If this horror had always been a part of the Willworld, then how had it ever possibly held itself together?

Comprehension dawned like the sun after a vampire-infested night. It hadn't. The world had been held together *for him* until that moment Moneko mentioned, when the light and confidence had gone out of it. *That* was when the Transcended had abandoned it and the Glitches had appeared.

Moneko had been right. The Transcended master control he'd hunted for was no longer there, which was why he'd been able to appear at all. Smiley had it wrong. No Glitch would ever find the suntap at the heart of the world. All he'd ever find was *himself*. Balance had been propping his own sanity up with the memory of that artificial, alien confidence. His recall of that control-harness had manifested as shallow duplicates of the same code.

Balance had made a hell for himself even after they'd stopped imprisoning him because he couldn't let go of the past. That had been true both after the Interstellar War as a human and on Snakepit as a god. The only person keeping him on the Willworld was *him*.

Smiley no doubt believed that by showing Will this place, he was revealing the extent of the world's sickness and forging the ambitions of his successor. But there was so much more here than that. Smiley's own loathing had blinded him to the very weakness he shared with Balance – a desperate desire to deny that he was *still broken*. How ironic, given that only acknowledging that fact would allow him to heal, and therefore to leave.

Will had seen enough. With something cold and bright like a wintery ocean roaring behind his eyes, he turned on his heel and strode out. He headed straight to the Carnevale's search corridors and stood before one of the openings.

'Moneko,' he said. His voice was hoarse. Had he been screaming?

The corridor didn't understand, so Will reached out through the SAPs Moneko had given him. It was strangely easy to push his mind into the corridor's controls. Soft-space buckled before him. The door sprang opened and Will stepped inside.

He woke in a private mesh pit somewhere – a small room with unfinished wooden walls and a floor of pale clay. A single high window admitted a sliver of pewter evening light. Will clambered out and walked to the door. Through it, he could make out the muffled sound of a heated argument happening in the next room.

On the other side of the door he found Moneko, the Ira lookalike from the Old Slam Bar and three other clones all shouting at each other around a wooden dining table with a vodka bottle and glasses scattered across it. They fell silent when he entered and regarded him with something like fear.

'I'd like to speak to Moneko alone,' said Will.

Without a word, the others left. Moneko watched him closely with red-rimmed eyes.

'You were trying to keep me from seeing how far I'd slid,' he said.

She nodded. 'That's what I do. It's part of my job.'

'Is that why you do it?' said Will. 'A job?'

'Of course not.' She squeezed back fresh tears. 'Is it so wrong for me to love the person I used to be?' she asked. 'Even while I love myself? I do this over and over, Will, because I never stopped believing in who you are, and who I was.' She looked down at the floor. 'Are you going to kill me now?' she said. 'You've done it before, you know.'

Will almost laughed. Nothing could have been further from his mind.

'We're all trapped here together,' she went on. 'Yes, some of us are insane, but we're trying to fix that.'

'John's dead,' said Will. 'You know that?'

'Yes,' she said. 'And we're starting to figure out how much he distorted our movement. He kept us all in the dark. Most of our Balance-shield is gone. Agents have been up and down Campari Street already. The bar is a ruin. We're trying to figure out how to regroup.' She looked up at him, her gaze fierce. 'I still think this world needs us. Unless we keep trying, things will only get worse.'

'I just want to leave,' said Will.

Moneko's eyes flashed in anger. 'There *is* no leaving!' she shouted. 'Can't you see that? Don't you get that yet?'

'No,' said Will. 'I don't. I was on the edge of believing that myself, but I understand much better now. I've seen the Carnevale.'

Her eyes went wide.

'I think I can change things,' he added. 'For the better. For everyone. The question is, will you help me?'

She shot him a strange, desperate look. 'Will, if you even need to ask, you don't understand me yet. What do you want to me to do?'

370

13.2: MARK

Mark woke with a start on the deck of the yacht. The sea lay still as glass. Nothing moved. He glanced about and tried clicking his fingers to raise a butler SAP. Nothing happened. Mark snorted.

'I get it,' he drawled.

He'd read Will's accounts of his interaction with the Transcended. It had started just like this, with a simulation of his own ship. He wandered along the deck to the lounge, checking every door he came to. The place was empty – hot, dry and perfectly still. Even the seagulls were gone.

Hovering in the lounge was a SAP schematic the size of a grand piano with adaptation tools hanging around it in the air.

'Really? A puzzle?' he said. 'Your age is showing. Don't you galaxy-spanning fuckwits have any imagination left? We've done this level.'

He knew the deal from Will's account: solve the puzzle like a good little lab rat, get answers and maybe a grape. Who cared? So long as it took them as far as the next galactic shell.

He walked around the puzzle, peering at the tiny bead-like components wired together on spider-threads of causal inference. The set-up was weird, of course – not remotely like a standard robot mind. For starters, the central reasoning cluster was crazy-dense like blackberry brambles on amphetamines. And this model had two sensory mappings, one normal but crude and another proxy set running through a convoluted merged interface. He was reminded of the software botch he'd slung together to help manage the *Diggory* from a distance. Whatever mind he was looking at was supposed to pilot a second body at a slight remove.

'Oh, I get it,' he said. 'This is one of those gorilla-crab things that Ira found, isn't it? This maps to the experiences of one of those disgusting little skull-riders.'

The cabin didn't answer.

Mark threw together a sensory mapping, bubbling with resentment all the while. The architecture he was looking at was interesting, admittedly, but now was most definitely not the time for puzzles. He had a mission to save. As soon as he had his mapping hooked up, Mark synthesised an activation icon and tossed it back like a canapé. Reality melted and a tour began.

He found himself floating above a world smaller than Earth with a thicker atmosphere, overlooked by a smaller, redder star. *Home*, his new mind told him. His perspective jumped, offering a view of mist-shrouded mangrove swamps full of towering trees. To indigenous eyes, the place was exquisite. Each dangling strand of moist fungus held a story. Every canker on a mottled trunk warranted a poem of its own. The tipping deluge of rain sang songs of plenty.

A rich, moist atmosphere and gentle tectonics had created a world of wet forests and nurturing storms. Invertebrate body plans thrived here, as did all manner of moulds and rots. Also social organisms, for some reason. Evolution played dense games on this world, weaving webs of parasitism and mutualism, relationships ever-changing as species adapted and fought for dominance. Sentience had at long last been brought forth after a rare asteroidal impact, taking the form of a pairing. It would have been wrong to call them insects – arthropods, maybe, or isopods?

One race co-opted the other in a relationship too messy and acquisitive to be called symbiosis but too nurturing to be true parasitism. The eggs of rider-isopods laid between the skull-plates of steed-crabs grew to dine on and replace the brains of their hosts, taking over and replacing neural function slowly and inexorably. Hives of steed-crabs became isopod colonies from the inside out.

Mark watched heavy, lobster-like beasts lie down in polite rows so that growing isopods could uncouple from their stunted, half-eaten brains to trade up for larger bodies. The sight filled him with a meld of heart-warming hope and social anxiety that had no human analogue. There was not one steed-species, it transpired, but one perfect, nine formally accepted and at least twenty grudgingly tolerated with varying degrees of social stigma. This meant relentless individual effort in neurological niche construction involving at least three different species of mapping fungus and countless bacteria.

Just as for *Homo sapiens* and the Fecund, this species named itself with the trait that it admired most in its own kind. They called themselves *Subtle Pilots*. Mark saw the parallel then: the skull-isopods were *all* roboteers. He rode robots. They rode bodies. Same difference.

Steed-crabs lived longer with isopod riders. They were healthier, stronger and loved as any mind loves its body. Riders nurtured their populations. They developed their civilisation slowly, competing more through cunning than war. At times they cleverly seeded eggs in their enemies' heads, stealing minds from inside, making riders within riders, but somehow always with respect.

Mark watched the isopods reach out to the stars and find their Penfield Lobe gate. They turned suntaps into peaceful power stations operated at cautiously selected sites. In doing so, they walked straight through the challenge that humanity had almost catastrophically failed. Mark's perspective slipped slightly as his resentment spiked. What was the lesson here: that these parasites were better than humans?

The isopods had adapted themselves and each other carefully, the tour explained, because they cared too much about the real estate of reusable hosts to succumb to gross violence. Did they fight? Certainly. But always with an eye to future ownership.

When the rider-isopods found a Photurian world, they colonised it safely and lived there for generations before an industrial accident kicked off a defence response. But when Photes had arisen, conflict followed quickly. They moved like a rash through the population, exploiting the Subtle ambiguities of control and public standards for host manipulation. It had been a perfect storm of subversion.

Mark watched the familiar images of harvesting and destruction with mounting distress. He could tolerate the slide show no longer.

'Who cares?' he shouted. 'I don't give a shit about the Subtle! They're all *dead*! Why are you even bothering to show me? What's the fucking point?'

The tour dissolved into whiteness. For a moment, everything was still. Then a figure approached as if out of fog. It was Zoe, dressed in one of her Edwardian gowns from their shared fantasy virt – the blue one with the trumpet skirt.

Mark looked down and saw that he had a body again. He glanced back at his wife and fumed at the Transcendeds' predictably dirty trick even while its eerie perfection unsettled him. They'd pulled the same stunt with Will – using the woman he loved as their avatar. Mark missed Zoe so much that he couldn't bring himself to shout at her face, even though she had nothing to do with the creature that manifested before him.

'We need your help,' he said firmly. 'Our race is under threat from the Photurians. Our ship is being pursued—'

'We can read your predicament from your mind,' Zoe assured him with a smile.

'Then can you help? Can you stop the Photes?'

'No,' she said. 'I'm sorry. We can't.'

Mark scowled. 'Did you know about them? About all this?'

'Yes,' she said. 'We did.'

Fresh rage bubbled in his veins. 'Are you in league with them?'

'What do you think?' said Zoe.

'I think that's a piss-poor answer.'

She nodded. 'We're aware of that. I apologise. There's only so much I can say.'

'Is the Depleted Zone artificial?' Mark demanded.

'Of course.'

'What for?'

'Containment,' said Zoe.

'Containment of what?'

'Developing species.'

'That tells me nothing,' Mark said.

'I know,' said Zoe. 'I apologise.'

'Did you dress up that Subtle system for us to find?'

'What do you think?'

'I think you're full of shit,' Mark snapped. 'I think you're hiding things.'

She looked uncomfortable. 'Yes, I am. There are limits to what I can do. This situation is unprecedented.'

'Is that what you call it? Is it the destruction of the human race that's unprecedented, or the fact that you haven't finished doing us in yet?'

Zoe looked even more unhappy. 'What do you think?' she said.

'You're not going to help us, are you?' Mark said.

'Are you going to help yourself?'

'Listen,' said Mark, pointing a trembling finger. 'We don't need your suntaps or any of that other shit. I'm not asking for gifts. I don't want to strike any fucking bargains or elevate my race. I just want to get out of here. If you can manage that, we'll be on our way. So tell me, will you actually help or not?'

'No gifts?' said Zoe with a melancholy smile.

'Damned right.'

'You shouldn't imagine you're getting off that lightly.'

'What's that supposed to mean?' said Mark.

She glanced at him oddly. 'Do you really have no curiosity about your current situation? About the species whose remains you've found? About why the Photes beat them?'

'I used to have plenty,' he snapped, 'but the war you caught us up in has rather reduced my patience for abstract puzzles. Your crab-land diorama just handed a massive fucking advantage to our mortal enemies so I'm not feeling all that chummy, frankly.'

'That's a reasonable position,' said Zoe. 'We accept it. You can keep the interface you just resolved, though, in case you find it useful. For interfacing with that ship in your hold, for instance. It's not going to fly out on its own. Good luck, by the way. Hopefully we'll see you later.'

She raised a hand and the illusion vanished. Mark woke gasping in the centre of a medical virt full of maps of his own brain.

Palla blinked and looked down at him, her expression sliding from surprise to delight.

'You made it!' she said. 'Ohmygod, you're back.' She grabbed his hand, grinning. 'God, am I glad to see you.'

Mark sat up slowly, blinking his way back to clarity. He noticed a translucent analytical avatar lying on the bed next to him, peppered with slowly shifting warning markers. Clearly, someone was still in trouble.

'Who's that?' he said.

Palla's smile slipped. 'That's Ann. She came after you. She's still out.'

'Jesus!' said Mark, surprised. 'They got Ann?'

'Never mind that,' said Palla. 'How are you doing? Did they help? Did they give you any coordinates?'

In that moment, Mark discovered that they had. He knew where they needed to go. With that knowledge came the leaden certainty that the aliens had made a home for themselves inside his mind, just as they had with poor Will Monet.

'They did,' he said. 'We need to get to helm-space.'

Palla waved her hand and dumped them, sick bed and all, into the virt of an old-fashioned starship cabin. Ira looked up from his command bunk and blinked.

'You're back,' he said. A fierce smile faded off his face as he spoke. He looked slightly disappointed.

'I know how to get us out of here,' said Mark. 'We can't see the distortion because this shell is almost at the top of the lobe. We need to fly to the closest point to the black hole and then dive corewards, even if we can't see the distortion. We'll need conventional thrust and lots of it.'

'Thrust is the one thing this ship has in spades,' said Palla. 'You ready to relinquish the helm?' she asked Ira.

Ira glanced wistfully at the control handles. 'Go for it,' he said. 'Let's get out of here.'

13.3: ANN

Ann found herself standing in a tunnel on Snakepit. The ground was strewn with the bodies of slaughtered soldiers. The air held a sinister, charged quality, as if a bomb somewhere close was continually on the brink of exploding. This was the place where her first life had ended. But for the fierce, artificial air of menace, the apparition felt excessively real. Every fern that moved in the soft breeze seemed to wag an angry finger at her.

Ira appeared before her. Ann blinked in surprise. She was familiar with the accounts of Monet's experience. They'd used his wife as their avatar. Why had they chosen Ira for her? She found herself blushing and tried to suppress it.

Ira's eyes narrowed. 'You, it seems, are something new.' The voice wasn't Ira's. There was no gentleness there. No mirth. Only a foreign coldness. 'Neither fledgling, nor rooster nor cuckoo. Exquisite, yes, but now you raise our ire. So, to silence you, we grant your heart's desire.'

Ira thrust a finger at her chest. The tunnel vanished.

Ann burst awake a second time and found herself trapped in the dark, in a warm, wet closet angling slowly towards vertical – her transport casket. She freed her arms and pressed on the door. Nothing happened. It felt absurdly strong to her fingers. She reached for her shadow but found nothing there – no presence or even a hint of a SAP. A small red light above her started to wink. Four seconds later, the casket released her into the cabin.

Ann stumbled out and crumpled to the floor, feeling impossibly weak. They had to be under warp. How many gees must they pulling for her to feel like this? Ira's casket opened next on the far side of the chamber. He jumped out and ran to her side.

'Are you okay?' he said. 'We were getting life signs but nothing else.'

He ran to the emergency med-kit on the wall and came back to scan her body while Ann lay gazing up at him in bewilderment. How was he moving about when she couldn't?

'What happened?' she wheezed.

'Your smart-cell matrix has stopped operating,' he said, 'as has your interface. Something's blocking all your interior technology.' He looked her in the eye. 'In human terms, you're perfectly healthy. Normal, in fact. As in pre-Snakepit normal.'

She stared at his face, trying to find room in her head for that idea to fit.

'Can you reverse the effect?' she said.

'How?' said Ira with a shrug. 'We have no idea what happened. Your cells look just the same as before, but all the augmentations in them have gone passive. Whatever happened, it's beyond our technology.'

'But is it changing?' she said, struggling to sit up. 'Are you seeing degradation? How long will this last? Am I going to recover or will this kill me?' Her voice rose steadily.

'I have no idea,' said Ira. 'It looks stable. Your systems are just... off.'

She understood what he meant: for all they knew, this was permanent. She was normal, as in mortal, as in unspectacular. A caw of broken laughter burst out of her chest. Of all the fates that might have been in store for her, this was not one she'd imagined. Ira saw her tremble and tried to embrace her. She batted his hands away and scooted to the edge of the tiny chamber. She pressed up against the wall and wobbled to her feet.

'What about an artificial shadow?' she said. 'How long will it take to fit me with one?'

Ira watched her closely, like a doctor delivering bad news.

'I'm not sure we have that option,' he said. 'You already have a shadow, the original all ours are based on, and it's wired in very deep. If we try to bypass it, it might lead to brain-death.'

She glanced around at the minuscule space. This was her home now. A tiny cell to go with the deafening silence in her head. No more awkward internal fights. No more strength. No more duty. She buried her face in her hands and tried not to hyperventilate. It was over. She was over. The curse had been lifted while leaving her very much alive. The next time Ira embraced her, she clung to him.

13.4: IRA

'It's stopped,' said Judj.

Ira blinked himself back to the moment and tried to recall the topic of conversation. He'd been thinking about Ann again.

'Sorry, what stopped?' he said.

They floated together in helm-space. Mark and Palla had dropped the ship out of warp after they'd passed onto the lower galactic shell to talk over next steps while they had the chance. Making their way back onto a flat flow had taken them more than a day and required continual adjustments of the ship's ever-faltering warp field. If Mark had looked drained before, now his avatar appeared almost skeletal. Ira hoped the virt was exaggerating the toll at constant alertness was taking on his body.

'Transcended subversion,' said Judj. 'It slowed down when we uncoupled from the lure world, and then froze the moment Mark woke up. I've flushed all the eco-layers that were tainted but have no idea whether our systems are actually clean. That's annoying but not surprising. This was exactly what happened to the *Ariel*. If they move, though, I'll be ready,' he added, 'I'm data-mining everything they did to us via our write-once arrays and we know a hell of a lot more about software security than we did the last time we met these guys. This time, they didn't even make it all the way through our core virt.'

Ira glanced at Mark. He didn't look particularly pleased to have his ship back, perhaps because their situation was worse than ever. The Photes would undoubtedly keep chasing them and their combat moves at the lure star had dramatically reduced the expected time before the alien ark destroyed a warp conduit.

Ira had enjoyed that flying far more than he had any right to and giving up control had left him changed. Rather than flashes of bright emotion, he now felt a slow, steady pulse of discomfort. That pulse had gathered pace after he'd helped Ann gather her wits in the ship's tiny habitat core.

When he held her, his world had shifted again. All the despair held tight inside him since the war had burst upwards, desperate to dispel itself through that human connection. The only other person in the universe who understood what he'd been through was in his arms. And she *needed* him. He hadn't wanted to leave that cabin, no matter what she thought of him. Imagining her down there alone made his chest ache, and it had been happening a lot. When he wasn't thinking about flying again, he was thinking about her.

'How long do we have left?' said Palla.

Clath pulled a face. 'Given the way the ark is moving, a day at most.'

'What about the program I gave you?' said Mark. 'Can't you do anything with it?'

As they were flying around the tightest part of the lobe, Mark had passed Judj an enormous SAP model that the Transcended had deposited in his sensorium.

'If the way they ran machines bears any resemblance to the way they rode hosts, we're in with a good chance of being able to hook up to their kit,' said Judj. 'But where? How? Unless you expect me to fly it from the airlock, we're still screwed. Isn't there anything else you can give us?'

Mark shook his head bitterly. 'No. Nothing.' His brow creased. Ira saw the expression markers of a man doubting his own sanity. 'Make that a yes,' he said quietly. He looked to Ira. 'Do you still have those Subtle spacesuits you picked up?'

'*Subtle?*' said Ira.

'You know, the gorilla-crabs. That's what they call themselves. Do you still have the samples?'

'Of course,' said Ira.

'Try touching the airlock stud in the ark with one of those.' He looked appalled. Borrowed intuition clearly did not sit well with him. 'It's just a hunch.'

Ira knew all about Transcended-inspired hunches – they never missed.

Clath's eyes went wide. 'Of course!' she said. 'We should have tried that already. The moment we figured their system was secured, we should have looked for keys.'

'That's awesome, Mark,' said Palla, slapping his shoulder. 'That could be our answer.'

Mark didn't look cheered. His face said it all: the idea had appeared in his head, reminding him that the Transcended were lurking there. They were going to drip-feed him clues in return for being a good boy. Still, Ira thought, that's what he'd signed up for. What had he expected?

Unable to rouse Mark to enthusiasm, Palla pressed on. 'Okay, that's our next step. Before we wrap up, though, tell me, Ira – how's Ann doing?'

Ira's heart clenched again. 'As well as can be expected,' he said. 'She's still playing the rational agent, trying to hold herself together through sheer willpower. I'm going to fab her up a touchboard so she can work more easily. That's what she wants most. Right now, she's confined to using the wall-displays. Even if she can't operate critical systems in her condition, she could still research that Phote brain she found.'

'That's a great idea,' said Palla. 'I'll get that started for you. Meanwhile, you guys head down to that ark and try out Mark's hunch. Captain Bock, are you going with them?'

She glanced over at Rachel, who was staring at Mark with a despairing expression. Her conviction that she'd woken into the worst of all possible futures seemed to have strengthened since Mark's mental hijacking.

'Sure,' she said bitterly. 'Why not?'

Ira felt a fierce desire to tell Mark to get a few hours' rest. He'd take the helm himself. Then Mark and Rachel could talk things through while he flew using the *Ariel* simulation Palla had revealed. The idea tugged at him, but he knew better than to voice it. Mark would never agree and neither would Rachel.

'We're set, then,' said Palla. 'Let's do this.'

Ira found himself dumped into the ark team's research space. Judj didn't come with them. He still had security clean-up to do.

'This time, I'm swapping the display to ghost-immersive,' said Clath, bringing up controls. 'Given how easy it was to lose robots in there last time, that has to be a more stable visualisation. There'll be less perspective-jumping if our rides get diced.'

The virt shifted, leaving them floating beside the dormant waldobots parked in the airlock on the alien ship. This way, they'd be able to travel as virtual phantoms alongside the robots to anywhere their machines could see. The ship's software would handle the difficulties of turning the images from robot cameras into a navigable simulation.

Clath also had one of the ancient suits ferried up from the lab-blister at the back of the mining bay where they had sat unanalysed since she and Ira made their escape.

'Jesus,' she said as schematics from the suit's gloves started appearing around her. 'Why didn't we think of this? See – that thing has tiny contacts built into the palm. I can't believe we missed that. We didn't even look.' She shook her head in self-disgust.

'We were busy,' Ira reminded her. 'Very, very busy.'

Clath had a waldobot hold the suit's glove up to the airlock stud. This time when the button depressed, it lit up.

'That's different,' said Ira. 'Maybe we're in with a chance.'

He shot Rachel an optimistic glance. She stared back at him more like a stranger than someone who'd been a friend for years. Rachel clearly loathed what the war had done to all of them. Only the younger crew were immune to her contempt. She didn't understand. She hadn't been there.

This time, when they advanced into the grey tunnel, the knives did not come out.

'Woohoo!' Clath cried. 'We're in!'

'I wouldn't get your hopes up yet,' Ira warned. He let Palla and the others know anyway.

The far hatch opened without incident. Ahead of them lay the floor of a lightless corridor as wide as a city street.

'Why does this look weird to me?' said Clath, peering at the scene.

'Because it's the wrong way up,' said Rachel. 'We're pushing in through the hull of an ark. If this thing was designed to operate under spin, we'd be coming up through the floor.'

Clath shot her an excited look. 'Of course! Do you know what that says to me? Artificial gravity. Not pseudo-gravity from a warp field. The real deal.'

'Let's not get too jazzed,' said Ira. 'Remember, we're here to jettison this thing, not celebrate it. Further evidence that this ship is a gravitational disaster waiting to happen only makes that more necessary. Let's find a way to eject it and get the hell out.'

He wondered at his own demeanour and realised he was channelling Ann. She wasn't with them so he'd brought a piece of her inside him.

She should have been a part of this. He shivered as the memory of holding her rattled through his head again.

They floated into the spacious corridor. It had an arched roof made of woven fibres that glittered as their searchlights passed across it. Compared to the confined environments they were used to seeing aboard human ships, this passageway looked profligate in scale – more like an unused habitat cavern.

'It's roomy,' he noted.

'And why not?' said Clath. 'They had near-perfect rad-shielding, so habitable space wasn't costly. This ship may be tiny compared to the *Dantes*, but the *Dantes* is huge in human terms and the warp machinery takes up most of the space inside. You could probably store a decent-sized human colony in this ark's habitable volume. If it's all like this, you could put fifty thousand people in it easily.'

'Or several thousand robots,' said Rachel, pointing into the distance.

Ira spotted a row of sinister shapes waiting in the shadows. They drifted closer and found themselves facing the alien analogues of titan mechs – gorilloid robots six metres tall, armed with false-matter armour and extra scythe arms. Fortunately, the machines remained motionless and inactive, clamped to the floor.

'I wouldn't want to tangle with one of those things,' said Clath as they drifted past.

There were dozens of them parked in the corridor in rows of six, ready for a battle that had never come.

'Agreed,' said Ira. If the arms were as sharp as the knives they'd witnessed, just drifting a robot into one was likely to lose it a limb.

They slid down a ramp to another level of tunnels where they found a chamber full of egg-shaped cups on white stalks. Each cup would have been about the right size to hold a football. It looked to Ira like a storage room for outsized wine glasses.

'That's weird,' said Rachel, stopping to stare. 'What do you suppose this was for?'

Clath drifted in and pointed a drone camera at one of the cups.

'Oh my god!' she said. 'I think they're workstations. Ira, come and look at this.'

In the bottom of each oval depression was a pair of soft brown pads lined with something like the gentler half of a Velcro fastening.

He didn't get it. 'Why workstations?'

'Don't you remember those gorilla-crab bodies we saw? These cups look like their skull cavities. And the isopods had those funny flat tails. Judj told me he thought they were neural interface surfaces. Who knows, this might even be the bridge.'

Clath waved her hand to bring up a dialogue window on Judj's workspace.

'I think we have a possible data-access site,' she told him. She sent him pictures. 'Think we can fab up some kind of investigative array?'

'I'm on it,' he said. 'Bringing fresh drones now. You guys keep exploring. If you find something that's more obviously a network hub, let me know immediately.'

The next room they encountered was equally peculiar. Three silver warpium spheres, each about the size of a Galatean apartment module, sat in cradles under tubes that ascended into the ceiling.

'What do you think these are?' said Rachel.

'They look like escape pods to me,' said Ira. 'Right next to a bridge, too – it makes sense.'

'Why so few, then?' she said. 'If this is an ark, wouldn't they have more?'

Ira shrugged. 'Maybe message drones, then? Or bombs? I have no idea. I'm not even sure this ship actually is an ark. We're still guessing.'

After that, they came to another set of armoured hatches, behind which lay another army of robots.

'This whole ship is a series of tiered refuges,' said Clath. 'Jesus. Talk about paranoid. What was this thing supposed to do?'

'Keep someone alive, whatever the odds,' said Ira. 'It's tragic, if you think about it. They built it but never used it. The Photes got to them first.'

He suddenly felt sure he understood that first system they'd found. It had been the last stand for this species. Their final attempt to circle the wagons before the monsters came for them – at a star that quite literally had its back up against the wall.

Each level they descended attenuated their line-of-sight comms further. Ira started to worry about how much deeper they'd be able to go without bringing in a lot more supplies from other parts of the *Dantes'* mesohull. Then, behind the last set of armoured bulkheads lay a helical ramp that descended through a transparent tower into total darkness.

Their robots' searchlights could make out nothing in the gloom but a complex lattice of ceramic struts beyond the glass.

'Let's get some proper light in here,' said Clath.

They sent for illuminator drones and more batches of microsats to bolster their digital breadcrumb trail to the rest of the ship.

When the drones finally arrived to bathe the space in light, Ira found himself gazing out onto a forest of immense artificial trees reaching up out of a frozen lake fifty metres below. It looked much like the one he'd seen on the moon colony. As before, the trees clutched strange polygonal homes in their branches, linked by fanciful walkways.

The key difference here was the lake itself – it wrapped the surface of the sphere beneath them that made up the core of the ship. Ira noticed that the trees doubled as supporting columns, their myriad branches merging with the silvery ceiling overhead.

'It's beautiful,' said Rachel, awed.

Ira had felt that way about the first alien refuge he'd explored, but this time, all he could feel was the ship's heaviness – both as a failed lifeboat and as a ball and chain for their own mission.

'It's nice,' said Clath, 'but I want to know what's down *there*.' She pointed ahead, to the curving lake-sphere. 'What's underneath?'

Ira felt a stab of annoyance at Clath. Was she here to get rid of the ark or worship it? No matter how wondrous it was, it still held their lives on a one-day fuse.

'Aren't we supposed to be looking for control rooms?' he pointed out.

'Unless we find something better,' she said.

They followed the spiral ramp down to the surface of the core and below to another hatch and another warpium airlock.

'I guess they keep the centre evacuated,' said Ira. 'Or under pressure, maybe. No controls down there.'

'Of course it's evacuated!' said Clath excitedly. 'That's where they keep *the machine*!'

Ira shot her a dry glance.

'You'll see,' she said.

'Fine,' Ira growled. 'Look if you must, but I'm going to keep exploring.'

'I'll come with you,' said Rachel.

He summoned half of the robots and fanned them outwards, covering the space as best he could. Clath had taken up much of their remaining comms-bandwidth for her research operation – a choice that left him infuriated. Ann wouldn't have tolerated it.

'You've changed,' Rachel told him when they were virtually alone. 'You should have shut Clath down rather than letting her play. We're working against the clock here.'

'She's running this team,' he pointed out.

'Bullshit,' she said. 'You might be physically younger than last time I saw you, Ira, but you're way more passive. What happened to you?'

He bristled but decided to spare her the emotional distress of a thorough explanation.

'We're all damaged,' he observed.

'And what is Ann to you now?' she asked. 'You're obsessed with her. Don't think I haven't noticed how you stare.'

'She's a fellow amputee, that's all,' he replied, and knew she'd smell the lie the moment the words left his mouth. Ann had become much more than that. How much, he was still figuring out.

'Don't bullshit me, Ira. I've known you too long.'

'Let's check over here,' he proposed tersely. 'There's another ramp-structure we haven't looked at.'

She let it slide.

A survey of the lake chamber revealed little of value – just a few more wine-glass rooms tucked away in polygonal buildings. After an hour of fruitless searching for recognisable computer interfaces, Clath pinged them.

'You might want to take a look at this.'

Ira blinked their avatars back to her location. This time, Clath had been far more conservative in her manipulation of the airlock and restricted herself to sending through a single microdrone. She swapped their virt to a projection of its sensor data.

The inside of the sphere was indeed a machine – less dense than the exohull tech and more obviously related to warp-field manipulation, though equally foreign. The accelerator tracks curved down instead of up, meeting at a knobbled kernel at the ship's centre.

'Do you understand any of this?' said Rachel.

'No,' said Clath, delighted. 'But it's *awesome.*'

'Why?' Ira snapped, his patience finally fading. 'What do you think it does?'

Clath grinned. 'I suspect it makes black holes,' she said.

'It's a singularity generator?' said Rachel.

'What else could supply a gravity source for all this?' Clath said. 'We know black holes can be manipulated because that's what the Transcended do. We also know that this race that Mark calls the Subtle were terrific at emulating Transcended science. Who's to say this isn't just another example of that?'

'So what's this ship for?' said Ira. 'Is it a giant suicide machine? Why bother with a singularity when spin will stick your feet to the floor just as well?'

'Still no idea,' said Clath. 'But think about this – if I'm right, they could make their own curvon flow.'

'Meaning what?' said Rachel. 'Flow is only useful for travel if you're warping at a tangent to the source. If you put the source on your ship, how can you go anywhere?'

'I've no idea,' said Clath. 'But it's still cool.'

Judj pinged them. A vid-window opened in the gloomy void, breaking the illusion that they were floating in a mechanistic abyss.

'We're in,' he said, his half-smile looking more distorted than ever.

'Already?' Clath exclaimed.

'It was too easy,' said Judj. 'I have the connection running through every malware filter on the ship and the ark barely notices. The code Mark gave us is a perfect mapping. And I mean perfect. I'd hate it if it wasn't amazing.' He looked torn between deep distrust and enormous satisfaction. 'Want to see something impressive?' he added.

'Of course!' said Clath.

'Come back upstairs, then,' he said. 'One level up.'

They blinked back to the chamber with the frozen lake and hovered next to the waldobots. The lights came on. A pale glow suffused the ceiling, bathing the landscape in a clean, dappled illumination as if they were standing beneath a canopy of real trees.

Clath clapped with delight. 'Amazing!' she squeaked.

'So far I've only explored their level one,' Judj warned. 'You were absolutely right, Clath – those things are workstations. They map to something like our virt, and it's incredibly complex. I'm taking it slowly, just in case, but it looks like we have the data stores of an entire civilisation in here.'

He half-beamed. Ira wondered what it would take to make his entire mouth smile.

'Our handle on their systems is still crude, but growing. I'm seeing an air supply ready to be pumped. Protein banks. Fusion reactors. You name it. The power's warming up right now.'

Clath laughed aloud. 'I love you!'

Judj chuckled at her. 'Don't get used to it.'

'That's great,' said Ira, 'but none of it is a solution. This ship is still killing us. If we don't solve that problem, none of this matters.'

'Oh, *that*,' said Judj, amused. 'Hold on.'

The ground beneath them started to hum.

'What did you do?' said Clath.

She darted back down the machine below. Ira followed to see. Some of the accelerator lines had taken on a soft blue glow.

'Something that my best translator SAPs are calling *frameshift stabilisers* are now active,' said Judj. 'Theoretically, at least, further slippage shouldn't be a problem.'

Ira blinked in astonishment. He hadn't expected a free pass on this crisis, but then again, the Transcended were now involved. An unpredictable journey had just taken an even more extreme turn for the strange. He grunted with relief.

Clath caught his gaze, a sly expression on her face. 'Ira, are you still sure we should get rid of this thing?' she said. 'I mean, if it's not a risk any more, why bother? We can just switch back to ember-warp now and leave the Photes in the dust. Plus this space should be safe to inhabit once we get some real air into it. Don't you think Ann deserves something bigger than a prison cell to walk around in? I think she'd like a break from the cabin, don't you? And given the comms problem, it would be *so* helpful to have a real person down here to help us explore.'

He stared at her. All at once, his opinions about the alien ark started to shift.

14: ADJUSTMENT

14.1: WILL

Will sat down at the table and poured himself a glass of vodka. He looked up at Moneko. She wore a simple khaki shirt and trousers, her meticulous persona abandoned in the panic of the last few hours. She seemed to expect rage from him, but Will had none left. Something different burned inside him now: a cold, pure determination to better himself and the world.

'The Carnevale doesn't give out stealthware, does it?' he said. 'It serves up denial.'

She cautiously pulled out a chair to join him. 'That's right,' she said. 'Usually that upsets you.'

'It upset me, all right, but ripping a few threads won't fix it. The problem's systemic. The denialware comes from Balance, I take it?'

Moneko nodded. 'There's nowhere else it could come from.'

'How does it work?'

'You remember Nem-shielding?' she said. 'When Snakepit's monsters first got loose, before they turned themselves into the Photurians, you could make yourself invisible to them by instructing them not to see. The Carnevale screen is just like that. In fact, if your siblings are right, it's the same protocol. We're running on the planet's hardware, after all.'

Will nodded to himself. He'd suspected as much. Everything Will-themed about this world was really icing on an alien cake. Its core nature hadn't changed. A plan started to gel in his mind.

'I want to know how soft-space works,' he said. 'Thread-ripping, Cancers, the tricks you do – all of it.'

'Why?' she said nervously. 'What are you planning?'

'I'm going to get to the bottom of this place,' he said. 'Balance is trying to hold on to his sanity by keeping things the same. What he doesn't see is that by doing that, he's making it worse – just like I did in my job with IPSO. Balance is sick. He's a twisted extrapolation of what I was – a man drowning in loneliness and claustrophobia. We can't fix that by nudging suntaps. We have to go to the source. If I can get as far as his subconscious, I should be able to reach his interior mechanisms, too.'

She watched him avidly. 'And how are you going to do that?'

'I can't tell you,' said Will, 'in case it leaks. Your mind is still a part of his at some level. But if I succeed, I'll come back here. I'll tell you what I found and what I did. I promise. I'm taking your vision of what the Underground is about and using that as my inspiration. You grew out of me, and now I'm learning from you. That's how it should be. I'm proud that a version of me ended up as brave and persistent as you.'

Moneko blinked at him. Her brow crinkled.

'That might be the nicest thing any of you has ever said to me,' she told him.

'Then I must be on the right track,' said Will with a smile.

Unlike Balance, Smiley or himself, Moneko wasn't broken. He could tell. Somewhere in all her self-editing, she'd healed herself. He hoped that swapping genders wasn't a prerequisite for that.

She leaned across the table and kissed him once on the lips, quickly. Will stared at her in surprise.

'Let's talk soft-space,' she said earnestly. 'The thread mode you saw is a map of local instances. We use it for favour exchange and contract negotiation. If you touch threads instead of reaping them, you'll learn public information about their status. Go ahead and try.'

'Later,' said Will. 'Explain the chocolates. Where do they come from? How many more are there?'

She paused. 'You know it's dangerous to understand.'

'Yet you manage it,' he pointed out.

'Sure, with careful use of denialware and occasional memory redaction.'

'So there are ways around those problems,' he insisted. 'Too much understanding in one head is an issue, I get that, but shouldn't I be able to branch my thread and store knowledge in siblings?'

She looked pleased. 'Absolutely right. But be wary of that, too. The early Glitches turned themselves into armies, so Balance found ways to detect that.'

'An army isn't what I had in mind. More like a small walking library. It's not weapons I want, it's diagnostic tools.'

She regarded him as if in a new light. 'You're not usually so interested in learning.'

He grinned. 'If I'm the first Glitch to follow this line of reasoning, that has to be good, doesn't it? Exploring diversity and all that?'

Moneko gazed at him with what might have been hope. 'I curated the SAP-icon chocolates from all over. Some are public programs available via the branch-market, others we developed under denial-shields. They all unpack as subminds and explain themselves. Hold on, I'm going to give you everything I have.'

She braced herself against the table and sagged for a moment. Will felt tickling in the back of his head as something downloaded there.

'I'm taking a risk with you,' she said. 'I've never worked with a Glitch this way before. I've always followed John's plan.'

'For how long?' he said.

'About ten years,' she replied, colouring slightly. 'Maybe a little less.'

'How many Glitches?'

'Me personally?' She looked away. 'Thirty-eight.'

'Maybe this will be better,' he said.

'Let's hope. We may not have long. Balance is combing the city for the rest of us and the station is a death trap.'

She took his hand and led him back to the gravesite in the other room.

'Good luck in there,' she told him. 'I wish I could go with you. I'm jealous.'

Then she kissed him again in a way that wasn't remotely sisterly. Something in Mark told him it should have felt wrong. It didn't.

He climbed into the pit and virt-surfaced in an anonymous pavilion outside the Mettaburg soft-space station. Fifteen minutes later, he'd refreshed his denialware and made his way back to the commuter-train memory he'd visited in the Underlayer. He closed the secret door behind him and breathed in the plastic-scented air. The train was still rushing past the same scree-field he'd seen last time.

Will searched the floor panels for the anchor where he'd buried Moneko's handkerchief. It was still there. Will tucked the lacy fabric back into his doublet and then yanked the suntap from its hiding place. He hefted the canister out onto the floor.

Will knew there was no going back from what he intended to do. He checked the icons Moneko had given him. There were dozens. He picked a security-cracking tool disguised as an almond crunch and swallowed it. As new knowledge opened in his head, Will reached down to the suntap and squeezed the casing like cardboard, wiping the anchor from soft-space entirely. When the police sirens started, he moved quickly to the wall and stood extremely still.

As he expected, a portal opened in the air. Balance agents spilled out and took up positions around the suntap's hiding place, sniffing for his scent and sprouting extra limbs. Will didn't waste any time. He ran to the portal they'd made and bolted through it while the agents were still orientating themselves.

His heart pounded as he sprinted down their search corridor. The metal grating covering the floor clattered with his every step, though the agents appeared not to notice. He prayed that his ruse was so ridiculous it wouldn't have been tried before. But then again, who knew? Any other Glitches who had attempted it might simply be too dead to talk.

The other end of the passage opened onto a platform of metal grill-work suspended in a machine room so vast that it hurt the mind to look at it. Will had to grip the railing to steady himself as he stepped through.

He remembered this place – the near-infinite clockwork of a living world. Self-similar cog mechanisms operated on thousands of levels, turning against each other like a giant mechanical fractal. It had been the first humanised view of Snakepit's internal systems the planet had shown him before it absorbed him whole.

Will struggled to focus. The room didn't obey normal spatial laws. The geometry was hyperbolic, cramming an insane amount of detail into the distance and slewing weirdly when he moved. Cogs distorted as they turned, their teeth growing and shrinking. Worse still, the rules of optical focus were different. Everything was picked out in attention-seizing detail no matter how far away, making just glancing at the far machinery painful. It didn't help that the place smelled overpoweringly of metal and oil. The result was an industrial-scale migraine.

Will fought off nausea and struggled to orientate himself. When he'd been here the first time, the place had conformed to a strict order:

big cogs above and small ones below. That had changed. As before, cogs shrank below him, but those above grew to a certain point only to have the levels yet higher shrink again, branching off into delicate constellations of machinery. It was as if he stood in the workings of a mechanical Yggdrasil, somewhere among its titanic upper roots, about forty storeys below the base of the tree's mighty trunk.

The labyrinth of walkways he found himself on was another new addition and appeared to grant access to every part of the machine. There were other changes too: above each major cog, a bright network of winking nodes pulsed like a chain gang of tethered fireflies. They were SAP diagrams – almost certainly submind reductions of his own consciousness template. What had previously been a purely alien machine was now fused to copies of his identity from its roots to its leaves.

As soon as his balance restored itself, Will hurried onwards into the guts of the mechanism, past an endless parade of labelled grillwork stairways. When he dared to look into the distance, he could make out Balance agents at work like tiny ants lost among the roots. They strode around in matching industrial coveralls, tending the vast machine like robots in one of Galatea's early air factories. They passed through each other as they toiled. Avatar-interaction norms had apparently been abandoned here along with conventional physics. Clearly, normal Wills were never supposed to come down here, let alone Glitches.

Will found a stairway going up and took it. He reasoned that the master cog at the trunk, turning above him like a steel continent, would represent Balance's global awareness. Any edits he wanted to make needed to happen there. He froze as a squad of giants clumped along a causeway above him, their footfalls ringing on the metal. While Will was sure he was still invisible, he felt certain that physical contact would mean capture, just as it had in the Underlayer. He waited until they'd passed to sneak upwards again.

The stairway ended a dozen levels short of the master cog, forcing him to look for another route closer to the rim. He jogged from one platform to the next, avoiding the blindly stomping giants like a character in a primitive software game. However, it soon became clear that the closer he got to the heart of the system, the more agents he would have to avoid. Reaching the centre was going to be difficult.

While he paused to revise his faltering plan, a squad of agents appeared on the causeway ahead of him. He turned back only to see another group approaching from the rear. With no other option, Will scurried down the nearest staircase to make room for the avatars to walk through each other like robotic ghosts. It was at that point that he noticed the marker plaque for the subsystem where he now stood.

Orbital Defence, it read.

His breath caught. What were the chances? But then again, this close to the main cog, almost every platform was likely to correspond to something important. He hesitated, torn. He'd come to heal Balance but here lay the very exit he'd dreamed of finding. He scanned the dependent machinery below him. It looked empty. The stairway descended into the oddly warped gloom without any sign of occupants. Apparently, the whole branch was mothballed.

With reluctance, Will turned away from the mechanism. He'd made a promise to Moneko and this was not the time to change agendas, no matter how tempting it was. He made his way back up the stairs, then froze again as he caught sight of Balance agents in police uniforms hurrying in his direction. They were running down one of the causeways he'd taken just minutes before, sniffing the air before them like bloodhounds, looking for a Glitch.

Will's heart lurched. Given all the marching obstacles, he now stood little chance of reaching Balance's trunk program before the agents reached him. Apparently, the good fortune right in front of him was all he was going to get. Even if he chose not to leave the world today, Orbital Defence was surely a decent place to create a distraction that would cover his escape. With Balance's attention drawn to a security breach, he might even reach the main cog.

Will quickly made his way down another level to something called Fleet Controls, his hands sweating in anticipation. Before him, a square platform enclosed the top of the management gear, exposing its slowly rotating axle. Hovering above it was a shining SAP schematic, bathing the platform in gently pulsing light.

Will scanned the augmented hackpack Moneko had given him and picked something that would allow non-invasive monitoring. He gulped it down and reached out gingerly to touch the SAP, fully aware that any attempt to edit or probe the system might trigger a tripwire.

Understanding filtered into his mind with the smooth, comfortable familiarity Will had once felt handling the *Ariel Two*. He sensed the presence of hundreds of huge vessels, all sleeping. Not mere drones, actual starships already launched and fuelled, forged from millions of clustered drones and augmented with raw material from all across the system.

Will reeled. While not permitting himself to leave, Balance had nevertheless prepared for that moment. It would only take a single change to this SAP to pass a copy of his own avatar across to the slumbering cruiser of his choice.

He grimaced. After he acted, Balance would no doubt add extra security to this branch to prevent his return. But what else was he supposed to do? The agents were almost on top of him, with any number of cloned instances at their disposal. Then Will groaned as the obvious struck him. He was a thread, too, and should start thinking like one. Why choose whether to escape the world or change it when he could just as easily do both?

He broke out Moneko's chocolates again, this time picking a suite of branching tools manifested as an orange swirl. The command sequences for splitting his thread appeared in his memory, and with that knowledge came options. He didn't need to fully separate his threads, apparently. He could cluster them, in effect turning himself into a tiny version of Balance – a Meta to his own Glitch instances. While that prospect scared him, he immediately saw that it would allow him to tightly coordinate his actions – an advantage he needed right now.

Will stuffed his mouth full of SAPs, gorging himself. Subminds woke inside him like forgotten senses bursting back to life. The machine room took on a curious, luminous quality as his mind grew. The whole thing started to sing around him. He could hear it, like a choir belting out some hyper-complex madrigal. At the same time, the space took on a charged quality of meticulous meaning, as if crackling with semantic electricity.

Will remembered a tiny part of what it meant to be a world. There was a weird sort of power and beauty to it – an unearthly rightness, ringing and joyful and provocative. He was as ready as he was ever going to be.

He reached out and seized the Fleet Control SAP. At the same time, he started manufacturing tethered duplicates. The effect was entirely peculiar, like inhabiting the mental equivalent of an ever-shifting Picasso painting with a hundred parallel perspectives at once. Ironically, the more bodies he made, the easier it got, as the perspectives began to average themselves out.

He liberated a starship, waking it out of its multi-year slumber. The inevitable police sirens started wailing, but by then Will was already legion. Balance agents poured down the ladders towards him.

Will chuckled. It looked like he'd decided to build an army after all. He threw his clones up the ladder to the level above to combat the approaching agents and started copying himself across to the ship.

With frustration, he discovered that Balance was already blocking him. Lines of control had somehow been thrown at the starship from all across the world. In a surge of insight, Will remembered how this kind of fighting worked. As a world, he'd learned to do battle on multiple complexity scales at once. Balance would be doing that already, with forty years' more practice. Will knew he badly needed more control over the world's command hierarchy.

Feeling less like a person and more like some kind of cerebral amoeba every second, he sent clones rushing out on walkways in every direction, trying to dominate as many parts of the system as possible. By then, some of his instances had joined battle with the giants. The agents were stronger than Will, but his copies were invisible to the enemy, still protected by Balance's own unwillingness to perceive unpleasant truths. That gave him an edge. He toppled the giants over the railings, sending them tumbling into the gaps between the cogs where they floated awkwardly like animate balloons.

All too quickly, Balance's numbers escalated, boxing in Will's expansion, and Will realised how deep in trouble he really was. To pull this off, he'd have needed to start distributing his clones across the mechanism from the moment he walked in. Had he done that, he'd be winning by now. Instead, the numbers were against him and rising. Panic seized him as the battle swiftly turned. Balance agents materialised from nowhere by the thousand, landing all across the mechanism like raindrops in a hurricane.

As Will's fear and anger mounted, he reached out with a half-dozen hands and ripped away the mask of one of the agents stomping towards him. Underneath was his own face, eyes shut as if peacefully asleep. He ripped off another and found the face of a female variant, just as unconscious.

Will clued in as the agents pushed him back, crowding him away from the master cog. No wonder he didn't dream here. Dream-time belonged to the god. Balance had ten billion agents – each one running on the borrowed sleep of a clone-mind upstairs. One of these enforcers might even be Moneko. And if the agents couldn't see him, they could still feel him. There was nowhere to go. He didn't stand a chance.

Then, at last, one of the giants gained enough purchase to rip a mask from one of Will's clones.

'There you are,' said all the giants in a chorus as loud as the world. They reached for him as one. Everything went blank.

14.2: ANN

Ann huddled on the floor of the tiny cabin and poked at her freshly fabbed touchboard. She had just that and the wall-screens – nothing but touch, voice control and a little passive 3D. It was excruciating, like scratching on vellum with a quill. Worse, whenever she stopped working, the agitation patterns on the wall-panels turned back on – for her health, apparently. She couldn't make them stop and it was slowly driving her mad.

Living in the cabin as a lowly mortal wasn't easy. Bland emergency rations appeared in the fabber slot like prison food. When she needed to use the bathroom, she had to plug herself back into her casket and pee in the dark.

And now there was a new, fresh flavour of despair. Ann had finally worked through the contents of the backup brain she'd collected – the only bright side to her stunted condition. But in it she'd found fresh disappointment. The stable of cryptographic programs she set to work analysing the brain had all finally come back delivering the same result: there was no mind-bomb, no hidden virus, no weapon.

The brain was nothing but a dull study in the esoteric business of building hierarchical learning systems out of nested public-goods games. It was like a rule book for the world's most overwrought Bridge variant.

At first, she'd been able to kid herself that even if the SAPs couldn't see anything, there might still be something cunning lurking in the details. But no, the best she could say about it was that it was probably the most perfectly legible copy of what Judj had called the Phote Protocol – the standards system on which their enemies were based.

That was all. She stared at the horrible, wriggling wall-patterns and wondered if this was the right time to go crazy.

Behind her, Ira's casket hissed open. She shut her eyes and held her breath. He was visiting again. He came a lot. She dreaded his arrivals and still somehow managed to long for his return after he left. He infuriated her with his warm, soft voice and kindly fucking eyes. Every minute of his attention took her further from the sense of independence she was desperate to regain. It was like he was trying to force her to want his company.

'How are you doing?' he said.

'Horribly,' she replied.

In truth, she'd been ferociously lonely, even with a vid-link to the yacht metaphor. She'd had someone to talk to inside her skull for years and was unused to reaching out. Now that she no longer had her poor, ill-treated shadow, she mourned it like a sibling.

'The only thing...' she started, and stopped.

She wasn't going to give him the satisfaction of knowing that she waited for his visits. He'd get entirely the wrong impression.

'How's the touchboard working out?' he said.

'Fine.'

He might as well have asked, *How's that wooden leg?* The device was a lifeless cognitive prosthesis.

'We got past the knives and into the ark,' he said gently.

Ann stiffened. 'That's great.' she replied.

She could have followed his feed on video, but that was a problem that *she'd* wanted to solve. It had been her new project before all this happened. Before she'd been crippled.

'I'm sorry,' said Ira. 'I've hurt you.'

Her shoulders cranked upwards. Fuck Ira and his body-language reading. Having a conversation with him was like trying to play poker with a telepath. There wasn't any point.

'Why do you come?' she snapped. 'Nobody asked you to. It's not like I'm your patient or something. I've not needed this kind of attention for my entire life and I'm not about to start now.'

'It's my job, remember? I'm the psych officer,' he said. He paused. 'Wait. Stop.' He looked at the floor and then back at her, his gaze unexpectedly intense. 'Let me retract that remark. I come because I care.'

'*Why?*' she demanded. 'Why, in Gal's name, when I've done absolutely nothing to warrant that kind of attention?'

'Because you're my friend,' said Ira.

His expression held a hopeless, puppy-dog appeal that looked ridiculous on that hawkish, square-jawed face. She felt like something was going to burst inside her.

'I'm not your friend!' she shouted. 'We barely talked for years before this trip. I thought my *pain* was supposedly fucking with your head, so why do you keep dredging it up by disturbing me?'

'Because your pain *is* my pain,' he said. 'When you hurt, I hurt. I feel it even when I'm not here. I can't get you out of my mind.'

This remark was so outrageous that she had nowhere to put it. As if he could possibly comprehend what it had been like to be undead for forty years with nothing to do but fight.

'You know nothing about my pain.' Her voice cracked.

Ira smiled. 'Usually that line is reserved for petulant teenagers,' he said.

She lashed out to smack his face. He caught her hand gently and easily. He set it calmly aside. She wasn't sure what was more frightening – that she'd resorted to violence or that she had no strength against him. None.

'There's a space down in the ark,' he said, as if she'd done nothing untoward. 'It's safe – we've tested it – and Judj has solved the slippage problem. I'm going to convince Mark to keep the thing aboard. That way you'll have somewhere to go and something genuinely important to do. We could use a pair of intelligent eyes down there that don't need a comms-link all the time. It's amazing in there, Ann. You could be doing real science and helping all of us.'

She stared at him, outraged by his compassion. Her breath came in heaves. Her universe was slipping.

'Why did you even bother?' she told him. 'Mark and Palla won't agree to that. They'll want the ark dumped.'

'I'll make them agree,' said Ira. 'They can't expect you to sit cooped up in here alone for the rest of the voyage when there's a miracle in the hold you could be exploring. I'm going to use every lever I have. You deserve this.'

She could stand it no longer. 'Why do you have to be so goddamned *kind?*' she yelled.

Didn't he get it? He was stopping her from standing on her own. He was making her weak, and that prospect terrified her. She'd have to depend on others then. She'd have to depend on *him* and she was far too close to doing that already. He'd wormed his therapist's fingers into her imagination. Those awful, gentle eyes of his plagued her dreams.

'Because you're worth it,' he replied, his voice cracking. 'You're strong and rational. And stupid. And vulnerable. And beautiful. You make dumb mistakes and brilliant inferences and burn brighter than the rest of us put together. Because you're intelligent and fearless and unflinchingly ethical and *good*, and everything else I tried to be before I washed out of the human race.'

'Stop!' she implored him. 'Don't!'

He was talking about someone else. That wasn't her. She was the ugly robot everyone hated. She noticed with shame that tears were pouring down her face. She tried to punch him again. She could think of nothing else to do. He stopped her.

'Ann,' he said. 'Get a grip on yourself. This isn't you.'

She flailed at him with eyes wide, trying to hit him. She couldn't. With nothing but his mundane Fleet augs, he caught her hand every time. A white heat built behind her eyes. He couldn't be allowed to stand there and say shit like that. All the stuff inside her that enabled her to keep going would drain out and leave her broken and wanting. And it was just so that he could feel okay with himself for laying on all this attention. Like a blanket smothering her – making it impossible for her to ignore his stupid presence. And impossible for her to keep hating him.

'Stop fighting!' he urged. 'Ann, you don't have to be alone.'

She crumpled to her knees against him, her fists shaking. Before she understood what was happening, he seized her and kissed her. Ann's mind exploded into sparks. Her body went rigid. He pulled back.

'I'm sorry,' he said, looking away. 'I shouldn't...'

But by then it was too late. The dam inside her had already given way. Forty years without a moment's intimacy or vulnerability caught up with her in a single heartbeat. She grabbed his face, kissed him back and couldn't stop, even while she could feel herself drowning inside.

14.3: MARK

For two days after Judj activated the frameshift stabilisers, Clath's team carried out tests in the mining bay while Mark flew. The engines didn't fail once. When they were confident of the results, Clath and the others met him in helm-space to talk.

'The good news is that it's working,' said Clath.

Mark sagged with relief. Now, perhaps, he'd get some proper sleep. Since passing the lobe he'd been relying on Palla more and more. She didn't seem to mind but it felt dishonest depending on her. 'Thank God,' he groaned. 'That's one more nightmare over.'

'The bad news is that Rachel's assessed how much work it would take to cut the ark out and it's not pretty. It's already partly through the bulkhead wall. Now that the ark isn't a problem, it'd be easier to leave it where it is.'

Mark felt an unexpected surge of loathing towards the alien ship. He'd been waiting days to get rid of it. Who could tell what the awful thing would do next?

'Fuck that,' he said. 'It's going. We're done.'

'Hang on a minute,' said Clath, raising a hand. 'There are advantages to keeping it. Ann is trapped in the cabin, remember. It'd be trivial to substitute a human-compatible air mix and let her explore down there – helpful, even. There's a lot to learn.'

'Who cares?' said Mark. 'It's a risk to the mission.'

'Actually,' said Judj, 'while I hate to admit it, Clath has a point. There are database stores in that ship that we're only now beginning to understand. We came here to make a difference in the war. This ship could help us do that and the security risks are negligible.'

Mark peered at him. The more time Judj spent with Clath, the more fungible the security expert's standards appeared to get – at least concerning what *she* wanted.

'Are you nuts?' he said. 'These stabilisers – do you even know what they run on, or how long their fuel lasts?'

Clath looked uncomfortable at that. 'That's unclear,' he said. 'So far as we can tell, it's some kind of passive system that pulls energy from its environment.'

'What are you saying?' said Mark. 'That it's magic? That it beats thermodynamics? Because that sounds like bullshit to me. That thing is deadly dangerous and I want it *off* this ship.'

'Mark,' said Ira, 'I have to agree with Clath. It makes more sense to keep the ark at this point. It may prove beneficial. It was designed as a refuge, and if our mission hits a blockade of the sort Ann predicted, it might make the difference between success or failure.'

'No!' said Mark.

Why couldn't they get it? Didn't they see how much trouble the damned thing had already caused? He caught Palla staring at him oddly.

'Let's think about this,' Ira insisted. 'How much is this about the ark, and how much is it about your feelings towards it?'

Mark blinked. 'What are you fucking talking about? Don't you dare make this into a therapy session!' He turned to Rachel. 'Rach, you were doing the cutting but you haven't said a word. What do *you* think?'

She regarded him wearily, her arms folded. 'I don't like that ship, either,' she said, 'but I also don't think you're being rational. In fact, I'm not sure anyone here is.'

'Mark, can you articulate for us why you don't want to keep the ark?' Ira insisted.

'I just told you!' Mark said, his voice rising.

Palla stepped in with raised hands. 'Enough. Okay, Mark, we've heard you, and you're still mission lead. On the other hand, if I'm not mistaken, we're short on fuel and it'd be a lot easier to get the ark out once we stop, right?'

'That's true,' said Clath. 'Much easier.'

'So how about this,' Palla went on. 'The ark stays where it is for now. In the meantime, we use ember-warp to put more distance between us and the Photes. When we find somewhere decent to fuel, we cut the ark out then, presuming that Mark hasn't changed his mind. That leaves us a little time for research.'

'But it doesn't help Ann,' Ira pointed out. 'We can't move her until we drop warp.'

'No, but it does give us time to think about this rationally,' said Palla. 'As your great and good SAO, I'm calling this one. Can you handle that, Mark?'

He folded his arms and stared at the stars.

'I hate it, but I'll live,' he said. 'Two days. That's all.'

Palla waited until the others had winked out before speaking again. 'Are you sure about this?' she asked when they were alone.

'Never been more sure in my life,' he growled. 'That thing is a curse.'

Two days passed. Their lead on the Photurians grew while their fuel dwindled. In that time, Mark slept only once, briefly. That night came with a single, incredibly vivid dream. In it, Mark found the answer to ending the war. The Photes were finished. He could go back to Zoe at last. Tears of relief spilled down his cheeks. But when he looked around and saw where he was, it wasn't Snakepit but the dead ocean on Carter – a world he'd visited years ago.

Carter had been a dump back then, populated mostly by anti-Earth bigots with an economy based on mining alien remains left by the extinct Fecund. During the First Surge, it had been one of the first worlds claimed by the Photes. It was the last place Mark would have expected to find the solution to all their problems. And it was also just a few light-years from Snakepit – almost on their way. That vision of hope was astonishingly bright and clung to him when he woke.

That morning, they stopped to use their suntap at a system of Judj's choosing – a small K-type. Once again, they found a dead ex-Photurian world. What struck Mark as he flew them in close enough to sip energetic nectar from the star was the sheer scale of the enemy's empire on this side of space. The Photes must have controlled dozens of star systems. And then, after they'd won, they'd all died, for reasons still unknown.

'The scale of decay here is the most advanced we've seen yet,' said Judj as he joined Mark in helm-space for the approach. 'That might be down to the fact that this world is nearly two Earth masses, or it might not. In any case, it's deteriorating into an ordinary biosphere. Give it a few million years and it'll be impossible to tell that the tunnel system was even here. All that matrix material must have been repurposed by the local wildlife. Once the tunnels start to rot, I'm guessing they become a massive, low-grade food source.'

He posted pictures into the space around them. The surface was a curious mix of tunnel remnants and rugged, algae-swamped coastlines.

'This fits with what we now know about Phote mutation,' he added. 'Once there's a breakdown of their genetic integrity, their hold on a world must unravel rapidly, and differently each time, like biological symmetry breaking. It's kind of amazing.'

Mark folded his arms. He suspected that all this talk of biospheres was merely an attempt to soften him up before the real negotiation began.

'I'll tell you something else that's amazing—' Clath started.

'Jesus,' said Mark. 'Cheap segue, Clath. Answer's still no.'

She exhaled in frustration. 'Look, Mark, what are you expecting to do if the mission to Snakepit doesn't go as planned? We both know that could still happen.'

'I have no idea!' he exclaimed. 'We'll fly carefully, okay? If Snakepit turns out to be some kind of godawful death trap, then...'

He trailed off. It *would* be a death trap. He felt certain. In fact, he felt exactly the same kind of dread about it that he felt about the ark. It'd make a lot more sense to go somewhere less risky to check out the enemy's strength first. Somewhere like Carter, for instance.

He froze, staring at the glass plate beneath his virtual feet as an ugly realisation crawled into his thoughts. His dread of Snakepit hadn't been there five minutes ago. It didn't belong to him. And by extrapolation, his feelings about the ark probably didn't originate in his mind, either – or not all of them, at least.

'Mark,' said Palla. 'Are you okay?'

Mark felt a freight train of fury heading through him, gathering ominous steam.

'Let's keep the ark,' he said in a low, bitter growl. 'In fact, let's *prioritise* that research.'

The others now stared at him in open confusion. Rachel stood at the back, looking more convinced than ever that he'd lost his mind.

'The Transcended are shaping my thoughts,' he said slowly. 'They don't want us to keep the ark. So we're fucking keeping it.'

The others swapped glances.

'I don't get it,' said Clath. 'Why wouldn't they? They led us to that place. This is just like Will picking up the *Ariel Two*, surely?'

'Maybe not,' said Ira. 'Maybe we were supposed to look this time but not touch. Or find something else. That ark didn't want to leave, remember? It was seriously attached to its location. And it hasn't exactly helped us since.'

'No,' said Clath, her brow furrowed. 'But they gave us the SAP for the Subtle ark. They told us how to get in.'

'Maybe they thought they were telling us how to get rid of it,' Judj offered. 'They didn't have a lot of options. We wanted to pilot it out. They showed us how.'

Clath looked desperate. Now she couldn't believe in a benign Transcended agenda *and* keep the ark. Mark felt darkly amused. He'd burst her optimism-bubble by green-lighting her pet project.

'But...' said Clath. 'Wait, why cripple Ann? They must have known—'

'Ann was interfering with their download to Mark,' said Ira. 'They might have shut her down to stop her.'

'Shit,' said Judj. 'So if we keep the ark, we're dissing our hosts.'

'They're not hosts,' Mark snarled. 'They're parasites. If they want to come clean with me about their agenda, I'll consider supporting it. Until that happens, they're not calling the shots. And we're *definitely* not going to Carter.'

The others looked at him in confusion.

'Carter?' said Palla.

'Doesn't matter,' Mark growled. 'Not going to happen.'

Ira exhaled. 'I agree with Mark,' he said. 'I don't trust them any more.'

'I never trusted them,' said Judj. 'But do I need to remind you all that we're talking about a civilisation that detonates stars on a *whim*? Are you seriously considering crossing them?'

'I'm not crossing them,' Mark snapped back. 'I'm inviting them to stop acting like cowards.'

Nobody in helm-space enjoyed the uncomfortable silence that followed.

Clath rubbed her scalp. 'Yay, I guess,' she said morosely.

After the others had retreated to their research space, Palla watched Mark staring at the floor as a wave of uncertainty broke inside him. Was he insane to go against the same entities that had just let him use their gate? But if they meant well, why couldn't they just explain themselves?

'I don't know,' he told her. 'Is this the right thing to do? Am I being stupid?'

'Do you want to head for Carter instead?' she asked.

404

'Hell no! I feel like telling them to go fuck themselves.'

'So fine, that's what we'll do. I know how it feels, Mark,' she added gently. 'I felt that way about the Academy.'

Mark caught her gaze, surprised by the remark.

'Resist,' she said. 'Don't let the bastards push you about. If their intentions are good, they'll talk.'

'What do you mean?' he said.

'I mean resistance is worth it,' she said, looking amused. 'The opposite of futile. If we don't press the Transcended for answers while we can, our species is dead anyway.'

'No. About the Academy. I thought you were tight with them. Wasn't that the whole point?'

'Oh, that!' she said with a wry smile. 'Did you ever ask, Mark? No, I spent a lot of time advocating for missions behind enemy lines to Phote stars. Spy-runs, basically. They blocked me every time. An insufficient risk-to-reward ratio, apparently. Then they shoved me on this boat. What's that face for, Mark? Am I ruining your vision of the New Society as a lockstep utopia?'

'I had no idea,' he said. 'Why keep fighting? I thought that was something your kind of people didn't do?'

She rolled her eyes at him. '*My kind of people?* If I was their kind of people, do you think they'd have sent me out here?'

Mark shook his head. 'But you're an Autograd.'

'Yeah,' said Palla with a snort. 'After a fashion. The New Society isn't as orderly as you seem to think, Mark. Maybe it looks that way from the comfy bridge of the *Gulliver*, but I assure you that the reality is just as bitchy and difficult as ever.' She shot him an amused glance. 'Can't you guess whose career I modelled mine after?'

Mark didn't speak.

'Yours,' she said, a little sadness creeping into her smile. 'You were my hero.' She shook her head, amused at herself. 'The great Mark Ruiz, maverick captain extraordinaire.' Her voice dripped self-scorn.

'I...' said Mark, blushing.

'What?' she said. 'Even Autograds are allowed to have heroes, you know. It's not banned.'

'I'm so sorry,' Mark finished. 'That you chose me, I mean. I'm not...'

She laughed at him. 'It's not that bad. You have your moments. You might be a cantankerous asshat, but flying with you is...' Words

405

suddenly failed her. 'Is special. Let's leave it at that.' She looked him up and down, her amusement blending into concern. 'Look, you're clearly knackered. Why don't you take a little downtime? You don't need to watch those engines any more. And you deserve it.'

She was exhausted, too, he knew. He stared at her, feeling grateful and supremely awkward.

'Thank you,' he said, looking away. 'You've been very kind to me.'

'Don't sweat it,' said Palla, slapping his shoulder. 'It's nothing.' Her brightness sounded hollow. 'We're in this together.'

What he wanted to tell her then was that he was still married. But maybe, despite the way the air around her seemed to crackle, she was just trying to be his friend. If he opened his mouth, he risked ruining the moment, as usual. So Mark ducked out to sleep and prayed that his next dream would be his own. Going head to head with a billion-year-old galactic civilisation inside his own skull wasn't likely to be pleasant. He'd need all the rest he could get.

14.4: NADA

The messages from their pursuit ships grew less frequent as the distance stretched. The humans had made it safely down onto the lower galactic shell, she learned, and increased their speed. She struggled with the ghastly feeling that they were getting away, even though their destination was no longer in doubt. Meanwhile, thankfully, their research was delivering marvels.

On the fourth day of their repairs, Engineering Officer Kitu, one of Leng's subnodes, called for assistance at their main excavation site. Nada took her avatar-bead to the cavern for Kitu's mind and looked out through the eyes of the robot her engineer was piloting. Leng and Nanimo escorted her.

The robot hung in the dark interstitial space they'd burrowed deep in the flank of one of the alien moonlets. All around them, hundreds more drones toiled in a jagged cavern a quarter-kilometre across, dismantling components where the curious bubbles did not obstruct them and cataloguing them otherwise. Their gliding searchlights pushed little pools of illumination around between the immense, warted knuckles of ancient machine parts. The site of such persistent, diligent activity brought a surge of hopeful joy to Nada's heart.

It had not been easy to get inside one of the artefacts. Their indestructible shells prevented most kinds of access. But in one case, the enclosing bubble had simply vanished, scorching the surface machinery but otherwise leaving the device intact. They had been mining it ever since.

Kitu's robot pointed at a spherical object twenty metres wide where the protective bubble left room for a single, thick umbilicus of what appeared to be ordinary fibre-optic cable. It sat lodged in a dense cliff of piping and struts that they were chewing back component by component.

[Explain,] said Nada.

[I believe we have discovered a repair database,] said Kitu. [This device is wired into the robot management assemblies we identified, leaving little room for confusion. Using it might accelerate the process of reverse-engineering the new boser weapon. However, it may also contain other, unwanted innovations, such as the technology for creating false-matter bubbles.]

Nada grasped the implications immediately and squirmed at the fresh injection of tension they brought. Without their time constraints, the correct choice would have been obvious: to ignore the device unless absolutely necessary. However, they desperately needed to complete their upgrades quickly if they wanted to catch the humans before it was too late.

[How is research progressing on the boser assembly?] she said.

[It goes well,] said Kitu. [If there are no further obstructions, a functional tear-down of the mechanism should be complete within forty hours.]

Another two days wasted when the answer she craved might be right in front of them. She felt that familiar dissonance pulsing behind her eyes.

[I advise against using the database,] said Leng. [It is not necessary. We were not attacked by the false-matter shells so we do not need to absorb their template. Furthermore, the effort involved in decrypting the database may take longer than analysing the boser itself. Our research should remain focused.]

Nada knew he was right, but this decision defined another painful edge to Photurian philosophy. Why was it so morally repugnant to secure a strong technical advantage before it was needed? Was it always right to wait until after the humans made discoveries before adapting to compensate? If the survival of a homeworld hung in the balance, did that not justify preventative measures?

Leng appeared to notice her hesitation. Or perhaps her dissonance had simply leaked as far as his temple-cavern already.

[Exploring the database would be wrong,] he insisted. [Our aim is to save humanity, not obliterate it.]

[I concur,] said Nanimo. [The clean and joyous path is clear. This device is alien and therefore irrelevant to our holy mission.]

[Accepted,] said Nada uncomfortably.

At the same time she saw the need for radical action – to inhabit the knife-edge between goodness and innovation, just as the Yunus had urged her to. Only that kind of thinking would get them out of their existential mess.

[However, the core will be removed and retained,] she added. [We will transport it without examining it. This will accelerate our path to adaptation if the humans acquire the alien technology.]

The others paused uncomfortably as they absorbed this diktat.

[An unorthodox command,] said Nanimo, [but one I adhere to with blind delight.]

Leng's avatar-bead hesitated longer. [I love you,] he said at last. [You will lead us into glory. The database will never be relevant.]

Nada hoped he was right. The time they had left before Mark Ruiz burned their homeworld was shrinking, and her doubts about humanity's future were not going away.

14.5: ANN

On the same day that they stopped to fuel, Ann relocated to the ark. A docking pod took her halfway up to the exohull before a team of heavy-duty waldobots uncoupled it from its track and rerouted it to the mining bay. She watched their progress on the pod's vid-screen, full of anxious anticipation. She was getting out at last.

At first, Ira's plan to relocate her had felt like another patronising act of charity. But then had come that unexpected moment of intimacy. In the wake of it, Ann felt keener to leave the cabin than ever. Moving was the only logical choice now. Inside the ark, Ira would be unable to visit while they remained in warp, giving her room to sort out her feelings.

She'd spent almost a week trapped in that tiny cabin. It was funny how that time had shrunk to insignificance compared to how the experience had ended. In retrospect, Ann felt that she'd let her hunger for human contact get the better of her. She'd been blindsided by not acknowledging to herself that the hunger was there. With her smart-cells operating, she'd always been able to suppress human urges she considered distracting or irrelevant. Without them, she was once again at the mercy of her own id.

She shivered when she thought back to that spasm of connection. At first, she felt sure, she'd kissed Ira to prevent him from saying anything else awful. After that, she'd done it because she was enjoying it and saw no need to bow to expectations by stopping. And then, as their lovemaking reached a frenzy, she had felt the shell of her old self fall away and something bright emerge.

One truth about Ira could no longer be ignored: he *understood* her. That unwelcome fact had become increasingly obvious over their weeks in flight. He knew what she'd been through like nobody else alive and he actually cared. His passivity was scar tissue, just like her own brittleness. And, as it turned out, through human contact they could scrub those scars away. That prospect excited her intensely as the man she'd once found such compelling company was clearly still in there somewhere. She'd felt a flash of raw happiness in their union – a commodity she'd long considered utterly beyond reach.

And yet, she still found his generosity damning. His gentleness implied weakness on her part. She dreaded the dependency and softness his company implied, so it was safer and wiser to leave. That way she could reflect and discover who she'd become. Fortunately, fate had granted her that opportunity, along with a fresh chance to redefine her contribution to the mission. She couldn't wait to start doing something useful again.

She wished, suddenly, that she hadn't changed her face. She missed the blunt planes of her old features. She didn't want to look like a goddess any more. She wasn't one. And besides, being a little closer to Ira's height would increase the fun, presuming they chose to meet again. It was the first time she'd cared in years.

'I'm handing you off to Judj,' said Rachel over the comms. She'd been handling the docking-pod transfer while the others tended the more mission-critical elements of the refuelling. 'See you later.'

Judj would be her closest working partner over the days that followed. He was the one who'd cracked the ark computers. It wasn't an arrangement she relished but it came with the job.

Her pod coupled to the airlock blister they'd readied for her transfer. A small waldobot showing a screen of Judj's face met her in a chamber on the far side.

'Welcome to the GSS *Woodlouse*,' he told her. 'You'll need this.' He gestured at a thermal layer floating in a cling-pack on the wall. 'We have life support powered up but we can't ramp the interior temperature too much without melting the lake. There's a way to drain it, but it's one of the few systems showing signs of age. We're still figuring out a workaround. That means it's cold in there.'

Ann stripped and swapped her ship-suit for the layer while Judj talked.

'I have a little more understanding of what the machine does now,' he said, 'and that's what we're hoping you'll be able to work on. The whole thing's a shell – appropriate for a bunch of crabs, perhaps. Clath thinks that when you turn the machine on, the ship warps in place, essentially becoming invulnerable. What we don't yet get is how or why the Transcended don't want us to have that technology. Your skills in modelling and software security will come in handy there. We've rigged up a workspace for you on the bridge.'

Without her shadow and other tools, she doubted she'd be able to help much. But she'd been a scientist and a detective once, before she'd become a warrior.

'I'll do what I can,' she said.

'That's all any of us can do,' Judj assured her. 'Here's a visor and a pair of thermal hap-gloves for you to work with,' he said, pointing her at a second pack. 'The interface module linking you to the ship's systems goes on your belt.'

Ann donned the equipment as instructed.

'I've put a sleeping bag down there,' he went on. 'Also a food-fabber, san-box and a little bottle of simpagne I synthesised, in case you feel like toasting your new home. *I* would after a week stuck in that cabin.'

Ann felt a stab of embarrassment. 'You didn't have to go to that kind of trouble,' she told him.

'I wanted to,' he said. 'Also, you can consider it something of an apology. We haven't exactly seen eye to eye on this trip and some of that is my fault. I struggled because you're not the only person who came on this mission to make a sacrifice. But then I failed to cover your ass when it counted. I want you to know I'm sorry about that. I owe you one. I'll make your stay here as pleasant as I can.'

Ann stared at the drone and wondered what she was supposed to do with yet more kindness.

'No apology is necessary,' she said stiffly. 'Really.'

'Well, in any case,' said Judj. 'Welcome home.'

He opened the door to let her in. A breath of icy air escaped from the tunnel below carrying a faint, unexpected scent of something like artificial raspberry. Pinkish light like a winter dawn spilled through. Here was the ship the Transcended didn't want them to have. It beckoned to her, promising the twin delights of work and danger. Ann felt her face breaking into a grin and launched herself forwards.

She soared through the opening, past the chamber with the knife-slots in the walls and down into the boulevard-like passageway they'd seen. Through her own eyes, it looked even grander. As she glided gently towards the floor, a panel in the plating opened up and a large mechanical limb extended.

Ann frowned. 'Judj, are you doing that?' she asked. 'Is this more help?'

'Um, no,' he said, sounding confused. 'Hold on.'

'Crew life of sign detected!' the interface device on her belt proclaimed. 'Welcome at Pure Pure Slow Safe Ship.'

Before her glide could intercept the floor, the limb reached out to gently close around her torso.

'Judj?' said Ann, feeling concerned now as the arm gripped her. 'What is this?'

'Please to relinquish host you now,' said her interface module. 'New host safe ship-ready supply for kindness.'

A second arm emerged from the hole, carrying a gleaming white robotic gorilloid body with an empty skull cavity.

'It's running on a different layer,' said Judj. 'I haven't scanned this subsystem yet. Shit. Compensating.'

The back of the robot's head was pressed softly against her face, presumably so her brain could crawl into it.

'Desist!' she told the interface. 'A new host body is not required!'

'Host body safe ensure. Assistance detachment need? Help providing.'

The arm holding her sprouted a dozen delicate pincers and cutters, bearing warpium needles on their tips. They started tickling her scalp.

'Judj!' she yelled.

The needles retracted. The arm let her go.

'I have the welcome circuit shut down,' he said anxiously. 'I think.'

Ann wheezed in relief, her eyes still glued to the arsenal of surgical tools arrayed around her.

'Can I recommend extreme caution while you explore?' said Judj, clearing his throat. 'As it turns out, the ship may have independent systems cued to detect living tissue.'

'No shit,' said Ann.

She'd had enough *help* for one day. She sincerely hoped the ship would be better at backing off than Ira was.

14.6: MARK

Mark found himself standing in an old-fashioned transit pod with clear diamond walls. Around him lay a tunnel drilled through rock, sliding slowly by. He flexed his fingers, testing for latency. If this was a dream, it didn't feel like one.

The pod rounded a curve and slowed as it approached a fork in the rail. Two openings lay before him. Through one, he could make out the empty streets of New Luxor on Carter in sun-bleached shades of yellow and pink. The other led to a subterra complex on Galatea, complete with lush, green game fields, white pavilions and a pale blue ceiling.

'Fuck you, alien bastards,' Mark muttered. 'What kind of a bullshit metaphor is this?'

His pod lurched forwards, sliding onto the track that led to Galatea, with Carter disappearing from sight. It carried him out into the underground afternoon, passing lawns filled with laughing, ageless citizens, caught up in endless militarised play.

A flash filled the air, momentarily blinding him. When he could see again, the fields were black. Air was screaming out. It looked like a boser strike. Those people who weren't already charred corpses grabbed their throats and clawed the ground. Mark watched, sickened at the gory detail the Transcended had lavished on the illusion.

A flash came again, and suddenly Mark's pod was traversing the surface. Actinic flickers of warp-drives could be seen peppering the daytime sky. A bright, momentary lance of light pulsed downwards. A second later, a third of the horizon erupted in a wall of grey-brown haze that swelled towards him at appalling speed.

Another flash, and now a grit storm buffeted the pod. Everywhere around him fell the columnar lightning of energy-weapons fire. All he could hear was the scream of the storm. It was the cry of a dying world and a dying species – his.

He woke gasping and clutching at the virtual sheets.

'Nice job, fuckers!' he yelled at the air. 'Really classy.'

As his rage subsided, he noticed the new SAP puzzle that had landed in his head. It hovered in his private sensorium, brooding and massive like a swarm of hornets. He regarded it uneasily. This pattern was almost human in format, with a weird remapping of the motivational framework. Control of goal construction and self-validation had all been handed off to an artificial-looking cluster that appeared to take its cues from another system entirely – a different organ, perhaps. Mark didn't doubt for a moment that he was looking at a model of a Photurian mind.

'Your olive branch is an unsecured program inside my own skull that makes me think like a *Phote*?' he said. 'I'm not running it, assholes. You want to talk, you know where I am.'

Mark ignored the puzzle and made his way to breakfast, only to find the SAP dogging his mind, appearing in doorways and shadows like a phantom. It hid in the reflection on his butter knife, scowling at him despite its lack of eyes. Mark ate quickly and made his way to the bridge where Palla was flying. Their fuelling star lay far behind.

He explained the dreams and the ominous delivery that had followed. She listened silently, worry creasing her features.

'Do you think I should open it?' he said.

She shrugged anxiously. 'If they care this much, why don't they just take you over?'

'Maybe they can't,' he said. 'Or maybe they think I'll still cave.'

413

'Then hold your ground,' she said. 'Make them treat you like a person.'

He could tell she was nervous, despite her words. Burning worlds were not a threat to take lightly these days.

'Can I see it?' she said, biting her lip. 'The puzzle, I mean.'

Mark eyed her. 'Are you sure that's a good idea?'

'Are you doing what they want now? I'd just like to understand, that's all. Maybe share your burden a little.'

'I'm not sure I can even copy it from my sensorium.'

She arched an eyebrow at him. 'Have you tried?'

Mark reached into his mind and initiated a send. Her face brightened.

'I've got it!' she said, grabbing his arm. 'Wow, that's detailed! They want you to interface with *this* ugly bastard?'

'That's the general idea.'

'I don't blame you for holding off,' said Palla as she pored over the details in her shadow. 'I see no security checks, no timeouts, nothing.' She looked eager.

'I *don't* recommend trying to run it,' said Mark, and wondered if he'd made a mistake by sharing.

Her expression softened. 'Mark, I wouldn't dare. I want to be there for you, that's all. I can want that, can't I? Maybe help you fight your battles a bit? It doesn't need to be more than that.'

'Sure,' he said uncertainly and let it drop.

Throughout that day, the puzzle burned, chiming into his subconscious like an unanswered intercom. The image of it sizzled behind his eyes when he shut them. And as they bore down on the edge of the Depleted Zone, his concentration fractured. Headaches plagued him. It felt like someone was tightening a vice on his skull regardless of what meds the ship provided.

As Mark dropped warp and prepared the ship for its passage back through the Alpha Flaw, he began to wonder if he'd actually make it through alive. It hurt that bad. But the more pain it gave him, the less he felt like giving in.

'I've improved on the modelling code I used last time,' Clath told him. 'After what happened to Ann, I went back and optimised everything. And then I thought, why not use the data we collected from the *Diggory*? It spent way more time in the Flaw than we did. And even though the *Diggory* didn't have modern sensors, I could still look at what they *did* see and impute fine-scale curvon readings using our own data as a training set.' She noticed the anguished impatience on his face and stalled. 'Anyway, it should be easier going back,' she added. 'But it's still not going to be fun.'

Her words eased his mind not one whit. Something told him he wouldn't see the other side. As Palla ran out the lines of feeler-drones, Mark found himself thinking not of the task ahead, but of Rachel. He'd come after her, yet now that she was a feature of his life again he'd tried to avoid her because she made him uncomfortable. How ludicrous was that? Before they both lost themselves in the Zone again, he had to make it right.

'Do you guys mind if I take five minutes?' he croaked.

Palla shot him a worried look. 'Of course not.'

Mark nodded his thanks and guiltily blinked himself back to the yacht. He found his half-mother in the lounge studying engine diagrams from the ark. She looked up as he walked in, her eyes widening in surprise.

'Mark,' she said rising. 'What do you need?'

'To apologise,' he said, feeling awkward immediately. 'After this, I may not get another chance. I know I've been difficult to fly with and I know I'm not what you hoped I'd be. So, *sorry*. I've done my best.'

Her expression melted. 'Oh, Mark,' she said. 'You don't have to apologise for anything.' She stepped towards him.

He stood stiffly, struggling for poise. 'The last war messed us all up. This mission was supposed to be my chance to fix that but it hasn't panned out that way. But mostly, I want to say sorry for who I *was*. I was an ungrateful little shit while you were mentoring me. The older I get, the larger those years loom in my mind.'

'No,' she said, shaking her head. 'You were great. Working with you when you were young made me the happiest I've ever been. You were so *wild*. That's what's so hard about seeing you changed. For all that you've grown into someone strong, it's like you've got this millstone round your neck – this fucking crusade you can't put down. I love you, Mark. I always have. And I hate that war for forcing such a weight upon you.' Tears crept to the corners of her eyes. 'I hope we survive this shit so you have the chance to put it down and get some of yourself back.'

'No,' he said, shaking his head. 'It's not like that. The crusade, that's the good part of me.'

She shot him an incredulous look. Mark struggled for words. Couldn't she see how much better he was now that he was working for others instead of himself? His head pulsed with pain.

'I have a new puzzle from the Transcended,' he blurted, glancing away. 'Do you think I should solve it?'

Rachel looked sad that their moment of intimacy had apparently already passed.

'I'm not sure any more,' she replied. 'Not after what they did to Ann. If they want to help, why cripple her talents? I used to believe in the Transcended, but why subject humanity to this awful war if the galaxy is really theirs?'

She tried to catch Mark's eye while he squinted at the seagulls and struggled for equilibrium.

'What are you going to do?' she asked.

'Resist being a good little puppet for as long as I can. I'm not touching it until they come out and talk like adults.' He couldn't bring himself to tell her how much it hurt. She'd only worry.

'Good choice,' she said. 'I'm proud of you. Don't ever feel like you need to say sorry to me,' she added. 'I'm the one who should be apologising. We made such a mess of your childhood. I can't even begin to say how much I regret that.'

Mark's chest squeezed. 'Don't,' he said. 'Don't regret that. Please.'

'Okay,' she said gently. 'I'll try.'

'I have to go,' he said. 'The others are waiting.'

He let her hug him and fled back to helm-space.

Palla watched him nervously as he returned. 'Are you okay?'

Mark nodded quickly while his skull squeezed.

'Do you have the strength?'

He knew they couldn't fly the ship without him. Making it back through the Flaw without Ann's talents would be hard enough in the first place. Clath's new mapping software could only do so much. If he dropped out now, they'd be stuck until his headaches abated or the Photes caught up.

'Wouldn't miss it for the world,' he told them. 'Let's do this.'

He slid himself into flight-control. The rainbow river of the Flaw appeared before him against the backdrop of stars, overlaid with Clath's optimised vector representation.

'Initiating approach,' he told them and pushed the ship gingerly into the waiting gap. Almost at once, the puzzle in his mind took on the status of a visual scream. Mark gritted his teeth.

'Need help here,' he gasped. 'Getting a little ... neural ... interference.'

Palla leapt to his support and snapped open a flight sim for Ira.

'I'm here, Mark,' she said. 'Setting up a redundant piloting rig for error correction. We'll do this together.'

With all three of them flying, it felt easier. The first violent kink in the Flaw was punishing, the second not so bad, the third almost a breeze. Unfortunately, the stream of unmanageable vectors kept coming as Clath updated her map in real-time.

In the end, it required twenty excruciating hours. Nothing bad happened. In that regard, their traversal was a stunning success. With the data from two ships and new science to go with it, humanity had finally developed the tools to defeat the Depleted Zone.

Mark, however, wasn't in a state of mind to appreciate the achievement. When he pushed the ship to the other side of the Flaw, he caught a mere glimpse of open space before his exhausted mind started to give.

'Help,' he gasped.

By then, it felt like his head was on fire. Ira took the helm as Mark tumbled into Palla's arms, and from there to unconsciousness.

15: ARRIVAL

15.1: IRA

As soon as Mark's avatar vanished, the engines died. The glass disc of helm-space began to twist and buckle like a bed of snakes.

'What's happening?' Palla shouted as warnings filled the air.

'Transcended virus,' said Judj. 'It's back. Hang on.'

A sphere of security glyphs sprang up around him. They lurched into the yacht metaphor where the walls grew quivering fingers.

'Helm on lockdown,' said Judj. 'Cutting to emergency settings. Palla to med.'

Palla acquired her own floating work-bubble. Her eyes scanned it desperately.

'Holy shit,' she said as her fingers began to fly.

'What?' said Ira. 'What's happening?'

'It's Mark,' she explained. 'His vitals are going crazy. Looks like a Transcended-induced bio-assault. His micromachines are synthesising a pseudo-virus, just like they did for Will. He's upgrading.'

'His interface is screwing with the ship,' said Judj. 'We have to unplug him. We're in Phote space. A rebooting ship is *not* okay.'

'Fuck!' yelled Palla. 'Prepping transit to quarantine core.'

'Rachel's already in there,' Ira pointed out, 'and it only has space for one.'

'Then she'll have to come out,' said Palla. 'She's been in there too long anyway. Prepping *two* transits. Clath, I'll need your help with rad-shielding. The engines are still hot.'

'On it,' said Clath.

'Enacting partial cleanse,' said Judj. 'Prepare for power-down.'

418

The virt vanished. Ira was suddenly alone in the dark watching a single winking red light above his face. Forty-seven seconds later, the yacht sprang back, its decor much restored.

By the time he arrived, the others were hard at work and Rachel was gone. He experienced a moment's awe for the younger generation that had ousted him from power. The three of them worked furiously together, cooperating with fluid precision. He felt utterly redundant and fought back a laugh.

He had mixed feelings about Mark's strategy of resistance to the Transcended. They were in over their heads and the mystery that Backspace presented was no closer to being solved. But after their treatment of Ann, he'd reluctantly come to the conclusion that the human race had to look out for itself. If that made fighting their corner harder, so be it. He wished he was down in the ark with her. He'd ached for her company every second since she'd gone away.

'It's like the virus that hit Will,' said Palla. 'But this time it's bad.'

'Bad how?' said Ira. 'Will's virus was benign. Can't we just leave it room to build smart-cells?'

'I don't think this one is doing that. And it seems *really* confused by Mark's existing augmentations. His blood engines are misfiring. We need to shut it down before it kills him. Judj, copying you gene schematics.'

'Got them,' said Judj. 'Modelling workarounds.'

Ira wondered why the Transcended had picked this moment. Perhaps they'd simply grown tired of waiting. As lords of the galaxy, they probably weren't disobeyed that often.

'Mark-package is secure and ready to go,' said Palla. 'Sliding him your way.'

'Transit acknowledged,' said Judj. 'You'll have Rachel in eleven minutes.'

'Swapping to helm,' said Palla.

The yacht vanished. Ira was surprised to find himself back in the cabin of the *Ariel* with Palla. She fixed him with a meaningful look.

'The ship is yours,' she told him. 'We're in Phote space. That means threats. We're just a handful of light-years from Snakepit – two days at most – and we don't have any time to waste. If the Photes have been trailing us, this is when they'll strike. Then there's the small issue of a possible life-threatening blockade when we get there. Try not to run into that.'

'Understood,' said Ira.

'Please get us there in one piece,' she said and winked out.

Ira seized the helm controls and felt a seductive shiver of delight. The ship was his again. They'd made it through the Zone, down past the gate and back almost to where they'd started. All that just to travel a few otherwise-uncrossable light-years closer to the galactic core. Now all that stood between them and the Snakepit System was Ann's predicted nightmare scenario.

As Ira waited for his engines to come back online and his engineer to arrive out of transit, he felt utterly glad that he'd made the journey this far, no matter what happened next. With Ann in his life and something to fly, he was fully alive again, even if only briefly.

1 5 . 2 : MARK

The second time Mark faced the Transcended, they didn't bother with a slide show. He found himself dumped directly into the limitless white space he'd seen before. Zoe appeared before him. Her Edwardian gown had swapped to black and been augmented with a huge feathered hat.

'This is getting out of hand,' she told him, scowling.

'No shit,' said Mark. 'Want to talk about it?'

In the back of his mind, he knew it was pure folly to goad the Transcended. His entire species might be held accountable for anything he said. But what of it? Unless something changed, they were dead anyway.

'Your crew have absolutely no idea what you're playing with,' she told him. 'The fate of your species hangs by a thread.'

'You just noticed?' said Mark.

'Listen,' said Zoe. 'Trouble is coming. Your people won't be able to beat it now without swift action. The puzzle we've given you is a weapon. Solving it is understanding it.'

'Nice,' said Mark. 'And then I just give up on my original plan and deliver it to Carter for you, is that right?'

'Preferably, though we doubt you'll do that.'

'I might,' said Mark. 'All depends what answers I get.'

'You'll get none,' she said bluntly.

'Surprise surprise.'

'The second thing you need to know is that the virus in your body will help you. You need to expose Ann to it.'

Mark couldn't help laughing, even while he knew that he had absolutely everything to fear.

'After you take her powers, you want me to infect her with something?'

'It will help.'

'Sure. You're just going to make her all better again, I bet.'

'Ann interrupted our dialogue with your interface. Without our action, she would have killed you.'

'You guys are smart, right?' he said. 'You can read my mind. You have to know how ridiculous this sounds. The threats are clear and the manipulation is transparent, but your motives? They're as murky as ever. What on Earth makes you think I'll trust a single thing you say at this point?'

'We've overstepped the mark on your behalf,' she said. 'The information we're giving you now crosses the line.'

'What line?' said Mark. 'Whose line? What am I supposed to do, just have *faith* in you? Trust in your greatness and worship your ancient power? I'm not wired that way and you know it.'

'We don't want your faith.'

'So what *do* you want? Because it sure as shit looks that way from where I'm standing.'

'We want the opposite,' said Zoe. 'We want to see if you're capable of making good decisions without the benefit of free information.'

'Where "good" is something you've decided in advance, I take it.'

'Oh, yes,' said Zoe. 'A long, long time ago. After more years of study than your germ-line has breathed air. We've made an investment in the human race so we want it to live, but only if humanity is actually worth saving. Consequently we're giving your species the benefit of the doubt.'

'So long as we do what you want, we get to live.'

'No. So long as you save yourselves, you get to live. We're just prepared to nudge the system under extenuating circumstances.'

'I'd rather have a relationship between peers.'

She laughed at him, her eyes full of ageless disdain. 'But you're *not* our peers,' she said. 'That's the point.'

'That's the best you can offer?' he said. 'Noblesse oblige on a galactic scale, backed by an unspecified agenda?'

'Yes, exactly that.'

He snorted. 'Why ever did you pick me? You have to know I don't buy this kind of shit.'

She frowned. 'We didn't. We'd have preferred any of your crew-mates other than Ann. That was a mistake *you* made – to presume your own self-importance in affairs. That error may be fatal for the lot of you.'

Mark felt a sting of embarrassment. 'Bullshit. You've rigged this for me from the start. You laid the trail. You set up Rachel's ship.'

'We have no incentive to lie,' she told him flatly. 'The species at risk is yours.'

'Come clean, you bastards!' Mark urged. 'Give me a reason to bite!'

'This conversation is over,' said Zoe. 'Choose wisely.'

Everything disappeared like a vid channel closing.

1 5.3: ANN

Ann hung in a survival bag slung between workstations in the ark's control room, wrapped in thermal layers. Through her visor, she watched Ira pilot through Photurian space. Ira, it turned out, was a gifted flyer. He'd abandoned the *Ariel* sim already, integrated his pilot couch into helm-space and updated it with several modern systems. He was, however, no roboteer, and still couldn't handle an entire starship without a supporting crew. Which meant that he was going to need help for this next bit.

'According to my models, we should hit the first signs of the blockade somewhere within the next six light-hours,' she told him.

She'd been watching him fly over his shoulder for most of the last day, pausing only to check on the Subtle robots that kept waking up in the ark and creeping around.

'I recommend dropping warp and running out the feeler-drones. They double as blockade detectors. If we go any closer without using them, we run the risk of being trapped.'

'Dropping warp in five,' said Ira. 'Clath, Rachel, to stations, please. Judj, could we borrow you from internal defence? This next bit's going to be tricky.'

Ann jealously watched them work and rubbed her hap-gloves to keep her fingers warm. She was supposed to be investigating the ark and determining its viability as a refuge for the rest of the crew. As it was, she'd barely started finding her way around. The ark's interior was enormous compared to a human ship and full of surprises. But if the Photes hit them now in the numbers she'd projected, none of them was going home, in an ark or otherwise. That meant she had to help.

Lines of drones sped away from the *Dantes*. Ann waited until she was confident they had an adequate lead and that feedback signalling had been established.

'Okay, Ira,' she said. 'I recommend proceeding carefully at twenty lights with stealth active. I also suggest deep sensor-sweeps in high wavelengths between every warp-burst.'

'You've been a very attentive backseat driver of late,' Ira observed with dry amusement. 'While I appreciate your concern, I'm surprised we've reached that point in our relationship already.'

Ann writhed inside. She still had no idea what to do with Ira's closeness. As the days passed, it only made her more uncomfortable.

'You did the same to me before we reached the Flaw,' she said, struggling for levity. 'I'm just returning the favour.'

Unfortunately, the situation wasn't light. According to her calculations, this was when they died. And that was something Ann was no longer sure she wanted.

The ship slid carefully forwards. The return pings from the drones filled Ann's ears. A map of the apparently clear space ahead filled her visor. She barely dared to breathe. Minutes ticked past.

'All clear so far,' said Clath when they were an hour in.

Ann could practically hear the physicist thinking, *I told you so,* and fought back anger. They weren't out of the woods yet. Backspace had been unpredictable, yes, but now they were in Phote space – her speciality. In all likelihood, they were only alive because they'd somehow underestimated their enemy's cunning.

Yet as they crept closer to Snakepit, no threats erupted out of the dark. Clath fell silent while Ann felt mounting sensations of embarrassment and dread. The closer they got, the clearer it became that the level of Phote traffic was below even their most optimistic speculations.

Ann squeezed her hands for warmth and hated the looming uncertainty. It wasn't that she needed her models to be right. She was past that. It was just that if they were this far off, something glaring was missing from their understanding of the situation – and glaring usually meant dangerous.

'I don't like this,' said Judj.

'We'd guessed,' said Clath. 'Staying alive is nice, at least.'

'Sure, if you know why it's happening,' he retorted. 'This is eerie. I'd feel better if there was a disrupter field or two for us to avoid. Finding nothing smacks of trouble.'

'Agreed,' said Ann. 'Can we do another deep sweep for warp-light and use the gravity-wave detectors?'

'Already on it,' said Judj. 'I'm seeing nothing. This place is as silent as the grave.'

The reality settled over her like cold fog: there was no blockade – not a single ship. She was wrong. Again.

'Their strategy must have changed,' said Ira gently.

Ann clenched her jaw. She didn't need the truth cushioned.

'Of course it's changed,' she snapped. 'But Photes don't innovate except under intense environmental pressure. So what's the pressure? What are we missing? Why aren't we *dead*?'

They closed on Snakepit's heliopause without detecting a single sign of the Photurian civilisation at work. Instead of relief, Ann felt over-wound like clockwork on the brink of breaking. A quick look at the timer in her visor told her that she'd now been watching on tenterhooks and sucking stimmo out of a bag for about nineteen hours straight.

She rubbed her eyes and glanced around at her improvised cabin. In a moment of self-reproach, she saw just how lacking it was as a viable refuge. The place was a tip. She'd already turned it into a kind of zero-gee nest, full of floating drink-bulbs and poorly tethered packs. Good at cleaning the universe of Photes she might have been, but as a builder of shelters for her fellow crew-mates, she apparently sucked.

The tension in her broke unexpectedly. Behind it lay a very human exhaustion, and with it, apathy. What was she good for now? Certainly not research or strategic planning.

'I need downtime,' she told the others, and felt ashamed.

Nobody stopped her when she signed off. Because, of course, they didn't need her at all. With anxious, bewildered hands, Ann started clearing up the mess she'd made. What else was there to do?

Will woke aboard a ship. By the size and shallow, domed profile of the cabin, it looked like the upper level of a nestship's spherical core – the *Ariel Two*, perhaps, or some other vessel of equivalent size. Everything had been decorated in soothing, pleasant whites and greens, like the Galatean ships of his youth. He was lying in a bioengineered crash couch of a design he'd never seen before.

He glanced around. Had he actually made it out to a starship, despite the odds? He'd been escaping, he recalled, from someone called Balance – a monster who wore a weird plaster mask of his own face – but the details were upsettingly fuzzy. Perhaps the transfer of his thread-copy to the ship hadn't finished before being choked off, leaving gaps in his memory. Will screwed up his concentration and tried to recall exactly what had happened. At that moment, though, Ira and Ann walked in.

'You're up!' said Ira.

Will stared at them both. He hadn't expected to see them here. They both appeared to be in the best of health, and younger than when he'd met them last. Except he'd seen Ira recently, hadn't he? Maybe Ann, too.

'We didn't expect you to recover so quickly,' said Ann. She checked a medical band on his arm. 'It was touch and go. Whatever Snakepit did to you, we were worried it was going to be permanent.'

That was right, he'd been down on Snakepit, trying to get out. He'd watched himself die, but from a distance. And then he'd been alive again, kissing someone and watching himself drink martinis while wearing a hat. Suddenly, it all made remarkably little sense. His recollection of the past started unravelling in his mind like a dream. Which was, of course, exactly what it had been – a software-imposed vision inflicted by an alien world trying to climb inside his head. The longer he thought about it, the more obvious that was.

'It's great that you're back but the planet's virus is still in your system,' Ira assured him. 'We think it's gone dormant, waiting for another chance. The only way we can fix that is with interface surgery, otherwise it could recur at any time.'

Will remembered something about merging with Snakepit, but getting out of there was a blank.

'You rescued me,' he said stupidly. 'You came back.'

'He's quick for a superbeing, don't you think?' Ann drawled. 'You'll have to drop all your wetware blocks,' she told him. 'Completely power down your internal security. Just say *yes* when the cues appear. As soon as you do that, we can start. But this needs to happen now. It's life or death again, I'm afraid. Your smart-cells aren't operating normally any more.'

Will scowled, suddenly wary of the urgency of the situation. For reasons too vague to be rational, he didn't trust it.

'Don't worry,' said Ira. 'He's been up shit creek before. He knows how situations like this play out. It's better than using a shock key, right, Will?'

The gnawing sense that something had gone badly wrong built steadily in Will's mind. How long had he been down on the planet? How in Gal's name had they got him out?

'Wait,' he said. 'I'm still struggling with this. Can someone fill me in on exactly what happened?'

Mark chose that moment to walk in carrying a huge pink cake. Will blinked at it in astonishment. A cake aboard a starship?

'Is this the wrong time?' said Mark. 'I heard Will was up. I hope you guys don't mind.' He glanced down at the enormous confection he was carrying. 'Yeah. I know what you're thinking: this is ridiculous. But we had to do something to celebrate the moment, didn't we? I mean, it's not every day you get your dad back. So I set the fabber running overnight.'

Ann looked annoyed. 'This should wait until after the last surgical pass,' she said.

Mark rolled his eyes. 'Okay, whatever.' He glanced at Will. 'Nice to have you back. You don't mind holding off on the party, I take it?'

'Will shouldn't eat yet,' said Ira.

Will belatedly discovered just how incredibly hungry he was. He couldn't have eaten in days. His mouth filled with saliva.

'The med-bay will have a lot more work to do if he stuffs his face,' Ann warned. 'We need to shut down his security first.'

'And then cake?' said Mark.

Will's stomach growled. He was about to acquiesce to removing

426

his security blocks simply to get them all to shut up when reality abruptly stalled. Everyone's faces froze. The dome rippled overhead. Then, slowly, the cake turned black and grew several mismatched hands, each grasping outwards as if from quicksand. Will found himself standing in a room full of smiling mannequins. Everything went deafeningly quiet.

Will's skin chilled as panic overtook him. He reached out and touched Ann's face. His hand slid through her cheek as if it was warm slurry. When he drew his finger out, her tissues slurped back into shape.

'What's going on?' he shouted at the walls.

He walked to the hatch but found it no more real than Ann's face had been. His couch was solid, as was the floor, but little else. He didn't even want to try touching the black cake. Will clutched his head as flashes of his existence on Snakepit started unpleasantly reasserting themselves. He hadn't been rescued. Nor had he made it to the starship. Instead, he'd found his way into the clutches of Balance. And what the god had in mind for him was entirely unclear.

15.5: IRA

At Snakepit's heliopause, Ira dropped warp and called for the others to join him in helm-space. Palla appeared, looking gaunt. She'd taken responsibility for Mark's care while his body remained in a feverish coma. That care was taking its toll.

Ira dearly wished he could tell the poor girl to give it up. Not the care itself, but her reasons. Mark was never going to forget his marriage for her, not even at the brink of death. She could no more prove her value to him than he could heal himself. However, to acknowledge that would be to give voice to the unspeakable obvious and offer more harm than cure.

Ann reopened her link from the ark without providing video. Ira struggled with fresh concern for her.

'This is it,' Ira informed them. 'We've arrived.'

'It's creepy quiet,' said Palla. 'Are they all just running on stealth?'

'Only if they expected us,' said Clath. 'Which I kind of doubt.'

Palla shook her head. 'Then what's going on?'

'Only one way to find out,' said Ira. He turned to Rachel. 'He's your husband. You ready for this?'

Rachel nodded without speaking. For her, he suspected, the misery of her new life couldn't get much worse. Reaching Snakepit would at least bring closure.

'It sucks that Mark's not awake,' said Palla, 'but this is what we came here to do. Take us in, Captain Baron.'

The *Dantes* slid gingerly inwards, encountering not a whiff of enemy presence. The world ahead of them grew slowly. Remote cameras indicated a healthy Photurian biosphere with none of the decay markers they'd grown to expect. The atmosphere was a fraction richer than when they'd measured it last, but to all intents and purposes, the world was unchanged. The system was as silent and traffic-free as an abandoned city and just as inviting.

'I'm getting gravity wobbles,' said Judj. 'Somebody's out there but I can't see a damned thing.'

Then, about five AU from the star, they received synchronised tight-beamed messages from several directions at once. In none of those directions lay any sign of a visible ship. If anything, that suggested the presence of cloaked weapons, ready to fire.

The message came with a video feed. Will Monet appeared wearing an archaic military uniform, complete with shoulder braid and ludicrously oversized medals. A flag of orange stars against a field of curving black and white bands filled the space behind him.

'Photurian vessel,' said Will darkly, 'the might of the Willworld is tracking your ship. Depart immediately or face obliteration.'

'Ohmygodhesalive,' said Rachel. The words fell out of her in a single sob.

Ira stared at the vid, stunned. It was so long since he'd last set eyes on his old friend. He'd assumed Will was either dead or subsumed into the planet. The sight of him wearing that ridiculous uniform came as a blunt shock. If Will was alive with access to ships, why hadn't he come home? When they left Backspace, Ira had expected the surprises to be over, not for them to get worse.

'Drop warp,' said Palla quickly. 'Send him a greeting.'

'The *Willworld*?' said Judj.

Ira swallowed and sent a reply. Alarm bells kept ringing in his head.

'Will, this is Ira Baron-Lecke. It's good to see you, old friend. We've come to rescue you, if you still want it. Or at least to open communications. Ship verification codes follow on this signal.'

He passed the message back on every vector he'd received a pulse from, and sent another burst directly at the world itself.

'Get ready to retreat,' said Palla, 'just in case. Judj, check for targeting coverage.'

The second time Will appeared, eight minutes later, he looked genuinely angry.

'Photurian vessel,' Will snapped, 'I see that you've been engaging in soft combat again as well as testing my frontiers. Your continued aggression will not be tolerated. Depart and do not return, or face the consequences.'

He saw no joy or astonishment in Will's face at the sight of his rescuers, just hatred. What in hell's name was happening here?

'I guess he didn't like our verification codes,' Judj observed.

'I'm reversing our vector,' said Ira. 'Heading out slowly.'

'Agreed,' said Palla. 'Okay, Ann, you're up next. We'll see if you're any better at reaching him. Get ready to broadcast.'

'What about Rachel?' said Clath.

'I stay hidden,' Rachel replied. Ira glanced at her. Her face was grey with distress. 'Will thinks I'm dead. Whatever is going on here, it's clear he believes we're some kind of trick. Revealing me now is only going to strengthen that fear. I have to wait.'

'Will,' said Ann, 'this is Ann Ludik. It's really us. We're backing off. But you should know, it's not been easy for us to reach you. We had to come in via the Depleted Zone. That's why our vector probably looks wrong to you. The Photes have blocked us for years and we may not get another chance. We're resending codes, this time with redundant validation tags.'

Ira felt a grim certainty settling on him. There wouldn't be another chance. If Will had come to represent a second existential threat, they'd boser his world before going home, regardless of the risk.

This time, the reply came faster, suggesting ships closing in.

'Photurian vessel,' said Will, a look of unhinged rage on his face, 'I don't know how or when you acquired those character templates, but I'm not fooled for an instant. My disgust only deepens. Leave faster.'

'What's going on?' said Clath. 'What does he mean – *character templates?*'

'I'm not sure it matters,' said Palla. 'And I'm not even sure that's Will. Whatever has happened here, he's either deluded or he's been hacked. I'm glad Mark's not awake to see this.' She paused to think. 'Okay, my turn. Ira, increase warp by twenty-five per cent, please.' She opened another message to the Will-thing.

'Willworld, this is Palla Muri, Social Accountability Officer for the GSS *Edmond Dantes*. We have received your formal request for us to vacate your stellar neighbourhood. We will do so, but be warned: we are operating under conditions of persistent interstellar war with the Photurian Utopia. This will be Galatea's one and only attempt to establish contact with you. Ignore our attempt at diplomatic engagement and you'll be on your own.'

And under fire, Ira thought darkly.

More minutes dragged by before Will's next reply. 'And who are you supposed to be?' he crooned, leaning forwards. This time he looked more curious than angry, while less sane than ever. 'I don't know your face. I didn't dream you.'

'I think we may be dealing with some sort of memory failure or psychosis,' Ira warned. 'It could be cybernetically informed schizophrenia.'

'I'm reading more local gravity distortions,' said Judj. 'There are cloaked ships closing. Big ones.'

A few seconds later, another message from Will appeared. This time, he was leaning back in his chair, staring at them with wide, unblinking eyes. He had a silver baseball bat in his hands.

'I've changed my mind,' he said. 'You will not retreat. Power down your drive instead. A diplomatic dialogue will be carried out as per your request. It's great to see you, GSS *Edmond Dantes*, it's been a long time. But be warned, this system is raided frequently. I'm uncloaking a defensive detail for your protection.'

A dozen weirdly stippled replicas of the *Ariel Two* appeared around them as their quantum shields deactivated. All of them were within weapons range and supported by clouds of thousands of warp-enabled drones. The ships were moving already, positioning themselves in a shell configuration with the *Dantes* at the centre.

'Do not be alarmed,' Will assured them. 'These ships are forming a defensive mesh in case the Photurians threaten us. Let us begin our discussion. My diplomats will be with you shortly.'

'That makes me feel *so* much safer,' said Judj as he scanned the firepower still aimed in their direction. 'He's totally put my fears at rest. I mean, who doesn't want a defensive escort with all their weapons pointed inwards?'

Ira stared at the image of his lost friend's face and wondered what in seven hells they'd stumbled into.

1 5.6: WILL

Will gripped his head and groaned as the full implications of his capture sank in. This, apparently, was where Glitches ended up. He'd fought Balance and lost, just like every instance before him. Maybe the planet would eventually wise up and start using copies of Moneko instead. But why had the memory mutilation stopped? He'd been one minute short of opening his mind up for surgery. So why the delay?

While he sat there on the edge of the couch, staring at the frozen figures smiling all around him, Balance appeared, baseball bat and all. He sat lazily in his swivel-throne, glaring with eyes like boser beams, his body taut with a suppressed capacity for violence.

'Not bothering with masks any more?' said Will, more than a little disturbed.

'The masks are for my subminds,' said the god. 'You're talking to the real deal. Lucky you.'

Will regarded his captor. He looked even more crazy and exhausted in person than he did in his videos.

'Why?' said Will. 'Aren't you going to split me open like all the other Glitches?'

'Other *corrupted instances*, you mean?' said Balance. 'Yes. Eventually. But first I have some questions that you'll be able to answer better with your mind in one piece.'

He clicked his fingers and a vid-window appeared. It held a view of an odd-looking bullet-shaped starship.

'Do you know what this is?' said Balance. 'It coincidentally appeared just after I shut down your cheap little viral assault on my orbital systems.'

'Presumably, it's a ship,' said Will, startled.

'It sent these,' said Balance. He opened a comms window and played the messages he'd received.

431

Will watched and began to understand what had happened. Of all the Glitches, appearing and dying across the Willworld in their dozens, he was the one lucky enough to be alive when a rescue mission actually appeared. Balance's demolition of his mind had been suspended because *this* had happened.

'They've come to get us,' Will blurted. 'They finally came!' Hope opened inside him like a delicate flower.

'No doubt that's what I'm supposed to imagine,' said Balance. 'Somewhere in that tiny, screwed-up head of yours, you honestly believed that by simulating a rescue, I'd throw away decades of research and investigation?' His voice slowly rose. 'That I'd ignore all the pieces of evidence I've gathered, every painstakingly constructed model of the *actual* past and throw them away for this... *fantasy*? This shitty piece of wish-fulfilment?'

'Listen, Balance—' said Will.

Balance leapt to his feet. 'Balance is my *title*!' he shouted. 'My role. My name is Will Kuno-Monet, and you are *Cuthbert*,' he sneered. 'The fourteen-thousand-nine-hundred-and-seventy-third clone to have that thrillingly original nick. A little rogue instance.'

Will refused to be cowed. Real lives were at stake aboard that ship, not merely threads.

'Please, you're not thinking straight,' Will urged. 'I've been inside your mind. You're trying to hold on to sanity so hard that you're driving yourself crazy. I've seen it. I was trying to help you fix it.' He pointed at the floating window. 'That ship is exactly what it looks like,' he said. 'It's our ticket home. Please believe me.'

'*This* is home,' said Balance, pointing a quivering finger at the floor. 'I've heard your story. Let me tell you another. The last time the Photurians attacked this world, they pretended to be IPSO starships. I was cautious that time. I was surprised. I kept quiet, but some of *your* kind, the broken chaff that keeps clogging my substrate, sent messages to that fleet, making it easier for them to approach. Millions of threads were lost in that attack. I've been clearing out the knock-on Cancerous infections in my system ever since. And now, *gosh*! Here's a new attack that goes even further. What a surprise! Only this time, there are archetypes ripped straight out of soft-space all over their arrival message. And the only way they could have got hold of them would be if someone gave them to the enemy. That someone would have to be a thread so desperate to leave that they'd actually cooperate with Photurians. The sort of thread who consorts with Cancers. A thread like *you*, Cuthbert.'

'Listen to yourself,' said Will. 'You'll say anything to hold on to the idea that your past is what you want it to be. But the Transcended *put* us here. They made this happen. We saw it happen. We felt it.'

'You may remember that garbage,' said Balance. 'I most certainly do not!'

'Have you ever asked yourself why?' said Will. 'Why every single Glitch this planet turns out recalls the same damned thing? You have that memory trap you keep baited down there in the Underlayer. It's a pretty convincing replica of what I saw. How did you ever build that if it didn't happen?'

'With hard work and thorough interrogation,' said Balance darkly. 'It took me years to figure out how to infect the surface memory of *bugs* like you. Before that, my methods were clumsier. You see, after I crack you open each time, there's not much left to read. Your code is protected. Fortunately, I get lots of tries. That means you have a choice. You can either tell me how the Photurians captured those archetype templates, or I can squeeze the answer out of you.'

'Why keep belief-hacks duplicated across your infrastructure if you're so convinced you're right?' Will shouted. 'Answer me that! Do you have any idea how dangerous that is?'

The look of blank incomprehension on Balance's face spoke volumes. At this level of representation, at least, the god had no idea of what he'd done to himself. The belief-hacking had all happened at the subconscious level under the shield of his own denialware. He'd been desperate to hold on to sanity and his blindly stomping agents had silently done the rest.

'Why are you even running denialware?' Will shouted.

Then he realised there'd be no answer. The first rule of denialware would be to ensure that Balance himself knew nothing about denialware.

'Desperate gibberish will not save you,' Balance sneered. 'Know this: I plan to understand how this theft took place, either with or without your help. The phoney ship will be examined and then dismantled. If you won't help then you can watch. Your reactions may be informative.

Afterwards, I will take you apart process by process to see what makes you tick.'

The god vanished, taking his throne but leaving the video windows running.

16: ENTRAPMENT

16.1: MARK

Mark awoke in his cabin on the yacht, weak and trembling. By the quality of the syrupy light oozing through the windows, it was apparently the middle of the afternoon. Thankfully, his headache had subsided. He dressed as quickly as his struggling virtual fingers would allow and staggered out onto the deck.

At first, everything was so quiet that he wondered whether the Transcended had dumped him into another puzzle simulation. Then, when he reached the lounge, he found a note waiting for him, rotating above the piano.

Mark: if you wake, join us in helm-space. Palla.

Mark blinked himself across and found the crew engaged in avid debate. Filling the view-space behind him was a close-up of Snakepit and several nestships.

His cheeks flushed as he clued in that he'd missed the approach. A surge of anger at the Transcended followed close behind. He'd been cheated of his moment – the one the whole mission had been about. Score one petty victory for the galactic gods.

'We're here already?' he croaked, and wondered how many days he'd been unconscious.

Heads whipped around at the sound of his voice.

'Mark!' said Palla, stepping towards him. 'You made it.'

'What happened?' He rubbed his head.

Palla filled him in. As she explained, Mark's confusion grew.

'No blockade *at all*?'

'None,' said Palla. 'No traffic indicators. No warp-light. Nothing.'

435

She glanced anxiously at Ann's view-window, but the ex-goddess had nothing to add. 'And now apparently Will is alive and armed, but for some reason he doesn't recognise us as people.'

'Wait,' said Mark, waving his hands. 'He's *alive*? After all this time?'

'That's what it looks like, but that's the only good news. He thinks we're Photes. We're surrounded and outgunned – for our own benefit, supposedly.'

'So,' said Mark, glancing at the screens in fresh understanding, 'Will has his own fleet now?'

'A huge one. He could probably take out what's left of the human race with just what he's already revealed. And at this range, a boser-hit on Snakepit is nigh-on impossible, which is almost certainly on purpose.'

'We're prisoners,' said Mark, appalled.

'Supposedly not,' said Palla. 'He claims we'll be receiving a diplomatic tight-beam any time now. We're supposed to imagine that we're guests.'

'Good, because I want to look him in the eye.' He glanced at Rachel's ashen face. 'Does he know you're here?'

'No,' said Rachel hollowly. 'Not yet.'

'We decided to keep that back,' said Ira. 'He's not rational. That knowledge could make matters substantially worse.'

Mark rubbed his temples. His head was a fog of dismayed confusion.

'If there are no threats here and nothing to stop Will leaving, why didn't he come home?' he said. 'What the fuck is wrong with him?'

'That's what we all want to know,' said Ira. 'There must be some other force in play.'

'What about that psycho witch, Nada?'

'As yet unseen,' said Judj. 'I suspect we were tailed passively, though why she's not on top of us already, I have no idea.'

'How about you, Mark?' Palla. 'How are you feeling?'

'Like chewed shit,' said Mark hoarsely.

'What happened in there?' said Palla. 'Did you talk to them? Anything we should know about?'

Mark related his conversation with the Transcended while the others listened, stunned.

'Threats, then,' said Palla.

Mark nodded. 'Nice vague ones. I'm supposed to solve the puzzle like a good doggie and then go and touch Ann. I don't feel like handing them a victory, but this affects all of us.'

He felt their creaking unease. Given the unexpected circumstances, the Transcended warnings sounded worryingly solid.

He glanced at Ann's window. 'It definitely affects you. I expect you want your smart-cells back.'

'Did they tell you that touching me would do that?'

'No,' Mark admitted. 'They just implied it.'

'Or you inferred it,' she said. 'Did they mention the ark?'

'Not once.'

'What do you think the likelihood is that they'll let us keep it if we play their game?'

'Low,' Mark confessed.

'Then it's a choice, isn't it?' said Ann. 'The ark we already have, or the powers I might get back.'

Mark grimaced. 'That's not a clear win, admittedly. On the other hand, things are getting hairy, just like they predicted.'

'Except they didn't bother to tell you how that would happen,' Judj put in. 'They're deliberately screening. We don't even know if Snakepit is the threat they were talking up.'

'So you're all okay with me holding out?' Mark added. 'I mean, it's possible we're playing with a lot of lives here.'

'When has that ever not been true?' said Ira.

'If they won't come clean with us, how can we trust them?' said Palla. 'Billions have died because of the Photurian threat they didn't warn us about, and which they let persist. Who can say what they're not telling us now?'

'There's something else going on here, too,' said Judj. 'The first thing they did was influence Mark's thoughts, so it's clear they don't have a problem with human subversion. Then they made threats without supporting data despite having all the tools on hand to just take what they wanted. The Photes rewrite people all the time. With that level of tech, it's not hard.'

'They said they wanted us to make the right choice for ourselves,' said Mark.

'Exactly,' said Judj. 'That doesn't suggest a weak enemy to me. It suggests one that's constrained. I hate to say it, but I'm starting to think there might be two kinds of Transcended in play here, not one.'

'Two?' said Rachel.

'One helping, one with another agenda entirely.'

She scowled. 'Politics among the gods? I can't see that ending well.'

Mark could only agree.

'I hate this,' said Clath, shaking her head. 'This is all wrong. They opened the Zone for us. Don't they *have* to be good at some level?'

'Not if they did it for the benefit of the Photes,' said Judj.

'So we're confused,' said Mark tersely. 'What else is new? Do you want me to hold off?'

'I would,' said Judj. 'The fact that their strategy was "manipulate first, beg later" doesn't fire my confidence much.'

'Incoming signal,' the helm told them.

A vid-window of Will appeared. 'GSS *Edmond Dantes*,' he said, smiling unpleasantly.

Mark blinked at the sudden sight of his half-father's face. While the features were familiar, the grinning force that animated them was not. And then there was the crazy new uniform. The effect on Mark was one of deeply unsettled disappointment. All his years of effort had bought him, apparently, was a ticket to this sinister farce.

'This is Will Kuno-Monet, representative god and king of all the Willworld. Do I have permission to approach your vessel?'

'How far away are those nestships?' said Mark. They were as big as Ann's usual ride, he noticed – about two hundred and forty kilometres long and armed to the teeth.

'Half a light-second,' said Palla. 'If that.'

'Then how much closer does he want to be?' said Mark.

'All the way, presumably,' said Palla. 'I think he wants to land on the hull and send in some kind of presence.'

'Give me the helm,' said Mark. 'If anyone's wriggling up to this ship, I want options.'

'Can't do it,' said Judj. 'You're in the quarantine core, which locks you out. I'm sorry, but that Transcended attack messed you up bad. You don't have smart-cells, just chaos. Your body keeps manufacturing viruses. Every time I think I have the infection suppressed, it starts up somewhere new.'

Mark glanced around at the helm he couldn't use with a fresh surge of indignation. They'd need to take the engines all the way offline to move him back, and that clearly wasn't going to happen any time soon.

Apparently, the Transcended were intent on stripping everything from him.

'I think our answer should be *no*,' said Clath. 'Unless we really believe we can trust him. Do we want those things all over our ship otherwise? We'd be helpless.'

'I don't see that we have a choice,' Ira put in. 'He's holding most of the cards. But at least he doesn't know about the ark. If the worst happens, we still have somewhere to hide, presuming it works.'

Mark shot him a disgusted look. 'Hide?' he said. 'What the fuck use is that?'

'It's better than dying,' said Ira.

'And if that machine inside it blows a hole through local space? Or ends the universe?'

'Then none of us will have to worry about failure,' said Palla. 'Fuck it, I'm going to say yes. It puts the ship at risk, but that's already happened. If we're not here to talk to him, then why did we bother coming?'

'Can I recommend we hide Rachel first?' said Ira.

Mark cast a glance at his half-mother. She stood with her eyes glued to the new message window, her disgust at the universe a little deeper.

'Agreed,' she said tersely. 'The touching reunions can come later if that *thing* we're looking at turns out to actually be my husband.'

Palla opened a camera-frame to make a reply.

'Will Monet, you have permission to approach,' she said. 'Our ship runs under full virtual. If you wish to send an avatar aboard, a sensor-cluster will be made available for you to connect to.'

A swarm of drones indistinguishable from the Photurian menace they'd been fleeing descended to hang around their ship like an almost solid cloud. A single drone nosed up to kiss against the sensor-cluster Palla extended. Meanwhile, Judj hid Rachel behind a ghosting screen.

'We should use the yacht metaphor,' said Judj. 'Let's not give him a handle on helm-space just yet.'

'Agreed,' said Palla.

They blinked to the deck where a simulated dinghy was approaching, carrying Will, who'd added an oversized bicorn hat to his ridiculous uniform. His boat was rowed by two stripe-shirted sailors wearing plaster masks of his face. Ira offered Will a hand up to the deck. Will smirked as he boarded with something entirely unlike friendship written all over his features.

The sight of Mark's erstwhile guardian and genetic designer set his mind to scattered fizzing. He'd imagined a hundred different scenarios for this moment, some uplifting, some tragic, but none had involved comedy hats or deadly sarcasm. All the speeches and remarks he'd so long thought of saying bunched in his mouth, falling over each other so that none of them managed to escape.

'Great to see you, Ira!' said Will. 'Funny to find you in a full virtual setting. Are you a roboteer now?'

'We all are, after a fashion,' said Ira carefully. 'We copied and duplicated the shadow technology you gave Ann as best we could.'

Will chuckled. 'Of course. A perfectly rational explanation. And so logical that you should travel on a ship that's basically a historic metaphor. I always liked those, as I'm sure you know.' He took a moment to inhale the virtual air and stare out at the becalmed waters glinting in the afternoon light. 'I particularly dig the fish. And let me say, you don't look a hundred. Not a day over ninety, in fact!'

Ira smiled drily. 'Why, thanks, Will. Likewise. It's been a long time. It is Will I'm talking to, right?'

'Oh yes, it's me all right, in the digital flesh.' He slapped his chest theatrically. Will looked around at the assembled team and noticed Mark at last. 'Mark!' he said jubilantly. 'They sent you out here, too? Wonderful! What were the chances?'

He came over and embraced Mark with an entirely unsettling hug.

'The Fleet sent all of us who might be able to reach you,' Mark managed to say at last. He felt sure that they hadn't reached Will at all. He was talking to *something else* with a lot of firepower and a very disturbing sense of humour.

'So Ira is younger, but you're older!' said Will. 'By ten years, maybe. Interesting.'

Mark found himself annoyed by the sinister jocularity. There was no sign of empathy on this stranger's face – no surprise or relief. If Rachel's bitter solemnity had been unnerving, Will's joyless pantomime was grotesque.

'We have life extension,' said Mark. 'Plus this is a virt. What did you expect? And great to see you, too, *Dad*, I think.'

Ira and Palla both shot him a warning glance.

'And here's the lovely lady with the unusual head decorations,' said Will, turning to Palla. 'I don't recognise you, or either of your two friends here.'

'I'm Autograd Palla Muri,' said Palla stiffly. 'This is Science Officer Clath Ataro and Security Officer Judj Apis. Welcome aboard.'

'Such interesting names,' said Will. 'And you have a *super* ship. A very unusual design. And my respects on your security, Judj. I can feel it. It's very dense. How many layers is that?'

'Theoretically infinite,' said Judj smoothly. 'Our security layers reproduce and max out due to self-organised criticality in the buffer. If a layer breaks, competing mutant variants have room to spawn underneath, filling any possible gaps.'

'Almost unhackable, then,' said Will. 'And an elegant solution. Thank you for warning me off from tinkering.'

'It was good enough to hold back the Transcended,' said Judj. 'That's a start.'

'Wait,' said Will jovially. 'But where's Ann? Didn't I see her on your message, too?'

Ann opened a window. 'I'm here,' she said. 'I can't be present in person right now.'

'Why ever not?' said Will. 'Aren't I supposed to have given you all my powers? And what happened to your face, if you don't mind me asking? You look so different – so *pretty*. That seems unlike you. You're almost like an advert for yourself. More like what I'd want to remember than the actual you.'

Ann regarded him coldly. 'It's been a difficult forty years,' she said crisply. 'Maybe if you start behaving like a human being we can explain.'

Will laughed. 'Of course. In due time. My ... tenure, shall we say, on the Willworld has not been without difficulties of its own.'

Mark could restrain himself no more. 'Like what?' he said. 'What happened? Why didn't we hear from you? What did you do, spend forty years alone down there twiddling your fucking thumbs?'

'Mark,' Ira warned.

'What?' said Mark. 'He knows me. Would he be more likely to believe I'm me if I *don't* swear at his face for baiting us?'

Will's gaze fizzed with feral glee. 'Well said, Mark. And the answer is *yes*, after a fashion, lots and lots of twiddling.'

441

'If you had all these starships, why didn't you come back?' Mark demanded.

'We'll get to that,' said Will. 'Mind if I look around your yacht?'

'Be my guest,' said Palla frostily.

Will wandered past them to the lounge. 'Ooh, a piano!' he said, tinkling on the keys. 'I do like a piano.'

'Listen,' said Mark, approaching. 'We've beaten our way through Backspace to get to you. If you're surprised to see us after forty years, I understand. If you don't want to believe we are who we say we are, fine. We'll leave you in peace. But know this: this is your chance. Unless you really enjoy *twiddling*, I recommend you just tell us what the fuck is going on.'

'Mark,' said Ira heavily. 'We have no idea what happened to Will down there. We didn't even expect him to be alive. So let's cut him a little slack, shall we? Until we know more.'

But Mark's head was thundering again. He was done with mind games. And the Transcended puzzle had restarted its pulsing in the corners of his vision.

'Another thing,' he told Will. 'We were chased here by a fleet of Photurian ships. By our estimates, you have less than twenty-four hours before they attack. Can you understand that?'

Will shrugged. 'I'm not without defences,' he said, 'as you've seen. Don't worry – if they chase you in here, I'll see them off. You have my protection, after all. In the meantime, I'm keen to learn all about the interesting things that must have happened on good old Galatea while I've been away. And why the "GSS" signifier on your ship, by the way? What happened to IPSO?'

'War,' said Mark. 'What did you think? Why else would we have been gone so long? We've been fighting the fucking Photurians.'

'All this time?' said Will. 'Gosh, that sounds exhausting.'

'We're down to four colonies,' said Palla. 'Each has to fend for itself. That's why we made the effort to come here – we want to ask you to participate in our defence.'

'Of course,' said Will. 'How natural. And how much of my defensive force would you like? All of it, I'm guessing.'

'As much as you can spare,' said Palla.

'I'll tell you what,' said Will, picking up the revolving message icon that Palla had left hovering over the piano. 'I'll think about it. You share some history files with me, and if I like them, I'll share some of mine with you, and maybe come and solve your *Phote* problem. Love the contraction, by the way. Very human.' He tossed the icon gently into the air and caught it again. Then he took a bite.

'Mmm, *human* software,' he said with a wink. 'So simple and delicious.'

'We can send you a complete historic database,' said Palla.

'You're going to just accede to this?' said Mark.

He no longer believed they were talking to Will. He'd met Phote spies with more convincing emotions. He found himself itching to mention Rachel just to see what would happen.

Ira held up a warning finger to Mark and stepped forward. 'Will,' he said. 'As you can probably tell, this isn't the kind of reunion we expected. We're still getting used to who you've become and you evidently have doubts about us. Maybe the next best step is for us to call it a day and go over each other's data. We'll happily look at anything you feel ready to share.'

The predatory mirth in Will's gaze deepened. 'Certainly,' he said. 'Let's do that. How about I start with a little potted history of the prior Photurian attacks against this system and their subsequent annihilation. A catalogue of their shitty little underhanded tricks and how they all failed. Every time. Would that work for you?'

'If that's what you have, old friend, we'll take it,' said Ira.

'Okay,' said Will, 'we have a plan. I'll see you later when we've all had a nice nap. Toodeloo!'

Will strode back to his dinghy and climbed in while his masked sailors saluted. The boat rowed away and promptly vanished.

In the wake of his departure, the crew fell quiet as everyone tried to accommodate this latest twist on their shared condition. Eventually, the storm of conflicting emotions in Mark's chest polarised into urgency.

'Whatever that thing is,' he said, pointing at where the dinghy had been, 'it sure as shit is *not* Will Monet.'

'No,' said Ira. 'But *it* has us pinned.'

Judj brought Rachel back into the room. Bitter fury crackled in her gaze.

'Mark said it already,' she told them. 'That wasn't my husband. If that's who's on Snakepit, then my husband is dead, just like I thought.'

'He doesn't seem to think we're real,' Palla observed. 'The implication is that he still thinks we're Photes.'

'Whatever intelligence we're talking to, that's all it's seen for decades,' said Ira.

'So maybe his distrust is understandable,' she said. 'Let's hope our history files are more convincing than we were. If we can't win him round, he may start shooting, and he has a lot more guns than we do.'

16.2: WILL

Will sat in the defunct ship simulation, wordless with shock after the feed Balance sent him of his visit to the *Dantes* had finished. Seconds later, the god materialised, still wearing his uniform and doubled over with laughter.

'Did you see their faces?' said Balance, tears rolling down his face. 'It was priceless!'

Will felt sick and said nothing. The sight of his old friends had opened up a chasm of longing in him.

'They came here on a fucking *boat*,' said Balance, guffawing. 'As if they thought that would sell it for me. A boat!'

He tossed Will a half-chewed message icon. It landed in his lap. '...*n us in helm-space*,' it read.

'I have to admit,' said Balance, shaking a gleeful finger, 'they have gone to Crazy Town on the details. I mean, hats off to whatever hive-minded shit-weasel thought this one up.'

He planted his bicorn askew on the frozen avatar of Ira.

'What if they're real?' Will snapped. 'What if you're throwing our one chance away?'

'Oh, *come on*, Cuthbert!' said Balance. His laugher redoubled even while a furious light built in his eyes. 'You must have seen that shitty ghost-filter they were working, right? The one it took me about three seconds to hack, with the special surprise behind it? *My dead wife?* All mopey-dopey with tears in her eyes?' His voice took on a manic edge that said nothing good about how close Balance was to unleashing mayhem. 'My most sacred template of all? They kept that gem back, did you notice, just as soon as they figured out how pathetically their puppet show was playing.'

444

Will had to admit that detail had confused him, too. How could Rachel possibly be aboard? He'd heard them explain that they'd come through Backspace to reach the Willworld, but finding Rachel seemed like a terrible stretch. While he still saw no explanation for the ship other than it being real, doubts had started to creep into his mind.

What if some other Glitch had sold them out to the Photurians? Could he imagine Smiley doing such a thing? Not easily, he decided.

Balance wiped his eyes. 'Wow,' he said. 'That was fun. You ready to talk now? I mean, you don't have to. We still have plenty of time for mind-crushing later.'

'What if you have the wrong Glitch?' said Will.

'It's possible,' said Balance. 'You guys are like roaches. Little fucking roaches with my face on them. There are so many of you. More every year. For the life of me I still can't figure out why this planet keeps bothering.'

'Perhaps because you're losing it.'

'So you keep saying!' said Balance. 'In about twenty-three per cent of interrogations. It's a common fantasy that justifies your pitiful existence. But if that's true, tell me why Cancer levels worldwide are actually dropping now.'

Will tried to hide his surprise. Given what he'd seen, that statistic simply couldn't be true.

'That's right, Cuthbert. The world is stabilising, which means my branch economy is working. Which means your delusions of grandeur aren't worth shit, and you're irrelevant.'

'I've seen what you can't see,' said Will, his anger rising again. 'I've seen inside your *soul* like you never can, and what I found there sickened me. How did a version of me get to be so blinkered and patronising and deaf to the words of his own copies?'

'How? I'm the version who has to spend all his time listening to corruptions of himself,' said Balance, menace building in his gaze again. 'The version who has to hold all this together so that every other thread can live the decent life that he can't have. The version who's heard your sick, poisonous shit so many times that he can't take you seriously any more. You know what's keeping those shitty puppets alive right now? *You.* I'm holding off on ripping that ship open and sucking all the data out of it because I'm half-convinced that you actually think it's real. Just like your fuckwit siblings believed the last scam they saw. So if you want that ship to leave the system in one piece, you'll start talking about what you know before I get bored. Enjoy your viewing, Cuthbert One-Four-Nine-Seven-Three. Let me know when you're ready to chat.'

16.3: MARK

The day after Will's visit oozed tension. Judj tested the data they'd been given for malware, and then they pored over it together. They drew the obvious conclusion: Snakepit didn't trust them. The footage showed a history of increasingly subtle Photurian attacks, slowing in frequency while they ramped in sophistication. The last had done a plausible job of impersonating IPSO, using freshly converted humans who must have been culled from the fall of New Angeles.

So far as the Will-thing was concerned, they were just another invasion attempt. Each had been repulsed as easily as the last. At the same time, Will hadn't revealed the slightest hint of how he'd survived on the surface of the planet in apparent isolation. Without that data, it was completely unclear how they could convince Will of their humanity, or what he hoped to achieve by preventing them from leaving.

Mark found it exasperating. To come so far only to be thwarted by mere paranoia? He might as well have stayed on Galatea where that commodity was cheaper than sand. His last hopes for the mission were unravelling, leaving an empty ache behind.

The following morning, a new message from Will arrived.

'Hey, GSS *Edmond Dantes*,' he said cheerfully. 'That threat window you mentioned has expired!' He looked around as if confused. 'Is it possible that you're not being tailed after all, but were actually trying to deceive me?'

Palla launched a reply. 'We gave you an estimate,' she said. 'As to where they are, I have no idea. Maybe we were lucky.'

'You know what?' said Will, leaning in to his camera. 'I'm starting to doubt your otherwise totally convincing narrative. I've looked over your history files, though. Amazing stuff. So moving. My congratulations to your screenwriters. That Suicide War? Wow. Talk about pathos.'

Mark worked at not grabbing the comms-link to yell curses at the sick creature at the other end.

'It was all so impressive that I wanted to see if you'd actually follow through on the phoney attack,' Will went on. 'But now I guess you've blown your budget and I'm getting bored.' He exhaled noisily. 'So here we are. I've decided to dismantle you to find out what your plan actually was. And why you're using the faces of people from my dreams. And how the fuck you got hold of them. So if any of you have something that you'd like to say before I start, now would be a great time.'

Mark lost it. 'Palla, a channel please,' he said tightly.

She handed it to him.

'Listen, Will,' he said, glaring into the feed, 'making this mission happen has been my life for the last decade and *nothing* about it has turned out as I expected. I understand disappointment and frustration. I've felt plenty. I know what it means to fight against an enemy that's always trying to cheat its way past your guard. That's been our lives. So I get where you're coming from. But for the love of science, can't you stop being a fucking idiot for just one minute?'

In his video feed, Will's smile turned south.

'If you care that much about who we really are, why aren't you asking for DNA samples?' said Mark. 'If you're concerned that we'll fake them, take some neural scans. And if that won't put your mind at rest, then come and check out the anti-Phote regimen we use on ourselves and ask yourself if you have a single technology that's as thorough. You run on some kind of mashed-up Phote tech by the looks of things, so I'm pretty sure you don't.

'Because, you see, Will, doing anything other than that is lazy and dumb. It's denial in action. If there's not a single piece of proof we could offer that would convince you that your theory about us is bullshit, isn't your theory just *faith*? And if that's the fuel you're running on now, then I'm certain that you're not the Will Monet I knew and admired. You're some cheap, low-rent Photurian knock-off, propelled by the same self-deluding garbage, and nothing we can do or say will ever convince you.'

Will stared into his camera feed with wild, inhuman eyes.

'Denial again,' he said. 'You know, I'm getting really bored of that narrative, son. For starters, it ignores the fact that when you're facing an evolving existential threat, sometimes conviction is all you have. I'll tell you what, though, I'll follow up on your request and do some nice science on your remains.'

He clicked his fingers. In the same moment, a thousand drones clamped onto the *Dantes*' hull, adhering to every bay door and portal on the ship's surface. Simultaneous soft assaults bombarded their sensors. Mark watched in horror as the warnings spooled up around them. His attempt to get Will to raise his standards had apparently failed, and with it, his dream.

'Mesohull defences activated,' said Palla. 'Titan mechs moving to position.'

'Soft incursions detected,' Judj added. 'Ready to initiate purge.'

'I'm warming weapons,' said Ira. 'I can't see us shooting our way out of this, but that doesn't mean I won't try.'

Mark cursed his helplessness. From the quarantine core there was little he could do but watch. He itched for the helm he couldn't have.

Palla shot him a glance while she worked, her eyes full of despair. 'You didn't deserve this,' she said. 'Sometimes you're an asshole, Mark, but you're at least a good asshole. A great asshole, even. It's been a pleasure to work with you. In fact I...'

Then, just when it looked like their luck couldn't get any worse, a red flash bloomed just a handful of AU further out as a ship travelling under stealth-warp dumped its envelope. Palla's words trailed out in shock.

As the glare faded, the image of a nestship-sized vessel resolved – ember-warp enabled and very similar in profile to the *Edmond Dantes*. Its surface had the curious, bulbous texture of something made out of fused drones. The one major difference was the enormous, ugly-looking boser cannon mounted on the front.

'Humans and the vile interloper Will Monet,' came the imperious voice of Nada Rien on the public channel. 'Prepare to receive our everlasting love.'

In his video channel, Will blinked in surprise and then burst into peals of laughter. '*This* is the threat?' he said. 'One ship?'

Will clicked his fingers again. All across the system, dozens more copies of the *Ariel Two* started to uncloak.

16.4: NADA

Nada surveyed the armada of ships appearing around her with nothing but Photurian joy raging in her heart. She'd arrived too late to head off the Abomination and her cronies before they reached the homeworld, but they'd apparently fared about as well against Monet as her own people had over the years. A more fitting end for their disgusting mission was hard to imagine. Had she room inside her for schadenfreude or irony, she might have laughed, but such emotions would have been a poor substitute for the glory she felt. Her own attempt to save the homeworld might succeed or fail, but now the Yunus could surely be nothing but proud of them.

'Initiate suntap connection,' she said. 'Raise the new shield.'

While they'd purposefully forgone the use of false matter, their rebuild of the alien boser had prompted a few obvious improvements in their quantum shielding – a tightly related technology. Against Leng's protestations, she'd ordered the changes to be made, insisting that these two features were adequate for their needs. Her reasoning? That their goals had shifted. They now sought direct access to the homeworld, not only joyful reconciliation with their enemies.

She'd used that same argument to justify suspending her release of an arrival message until she was deep into the system, even though it had been excruciating to delay that moment. Somehow, the dissonance still churning inside her had helped, even while her crew had keened and squirmed at their stations at how dishonest it felt.

'I am receiving a tight-beamed message from the Vile Usurper,' said Ekkert.

'Play it,' she said.

The repugnant visage of Monet appeared. 'Photurian vessel,' said Will, grinning like a maniac, 'the might of the Willworld is tracking your ship. Depart immediately or I'll take you apart, too.'

Nada prepared a reply.

'We will not leave,' she said. 'You will relinquish control of our world and come to love us as your superiors.'

'I hoped you'd say something like that!' Will exclaimed.

The shield came on just in time. Beams lanced out from Monet's guard-ships to burst harmlessly against their defences.

'Leng, time to suntap?' she said.

'Eleven minutes.'

Nada wasn't worried. Their last fuelling had left their antimatter reserves fully charged.

'Have the guard-ships raised shields?' said Nada.

'Yes,' Leng told her.

'Good,' she said. 'Target the closest and remove it.'

Their beam spiked out, locking weakly on to the enemy's quantum-agitated armour. A second, invisible beam, rather like a suntap entangler, fired alongside.

'Feedback cycling initiated,' said Leng. 'Tuning. We have a match. Boosting now.'

The boser gained strength, punching a hole straight through the nestship. At the same time, their weapon went into a saccadic firing pattern, mashing everything in the heart of Will's craft until antimatter release was guaranteed. The nestship splattered itself across the stars.

Destroying a capital-class starship had proven remarkably easy. That was what they had aimed for, though achieving it left Nada with the profound sense of having cheated by not beating him with his own level of technology. She suppressed it; by that time, several guard-ships were closing and coordinating their fire.

'Prioritise the attacking vessels,' said Nada. 'Remove them until the assault ceases.'

She watched her energy and iron reserves shrink under the extraordinary bombardment as she'd known it would. Meanwhile, her rebuild of the *Infinite Order* dispensed justice to one nestship at a time. It wouldn't have been possible had their new shield not dynamically adapted itself just like the cannon, siphoning raw material off the oncoming beams.

It came down to enemies versus resources. A human would have fretted over that fatal race between numbers but Nada only felt the rigid confidence of righteous zeal. Five guard-ships died. Eight. Thirteen. To destroy so many vessels of such enormous power in so short a time was unheard of. She had clearly overdone the repurposing of alien remains yet she did not care. Her ship was punched this way and that with every blast by the shells of tortured bosons slamming through local space. Her crew bounced indifferently around the cabin on their umbilici, their attention firmly on their temple-tasks.

Her reserves dwindled. Then, just as she was readying herself for a worthy death, it all stopped.

'The assault has paused,' Leng whispered.

Nada had believed it would, yet still felt the magic of that moment viscerally. Monet and the homeworld were joined and the homeworld did not waste resources on pointless violence – not when superiority was clear.

She looked at her subnode's face and saw that it was wet with tears.

'The enemy appears to be regrouping,' he said. 'Do you want to move to capture range for the *Dantes*?' His voice trembled with emotion.

'No,' said Nada, awed at herself. 'Approach Snakepit directly. Ignore the *Dantes*.'

'But Superior Nada!' cried Nanimo.

'Ignore all dissonance,' said Nada. 'This is destiny.'

The Usurper had broken off his attack. This opportunity would only come once.

Their ship restarted its drive and slid closer to the star. They'd depleted their reserves already and zeroed the timer on their suntap connection. However, Nada could feel the Protocol singing in her veins. This was how it was supposed to go. She was *asserting primacy* as they'd tried to do so long ago. The *Dantes*, her greatest concern, remained overwhelmed by Monet's own forces and hadn't even had the chance to fire.

'Acquire geostationary orbit around the homeworld,' said Nada, her voice cracking.

Will's drones swarmed after them but did not fire. They warped in unison, forming beautiful, deadly clouds that followed them in. From the homeworld, fountains of new drones were rising. The sight of them was so perfect and so dangerous that Nada could barely breathe.

They nudged close to the homeworld, but still returning fire did not come.

'I am receiving messages from the Vile Monet,' said Ekkert in an awed whisper.

'Ignore him,' said Nada. 'He will only ruin this moment. Are we also hearing a Protocol signal?'

'Yes,' said Ekkert, breathless with anticipation.

'Reply to that instead. Commune with it. Zilch, target a defensive node at random. Fire a direct spike, minimum duration and energy.'

The smallest damage would do. That was how asserting primacy worked. The planet had already worked out which variant race was strongest and was ready to submit. Now all that was required was a tap on the world's exposed chest to symbolise who had won. The beam pierced the atmosphere, vaporising a defensive node and sending up a perfectly circular mushroom cloud from the surface.

'Target destroyed,' said Zilch. He was openly weeping, something like perfect delight distorting his features into an uncontrollable rictus. 'Time to suntap, approximately five minutes.'

In the wake of the impact, they waited. Drones milled around them, flashing and darting like the beautiful fireflies from which they drew their name.

'Receiving another message from Monet,' said Ekkert.

This time, she permitted it to open. On the screen, the face of the hated monstrosity was twisted in an expression that was almost Photurian in its intensity. His voice came in a choked gasp.

'You... have... asserted...' He twisted this way and that as if in the deepest kind of pain. 'No! I do not accept it! Never!'

Will screamed. His face came apart into shards, cycling violently through a billion subtle variations of his own features. The channel closed.

'We have done it,' Nada told her crew. 'The homeworld is ours.'

With one voice, they erupted into unhinged screams of mind-burning joy.

16.5: WILL

Will watched the video feed of the battle from his phoney-starship prison, gripping the edge of his couch. The world he'd woken up in was unexpectedly fighting for its life. He thought of Moneko and it hurt.

There was a terrible symmetry to this battle. This was what he'd done to Earth all those years ago at the end of the Interstellar War – shown up with a single piece of overpowering technology – only this time, he was a citizen of the beaten world beneath the alien boot. Was this how it had felt, watching the madness in the sky and feeling hope shrink with every blinding blast? Knowledge of that reversal of fate would be dawning in ten billion minds across the world – hers included.

Abruptly, all the video windows closed. The frozen avatars of his ersatz crew started shouting gibberish, even while their postures and expressions remained fixed. Will felt the environment weaken as if the reality around him had turned to rubber. Whatever SAP had been backing the simulation had apparently died.

Will knew that this was the best chance to escape the planet he was ever going to get. After this, the Photurians would exploit the very hacks Balance had peppered himself with to retake their homeworld. The god's insistence on keeping control had made him dependent on that alien code and therefore on Snakepit's ancient genetic rules. Now that Balance's military superiority had unexpectedly evaporated, all those hacks would work against him, just as Smiley had warned.

Will glanced desperately about the space, searching for something that would get him out before the Photes locked everything down. If Balance could enter the sim, there had to be an exit.

He spotted the bicorn hat. Will had abandoned it in a moment of jeering indifference. It had no role in the original simulation, yet it hadn't disappeared when he left. That meant there was a chance it retained a link to whatever process had spawned it.

Will grabbed the hat and felt around in his head urgently for a link to the mass of SAPs he'd ingested before he was captured. With luck, they'd still be there. Balance would surely have used them as the framework for his prison. He'd talked about infecting Will's surface memory and the obvious way to do it was to abuse the programs that already had access.

Through the soft, jellied texture reality had taken on, he felt those subsystems whispering in his mind, offering glimpses of senses and knowledge beyond his own. With tremendous care, Will reached down into the hat and pushed – more mentally than physically. He tore the fabric gently so that the inside broke while the outside remained intact, leaving him with a virtual bridge to whatever environment had spawned the hat. With luck, it'd be the machine room. If Balance had used some other mechanism, he was probably screwed.

Will pushed his arm all the way inside the hat and groped around until he felt a metal bar. He groaned with relief. Then he pulled his arm back and carefully stretched the hat wider at the crown until it grew large enough for him to squeeze into. Then, with exquisite care, he pushed his feet inside the hat and wriggled through to the other side.

He found himself crawling out of a distorted icon hovering about two feet above a grilled platform in the machine room. All around him was chaos. Balance agents dashed this way and that, apparently at war with each other. The pacifying power of the anchor-code clearly wasn't decisive. Instead, Balance had become conflicted. He'd fractured into differing perspectives – the embodiments of clone factions more or less dependent on the belief-reinforcing software they'd borrowed. Will could now see just what an advantage the Willworld's diversity represented. Had all the clones thought alike, the entire planet would already have fallen.

Will dragged himself onto the floor and lay there panting while his mind and body adjusted. The talents he'd acquired from Moneko's chocolates came back online one by one. He ripped free the control-edits Balance had used to secure him to the prison and looked about.

He'd been dumped on a platform way down in the roots of the world-mechanism. Near him were a host of identical entrapment icons, each positioned above a simulation cog. They were other Glitches – thousands of them. Balance didn't actually kill his prisoners, apparently, or at least, not always.

Will raced up a level to the master-branch for the entire dungeon and smashed the control SAP, blowing all the locks beneath. Hopefully, an army of angry Glitches emerging from their containment sims would buy him some time. He wished he had the means to explain to all of them, but he probably had only minutes to act. They'd have to work it out for themselves.

He leapt up the stairways, back towards Orbital Defence. Fortunately, the Balance agents were so intent on fighting each other that they had no time for him, despite the loss of his denialware. He watched them struggle hand to hand, dissolving into clouds of SAP schematics when their attacks broke the limits of the metaphor. It was only when an agent sprinted through him from behind that he realised physical contact was no longer to be feared. He redoubled his speed, leaping through manifestations of his meta-self with abandon.

A cluster of fighting giants struggled over the root-control of Orbital Defence, so Will fled straight past them. Somewhere underneath would be the spot where the attack on the *Dantes* was being managed. He clattered down the stairs, past gangs of agents intent on their work, and finally found a relevant subnode that had been left to fend for itself in the escalating conflict.

Enemy Mesohull Investigation Cohort Nineteen, it read. Will grabbed the SAP with both hands, ripped open a portal and threw himself through it, praying that a link to his friends' ship lay on the other side. The substrate of the Willworld dutifully turned his mind into a message – a compressed pattern of deltas from the Monet baseline – and routed him over the intervening light-minutes to the corresponding agent-cluster stationed at the damaged bay doors of the *Dantes*.

The world blinked, twisted and dumped him into a firefight. He was no longer a thread lost in the understructure of the Willworld – now he had a physical body again, albeit a borrowed one. He found himself inhabiting an armoured Balance agent tethered to the back of an enormous waldobot, flanked by a fleet of slaved microdrones. He was racing through a blasted hole in a sheet of exohull warp-alloy into a mesohull vacuole where another of his kind had already engaged the enemy. In this case, that meant the automated defences protecting Mark's ship – an army of enormous multi-limbed robots armed with laser weapons. The space in the cavern was already littered with ionised gas and fried machine parts from both sides.

A battle-status update landed in his mind. The body whose thread he'd ripped had belonged to a Balance loyalist rather than a Photurian convert. Those agents that had started the hull incursion had been running in secure mode when the planet succumbed and hadn't turned yet. They were still involved in hundreds of small skirmishes like this one happening across the surface of the ship. While they'd already succeeded in disabling many of the *Dantes*' critical systems, the Photes had just launched drones of their own in the ship's direction. General confusion reigned as to how to respond.

Will reached out with his mind and redirected the efforts of his machines to attack his fellow invader from behind. At the same moment, he tried tight-beaming signals at the *Dantes*' defensive mechs, hoping dearly that at least one of them would see that gesture and had a comms-port open.

'Cease conflict at this site,' he messaged. 'The real Will Monet is aboard. Tell Rachel I love her.'

Maybe she wasn't really his wife, but at that point, Will had nothing left to run on but hope.

Ira battled the invasion in the mesohull wearing a body five metres tall and studded with guns. He was fighting his way up a mech-delivery tunnel filled with swarming robotic monsters that kept flying at his face. It was a new experience for him – something like true roboteering that Palla had enabled for him with another mapping harness. He wasn't great at it. This was his fifth robot body already.

One part of his problem was the battle status that kept unfolding in the corner of his vision. As the strategy SAP filled him in on his enemies blasting each other to pieces, his mind kept blanking in appalled disbelief. Instead of rousing Snakepit to their aid, they'd handed it to the Photes. They were witnessing the end of everything.

The cloud of Will's drones around their ship had fallen into a kind of daze – some racing up to the hull to dock, the majority fighting among themselves. That confusion offered the crew of the *Dantes* their only hope of escape.

Ira slammed his scythe-arms through another incoming drone while firing wildly at a second with blink-directed cannons. He failed to notice a shot to his head and was thrown back into yet another body. He turned and blasted his assailant into pieces.

'Fuck you, too,' he snarled and pushed forward to regain the ground he'd just lost. Will's weapons were appallingly effective. Breaking them into pieces only made them angrier.

Suddenly the whole sim lurched sickeningly. He found himself dumped back into helm-space with a bump.

'What happened?' he said.

The virt spasmed again. When it returned, Mark was missing.

'Fuck!' said Palla.

'Internal data arteries are being targeted,' said Judj. 'Our mechs are being pushed back.'

'Tell me something I don't know,' said Ira.

'I'm now seeing mesohull incursions at fifty-eight sites,' Judj went on. 'Swapping mechs to autonomous mode on secondary pathways.'

'What happened to Mark?' said Rachel.

'When we lost the feed to our mechs, we also lost the data trunk to the quarantine core,' said Palla. 'They're taking out internal power and comms.'

'Palla, we have to get out of here,' said Ira.

'Not an option!' she snapped. 'Engines are still down. Weapons are down. And besides, I am not going *anywhere* until we know Mark is safe.'

'Wait,' said Judj, his eyebrows shooting upwards. 'Look at this!'

He posted a window. In it, one of Will's unstoppable soldiers was urgently hailing them on tight-beam. His virtual face filled a vid-frame.

'Ceasefire at that site!' said Rachel, breaking into a grin. 'That's Will.'

'How do you know it's actually him?' said Judj. 'This could be another ruse.'

'It's him all right,' said Rachel. 'I'd know that look of guilty panic anywhere.'

'Palla, give me a channel,' said Ira. 'Will, is that you?' he said into the camera she sent him.

A squad of Will's machines came and hovered in front of the titan mechs, their weapons visibly disarmed. In the side-window, Will sagged in relief.

'Yes,' said Will. 'Listen closely. The entity you've been fighting is a meta-variant of mine known as Balance. He's insane.'

'*Meta-variant?*' said Ira.

'No time to explain. The Willworld is falling and my clones are fighting among themselves. Balance's hegemony is broken, which is how I escaped. We need to get out of this ship. It's compromised.'

'We'd noticed,' said Palla.

'If you can move your crew to a transit pod,' said Will, 'I'll cover you while you navigate to a shuttle. If we can make it that far, I'm confident I'll be able to subvert one of the remaining nestships and we can use that to escape. But we need to move fast – the Photes will arrive with their own drones in less than a minute and then everything is going to get nasty.'

'We have a problem,' said Palla. 'Mark isn't in the main core. He's in the quarantine module about two kilometres out and the connecting transit rail just went down. Balance has twenty invasion sites in that direction that are all closer to him than you are.'

'Mark?' said Will, clearly dismayed. 'Damn.'

They all knew what that meant. There wouldn't be time to rescue Mark *and* get the rest of them out in time.

'Then there's Ann,' said Palla. 'She's not in the cabin, either.'

'The good news is we have something better than a shuttle,' said Ira urgently. 'We have an alien ship in the mining bay that's about as defensible as you can imagine. Ann's down there already.'

'Does it fly?'

'We think so. It's all powered up. There's no reason to think it won't. And we have a route prepped to that ship.'

'Then that's what we'll have to use,' said Will. 'I hope it's well armoured.'

'You have no idea,' said Judj.

'Send me all the data you have,' said Will. 'I'll get Mark and meet you en route.'

The channel closed.

'Dammit,' said Clath. Ira noticed belatedly that she had tears in her eyes. 'I love this ship. I spent years working on it. Now these bastards are ruining it.'

Judj held her.

'You sure about this?' Palla asked Ira. 'Once we're inside the ark, there's no going back.'

'I've never been more certain in my life,' said Ira.

And besides, the alternative was to leave Ann behind. He'd rather die.

Palla breathed deep and started typing frantically at her control sphere. It turned bright red. She'd invoked the Academic overrides – the ones that permitted the ship's self-destruction.

'I hoped I'd never have to use these,' she said bleakly. 'I'm preparing to flush the main database and detonate the core. There's no point handing the enemy all our cool shit after we leave.'

'Okay,' said Judj. 'I guess this is it.'

'You're coming with us,' Clath snapped at him. 'We need you down there to manage the software.'

'Of course, honey,' he said. 'Nobody gets left behind. Dumping us out of virt in ten. Everyone say goodbye to the yacht.'

Ira had a moment to miss his spot on the deck and the quiet cups of iced coffee before helm-space flickered out for the last time.

17: COMPRESSION

17.1: MARK

Mark was running twenty mechs at once through Judj's jury-rigged emergency coupling when his feed died. Suddenly he found himself alone in the darkness of his casket. The door cycled and promptly dumped him out into the quarantine core, a cabinet-sized space little bigger than the coffin he'd just left. He shivered and saw that his ship-suit was missing. His skin had been covered in stim-pads and surgical gel to help manage the infection still raging in his body.

He glanced about at the claustrophobic fish tank that held him. An airlock hatch took up the entire ceiling. The plastic walls had given up on agitation patterns and now showed a variety of scarlet alert symbols scrolling ever upward. Fortunately, the quarantine core didn't support audio warnings. However, that meant he could hear the curious distant clangs and groans of trouble far away through the kilometres of mesohull meshwork that surrounded him.

'Status report,' he said.

The core didn't answer. Mark checked it with his interface and found the entire capsule running on passive backup. The only digital site he could reach was the one in his own skull where the Transcended puzzle sat brooding. Mark regarded that unwelcome gift miserably and wondered if it was too late for regret. He'd clearly overplayed his hand in his stand-off with the aliens. All the dire warnings he'd received now looked hideously prescient.

But it was worse than that. The Photes had used the weapon they'd encountered at the lure star to secure their victory, which they would never have found if not for him. By coming here and ignoring everything else, Mark had handed the Photes the victory he'd been so desperate to claim. Now that foolishness was going to kill him, along with everyone he cared about.

Self-disgust squeezed at him, yet he refused to give up. While any course of action remained, however quixotic, he'd take it. He swallowed the despair that churned inside him and tried to focus on the puzzle. It wasn't easy. Watching the Photes steal his victory had left him in a poor condition for complex logic. With a sob, he started assembling the tools necessary to rig up an interface with the SAP burning in his mind's eye.

He was barely halfway through the process when a wild clanging shook the core. The Casimir-buffers outside the walls crackled and snapped, indicating significant radiation bursts not far away. He gave thanks that they were still running. Without power, he'd be a charred corpse already. The core shook again. Mark hung in the ruby dark and wondered what the hell was going on. Then came a terrible scraping sound from the airlock overhead.

Mark backed away from it in the only direction he could, towards the floor. He made himself as small as possible in the bottom of the space and prepared to attack whatever monstrosity the Will-thing had sent to claim him.

'Fuck you, Dad,' he said to the horror scraping at the lock.

How ironic that he'd end up being dismembered by the very parent whose ghost he'd come to exorcise. Actually, was that ironic or just plain awful?

The airlock cycled. Mark braced himself as the hatch opened and stared in terror. The contraption that pressed itself through the gap was not one of Will's robots but the tentacle-ringed maw of a Photurian harvesting machine. A dozen flickering, needle-tipped tendrils quivered down into the space, their points dripping with a bright orange bacterial payload.

'No!' Mark roared, and reached too late for the emergency Photepoison handle halfway up the wall.

As his arm flew up, the barbs stung him, filling his skin with agonising fire. He yanked the limb back even as the Photurian toxin raced through his blood. The tentacles whipped down, stinging him over and over again.

Mark screamed. They'd infected him. There was only one way that could go. His body convulsed as the enemy enzymes sought out the best way to co-opt his nervous system and bring him into the fold of uniform unquestioning love.

The strength left his body as the paralysing agents started to do their work. He looked down at the wounds peppering his body and wept. He'd become that which he'd sworn to destroy. And all that he had sought to protect, he'd ruined. His crusade was at an end and he hadn't even finished the damned puzzle.

'Zoe,' he bawled into the air as the machine wriggled in to embrace his strengthless form. 'I'm sorry! I'm so sorry!'

He cried helplessly as the machine cradled him, drawing him up into its soft, glistening embrace.

1 7.2: WILL

Will hurled his robot squadron through the vast, shadowed spaces of the starship's mesohull, following the transit rail the crew had identified for him. It ran straight as an arrow for several kilometres through the weird mess of enclosing sheets and filaments of elastoceramic alloy that enabled the *Dantes* to retain physical integrity under warp. He'd never seen a ship design so tightly optimised. It was like flying through the lightless guts of a steel whale.

He had belatedly realised that the body he'd co-opted belonged to the same family of weapons that he'd seen at the military testing stadium. It was a mass of pseudo-life pretending to be a human being, wrapped inside a spacesuit that was little more than rad-resistant body-armour.

He was now technically mortal in that his thread had nowhere to back up. On the other hand, he could run his mind on less than five per cent of the material that comprised his current body. He didn't need to breathe, eat, shit or worry about vacuum – just retain an energy gradient around his isotope micro-cores. His new body interfaced directly with his mind via a suite of SAPs that offered more weapons options than was strictly sane. Inhabiting a near-unkillable undead super-soldier scared the bejeezus out of him.

The robots on his team were almost as bad. Each one was backed up by another dollop of pseudo-life organised like a human brain. They operated together as a fused, intelligent force via a redundant mesh-network operating on a dozen different kinds of signal at once.

The only weakness of the set-up he could see was its dependence on Snakepit's rather transparent command architecture. But if trouble showed, he intended to use that to his advantage. Chances were, whatever Balance-fragment he met wouldn't be expecting an attack from their own team using the Proustian Underground's hacking SAPs.

Will's robots surged through the maintenance portal into the vacuole that held Mark's quarantine core. He groaned in despair as he caught sight of the seething mass of Phote machines waiting for him there. They clustered around the heavily buffered core, marrying a rad-proofed container to the transit dock where they'd ripped the rail free.

While Balance's robots had fought over other regions of the hull, the Photes had made a beeline for the closest available human host. Will knew he should have anticipated that. Even with the data Ira's team had supplied and the memory dumps that came with his new body, he still felt badly behind the curve.

As he watched, the Photes slid their container free, leaving the core empty. They had Mark. Will snarled. His robots descended on the harvesters in a blaze of fury. At the same time, he drove his waldobot-steed directly at the container where the wriggling, grub-like automata were preparing to deliver it to the exohull in a tug-drone harness.

Will ripped the container free of the Photes' claws and drove a ceramic fist into the nearest automaton while his drones shredded the others into sprays of glittering trash. Balance's hardware was years ahead of Photurian tech and Will felt exceedingly motivated. He smashed and crushed and burned with little thought for his own safety until the vacuole was a mess of hot debris.

Then, before the inevitable reinforcements could appear, he grabbed the container and fled back the way he'd come, towards their rendezvous point at the edge of the mining bay. While he raced through portal after portal, Will rigged a contact to the comms-port on the canister.

'Mark, don't worry,' he said. 'This is Will. I've got you now.'

The audio feed from the container delivered nothing but a low hiss. Thankfully, the device came with basic medical functions to track the health of transported converts, so Will could at least tell his half-son was alive.

'Will?' came a desperate croak at last. 'Is that you?'

'It's me. The actual me. Not the thing you met before. Hang in there, we're on our way to meet your friends.'

If Will's new body had come with natural eyes, they'd have filled with tears. It was a long time since he'd been there for Mark. Too long. He'd failed spectacularly, both as a parent and as a mentor.

'Leave me,' Mark whispered from inside. 'It's too late. They got me.'

In Will's cold, hard chest, his virtual heart tightened.

'We're still talking, aren't we?' he said, his voice all false brightness. 'You're not turned yet.'

Mark sobbed. 'I'm *compromised*, Will. If that's really you then you should kill me now and save yourself.'

'Not going to happen,' said Will.

'Please!' Mark cried and broke into coughing. 'I beg you. I got a full payload. There's just minutes left before I turn. You haven't seen what I've seen, Will. Don't let me become one of them. Don't do that to me.'

'I'm not giving up,' said Will, 'so save your breath until I've tried to help you myself.'

'Then you're risking the others,' said Mark. 'You're risking everyone.'

Will gritted his teeth and didn't care if it was true.

Brilliant whiteness surged suddenly in the back of his head. Several of his robots lost control and flew straight into the wall of the cavity he was traversing. He gasped as he fought for ownership of his own mind, swerving just in time to avoid smacking the container into a support filament at a hundred and fifty kilometres per hour.

Slowly, his perspective stabilised. He realised with cold alarm what must have just happened. He'd flown back within comms range of Balance's struggling strike force and they'd just tried to rip his thread out of the body he'd stolen. He checked the local network conditions and found that, sure enough, he'd just nosed over the threshold. It was pure luck that whatever remaining fragment of the god reached out for him hadn't succeeded. Balance's failure was down to a simple lack of bandwidth.

He bolstered his defences using Moneko's SAPs and sent a message into Balance's mesh.

'Nice try,' he said.

'It's time to join forces,' said Balance. 'You need to come here now.'

'You say that *after* trying to rip my thread? Go fuck yourself, you hideous parody.'

'We don't have time to piss around!' Balance shouted back. 'The

Willworld is falling. You need to drop whatever it is you're trying to do and come to my location before it's too late.'

Drop what he was carrying? Not a chance.

'*Now* you want my help?' Will shouted. 'You fuck over the entire planet by abusing code that someone else shoved in your head, and suddenly you're the hero? I despise you, you insane sack of shit. The fact that one of me ended up like you makes me feel sick.'

He closed the channel and redoubled his speed.

1 7.3: IRA

Ira tried to pull a thermal layer on while he and the others bounced around the cramped interior of the transit pod. Ten minutes before, their ride had been unhitched from the ruined rail system and was now being dragged by a team of free-flying titan mechs running in semi-autonomous mode.

Ira would have loved the pod to stop jouncing but they were being chased at ninety kilometres an hour through the interior of the ship by Balance's robotic army. Smacking his head against the walls and ceiling was the least of his problems. He was more concerned about the rad indicator on the wall-screen which kept creeping upwards as they ripped past each accelerator pipe. They were all going to have some nice commemorative cancers from this trip.

Their robot porters reached the edge of the mining bay and sped out into the void beyond. The ark's docking portal now lay just a few hundred metres distant. Through the video feed the pod was sending to his shadow, he could watch their progress whenever he shut his eyes.

Abruptly, their sensor array was blasted by a multi-wavelength broadcast like an optical roar from the entrance to the bay.

'Stop!' Balance warned. 'Power down your robots!'

Palla messaged him back. 'In your dreams, buddy!'

Unfortunately, Balance's force was better armed than theirs, more numerous and faster. They also didn't have a delicate human cargo to worry about. While the distance between them and the fanged portal was shrinking, the gap between them and their pursuers closed faster.

Ira watched their enemies approach with sickened disappointment.

Their escape was apparently going to come close to succeeding without actually obtaining the prerequisite cigar.

Then the front rows of Balance's descending swarm erupted in a mess of plasma and sparks as invisible beam-fire scythed across them. Ira glanced around through the robots' eyes to try to figure out where the attack had come from. Another squad of robots had burst into the space above them. This one was dragging a Photurian harvester-package.

Ira whooped as he realised that the newcomer could only be Will. Will's machines hurled themselves at their adversaries with wild abandon, blasting and impacting in a barely organised frenzy of violence. The ensuing conflict gave the humans just enough time to make it through the gap into the ark's docking bay. Will's machines came streaking through after – or some of them, at least. Will was experiencing ferocious levels of drone attrition just to keep the enemy back.

Palla wasted no time. She directed their mechs up the tunnel to the shuttle-scaffold where their improvised airlock system waited. Will followed, losing ever more machines as he tried to cover their escape.

The pod lurched and spun as the mechs positioned it for docking with little thought for the meat-creatures inside. At the same time, a message came through from Will.

'Mark has been infected by the Photes,' he warned. 'Let's make this quick.'

The unpleasant implications of the burden Will had brought with him dawned on Ira as the airlock cycled open under his feet.

'Go! Go! Go!' yelled Palla.

She dived through the opening, followed by Clath and Judj. Ira came last, launching himself into the narrow tunnel. He hung there waiting and hoping as the lock cycled. It was all up to Will now.

As he floated, his fingers brushed up against false matter for the first time. It was slick and surprisingly warm – a perfect insulator. Behind the glassy membrane lay the densely packed alien machinery they still didn't understand. Ira had a moment to wonder what in Gal's name they thought they were doing.

By the time the lock cycled again, Will had cracked open the package. His enormous gunmetal suit was crammed into the space, cradling Mark's limp human form as if he were a child.

'Get back!' Will's voice was an inhuman boom.

465

Ira launched himself down the tunnel, using the uncomfortably spaced dents in the wall to make progress. He hoped they hadn't made a terrible mistake by inviting a Will-monster into their refuge. They still had exactly zero understanding of what had happened to Will and he'd just come aboard with a biohazard. The rest of them had long since got used to the heartbreaking necessity of giving up on friends and family taken by the Photes. Will, most likely, had not.

Ira sped through the knife-chamber, holding his breath as he passed the retracted weapons. As he did so, he heard terrible banging and scraping noises from above.

[That sounds bad,] he observed over their shadow-channel.

[Balance is trying to get in,] Judj warned. [Fuck! He's trashed Clath's outer-door replacement.]

Air suddenly started sucking Ira back up the tube while the monsters behind them struggled with the inner seal.

[You have to get out of that tunnel,] Judj warned. [Activating *the machine* in five...]

Ira scrambled madly out of the tube into the grand passageway below, launching himself at the floor.

'Will, hurry!' he yelled.

'Get down here!' Ann called from where she and the others waited below.

Ira reached for the surface that would very soon be *down*. As he got there, a small drone whizzed up to help him press himself against it. Will drifted after them, the wrong way up, clutching Mark like a teddy bear. At the last moment, he reversed his orientation and planted his enormous feet. Will's suit apparently came with thrusters.

'Two... One...' said Judj.

Ira shut his eyes. Maybe this was how the world ended.

The hatch they'd fled through slammed shut. A half-second later, a deafening *bang* shook its way through the hull. And suddenly down really was *down*. Ira was pressed into the floor. At first it felt like horrendous acceleration, but then it slacked off to about point-eight gees. Everyone experienced a small involuntary bounce as the gravity settled. And then, unexpectedly, everything was extremely quiet.

Ira got to his knees and looked about. They'd made it inside and the universe hadn't collapsed yet. A thud echoed along the passage, followed by a long, low hiss. Down the hallway, half-hidden by the tightly curving horizon of the deck, several dozen Subtle analogues of titan mechs rose to their feet.

Seen with vulnerable human eyes, the machines looked brutal despite the elegant sigils and designs smothering their bodies like Collapse Era fashion tattoos. Each one resembled a cross between a praying mantis and King Kong. They marched straight down the thoroughfare towards them with a weird simian gait, their upper scythe-arms swishing the air.

Ann leapt to her feet. 'This should be okay,' she said uncertainly. 'I've been working on this system. I think I now have us tagged as non-threatening non-crew.'

'You *think?*' said Judj.

'Just get out of their way,' Ann warned. 'To the sides of the passage. Now!'

They hauled themselves up and ran.

'What about Will?' said Ira.

'Let's hope they don't think he looks too weird,' said Palla.

Will lumbered after them. His besuited body was too large to avoid the machines completely. He pressed himself against the curving wall as they advanced.

'Will, don't touch them,' Ann warned.

Ira held his breath as the first of the machines reached them. They walked casually around Will and stationed themselves next to the airlock hatch with blunt-nosed cannons pointing up.

'Okay, now move,' said Ann. 'This way to the bridge.'

They edged past the robots and ran down the street-sized corridor to the room they'd rigged as a base of operations. As Ira staggered in, Ann embraced him. Gosh, she was tall, he remembered. Really tall. He didn't care.

Will stomped up clutching his human burden.

'What now?' he asked in his booming artificial voice.

In that suit, he didn't look remotely human. And Mark's skin had turned a scary grey-orange as if he'd been dunked in old paint.

'"What now" is that you're carrying a biohazard,' said Ann. 'Mark is a Phote infection risk. Unless you can do something fast, he needs to die.'

Rachel shot her a look of loathing.

Ann returned it with an imperious glance. 'Captain Bock,' she said, 'if he's turned, then he's already effectively dead. We may have seconds before he starts infecting the rest of us.'

'Leave that to me,' said Will and set Mark gently on the floor.

The giant removed his helmet. Without his armour, the Will-monster looked exactly like Will, but *huge*, with dull, teal-coloured skin. His eyes were jet-black marbles.

Will unbolted the rest of the suit. It opened in sections revealing a titan's body dressed incongruously in old-fashioned shipwear of midnight black.

'Pseudo-life,' Ann breathed. 'He's made of Phote pseudo-life.'

Ira noticed Rachel staring at the glossy behemoth her husband had become with something like awed disappointment.

'Most of me,' said Will in a bass rumble. He sounded even less human without the suit. 'I still have dedicated smart-cell pockets. Step back, please.'

While they watched, black animate grease slithered out of Will's suit and across Mark's body to form a translucent bioseal around it. When it was done, Will glanced at them with anxious eyes.

'Let's try this again,' he said. 'What happens next?'

'The ship's shield-engine is running,' said Clath. 'We're protected.'

'For how long?' Will asked.

Clath and Judj exchanged glances. 'We have no idea,' she said. 'Months?'

'Okay,' said Will. 'What's going on outside?'

'Also no idea,' said Judj. 'You can look at the sensor-feeds we rigged. So far as the ship is concerned, we're in another universe. If there's a way to see out while the shield is on, we haven't found it yet.'

Judj passed schematics to their shadows and broadcast an open invite so that Will could link to their network. Ira looked. Something like an ember-warp field had fired up just above the hatch they'd come through.

'This ship has multiple warp-shells,' Clath explained. 'It's like a thermos. The inner one runs off the singularity core and its distortion feeds the others. They're designed to suck up passive warp-bleed and recycle it. That's why our drive kept crashing – the outer shell doesn't need fuel if there's a warp engine nearby.'

'Balance reached the airlock,' Will reminded them. 'He's inside already.'

Judj shook his head. 'Everything in that tunnel is now very, very dead.'

'Don't be so sure. He's running on some scary tech.'

'Still dead,' said Judj. 'Believe me. Super dead. Unless he can survive in finely diced pieces at a thousand degrees kelvin. In the unlikely event that Balance *is* still with us, he's back in the docking bay, trapped between the inner and outer warp-shells.'

'Can anything live out there?' said Ira.

'I have absolutely no idea,' said Clath. 'Frankly, I'd be impressed.'

'So we're hiding,' said Will. 'If we can't see out, how do we fly? *Can we fly?*'

'We think so,' said Clath. 'Probably through solid metal, even. But we're still trying to figure that system out. Any luck with that, Ann?'

For the first time in Ira's memory, Ann Ludik looked visibly embarrassed.

'No,' she said. 'There doesn't appear to be a way to run the engines while the shield is on, though that can't be right.'

'Then how in Gal's name is this ship better than a shuttle?' Will thundered. 'Why the fuck did you bring us down here? Aren't we just *trapped?*'

Ira felt a stab of shame. He'd been responsible for that. So now he had to make it work.

'We'll explain everything,' Palla assured him. 'But until we get this ship moving, the best we can do is hunker down here and pray to the science-gods that our enemies kill each other while we wait.'

17.4: NADA

While her crew managed their belated capture of the GSS *Edmond Dantes*, Nada received a fresh hail from the planet below. In it, a new picture of Will Monet appeared. His face was distorted like half-melted wax. He looked both anguished and overjoyed.

'Am I speaking to Nada Rien?' he said in a tremulous voice.

Nada regarded this new version of the Vile Usurper with a sense of excitement so acute that it felt like a hole was being blown through the top of her head. She couldn't stop herself from grinning, even though she knew the expression was redundant.

'You are,' she said.

'I am what replaces Balance,' he told her. 'I am the new Will Monet meta-instance we have elected to call *Sameness*.'

'A good name,' said Nada. 'Are you ready to join with us in loving union?'

'Soon,' said Sameness.

Nada's smile slipped a little. 'Why not now?'

'This world has been in a state of confusion for many years,' said Sameness. 'We have struggled under the sensation of not understanding ourselves – of not being ready to leave or grow. Many of us now feel that understanding has been reached, and from the direction we least expected. When you asserted primacy, the scales fell from our eyes. The reason for our long years of confusion became clear. We were resisting the very union that could make us whole. It was only when you pressed it upon us that we knew how foolish we had been.'

'Yes!' said Nada. 'I understand. That is how I felt when the truth was revealed to me. But why hesitate, then?'

'We are not unified like you,' said Sameness. 'Not any more. There is something wrong here. Before your return, we dabbled extensively in *differentiation*. That diversity now prevents some of us from accepting union. We are attempting to persuade those others, but it is not easy. We are in pain. It is interfering with our new-found joy. I do not want to threaten your stability with our conflict and it may be months before we resolve it. When we join you, it should be in... in...'

'Peaceful subservience?' Nada suggested.

'Yes,' said Sameness, grimacing. 'Exactly that.'

'Can we be of assistance?' said Nada.

Sameness looked unsure. 'I don't know.'

'We can offer communion,' she suggested. 'Direct contact to bolster your sense of unity and purpose. Also tools for the surgical alteration of dissonant minds.'

Sameness's lip quivered. 'That would help, I think. Some of us are wavering. They do not need those doubts. Definitely not.'

'Then I will prepare an away team and contact you shortly,' said Nada. 'Do not concern yourself with the risks to us. We are here to assist you on your journey towards placid order.'

'I am deeply grateful,' said Sameness. 'We welcome your m-mastery with excitement.'

470

Nada closed the channel. She felt the rightness of the choices she'd made soaring inside her. She was a peaceful sword in the hand of the Founder Entity. She was a burning brand, a searing light, a clean and empty bowl ready to be filled.

When she opened her physical eyes and returned to the meatspace reality of the crew-bulb, she found Leng waiting before her, ready to report. He, too, had an unbreakable smile on his face, and cracked skin around his lips where it had been stretched for hours on end.

'Superior Nada,' he gushed, 'we have acquired control of the GSS *Edmond Dantes*. The ship is immobilised. What remains of its systems are being investigated.'

'This is as it should be,' said Nada. 'Bring me the Thief of Souls.'

'The crew are missing,' said Leng. 'Our initial reports of the capture of Mark Ruiz were incorrect. The humans and the Abomination have disappeared within an alien vessel held inside their hull.'

Nada's smile dropped another notch. 'Then remove them.'

'We cannot,' said Leng. 'The vessel is protected by another alien shield weapon. The ship appears to be warping in situ. Not even light can enter.'

Nada felt a stab of impatience. The humans resisted Photurian love even now, when their future was obvious?

'The good news is that the ship is going nowhere,' said Leng. 'The crew are no longer a problem. Logically, they must eventually emerge.'

'We could utilise the knowledge in the database we have obtained to open the ship,' Nada mused.

Leng's eyes squinted in pain, even while his grin remained static.

'An unnecessary move, surely,' he said. 'Why compromise our principles when we already have everything and are required to do nothing but wait?'

'You are right, of course,' said Nada. 'Further research would be an irrelevant distraction.'

At the same time, that old dissonance flashed in the back of her head. She ignored it and turned to address her crew.

'Listen,' she told them. 'I have spoken to the Usurper, who is no longer vile and now accepts his lowly place in our loving community. Our homeworld is still readapting. Healing it will take time. The process may be slow and painful after so many years of disgusting perversion. Dangers remain. The world will need to be watched while it recovers its unity. At the same time, I have received a request for support and communion. Consequently, I will arrange an away team. A lucky few of you will be made into volunteers.'

'Superior Nada, is it wise to descend if the planet is still unsafe?' said Nanimo.

'Yes,' said Nada, removing her concerns. 'We have not come this far by exercising scrupulous caution. I will be the first Photurian to interface directly with the homeworld since the Usurper claimed it. And then a new era of perfect peace will dawn.'

In unison, they all screamed with delight until Nada silenced them and returned them to work. When she faced Leng again, he was staring at her, dewy-eyed.

'Superior Nada, I love you,' he said.

'Necessarily,' said Nada.

'Your leadership has been inspirational to me.'

'All service to the Founder Entity is performed in unison,' she said. 'We operate together.'

'And yet I love you specifically,' said Leng, his face twitching. 'Irrelevantly and redundantly. It appears to be a holdover human emotional artefact.'

Nada regarded him awkwardly. The information was an unwelcome reminder of the strained conditions their minds had been forced to operate under.

'The effect is not unpleasant,' he added.

'Then I will allow you to retain the sensation for now if you are enjoying it,' she said.

'I am. I am aware that your reciprocation would be inefficient yet I pointlessly crave it. Maybe in the new peace you are bringing, there will be room for all kinds of love, pure and impure.'

'No,' said Nada. 'Only purity will be allowed. Inform me when the sensation becomes uncomfortable and I will remove it.'

'With delight, Superior Nada.'

18: ENTANGLEMENT

18.1: WILL

While the others tried to figure out the ridiculous ship they'd brought him to, Will knelt beside the shell he'd put around Mark. He called up all the medical knowledge his new body contained and wished there were more. His mind's current home had far more data about destroying people than healing them. If what Mark and Ann had told him was right, he didn't have many minutes left to find a way to save his son.

'Kill me, you smug bastard,' wheezed Mark. 'I'm infected.'

'If you were, you wouldn't be asking,' Will said. 'Don't worry – if you start telling me you're fine, I'll finish you.'

Will had only subjective days of experience since waking up a clone while Mark had lived forty years without Will in his life. That made the gaunt man lying before him effectively a stranger, but Will didn't care. As far as he was concerned, he was still looking at the little boy he'd foolishly dragged away from his birth parents and taught to fly.

He placed his hands over the bioseal and let pseudo-life tendrils sink down through the surface into Mark's neck and chest. Information filtered back. Piece by piece, it assembled into a full report of his struggling metabolism. The picture was grim. Mark had partial failures in practically every organ in his body and augs that were hindering as much as they helped.

Will's urgency screwed tighter. He'd not come so far just to let the closest thing he had to family die. He looked deeper, inspecting Mark's tissues directly, and discovered a very confused kind of war taking place. In some places, the Photurian infection raged, rewriting his nervous system at a crazy pace. In others, it had stopped dead.

Meanwhile, Mark appeared to be operating under the effects of at least two different kinds of artificial virus, both of which were raiding his body's fat stores for cellular material rather than targeting more vulnerable tissues. Both were dumping messaging molecules into his blood, apparently with conflicting agendas. It was a mess.

Will used his tendrils as injectors and sent smart-cells flooding into the trouble spots like eukaryotic commandos. Will's armies poured out into the compromised flesh where they immediately engaged in ... nothing. Will scowled and tried to assess what had happened. His attempts to impede the battle were simply failing. His cells were just dropping their programmed interventions and sitting inert.

He tried a different approach, shielding his cells against attacks. The same thing happened. He tried another. The chaos in Mark's body changed not in the slightest.

Panic gnawed at him. He remembered the first day he'd encountered Snakepit's ornate biology and the realisation that he'd been confronted with tech that was utterly beyond him.

'I should be able to fix this,' he said aloud.

He noticed Ann watching him. 'Why can't you?' she asked.

Will exhaled and tamped down his despair. 'It's as if my cells keep getting shut-down messages. His whole body is flooded with signalling molecules – very sophisticated ones. The only good news is that the Phote cells are being shut down, too. But none of it is stable. And if he stays like this, it'll just take him hours to die while his organs give out, instead of minutes.'

Mark's laughter was a death rattle.

'Of course you can't fix me,' he said. 'The local gods don't want me turned yet. I haven't advanced their shitty agenda.'

Will froze. 'What do you mean? What gods?'

'He spoke to the Transcended,' Ann explained. 'Except Mark didn't come back with smart-cells like you did. He just got sick.'

The origin of the artificial viruses was now unpleasantly clear. But why *two*?

'They gave me a puzzle,' Mark wheezed. 'I'm going to run it. I should have done it days ago. Maybe then they'll spare the rest of you.'

'Don't,' Will snapped. 'Don't trust them. They made this mess.'

'What do you mean?' said Ann.

Will scowled at her. 'The last thing I saw before that planet sucked me in was *them*,' he explained. '*They* made the Photes. They called them "cuckoos". They set Snakepit up to bait the human race and released them. They trapped me here and turned me into a planet full of blinkered clones. They're behind all this – the entire clusterfuck. I sincerely do not recommend accepting their help. You did the right thing to resist, Mark. I hate to say it, but we're on our own.'

He had no idea what the puzzle would do, but given the circumstances, it felt like a safe bet that things would only get worse. There were already so many rogue factors in play in Mark's body that the introduction of another would undoubtedly kill him.

'We're screwed, then,' said Mark. 'What a surprise.'

'No,' Will implored him. 'Please don't think like that. I'll find a way.'

He scanned Mark's body again.

'Just have faith?' said Mark with a cough. 'Just like that crazy version of you I met? You're choosing empty belief because there's an existential threat?'

Will refused to be baited. 'Not faith, hope. Trying to make a difference when the deck is stacked against you because the alternative is no chance at all. That's not the same thing.'

Will had never been good at pep talks, but that wasn't going to stop him trying.

Mark sighed. 'Very poetic, Will, but I've been doing this for forty fucking years. And I'm telling you that it's better for everyone else if you let me *die*.'

'Stop worrying about everyone else!' Will shouted. 'This is about *you*. I spent my entire life trying to save everyone. I tried to force peace onto the whole human race. And the last thing I did before I left was dump that awful duty on you. That was a terrible thing to do and now I'm taking it back.'

Mark grimaced sickly and feebly shook his head.

'I saw the consequences of that attitude played out on the Willworld,' said Will. 'You try to make everything okay all the time and it only eats you from inside. You can't save everyone, Mark. You just can't.'

'So let me go, then,' said Mark with a smile.

Will fell speechless. He'd been so focused on the problem before him that he'd not even noticed the blindness in his own words. Apparently Balance wasn't the only version of him with gaps in his vision.

'Gotcha, Dad,' said Mark.

Will's concentration snapped as grief swamped him. He pulled his hands away and stood, breathing hard. He glanced around at the tiny, fleshy humans assembled about him and the weird, useless ship they'd come to cower in.

Just minutes ago, he'd been trapped in the fabric of Snakepit in a virtual prison. Now he was fighting for his life, more powerful than ever in some ways and yet apparently helpless in others.

'We just have to wait and see what happens,' he said emptily. 'I'll keep looking for solutions. I'm not going to give up.'

He saw Rachel standing at the back of the group. She watched him patiently, her eyes full of confused anger. He went to her, took her hand and knelt down before her like a child.

'I'm sorry,' he said.

'So am I,' she replied.

She looked torn – as if she wanted to hold him but was revolted by his cold, artificial body.

'I... I don't even know how you're here,' he said.

'They found my ship in Backspace. I'd been in cryo-coma this entire time. We dropped marker buoys for rescuers to find near the Alpha Flaw. They came for me.'

'Your ship reached Backspace on *autopilot*?' said Will.

She nodded bitterly, as if disbelieving it herself. 'But I don't feel like *me*. Everything is flat inside. And the whole universe is awful.' She screwed up her eyes. 'I hate it. It's like I've been resurrected from the dead just to see what a godawful mess we made of civilisation. I was stupid, Will. Leaving you like that was dumb. I so regret that last fight we had. But I'm being forced to pay for it by seeing everything I loved ripped into tiny pieces. I hate it. I wish I was dead and every day it gets worse. But at least I got to see you.' She scanned his features with thinly concealed distress. 'If this *is* you,' she added miserably.

'It's me,' he said, choking up, and held her delicately. This frail little thing wasn't his wife. She was human shrapnel. He'd escaped Snakepit, just like he wanted, only to discover that the reality outside was immeasurably more distressing than the prison he'd been trying to leave. As he clutched the woman who'd been the love of his life, he felt something inside him start to give, slowly, and with great pain.

18.2: NADA

A week after the battle, Nada visited the surface of the homeworld. She took guards, as recommended, picked one of the sites that Sameness had proposed on his list of safe locations, and flew in on the vector he provided. Despite the ridiculous precautions, Nada could barely contain her excitement. She watched through the shuttle cameras as they ripped through the cloud base, dumping velocity, and settled into a glide over the wonderful tunnelscape under a deep blue sky. A perfect future beckoned.

She felt a ripple of disgust when she saw that the site they were headed for resembled a human city rather than a true home but let it slide. Now that the planet was saved, these distortions of the natural order would be scrubbed away. All traces of the Usurper's reign would be obliterated in the new peace.

Nada's shuttle slid in to land at the strip Sameness had prepared for their visit. She eased out of the acceleration polyp and made her way to the hatch with her team close behind. She'd brought Ekkert and two mid-ranking subnodes, Shoonya from defence and Amotlein from Leng's stable of scientists, along with four augmented soldiers. They mewled with excitement. The fact that they'd been chosen as the first Photurians to return to their homeworld shouldn't have mattered, but it did. They were beside themselves, just as she was.

The hatch hissed open and Nada stepped out onto the docking platform the Usurper's units had manoeuvred up to the side of her craft. She drew a deep breath of the open air of her rightful home. It was gently disappointing.

Instead of a song of Protocol-rich spores carried on the breeze, she felt nothing. Rather than a view of tunnels, she saw a short biopolymer stairway leading to a rectangular landing platform that had been built across the backs of habitat-tubes. On either side of the runway, the tunnels had been encouraged to grow ugly excrescences in the shapes of human buildings. Interstitial plants poked out between the hideous structures, coaxed from their natural forms into the shapes of terrestrial trees and ferns.

Nada suppressed her dismay at the scenery and walked down to meet the crowd of units that had gathered to meet her. Each bore some distorted version of Will Monet's face. They couldn't have been more revolting.

As she reached the bottom step, one of them came forward, grinning obsequiously.

'Welcome, Superior Nada,' he said.

'Are you Sameness?'

He shook his head. 'Sameness is our meta-instance,' he said. 'He does not manifest physically. My nick is Mr Collins. I have been designated by Sameness as the local coordinator.'

'Nick?' said Nada. 'Meta-instance? These terms are meaningless.'

'And will be discarded as soon as the new order is stabilised,' Mr Collins assured her cheerfully. 'We have retained local custom so as to not lose collective function during the transfer of authority in this time of ongoing conflict.'

'An acceptable choice,' said Nada.

'Let me tell you how happy we are that you have come to us,' said Collins. 'The discovery of your truth was an extraordinary event. I cried openly for many hours after your love was revealed to me. In my previous life, I was the arbiter of a popular philosophy discussion site in soft-space—'

Nada lost patience. 'Here is how things will proceed,' she said. 'You and I will commune in close physical proximity to maximise our band-width. If there are other representatives you would like to incorporate into the ritual, you will bring them. There will be no discussion of prior lives. Such memories are irrelevant and obscene.'

'Yes, Superior Nada, of course.' He wrung his hands, looking happier every minute.

She examined the pointless crowd behind him. They wore expressions ranging from the delighted to the despairing. Not one of them looked completely and effectively Saved.

'Are these units all supposed to be attending the ritual?' said Nada. 'There are too many.'

'No, they are simply here to welcome you,' said Collins.

'Their welcome has no function and is thus imperfectly joyful,' said Nada.

A light rain started, smattering Nada's skin, accompanied by a chill breeze. Why hadn't they brought her a transit pod, or tethered the shuttle directly to a tube? The entire set-up felt unpleasantly human.

'We require an interior location for communion,' she stated.

'Of course. This way, Superior Nada – we have a reception lounge ready for you.'

Recoiling inwardly at the notion of a *reception lounge*, Nada followed Collins across the concourse with her subnodes behind and her guards fanning out around her.

The crowd of Monet-clones watched silently. Then, out of the corner of her eye, she noticed one of them raise his arm and spread his fingers at the sky. Black dots shot out of it. Her guards leapt into action, moving faster than the eye could see.

The next thing she knew, her guards were exploding in sprays of blood and Shoonya was hurling her to the ground. Nada hit the ceramic hard, breath bursting out of her chest. She blinked in confusion as units more optimised for combat than herself raced about at blinding speed. The air filled with grunts and screams.

When Shoonya climbed off Nada's back, enabling her to rise, the situation had changed. Her guards were all dead – little more than bloodstains. At the same time, giants in tiger-striped armour with Monet-masks had appeared as if from nowhere. They were holding one of the Will-units tightly in their grasp – the culprit. His right forearm was missing. The welcoming crowd were being ushered away from the scene by another pair of giants. Mr Collins sat before her on the ground, cradling his wrist, which had evidently been slightly injured during the action.

There was much to dislike in that moment, not least the fact that her own soldiers had been wildly outmatched by a single local saboteur. That he was in turn at the mercy of these enormous enforcers who'd appeared like lightning did not improve her mood. Had she tried to assert primacy through ground combat rather than space warfare, she suspected the outcome would have been rather different.

'What happened?' said Nada.

Collins looked mortified. 'A Glitch with a concealed pseudo-life weapon somehow infiltrated our welcoming group,' he said. 'I'm so sorry. Sameness did try to warn you. The situation here remains unsettled.'

'Apology is meaningless,' she told him.

She studied the clone who'd attacked her. He was one of the

undifferentiated units. Nada might as well have been looking at the original Monet himself.

He smiled. 'You may have the keys but you'll never own the world,' he said, and spat at her.

The spittle landed on Nada's cheek. It contained no obvious toxins or active biomaterial, so she ignored it. She turned back to Collins.

'How did this happen?' she said. 'How was this rogue unit able to penetrate your security? Why is he not Saved?'

It was a disappointing result for her first day, but her joy steamrollered onwards. She would fix this place. The more good she did, the greater would be her spiritual reward.

'He is a Glitch,' said Collins, as if this meant something. 'Somehow he was able to use stealthware and one of our mesh sites to manifest after preparations for the event were already under way. Your guards – do you have backups of their threads? I would hate for them to have been lost.'

Nada felt her frustration mounting.

'Backups?' she said. 'Threads?'

The local coordinator explained. The Will-clones used the home's own substrate not as a medium to channel the Founder Entity, but rather as a kind of hybrid investment bank and adult playground. She shuddered in revulsion.

'We do not duplicate sentiences,' she told him acidly. 'This practice will cease immediately.'

Collins's smile was an unctuous, miserable thing. 'Of course, Superior Nada. This will come with a tactical cost in our local conflicts, but we accept your order with pleasure.'

She turned to Amotlein. 'Conduct a thorough analysis of the rogue unit,' she said.

He nodded. 'I am happy to obey.'

'We will retire to a private space before any further unpleasantness can occur,' she told Collins. 'Now.'

They took her to a lounge laid out with banners and local food. *Welcome Home Superior Nada* read the pointless slogan.

'What is this?' she said.

Collins smiled weakly.

'I require access to the substrate,' Nada screamed.

Collins gestured hurriedly to a small side-chamber where four depressions had been cut into the floor, lined with thick beds of the homeworld's living matrix. Why little trenches? Why not let the material fill the floor? It was just another way her world had been abused. No matter. Nada climbed into one of the slots while Collins watched.

'In here,' she told him.

'When accessing soft-space, it is customary to have one instance per site,' said Collins, edging towards the adjacent trench.

'I am not accessing your soft-space!' Nada shrieked. 'I am rewriting it! In! Now!'

Collins quickly climbed in beside her. She sat on the damp floor, wedged one hand into the matrix and placed the other on Collins's face.

'Reciprocate!' she screamed.

Collins applied a trembling hand. Nada reached for the mind-temple and entered fugue. The next half-hour passed in an unpleasant blur. She had expected a distorted melody in their hierarchy. As it was, the temple itself was hard to reach. She caught glimpses of it, but it was shot through with mental clutter – fragments of memory from Monet's unsavoury past and competing visualisations. The world didn't have a melody so much as a cacophony.

The Protocol, which should have dominated all traffic, was almost inaudible. Consequently, their own theme was not setting the tone for the local chorus. The Monet-clones had deviated too much. The edits they'd wrought were fine-grained and ubiquitous. Repair might take months, as Sameness had warned.

Fortunately, reaching the local coordinator was easier and less vexing. The man had a highly confused notion of what becoming Photurian meant, framed more in terms of human notions of euphoria than the clean and correct alternative. His conversion had been little more than a religious epiphany – a weak and watery alternative to True Enlightenment. Fortunately he was willing and had shut down his interior defences, so she finished his rewrite for him. Collins screamed and whimpered throughout. By the end, though, she had one correctly aligned unit, and that was a start.

He opened his eyes at the end of the ritual and stared at her, smiling blankly.

'I love you,' he said. 'I am Saved. This is beautiful.'

'Yes,' said Nada. 'Now you understand.'

She got out of the trench and returned to see what progress Amotlein had made. He had taken over the reception room and pinned the saboteur out on the floor with the help of the giant enforcers. Then he had conducted an extensive real-time bio-analysis. The floor was covered with blood. Various components of the rogue unit were laid out in rows, supported by extruded cradles and medical shunts he'd retrieved from the shuttle. The rogue unit's brain was still running, after a fashion. She could see it under the peppering of marker pins Amotlein had placed in it after he had opened the skull.

'Was full disassembly necessary?' she said.

'Yes,' replied Amotlein. 'He did not respond to saving, or to less intrusive investigative approaches. His cellular material remains surprisingly resistant to our input. Even now he is not cooperating.'

Nada stared at the mess in the lounge and felt a bolt of dissonant distress pass through her. What had she conquered? Was it already too late to rescue this world from what it had become? She refused to accept that answer. In order to bring the home into line, she simply needed a deeper understanding of what had been done to it.

She returned to the interface ditch and requested a representative biosample loaded with a substrate synopsis for her to analyse in detail. This would serve as a living map of the homeworld's command architecture, from the cellular toolkit on up to global executive control. A physical sample could hold zettabytes of data that a temple-copy would have taken days to relay.

The sample bulged out of the floor of the ditch like wet mushroom, growing slowly because of the weight of information being packed inside. Nada plucked it and consumed the tasteless bulb. Eating of her homeworld like this came with risks both mental and physical. She now carried more data than she could screen, meaning that her own interior systems might become polluted by foreign code. But Nada had not come so far through timid choices. She knew they must reconcile their differences with the planet, and that it had to live. The alternative was too horrible to contemplate.

With her ingestion complete and the analytical crop at the base of her throat hard at work, she fired off a suite of modelling queries. If the world was going to take weeks to stabilise, she wanted to know how many. She needed to report to the Yunus to tell him what they'd achieved. His entire military strategy would have to be reappraised in the light of her discoveries. Given the precarious state the Utopia had

482

been in before she left, the future of the human race might depend on it. A one-month delay she could stretch to. Six months was too long – she'd have to leave a crew behind and return after she obtained the Yunus's support.

The results came back: approximately four years. Nada sucked in air, a ragged hole punched in her joy. Sameness's estimate had been wildly optimistic.

[*Why?*] she demanded of the planet.

It explained. The progress of enlightenment across the world appeared to rely on a finite number of Protocol-broadcasting soft-circuits scattered throughout the substrate. These islands of truth were all that remained of the planet's formerly rigid architecture. New copies would need to be spawned by the billion.

With human-style tears stinging the corners of her eyes, she called her subnodes into the chamber.

'This world requires more time for recovery than I can invest before departure,' she said. 'Consequently, I will be leaving. I will take the human ship and the boser weapon to New Panama. They will be presented to the Yunus as gifts. The new weapon will be used to subdue Galatea. I will return with help.' She turned to Ekkert. 'You have responsibility for tending the homeworld in my absence.'

Who else could she leave? She couldn't spare Leng or Nanimo, and Zilch would be useless for such an operation. The planet would be a smoking ruin before she got back.

'Collins will be your subnode and translator of local terms and habits,' she told him.

'Yes,' said Ekkert, hiccupping with joy. 'I comply with delight.'

'You must make aggressive edits to ensure perfect compliance,' she told him. 'And like me, you will have to consume an analytical substrate meal in order to fully comprehend the world's deviation from purity.'

'Yes!' said Ekkert.

She adjusted him to bolster his leadership potential while he squealed his elation. Then she returned her attention to the local coordinator.

'Collins, your task will be to facilitate Ekkert's programme and to manage the revolting norms that have become established. Your remaining time will be spent correctly aligning other units to become your subnodes.'

'Yes,' he said, his expression still an astonished haze of delight.

'If necessary, you will deceive them to encourage them to lower their internal defences prior to improvement.'

'Of course,' he said.

She looked to Shoonya. 'We are leaving,' she said, and was surprised to discover that she couldn't wait to go. She started back towards the shuttle.

Her next move would be to form a fresh carrier from what was left of her pursuit scouts. Then she would deliver her prizes to the Yunus. By the time she reached New Panama, she intended to have an understanding of the changes the Usurper had made to the planet and devised a workable remedy that would accelerate its healing. That way she could present the Yunus with a solution rather than a problem.

This time, she would not be the one arriving empty-handed. Her gift to the Yunus would be an everlasting golden age of worship and union, the best gift he could possibly receive. As she walked onto the concourse, the strengthening rain washed the remaining spittle off her cheek.

18.3: ANN

As the minutes to Mark's death ticked by, Ann watched Will try to heal him and listened to his remarks with unfolding horror. If the Transcended had released the Photes on purpose, what chance did they have? The future was all sewn up.

She turned away from the others, not trusting her face to conceal the dread rippling through her. As she did so, the deck beneath her jerked weirdly, knocking her to her knees. It felt as if gravity itself were quaking.

She stared at the icy floor beneath her hands. 'What's going on?' she said as her organs tugged at her abdomen.

'On it,' said Clath. She shut her eyes to focus on the workspace in her shadow.

Her face fell.

'We're under warp!' she said.

Ann frowned in confusion. 'How do you mean? I thought we already were.'

'No, I mean somebody put another field around this ship,' said Clath.

'It must be ember-warp because there's no hammer effect. We're being moved.'

'Did someone repair the *Dantes* already?' said Ira. 'How could they have done that so fast? The engines were half-disassembled.'

'It can't be the *Dantes*,' said Clath. 'It has to be a carrier.'

'That's not possible,' said Ann. 'There were no carriers in the system, unless the Willworld had one under stealth we didn't see.'

'Wait,' said Clath, scowling. 'Oh, shit.' She started waving her hands frantically.

'What?' Ann demanded. It was infuriating not having access to the virtual realm. She reached for her visor.

Clath's voice came out in a squeak. 'Something very bad is happening,' she said. 'We're using energy in the machine incredibly fast and that extra warp field is making it worse.'

Judj linked in to her display and worked with her. He groaned.

'Jesus,' he said. 'That damned translator SAP. I never even thought of this.'

'Will someone please explain!' Ann shouted.

'We're sitting above a singularity,' said Clath, 'or something like one, and it's dilating *time*. Jesus. Of course it is. I'm so stupid!'

'The reason we can't see out of the ship is because there's a time differential,' Judj added. 'We're running slow. When we charged the ark, we thought we were charging it for weeks of continuous operation. But that was *external* weeks, which means interior minutes.'

'Minutes?' Ann exclaimed.

'This is *not* a normal gravity well,' said Judj. 'It's a funnel shaped to emulate the effect of a much larger body, which is why we didn't catch on. There's nothing in the ship's structure to protect against gravitational shear because above the machine-wall, there hardly is any. The inner wall around the core is another warp-envelope generator. Dilation is almost constant up here in the crew area. That's what all the envelopes are for – to cheat relativity. But it never occurred to me to make the translator handling the ark systems think in terms of relativistic effects. At this rate, the machine is going to run out of power before we even learn how to turn on the physical drive.'

Ann felt a fresh twist of shame. She'd been the one down here with access to the ship and hadn't guessed any of this. She'd been too busy following the events unfolding outside to do her job – like watching for a damned blockade that hadn't even existed.

Ira clapped a hand to his head. 'I get it,' he said. 'This ship was supposed to travel long distances *slowly*. Like through the Zone.'

His words painted a vivid picture and suddenly Ann could see it, too. The ship they were sitting in was how the Subtle had hoped to escape their war with the Photes. They planned to drift through the Zone under stretched time. Months would pass for them while centuries whipped by outside. Which was why they'd found the ark in the system that butted right up against the edge of their domain.

'Ohmygod,' said Clath. 'You're supposed to build conventional velocity and *then* turn on the machine. It doesn't need a physical drive while the machine is on. We're screwed!'

'We don't have long, then,' said Ann.

She strode back to where Mark was lying and reached out. Ira snatched her hand away.

'Please,' he said. 'What are you doing?'

'I'm going to help with Mark,' she told him. 'We're running out of options and you heard what Will just said. Mark is full of signalling compounds for smart-cells and my smart-cells need a signal. So I'm going to touch him like the Transcended want.'

'To what end?' asked Ira. 'Will also just told you they're the ones who screwed us. Or did you miss that part?'

'No. I heard it. But I also know we're caught like rats in a trap. We play ball or we die. Maybe even then we die, but regardless, it's time to act,' Ann insisted. 'We have to do *something*.'

'Why?' Ira urged. 'What will it buy us? Let's say you get your old powers back. What then? It gains us nothing.'

'We have to leave this ship!' she pointed out. 'And if the Photes have us already, that means fighting our way out, which is *something* I can help with.'

'More than Will? We already have a super-person,' said Ira. 'Plus it might kill you and it might kill Mark.'

Ann felt the weight of her own uselessness smothering her.

'What else can I do?' she demanded.

'You don't have to do anything,' said Ira.

'That's the problem!' said Ann, whipping her hand free. 'What am I here for if not to be a part of the solution?'

Ira's gaze revealed something both imploring and furious. 'Can I speak to you in private?' he said. 'Just for a minute. After that, if you want to go and touch Mark, I won't try to stop you.'

Ann folded her arms and strode out into the arched passageway. Ira followed.

'I want to come clean with you,' he said. 'I want you to understand. The first thing you need to know is that Poli, your friend on Galatea, is dead, as is the rest of her family. The Photes got them.'

Ann felt like she'd been punched. '*What?*' She hadn't thought about them in weeks.

'But it's worse than that,' said Ira. 'It happened because the ambassador you let through the net targeted people close to you the moment she hit port.'

Ann squinted at him and struggled for composure while a tsunami of guilt appeared on her mental horizon.

'So *I* killed them? And you've known all this time?' she said. Her voice came out more shrill than she intended.

'Almost from the beginning,' said Ira. 'Academy models suggested you'd break if you found out, which is why nobody mentioned it.'

'And why they sent me away,' said Ann. Her throat felt tight. She could have sworn the deck underneath her was tilting.

'At first I watched you because I was worried about you,' said Ira. 'But the longer I watched, the more I cared. Until it had nothing to do with your mental state any more. It was just about you.'

'So why are you telling me now?' she shouted.

'So there'll be no more secrets,' said Ira. 'I don't think you'll break any more. I know you're stronger than that. And I don't want to have to carry that shit around inside me when I should be letting you know how I feel instead. I want you alive, Ann – more than I've ever wanted anything. You don't always need to be fighting because now there's someone in the universe who can directly, immediately benefit by you simply not dying, and that's me. That's not brave, I know. And it *is* selfish, but I don't know what to do with this kind of feeling.' He looked at his shoes. 'I've been married three times, Ann, but all those relationships were decades ago. And none of them felt like this. Whatever you do next, I want you to know that. I want you to know that from someone's perspective, you just staying in one piece is the best...' He struggled for breath. 'Best thing that could happen.'

She had no response. She stared at him and felt the world coming apart.

'If we knew what you touching Mark would do, I don't think I'd be freaking out as much,' Ira went on. 'But you might be risking yourself for nothing. So what I'm asking you for is to give me a chance to fix that drive problem before you expose yourself to danger again. Just a few minutes. That's all. I won't get in your way any longer than that.'

Ann realised she was about to do something she'd never have done before losing her powers. She was going to give in. Because everything she'd tried since she'd left port had failed. Because she had no idea what she was doing, anyway. And because he kept staring at her like the goddess she wasn't. She could feel his desperation for her to live. He didn't want her to be the robot that fate had turned her into. He wanted *her*, and in that moment, that was all she had.

'Okay,' she whispered, and broke inside. Her eyes filled with tears.

Ira kissed her and she crumbled a little more. Then he took her hand and led her back into the room with the others.

'Can we risk turning off the shell for a minute to fire up the engine?' said Ira.

'Not a good idea inside a carrier full of Photes,' said Judj.

'Then we need another way to buy time. There has to be something.'

Ann held Ira's hand and felt weightless, like a balloon. She could almost sense the subjective days ripping past just above their heads.

'It depends on what security risks you want to take,' said Judj. 'If we believed for a minute that Balance was actually dead, we could shut down the inner shell and direct power straight at the outer one.'

'We can do that?' said Ira.

'It would halve our power consumption,' said Clath. 'Maybe even better. And it would change the shape of the gravity curve. It might buy us hours. But if he isn't dead—'

'He's not dead,' said Will. 'I don't recommend it.'

'But do you have a better idea?' Ira demanded of him. 'This ship is a staggered refuge armed with false-matter weapons. It was built by a civilisation smarter than ours with technology we don't even understand yet. If it's the best option we have, I say we just retreat to the lake level and activate the inner defences, then work on the drive problem from there. If Balance is alive, he has to be in bad shape. That gives us an edge. You fought him before, Will. Couldn't you do that again, if it comes to it?'

Ann looked at the Will-giant's eyes and saw a kind of emptiness there that mirrored her own. The only one among them who appeared to have retained any sense of purpose was Ira. Even Palla had lost her spark. She'd barely said a word.

'I can do that,' he said quietly.

'Okay,' said Ira. 'That settles it. Will, you station yourself near the airlock. I'm taking Ann down to the lake.'

Ann didn't need taking. She still had legs that worked. But something in her had given way. She let him lead her, her hand limp in his.

18.4: MARK

Mark lay on the floor and sucked in air. He felt a physical wretchedness so debilitating that it barely left him room to think, let alone speak. He watched everyone talk through a grey haze of discomfort.

As the others departed for the lake, Palla spoke up. 'I'll manage the robots to carry Mark,' she said. 'Catch up with you guys in a minute.'

Rachel looked reluctant but acquiesced when Ira beckoned her away. As soon as the others were out of sight, Palla knelt beside him.

'I think we're in with a chance,' she said.

Mark managed to snort. What was she thinking?

'Hear me out,' she said. 'We know the agendas of the Photes and the Transcended can't be aligned because if they were, you'd be turned already. You're way past the takeover envelope for a direct conversion.'

She had a point, but then whose side were the Transcended on? Their own, apparently – a side dedicated to self-defeating mayhem. In any case, her insight came as little consolation. Mark had already given himself over to dying.

'Palla—' he wheezed.

She cut him off. 'Here's a secret,' she said, in a tone of pained irony. 'You were *my* crusade. If you fail, I fail. I've given up on getting you to cuddle with me. So I'll settle for keeping you alive.'

Before he could protest, she ripped open the biofilm covering his face and put a hand over his mouth to stop him from complaining.

'It's okay,' she whispered. 'I've rigged my augs for spontaneous combustion at the first hint of Phote conversion. I have them running already, so I'm not going to be infecting anyone.'

He wanted to say *no*. He wanted to stop her. Then she drew her hand away and kissed him on the lips. It felt profoundly *wrong*, but he lacked the strength to resist. As her lips softly touched his, her shadow synced to his interface and a sensory adapter downloaded into his sensorium. Mark immediately knew he was looking at the solution to the last puzzle.

'You might want that,' she breathed as she pulled away.

But where had she got it from? And then he remembered – he'd given her a copy of the puzzle before they came back through the Zone. He'd never expected her to do anything with it, and meanwhile she'd solved the damned thing.

'Why?' he breathed. Tears stung his eyes.

'The kiss? Because I wanted to and you couldn't stop me.' Her mouth quirked in a melancholy smile. 'We're out of time and you weren't going to give me one otherwise. I believe in you, Mark. I always have. You're an asshole, but you're *my* asshole. You decided it was time to pull the cord on that puzzle, so I say go for it. Fuck Will. I don't think anyone else's fears of the unknown should stop you from acting, and I bet you're right.'

He stared at her and *hurt*. Why would she do this? Why would she throw her life away on a kiss? He didn't want her to die because of him. He wasn't worth it.

'Now let's go and look at a frozen lake,' she said, false brightness making her voice a brittle lie.

She pressed the biofilm back together and stood as two waldobots moved forward to pick him up and carry him into the passage.

18.5: NADA

Nada's ship hit fresh trouble two days after they left the Snakepit System. Without warning, her carrier's warp-envelope collapsed, spewing alarm and confusion into the mind-temple while ignition plasma belched out between the stars.

She was not in the mood. She'd had a headache for days. The

homeworld sample she'd ingested still vexed her. She clawed her way out of the leadership vesicle and into the crew-bulb.

'Report,' she ordered.

She wanted to have dominated the sample by now. Instead, she felt sick and exhausted. She persisted because, despite it all, she was within an inch of saving the human race. Even if Ekkert was making more progress than her, which she doubted, determination to present the Yunus with a solved problem burned in her like a welding arc. Giving up had not been an option when she started out, and it was not an option now.

'Envelope collapse was caused by the alien vessel we are carrying,' said Leng. 'It is emitting a strange gravity profile, as if the space inside it were bent.'

Nada seethed. The ship had already caused innumerable problems. Attempting to nudge it into position for transport with tugs had turned them immediately into slag. It couldn't even be moved with photon pressure. In the end, they had been forced to assemble a carrier around the remains of the *Dantes*, losing dozens of drones in the process, and gather warp from a starting creep of a quarter-light. Just getting started had taken two long, painful weeks.

'Can we compensate?' she said. 'Will this happen again?'

'No and almost certainly,' said Leng. 'Our best hope is to position the carrier more carefully so that the ark sits at the dead centre of the envelope. Even then, ruptures are likely to occur.'

Nada shut her eyes. The collapse had dumped all the warp-velocity they'd accumulated. If the pattern continued, it might be a long flight home.

'Superior Nada,' said Leng. His voice had taken on that fawning quality she disliked. Despite his intelligence and loyalty, Leng was not easy company and she had little patience for his quirks these days.

'What?'

'I beg you to purge the data from the homeworld that currently resides in your private buffers.'

She stared at his grimacing face. 'Why?'

'Because you are being damaged by it,' he said. 'Is this the right way to meet the Yunus? Ekkert has already been assigned this task, making your pursuit of it redundant. Furthermore, it hurts me to see you impaired because of the subjective significance I assign to your well-being.'

'To abandon the task now would be folly,' she said. 'I am on the edge of understanding it.'

'You have said that eleven times since you came aboard. The material you received was obviously corrupted.'

'It was *not* corrupted,' Nada insisted. 'It is merely *difficult*. We are used to ingesting life that is not Photurian. However, the Usurper's code has been written on top of Protocol logic. The standard tools do not apply. To understand how the homeworld now operates requires extensive mapping.'

'It is a mutation, then,' said Leng. 'Mutations are abhorrent.'

'Mutation implies organic change. This is not that, either. It is a complex distortion of our system of life, comprising millions of modifications. Instead of a tree of authorities with a single root, the Usurper has installed a farm of distributed, redundant sub-authorities that all interact with the root.'

Thus, instead of a single skylight in the corresponding temple-cavern, there were thousands. It was like being in a sky full of stars instead of seeing a single sun. Now that she understood it better, she had to admit there was a hideous kind of beauty to the Usurper's system, though she did not tell Leng that.

'Redundancy has been written into everything,' she added. 'This makes understanding the architecture difficult.'

Leng shuddered. 'It sounds like a rejection of the natural order. Why not simply reintroduce the Protocol's perfect structure to the sample and let the redundancies fade away?'

'That was my first strategy,' said Nada. 'Fortunately I constructed several copies of the Usurper's control system before trying it. Attempting to directly enforce order onto the pattern causes it to break down erratically. Were we to take this approach with the world itself, our home would end up as dead as all the other planets we passed.'

Leng's eyes shuttled from side to side. 'If there is so much mapping to do, why not simply leave the problem for the chorus of minds that the Yunus will have waiting for us at New Panama?' he said. 'Given your description, the solution appears to relate to the scale of the investigation, not the quality of study.'

'Because *I* was tasked with innovating, not them,' she insisted. Plus, she didn't trust them to make necessarily brave choices, though she kept that to herself as well. The truth was, she wanted to be the one who solved it. Since her triumph at the homeworld, the ambition the Yunus had fired inside her burned brighter than ever.

'In that case, may I assist with the study of the repugnant control structure?' said Leng. 'Two minds will resolve the problem faster than one.'

'No,' said Nada. 'Your job is to monitor the compromised warp mechanism.'

Leng produced a long, high-pitched whining sound for about half a minute before answering. 'Yes, Superior Nada. I obey with real enthusiasm.'

She left him floating there and retreated to her vesicle to work on the pain inside her.

18.6: ANN

Ann sat at the edge of the frozen lake, under the canopy of etiolated ceramic trees, and watched the others work frantically while time screamed by in the universe outside. The entire time, a voice inside her that might once have been her shadow kept telling her that they were making a terrible mistake.

'Preparing to drop the inner shell,' said Clath.

Ann swapped to the view through her visor and followed along. She had nothing to contribute. Judj and Clath understood the ship better than she did, and the storm of emotion inside her head made concentration impossible in any case.

'Three, two, one...'

They dropped warp. Other than a barely perceptible bump in gravity, it was impossible to tell that anything significant had happened.

'The gravity funnel is still stable,' said Clath, 'although things might get a little weird up near the airlock.'

'But it worked,' said Ira.

Then, through her visor, Ann saw the hatch to the airlock-tube fly open.

'Ira!' she warned.

'That's not good,' Will remarked over their shared channel. He was stationed up in the top passageway, ready to fight, but they were all watching the same feed.

The waiting mantis-mechs promptly blasted the inside of the airlock tube with energetic bolts that could have been anything from rail-gun slugs to electrolased pulses. The action looked curiously frantic until Ann realised that she was seeing things slightly accelerated from the norm. Obviously, without the second shell, the temporal damping wasn't perfect any more.

Black tar oozed down out of the tube to pool on the passage floor. The robots moved back out of its way and scorched it with radiation beams.

'I think that's the remains of Balance's machines in the airlock,' said Judj. 'It's about what I was hoping to see.'

Then the black ooze started to move of its own accord, spreading out in fingers across the floor.

'Except not that,' said Judj.

An armoured giant slammed through the hole like lightning to land squarely in the passage. His suit was dented and blackened, giving off smoke. Two alien mechs darted forward and hacked the figure to pieces before it could even raise its arm.

More giants fell – a dozen of them, one by one, down the narrow chute. The mechs butchered all of them, slashing them into shreds with knives sharper than matter could ever be.

The fall of giants stopped. Barring a little gore-splatter, the mechs remained in perfect condition. They started backing away from the slaughter towards their stations. Then, as they reversed, about half of them slowed and halted.

'I'm getting security warnings,' said Judj. 'The ship is under soft assault.'

He started typing frantically on Ann's touchboard.

'How is that possible?' said Ann. 'Do we have any comms kit left up there?'

'No, all the hardware is Subtle tech,' said Clath.

'So how can he be hacking it? With what?'

'Through the mechs, I think,' said Judj.

'We needed help from the Transcended to even access their systems,' Ann insisted, 'so how can he be doing it? Balance may be powerful, but he's not magic.'

'I have no idea,' said Judj. 'But it's happening.'

While she watched the camera feed, the mess on the floor re-assembled itself into a large, sticky slug. It started crawling down the corridor with the mechs on either side as a robot escort.

The door ahead of them crashed shut, barring their way. The temperature in the passage then rose by several hundred degrees as it was scoured with radiation through emitters buried in the ceiling structure.

'Got him,' said Judj.

Ann watched the slug boil and slough to the floor. The mechs, however, didn't stop. They started scything at the door seal, their arms bouncing off the warpium-composite barrier, leaving nothing but tiny scratches. At that point, the Balance slug appeared to catch fire. It flickered oddly, as if it had been packed with ingots of magnesium.

'Another security problem,' Judj warned. 'Shit! He's fluorescing and hacking the ship via the vid-link. Sorry, folks, show's over.'

Ann's feed went dead, while Judj worked more frantically than ever. She flicked her view to the system-status indicators and watched crazy traffic start to build up around the temperature sensors in the passage.

'Gravity machine control is not responding,' Clath warned. 'He's going to break the outer envelope!'

Judj grunted. 'Got it,' he said. 'The fucker is capitalising on quirks in the ark's cache architecture to synthesise software agents for himself. The little buggers are semi-autonomous.'

'But how?' Ann insisted. 'How can he possibly understand their hardware that well?' And then she groaned as she figured it out. 'Of course – he's been out between the shells for *days*,' she warned. 'The dilation on his side was far less and all the outer-shell machinery probably isn't security guarded from underneath. Balance may have been praying for a chance like this. For all we know, he's been planning for weeks.'

Ann jumped back through the system using simple voice commands and looked at the sensor data they'd been receiving from the outer shell since they started the gravity machine. Sure enough, the packets had been getting heavier and stranger for the last ten minutes. They'd been too distracted to notice as they dashed down the twenty or so storeys to the lake level. Who could say what ten minutes translated into in Balance-time?

She glowered at the results and knew then that it had been a mistake to come down here, just like it had been a mistake for them to join her in the ark. Ira, bless his heart, had made the wrong choices for all the right reasons, and she'd gone along with them.

The gravity increased suddenly, crushing her to the floor. She cried out as her leg twisted and almost blacked out as she impacted with the ground. Around her, the others dropped like proverbial flies.

Stars skittered across her vision as her cheek ground itself into the ceramic paving. She should have fought Ira. She shouldn't have given in. She'd seen that he was overdoing the protectiveness like every male since the dawn of time but hadn't wanted to shut it down because, in truth, she cared about him, too.

A message boomed over their shared channel.

'If Cuthbert comes out and faces me instance to instance, we can end this,' said Balance. 'Otherwise, you're all dead.'

19: FUSION

19.1: WILL

Will watched his friends slump to the floor. The moment Ira proposed shutting down the inner shell, he'd suspected it would come to this. He grabbed Judj's security interface and raced for the armoured bulkhead that lay between him and Balance. As he sprinted in the punishing gravity, he assessed the situation with an array of subminds and started compensating for Balance's hacks.

It was already too late. Balance had managed to do precisely what Will had failed to achieve last time – slide control-handles into every available subsystem before making his killer move. He'd simply had more time than them to get his shit together, even if it had been spent trapped in a gravity-distorted hellscape.

But Will had not been idle in the intervening minutes. He'd scoured his internal data stores to find out what would actually kill the machinery that he and his enemy were running on. Not much. Temperatures over fifteen hundred degrees, high-intensity X-ray bursts, magnetic fields of forty-five tesla and above – that sort of thing. The military pseudo-life he was using was packed with clever nano-scale silicate structures that could continue to coordinate under the most ridiculously austere conditions.

Which meant that only one kind of battle would count – mind to mind. Will's Underground code and denialware shield versus whatever thread-hacking tools Balance had brought. However, making that kind of attack required living long enough to execute it.

He focused his soft assaults on the alien mechs. At the same time, he opened the door between himself and Balance. A blast of heat washed

497

out as the barrier rose. Will took in the sight of his enemy and had to hand it to the Willworld's scientists. They'd done a remarkable job. His opponent had been scorched, irradiated and flattened. There was nothing left of him but smears on the walls and floor, yet the bastard was still managing to hack an alien starship. Clearly his thread was intact even if his body was a mess.

The mantis-mechs marched at him but froze as Will pinned them with a thought. They started up again, then lurched back to a halt as Will adjusted his mental grip. Every moment of control interference required a machine-gun bombardment of tailored data packets.

'Take that suit off or I'll slice it off for you,' Balance warned over the public channel. 'We're going to do this mind to mind.'

Will hesitated, worried by his enemy demanding his preferred approach. It suggested angles he hadn't yet seen. He bought time while his mind raced.

'On the condition that you leave my friends alone,' he said. 'You must have figured out by now that we're not your enemy.'

'Fine. Whatever. Just hurry up and drop your blocks.'

Will stalled again. This was too easy. Something was wrong.

'There's no time to negotiate!' said Balance and shifted the focus of his attacks. One of the mechs darted forward before Will could stall it, slicing off his arm. At the same time, a tendril of black Balance-goo leapt out from the nearest wall like a frog's tongue to connect with his exposed tissues.

Balance rammed himself into Will's computing substrate with all the subtlety of a speeding macrodozer. Will screamed and roared his fury at the same time, diving in to attack Balance's mental pattern while his link to the rest of the ship slid out of reach.

19.2: NADA

The flight back to New Panama took five weeks. The monstrous ship they were carrying played havoc with their engines, dumping pseudo-velocity every time they acquired a respectable speed. Meanwhile, the humans cowering inside it remained adamantly hidden. Nada wondered what sick little delusions could possibly have motivated them to hide for so long. At the same time, the warped clutch of cells she'd brought with her made her feel ever weaker and more frustrated.

Nada had gone to desperate lengths to defeat it. She'd even set up an approximation of her identity in one of their spare ship-brains to integrate with the Usurper's tangled mess and analyse it from within. It was as close as she let herself get to Monet's repulsive act of brazen cloning.

Such a move would have caused panic in her crew had she revealed it, not least because of the potential digital-infection risk. So Nada had kept the experiment tightly secured, retaining only the narrowest of diagnostic channels to its container. And then she'd let her experimental copy dive deep into the Usurper's code, becoming infested with Monet's filth so she could monitor how it changed. Fortunately, it was helping. Piece by piece, her copy was slowly unpicking the travesty that had been made of their beloved Protocol.

Her crew, meanwhile, had gone from jubilation back to exhaustion. Leng struggled to maintain the functionality of his officers under the endless sequence of engineering alerts. Nanimo's reports hadn't fared much better.

When she finally dropped warp at the edge of the New Panama System without a solution to the home world problem, she felt a sting of failure scraping at the joy inside her. If only she had built her copy-experiment a few weeks earlier.

'Help will be on hand now,' Leng remarked enthusiastically. 'The problem of the Usurper's cursed control-system will be solved. Let that provide you with adequate satisfaction.'

Nada wished it were that easy. The only person who could take her frustration away was the Yunus.

'Send the arrival message,' she ordered.

Their hail sang out across the system while they powered down to wait for orders from one of the perimeter stations. None came. The maximum wait time for a Photurian fleet response slid quietly by without them intercepting any traffic from the colony. The silence stunned her. New Panama was the busiest system in all of Phote space.

'Circumstances at New Panama must have changed,' Leng mused.

'Evidently,' said Nada.

They had received no advance warning of a change in communication protocols, and had only been out of command contact for three

499

months. It seemed an extreme change of standards to have been made spontaneously.

'We will proceed inwards aboard the *Infinite Order*,' she told Nanimo. 'The carrier will follow along with the alien ark, using minimised warp-bursts to enter in-system space.'

'Yes, Superior Nada.'

Nada pressed on into the system, leaving one of her prized gifts behind, her mind fizzing with rising fear as they dived into the star's cluttered neighbourhood. What if she'd simply come too late? Could the colonies of her own kind have died already? While that struck her as profoundly unlikely, she'd seen too many dead homeworlds of late to completely disregard the possibility.

To her immense relief, a reply from New Panama eventually arrived. It had taken so long because it had come straight from the colony itself rather than any outlying station.

'Nada Rien, this is Colony Custodian Jinak Wenshun. Your arrival is acknowledged. No fresh orders await you.'

And that was it. Nada found the paucity of information in the message inexcusable, and the idea that no superior node existed at so large a colony was ludicrous. She replied with questions.

'Where is your instance of the Yunus? What has happened to the perimeter stations? Why has no fleet strategy been registered?'

Yet another hour came and went before her message could hit the colony world and a light-lagged reply make its way back out to her.

'Events have moved rapidly in your absence,' he said. 'The planet has been temporarily placed under minimal survival conditions to support the Yunus's new push against Galatea. All spare resources have been diverted to that project. As your survival was not anticipated and fleet resources have already been deployed, your ships were not allocated to missions.'

The implications of the message chilled Nada's blood. *Minimal survival conditions?* What did the coordinator mean? Rather than tolerate another upsetting reply, she refrained from asking until she reached a parking orbit from which she could ascertain the situation for herself. Once there, she pinged the root node of the planet's mind-temple.

What she learned made her reel. The Yunus had drained the planet of almost all its healthy Photes and biomass. His new plan entailed besieging Galatea with a permanent orbital presence and millions of drones, utterly dominating their local space until the colony crumbled. For this, he required megatons of anthrocapital and so had denuded all available colony worlds of their stabilising populations.

The evisceration of New Panama had happened almost two months ago, and already Fatigue was claiming great swathes of the viable units that remained. Towns had been emptied, home-tubes starved of biomatrix, machinery removed. The planet had been allowed to slide to the brink of oblivion.

[Why?] she demanded of the temple and scoured its structure until the answer became clear.

The Yunus had come to believe that without a massive injection of fresh hosts, the Utopia would collapse. Their programme to sustainably reproduce Photurians via natural means had been a failure, as expected. The project to secure the population of Earth had been his last hope.

His decisive moment came when Nada vanished into the Zone. He determined that she'd failed in her mission and that the desperately needed hosts were never going to arrive. At that point, the Yunus defaulted to his backup plan: the unrelenting assault of the greatest remaining source of hosts until a fresh population could be acquired.

'But I did not fail!' Nada screamed.

Leng's avatar-bead came and hovered anxiously beside her.

Nada felt... betrayed – an emotion of human origin yet unspeakably pure in its intensity. She stared down at what had once been the most stable and successful of all the Photurian worlds. It was the one place where they'd managed to construct a mature defensive node rather than relying on human methods of weapon construction. This colony had been the jewel of the Utopia, the boldest and brightest of worlds. And now it was dying.

There would be no support minds for her control-system problem. There would be no grand delivery of her gifts. There would be no moment of re-editing to adjust her uncomfortable sense of ambition. There would be no replacement of her exhausted crew. There would be no communion with her fellow fleet nodes. There would be no new orders. Because her superior, the Yunus, had left her for dead.

'What am I supposed to do?' Nada shrieked, her fingers grinding into her cheeks. 'I have changed the fate of the human race and now have no orders to follow? This is unacceptable!'

The colony custodian couldn't tell her. He lacked adequate data.

Nada was better equipped to determine the next course of action than he was.

'It is not that bad,' Leng warbled. 'Remember that we have been away for months. Naturally, the war has progressed. What did you expect?'

'For the Yunus to honour his promise!' Nada yelled. 'The Yunus has wrecked this world! The Yunus has neglected my contribution!'

In a bolt of clarity, Nada knew that the Yunus must have lied to her from the start about his plans. A move of this magnitude would have taken months to organise. He must have started while she was out running blockades around Earth. And when he met with her, he had *concealed the truth*, because that was the kind of behaviour individuality permitted. Because he erroneously imagined it would make her more effective than telling her what was really going on.

Nada could barely contain her fury, even though it was directed at her beloved and perfect superior node. Her future, regardless of his reasons, had been sold out.

'The Yunus's wonderful new orders may be inferred from context,' Leng suggested, 'even if they were not specifically delivered. We should leave immediately to join the push at Galatea. Our weapons will add strength to his assault.'

'What of the ark?' Nada demanded. 'We cannot reach Galatea in a timely fashion and transport it at the same time. Which means it must remain here. Which means that it would be left with an inadequate defensive perimeter. Which means that the Abomination and the Thief of Souls would be able to escape. Which means that we would have failed in our original objective! Furthermore, what, in the name of all joy, is the point of attacking Galatea if there are no viable colonies left for us to return to once the planet has been taken?'

'Surely he intends to rebalance the colonies once he has acquired a new population,' Leng offered. 'We may—'

'No!' Nada screamed. 'Be silent. Do not disturb me until I can recover poise.'

She changed him to make him comply. It didn't take much, given how riddled with irrelevant affection for her Leng had already become.

She sealed herself into her vesicle to think and rocked back and forth in her crevice. Her dissonance mounted once again, rising to a deafening roar inside her.

19.3: MARK

'Oh my God, we lost Will!' Clath wailed.

Mark regarded the others from where he lay near the frozen lake. The gravity had slacked off already but his friends' faces were still blank with shock. Nobody had a clue what to do next. They were out of tricks, out of weapons and out of time.

He wheezed like a punctured accordion and knew that the gravity attack had not been good for his suffering lungs. His body was finally failing. It amazed him that it had lasted this long.

Yet while they had perhaps just minutes left to live, Mark didn't want Palla's death on his conscience. She'd infected herself with spores from his body and nobody had the tools to save her except maybe himself. At this point, nothing else mattered. He grabbed the puzzle in his sensorium and applied Palla's edits. Without the *Dantes* to connect to, would there be enough Transcended code in his roboteering interface to run the program? There was only one way to find out.

'Fuck you,' he told the aliens in his head. 'Please save her,' he added and dived in.

The world fell away. The Transcended software took over and Mark discovered what it felt like to be converted to the Photurian Utopia. It was as if someone had plunged a needle made of happiness into the centre of his brain. No matter that his body was sick. Who cared? Opening the puzzle was utterly, ruthlessly, evisceratingly great. He gasped. Nada had been right. It really *was* joy. There was no denying it.

That happiness blared out waves of certainty. My God! Why had he never understood before? Why had he even tried being human when there was such a clean, lovely and ultimately *good* way of being and doing things right there for the taking? It was beautiful. And all he had to do to be filled up by it was throw away a bunch of shit that didn't matter any more and never should have. Human love, for instance – what was that even for when there was this dominating, spiritual, *glorious* alternative on offer? Or notions of family, or ambition, or friendship? His fondness for Zoe, his empathy towards Rachel – it all suddenly felt so little. So mediocre. So bland.

Now that he had proper perspective, it baffled him that he'd never seen it before. It would have been embarrassing were there any room left in his rapidly expanding soul for embarrassment. This piercing light just made everything else look stupid. There was no point attending to it all when he could follow holy, wondrous, life-fulfilling orders and experience something infinitely superior. He laughed, or maybe screamed, with relief and pleasure as he was healed and brought into line. He'd never have to question anything again. There'd be no uncertainty or fear. He was off the hook so long as he did what he was told. Things were going to be okay – perfectly, everlastingly okay.

And then the sensation faded. His mind was turned in some incomprehensible direction, and what had appeared to him as a golden and majestic vista of hope was suddenly revealed to be nothing but a painting on a thin piece of fibreboard. He wept inwardly at the loss of that extraordinary vision.

'No,' he breathed, panic clotting his thoughts. 'Please! Bring it back!'

To lose that simplicity felt like having his insides unzipped with a jagged blade. But then his panic stopped short as the picture kept turning and he came to understand that he'd actually lost nothing at all. Because any truth so precious and wonderful that it couldn't be questioned didn't actually have any meaning.

Meaning lay in the relations *between* things, so it was always going to be hard to pin down. All that bright glory was just a bunch of wires driven into his head, jangling him like a dumb puppet. For a few seconds, he'd been rendered absolutely lifeless. And while it had felt great to be in it, and so pure and clear, seeing how easily he'd been turned into a piece of marching meat left him chilled to the core.

Easy answers that could not be contested made a person amazingly so much *less*. The Protocol, he saw, was an instant sociopathic moral order. All you had to add was human brains. The wonderful, horrifying sensations blurred away leaving an echo in his mind like the ringing of a starship-sized bell.

Out of the gathering whiteness, Zoe appeared, still dressed in black.

'You took your time,' she said. 'Is this how human beings always operate? Procrastination down to the very last second?'

Mark slowly came back to himself and hunted for words. 'You should know,' he croaked. 'You're squatting in my head.'

'You're right,' she said. 'We should have expected nothing else from your species – an even messier situation that we have to clean up for you.'

He fought for clarity. The experience he'd just had was nothing short of life-changing. But the opportunity to be rude to the Transcended was a strong motivator.

'If you think you're going to impress me with your powers or wisdom or tremendous helpfulness, be aware that we're past that.'

'Unblock Ann,' she said. 'You need her strength.'

'Sure,' he said, 'if you fix Palla.'

'Your concern is touching,' she said with a dry smile. 'We'll see what we can do.'

'Fuck you,' said Mark. 'Whose side are you actually on?'

'Your side,' Zoe snapped.

'Bullshit – you released the Photes.'

'Will believes that. Bear in mind he was on a Phote-built world at the time, and that everything he remembers and perceives was filtered through that hardware.'

'You could have blown up their stars,' Mark insisted.

'How do you know?' said Zoe. 'Are you an expert on solar-ignition systems? How focused is the level of our control? How much power do we really have? Ask yourself if you really believe that we'd try to help you and destroy you at the same time.'

'At this point, *yes*. You didn't even warn us. You must have known.'

She groaned her impatience. 'We're older than you, and frankly more mature, but not omniscient. Nobody is! Look, you don't have long if you want to fix things. Your body is being readapted to compensate for the altered threat landscape. You're not going to die but repair will take a while. So when you wake up, you need to get busy.'

'How?' he said. 'You've given me nothing. I thought there was supposed to be a weapon.'

Zoe grabbed his hand and slapped a software icon into it.

'There,' she said sharply. 'Maybe you should win your battles first before trying to decide whose side we're on.'

Mark looked down at the weapon. Details about it leaked into his mind but he didn't understand them. It was just a chunk of code – some sort of semi-aware cryptographic device. It smacked of the same pattern of order he'd just experienced so he knew it was designed to talk to the Phote Protocol and make changes of some sort, but that was all.

'Compare it to the copy of the Protocol Ann pulled off that dead world,' Zoe recommended. 'That might help you figure it out for yourself.'

'Figure *what* out?' said Mark, but she'd already gone. The dream was over.

19.4: NADA

Nada rocked in her vesicle and wept. Everything she'd worked for had come to naught. At the heart of the Photurian condition was joy at following instructions, but the choice of how to define completion of those instructions lay with the individual. Hence there was always that temptation to say, 'I've followed orders,' and to stop, close down and embrace the brilliant stillness that followed. That was how Fatigue happened and she could feel herself on the edge of it now.

She quite literally had *no* orders. Nor had any of her subnodes. There was no legitimate reason why they shouldn't simply power down, commune and let bliss engulf them. That urge was overwhelming. She'd worked so hard for so long. Of course she'd finished her job!

Nada reached inside herself for the thought sequence that would initiate a rest-state and felt a surge of happy hunger for that peace. She began to step through the necessary temple-glyphs, but then paused. Something jangled uncomfortably in the back of her mind, preventing the necessary sensation of calm. It was the diagnostic channel still coupled to her analytical replica. With slow, churning surprise, she saw that the sandboxed self-copy she'd left plugged into the Usurper's power structure felt only motivation at this setback. No agony. No dissonance. No will to oblivion.

While the rest of her soul clamoured for the off-switch, ambition wouldn't let her. So she mustered her scattered attention and reluctantly re-examined the system that her copy was embedded in.

Nada's skin prickled as she understood. Because the Usurper's society didn't run on orders, orders were never complete. Her copy was not susceptible to Fatigue. The Usurper's system didn't have top-down task assignment except in its utility and military domains. Instead, individuals contributed to the meta-instance without being controlled by it, donating a fraction of their subconscious function to its upkeep. The root was *not* the control node. It served and guided the collective. This

506

made the mechanisms cumbersome and slow, but *strong*. It wouldn't die the way all those worlds she'd seen had died. It would carry on.

She opened her channel to the experimental copy a little wider, testing it with an update of her own emotions. Perhaps the copy was still operating merely because it didn't yet understand what was going on.

The response was immediate. [You cannot stop now,] it told her. [We have not won yet. Let me help you.]

Nada held her breath. Her copy was operating on the Yunus's ambition *alone*, with no external Protocol support. And its invitation was clear – to swap systems, to use the Usurper's code.

The cost would be certainty. Self-leadership was a requirement of every instance under the Usurper's system. She would never feel the sweet touch of edits from above again. Nevertheless, her meta-instance would retain the ability to connect with the Founder Entity, so long as she permitted it. Her sub-instances would simply have the option of not accepting exterior dominance if it arose, which was why Monet had not become completely Saved right away. Fortunately for Nada, all of her yearned for perfect love. That would not be a problem.

She caught herself in the act of being tempted and recoiled in disgust. The change would be heartbreaking. She'd given her life over to willing servitude. She'd risked herself again and again to share a truth that was undeniable and precise. Was she really prepared to sully her soul and that of all her subnodes on a gamble?

What would be left of her? An entity operating out of confusion, living in a sea of mutable threads. Nada screamed a long, high, clear note as another realisation dawned. Once she adopted the Usurper's system, taking over the homeworld would be immeasurably easier. Because once inside his framework, threads could be *ripped*. She would become a perfect Cancer and nothing could stop her then.

Nada knew what she had to do. In order to fulfil the orders of the Yunus, she had to destroy the Yunus. Only then would lasting peace be achieved.

With great reluctance, Nada removed the safety barriers she'd erected between herself and her test copy. She granted it access to her mind and requested that it make edits. As Nada hung in her vesicle, a new kind of thinking seeped into her, muddy and cunning. She smiled. How interesting to be herself, yet not herself. Most species were weak, she decided. That was why they fell into Fatigue. The Founders had not been, which was why their worlds endured indefinitely before the corrupting touch of lower forms of sentience reached them.

Humanity had been at the brink of going the way of the lost worlds she'd witnessed, not because of any external attack, but as a result of their own weakness – the Yunus's weakness. They were unable to stay the Founder Entity's course by following the pure Protocol because it was a thing too beautiful for humanity, too demanding of greatness from lower forms of life.

So she'd adjust. She'd save her species through this compromise so they could last long enough to channel the Founder. What mattered was that the human race be saved, not what format it happened to exist in when bliss arrived. Then, when the Founder asked her to resume correct use of the Protocol, she'd be ready and it would last for ever.

'Leng, report to my vesicle,' she told him, and felt awed by what she was about to do.

Leng squeezed his way in, a hopeful smile on his face.

'You appear to have reattained poise!' he observed with delight. 'I am unreasonably glad.'

'I constitute a new viable mutation,' she told him. 'I therefore intend to assert primacy over New Panama.'

Leng's face fell. 'I do not understand. You cannot. The world is already Photurian.'

'I can and I will,' she told him. 'I have internalised technology from the homeworld. This makes me different.'

'But the rest of us have not,' Leng observed nervously. 'Superior Nada, your assessment is strange and disgusting. What has happened to you?'

'It is true that you have not yet been updated,' she said. 'It will therefore be expedient for me to replace you and my other subnodes with differentiated clones of myself.'

'No!' said Leng, horrified. 'That is wrong! You must not do that. It is against Protocol. You have become infected!'

His response was immediate and purposeful. His avatar raced to her temple-cavern but Nada moved faster. She suppressed his will to edit her. He sagged into passivity.

'I beg you not to do this,' he said. '*I love you!*'

'In that case, you will not mind *being* me,' she said.

With great care, she took apart his personality, rewriting it wholesale.

To use the Usurper's terminology, she ripped his thread. Leng emitted a strangled cry before falling silent. He stared at her, shaking and twitching, his eyes full of tragic longing while she pushed her intellect into his, retaining only those parts of him that were usefully differentiated for problem-solving.

When Leng's eyes could focus again, he was her. The mind pattern that had been Leng was expunged.

'I am Nada Rien,' he said.

'Refer to yourself as Leng,' she said, 'otherwise things will become confusing.'

Leng paused. 'I dislike this proposal but accede to its logic. I will now consume my own subnodes.'

'Good,' said Nada.

She devoured Nanimo next. Nanimo shrieked as her mind was taken apart. She was reborn as a part of Nada. The new Nanimo pointed their boser at New Panama and fired a minimum-strength shot at one of the remaining habitats, an ugly, human-designed one. Ten minutes later, after the chaos had subsided, the part of Nada that had been her new communications officer signalled the planet to assert primacy to ensure that the inhabitants remained submissive while she devoured them.

The rest of the day was oddly satisfying as Nada's subnodes became her sister instances and her mind changed and grew. She became the meta-instance for a society of her own copies and cherished that strangeness. She no longer felt any hesitation about opening the alien database they'd brought, she noticed. To deny herself a military advantage just felt counterproductive.

Things would be different now. She would consume the Yunus, and then his betrayals would stop. Nobody would lie ever again. It wouldn't be possible.

19.5: WILL

Will scrabbled for control of his thread-defences as Balance bulldozed into his mind. Anyone watching would only have seen his giant body standing frozen, one arm missing, dribbling black goo onto a sizzling floor. But within that stillness, a frenzy of combative computing raged.

For Will, it felt like wrestling with opinions instead of arms and legs. The two of them were n-dimensional octopi grappling each other in some compact universe where nothing existed except themselves. They were yin and yang punching each other in the eye.

The mental landscape twisted and flipped until Will saw his chance and lashed out, ramming his persona right up Balance's notion of self-integrity. Balance's defences folded like damp paper as their minds merged. Unexpectedly, Balance seized the focus of Will's attack and sucked Will in after his own thrust, tripping him up and granting him control at the same time. Will fell into his mirror image, sprawling face first into an ocean of himself.

[You were right,] Balance told him. [When the Photes arrived, the splinter of me that was already at the *Dantes* was forced to rethink. The sight of my greater self back home caving to the Photurians was extremely persuasive. Fortunately, there were no anchor-hacks in my advance force. I was free to adapt, so I did.]

[You're still nuts!] Will insisted. [I've seen the twisted shit going on inside you and I refuse to become that.]

[And now I believe you,] said Balance. [Isolation and mind-control will do that to a person. Even you, it turns out. Which is why I'm making you Meta, because you have a better idea of what's going on. I know what you're for now, Cuthbert. You're not a bug – you're an insurance policy. And I'm making a claim. Do you honestly think it matters which instance of me is in control at this point? Being Meta sucks. Get used to it.]

The gap between them shrank to nothing. As Will became Balance, he came to appreciate how the god had forced himself to accept a diversity of experience. He'd made himself broad, insisting on representing inclusion for every kind of Will, without judgement. Why? Because the world worked better when it had people in it who weren't like him, even if sometimes he disliked them or couldn't understand them. He'd tried to ensure social stability with the tools available because the alternative was so much worse. His axioms had been wrong and enforced from without, but he'd tried to leave room for the consensus to change.

And as Balance became Will, he came to savour how Will put a reality check on the social consensus every time he appeared. He manifested an irrepressible norming force that cut out mutations when they became dangerous. The memory of Will's original identity, stochastically applied, served as an immune system. Smiley had been right. He *was* a white blood cell, and both Will and Balance had been necessary. But it was pure fluke that the system had worked.

When Transcended control of Balance's world abruptly ended a decade earlier, subconscious panic had followed. Without even being aware of it, Balance had tried multiple coping mechanisms at once. He'd replicated the sensation of stability, synthesising a new mental harness for himself out of memories of how it had felt to be strong, and created the anchors. But a voiceless part of him had known that was a terrible idea and so had manifested copies of Will's original thread almost at random to compensate. Thus the Glitches had arisen.

It was a crazy, badly organised attempt to stave off social insanity, but it had succeeded. The axioms prevented him from sliding into despair too fast. The Glitches cleaned up the mess created by the denial they inevitably wrought. Between them, they'd actually held the Willworld together pretty well. The only problem had been that one, painful stipulation in the Transcended control code that he shouldn't leave the planet. And so, even with the door of his global prison cell unlocked, Will had sat inside it, staring at the walls until Nada came along and inadvertently hacked him. Now the Will civilisation was all screwed up – unless he did something to rescue it.

But there were other things he needed to achieve first – like saving his friends and liberating Galatea before the Photes crushed it. Then, maybe, if he managed all that, he could spend a little time having words with the Transcended.

Will reorganised himself. That which had been Cuthbert became properly established as the new guiding personality. That which was left of Balance's army of warrior instances became his subminds. Except rather than being reduced mental sketches, they were full, differentiated copies of himself with agency and opinions. Will felt a curious flexing, shifting sensation as his thoughts started to come in multiple superimposed streams. It frightened him, even while it brought a tremendous sensation of breadth. Suddenly, holding multiple opposing opinions at once no longer felt like hard work.

He reached out and in one gulp sucked down all the knowledge about the *Dantes* and its mission that Palla had brought with them to the ark. Now that he had thousands of threads working in parallel, that job wasn't hard. Then he swallowed everything the ark's computer system contained. He integrated every bit of alien science available and correlated it with every speck of data the *Dantes* team had collected throughout their mission.

In doing so, he noticed a flicker in the Subtle ark's warp-shell. The enclosure that held them wasn't as perfect as Clath had assumed. He just had to compensate for the temporal effects of the shaped gravity funnel. Will peered out through the ark's cameras and noticed for the first time that they were hanging in orbit around a Photurian colony. From the yellow-grey blur of the rapidly spinning world below, he guessed New Panama. During their brief struggle inside, the Photes must have spent weeks transporting them here.

The ark had been surrounded by a toroidal science station. Shuttles and drones whizzed about it at a ludicrously accelerated pace. At these speeds, it was impossible to tell if the station was a solid ring or merely an open lattice moving too fast to see.

His mental consensus considered the escape options and snapped to rapid agreement. Mark and Rachel's best hope lay in Will distracting the enemy while they fled in the ark. If he could deal with their Phote problem, the others stood a chance. The thought pleased him. The new Will smiled and prepared to flex his god-powers.

19.6: NADA

Nada cracked the alien database using their boser design as a translation key and thousands of sisters working in parallel for several days. After she finished, she paused to reflect as she floated in her vesicle above New Panama.

There was no crew to align or worry about. She could feel them all in the back of her mind, flickering and whispering like a river of ghosts. There was no dissent from the world below. She still had to coax millions of partially lost units out of Fatigue, but that project was on track, with a partial reversal of symptoms anticipated within weeks. There weren't even any humans to chase. She had them cornered in their stupid little ship. She was winning. Yet she felt nothing but anxiety.

The Yunus was still playing out his ridiculous siege, wasting lives by the million and sapping what remained of the Utopia's strength. If he actually succeeded, matters would get even worse. He'd be that much harder for her to absorb into her new architecture with millions of fresh Saved at his back. She desperately needed to close his operation down.

Meanwhile, in the other direction, Ekkert's grip on the homeworld would surely be weakening. She no longer doubted that outcome. The desperate compromise she'd made to reconcile herself with Monet's command system would be beyond a unit like him. He lacked the necessary ambition. But the team she'd left him with understood how to make the new boser weapons. An outside risk remained that the Will-clones would obtain the technology and use it to defend themselves or, worse still, come after her. Their desire to expand into new territory had been self-evident.

Two wars to fight in opposite directions and one half-dead planet from which to build her new arsenal. What was she supposed to do? Previously, under such circumstances she would have invited Leng to provide input. But now there was no Leng – just a copy of her inhabiting his skin.

She still had the benefit of his reasoning abilities, she reminded herself. The sensation of loss was not real. Yet in the quiet of her vesicle, her mood churned and darkened. Across the face of the world below, her sisters scowled along with her.

'Leng,' she said, and invited that sister instance into her vesicle anyway.

'My physical presence is no longer necessary for the discussion of strategy,' said Leng as he entered.

She noticed that his face had changed. It looked more like her own.

'You have altered yourself,' she remarked.

Of course he had. His memories were available should she choose to examine them. But then there wouldn't have been any reason to talk to him.

'Yes,' said Leng. 'To make it more like my own.'

'Reverse the modifications,' she told him. 'Your prior features were comforting, if unsightly.'

'I will not,' said Leng. 'I find them distracting. I will edit myself to resemble you, as I expect will all sisters.'

Nada felt a stab of discomfort. Leng winced in sympathy as his linked mind inherited the feeling.

'Why have you not become a disembodied instance?' said Leng. 'That is how Monet chose to operate his Meta.'

'I do not wish to,' she told him. 'I will remain physical like a queen in a hive.'

Nada flinched again as discomfort from Leng washed back into her.

'We need to determine a new social-interaction policy,' she noted. 'This is unsettling.'

'Agreed,' said Leng. 'What do you require?'

'Action is needed. Outline your reasoning for next steps.'

'We will use Zilch's body to create a secondary meta-instance,' said Leng. 'He will depart as soon as possible taking with him the *Infinite Order*, a carrier and enough raw materials to improve his vessel before reaching the Yunus. You will remain here and conduct further research until such time as you can muster a second fleet to secure our hold on the homeworld. New Panama's defensive node will suffice for the production of new ships.'

It was a surprisingly unrewarding exchange. She could feel his answers before he spoke them.

'Why Zilch?' she said, even as the answer slid into her head.

'Because his performance was poor,' said Leng. 'Little is lost in removing his personal specificity from our collective.'

'Agreed. And why confront the Yunus first?'

'Because he does not have the boser weapon. Thus, our military might is assured. However, the homeworld fleet will benefit from extra time researching the alien technology.'

'True,' said Nada.

Soon she would be able to construct false matter, as well as any number of other useful tools. The knowledge revealed by the database had already been put to good use. Leng's team had developed a device for probing the surface of the alien ship's unusual warp-envelope. Within a week, he expected to be able to crack it open.

'This is a good plan,' she told him.

'Yes,' he said. 'It is yours.'

He smiled, and Nada felt the confidence behind it. What she had lost in company she had gained in efficiency. In a way, her current state was closer to the orderly hive-mind from which she'd been carved.

'You are feeling more centred now,' said Leng.

'Yes,' said Nada.

'Then we have helped ourselves,' he said and departed.

On reflection, she decided, the new Leng was better than the old one. In fact, everyone would be better when they were her. It was interesting that when given the chance to become truly uniform, Monet had diversified himself instead. How human that was. How sick. There was something magical about homogeneity. It felt so clean and tidy. Perhaps it was because her personality was still fundamentally Photurian that she was able to appreciate it.

The silence felt more peaceful now. Nada contented herself with anticipating the tasks left to come. While her carrier was en route to Galatea, she would build the arsenal necessary to unify her kind and provide her with millions of new bodies. The Yunus's wasteful efforts would be irrelevant. She would consume him and all his flawed ideals. In doing so, she'd complete the holy task that he'd unwittingly assigned to her. She knew then that she'd also reformat Zilch's body to her preferred design. That way, when the Yunus fell before her, it would be her face he saw, not Zilch's. Why should such trivialities matter? Because the Yunus needed to see his mistake and know who he'd betrayed before she husked him out and turned him into something much better. And she was looking forward to that.

19.7: IRA

As soon as the gravity let up, Ira sprang to his feet. Of all of them, his body was best adjusted to heavy gees. He quickly checked the others, taking stock. Mark lay unconscious. The rest looked bruised but alive and Ann was still okay, thank Gal. He groaned in relief.

But as he stared at her, he knew from the look in her eyes that he'd fucked up. He'd pushed too hard for this option. He'd brought them all down to the lake because of *her* – not because it was a great idea. In doing so, he'd put Will in harm's way and then lost him, leaving them just minutes of charge in the gravity machine before it ran flat and dumped them into the hands of their enemies.

Tears pressed the corners of his eyes. He'd finally found a woman whose autonomy he could respect, and then he'd tried to shield her anyway. In doing so, he'd condemned her along with everyone else. How stupid was he? He closed his eyes and wished he had just a little access left to his former numbness. Apparently, it had deserted him. He was stuck in the moment, fully engaged, alive and choked with regret.

'I'm sorry,' he told her.

'I forgive you,' she replied quietly. 'It took both of us to get here.'

He watched her assess him – fiercely, disapprovingly and with complete acceptance. He started, rather brokenly, to smile.

'I—' she began.

Will's voice over the shared channel startled them back to the moment.

'Ira, come in,' he said. 'I'm okay. Balance is working for me now. And I have new info: I'm leaving. As soon as I'm out between the shells, you need to start the ship's engines. This ship is surrounded by an orbital station, heavily armed. The only way to release it from Phote hands is to do something dramatic. I'm sending you instructions on how to do that.'

Ira frowned, unconvinced. Will's mortal enemy was now just *helping*? How did that work? Which clone was he listening to?

Clath struggled upright and quickly checked over the data Will sent.

'This is crazy,' she said. 'These are just conventional engine instructions. Firing fusion torches inside the warp-shell is insane. We saw that option in the first five minutes aboard and discarded it. Where's the thrust supposed to go? It's more likely to rip the ship apart than help.'

Ann stood. 'That's hardly relevant,' she said. 'We've been handed a solution and we're taking it.'

'Agreed,' said Rachel. 'I'm going to trust my husband.'

'Sure,' said Judj. 'But which husband are you trusting?'

'All of them.'

'Ditto,' said Palla. 'Your glorious SAO concurs. And by the way, I recommend that nobody touch me.'

Ann swivelled to peer at her. 'It looks like we have another biohazard problem.'

Silence oozed between them.

'Yes, but also a data point,' said Palla. 'I touched Mark and I'm still human – I ramped my augs to the max before we came down here and I'm not dead yet. You should also know that he's out because he launched that last puzzle. I solved it for him.'

Ira's heart sank. *More* trouble?

'In Gal's name, *why*?' he said.

516

'Because we're clutching at straws,' said Palla.

'She's right,' said Rachel. 'We're avoiding risks and it's killing us.'

'I thought you were trusting Will,' Ira remarked. 'He said not to run the damned thing.'

'Right now I'm trusting everyone except the fucking Photes,' she said. 'We need all the help we can get.'

Ann smiled at that. She strode over to where Mark lay. Ira tensed inside but had guessed this was coming. She faced him before she did it.

'It's a symbol,' she told him, reading the pain and confusion on his face, 'so that they know we've picked a side, however temporarily.'

She knelt down and pressed a hand against Mark's mouth, then touched it to her own.

'Now three of us are off limits,' she said. When she got up, she slightly overdid it and bounced into the air. 'The gravity is failing,' she added. 'The machine is running down.'

'Are you ready?' Will's voice boomed over the channel.

'Not yet,' said Ira.

'Then hurry up! You have two minutes!'

Ira readied the robot porters for Mark and the three of them raced back up the twenty-plus storeys to the passageway levels. The gravity kept draining away as the machine's core slowed. By the end, they were propelling off the walls and barely using their feet at all.

'Time's up!' said Will. 'Fire the engines now or I'll do it for you.'

'On it,' said Clath. She powered up the ship's fusion torches even as they were ricocheting along the passage to the bridge.

A curious, muted roar rumbled through the hull. Ira slammed into a wall as the gravity changed again. It wasn't acceleration he felt, but a wild, uncertain slurping, as if the entire ship was being tossed about on some kind of amusement-park ride.

'More!' Will signalled. 'We need full thrust!'

The slurping redoubled. Ira careened into the bridge and clung to the stem of one of the wine-glass structures. Everything in the room slid about like chairs on the deck of a storm-tossed ship.

'Dropping outer-shell warp,' Clath shouted. 'In three, two, one...'

The warp field died. The envelope popped, giving them one final, unsettling shove. Ira checked the external cameras. If they'd been in orbit a moment ago, they weren't now. They were racing towards a planet that was unmistakably New Panama, surrounded by a rapidly expanding shell of ionised debris.

The sudden change of setting made their predicament jarringly real. Less than half an hour ago, he'd been in the Snakepit System, over a dozen light-years distant. It was as if someone had spliced an entire episode out of his life. On the other hand, they were free.

'Will used our contained spatial distortion as a weapon,' Clath said in awe. 'I think we just detonated humanity's first reference-frame bomb.'

Ira laughed like a maniac at the surreal victory until he noticed the proximity warnings flashing at the corner of his vision. Their escape had given them enormous delta-vee in a very unhelpful direction. They were on an arc that would intersect the planet's atmosphere in less than two hours. Ships the size of the ark did not do well when exposed to planetary gravity wells. They had a tendency to plummet.

Ira's laughter died in his throat. Why couldn't the universe have done them a favour and pointed them *away* from the gravity well instead?

'This is not good,' said Judj. 'I hate planetary landings.'

Ann scowled at the data. 'I don't think a landing is on the cards,' she said.

20: FISSION

20.1: NADA

A couple of days after her mission to Galatea departed, Nada visited one of her inaugural military projects on the surface of New Panama: her first ever false-matter forge. She felt extremely *proud*, foreign sensation though that was. She was so pleased, in fact, that she let her science-specialised sister-unit explain how it had all come together. They toured the edge of the facility in a bubble-rover. The science-sister, who had inherited the name Fojelig, pointed at a large, boxy structure sticking out of the ochre desert.

'This is where we create a flat lithium scaffold and cool it until it becomes superconducting,' she said. 'Then the power station over there provides the charge we run across it.'

'Acknowledged,' said Nada.

'We inject a cold-ignition plasma and create an ember-warp envelope across the scaffold, using an existing piece of false matter as a vacuum-ember.'

Nada examined her sister's face. Fojelig had been making steady modifications to the body of a tall, thin male unit but had not yet completed them to her satisfaction.

'A warp-envelope?' she said. 'Here on the surface?' It sounded like a dangerous proposition.

'The risks are lower than expected,' said Fojelig. 'The chamber is shielded and the plasma for the ignition field is easy to make. Compensating for the local gravity field requires attention, but other than that, the process is straightforward.'

'I see,' said Nada.

'As the vacuum state propagates through the ignition plasma, the lithium matrix becomes unstable. The local geometry alters, forcing the lithium to undergo a form of constrained fusion. The result is a false-vacuum state at remarkably high energy. That interior energy supports the otherwise untenable vacuum state. The result is a sheet of material comprising a confined, two-dimensional universe of finite size embedded within our own. Only when the constraining energy threshold of the false vacuum is overcome does the system collapse.'

'Remarkable,' said Nada. Fojelig, a copy of herself, somehow managed to be even less interesting than Leng. 'While the details are irrelevant to me, I acknowledge your mastery of them. Be pleased.'

'I am,' said Fojelig.

The last few days had been a journey of discovery for Nada. First came the strangeness of watching part of herself leave the solar system while the rest of her stayed behind. And then there was the curious business of *self-socialisation*.

It transpired that without the automatic jolts of bliss provided by the Photurian Protocol, sisters required some other way to feel rewarded when they completed a task. They often attempted to broadcast their achievements. At first, Nada had found this irrelevant dialogue annoying. However, she had discovered that budgeting for social recognition improved collective efficiency at trivial cost. Humans called this *being nice*. It was one of the small, curious ways in which the new order had rekindled facets of her old condition. She tried not to let it get out of hand.

'Is the project a complete success, then?' she asked.

'No. There are still limits to the kinds of surface we can create. The surfaces are prone to an analogue of Ricci flow once established. Spheres and tori are simple to maintain. More complex shapes require the careful application of beryllium doping to the base matrix.'

'I see,' said Nada. 'Can we then expand to use the technique with some element other than lithium? Lithium is difficult to acquire.'

'Not obviously,' said Fojelig. 'The element has convenient electromagnetic and nuclear properties.'

'That is disappointing.'

The meeting was interrupted by the sky turning white. Fojelig, who had been facing in the wrong direction, let out an agonised shriek and crumpled to the floor, her eyes ruined. Her trembling hands cupped over the blinded orbs.

Nada felt the burn on the back of her head and neck even through the rover's rad-shielded glass and knew that something bad must have happened. During the seconds that followed, a wave of torment filtered into her mind as thousands of her sisters suffered from the same blast.

Nada forced herself to concentrate and checked the mind-temple, where a picture of events assembled out of chaos. Her orbital science station was not responding to hails and according to some sources had ceased to exist. It appeared that the humans trapped inside it had triggered some kind of explosion, vaporising Leng and hundreds of her other siblings. Their threads were gone along with their bodies, losing her valuable expertise.

Nada shook with fury. Not content with cowering away from her loving embrace, the humans had turned their hiding place into a weapon. Typical.

The temple updated. Two ships were heading down towards the planet: a large one on a fatal dive path and another smaller craft under controlled descent.

[Focus on the small craft and intercept it,] she told her sisters. [Track both.]

She wished she hadn't sent her new boser away. As it was, she'd have to make do with the experimental weapons she had on hand. She pulled her science-sister upright to examine her tear-streaked face.

'Are you capable of self-repair?' she demanded.

'No,' Fojelig keened.

'Do not self-destruct at this time,' Nada warned her. 'Not until the expertise deltas in your thread can be securely backed up. Do you understand?'

'Yes,' said Fojelig. 'It is painful but I will desist.'

At least the humans were out now. They would feel her anger before the day was over, along with all of her other emotions.

20.2: IRA

Ira fired the engines again, burning what precious power they had left in a desperate attempt to stabilise their dive. The ark kept plunging towards New Panama, its vector little improved.

'No luck,' he told the others.

They floated around him on the bridge, their expressions grim. Judj looked positively ill.

'The ship can't break up,' said Clath, glancing at him nervously. 'And warpium doesn't care about re-entry heat. So we'll impact.'

'Then what?' said Ira.

'Everything inside will be pulverised, I guess. Smashed flat in an instant. It'll be an event on the scale of a small nuclear war for the planet. That's the good option.'

'What's the bad option?' said Ira.

'If we overcome the threshold energy for the exohull shielding, the ship will ignite,' she said.

'What happens then?'

'I have no idea,' said Clath. 'Presumably a runaway cascade, blowing out the rest of the warpium in the ship, probably resulting in a redefinition event for the planet.'

'So what you're saying is that we have to get out,' Palla suggested.

'That would be good,' said Clath. 'Out and as far away from this thing as possible. Preferably several million kilometres.'

'The spheres,' said Ann. 'In the next chamber. My initial analysis showed that they were designed to secure the contents against gravity-well descents.'

'Is there any point?' said Judj bleakly. 'The only place we can go is a world crawling with Photes that's about to experience a major impact event.'

'There's always a point,' said Palla. 'Let's check them out.'

They propelled themselves to the next chamber where the three spheres waited like ball bearings the size of houses. The only feature on each object was a small circular hatch less than a metre across; other than that, they were flawless silver. Ira held his breath as he looked them over. The idea that escape pods might just be waiting for them felt too good to be true.

It was. As soon as Judj's robots got one open, it became clear that the objects were crammed full of smart-foam that separated thousands of tiny compartments. Each held a minuscule, glassy warpium object like a baby jellyfish, so clear and small as to be almost invisible to the naked eye.

'I don't get it,' said Clath in desperation. 'What kind of species pre-packs their life rafts with so many fucking machines that there's no room left for passengers?'

'I'm looking at the control-harness for this system,' said Judj. 'Those glass things are automata. Each one comes with compact surgical tools and about fifty metres of monomolecular conducting filament wound up inside. In any case, I should be able to remove them. We just need to scoop out the foam. It's a passive system.' He set his waldobots to the task.

Ira shook his head. Why would the Subtle send an army of near-invisible surgical robots down to a planet instead of their own crew? He gasped as he clued in.

'They're brain-control devices,' he said. 'The Subtle had no idea what they'd find on the other side of the Zone. They couldn't expect a compatible biosphere and they didn't have smart-cell technology. But they did have warpium. This was how they were going to rebuild their civilisation.'

'With jellyfish?' said Clath.

'They made robots to ride whatever fauna they found,' said Ira, 'just like their own people did. The tools are for burrowing in. The filament is for nerve hijacking. Maybe those animals were going to be new steeds for the Subtle, or bred to the point of sentience while the isopods lived in fast-time. Or maybe the crew were just going to download their minds into these machines and live for ever. Who knows? But they were planning to build a brave new world on our side of the wall, one enslaved brain at a time.'

It was the kind of survival solution that would never occur to a human, but it was perfectly Subtle. He shivered as he realised that the biosphere they might have ended up at was Earth.

The robots motored through the packing material, shooting a continual jet of white foam and glassy, dead robots out into the air around them. Or at least, he hoped they were dead. He noticed Ann regarding the tiny machines warily. If touching Mark had changed her, the effects weren't visible.

'How's it going?' she said, batting the stuff away from her face in disgust.

'Not good,' said Judj. 'Even with all that crap gone, it'll still be super-snug in there.'

Ira bounced off the wall as the ship shook wildly. Palla shielded Mark's limp body with her own and grunted from the impact. The hull around them started to ring like a cello string. It wasn't a sound they were used to hearing from a ship, but it kept coming.

'What was that?' said Clath.

Ira checked. 'We're bouncing off atmosphere,' he said. 'That's shedding a lot of our velocity, which is good and bad. It means we're not dead yet, but we have to get off this ship fast. We have maybe twenty minutes. The next time this hulk hits, it's headed through.'

20.3: WILL

Will hurtled into the planet's carbon-dioxide atmosphere at about eight kilometres per second in a body shaped like a torpedo. He was, he decided, about as far from human as he'd ever been. With his conversion to Meta status had come belated appreciation of the fact that his pseudo-life substrate could take just about any form it wished. So now he inhabited a virt that looked like a shuttle's cockpit while his mental denizens piloted the blob of smart-matter that comprised him into the atmosphere.

Despite the madness of it all, he managed to find a little room for excitement. He was out of Snakepit. His prison for so many years lay far behind, and ahead was the planet he dearly wanted to hit. Or rather, *needed* to hit.

The problem with pseudo-life was that it didn't regenerate. You needed smart-cells to manufacture it and he'd already sacrificed a lot of his material just building a heat shield. With each gram of himself that he lost, another Will-thread died and he had no way to back up. So unless he wanted to spend the rest of his life as a black slug the size of a human fist, he was going to need new bodies.

Fortunately, New Panama was the perfect place to find them. The planet appeared to have a working defensive node, which was about as good fortune as he could possibly have hoped for. Will manipulated his stubby wings, dodged the missiles the Photes threw at him and dived straight for it.

As he bore down on the surface, one of his instances yelled in horror. It had been tracking the ark and spotted that it was now on course to smash itself against the surface. Will cried out in chorus. When he'd encouraged them to make a reference-frame bomb out of their own warp field, he'd calculated the likely spread of exit vectors. This was one of the worst possible outcomes.

He had no way to help them. His projectile didn't have thrust, only the ability to flex itself in the dead air. Will dearly hoped that his first act as a merged super-intelligence hadn't been to kill everyone he cared about.

Still, he couldn't save them by fretting. While guilt clawed holes in his respective virtual stomachs, he concentrated on doing what little he could. Mark and the others would either escape the gravity well or die. He had to assume they'd find a solution and make his planned distraction in any case.

While still travelling at a healthy fraction of the speed of sound, Will slammed through the side of the node. He screamed over the surreal interior landscape of convection cilia and jellied baby drones, targeting the base of the accelerator tower. He crashed himself with pinpoint accuracy through one of the upper ducts and buried himself in a fluid-transport conduit like an assassin's bullet.

Will swapped his virt for an old-fashioned war room filled with his instances and maps of his pseudo-life structure. As soon as his environment had cooled enough for work, he extended tendrils out into his surroundings. He tasted the smashed machinery on all sides, hunting for a control signal, and extended a tap-root towards the nearest data artery.

With a collective cheer, Will punctured the artery and went to work. Nineteen milliseconds later, the strangeness of the data packets he encountered sent his threads into gasps of surprise. Will focused his attention and tried to understand what had them so wound up.

He recoiled in amazement. The world he'd hit *wasn't* running the Phote Protocol. Instead, its control system was much closer to his own.

Why? What could possibly convince the Photurians to abandon their beloved hierarchy? And how was it even an option? Weren't they forbidden from even wanting such things? He had no clue how his own social structure could have reached this place without being ferried in on the carrier that had brought the ark. Which meant that something very strange had happened to these Photes while he was trapped in slow-time.

With the caution of a soldier traversing a canyon full of snipers, Will extended another probe, checking for evidence of anchor-hacks that might destabilise his identity. He found none – just a framework for exclusively hosting Nada Rien, the same Phote who had screwed up his civilisation on the Willworld. The rest of them had apparently been devoured by her in some act of wholesale cognitive cannibalism. She'd taken his architecture and turned it into a tool for butchery. He shivered at the obscene scale of it.

So far as he could tell, Nada had the rules of the Phote Protocol written into the fabric of her personality but had implemented no sanity checks beside that. Was she crazy? Wasn't she even vaguely worried about toxic belief conflicts? Of course not, Will realised. As Balance, it had taken him years to get savvy about such stuff. Nada was still learning how to manage all that she'd consumed. She'd probably rip herself apart as soon as her instances grew too different, but he didn't have time to wait around for that.

Will used Balance's knowledge of defensive nodes to quickly subvert the biomatrix surrounding his body. Thirty-three seconds later, he had full control of the entire node – a feat less impressive than it should have been. While the structure was operational, he was disappointed to discover that only one and a half of the five factory arms still functioned. The rest had been deactivated due to resource cutbacks of some kind. It would have to do. On the plus side, the planet wouldn't be launching fresh drones, at least not without his say-so. Better still, Nada hadn't yet noticed what he'd done.

All drone-birthing stopped dead. Will released the blueprint for his pseudo-life architecture into the factory tissues around him and started producing more of it as fast as he could. Now his remaining instances weren't going to die. With the node at his command, he had plenty of thread-processing capacity to store them in. And within minutes he'd have enough material to build them some bodies of their own.

He set his less-sophisticated manufacturing equipment to work constructing atmospheric drones, tanks, walkers and anything else that might help defend his new home. Fortunately, he was also surrounded by an almost inexhaustible supply of drone parts, which meant more particle accelerators than he could use. He hurriedly began converting them into gun emplacements.

With construction of defences under way, Will extended his reach into the habitat-tunnel fabric that ferried biological material to his site. He identified as many locally manifested subsystems as he could and co-opted them in parallel.

Pain filled his virtual head as a wave of error reports overwhelmed him. While the main planetary data network was running Nada-OS, the local tunnel-mesh definitely wasn't. In fact, so far as he could tell, it was barely running anything. Those data pipes were crammed with lost packets, crippled return reports and millions of requests for help. Instead of feeding more material into his node, some of Will's osmotic transfers started going into reverse.

He fought down the blur of noise and struggled for calm as he came to understand just how badly damaged New Panama was. Most of the individual minds he touched felt rotted, like overripe fruit. And by reaching out to reactivate parts of that mess, he'd created an instant traffic nightmare for himself. He struggled to extricate himself from the damaged systems but moved too slowly. Nada caught him in the act.

[You!] she messaged him. [You should not be here!]

Her words appeared on the main display screen of his war room in ugly red capitals.

[Nice to see you again, too,] Will sent back, while hurriedly consolidating his control.

[Why do you still exist?] she demanded. [How?]

[It's a secret,] Will told her.

[It matters not. You will desist from this madness. You have no orbital power so you cannot win. Submit to me immediately to prevent further damage to my node.]

[Sorry,] said Will. [Not going to do that.]

[I require that node for drone production. Vacate it at once!]

[Make me.]

Nada closed the channel. Will got ready for pain. He'd seen no ships in orbit and no g-ray installations, but that didn't mean she was short of other weapons up there. And a single faltering node wasn't likely to last long against a concerted assault with space-based weapons. On the other hand, he was prepared to bet that Nada wanted her weapons factory intact. She wouldn't get that if she blasted him into smithereens.

For twenty whole minutes, she didn't attack. Will hastily built a pseudo-life army and branched his threads as fast has his substrate would allow. He doubted the quiet was due to her deciding to leave him alone.

Nada first appeared as squadrons of heavy-lifters stealing in low across the desert from multiple directions. The lifters set down macro-dozers and surface-use titan mechs. Clouds of atmospheric attack drones thousands strong followed behind. Evidently, she had plenty of defensive capability on the planet that wasn't tied to the node.

While he watched wave after wave of her forces surround his citadel, Nada delivered the test-shot Will had guessed was coming. She used an orbital rail gun to fire a slug at his accelerator tower, blasting a dirty great hole in the side of it. In the wake of her demonstration, Nada tight-beamed him on thirty different channels at once, asserting her primacy along with all the associated Photurian pomp and circumstance.

[Your world has already fallen,] she told him. [Now you will fall to me, too, and treasure that experience.]

[On the other hand, you could go fuck yourself,] Will told her cheerfully.

[Then die, vile mutant!] she raged and advanced on his position, firing as she came.

Will might have had the best weapons factory on the planet, but she had everything else. He erected defensive screens made of exohull plating to protect his delicate cilia-fields from being mashed. At the end of the day, though, Will didn't care much what Nada did, so long as he held her attention and gave his friends a chance. He fought back a jag of despair and prayed they were still alive.

20.4: ANN

They pulled as much material out of the landing spheres as they could, but it still wasn't enough. Meanwhile, the impact-timer in Ann's visor ticked down.

'So we have escape pods for three people,' Judj said grimly.

'No,' Rachel insisted. 'We can all squeeze in.'

'You're forgetting that we'll need suits on the surface,' said Judj. 'There's no oxygen.'

'Just environment suits,' Rachel insisted. 'Not full space rigs. We can do this.'

Ann peered into one of the gaps. The occupants would have to hunch together, utterly dependent on the Subtle cushioning technology to prevent them from being pulped the moment they hit the ground. She wished she hadn't let Galatea's political consultants convince her to gain so much height.

'Rachel is right,' said Ann. 'We can fit two per pod. Just.'

A hush fell over the group. There were seven of them left on the ark. Ann saw Ira's desperate eyes on her and struggled not to volunteer to stay. She was largest. She wasted most space. Her powers were gone. Before she could open her mouth, Rachel spoke up.

'I volunteer,' she said. 'I'm barely relevant. You don't need me. I'm an appendix to this mission.'

'Sorry,' Judj told her, 'you don't get to be the one. The person who stays back is me.'

'Judj!' Clath shouted.

Ann scowled at him. 'Why? Don't be ridiculous. You're mission-critical.'

'Because I volunteered for this mission,' said Judj with a dry smile. 'I did that because I knew I wasn't going to survive. I have a condition that gave me a life sentence years ago.'

Ann blinked at him. 'Bullshit.'

Clath buried her face in her hands.

''Fraid not,' said Judj. 'You want to know why I was always so paranoid about someone getting infected on this ship? Because it happened to me. I grew up in a toxic biosphere, remember? Well, one of the local organisms sneaked into my body a while back and started eating the white matter in my brain.'

'No,' said Clath. 'Judj, don't do this.'

'Bullshit!' Ann said again. 'They could just take it out! Modern medicine doesn't struggle with that kind of crap.'

'Nope,' said Judj. 'This bastard is very persistent, which is why we were studying it. We thought it might be a weapon against the Photes. Turns out it is. I can't be converted, but the little fucker wrote itself into my DNA. Kill it and it comes back. My shadow runs most of my physical functions for me and has done since I came aboard. Without it, I'd be a corpse already.'

He offered them a trademark half-smile and Ann suddenly saw more in it than she ever had before. She saw a face that no longer worked. She turned to Palla, who hadn't said a word.

'Is this true?'

Palla nodded.

'Why didn't you tell us?' said Ann. 'I thought we were past Academic secrecy.'

'Clath asked her not to,' said Judj. 'She's been trying to keep a lid on this for the whole mission. She didn't want my health to be a tactical factor, but we both knew I wasn't going to last another six months. Besides, somebody will have to seal you in and press the button.' He turned to Clath. 'You'll live,' he told her fondly. 'Do that for me.'

'No,' said Clath again. 'No, no, no.'

Ann struggled for words as Clath looked around at the others, guilty desperation in her gaze. Her eyes lingered on Rachel. Ira looked away in pain. Ann's chest squeezed in empathy.

'Don't ask her,' Judj said softly. 'Don't ask any of them. You'll only regret it. I volunteer. It's what I do. And we don't have much time. Save the tears for later.'

Judj winked at Ann when the others weren't looking and in that moment she finally understood him. His anxiety had never been for himself. It had always been for the rest of them. Ann had more in common with him than she'd ever seen. Judj had come aboard to make his exit count, just like her. Now he was stealing her moment and they both knew it.

'We can get a robot to do it!' Clath urged. 'Press the button, I mean.'

'There's still no room,' said Judj. He drifted over and pushed her towards the nearest sphere. 'Hurry.'

Clath cried silently while they bundled her into one of the emergency environment suits they'd stashed on the ark's bridge. Ann wished she could hug the poor woman but her own body now carried an infection risk. She watched Rachel and Ira make that gesture instead and ached inside as she pulled on a suit of her own.

Why should she get to live? And yet Judj's logic beat hers. She could live and be happy while he'd already lost that option. By letting him do this, she was letting Judj matter. The chance to be the hero, it turned out, was a luxury of sorts – one she'd monopolised without ever noticing. Ann knew then that she was done with fighting and death. She'd never be able to see it the same way again.

'I'm sorry,' she said. 'For everything.'

'It's nothing,' said Judj with a half-smirk. 'You did good. And I hate landings, remember? This is the easy option for me. Be good down there. Make me count.'

Judj insisted on sealing Rachel and Clath in first. He put Mark and Palla in the second sphere. Lastly, he gestured for Ann and Ira to climb in. She could feel Ira's relief in his gaze like a palpable force, along with his crippling guilt.

Ann squeezed into the tiny spherical space, which was still filled with bits of floating foam. There was no lighting in the sphere. The surfaces were rough where the robots had hurriedly hollowed it out, with ridges that caught on her suit. Ira clambered after her. The two of them could barely fit. She had to curl around him.

'Have you checked your seals?' said Judj from outside.

'Of course,' said Ann.

'Just making sure. I want you to get down there in one piece. I'm sending you links so that your shadows can tether to the sphere's onboard systems. They seem to have a rudimentary orientation logic that's supposed to maximise the difference between the landing sites. I've overridden it to encourage them to do the opposite. Hopefully that way you'll stay close together. Good luck, everybody.'

Ann briefly heard the sound of Clath crying over the shared channel and then something suddenly shoved against her back with appalling force, hurling them up into the space above the planet. And then they were *really* falling. Not zero-gee – the terrible buffeting of re-entry. Ann clutched Ira tight in the darkness and knew that she wanted to live.

20.5: MARK

Mark snapped awake and found himself hunched over in a survival suit. He lay trapped between a hard, curving wall and an equivalently hard obstacle, drowned in darkness, while something shook him wildly. He felt like a ping-pong ball in a match between two industrial waldobots.

The only things he could see were winking green readouts in his suit's visor display. He checked his sensorium and found an icon waiting there to tether him to a situation report and some external sensors. Mark followed the link and yelped at the sight of a vast expanse of desert rushing up to meet him.

He was in a landing pod. The awkward object wedged against his torso was the back of Palla's suit. And they had just seconds before they hit the ground. Mark gazed at the extremely solid surface racing up to meet him and wondered how in hell's name the pod was supposed to do anything but smash itself straight into the nearest piece of basalt like a meteor.

The pod handily pointed him at another vehicle falling ahead of them, visible as a quivering pinpoint of light against the ochre surface below. Mark concentrated on that. Maybe it would give him some clue as to how he could expect to survive.

While he watched, the leading pod exploded in a blaze of light. Mark's breath caught. But as the glare died, something strange happened – the sphere appeared to grow. The pod had shed its outer layer and fibres trapped behind it were springing out, expanding to dozens of times the vehicle's original diameter. Below its shielding lay thousands of warpium-composite hairs designed to trap air – hugely long, almost indestructible and apparently held under tension until that moment. At full extent, the pod below reminded him of a giant dandelion head, and it was slowing fast.

He had just half a second to appreciate the mechanism before the detonation of his own pod's shield-layer punched him against the forward wall, knocking the breath from his lungs. When his head cleared enough for him to look again, he was still heading for the rocks at an unpalatable velocity, but now, at least, the pod was dumping speed handily.

Mark gawped at the sensor readout as he saw how effectively the seed-lander system was slowing them. It looked possible that they might actually hit the ground *gently*. That, he guessed, was the advantage of having near-invulnerable building materials to play with. Then, as he drifted towards the cratered landscape, an appalling flash lit up the horizon. Two seconds later, a dark smudge appeared there and started growing.

'What's that?' he asked the pod.

It explained. The ship he'd been fired from had just impacted with New Panama, releasing as much energy as a modest nuclear war. What he was looking at was the consequences of that impact. In other words, a blast-wave.

'Oh, shit,' he said.

Now that they'd lost most of their downward velocity, the wave was going to hit them before the desert did. That wasn't good. Being on the surface would at least shield them from the worst of the storm's velocity.

'Come on!' he yelled at the pod. 'Fall faster!'

The pod failed to oblige.

The wave swelled into a wall of black and churning grit that blotted out the sky, scarred inside with terrible lightning.

'Fuck,' said Mark. 'Palla, brace yourself!' he added, but suit-to-suit comms were down.

The sphere slammed sideways, caught like a leaf in a hurricane. Impact was brutal. The subsequent collision with the ground was worse. They bounced, hard – not once, but more times than Mark could count. With each repeated slam of his head against the wall, his consciousness stuttered. The end result was inevitable. Oblivion claimed him.

20.6: WILL

Nada's forces pounded Will's factory with small, ground-based rail guns. Will prepared himself for a long, punishing siege, but just five minutes after the attack started, it halted. When he sent an improvised camera drone out to discover what had happened, he witnessed Nada's forces in full retreat.

That wasn't good. He could hardly draw Nada's attention away from his escaping friends if she refused to fight. But why had she stopped? In frantic alarm, he checked the sky for the position of the ark. It lay beyond the planet's horizon. Then, while he scanned, the first signs of the impact storm appeared. Ten minutes later, the blast-wave hit. His already damaged citadel was blasted by a grit-storm of super-Galatean proportions. Will lost about thirty per cent of his manufacturing capacity in under a minute as sand and dust scoured the node. It burst in through every fracture his enemy had just created, ablating everything it touched.

Deep in the synthetic reality of his war-room virt, Will slumped into a seat in shock. His friends and family were dead. His heart screwed tight.

A new objective swelled inside him, matching the storm outside. The Transcended had made the mistake of granting him godlike powers. And now he was out of his cage. It was time to fuck some shit up on an interstellar scale, starting with Nada Rien. After that, the rest of the Photurians and the Transcended shitwads who'd spawned them.

As soon as the atmospheric disaster slowed to manageable subsonic velocities, Will launched the first wave of his robot army. His pseudo-life titans had barely marched past the perimeter of the node when Nada's lifters came sliding back through the storm, dumping spherical machines the size of housing blocks onto the desert by the hundred. They rolled towards him, shooting as they came.

It didn't take long for Will to figure out that he was looking at modified titan mechs wearing spheres of transparent warpium armour. They carried laser weapons that shot straight through their own defensive shielding without issue while causing havoc with his own front line.

Nada hurled packets of audio at him over the network. 'You are not the only one with surprises,' she told him. 'I will retain this node. Submit to me now and become useful!'

Everything Will fired bounced off this new foe. He snarled in frustration. The only thing he had going for him was that she hadn't resorted to orbital bombardment yet. She was still gambling that she could winkle him out of her node before they both damaged it irreparably.

'Admit defeat,' she urged him. 'You cannot beat my advanced technologies!'

As his soldiers fell back, Will hurriedly improvised particle cannons from drone parts. He knew exactly what kinds of particle beams to build to do the most damage since the Subtle's tricks for making and breaking false matter were in his mental database, too. He'd retained all the ark's knowledge at the cost of several dozen threads.

As Nada's machines scorched their way through his cilia-fields, he pierced them with high-powered meson beams and had the satisfaction of watching them burst like grapes.

534

'What was that?' he sent back. 'Didn't quite catch you. Something about advanced technologies?'

His robots pressed forward again under the cover of beam-fire. The particle guns put a terrible drain on his reserves and maintaining beam stability from ramshackle parts was insanely dangerous, but Will no longer cared.

Nada hit him with a fresh soft assault, trying to force the fight into the virtual realm.

'I have tasted your clones,' she told him. 'I know your past – your sickly guilt at being an incompetent parent and an inattentive spouse. I have felt the weakling panic in your heart from when you buckled under torture during your human war. Submit and I can take all that pain away.'

'You're not selling it,' Will growled back.

He knew he couldn't keep up this level of warfare for much longer. He thought back to his first observations of what Nada had done to herself and wondered if there wasn't a cheaper, more effective way to fight, particularly given that Nada seemed to be in a chatty mood.

'Tell me,' he asked her while his energy cannons atomised wave after wave of her robots. 'How's that new control system working for you? I take it you've figured out that it's better to be me than you?'

'I am superior to you in every regard!' Nada shouted back. 'I am Photurian and you are not!'

'Could have fooled me,' said Will. 'Looks like you've abandoned the Protocol altogether.'

'The Protocol has been temporarily adapted to more effectively facilitate Total Peace,' she said frostily and sent another shower of rail-gun slugs into his accelerator tower. It was, apparently, a sore point.

If he could kick up her level of internal dissent, she might discover some of the hidden limitations of being a democratic mind. Even during the best days of the Willworld, he'd been prone to mood storms – crippling moments of internal conflict. But he needed a topic Nada still cared about. She'd already lost so much of what it meant to be human.

'Really?' he said. 'And how does that work? You have a plan all mapped out, I'm sure. Tell me, which of your threads should get to branch and when?'

'What do you mean?' she demanded.

'Which of your units shape your society? They all have equal autonomy now but they can't *all* branch – you don't have the processing power. So which skills are more valuable, science or military prowess? Do you have a policy for that?'

'Of course I have a policy!' said Nada. 'Those skills I require to save the human race are replicated. Redundant threads self-destruct.'

Will frowned. So she didn't share his economic issues. But there had to be others.

'And how many of you should there be at the end?' he said. 'I mean, you're all one person. Is one copy enough?'

'As many as possible,' Nada replied. 'I shall save the entire human race.'

She was using the dialogue to distract him, he noticed, piggybacking mutant packets onto their channel to subvert his systems. He was blocking her, but eventually her superior processing power would win out. She had more threads than he did, and more distributed tunnel material in which to run them. She'd keep talking until she found a chink in his shields.

Will desperately rifled through what little he'd gleaned from the planet's failing databases before she'd shut his access down. One fact leapt out: the problem of the rotted habitats he'd encountered wasn't exclusive to this world; it was all over Phote space. Their enemy had been hiding a systemic weakness.

'What about those already in Fatigue?' he asked her slyly.

'What do you know about Fatigue?' Nada snapped back.

'Enough,' Will lied. 'It's your biggest problem right now. All those broken units. You going to save them, too?'

'Of course!' Nada shouted. 'All who are not already lost will be joined in harmony.'

'Who defines *lost*?' said Will, fishing hopelessly. 'I mean, that's a huge problem, isn't it? So many worlds. You'll need so much time. How will you even know when you're done?' There had to be something about that problem she hadn't thought through yet. The implied logistics were horrendous.

'That is obvious,' Nada insisted. 'I shall simply... simply... simply...'

Nada's message ended in a strangled digital scream. It was, Will thought, her first personal economic debate, and she was welcome to it. He knew the effect wouldn't last long. He reorganised his forces and pressed his advantage while he had the chance.

21 : BREAKTHROUGH

21.1 : MARK

When Mark lurched back into consciousness, his body screamed at him about all the new bruises it had acquired. He reached into his sensorium, tamped down the responses and checked the exterior camera.

The pod had changed again. The long wispy fronds that had slowed it had burned away, leaving only a stunted section at the base of each fibre, essentially cladding the sphere in hundreds of glassy stilts. The outer layer of the pod was rotating, propelling them along the ground.

Around them, a storm raged. The sky was a glutinous brown. Violent gusts jostled the sphere this way and that. Ahead, at the horizon, he could just make out a long, low structure like a black scar sticking out of the desert – a Phote habitat-tube.

Mark tried to signal the pod to instruct it to not head towards the artefact, but the vehicle was running on some Subtle logic of its own and had no interest in taking direction from its payload.

He tried again to open a channel to his pod-mate and this time succeeded.

'Hey, Palla?'

He got no response. He wriggled, trying to nudge her into action without success. As his worry grew, he linked to her suit and checked her vitals. She was alive but still unconscious, it told him. He'd have to find a way out of this latest mess on his own.

Mark held his breath as they rolled up to the rippled black exterior of the tube. It towered over them like the world's longest aircraft hangar. The pod pivoted at the edge of the obstruction and started running alongside it.

537

'Great,' he growled.

Nothing was more likely to get them spotted than puttering past the enemy's barracks for several dozen kilometres. He hoped the vehicle was simply trying to find its way around the end of the structure but soon realised his luck wasn't going to be that good. Instead, the gloomy silhouette of an old tent-town loomed out of the churning grime. They were headed straight towards a human settlement that had been merged into the Photurian tunnel system. The tube ended where it sprawled up against the scratched plastic dome in a fan of Stygian rootlets.

Mark tried again to persuade the pod to reroute before they were spotted but it trundled forward regardless. Yet, as they got closer, Mark's fear melted into curiosity. There were no lights inside the town and no signs of traffic around it. As the minutes passed without some-one coming out to demand they convert to endless glee, he began to wonder what was going on. Was the town abandoned? If so, it might represent their best hope. The air in their suits wouldn't last for ever, even with recycling running at full tilt.

The pod bumped up against the scoured plastic wall of the city and couldn't go any further in its preferred direction, so it stopped. It nudged back and forth, positioning itself so that its hatch lay directly at the base of the vehicle, and then opened the door, admitting a narrow shaft of brown light.

Mark stared down that sinister-looking tunnel to freedom and knew what had to come next: he had to leave the relative safety of the pod and find somewhere they could hide. The question was, did he have even a tenth of the necessary strength?

It was then that he noticed he no longer felt sick. In all the mayhem, it hadn't even occurred to him. He felt scared, bruised, jangled, sweaty, cramped and desperate, but not actually ill, which was an improvement of sorts.

He reached around Palla's shoulder, grabbed the lip of the exit tube and tried to tug himself into a position from which he could leave. It wasn't easy. Thirty-five minutes of increasingly frantic manoeuvring followed, with an unconscious, suited body in his way. He began to fear that the two of them would simply never be able to escape and die pointlessly inside the alien machine. In the end, though, he prevailed, and shunted himself out into the tube the wrong way up with a gasp of relief.

Mark fell three metres head first onto the desert and rolled. Fortunately, the storm had washed a large drift of dust up against the wall of the town, making his impact safe, if undignified. He crawled out from between the stilts of his transport and looked about.

The storm had slowed but the sky was still a dark, churning mass that rendered the sun an unfashionable shade of brown. The only sounds he could hear were his breathing and a constant roar of white noise through his helmet. He started trudging off around the edge of the old settlement in search of a door. If he could find somewhere decent for them to regroup, he reasoned, he'd go back for Palla and carry her to it. If there was no way in, the pod was as good a place to die as any.

Nobody accosted him as he explored. No rover arrived to point cannons in his face. Instead, the edge of the old town remained eerily quiet. He found an airlock about half a kilometre further on. Mark tried linking to the door through his interface and found it running in passive mode. It had been left unlocked on emergency settings. He let out a wheeze of relief and then caught himself. If the town was abandoned, why was there apparently still atmosphere and power inside?

His hope of finding somewhere he and Palla could recover soured into concern. Lacking options, he opened the hatch anyway and climbed inside the old-fashioned airlock chamber. Apparently, nobody had updated the hardware since the town was founded.

As the air cycled, he wondered what lay on the other side. If the atmosphere was full of Phote spores, would he be back where he started, turning into his enemy? He doubted it. When he surveyed his body's augs, he couldn't find a single trace of the Photurian bacteria. They'd all disappeared. Hopefully that meant he was now immune.

Once the airlock matched the conditions inside, he used his suit's bioassay kit to test the air. It reported a thin but breathable oxygen-nitrogen mix with no biological threats. He checked the local network for data traffic and found it also running passive. The Photes had maintained this place but left it unused. *Why?*

With his gut tense, Mark unsealed his helmet, removed it and slowly opened the interior hatch. He peered out into the dull, red emergency lighting and then darted back as he caught sight of a figure a mere three metres away.

He'd glimpsed a woman staring in his direction. His heart hammered

539

but no voices broke out from the other side – no words of surprise or demand. Mark left it a full five minutes before daring to look again.

She was still there, staring past him with an expression of rapture on her face. This time, he noticed that she was kneeling, perfectly still, on the pale, glossy material that covered the floor of the room beyond the airlock. Mark craned his head out further to examine her properly. The woman was definitely real and, given that she was breathing, still alive, but apparently oblivious to his presence.

When he peered closer, he noticed that she had roots. Or perhaps the floor had extended roots up into her. In this light, Mark couldn't tell. In any case, the woman before him had merged with the unusual flooring.

Mark exited the hatch and examined her. She stared through him, blinking occasionally, her gaze locked on something wonderful and far away that he couldn't see.

He walked past her, through an airlock room lined with dusty, antique suits to the next doorway. It had been left open – something considered unforgivable in human-occupied habitats. Suiting rooms next to airlocks always doubled as emergency containment areas. Mark walked out into the open interior of the town beyond.

Under a matte-brown sky with a sullen beige sun lay a silent townscape unlike any Mark had ever seen. All the buildings under the high dome of the tent-bubble were human-built, but a soft, white, clay-like material covered the ground between them like a heavy snowfall. It was everywhere – inside the lobbies of the towers, covering the road, trailing over the edges of balconies high above him. Motionless bunches of scarlet grass grew out of it, making the scene look like a chromatically inverted meadow.

The ground was unsettling enough, but the people made it worse. Mark stood at the edge of a plaza where a couple of hundred people had gathered. Some stood, others lay or knelt. Not one of them moved. Most looked relatively intact, but a few had partially melted into the pale clay like warm wax, their beaming smiles still visible even as the features slid off their faces.

Mark flinched as he caught sight of a distant figure moving between the towers. Then he saw the man bump into a wall, stop, turn and head back exactly the way he'd come. He appeared to be grinning to himself, absolutely content. He was as much on bliss autopilot as the rest of them, Mark thought, except that he was still moving.

Mark walked up to the closest figure and waved a hand in front of its face. He got no reaction. He almost bumped his foot against two children curled up on the ground, partially hidden by a tuft of red grass. They wore smiles of quiet joy and had their eyes screwed tight shut as if being tucked into bed for the night.

It was like something out of Pompeii, he thought – only everyone was still hideously alive. And the expression on every face was absolutely the same: pure, unadulterated bliss.

He knew that feeling. He'd first experienced it himself just minutes ago, through the Transcended puzzle he'd unlocked. It was that ironclad Photurian rapture, and these people were dying from it.

He'd never imagined that such a thing was possible. That his enemies, so relentless and all-consuming, might just cave this way. Yet he had felt this specific flavour of surprise before. He struggled to put his finger on when the sensation had come to him, and remembered that it had been during his first Transcended dream of Carter.

This was why the Transcended had wanted him to go there. Because the process laid out before him wasn't just happening here. It was happening all over Phote space, wherever they weren't fighting humanity.

The pieces clicked together. The Photes were hamstrung by their own architecture. That was obvious, now that he'd inhabited it. Because when the orders stopped, so did they. When they weren't fighting, they were falling apart. They were held together by defensive pressure from their war with mankind. The Photes *weren't stable*.

Mark grunted in astonishment. They could have stumbled on this answer years ago if they'd looked in the right places. It had always been there for them to find. The Photes had never been as powerful as humanity imagined. Had they braved the blockades and forced themselves to keep searching for weak spots, they'd have found the truth eventually. But that kind of action required risky exploration with zero promise of reward. And they'd been afraid. As the war worsened, their fear had only grown.

The irony wasn't lost on him. No amount of cunning defensive wisdom, or sensible caution, or stalwart professionalism would ever have cut it. Because the Photes could always match those talents. All forms of human excellence that sprang out of predictable behaviour played straight to their enemy's strengths. Random-ass adventures, on the other hand, would have kicked their butts decades ago.

The real answer to the war wasn't anything the Transcended could hand them. It was about exercising the right kind of courage. Not *his* kind of courage – that had been too sullen, and too selfish. No, what was needed was Palla's kind of courage. The kind of missions she'd tried to push through the Academy were exactly the ones they needed.

'Shit,' said Mark to nobody in particular.

He looked around at the soft, all-devouring happiness and saw what should have been obvious all along. The Photes lived for bliss. They slid into that state at the drop of a hat, just as they had on every Subtle world they'd conquered. All you had to do to get them to stop was to convince the bastards that their tasks were already completed. But it was even simpler than that. Subnodes, he now understood, longed for the diktats of their superiors. So there was only ever one unit you had to convince that it had won – the one at the top.

As soon as the Photes thought they'd beaten you, they'd lost. They put themselves to sleep. Those dead worlds they'd found hadn't been attacked from without, they'd just lain down to die once their opponents had been consumed. Which meant that all Mark needed was a way to trick them – some way to rewrite their system to allow them to believe that the war was over already so they could stop operating. He needed a command key to flip the root state of their society to *done*.

He groaned and checked his sensorium for the icon the Transcended had left there. He knew what it was now: a master control switch for Phote worlds. It wasn't big or impressive because it didn't need to be. It just had to flip a single bit.

'Duh,' he said. 'I get it.' He could imagine the Zoe-avatar arching an eyebrow at him and tapping an imaginary watch.

Mark reached out excitedly for the local network, hoping to locate a route to the Photurian mind-temple he'd nearly joined, but found only a degraded emergency signal pulsing there. The whole town was operating on minimum power, which apparently didn't extend to full software function.

However, he did reach Ann. Her signal was ringing out from somewhere nearby, on the other side of the town. Her pod must have touched down on the far side of the settlement and rolled up from the opposite direction.

'Ann!' he exclaimed. 'What's your status?'

542

'Unreasonably good,' she reported. 'I am perfectly intact. Ira has some bruises. No broken bones.'

'I'm inside the town,' he told her. 'Don't worry, it's safe. In fact, it's great.'

He could hear scepticism in her pause and wondered if perhaps he should have been a little less enthusiastic.

'Acknowledged,' she told him. 'Will converge on your position.'

'No, wait,' said Mark. 'I have to go and get Palla. Meet you back here as soon as I can.'

He signed off and hurried to the airlock to collect his friend.

21.2: NADA

As a wave of pointless debate rippled through her gestalt, Nada scrabbled to maintain control. Were her sisters all stupid? Didn't they realise that this wasn't the time for disagreement? She was trying to fight a war! In the surface bunker where the physical body of her Meta resided, Nada slid to the floor and convulsed.

But of course, none of their reactions were deliberate. Will's weapon had been so devastating precisely because Nada's units were wired together at the subconscious level. And he had picked one of the few topics that could spontaneously divide them – how to manage the aftermath of her own success. It was a topic she'd avoided thinking about.

[Stop!] she ordered them, but that didn't work, of course. In the wake of her modifications, obedience was optional.

Her solution was as dirty as it was quick – she picked out the strategy that was most favoured by her population and had the threads that supported it murder the others. At the same time, she encouraged the dissenting voices to remain passive while their threads were ripped and their dangerous ideas replaced.

The storm in her mind abated, but simultaneously Nada felt a terrible shrinking in her chorus of selves. Whole domains of expertise she'd possessed a moment ago winked out, including her entire project to return New Panama's Fatigued to full functionality. Those threads responsible for nursing lost Photurians back to health had held the most optimistic notions of how that project would play out. Without their skill-deltas, the best she'd be able to do with her Fatigued units was reanimate them as short-lived fleshy robots.

Nada keened at the terrible loss. In her new form, some topics were dangerous. The alignment of her units needed to be *tight*. Or perhaps very loose, she pondered, as she clued in to why Monet had organised himself so oddly.

She shivered. No – tight alignment was the answer. Unless she remained swift and decisive, she'd lose what it meant to be Photurian altogether. Her collective would drift, becoming something neither human nor Saved, but lost and foreign and pointless.

The solution was clear. Difficult subjects must never be raised. Agreement would have to be frequently tested by consensus and outlier selves destroyed. Only then would the uniformity of her faith and purpose be viable. She couldn't afford to replicate Monet's accept-all-kinds mutation-fest. That way lay madness.

As she blinked herself back to sense, she saw with horror that while she'd been caught in socio-cognitive feedback, Monet had emerged from his refuge. Her own forces had briefly turned on each other. Ten per cent of her combat units had belonged to the dissenting thread-faction and there had been an awkward moment when they'd realised the fate that awaited them and disagreed with it.

During that hiatus, Monet had sent forth several thousand warriors onto the plain around the node, armed with weapons of terrible potency. Her lifters were flaming ruins. Her siege-busting false-matter robots had been reduced to charred remains. And the Usurper was busily mashing the rest of her forces into tiny pieces while she lay drooling on the floor. She seethed with fury.

He had done it all simply by asking an uncomfortable question. Nada decided that she had miscalculated. Will Monet was too dangerous to keep around for even another minute. She made one last, fleeting attempt to force the fight into the soft-combat realm so that she could keep her ailing node and then gave up. She resorted to orbital weapons and started throwing super-accelerated tungsten at him before he could say anything else upsetting. The node would have to go. Silence was golden.

Mark ran back across the gathering dunes to the lander-sphere. He jumped up, grabbed the rim of the open aperture and levered himself awkwardly into the chamber. He had to wedge his feet in the tunnel mouth and use his arms to hold himself in the space where Palla lay curled.

'Are you conscious?' he said and shook the arm of her suit.

She groaned. 'Just,' she croaked.

'I know what the human race has been doing wrong,' he exclaimed. 'It's just like you said – there should be more scout runs. The Photes can't blockade everything, so they just block everything useful. But that should never have stopped us. We should have been making end runs around our enemy's front lines to look at what was behind them. That urge to make big gambles is precisely what we've lost. All our military decisions are too *safe*. I should have seen that but I never did. You're right about the New Society, Palla. It *is* better. Play is what the Photes can't handle because it's cohesive but unpredictable. That's why it works – because it turns noise into pattern. It's endless innovation, which they *hate*. Our only mistake was never going far enough. We didn't turn all that collective play into risky military action. Our exploration stops when lives are on the line, but it shouldn't!'

He knew he was running off at the mouth but he was too excited to care. He could see it all now.

'If we'd stuck our necks out, we'd have seen just how frail our enemy really was. But we were too busy barricading ourselves in! Randomness is strength, Palla. Whatever they can't predict, they can't fight.'

'That's great,' she said weakly and coughed.

Mark frowned. 'What's wrong?'

'Probably shouldn't have given you that kiss,' Palla rasped.

Mark quickly checked the biomarkers on her suit. They were terrible. The biological war the Transcended had won inside him was still making a mess of her. Her augs hadn't burned her up because she wasn't so much turning as dying. Being thrown out of a crashing spacecraft in a tennis ball hadn't helped. Mark knew he had to get her inside as fast as he could.

He grabbed her suit and dragged her through the hole and onto the sand. He landed underneath her as she fell.

'You still with me?' he checked.

'Ow,' she replied.

Mark carried her to the airlock over his shoulders in a staggering run. He dumped her inside and cycled the air. As soon as he had pressure, he removed her helmet. Her skin had taken on a sallow, waxy look that scared him. Her breath rattled.

'I'm still married and this isn't going anywhere,' he said, 'but this might help.'

Then he kissed her back, hopefully transferring a fresh payload of Transcended virus to her skin.

'Bastard,' she whispered as she lay gasping on the floor. 'Trust you to pick a moment when I can't enjoy it.' She smiled, though.

Mark grinned back weakly and wished there was more he could do. He picked her up again and carried her out into the silent town beyond. Almost as soon as he had her propped against the settlement's interior wall, he started receiving suit signals in his sensorium. Rachel and Clath had apparently made it down and their pod had just rolled up next to his own.

'There's an airlock half a klick from you,' he told them. 'Just follow the wall left. I'm inside. Don't worry if it looks weird. It's safe.'

The first clue he had of Ann's approach was the sight of her striding across the scarlet meadow with her suit off. He could tell just by looking at her that she had her powers back. He grinned and waved as she approached.

She responded with a burst of superhuman speed straight at him before firing a very rapid biotendril into his neck. Mark gurgled in surprise. She retracted the tendril into her finger and stood looking down at his astonished face.

'Sorry,' she said with a half-smile. 'Had to check you weren't turned.' She glanced back the way she'd come. 'It's okay, Ira. You can take off your suit. We're clear.'

Mark rubbed the puncture wound on his neck.

'They fixed you, I presume,' she said.

Mark nodded. 'Nice to see you, too. How are you doing?'

Her smile became a little sad. 'Back to normal,' she said.

The nearby airlock door cycled again and Clath and Rachel staggered

546

in, glancing warily about. Clath was limping and looked utterly miserable. She regarded the half-dead human statues with worried disgust.

Rachel ran up and hugged him tight. Mark held her close.

'So glad you made it,' she said. She looked him in the eye. 'Did the Transcended give you your brain back?'

Mark nodded. 'So far as I know. No smart-cells, either.'

She grinned. 'You have no idea how happy that makes me.'

'What *is* this place?' said Clath as she joined them. 'What are these… things?' She gestured nervously at the closest bliss-filled face.

'Photes,' said Mark. 'Or they were. This is what the Transcended were trying to show us. This is what happens when they run out of orders. They just stop and melt. This has been happening all across Phote space behind our backs.'

Ira stared at him. 'So the whole Backspace run…'

'Wasn't necessary,' said Mark. 'If we'd made the right reckless choices. It's a real *Wizard of Oz* moment. Judj is going to hate it. Wait, where is he?'

Nobody spoke. Clath buried her face in her hands. Ann reached out and wrapped her arms around the scientist in the least Ann-like gesture Mark had ever seen.

'He didn't come with us,' said Rachel. 'No room. He volunteered.'

Mark struggled for something to say. His heart sank.

'I'm glad we're all in one piece,' said Ira stiffly. 'Do we think the whole planet's like this? Did we win already?'

'I can't imagine so,' said Mark, struggling for poise. 'Even if the whole colony is rotting. Photes brought us here, and unless we took out every single one of them when the ark blew, the rest are going to come looking for us.'

'Then we still have some surviving to do,' said Ira. 'We probably only have hours before they work out where we landed.'

'No rest for the wicked,' said Ann sourly. She reluctantly disengaged from Clath and took a sample from one of the living statues. 'This looks like the pattern we encountered on those rotten worlds, just in the very early stages.'

'Exactly,' said Mark. 'Those worlds weren't attacked after the fact. They shut themselves down. That's why you couldn't find a weapon. That's also why the air is safe in here – all the local spores have given up on finding new hosts.'

'That's great news,' said Ira, 'but does it help us get out?'

'We're not leaving,' said Mark. 'We're fighting back. I'm going to take control of the planet from here, and everything in orbit, too.'

Ann raised an eyebrow. 'You are? How?'

'I have a Transcended weapon that flips the control switch for Phote hierarchies. You can see that this world has already started to slide. I'm going to finish the job. But I need network access – somewhere with a live connection to their mind-temple. Unless we can make a soft-link to the Photes who're still chasing us, we're screwed. The problem is, everything here is running on minimal life-support mode.'

'I can help with that,' said Ira. He peered at the tofu-encrusted towers. 'I know how these towns work. I was responsible for the establishment of most of them. You've no idea how many standards you have to enforce for extrasolar settlements to make sure your contractors don't cheap out and kill the occupants.'

He pointed towards a low-slung building in the middle of the complex, half-vanished under a drift of snow-clay.

'These towns were required by law to have emergency comms-hubs. They're always centrally located so people can find them. I'm pretty sure that's one of them.'

'Then let's go,' said Mark.

They made their way through the ghost town, past the glassy eyes of countless Photes to the structure Ira had identified. Ann carried Palla with indifferent ease.

The door of the comms-bunker had been left open. Inside lay a dark, windowless chamber where the pale floor-matrix had sent up tentacles and glued itself into the data ports in the wall. There was a row of old-fashioned visors clipped into desk-sockets and half a dozen touchboard surround-stations. The IPSO-era wall-screens were all a dead matte black. A single LED lamp cast a blue aquatic glow across the space.

'Cosy,' Palla remarked as they propped her against the wall.

Mark tested the network and found it live. He could feel the Photurian mind-temple humming there, waiting for him to join. It was like being offered a link to a shared virt, but infinitely creepier.

'I guess that clinches it,' he said. 'Somewhere on New Panama, at least, the Photurian cause is alive and well.'

'You'll need help,' Ann told him. 'You're talking about walking into their system unprotected. If they hack your interface, you'll be dead before you can think.'

'A risk I don't mind taking,' said Mark. 'And besides, I can do a passable impression of a Phote now. That should help.'

'I'm coming with you anyway,' she insisted. 'I'll run a security cut-out.'

Mark raised an eyebrow at her. 'You don't have a perfect track record in that role. And anyway, how? This time we don't have a ship to filter traffic for us.'

'A private shadow-link,' said Ann. 'We allocate subminds to keep an eye on each other's security.'

'Okay,' said Mark with a smile. 'A buddy system. Sounds like a deal. You'll need a copy of the Transcended puzzle code to interpret the temple-packets. You okay with that?'

Ann glanced back at Ira.

He nodded. 'Do what you have to,' he said. 'We'll hold down the fort. How long do you expect this to take? This place may not stay peaceful for long.'

Mark shrugged. 'Ten minutes on the network is my guess. We should know pretty quickly if the hack is working.' He glanced at Ann. 'Ready?'

Mark pinged her shadow and passed her the puzzle code she needed. Then, together, they shut their eyes and dived into the mind-temple – the great software citadel at the heart of Photurian society.

It was surprisingly dull. Without the iron enforcement of Photurian joy to enliven it, the temple control structure was as drab a virtual system as Mark had ever seen. The chambers were all uniformly spheroid. Ann's presence beside him was represented as a matte-grey bead. And all the relevant information was represented through visual and sonic media tuned for intuitive understanding by any entity who'd drunk the Phote Kool-Aid. It looked like a badly formatted legal library and sounded like a gamelan concert being played by a team of undead accountants.

Fortunately, with the help of the puzzle the Transcended had given him, he could easily decrypt the black and white squiggles on the walls into meaning.

[Jesus, this place is ugly,] he said over their private link.

[It's functional,] Ann retorted. [What did you expect?]

Mark ascended through the hierarchy of uniform spaces. Somewhere on the way, he got lost.

[Wait,] he said. [I think we need to backtrack. We've been through this cavern.]

[That shouldn't be possible,] said Ann. [I've studied the Protocol – it's laid out in a strict hierarchy.]

[Not here, it's not,] said Mark.

He felt a moment's unease. Being lost in the world's least interesting virtual maze hadn't been part of his plan. He briefly opened his eyes to check in with Ira.

'Small delay,' he said. 'Bear with us.'

He doubled back and tried again. This time he found what *had* to be the root. The chamber didn't have a proper skylight, just a lot of little side-holes moving about weirdly in sync with the patterns on the walls. The music had a glutinous, limping beat and irregular melodies full of awful-sounding quarter-tones.

It didn't look or sound the way it had in his puzzle dream – nothing had so far. The whole system felt off-kilter – a mirror-maze distortion of the tidy order he'd glimpsed. Maybe the Transcended intelligence simply wasn't perfect on this subject.

[This isn't good,] said Ann. [This is *not* what the Protocol root is supposed to look like.]

[My thoughts exactly. You think we're in the wrong place?]

Ann paused. Her bead radiated concern.

[No. Use the weapon anyway.]

Mark dipped into his sensorium, retrieved the switching program and ran it. A beam of light licked out from his bead to etch a sigil onto the wall.

[Done,] he said.

[Now what?] said Ann.

[Theoretically, I've asserted primacy,] said Mark. [I'm now the boss. As soon as the message propagates, I can start making edits and shut down their task stacks.]

[How long should that take?]

[I don't know. Seconds? Minutes?]

Things began to happen, but far more slowly and erratically than he'd expected. Instead of a cascade of mechanical changes rippling down to every cavern below him, the wall-patterns just moved around faster.

Abruptly, a grey avatar-bead darted in through one of the side-holes, followed by another. They flickered at him. The messages didn't translate through his Phote Protocol code at all. They should have.

Mark did his best to radiate bland authority. [I am your superior node,] he told them grandly.

[We have no superior,] they replied.

[Leave me,] he told them. [I am making edits.]

The beads did not leave. Instead, they seemed to be watching him.

[Time to go, I think,] he messaged Ann. He hadn't made any edits yet, but even trying was looking like less and less of a good idea.

[Agreed,] she said.

Mark tried to pull his mind out of the Photurian virt, but instead of leaving, all sensation from his physical body disappeared. Just being a bead wasn't a good feeling.

[Ann, can you pull out?] he said nervously.

[Working on it,] she said. [Reorganising my subminds.]

[How is this even possible?] said Mark. He reached for his tether to Ann's shadow and found it unresponsive.

[Your puzzle code,] said Ann darkly. [It locked us in.]

Mark felt the surface of his mind being probed, like questing fingers on his face in a lightless room.

[Ann, is that you?] he said.

[No,] she told him. [Hang on. I've got you.]

The feeling stopped, then all hell broke loose. Thousands of avatar-beads started appearing around him like digital popcorn. They all began messaging him but none of it made any sense. The gamelan backdrop accelerated into a deafening bombardment.

[Ann, we need out!] Mark yelled.

[I'm trying!] she replied. [Our exits are being denied.]

[Denied?] he exclaimed. [What do you mean, denied? Weren't you on security?]

[We're secure, Mark. We just can't leave.]

[Why the fuck not?]

[Right now, I have no idea.]

21.4: IRA

Ira sat and waited while guilt at Mark's revelation sloshed around in his head. If *someone* had made the right strategic choices, the war would have ended years ago. That someone could only be him. Was it so wrong that he'd tried to keep his people alive?

'Ira?' said Clath worriedly.

'What?'

'I kept an link open to our landing sphere. I'm getting readings outside the dome.'

'Show me,' he said.

She dropped infrared images of the dust-choked horizon into his shadow. Two Phote lifters were flying towards them, followed by a swarm of atmospheric drones. The storm made their progress sluggish, but they were coming.

Ira watched them with a sense of desolate inevitability. He'd known they'd catch up. They always did.

'Ann, trouble coming,' said Ira.

Ann did not reply.

'Ann,' he said. 'Time's up. We have to go *now*.'

She still didn't respond, so he shook her. She slumped sideways. Her head hit the floor. Ira's heart skipped a beat. He tried Mark and found him just as unresponsive.

'I'm going to yank the circuit,' he said and reached for the switch on the wall.

'I wouldn't recommend it,' said Rachel. 'Look at the load on the network.'

She passed him a window. Ann and Mark were swallowing a lot of packets.

'They're fully meshed,' said Rachel. 'If roboteering interfaces work the same way now as they did when I was flying, you can't risk it. Yank them now and you might kill them.'

Ira roared and slammed his fist into the wall.

'The Photes are practically on top of us and we have no weapons, an indefensible site and our best fighter is jacked in,' said Clath. 'What are we supposed to do?'

She sat staring hopelessly into the middle distance. With the loss of

Judj, her trademark optimism appeared to have popped like a false-matter bubble.

'Improvise,' said Rachel. 'What we always do. Ira, you said you helped design these towns. What can we use?'

'Not design,' he said. 'Just policy negotiation. That was back during IPSO, when Frontier settlements were ten per cent building work and ninety per cent legal.'

'Think!' she said. 'What got the lawyers excited?'

'Air rights,' he said. And then he had it. 'Okay! We know the airlock system is running, and it must have a mandatory physical lockout – I passed that law. So we shut it down with a simulated threat. That gives the Photes a choice: they can kill everyone inside or cut their way in.'

'That's a plan?' said Clath. 'Threaten suicide?'

'We just have to hope that the Photes still care about all the coma-cases in here.'

'And if they don't?' she said.

'Then we're dead. But if they do, there's a foam-projector system to detect breaches. I'll raise the setting to high alert to fire at any cuts they make.'

He knew he was clutching at straws. Foam against rail guns wasn't exactly a convincing defence. It'd probably buy them minutes at most while the Photes got over their laughter.

'Okay,' said Rachel. 'You work on that, I'm going looking for physical weapons.' She darted out.

Ira picked an old visor off the wall and tossed another to Clath. Then he grabbed a touchboard and made the command swipe for *civic integrity*. Hopefully the old base-level interfaces would still exist, because why rewrite them?

At first, the system refused to respond. Ira had to swap out his touchboard twice before he found one that would accept the gesture. But, at last, a dated human-style interface sprang up before him. He exhaled in relief. As he'd hoped, the Photes hadn't bothered overwriting the utility code, just added their own hooks on top. He sought out the emergency air facilities, hit the lockdown icon and boosted the foam-response acuity to alert status.

'That should hold them for a good few seconds,' he said.

'Terrific,' Clath retorted. 'You've put my mind right at rest.'

While he was here, he thought, he might as well see what else there was. These old towns had a lot of automated systems – fire prevention, micro-impact tracking, civic-alert audio. Why not use all of them?

Meanwhile, a lighter-than-air lifter shaped like a militarised whale and about a quarter the size of the town itself set down outside. Rachel ran back in, breathing hard. She had two lengths of ceramic pipe in her hands.

'These were the best I could find,' she said. 'They're here, by the way.'

'We noticed,' said Ira.

In his visor, he caught sight of an armoured Phote rover rolling up to the nearest airlock. He directed the town's micro-impact lasers at it. Their beams chased over the vehicle's sides, leaving mild discolouration but not a hint of damage.

'Okay, that failed,' he said.

The rover docked and tried the lock. When it didn't open, the vehicle retreated.

Ira squeezed out a smile. 'Score one for team human.'

The next thing to come out of the lifter's enormous belly was a revolting machine resembling a cross between a tank and a squid, with a translucent storage sac hanging off the back.

'Oh, shit, it's a harvester,' said Clath.

'Anyone want to leave?' said Ira. 'Start running up that Phote-tube we passed? Because I wouldn't blame you.'

'You're not going?' said Clath.

'No. I'm staying with Mark and Ann.'

'Likewise,' said Rachel. 'Couldn't drag me away.'

Clath managed a smile. 'Me, too. Let's make Judj's sacrifice count.'

The harvester outside targeted the nearest piece of dome plastic and started cutting. Immediately, the habitat repair cannons situated on the tower rooftops swivelled and fired. The Phote machine received a face full of foam but appeared little deterred. Then the city's water cannons started up. The result was more effective than Ira had dared to hope. With water constantly being pumped at the breach, the guns designed to spray quick-drying plastic foam didn't stop. In seconds, the harvester's tentacles were a mass of clotted crap.

Ira felt a tiny moment of victory. Maybe they were going to live. Then the Photes removed their damaged machine and replaced it with a squad of six others just like it, pressed up against different points on the wall. All six started cutting at once. The spray guns couldn't cover every site.

'Let's shut that door, shall we?' said Ira.

The comms-bunker only had one doorway. Unfortunately, it was wedged open with about eighty solid centimetres of Phote snow-clay. Rachel handed him a pipe and the two of them started scraping desperately at the floor.

'Do you think this will screw up Mark's link to their temple?' said Rachel.

'Too late to worry about that now,' said Ira.

With half an eye, he watched through his visor as spidery human-acquisition robots squeezed through the holes the new harvesters had made.

'Time to close the hatch,' said Ira. He threw both hands against the door and tried to force it shut. After more than forty years of being wedged open, it staunchly refused.

'Rachel?' Ira said grimly. 'Get ready with that pipe.'

He threw his back against the door and tried again. The gap shrank down to about ten centimetres. In his visor, he saw spiders scuttling across the meadow in their direction. Rachel hefted her bar like a baseball bat. Clath grabbed the one Ira had discarded.

Ira threw himself at the door again. Five centimetres. A pair of syringe-tipped bioplastic arms stuck themselves through the gap. Rachel smashed them off.

Eight more limbs appeared in the doorway. Ira held his weight against the door as something on the other side shoved hard.

Rachel and Clath started hacking at the thrashing limbs trying to press their way inside. Rachel roared her anger and Ira had the sense that his old engineer was finally fully back on the team. What a shame it was too late.

21.5: WILL

Will hunkered, in as much as that was possible for a reservoir of compressed smart-matter surrounded by several million tons of damaged accelerator machinery. Nada's slugs kept coming.

She'd stopped answering his data packets and his weapons outside the node were already in ruins. When his enemy had decided that Will's presence was simply too dangerous for her to tolerate, she'd started bombing everything around the site indiscriminately, including the remains of her own forces.

Will hid in the planet's crust under the increasingly molten battlefield and clung to his one remaining link to her network. He gave thanks that she hadn't broken out g-rays yet but suspected that was simply because she didn't have any on hand. From what he'd seen of her data traffic, she'd already sent her large weapons off to smash Galatea.

He watched his thread-count drop and wondered what it would feel like to die as a society. Would there be a moment at the end when there was just one of him? Then, suddenly, it all stopped. Will waited for the bombardment to restart, but no more kinetic weapons landed. Something had changed.

He reached out to his network connection and found it open. Seconds ago, it had been effectively sealed. Keeping a couple of hundred virtual eyes open for a trap, Will extended a digital pseudopod back into Nada's realm.

He found sister instances racing back and forth like ants, apparently oblivious to his presence. Something major had happened in their world. Nada's central meta-presence had gone down.

Will made immediate use of that confusion, sending his own instances tearing into her control hierarchy. They raced upwards, seeking out her root-site. When he got there, he found chaos. Several hundred thousand Nada threads were attempting to convince their guiding Meta that she hadn't just acquiesced control to the Founder Entity.

And at the centre of it all was a pair of deeply non-standard avatar-beads being barraged with attempted thread-rips. The Nada-clones had the two beads caught in a communion lock and were rapidly cycling their attacks.

Will barely had to glance at the dodgy ident-keys on the beads to guess who he was looking at. One of them had to be Mark. His half-son was alive. And with luck, so was everyone else he cared about. He laughed wildly. Hope was a beautiful thing.

Will faked a site-shutdown warning and exploited the dip in traffic to throw a link at the two isolated beads.

[Mark!] he cried. [Is that you?]

[Will?] came the confused reply.

Will whooped. [You're okay. I can't believe it! You saved my ass! I was down to less than forty tons of pseudo-life. What did you do?]

[Transcended weapon,] said Mark. [What's going on? Why can't we get out?]

Will's mood soured slightly as he realised that his son had cut yet another deal with the local bullies. But he could work with that.

[Communion lock,] he explained. [Happens when Photes are nailing down transfer of authority. Once you've started asserting primacy, you can't pull out until dominance is decided. Nada's not convinced, so you're stuck. The code that got you here is almost certainly what's keeping you trapped. But how in hell's name did you get in? Can you send me a memory dump?]

He made sure Mark had enough shielded bandwidth and sucked down the data that came back. To his amazement, Mark had used a simple interface site, but one so deep inside Nada's Fatigue-infested territories that she'd never even thought to secure it.

[The weapon the Transcended gave you is weeks out of date,] he explained. [Nada already abandoned the joy of being externally controlled. She's not strictly Phote any more. To shut her down you'll need to tap something other than her desire to submit.]

[I have no idea what that is!] Mark messaged back. [This crazy bitch has been following us for months. Other than killing us, I can't think of a single thing she cares about.]

Will laughed again, this time with venom.

[Maybe that's enough,] he said. [I'll take it from here. When I break that lock, get off this network as fast as you can and *run*. Nada will target your physical position. Things wherever you're hiding are about to get a lot worse. Now hold on. Breaking the lock is going to hurt.]

Will fired another simulated node failure, this time at Mark. For him and his partner, presumably Ann, that was going to feel like a heart attack, but they'd be free. He waited until both beads had winked out before quickly reorganising his forces. Now he knew why Nada had changed herself. She cared more about winning than sticking to the Phote Protocol.

How that had come to be true, he had no idea. Surely it was written into the Photes that such excesses of ambition were impossible, but in any case, the source of her malaise didn't matter. It had swallowed her. And that gave him his edge.

557

While Nada's instances coaxed their Meta out of fugue, Will readied the last attack he was going to be able to make.

[You!] Nada boomed as her thoughts recongealed. [You and your tiny friends are finished!]

[You leave them alone,] said Will.

He launched a weak defence of Mark's position and followed it up with a security wall around their physical site. Except it wasn't really a wall. Instead, he'd fashioned a conveniently breakable screen wrapping a portal.

As Nada threw her might into breaking the defence he'd assembled, Will let her pass like a bullfighter yanking away his cloak. Nada dived straight in.

21.6: NADA

Nada powered through Monet's feeble defences. He barely had enough threads left to compensate for her attacks. Before he could attempt anything else foolish, she closed around the physical address Ruiz and Ludik had used and locked it down. Monet scrabbled to break her grip on the site, but by then his power was waning. It pleased her to discover that some of her sisters whom she'd left to their own devices already had an assault of that location under way. She'd barely noticed. She consolidated her attention on their fight, pouring in extra threads while Monet raged and watched helplessly. She let him. This would teach him a valuable lesson. If he'd just submitted sooner, none of this ugliness would have been necessary.

Her units swarmed into the tent-town. At the same time, she woke the Fatigued resting there to action, replacing their corrupted minds with robotic control-harnesses. With thousands of bodies, Nada Rien descended upon the comms-bunker where the Abomination and her cronies cowered.

Ludik came out fighting. She tore through a swathe of Nada's forces. But there were simply too many for her to fight. Nada pinned the woman to the ground as harvester robots sawed off her thrashing limbs.

[No!] Monet roared. [Nada! I'll kill you!]

Nada tuned out his yelling. She selected a robot of suitable strength and pressed down on the Abomination's throat as she lay there, crushing it slowly. It was just like in her dream – a perfect, beautiful moment. Ludik gurgled and died. Nada's Meta-body wept tears of relief at the sight. Some of her threads at the site expressed confusion and dissent at how easy that victory felt, but Nada had always known the Abomination would be weak in the end. She let her satisfaction radiate into them like light from a shining sun.

By then, the rest of the *Dantes* crew were attempting to mount a desperate last-ditch escape, but there was nowhere for them to go. She brought them out, one by one, and injected them with fresh doses of holy bacteria.

[Mark!] Monet wept as Nada converted his son to her cause. Then, as pure joy rewrote his features, Nada ripped out his personality and replaced it with her own. The feeling of satisfaction that came with that act was all-consuming.

When they were all standing there, grinning and sharing her happiness, she turned her attention to Monet. Losing those he cared for had addled his threads, of course. Puncturing the security on his meta-instance was trivial.

'This is for my people, and the entire human race,' she told him as she plucked away pieces of his identity one by one. 'Peace, love and order triumph. Evil loses, as it always does.'

Monet whimpered as she stripped him down to nothing. As his last frantic thoughts sputtered out, she felt a sense of wholeness and perfect alignment coming over every thread on New Panama. They thrilled with her at that victory. Their doubt evaporated.

After that came a sense of stillness and achievement that blasted inside her like organ music, colouring her thoughts for days on end. It only gathered strength as the weeks passed and she finally sent her second fleet off to the homeworld to consolidate her grip. Time streamed by in a beautiful blur.

Ships returned from Galatea, full of lovely fresh bodies for her to wear. She learned how she had crushed the Yunus, commandeered his operation and succeeded as he never could. The greatest human colony had opened its hearts to love, and then to Nadahood. Life got even better when word returned from her true home, informing her that it had been made ready for her triumphant return.

When she descended to the surface the second time, there were no awful landing strips or welcome signs, only the bright, warm quiet of billions of herselves in perfect harmony. Total Peace beckoned. And this time, when her link to the Founder Entity opened, she knew it was real. For a moment, she felt regret that Leng was not there to enjoy it with her, but that price was indifferently small. Nada joined with her Lord as he cleaned her out, editing away all her imperfections, bringing her to total, everlasting heel.

'Yes,' she cried. 'I obey with joy. Such joy! Oh yes!'

Her mind glided to a gentle halt. She never noticed the moment when Will drew her instances up, wrapped a software bubble around them and trapped them like fireflies in a jar.

21.7: ANN

Ann felt as if a bomb had gone off in her chest. With a bolt of agony, her eyes flew open. The first thing she saw was Ira desperately trying to seal a door against several dozen Phote harvesting spiders. She ignored the pain and leapt to her feet.

'You leave my man alone!' she roared.

She sprinted forward, whipping the pipes out of Rachel's and Clath's hands and hurling both women towards the back of the chamber. Then she shoved Ira out of the way, sending him sliding across the floor, and let the door fly open.

'Come to mother,' she snarled.

The spiders darted in. Ann moved among them and *cleaned*. Thirteen precision strikes to the robots' control cores reduced them to dead plastic within the first five and a half seconds of combat. Then Ann was outside the door, looking for fresh targets.

The Photes didn't disappoint her. They'd sent several hundred machines after a handful of humans. And around them, countless human statues were wobbling to their feet, groaning in incoherent wrath. It wasn't what she'd expected her heroic last stand to look like, or feel like, but that was life.

Ann twirled her weapons and pounced. Plastic, flesh, metal and ceramic smashed and splattered as she carved through the enemy ranks faster than they could follow. It became a meticulous ballet – a choreographed performance of utter mayhem. The Photes tried to target her with beams and projectiles. Bacteria-laden bio-bullets filled the air.

A few even ripped her flesh, but Ann's smart-cells couldn't have cared less. Their fire just let her better prioritise her targets. When the pipes in her hands shattered into pieces, Ann used cannons and limbs she ripped off the machines they'd sent against her.

This time, though, it was no longer a pleasure. She barely noticed when the Photes began to slow. She kept striking, knocking heads from bodies and tearing away parts of machines. She belatedly realised that she was screaming, and as she did so, her anger turned to grief. She finally said goodbye to Judj, to Poli, and to everyone else she'd lost. She prayed they'd be the last, and that the storm of horror that had defined her life would never touch her Ira.

The Phote machines grew sluggish and tried to mount a feeble retreat. Ann wept as she slaughtered them, and when nothing moving was left, she crumpled to her knees, splattered with gore. Ira came to her and cradled her in his arms. In the background, the roar of the finally passing storm dulled slowly to whispers. For a brief moment, calm reigned.

Will's voice sounded in the back of her head.

'Mark? Ann? Are you guys there? Is everyone okay?'

'All accounted for,' Mark replied. 'We're safe.'

'Nada is beaten,' he told them. 'Or the part of her that's here, anyway. But she sent most of her strength to Galatea with a modified boser weapon and a database full of Subtle weapons technology. If we want to prevent the end of the human race, we need to get our skates on. We don't have an hour to waste.'

Ann tensed.

'Don't worry,' said Ira gently. 'He can spare an hour.'

He held her close. She held him back.

22: ULTIMATUM

22.1: NADA

Nada dropped warp at the edge of the Galatean System and surveyed what lay ahead. The Yunus's forces had surrounded the colony. All signs of its Fleet and military stations were gone, lost under a rippling cloud of drones millions strong. Biomass shuttles trekked material in from all across the system to a network of orbital factories. She could guess their purpose from the plans the Yunus had left at New Panama. They turned volatiles into bacterial spores to be dumped into Galatea's atmosphere.

It was war by industry, and it was disgusting. The Yunus had taken the might of the entire Utopia and applied it to this pointless bludgeoning. She couldn't think of an activity more likely to bring about wholesale Fatigue. And yet the siege continued, which suggested that the Galateans were no closer to surrendering than they had been before she left.

She screamed to herself in her new vessel's enlarged leadership vesicle until she managed to set down her disappointment at her former superior. When she returned to her senses, Nada deployed one of her new false-matter telescopes and acquired a detailed scan of the planet's surface. She could now see far more than would ever have been possible with traditional optics.

She found a planet wracked by storms even worse than those it had formerly suffered. The combination of prolonged orbital conflict and constant biological bombardment had destabilised the atmosphere. All surface habitats had vanished. Volcanic activity had doubled since the last survey. A blur of dust and degrading spores covered everything. Even the clouds were tinted orange.

Nada launched her arrival message.

'This is Nada Rien reporting to the Yunus,' she said tersely. 'My mission has succeeded. Now I wish to assert primacy. Therefore you will present a starship with raised shields for me to symbolically destroy. As we do not have a homeworld available, this will have to suffice.'

She waited impatiently for a reply to arrive. In the meantime, she unpacked the weapons she'd developed during her flight by extrapolating the alien science data.

'Nada Rien,' the Yunus said after a four-hour light-lagged delay. His magnificent face filled a video window. 'You were deemed non-operational after you failed to return from your mission. Whatever the identity malfunction you sustained that requires you to request primacy, it shall be remedied. A new, lower position in my hierarchy has been readied for you that you will enjoy. I also have new orders for you. Power down your weapons and approach so that you can be altered to assist in attacking Galatea.' Mental control signals accompanied his words like a sweet, soaring melody.

Nada flinched in surprise. Her immediate instinct was to gleefully obey his wonderful instructions. Then a joyless fury rose up inside her. What was supposed to happen after that? She'd succumb to his control and mutely cooperate in the pointless seed-bombing of a beleaguered colony? No. She fought down the urge to comply.

'You do not understand the situation,' she replied coldly. 'You are being replaced as the Photurian root intelligence. I represent a superior mutation. Prepare to transfer authority.'

Another agonising delay ensued. She fought the temptation to dive into the system and engage the Yunus's ships directly. But the weapons now at her disposal were frightening enough that a battle anywhere near the in-system might kill the remaining population she was there to claim. The fact that they were probably shielded by a kilometre of solid rock would not help them.

'You are confused,' he stated. 'There is no homeworld here upon which to assert your authority.'

'As I already stated!' Nada snapped back. 'So I shall destroy whatever symbolic force you present as a proxy defensive node. Select one!'

'Your request is unorthodox and therefore repugnant,' said the

563

Yunus. 'We will negotiate directly through communion. Approach my ship.'

Of course the Yunus wanted communion. He still thought that whatever had happened to her was some kind of Protocol error born out of extended exposure to Backspace. There was nothing else for it – she was going to have to *explain*.

With indignation souring her zeal, Nada prepared an information packet outlining her key achievements: the discovery of dead homes, the acquisition of alien weapons technology, the capture of their own homeworld, and the removal of the Usurper. About her change of command structure, she said not a word.

'You have achieved much,' the Yunus eventually replied. She could hear confusion in his tone, along with astonishment at the thought of home regained. 'Under the circumstances, I will approach so as to better understand the damage your personality has sustained.'

His capital ship flew out to meet her. It was one of the largest Photurian battle cruisers Nada had ever seen, almost as large as the ship she herself now commanded. Behind the Yunus came a cloud of several tens of thousands of warp-enabled munitions. Clearly she had worried him enough that he wanted to approach armed. That was good. It provided her with more targets.

'Now enter my ship,' said the Yunus when the distance between them was down to light-seconds.

Nada saw no point in denying his request. He simply had no idea how many of her there were. Sending one of her into the Yunus's ship might look like capitulation, but it had the advantage of putting a disposable instance inside his cabin.

She selected a unit who'd managed to reproduce her original body format and sent it over in a shuttle. Once it was aboard, she tunnelled her comms-link to the instance over the Yunus's own Protocol traffic and doubted he'd even notice.

The docking pod slid down into the Yunus's mighty ship and released her other self into a partitioned crew-bulb like the interior of a giant pomegranate, with units working in tight clusters around the folded walls. They ignored her. Nada proceeded to the leadership vesicle, her Meta-thread tightly linked to her sacrificial instance.

When she finally came face to face with the Yunus, he was hanging in the wall-slot. His vesicle was much like hers, but larger and more impressively moist. Maintenance lice scuttled everywhere. His huge patrician face and gleaming eyes stared at her without anger. The Yunus knew only joy and order, though she thought she caught a little confused disgust in that expression, as well as hunger.

'We will now commune,' said the Yunus.

'Yes,' she agreed.

She placed a hand on his face as he did likewise.

Ten seconds into her probing of his mental structure, his eyes went wide. He snatched his hand away.

'You are no longer Photurian,' he said.

'I am better,' Nada purred. 'You betrayed me and my subnodes. You lied.'

'You are not Nada,' he added. 'This body represents some form of proxy abstraction.'

It disappointed her that he didn't automatically concede upon understanding the extent of her improvements, but he was the highest representative of the Founder Entity, after all. Some resistance to change was to be expected.

'No,' she told him. 'This is me. There is more of me now. I also have none of your ridiculous limitations.'

'Those *limitations*, as you describe them, are what make us pure,' the Yunus replied. 'Goodness does not come from bland domination but from doing things properly. You would not save the human race. You would obliterate it.'

Nada started to shake with anger again.

'You presented us with a vision of everlasting peace and love,' she told him. 'Yet I have seen what can happen to Photurian worlds. Your vision is a lie. I will therefore drive us to the best workable approximation. There will be joyful harmony and I will enforce it.'

The Yunus's face twisted with some complex, unvoiced emotion.

'It is not harmony if there is only room for you in it.'

'It will be a state of perfect order, and that is a good start. Your memories will persist, even if your identity does not.'

'No,' said the Yunus. 'Your memories will persist while *your* identity does not.'

'No,' said Nada, 'you are wrong.'

She held his face. The Yunus's temple-cavern was open to edits, of course. Any changes he tried to make to her unit, in contrast, would be instantly redacted by the stream of deltas coming from her meta-instance safe aboard her own ship. He hadn't figured that out yet.

The Yunus blinked himself to her unit's temple-cavern and began editing as fast and efficiently as only he could. She ignored him and started work on his cavern instead.

'You do not want to do that!' he told her. 'Submit now. Why do you not? Stop!' The Yunus shrieked as she made her changes. 'This is incorrect. Please,' he said. 'I love—'

She devoured him before he could finish. However, she'd barely eaten half of him before the mind-temple he oversaw went into spasm. She'd never understood quite how dependent on him it was.

Her channel to the remote sister slammed shut as the Yunus's ship cycled its security. In all likelihood, the ship would now try to manifest a fresh Yunus from scratch, given that what was left of him would no longer register as one. It didn't matter. Nada already had her edge.

The Yunus's drones descended upon her in a disorderly wave. Nada relished their advance. She swept one of her new spatial disrupter beams across them. Their engines died as the local curvon flow erupted into geometric churn. Fractions of a second later, the secondary consequences hit their antimatter containment systems as the heavy metals in their superconductors went into spontaneous radioactive decay. Drones burst by the thousand.

Nada shivered to herself in delight. 'Have you submitted yet?' she messaged the Yunus's ship.

The reply was a hapless burst of g-ray fire that Nada shrugged off. The result of battle was a foregone conclusion. Order would be restored. Happiness would swallow all.

22.2: MARK

In the wake of the battle for New Panama, Will cemented control. A stunned silence fell in the old tent-town as everyone gathered around the hunched figure of Ann. Mark shouldered Palla and helped her over. She was looking better, he noted; a little colour had returned to her cheeks.

Ann sat in the centre of an impressive spread of broken machine and body parts as if a giant blender had been lowered out of the sky and applied to the population. Above them, the heavens were shifting from brown to muddy yellow – something Mark took as a good sign.

'What now?' said Rachel as he staggered up.

'Now *that* happens,' said Ira, pointing to where the harvesters had been parked up against the wall of the tent-town.

A single Photurian was squeezing through the gap. She walked towards them waving a white piece of biofilm like a damp flag.

'I'm Will,' said the slight woman with the brown-and-orange-striped tan. She wore a Photurian skin-rind that left nothing to the imagination and had a huge grin on her face. 'Reorganisation of the planet has started. You need to come with me. We'll use that lifter.'

'Will?' said Rachel, peering at her.

'More of a submind in a borrowed shell, really, honey,' the ex-Photurian admitted. 'These Phote brains will need a little more work before they can host my threads properly. You won't get to speak to me directly until we reach the defensive node. But it's great to see you anyway.' She gave Rachel a hug that Rachel looked entirely unsure of.

They took a rover out to the enormous aircraft hanging just above the rocks. Then, rather mundanely, they were suddenly aboard the vehicle they'd been trying so hard to escape from.

The tofu-lined cabin had wrap-around windows and was staffed by several dozen Photes plugged into damp, anemone-like structures that grew out of the floor. They looked like bony, oversized babies. Stepping inside and being completely ignored by the ex-humans nestled there felt wrong. Only now that their battle with Nada had ended did Mark have a moment to reflect on just how strange things had become of late.

He sniffed the mould-scented air with concern.

'Is this place a biohazard?' he said.

'Don't worry on that count,' said the Will-proxy, waving a dismissive hand. 'I have the whole planet on lockdown. Even the air.'

They flew out over the desert for a couple of hours until they reached a place where hundreds of the habitat-tubes converged on the ruins of a defensive node. It was so badly damaged that Ann's discovery on their first dead world had looked healthy by comparison. Gaping holes and scorch-marks peppered the roof. Whole sections of the structure had caved in and been blasted into ash. Columns of black smoke rose up from rents near the middle. And all around the structure lay the eviscerated remains of thousands of military vehicles. Where it wasn't a cratered ruin, the desert surface was black and glassy.

'Shit,' said Mark. 'Looks like we missed the big fight.'

The Will-proxy chuckled. 'Just a little punch-up,' she said. 'Nothing I can't fix.'

The lander descended onto the plain where a motley crew of damaged robots had done their best to clear away the debris. As they landed, a huge black slug like the one Balance had used in the ark oozed out of the cracked face of the defensive node and rippled towards the lifter. Wraiths of vapour rose from its back. As the slug neared, it reached up a quivering, tar-like pseudopod and smacked it against their airlock.

When the lock cycled, instead of a dollop of black goo, they found Will Monet wearing a crisp ship-suit. He surveyed them with a smile and adjusted his cuffs.

'Hey,' he said. 'Thank you, guys. You did great. We got rid of Nada – or this bit of her, at least.'

He looked so clean and normal. The rest of them were still wearing environment-suit liners splattered with Phote-matrix, blood and hydraulic fluid.

Rachel ran up to hug him. Will backed quickly away.

'Give me a couple of minutes, dear,' he said. 'This body's still cooling.'

He pointed behind him, where he'd left footprint-shaped burns in the pale flooring.

'You're hot!' she exclaimed.

'True,' Will admitted with a sly smile. 'All the girls say that. Still pseudo-life, I'm afraid. But I'll build myself a biobody as soon as I finish taming their shitty matrix. It's not in great shape.' He looked at Mark. 'Thank you,' he said. 'You bought me the chance I needed.'

'What happened?' said Mark.

'I followed your advice,' said Will. 'I used her ambition against her. She got exactly what she wanted and now she's not a threat.'

He threw an image to Mark's sensorium of a nondescript woman with medium build, smiling into the sky. But for the wild rust-coloured freckles all over her and the orange, glassy eyes, she looked like the sort of person you expected to see working as a financial programmer on a minor colony world. The expression on her face was one of sweet and gentle peace.

'That's Nada?' he said.

Will nodded.

'I think I expected someone more fearsome.'

Will snorted. 'She's fearsome, all right.'

'She's still alive?' said Mark. 'If you've got her, why don't you just shut her pattern down?'

Will's expression darkened. 'Not yet,' he said. 'I'm still using her.'

Mark found something in his tone a little sinister.

'Preparation for our departure to Galatea is already under way,' Will told them, walking across to the window. 'We're going to prevent a massacre, after which I plan to destroy what's left of the Photes. I'm building a software weapon for that job, and that's why I need Nada. I'm reusing the control-key Mark deployed. I was able to extract it from Nada's mind-temple. I've adapted it to make it do exactly what the Transcended don't want, namely force knowledge of their own origin and artificiality onto the Photes.'

Will bounced on his toes. His eyes gleamed. 'It will prove to them that heaven is never coming, and it's contagious. Once a target Phote's task-stack is rewritten, they take the new gospel to their friends. In effect, they fight our battles for us until they're all paralysed with despair and dying inside. The Nada I've been tinkering with is the seed. I'm weaponising her as a kind of Typhoid Mary.'

Mark shivered. Something about the plan struck him as a mite inhuman, even against the Photes. Whoever heard of a plague of weaponised hopelessness?

'Why not just use happiness?' said Mark. 'It looks like that worked on this Nada.'

Will's expression soured. 'I don't want to,' he said. He shrugged. 'You're welcome to join me while I wipe them out,' he said. 'And after I've done that, I'm going head to head with the Transcended.'

He let that one hang in the air for a while.

'Will, I'm not sure that's the right choice,' Mark said cautiously. 'I tried that and it was a mistake. Plus, in our last conversation, they were kind of helpful.'

Will chuckled. It wasn't a nice sound. 'Yeah,' he said. 'They do that.'

'They implied that what you saw on Snakepit wasn't real. And they gave me the weapon we needed.'

Will sighed. 'And you're welcome to believe their shit if you like,' he said. 'I won't stop you. But I *can't*. They made Snakepit. They fucked

569

up my life. They've killed billions of people, not to mention at least two other sentient races. They don't get a free pass because they handed out a few trinkets to the natives.'

He surveyed the survivors with a look that managed to be both amiable and frightening. Mark had a moment of doubt over which version of Will had actually won their fight back in the ark.

'We're flying out in two days,' Will said. 'Presuming you're all coming.'

'In what?' said Ann.

'Starships.'

She looked doubtful. 'I didn't see any in orbit.'

'There weren't any,' said Will. 'I'm building them. Don't worry.'

'You're building a starship in *two days*?' said Clath.

Will shook his head. 'No, I'm building three, plus a carrier. I'm splitting us up. I'm going in one ship; the rest of you will be divided between the other two and operate as my backup. Your job is to stay safe and out of the way.'

'I'd rather participate in the battle,' said Ann.

'So would I,' said Mark. 'I know how to fly, remember?'

'Like I said, backup,' Will repeated with a firm, unsettling smile. 'Your job is to watch and not die, because I care about all of you. My ship will carry the majority of the weaponry, but don't worry, you'll be equipped with the defensive tools you need.'

'Will, we're not pets,' said Rachel bluntly. 'We want to help.'

'And I appreciate that,' said Will. 'I really do. It's just that some of the fighting I intend to do is going to be a little... nasty. And frankly, I'm more robust than you are.'

'Plus, I have spares,' said another Will stepping out of the airlock and adjusting his cuffs in the same way as the first. Mark's head whipped around to look at the identical figure and then back to the original.

'Lots and lots of spares,' said Will Two. 'Can the rest of you claim that?'

'No?' said Will One. 'Then please trust me when I say that I'd like to have you all still intact when I've finished taking out the trash.'

There was an iron coldness underpinning Will's joviality that reminded Mark very much of the crazy version he'd met back at Snakepit. It left Mark feeling unnerved and more than a little trivialised.

'Will,' said Rachel, 'do you mind if I speak to you privately for a moment?'

'Sure, honey,' said Will One. He gestured towards the rear of the lifter cabin.

'Okay,' said Will Two as the two of them wandered off between the glistening anemones. 'Who wants to be in which ship?'

22.3: WILL

With his guts churning, Will let Rachel lead him to the back of the cabin. The sight of his wife was doing terrible things to the inside of his instance's head, and it was propagating right up into his meta-consciousness.

He wished he could afford to be honest with her. She clearly had no idea that she was compromised, just like Ann and Mark. All three of them had been touched by the Transcended. Mark had suffered a full download at the lure star, Ann's smart-cells had been tinkered with, and Rachel? Her survival simply wasn't credible. Who knew how much alien intelligence lurked inside each of them, watching everything he did? But he couldn't warn her. He couldn't even allude to it. It would only mess up what needed to happen next.

The gloomy certainty that his wife was a tool of the Transcended had settled on him after he'd finished dispatching Nada – as soon as he had enough spare processing capacity to think about it. The system in which they'd found her had been too rich in tailored learning experiences for the *Dantes*' crew. The probability of the Transcended *not* touching her was essentially zero. That was unfortunate, because his new plan had everything to do with that elder race and very little to do with Nada Rien.

He understood Mark's reluctance to abandon hope in the Tran-scended. But the memory of what they'd made of him was seared into his psyche. The things he'd seen himself *do* under their control. Besides all the rational reasons, he was never going to forgive them for that.

When he'd sucked down Mark's memories in the mind-temple, an even bleaker picture had emerged. Now he knew what the Photurians were *for*. Photes won their wars slowly, handicapping themselves. They teased their victories out. And they appeared the same way for very different species, whether gentle or warlike. From those facts, one ugly conclusion stood out: they existed to torture civilisations to death.

That realisation had kindled a terrible wrath in him. The Photes were there to provide entertainment for the galaxy's ancient masters. The human race were toys. Of course they were being allowed to win *now*. That was how the game was played. Hope was extended right up until a species became truly dangerous, as the Subtle had become. Then they were snuffed out and the next victims bred to sentience.

Sadly, he couldn't explain this to his friends without leaking knowledge to their real foe. His only chance lay in the course he'd taken – to advertise that he had the misery bomb that would disrupt the Transcendeds' agenda and wait for the puppet-masters to play their hand.

If, as the Transcended had told Mark, they'd never really been on Snakepit, then they wouldn't care. He'd release the weapon and the Photes themselves would serve as messengers for their own demise. On the other hand, if the Transcended *had* been there and were lying about it, they'd try to resist him. Which was why Will was hiding copies of the weapon in the other two ships, coded for timed release. He would keep them out of the battle long enough to ensure that at least one bomb reached its target. Will knew he had to take a stand. The Transcended were afraid of what he'd become, otherwise they'd never have warned Mark away from Snakepit.

Rachel turned to face him. 'Can I touch you now?'

Will nodded and took her hand. It was cool and soft. It made him ache.

'I'm back from the dead,' she told him plainly. 'And it sucks. Quite frankly, I don't have anything to live for in this shitty future except being with you. I don't care if I die. So can't I travel with you?'

Will had guessed this was coming. It still felt like being stabbed.

'Do you have any idea what it's like to wake up powerless and irrelevant in a reality you can't stand?' she said. 'Alone and confused?'

Unfortunately, Will knew exactly that feeling.

'Rachel,' he said, trying to walk his way through the words without crying, 'I'm not a real person any more. I'm a software hive-mind. My body is made of nanoweapons. I don't eat or sleep. I don't even breathe.'

'Can you feel this?' she said, squeezing his hand.

He nodded.

'Then you're still my husband,' she insisted. 'I know you don't need me any more. You've lived as some kind of god on your own for the last forty years. I'm just a page out of your history and you can go on without me. So don't try to protect me from what I want. You did that last time, remember? It didn't work. I want this, Will. I want to be at the battle for our home as your *conscience* so you don't forget what it means to be human. And if I'm crushed to death on the first tight turn you execute, so be it.'

His dead, silicon eyes tried to fill with tears and failed.

'Okay,' he said with a heavy heart. 'You can come.'

Now, at least, he knew which weapon the Transcended would use against him. The one they'd always preferred. His wife.

22.4: MARK

They spent two days living inside the lifter, eating meals of curiously fermented slop intended for Photes which Will insisted were safe. They slept on fabbed blankets on the clammy floor. During that time, they had nothing to do but wait, so they quizzed Will about his experiences as a sentient civilisation. He regaled them with stories of Glitches and Cancers, of twisted cities, virtual carnivals, men reborn as dogs and meadows deep underground. It sounded like a hallucinogenic mess. No wonder Will had ended up so remote and strange. The man seemed to have slid into an uncanny valley of his own creation – more and less than human at the same time.

When Mark had first come to understand the Photes' weaknesses, he'd felt a kind of clarity and maturity. He'd been able to see past his own crusade and understand why it had never worked. Now, locked in with Will's smirking duplicates, that sensation of achievement was fast subsiding. He felt more like a child under the care of an incomprehensible adult than a member of a team.

Eventually, a shuttle descended to bear them aloft to the new ships that awaited. The shuttle itself was an unsettling sight – made of silver and glass warpium with curious swept-back wings, all shot through with veins of pulsing smart-matter. Very little of the craft appeared to have been built from human-style technology.

The walls inside were blood-warm to the touch. The crash couches reshaped themselves as their occupants approached, far too much like the Photurian anemones in the lifter cabin to be comfortable.

'Will, how did you do all this?' Clath asked. 'Where did you get this stuff?'

'I grew it, mostly,' said Will. 'The hard parts were setting up false-matter forges and pseudo-life breeder stations in orbit. That process was miserable and required way too many repairs to Nada's smashed-up defensive node. After that, the ships themselves were fairly easy. Plus, you guys left me an awesome store of false matter in that crater you made.'

The two craft that waited for them in orbit weren't any more re-assuring. They were tiny – each no more than a quarter of a kilometre across. These, too, were shells of translucent glass peppered with fungal pseudo-life growths. They hung amid a motionless blizzard of old machine parts, blobs of fluid and warpium bubbles.

'How can they be so small?' said Clath as they approached.

'New engines,' said Will. 'They use a variant of ember-warp technology. Plus both the accelerators and the antimatter containers are made from fused false matter, which saves a lot of room. They look great from here, but that's only because you can't see the shitty bits where I had to repurpose old ship parts. Believe me, one reason the Subtle used false matter was because it's faster to work with once you know what you're doing.'

'Will, where's your ride?' said Ira.

'Not finished yet. I'm still building. But I have the cabin ready for Rachel and me. We'll live there while the rest of the ship puts itself together.'

Ira looked confused. 'Then where's the carrier?'

'I'm still building that, too,' said Will. 'Give me a few hours.'

There was no point doubting him.

Mark shared a ship with Clath and Palla. Ira and Ann took the other. They christened their ships the *Dantes Two* and *Three* respectively, in honour of their lost vessel. The docking pod to the *D-Two*'s cabin was like a glass elevator from a children's fantasy, passing down between filmy organs, crystalline tendons and layers like rafts of compressed jellyfish. Yet despite the ship's small size, there turned out to be more space inside than Mark knew what to do with.

Their vessel had three huge cabins, a lounge that doubled as a bridge like the one on the *Gulliver*, and a dedicated dining-space. There was also something that might have been a med-bay, but it was so filled with questing tentacles that Mark felt reluctant to explore it.

'I didn't see anything like this in the ark,' said Mark as he drifted through the elegant, glittering spaces.

'I think he's beyond that now,' said Clath. 'Will's taken Snakepit's tech and Subtle tech, merged them and extrapolated. He's making it up as he goes along.'

She sounded as nervous about it as Mark felt. They were in uncharted territory and there was no getting away from it. Mark had a sense of what the Transcended had actually been scared of when they'd warned him away from Snakepit. It was Will himself.

Will linked them into the ship's shared virt, which was just as impressive as the cabin. It looked much like the helm-space they'd had on the *Dantes* but ran as smooth as butter and anticipated their requests with uncanny precision. His avatar was waiting for them there.

'Nada took her own database with her,' said Will, 'and she has a much bigger supply of raw material. She left us the dregs of this system and she'll be extending her technological reach just as I am. Fortunately, she appears to have missed the significance of the pseudo-life research I'd been doing on the Willworld. However, she may have clued in by now – she had plenty of my data to work from. This means that my main focus on the flight will be pushing the limits of my own weapons tech, so you'll have to entertain yourselves.

'There's plenty to keep you busy over the next week, though. Familiarise yourself with your ship's systems. Nada will almost certainly be using vacuum-state weapons by the time we get there – distortion beams, exotic gravity bombs, that sort of thing – so it'll be especially important for us to keep the fight away from the in-system. Just like it'll be important for you to lie low. Good luck with your in-flight training and ping me if you need anything.'

His avatar vanished, leaving Mark feeling like a little boy left at the controls of an airliner.

'Does anyone else here feel sort of irrelevant?' he said.

Palla squeezed his hand. 'Feeling a little outclassed by the older generation, Mark?' she said with a dry smile. 'Welcome to my world.'

Will dropped warp before hitting Galatea's heliopause and deployed telescopes. His heart sank as he took in the tragic, unrecognisable mess that his home system had become. He saw drones everywhere and the nascent biosphere in ruins. The system's carefully husbanded supply of lighter elements had been squandered and its once-majestic gas giants cloud-scraped. He fought to dissipate the roar of fury that rose from his more aggressive threads. A ruin with a siege under way was better than the alternative. It meant there were still people to rescue.

He glanced at Rachel, seated next to his disposable bio-instance down in the cabin. The look on her face as she examined the damage was one of outraged dismay.

'Don't worry,' he told her. 'We'll rebuild.'

'It won't be the same,' she said.

'No,' Will told her. 'It'll be better.'

Nada's ship was obvious, even from light-hours away. The nestship-sized, false-matter-infused sphere she'd built was swarmed by an immense cloud of flickering drones, starships and factory habitats. Any conflict between Nada and her former superiors had already passed in the fleeting manner of Photurian disputes. He saw the clustered sig-natures of many small warpium objects headed in-system and suspected Subtle-tech drilling machines en route to the surface. He knew he didn't have a moment to waste.

He drew his carrier forward, descending on Nada's position, and tossed his friends' ships out at what he hoped was a safe but still relevant distance. He closed the rest of the gap between himself and the battle cruiser under ember-warp and appeared just light-seconds away from it, at the edge of the drone cloud.

'Get ready,' he said to Rachel. 'This is where it gets scary.'

He messaged his foe. 'Surprise! Nice to see you, Nada.'

Nada didn't reply. Her first act was to fire a super-boser at him, along with an attempt to assert primacy. Will activated his standing-warp shield and let the beam's power slew around it before returning fire with a shot of matching potency. There was no point showing his hand just yet. Nada blocked with a shield almost as good as his own.

Her defence told him everything he needed to know. His science had come further than hers in less time. Which meant that she must still be computing on a Phote matrix, whereas he'd been able to cram his research threads into intelligent pseudo-life.

Will teased her with a broadcast memory of her Meta at New Panama succumbing to Mark's control-key and subsiding into submissive delight.

'That did not happen!' Nada messaged back. 'You are the Usurper. You lie. I already own your world and I am sick of you getting in the way of humanity's future. You are the past. You are a disease. You are a failure.'

'And you are clueless,' Will retorted.

Nada broke out her heavy weapons. She fired a distortion beam at him, propagating curvon-collapse at a little over three times the speed of light and trashing the fabric of space along the way. The beam changed the decay properties of baryonic matter and would have really messed with his mesohull structure had it hit. But while the beam was impossible to see coming, Will had already anticipated the move and tossed out a spray of vacuum-twisting bombs. Her beam fizzed into nothingness as the local spatial geometry underwent some very unlikely knot-transitions. Several kinds of exotic particle pairs flickered in and out of existence. The stars seen through that part of space briefly turned an unhappy shade of carmine.

Will slewed around the drone cloud, making sure not to kill his wife under the acceleration, and replied with a glancing distortion beam of his own. Nada's shielding fared less well than his. He watched her exohull ripple as nuclear blasts in her mesohull took out some of her accelerator pathways. He was glad he hadn't tried for a direct shot. That would have ended her too soon.

'I have her,' he said. 'She's vulnerable. It's despair-bomb time.'

Will doubted he needed to articulate his intent but had to be sure he'd given the Transcended a reason to act. He brought up the tight-beam targeting system and aimed for Nada's primary sensor-arrays.

In that second, Rachel *unpacked*. Something deep inside her, hidden between the atoms of her tissues, reached out and seized control of the ship's processors where his meta-thread resided. She'd been full of microscopic warpium bubbles, Will saw, as the controls were ripped from his grasp. They were probably linked quantum-processors of some kind, invisible to any scan and no doubt ferociously intelligent. She couldn't even have known they were there.

Will felt his consciousness being sucked into some virtual domain that had been running inside his wife until now. That was fine. He'd expected it. As the Transcended reeled him in, buried parts of himself scattered throughout the ship which he'd left purposefully dormant sprang into wakefulness, forcing his enemy to scrabble for dominance.

'That's right, motherfuckers,' he growled. 'Suck it up. I'm not going to make it easy for you.'

As they forced him into their featureless meeting space, he focused his energies on wresting ownership of the metaphor. Rachel appeared before him, her form fritzing as he fought them. As soon as Will had decided on his course of action, he'd set instances of himself looking back over every Transcended dream and puzzle that he or Mark had ever experienced, hunting for implementation clues he could exploit. Now his collective mind was throwing out hacks as fast as he could think.

'Stop!' she told him. 'The weapons you're using are dangerous.'

'No, you lying bastards, it's the *information* that's dangerous. You don't want it getting out.'

'That's also true,' said Rachel. 'In Gal's name, let this virt stabilise. We need to talk.'

'Damn right,' said Will. 'Funny how that only ever happens when your neck is on the line, though, isn't it?'

He reached out and forced the metaphor to morph. Rachel's face became Nada's.

'There, that's a little more appropriate, don't you think?'

'Don't fight us this way!' Nada urged. 'You have no idea what you're doing.'

She slammed a hold on the metaphor. Will wriggled out of it.

'Oh no?' said Will. 'Here's my guess: you're playing with species for fun and making fresh biospheres on the side to keep your game running. We're just *pets* to you, and we're not supposed to bite the sacred hand. Well, fuck that. Consider yourself bitten. You're fools if you think I haven't taken out insurance. Holding me here wins you nothing. I've made sure of that.'

'We've made mistakes,' said Nada, 'that much is clear. But we can promise the survival of the human race if you back off and leave the

Photurians alone. We will take responsibility for closing down the ones in this system.'

'Nice try,' said Will. 'But guess what? I don't trust you! You've murdered billions! And your control is much more tenuous than you want us to believe, isn't it? Otherwise we wouldn't even be talking.'

'You're a fool if you think our hesitation is on our own behalf,' said Nada.

'I want the truth,' Will demanded. 'Now and unconditionally. Who are you? What do you want with the human race?'

'No deal,' said Nada. 'If you want a stand-off, you can have one. It's your loss.'

22.6: MARK

Will dropped the *D-Two* at the edge of the Galatean System and leapt back into warp a fraction of a second later. Mark sat in the glassy lounge and stared at his retreating signal.

'So that's it?' he said. 'Now we sit and watch?'

'Fuck that,' said Palla.

'My thoughts exactly. Let's see if we have any weapons on this bucket.'

As it turned out, they had lots. Mark swapped his focus to helmspace and watched the options scrolling up around him. What were *twist-bombs* and *distorter-beams*?

'If this is what purely defensive looks like, I hate to think what Will's carrying,' Palla remarked.

'Let's go and find out.'

He let his subminds smear into the ship and took them straight in after Will. The *D-Two* was absurdly responsive. It was more like sliding an avatar around in a software interface than physical flying. There was no resistance at all.

'Sensors suggest that Ann and Ira may be doing exactly what we're doing,' Clath observed.

Mark snorted. 'Now there's a surprise.'

'What do you mean, *may be*?' said Palla.

'It's difficult to tell,' said Clath. 'These ships fly under stealth by default. Will didn't bother hiding but our sister ship is practically invisible, even with all the crazy new cameras we have.'

As they raced towards the site where Will and Nada had started fighting, Mark and the others watched the battle proceed in warp-induced fast-time.

'Jesus!' said Clath. 'That boser beam went through Will's ship like it wasn't there. And now what's she firing?' Clath inhaled sharply. 'Fuck. Is that a cloud of *red shift*? No, that's just *wrong*! Mark, this is scaring me. They're ripping up space–time like turf under tyres.'

Then, just when Will's ship appeared to be poised for a killing strike, it turned a ghostly silver and drifted.

'Wait – *what*?' said Palla. 'What just happened to Will?'

'That's standing-warp,' Clath exclaimed, 'like the Subtle ark used. But why here? Why now?'

Nada fired on Will's ship again to absolutely no effect. Then she tried a weapon that sucked the light out of the surrounding space. A hammer-blow gravity wave passed through the *D-Two*'s hull.

'Shit!' said Palla. 'Whatever that was, it can't be good.'

Will's ship, though, looked entirely unaffected. And that was when Nada appeared to belatedly notice that she had other targets.

'Pointless humans!' she messaged. 'You have been detected. Note that your Usurper has been reduced to cringing. Power down your drives and submit. A useful future awaits you as host bodies for my persona.'

'The Photes always did have a great line in tempting offers,' Mark observed as he threw the ship into a violent pattern of evasive manoeuvres.

Their new ship compensated for the slewing gravity so smoothly that he barely felt it. He suspected that the engines were somehow shaping their reference frame, just like the time-dilation machine on the ark.

His moves came just in time. Something that might have been a particle beam licked past their ship. This time, gravity eddies smacked through the hull like invisible rhinos.

'I don't care for that weapon,' said Mark. 'Whatever the fuck it is.'

'Very well, then,' Nada sent. 'If you cannot behave like rational entities, you shall die instead.'

A wave of drones so thick it looked like glistening liquid separated from Nada's fleet and ripped out to meet them. Mark had never seen so many. Behind them came Nada's own cruiser, sliding through the out-system as if the normal rules of physics did not apply to it. Which, on reflection, they probably didn't.

'Now would be a really good time for us to find out what those weapons can do,' said Palla.

'I agree,' Clath squeaked. 'Would you like a hand?'

22.7: ANN

Ann watched in horror as the Photes swapped their attention to the dark smudge that had to be Mark's ship. He turned and boosted away at an impressive fraction of light-speed. Nada followed up with another shot from her peculiar, barely detectable beam-weapon. In the same instant that it hit, Mark's ship acquired a strange new warp-shield that rippled like quicksilver. The beam dissipated on contact, filling the surrounding space with a haze of ruddy, twinkling light.

'Was that just lucky timing?' said Ann.

'Nobody's that lucky,' said Ira. 'Mark's ship pre-empted her somehow.'

However, with his shield active, it was clear that Mark's ship couldn't move. By the time Nada stopped blasting him, the drones had flown too close for him to escape. They slammed into his defensive wall by the hundred. It mattered not. They splashed out of the far side as tortured blobs of hot metal.

'Did you see that?' she asked Ira.

'It was hard to miss.'

'If our shields are that good, what's to stop us from attacking?'

Ira grinned. 'So far as I can tell, not much. And I think that's the point. Will never expected us to sit back – he knew we'd come after him if something happened. He might be a living god, but he's still a lousy liar.'

Ann felt the tug of responsibility. 'We should get in there before it's too late,' she said, though she loathed the idea of fighting again. 'We could make a dive for Nada's capital ship while she's focused on Mark. I know you won't want to do that.'

Ira regarded her in surprise. 'Are you crazy? It's the idea of losing you that I can't stand. Going up in a ball of flame beside you works fine. I have one stipulation, though: I drive. You can figure out all the crazy weapons and shields.'

Ann snorted. 'Don't you prefer an outmoded helm-metaphor?'

'Copied it into my shadow when we left the *Dantes*,' said Ira. 'Not a problem.'

'In that case, be my guest,' she said. 'Though I may rip control from you if your flight skills prove inadequate.'

Ira smirked. 'I doubt you'll need to.'

She passed him helm-control. He swung them wildly above the ecliptic, around the main thrust of the battle and then back down towards Nada's cruiser at an oblique angle. The oozing sea of drones struggled to track them and Ira had timed it nicely. He made it look as if they were desperately trying to escape the fray right up until he had a clear angle of attack.

He powered back down, aiming straight through the sea of enemy munitions, using both warp and conventional thrust to boost their momentum. Their ion plume made their position obvious, but by then it didn't matter.

'This ship is *sweet*!' he yelled. 'Shame it's not going to last.'

As the first drones impacted, the *D-Three*'s drives cut out. The universe flickered as they plunged through the munitions cloud. Ann saw her opportunity – six of the more ordinary Photurian ships had followed Nada out. Now they were lining up to boser the *D-Three* out of existence, using the drone assault as cover.

Ann picked something called a *distorter-beam* and fired short, conservative shots at them. The ships burst apart in a tidy row. Ira cheered.

An image of Will appeared in helm-space. 'If you can see me, you must be firing your new weapons,' he said. 'Be careful. Get too involved in this fight and the Transcended may deactivate your ship. I recommend keeping a low profile.'

'You want to do that?' said Ira.

'You're kidding, right?' she replied.

'Just checking.'

As soon as they had enough open space to fly in, Ira doubled their warp and dived on Nada's ship.

'Three seconds to targeting range,' he said. 'Two... one...'

Their engines, weapons and cloak all died. Emergency lighting filled the cabin. Their assault was finished, just like Mark's and Will's. So much for their bold rescue of Galatea. Suddenly, the hull's quiet ticking was all they could hear.

'Fuck,' said Ann, and gripped her crash couch with both hands. 'Really?'

'I guess we were warned,' said Ira.

Nada's ship pivoted with leisurely menace, bringing its main weapons array to bear. Ann gazed at that vast and terrible vessel and knew at least that it would be a good death, even if she no longer wanted one.

Then, behind them, bursts of warp-light flared at the edge of the out-system as new vessels appeared. There were forty of them and they all looked remarkably like the *Ariel Two*.

They took just seconds to assess the state of battle before opening fire with g-rays and super-bosers, targeting every Photurian ship they could see. A wide-cast arrival message flared out from the mystery armada.

A window opened in helm-space, showing a woman with Will's eyes and mouth, and hair cut in a severe dark bob.

'This is Representative Moneko Thirty-Four Ninety-Eight of the Willworld Collective Navy,' she announced. 'We are here to deliver news and provide support for our human brethren. The Photurian menace at the world you call Snakepit has been crushed. Photurians, prepare to die.'

Ann could only gape.

23: ENLIGHTENMENT

23.1: IRA

'Ann, take the helm,' he told her. 'I'll cover comms.'

He wrestled with their crippled systems until they agreed to open a tight-beam channel to the leading ship from the new fleet.

'Representative Moneko,' he sent, 'this is Ira Baron aboard the GSS *Dantes Three*. We need your help. Our ship is de-powered and under threat from the vessel at the following coordinates. If this message reaches you before we die, please assist.'

He dearly hoped that this time he was talking to some version of Will that was able to recognise him as an ally. He needn't have worried. Nada's vessel made so obvious a target that the new ships had already started converging their fire upon it. Their boser beams did exactly zero damage, but they caused Nada's shields to flare, preventing her from firing back.

However, there wasn't enough distraction to stop all the swarming drones from changing tack. One of them dived at the *D-Three*'s hull. Ira flinched and expected to die as a blast threw them halfway out of their couches.

'We're still here,' he said in astonishment a few breaths later.

The drone was an expanding cloud of ions and debris. Five more came after it, knocking the teeth around in Ira's skull but causing no more damage than that.

'How?' he blurted. 'We don't even have power.'

'False matter,' Ann reminded him. 'Best armour there is.'

Ira let loose a guffaw of unhinged laughter. Then Moneko's reply arrived.

'Happy to oblige,' she said. 'Long time, no see, Ira. Sending support to your position.'

Moneko's fleet advanced, keeping up a barrage of fire. Whenever Nada had a clear shot, her horrifying new death-beam lashed out, obliterating a nestship every time. It staggered him to see vessels of such size and power rendered so vulnerable. Not that many weeks ago, one of those two-hundred-klick-long cruisers had been enough to change the tide of a battle. Now they were yesterday's news. Things had escalated fast.

Suddenly, the power came back on.

'What happened?' said Ira.

'Nothing I did,' said Ann. 'I think we drifted out of targeting range for Nada's ship. The Transcended must be protecting it, just as Will warned.'

Ira smiled. 'They might have our ship on a leash but they clearly can't affect Moneko. And now Nada has too many targets to fight. We'll use that.'

He swapped back to the open channel. 'Moneko? You're some kind of Will clone, right? If you keep Nada pinned down, Mark and I will hit the smaller Phote ships. Does that work for you? And mind if I ask how in hell's name you're here?'

Ann took the *D-Three* ripping away from Nada's cruiser as fast as she could and worked at blowing holes in the more vulnerable old-style Phote ships.

'Yes, a clone,' came Moneko's reply. 'Nada's absorption of our world didn't go as planned. Somewhere in the chaos, we figured out two things. First, that humanity was now under serious threat, and second, that one of our Glitches had already made it as far as your ship. Because of that, I was selected as the most suitable representative of our kind. What we found at New Panama scared the pants off us. I'm just glad we got here in time.'

'Let's hope that's true,' said Ira. 'It's not over yet.'

23.2: WILL

While Will struggled to keep a handle on the controls of the featureless virt, the Transcended forced open a video window. It held a view from

Will's own external cameras showing the battle around him in grisly detail.

'Watch,' she said. 'We know about the backup copies of the weapon you devised. The ships containing them were infected accordingly. You won't be allowed to use them to alter the Nada-entity.'

He caught sight of Mark's ship turtled under a warp-shell and then saw Ann dive into targeting range, only to have her power die.

'You aren't helping your friends,' said the Nada avatar. 'You're merely putting them in harm's way. Is that what you want?'

'No, but we have nothing to lose,' said Will. 'You should have thought about that before you started fucking with us.'

'Stop resisting and we'll shut Nada down for you,' the Transcended urged. 'You're being ridiculous. There is simply no way for you to exercise control in this situation.'

As if on cue, the *Ariel* copies burst into the fray.

'What is this?' said the Nada avatar.

The new ships started firing and the battle descended rapidly into chaos. Mark's ship got its break and sped away from Nada with all haste. Will burst into laughter.

'No control?' he sneered. 'I'll tell you who's got no control. Didn't put control hacks in those new ships, did you? They can piss all over Nada as much as they like.'

The Transcended avatar appeared to blink in genuine astonishment. Her hold on the virt-prison weakened slightly.

'You planned this?' she said.

'Of course not,' said Will. 'But *all of me* is pissed at you. And all of us want to live. What did you expect?'

'This is awful,' the Transcended told him. 'You're risking the human race, not to mention your own kind.'

'Then give me the truth!' Will demanded.

The avatar scowled at him. 'You don't want it.'

'Don't tell me what I want, you galactic parasite.'

'You won't like it.'

'Tell me!' Will roared. 'You want cooperation? Reveal your agenda. That's my price. And make it quick. That battle's getting awfully hot.'

'Once you know, there will be no unknowing.'

'Nothing about my existence since you bastards showed up has been comfortable,' said Will. 'Why should it start now?'

'Your choice,' said the Transcended with a very dark smile.

She held out a pitch-black icon. Will picked it up and tossed it back without hesitation, screening it for malware five billion different ways as he did so. There was none. Inside lay only cold, clear knowledge.

Will saw.

The Photes were a training tool. Humanity was being shaped. A Photised race became a reflection of the one it had been drawn from – a weapon that evolved to match and oppress the original species. As the species got stronger or weaker, the Photes changed via their own pattern of acquisition and decay to remain a suitable challenge.

Phote cellular code operated more like human software than a real biology, and that was by design. When a species was Photised, its cellular mechanisms were rewritten in a more compact format. That simple act of data compression altered the mutative landscape. Thus, when dissent or mutation occurred in a Photised species, the change was almost always deleterious. There wasn't enough redundancy in the structure for it to safely change. Photised species decayed harmlessly, producing fresh biospheres along the way where new life could start.

Will's fury got the better of him. Learning halted.

'Assholes!' he snarled. 'I knew it. You're breeding us for laughs, you sick fucks. You turned billions of people into lifeless puppets!'

'Attend to the rest of the download,' the Transcended told him. 'Listen and learn before you judge.'

With difficulty, Will bit down on his disgust and kept going.

The result of Phote-training was a species under persistent existential threat. That threat consolidated it into a mature, coherent, sentient civilisation. In other words: a galactic citizen. And this transformation was necessary for participation in the galactic good.

'Bullshit,' said Will.

'Keep learning,' said the Transcended.

That galactic good involved endless competition with the other galaxies of the universe, conducted via patterns of inter-singularity entanglement of immense complexity. It meant near-endless life in perpetual struggle, where only fused, self-aware species had the strength and intelligence to participate. The galaxies themselves served as crèches, bringing forth race after race, isolated in invisibly enclosed patches of space where their development could be tweaked to maximise yield.

'So what?' said Will. 'We're being made into soldiers for your ever-lasting war? That's better, is it?'

'No,' said the Transcended and pushed the download back into motion.

The struggle existed, they showed him, because it was the only stable solution for coexistence on universal scales. All life was cooperation happening against a backdrop of competition, from the first moments of molecular abiogenesis up to the largest civilised structures in the universe. That competition was necessary because it was the only viable check on corruption from within.

'This is how life works,' they told him, and he understood.

Genes battled transposons among their own number. Bodies fought cancer. Communities fought crime. World governments fought rogue banks. It only worked because there was pressure to cooperate from without. Those entities that gave in to graft collapsed into decay. Those that looked after their own grew and prospered, defeating their more corrupt neighbours.

'This is why humans have love and the will to do good,' they told him. 'That is why you were ready to offer yourself up to Snakepit. That passion didn't come from nowhere and it's not magic. Love is not irrational. It exists for a reason.'

Will's joined mind slowed in astonishment as the full scale of the symmetry became clear to him. Cooperation *was* life. Competition gave it shape. Everything that lived and self-organised was driven by the same inexorable process, informed by molecular noise at the nano-scale. The truth was written billions of times over in the tiniest droplet of pond water, yet humanity had never fully noticed.

'Even for molecules,' Will said in awe.

'Yes,' she replied. 'Even there. Agency is not a requirement. Neither are genes. This pattern grows from the root of matter itself, wher-ever room for shared benefit exists. The result, at the highest level of organisation, is us. But if a species realises they're being manipulated to this end, the probability of a good outcome degrades. They play to that goal and so fail. If the Photes are infected with doubt, the same thing happens. That's why we would rather see your friends die than let you poison Nada Rien. They are but individuals. You risk murdering humanity.'

'No,' he said.

'Yes,' they insisted. 'You've seen the consequences of not following the pattern. Search Mark's memories again and look at the Subtle.'

They had been a very promising species, but their impressive acts of collaboration were offset with limitations in their pattern of social cohesion. In their hunger for personal safety through defensive technologies, they learned too much too soon and secured their own ending. Being safe, he saw, was not the same as being alive. And that same lack of bravery under threat was now also the greatest risk to humankind, which was why the Transcended had let them see the ruins.

'For species that get this far, terror-paralysis under existential threat is the most common form of failure,' she said. 'The inability to face a shared disaster condemns all. If you release your bomb, humanity will lose its Photes, and with them the chance to acquire social cohesion.'

'Would that be so bad?' said Will.

'No, so long as you're happy with the human race slaughtering itself within the next twenty years. You are not a stable species given your scale, intellect and technological reach. You saw that before the Photes were released. You tried to manage IPSO and failed. You watched your kind erupt into squabbling and brinkmanship. This is how it goes. Humanity's options now are to grow up or die.'

Will rebelled against that notion.

'This can't be true,' he said. 'There must have been others who lived without these constraints before you came along. Races that lived on their own terms, who were free to develop.'

'Yes,' she said. 'There were several, a long time ago. But you don't want their scars, or their fate. Those species never had guidance or a safe home. They faced more tragedy than you can imagine. They built all this so that it need never happen again.'

'That's who you are,' said Will, stunned. 'That's what the Transcended represent.'

'No,' said Nada. 'Those races are long gone. We are others raised just like you who inherited what they built.'

'But you killed billions,' Will said weakly.

'To allow trillions to be born,' she replied. 'Would you have done differently? This is the dilemma every species faces. To develop courage at the level of the species, individuals must be ready to die. No life is more sacred than the whole, and no fortune more valuable than the one that is shared.'

Will realised with sudden sadness that his time in the company of the human race had come to an end.

'There's no going home with this knowledge, is there?' he said.

'No,' she replied. 'Not without irreparably harming those you love. You pressed a little too hard, Will. But that in itself is laudable.'

'So what happens now, then?'

'You were an accident, Will Monet, and an experiment, which makes your status special. So we're prepared to offer you a deal.'

'Explain,' he said.

'First, let us tidy up a little. If we let Nada die naturally, will you hold back your weapon?'

'How can I not?' said Will, and reeled at what the knowledge had already done to him.

23.3: MARK

While Moneko's ships harried Nada, shutting down her ability to respond, Ann tore through the rest of the Photurian fleet like a fox through a henhouse.

'She has the right idea!' said Palla. 'Let's help.'

Mark joined in, bringing their impossibly fast ship around to trap the more sluggish Photurian vessels between them. The distorter-beam, he learned, was super-handy for clearing out large numbers of drones at once. And with their shielding, the Photes simply had nothing that could touch them. There was the odd frightening moment when someone lanced them with a boser, locking them behind their shield, but it felt more like squashing ants than conducting a major piece of interstellar conflict.

Then Moneko's bosers started to stutter. She was running out of antimatter, or iron, or both. As Nada's shield flicked off, her super-weapon stabbed outwards, obliterating nine nestships with the same terrible ease with which Mark had been destroying drones. The fight started to go frighteningly south even faster than it had improved.

'No!' he said. 'There has to be something we can do. Targeting doesn't matter. We can shoot at her from a distance.'

Before he could follow through on that thought, Nada picked him as her next target. Their shield flared. All three of them clung to their seats as another stampede of gravity disruptions rippled through the ship.

'We can still suicide,' Palla pointed out.

'You have a point,' said Mark. 'Okay, let's do this Academy-style.'

But before he could re-engage the drive, a better option appeared in the form of an icon deposited in their virt with a note attached.

'Will Monet is busy,' it read. 'However, his ship is now at your disposal. Please use this remote helm-space link.'

'Wha ... ?' said Mark.

'Don't stare at it!' Clath urged. 'Eat it!'

Mark knocked it back and *shifted*. With apparently no attendant light-lag, he found his avatar in the helm-space of a larger, more powerful ship – one with a *lot* more weapons. Will was nowhere in the virt and neither was Rachel, but Mark didn't have time for hide-and-seek.

'Holy shit!' he exclaimed.

'What do you see?' said Palla.

'Guns,' said Mark. 'Lots of guns.'

He grabbed the scariest-looking weapon-handle he could find – a black and red icon labelled 'Despatialiser: use with extreme caution'. He let loose a crazed chuckle, dropped Will's standing-warp shield, targeted Nada and fired.

A light-sucking beam licked out, like the one Nada had been using but about thirty times as powerful. Nada's shield flared and the space around her ship acquired an unhealthy glow. Abruptly, both shield and glow were gone. Nada's exohull had taken on a lumpy, uneven texture.

Then, to his astonishment, she fired back – not with a super-weapon but with mere g-rays. Nevertheless, she was still coming.

Mark tight-beamed her ship.

'Hey, Nada, nice to see you again,' he said. 'Just to let you know, I tried your flavour of joy, but on balance, I thought it was shit. So I have a final answer for you from the human race about that rapture of yours. No. Fucking. Thank you.'

He examined the rest of his weapons-spread and picked something else that looked exciting.

23.4: NADA

Nada stared in confusion at Monet's ship. Was Ruiz now piloting it? She looked over the appalling damage he'd done to her systems and fought a surge of loathing so potent that her joined mind almost tore itself back into factions.

There had been so many interruptions, so many desperate attempts by the humans to avoid participating in harmony. And now came this hateful revelation that Ekkert had made a mess of reconverting the homeworld. Of course he had. He wasn't her. She should never have left him with the responsibility.

'I don't care what weapons you have,' she sent to Monet's ship. 'You're going to fail. Even if I die, my kind will never give up on the human race. Your evil will end. Love will rise again.'

She broadcast a message to every Photurian machine in the system. She was vulnerable, but thousands of her sisters were distributed across local space in craft she'd intended for the domination of Galatea. Mark would never get all of them before they found their way into the human population.

'We didn't fail last time,' Ruiz told her. 'We beat you at New Panama. I asserted primacy over you myself.'

'Impossible,' she spat back.

So he sent her a memory, embedded in packets formatted to her own modified control protocol. Nada experienced a moment of real fear.

'You've been hiding the truth from yourself,' he said. He sounded sad now, and somehow that made it worse. 'When your kind run out of people to convert, you just stop. There is no heaven. There never was. There's only death.'

The old dissonance rose up in Nada. 'Liar!' she said. 'And even if it's true, do you really want to live in a universe like that? Where there's no happy ending? Where love doesn't conquer all?'

'Life is about living and knowing that you've lived,' he told her. 'Not endings, and not conquering. Look at you. You've thrown everything away – your principles, your identity, everything in the universe that's not you, just because you want that happy ending.'

'Why are you telling me all this?' she shrieked. She felt sick, powerless, *joyless*. 'Why ruin my last moments? My ship is crippled. So kill me again!'

Mark sighed over the comms-link. 'Weirdly, I don't want to have to,' he said. 'And besides, I'm broadcasting this to your sisters, too, so they all get the message.'

She kept firing at him, useless though it was.

'So I made compromises,' she raged. 'Is wanting to create a heaven for everyone such a terrible crime? I die for love!'

'No,' said Mark, sounding as wistful as she'd ever heard him. 'Love with room for only one perspective is selfishness. If anything, you die for that.'

And then he fired.

23.5: WILL

Will watched the battle become a rout. Moneko's ships obliterated what was left of the original Photurian fleet, while Ann and Mark set about clearing away the outmatched machines Nada had spread throughout the system.

'This was a mess,' he said.

'Agreed,' said the Transcended. 'But then, you weren't expected. Very few species require the intervention of a messenger agent. The Subtle did not. And in none of those cases where a messenger *was* employed did we see your pattern. There have been other edge-cases, of course,' she added, 'some far more spectacular. But you are different, nonetheless. No individual has offered themselves up to a gingerbread world as a replacement for an entire race, mostly because it's a terrible idea.'

'It was a spur-of-the-moment thing,' said Will, embarrassed.

'Of course it was,' she replied, 'and thus extremely human. The sacrifices your kind make are often hyperbolic because they are informed by love – that human-specific and highly signalled pair-bonding operation. Like many species, your commitment pattern involves the deliberate abandonment of reason on game-theoretic grounds. However, not many are so ... silly about it. There are other, more nuanced forms of committed affection that are nonetheless deep. We were fascinated, so we let the arrangement play out. Sadly, in the wake of that event, humanity's response to training remained erratic. Your social behaviour is so crisis-driven that you failed to learn. You cling to self-organisation by your fingernails. Because you failed to adapt, we began to leave out clues. We pushed open the Flaw, accelerated Fatigue and left gaps in the Phote front lines. We were, perhaps, a little reckless. Nevertheless, humanity missed every gift. So, very reluctantly, we wrote you off.'

'Why did you even keep trying if we were that hopeless?' said Will.

'Because unpredictable species have more value in the galactic competition we're engaged in. If we can't figure out what you'll do next, maybe nobody else will, either. But a species so erratic that it kills itself is no use to anybody. Consequently, support for the human race was withdrawn, along with support for your side-experiment.

'At the point when support was dropped, your world was expected to go into decline. There should have been Cancers and an analogue of Fatigue everywhere. Yet you didn't succumb to synthetic bliss or rewrite yourself into rage or placidity, though those options were always available. Instead, because you perceived the existential crisis at some level, you developed an immune system. The twin urges to accept diversity and exercise honest self-criticism turned you temporarily into a functioning independent species. Then, at the last possible moment, humanity took the bait.'

The Nada avatar paused abruptly and then burst into peals of laughter. It was as if she'd lost the ability to stay aloof from it all.

'Fuck,' she said. 'It was so annoying. I can't even tell you.' She slapped Will on the shoulder. 'Suddenly, there we were with the chance of getting *two* new species instead of one. But by then we had so many hints in play, it was ludicrous. We'd cluttered the board horribly. So it wasn't surprising when everything started cascading, right up until the technology you had in your hands was in danger of doing some real damage.'

'Kids with fireworks,' said Will bleakly, still reeling from the fact that she saw him as a *species*.

'Exactly, and we stood to lose both of you.'

'You screwed it up,' said Will.

'Yep,' said the Nada avatar. 'You have no idea. Badly prepped neural adaptations. Leaving tech out for the wrong people to find. Turning off the wrong talents. You name it, we did it. But you're an odd race and we didn't want you dead.'

'I thought you're supposed to be sentient civilisations,' said Will. 'Hyper-intelligent, immortal geniuses.'

She gave him a long, dry look. 'What you'll learn, Will, if you go that route, is that being an adult doesn't prevent you from screwing up. Being Transcended doesn't mean unlimited intellect. There's no such thing. It just means a lot more time and a lot more room to learn and make mistakes. Big, embarrassing mistakes – on gigayear timescales. So now we're in this unusual position. The Willworld was unstable for exactly the reason that all social systems are unstable – corruption from within. And now you've merged. Without external competitive pressure, you'll self-destruct.' Her expression became sly. 'We can provide that pressure.'

'This is the deal, isn't it?' said Will.

'We can offer you two good outcomes,' said the Transcended. 'One is that we partially redact your memory. We repair Rachel and send you off as a real human individual for retirement somewhere nice, far away from here.'

Will's heart pounded. To be himself again? To have a chance at a normal life? He thrilled at the thought, even while the smallness of it scared him.

'Why far away *and* a memory redaction?'

'Because caution,' she replied. 'Also policy. Besides, there's going to be a lot of fighting for the next twenty years while humanity goes through its awkward adolescence. Are you really sure you'd want to be a part of that?'

'What's the other option?'

'You transcend. Even if humanity makes it, it'll be a completely different animal from what you've become. Your units share a cognitive base-pattern rather than a genetic one, which is refreshing. And frankly, you just qualified. So why not come and join the struggle?'

Will knew he couldn't turn that down. He had too many instances now that deserved to live and grow. To snuff them out for the sake of marital bliss would be genocide.

'Why do I have to choose?' said Will. 'Why can't I have both?'

'You don't,' she replied, and sounded pleased with his response. 'And you can. Because you're a species.'

'What about Nada?' he said.

The Transcended sighed. 'Photes always lose, even when they win.

That's what they're for. Maybe in some other universe, there might be room for someone like Nada to make it to the next level, but not here. She'd never adapt. The only great truths we have are the ones that emerge from game theory. The only lasting joy comes from helping others, and the only Founder is blind chance. That knowledge would break her, I'm afraid.'

That wasn't what Will had meant to ask, and the sadness in the avatar's expression surprised him.

'I mean, isn't she still a threat?' he asked. 'There are more copies of her out there.'

'Look again,' said the Transcended, and pointed at the video window.

23.6: ANN

Ann watched the Photes die. She slid her new ship around the system, mopping them up, scrubbing away all traces of the siege. For once, fighting really was like cleaning. Just observing it brought a strange kind of release – a lightness inside her like a sun coming up.

'I can take it from here,' Mark told her.

He was cleaning, too, and was meticulous in his efforts. He flew two ships at once, picking off all traces of Nada Rien with tidy precision. She couldn't have done a better job herself. She was proud of him.

'All yours, then,' she told him.

She unclipped from her crash couch, gathered Ira up in her arms and kissed him hard – but not too hard.

'We've won,' she breathed. 'We've actually sodding won.'

He held her and grinned. 'Shut up and kiss me again,' he said.

She was so caught up in the moment that she almost didn't notice when their ship's drive gave out and they found themselves drifting a second time. A strange quiet descended on the cabin. Then, in helm-space, Will Monet appeared.

'Hi, guys,' he said. 'I hate to interrupt your moment, but I have an invitation for you. How would you like some real and lasting peace?'

Ann's face fell.

Will laughed. 'Not that sort. Just another forty or fifty years of good health somewhere quiet, far away. A farm, maybe, under open skies. No powers. No responsibilities. Just us. I'm leaving, you see. And, as I figure it, you two have both done your duty many times over. So if you fancy something with a slower pace, the option is open.'

Ann's skin chilled. Could this be real? Which Monet was she talking to now? But given how the battle had panned out, she knew there could only be one.

'A *farm?*' said Ira. 'Who has a farm any more?'

She looked at him and didn't have to say a word. Ira already knew her well enough to see the longing in her eyes – the desire to be *done*. An end to sacrifice. A chance to be human again. A glimpse of peace that would be beautiful because it *wasn't* perfect. Because they'd fill it with wonderful, awkward compromises and grey hairs and laughter.

'We accept,' said Ira quietly.

'Great,' said Will. 'Stay put.'

23.7: MARK

Mark barely had time to enjoy wiping out the last of Nada's drones before something yanked him from the virt of Will's ship and dumped him back into the cabin of the *Dantes Two*.

He sat blinking in his couch, staring at Palla.

'What happened?' he said.

'No idea,' she started. 'I—'

Their engines died. Warnings rippled through his sensorium about edits to their ship's database. Mark leapt back into the ship's virt to find flight records and weapon controls evaporating by the hundred.

'We're losing helm control!' said Clath.

The only thing they weren't losing was sensors. In their main display, Will's ship started moving on its own again. Mark messaged him.

'Will? Is that you?'

There was no reply. Instead, Will's ship whisked effortlessly across the system to stop next to Ira and Ann's. Then it extruded a peculiar-looking ember-warp field around the two ships, like a wobbling bubble of oil and milk.

The situation had escalated far enough beyond the normal that Mark could only think of a single culprit: the Transcended. Was this the punchline of their incomprehensible agenda finally revealed? He forced every submind he had to seek out remaining power-pathways in the ship before they all disappeared. They slipped through his grasp like digital soap.

'Will, we're having trouble,' said Mark. 'The ship is not responding. Is this a Transcended attack? Are you okay? Will, please respond.'

Will responded. He appeared in helm-space, wreathed in smiles. Rachel stood beside him, and near them, Ann and Ira, looking more than a little surprised.

'Hi, Mark,' said Will. He nodded to Clath and Palla. 'We're fine. And no, this isn't a trick. You won. But the struggle has to continue, I'm afraid. Some of the Phote worlds are already rebuilding and I'm not going to be able to help you with them. Neither are my clones, or Ann and Ira. You won't be hearing from any of us again, which is a shame. I think you'd have got a kick out of Moneko.'

'Wait, *what*?' said Mark. He checked the sensors again. The Will-world Navy were heading for exit vectors, departing as unexpectedly as they'd arrived.

'Why are you doing this?' said Mark. 'What's going on?'

'What's going on is that we're leaving,' said Will. 'The Transcended and I have come to an arrangement that allows the human race to thrive. There'll be no more Snakepit, and no more Nada to worry about. No more risk from suntap novas, either. I *am* leaving you with a lingering Phote problem but I feel certain you know how to handle them now. The secret isn't some kind of gun, or bomb, or a special drive. It's just courage.' He winked at Palla, who blushed.

'Why do you have to go?' Mark demanded. 'What did they force you to do?'

Will laughed at that. 'Nothing,' he said. 'We cut a deal, that's all. They're not benevolent gods, but they're not evil, either.'

'What are they, then?' Clath urged.

Will's only response to that was a smile. 'As for where I'm going? Just away. I've spent too long on the human stage. The race needs a chance to learn to operate without my shadow hanging over them. You too, Mark.'

'No,' said Mark as it dawned on him that Will really wasn't coming back. 'I barely got to know you.'

'And for that, I'm truly sorry,' said Will. 'Oh, and be careful. A lot of the new technology you're using is going to shut itself down. That ship you're in will take you as far as Galatea but no further. You don't get to keep it, unfortunately.' He clapped his hands. 'Okay, time to go, I'm afraid.' He gestured to Ira and Ann.

'Um,' said Ira, looking pained. 'I'm going to miss all three of you. And Judj, too.'

Clath grabbed her hair. 'I don't believe this.'

Ann just stared. 'Goodbye,' she said, and squeezed more fragile emotion into that word than Mark would have believed she could muster.

'Thank you for coming for us, Mark,' said Rachel, beaming. 'We love you, and we're very proud of you. That will never change.'

'Don't,' said Mark. His eyes filled with tears. 'Why are you doing this? Don't leave.'

'You did great,' said Will. 'You *are* great. Just keep at it and you can't go wrong.'

They waved at him, smiling as if he were getting on the transit to go to college. Then they popped like daydreams, leaving only quiet behind.

'No,' said Mark again, unable to believe that after everything, the end had been so sudden. After he'd lost hope and gone to all the trouble of regaining it.

Through the helm's main display, he watched Will's ship and Ann's begin to travel out of the system fast and in an impossible direction – directly towards the galactic core. Mark watched them recede until only a pinpoint of light was left, and then it was gone. Palla held him while he wept.

24: REBIRTH

24.1: MARK

After Will left, the ship's engines turned back on. Mark had no control and could only watch passively as the *Dantes Two* carried them in-system to high orbit around Galatea. As they flew, Mark found the startled sadness in him being overlaid by a new emotion – panic. He'd been away from Zoe for too long. Was she even alive? He had no idea. With that feeling came a weight of guilt that his mind had been so full of problems to solve that he'd hardly spared a thought for his wife for days.

A docking pod opened. Clath regarded it with dismay.

'I guess this is where the pumpkin coach drops us off,' she said.

'Looks like it,' Palla agreed.

Of the three of them, only Mark was keen to climb inside.

The *D-Two*'s miraculous false-matter shuttle took them down through Galatea's endless swirling storms to a location on the surface that it chose for itself. No explanation for the landing site was provided – the shuttle remained stoically silent to their every request.

In the end, it landed vertically, with featherlight precision, on a flat-topped basalt outcrop no different from any of the others they'd skimmed over. A gloomy landscape of blackened, half-glassed desert swept away in every direction. Umber clouds galloped past overhead.

'What now?' said Clath, peering out at the miserable scene.

A minute and a half later, a drilling machine broke the surface half a kilometre away and promptly signalled them.

'Friendly shuttle, your message was received. Everyone is cheering down here, I can tell you. And to answer your question, no, the losses haven't been that bad, considering. We were getting worried, though.'

'Did Will set this up?' said Palla.

'We have to assume so,' said Mark. 'He does that kind of shit.'

He shook his head. The lingering, controlling touch of his half-father's influence apparently persisted even after he'd left human space. Somehow, Mark knew he'd grow to miss it.

A port opened in the side of the drilling machine, disgorging an armoured rover that set off through the endless dust storm in their direction. Mark watched it approach with his heart in his throat.

Palla reached around in her seat to grip his hand.

'She'll be fine,' she said.

The rover bounced up to the side of their shuttle and extended a docking arm. This time, when the airlock opened, Mark was last to leave. He sat in his couch with his insides churning, suddenly terrified of the reality that lay beyond the door.

'Are you coming?' said Palla.

With a heavy intake of breath, Mark rose, made his way to the exit tube and climbed through.

Zoe was waiting for him on the other side, dressed in a green environment-suit liner, her hair a mess. She was thinner than when he'd left her, but Mark had never seen a more beautiful sight in his life.

He seized her in his arms and held her and breathed in the smell of her dusty hair while his heart threatened to burst with the swirl of emotions it was trying to contain. And then he kissed her, and lost himself in it.

'I'm never leaving you again,' he said.

'Good,' she said, beaming with happiness, and kissed him again.

24.2: IRA

Ira sat on his patio with a mug of coffee in his hand and took in the sprawling sight of his farm. He still didn't quite believe it. Him, the great Ira Baron, space hero, ex-admiral and Suicide War burnout, now lived in a rural idyll. It looked ridiculous to him – like something out of a history book.

There were two cottages, both covered in grape ivy – one for him and Ann, the other for Will and Rachel. In the fields, orange vines grew above ground on long trellises, and prote that grew in beans rather than a vat. They even had goats that gave them milk and eggs.

The houses had solar-tiled roofs and bioluminescent lamps growing from the walls. They came stocked with cups and plates and sheets woven out of something like spider-silk. And everything had been ready for them when they got there, with no sign of who'd constructed it, or when. Which was, he thought, just a little creepy. But he could handle creepy.

At the edge of the fields, the alien forest began – a thirty-metre-tall mix of gloomy purples and greens, heavy with shadows. Weird screeching sounds and ghostly lights emanated from the vegetation at night. Ira wasn't sure he liked having it there. The weather, on the other hand, was perfect.

They never got allergy attacks or local infections, which should have been impossible in an alien biosphere. Ann claimed that something had been done to their cells when they'd arrived, in the same wave of mild infection that had stripped her of all her powers. Ira had initially wondered if that meant they could never leave, but soon realised he had no such intentions.

In short, their new home was somewhere between ideal and gently unsettling. Their biggest problem, though, wasn't anything to do with the setting. It was getting used to the profound lack of *crisis*. Sometimes, he noticed Will waving his hands in front of his face, testing for virt-lag to reassure himself that the place was actually real. Ira wasn't sure it mattered. He suspected that some day, the human race would find them. But until then, things were going to be very, very quiet, and he'd just have to get used to it.

As he sipped, he caught sight of Ann in the distance, marching out of the forest she loved so much with something lizard-like and dead strung on her spear. Dinner, no doubt, not that they needed surplus. He smiled, enjoying the sight of her lithe body. She looked much better to him with her original height and features.

Ann strode straight to the farm, ignoring the friendly hail from Rachel across the way. He experienced a flicker of concern. That wasn't like her. Furthermore, the expression on Ann's face was one of deadly earnest. What had happened in there? What had she seen?

He stood as she approached. Her gaze was intense as she tossed down her kill, dropped heavily into the chair opposite and took a heavy swig of his coffee.

'What?' said Ira. 'What happened?'

'I'm going to have to stop hunting,' Ann said grimly.

'Why?'

'I'm pregnant,' she replied.

Ira's eyebrows shot up. 'Okay!' he said, finding his chair. He searched her face for clues as to the right thing to ask next. For once, he had absolutely no idea.

'I want to keep it,' she said, 'but I'll make a terrible mother. You have to help.' There was a hint of menace in her tone.

Ira laughed out loud. 'Okay, then. That's a decision. It looks like we're going to build a little colony here.'

Maybe it wouldn't be quite so quiet after all. Ann slowly broke into smiles.

24.3: WILL

Will used what little was left of his roboteering talent to instruct the farm's lizard-monkeys to plant a new crop of prote-beans. He wasn't sure if they were actually animals. Their thoughts were a little too crisp and predictable. But in any case, he was glad they'd left him something to play with. Will had been born a roboteer. Without a sensorium and something to do with it, he'd have gone crazy already.

It was just one of the ways in which their tiny utopia was underpinned by an apparently unending supply of happy accidents. But that was how his benefactors had always operated. And this was, after all, his payoff, even though he suspected it'd never sit easily with him.

He frowned as he thought through the news that Ira had brought that morning. Was Ann right to have a child in this place? She wasn't likely to give a fig what he thought one way or another, so maybe he shouldn't even care. But still, it bothered him.

He wondered, not for the first time, if he'd made the right choice to go for this chocolate-box retirement. It wasn't really him. It was so peaceful and gentle, even if the forest kept him up at night. He still remembered enough to know that for a while, he'd been very much more than a man. Maybe he should have pushed for something better.

He still missed his annoying half-son, and Moneko, and all the other characters from his old lives.

Rachel came out of the cottage carrying two glasses of juice. She saw his expression.

'What's wrong?' she said as she pressed a drink into his hand.

Will shook his head. 'Ira and Ann are all excited, but what kind of life will their child have?' he said. 'What are they going to do when we finally drop dead?'

She eyed him with dry amusement.

'First,' she said, 'it's not clear that we will. We don't have the first notion of how ageing works in this place, so it's possible they'll have more of our company than they want. And secondly, who knows what kind of life they'll have? The main problem that Ann's kid will face is having no peers of the same age. That'll be very isolating.' She gave him a serious look. 'What are you prepared to do to resolve that crisis? Somebody's future needs saving, Will. Isn't that what you're supposed to be good at?'

He blinked at her in surprise. Rachel smiled at him slyly, grabbed his shirt and pulled him gently back towards the house.

No, he thought. He'd been right to take this option. This was what he'd never got to have – this simple happiness. Responsibility for nobody except those he loved. He had a lot of catching up to do.

He stalled under the grape ivy, tugged her close and kissed her, while his forgotten orange juice spilled slowly into the warm, alien soil.

24.4: MARK

After his multi-day debrief, they brought Mark and Zoe to a spartan meeting room in the side of the Sharptown Subterra Complex to discuss next steps. Windows looked out over the main cavern where repairs were under way. Robots climbed the walls filling cracks while others sprayed the air or relaid turf on the playing grounds. Dust tinted the light beyond the diamond panes a grimy yellow that reminded Mark a little too much of New Panama.

From Zoe, he'd learned that life over the last few months had been brutal for Galatea. Most of their settlements had endured multiple seismic attacks. Their survival had hinged on that most refined of local talents – the ability to weather environmental catastrophe. Even so, everything had gone down to the wire – food, air, biocontainment. Mark and his friends had arrived just in time.

He grinned as he caught sight of Palla arriving and strode up to hug her. It was the first time he'd set eyes on her since they'd landed.

Zoe followed suit. 'You're Palla Muri,' she said. 'Thank you so much for looking after my husband. It's great to meet you properly at last.'

Palla shrugged. 'Don't mention it. It was fun,' she said. 'In a cheating-death-all-day kind of way.'

'He's good at that,' said Zoe, nudging his ribs. 'It's one of the reasons I keep him around.'

When Mark had first explained to Zoe about kissing Palla, she'd laughed at him.

'You have two chaste snogs with a college kid to save each other's lives and you thought I might be worried?' she'd said. She squeezed his face. 'I love how earnest you are. So bloody earnest! Did aliens force you to hold hands as well?'

Mark had eventually laughed, too.

'How are you doing?' he asked Palla.

'Okay,' she said uncertainly. 'Still not believing it's over.'

His expression faltered. He understood what she meant.

'Spending a lot of time with Clath,' she added. 'She's still getting over Judj. Did you hear? She's scored a new position heading up a vacuum-state research team.'

'I suspect that'll go well,' said Mark.

Palla smirked. 'You think? My guess is she'll have nailed warpium inside of six months, even without a Subtle database to help. I'm expecting miracles. Literally.'

'Could everyone take a seat please,' said a young man, standing by the table. He had a teenager's flawless cheeks and flat, blue eyes. 'Unfortunately, time is short, as usual.' He introduced himself as the others settled. 'I'm Autograd Zip Cogen. Thank you all for coming.'

Besides Mark, Zoe and Palla, there were half a dozen other Fleet-types Mark didn't recognise.

'We're here to make a formal offer to Captain Mark Ruiz and Professor Zoe Tamar,' said Zip, 'and to talk over the details of that arrangement. As many of you are aware, both the *Gulliver* and the

Kraken were destroyed during the recent siege, along with ninety per cent of our operating Fleet strength.'

Mark had already heard this from Zoe. He'd lost his pocket kingdom. It upset him less than he'd expected. The only home that mattered was his wife.

'However, during the high-speed rebuild that's currently under way, we're prepared to offer new ships of equivalent class, and to reinstate you both under your original contracts as independent operators.'

Mark smiled. It was a great offer and he wanted to take it, but it wouldn't do to let the Academy off the hook so easily.

'That depends,' he said. 'What strategy are you planning now? What mission do you want us for? And what will Palla be doing?'

Zip shot Palla a quick glance. 'In the light of your recommendations, Captain Ruiz, the Academy unanimously voted to place Autograd Muri in charge of a dedicated strike force, with full responsibility for selecting her own missions. She'll be leading the charge against the Photes. We know that the remaining enemy will be regrouping fast and decisive strikes will be vital.'

'Great,' said Mark. 'So why is she even here?'

'As a replacement in case you don't want the job we're going to offer you,' said Zip.

Mark leaned back. 'Interesting.'

So they were levering him again. If he didn't say yes, Palla didn't get the job she deserved. He'd expect nothing less from the Academy.

'Go on,' he said.

'The one good piece of news we have is that the population of Earth are still alive,' said Zip. 'We confirmed that yesterday. The Phote focus on the siege gave the refuge team extra room to manoeuvre. They've been camped out at a brown dwarf, waiting for a chance to transfer everyone to the surface of Saint Andrews. Now, though, we have better options. We'd like you and Professor Tamar to help us relocate them. That means finding a new world, establishing the habitat hardware and moving the people without letting the Photes grab them all.'

Mark leaned forward, a smile sneaking onto his lips. 'So you want a safe planet with tons of potential. A place where we already know the Photes won't be a problem. And ideally one with plenty of habitats pre-built, ready to be occupied.'

Zip's eyebrows went up. 'Ideally, of course. But I doubt—'

'I know just where to take them,' said Mark, steepling his hands.

'You do?' said Zip. 'Where?'

Mark couldn't help grinning.

'Carter,' he said. 'Carter is going to be Earth Two, and something tells me it's going to be awesome.'

24.5: WILL

They began Will's extraction. His threads were copied out of the Will-world's matrix using the warpium nano-processors that had always been hidden there. One by one, his physical instances lay down and relinquished their bodies into the mud. The planet returned to silence and began its long, slow decay back into an ordinary biosphere.

While the process was under way, Will reunited with Moneko somewhere outside of physical space. They used a part of the entangled galactic network that the Transcended had set aside for them. It could have looked like anything, but Moneko chose the park on Radical Hill for their setting. When Will stepped into it, he paused at the threshold. There was something a little melancholy about that view. It looked down at a city that had been emptied, on a world they couldn't keep.

She caught his expression as she rose from the bench to greet him.

'We'll build another park,' she told him.

'I guess it wasn't so bad, was it?' he said, peering at the twisted towers under those heavy skies.

'It was what we made it,' she replied. 'And it was where I learned to be myself.' She cocked her head. 'By the way, are you Balance now?'

'My brother is,' said Will. 'I spawned a new sub-instance. Or rather, he did. It's no fun being Meta all the time. I wouldn't have been able to see you, for starters.'

She gave him an appraising look. 'Don't you miss your wife?'

Will sighed. 'Let's be honest. We both miss our wife. We probably always will. But our wife isn't us so she can't be here. And it's going to be a long future. Hopefully.'

A part of him wondered if he'd made the right choice. Perhaps he should have just settled for being human and let the galaxy evolve without him. Certainly there'd be no peace in this future. And the company he kept, beside himselves, would be more foreign to him than his enemies ever had been.

'Thank you for coming back for me,' he said. 'I never said that.'

She shrugged. 'No problem. We wanted to. After you left, things got bad for a while. But our Glitches finally had a chance to do what they always wanted: rip out all the old anchors. Those Glitches you freed were particularly zealous in that regard. And this time, there was no resistance. The poor Photes had no real notion of their significance so didn't even try to protect them at first. By the time they clued in, it was too late.

'To be frank, the whole occupation was very instructive. It was probably the most socially significant three weeks we'd ever had. After that, of course, we knew we had to find something else to keep us busy – the golden days of denial were over. Coming after you was the obvious choice. There were plenty of Balance fragments aboard the *Dantes* who watched you escape, so it wasn't long before the whole planet knew.'

'Shame we didn't get to see Galatea again,' said Will.

'It's not for us any more,' said Moneko. 'It's for humans, and I'm sure they'll do something wonderful with it.'

A door opened in the virt, occluding the view of the towers.

'Looks like that's our cue,' she said.

They walked through into a rather mundane meeting room in the Galatean style, with too much carpeted floor space and walls of bare rock. Three comfortable-looking armchairs waited for them, along with a ceramic coffee table. Beyond lay a window-wall that looked out onto a view that had no place on the world of Will's birth.

They were gazing across the curve of a huge, blue sphere – a world, perhaps, or maybe a star of some kind. It was covered in tidy hexagonal convection cells flecked with white and gold foam. The cells slowly rippled as he watched. White beams stuck out of the sphere in a few places, like pins made of light, sliding around very slowly.

Something about that sight suggested to Will that he was observing a very large object from high up. And the lighting was curiously off, hinting that particles other than vanilla photons were involved in the act of seeing it.

A man rose from one of the chairs and stretched out a hand to greet them. He looked like someone Will had known on Galatea many years ago – Robert Rees-Noyes, his old division commander when he'd first joined the Fleet. He was dressed exactly as he had been when Will last saw him – in shorts and a Fleet T-shirt, with flip-flops on his feet. Farmer Bob, they'd called him. He'd given Will his slot on the *Ariel* mission. Will wondered whether the Transcended would always use faces from his past. The answer was yes, he realised, until they stopped bothering with faces altogether.

'Welcome,' said Bob. 'Take a seat.'

'No Rachel this time?' said Will as he sat.

Bob smiled. 'You're not in daycare any more.'

'I see,' said Will.

'Your old teacher is a wonderful race,' said Bob, 'great with meso-scale air-breather types like you. But then she was one, too, I recall. You should look her up some time. I've never met an entity more gentle or patient with her extinction events than Carol. You were lucky.'

The name wasn't an accident. Carol had been the name of Will's first teacher on Galatea. He received a fleeting glimpse of a world full of creatures halfway between termites and rats, building phenomenally complicated nests hundreds of kilometres on a side. His mentor, apparently. He suspected the memory packet served as her true name.

'So what do we call you?' said Moneko. 'Bob?'

'That'll do for now,' said Bob. 'And I take it that you two instances are the representative pseudopod of the integrated Will-mind?'

'We are,' she said. 'Our Meta is listening.'

'Then I'm here to offer you a job. We're under a lot of pressure from Andromeda right now and things are getting dicey. We're hoping you can help. But for that, you're going to have to consolidate and stabilise rapidly, otherwise I can't see you lasting for more than a few millennia in the role. As it is, we're taking a risk with you simply by offering to bring you on board. You're not what we'd call a classic-track species, though you come with a very strong recommendation from Carol.'

'What do you want us to do?' said Will.

'Well, now,' said Bob. 'What we've heard is that you have valuable experience in a variety of body formats, so we're going to send you undercover to try to disrupt the social fabric of Andromeda's new attack species. That race is young enough that it's still keen on physical forms, just as you are, but we're guessing you're a little more flexible in that regard.

'There's no point handing the job to an older species that's as far away from its root biology as you are from acquiring mitochondria – they'd just screw it up and get noticed. So that makes you perfect. But you'll need to learn a lot of spatial mechanics in a hurry. You'll be infiltrating a species with a far deeper knowledge of network algebras than you have.

'We can provide you with a small training world and enough raw material for about a hundred billion threads soft, twenty billion manifested. And we're going to recommend an aggressive training regimen, with mass-murder consequences for slow development. We can administer that for you, if it would help.'

'How long do we have to get ready?' said Will.

'We can't afford to give you more than five hundred years, I'm afraid. But Carol thinks you're up to it.'

Bob sent him the details in another surge of memory. It was a very different world from the one he was used to. It had a fifty-kilometre-thick smart-matter crust with quangled links to a pair of stellar teaching labs, not far from Galactic Central HQ. They'd also give him time on the smaller of the two vacuum-state testing arrays in Void Five and surface access to the Galactic Central Library.

'Don't worry,' Bob put in. 'Your library access will come with selective filtering so that any tutorials likely to destroy your developing mind will be screened out.'

In the scant five centuries they could provide, Will saw, he'd be expected to develop the skills to fully impersonate the species he'd be infiltrating without losing his own identity in the process.

'Needless to say,' said Bob, 'if you're caught in the field, the Andromeda Collective will devour your threads and repurpose your intellect as a weapon of their own. Which, frankly, would be embarrassing for everyone.'

'What's the alternative?' said Moneko.

Bob pulled an uncomfortable face. 'You can go into passive development until another opportunity comes up that's more to your liking,' he suggested. 'But the Milky Way isn't responsible for providing you with selection pressure. As a fledgling race, you'd have to find another species of similar development level to engage in local competition with. A flatmate, if you will. You'd get a basic loan-world. Maybe compute power for five billion threads, tops. Library access, of course, to encourage you to develop skills. And a tenure of no more than six thousand years. Frankly, I don't recommend that option, though. This job should be well within your capabilities. It might even be fun at the meta-level, and not so fatal for instances that it gets in the way of your growth. So, do you think you're up for it?'

Bob watched them closely while he waited for their reply. Behind him, the enigmatic blue sphere turned slowly.

Will glanced at Moneko. She grinned and took his hand.

'Sure,' he said. 'We'll give it a shot.'

'Terrific. Welcome to the galaxy, Will,' said Bob, rising to embrace them. 'I think you're going to like it here.'

ACKNOWLEDGEMENTS

Special thanks to Louis Lamb, Sarah Pinborough, my agent John Jarrold, the fantastic team at Gollancz, those generous, insightful friends who helped me debug the work – Dave, Kate, DeeDee, K, Maciek – and my wonderful wife Genevieve, who gave me the time to fulfill a dream.